The Scarlet Pimpernel **OMNIBUS**

Volume III

The Scarlet Pimpernel
OMNIBUS

Volume III

The Way of the Scarlet Pimpernel • Mam'zelle Guillotine • Eldorado

by Baroness Orczy

Originally published 1933, 1940, 1913.
Reprinted by Cavalier Classics in 2014.

Contents

THE WAY OF THE SCARLET PIMPERNEL

CHAPTER I

At an angle of the Rue de la Monnaie where it is intersected by the narrow Passage des Fèves there stood at this time a large three-storied house, which exuded an atmosphere of past luxury and grandeur. Money had obviously been lavished on its decoration: the balconies were ornamented with elaborately carved balustrades, and a number of legendary personages and pagan deities reclined in more or less graceful attitudes in the spandrels round the arches of the windows and of the monumental doorway. The house had once been the home of a rich Austrian banker who had shown the country a clean pair of heels as soon as he felt the first gust of the revolutionary storm blowing across the Rue de la Monnaie. That was early in '89.

After that the mansion stood empty for a couple of years. Then, when the housing shortage became acute in Paris, the revolutionary government took possession of the building, erected partition walls in the great reception and ballrooms, turning them into small apartments and offices which it let to poor tenants and people in a small way of business. A concierge was put in charge. But during those two years for some reason or other the house had fallen into premature and rabid decay. Within a very few months an air of mustiness began to hand over the once palatial residence of the rich foreign financier. When he departed, bag and baggage, taking with him his family and his servants, his pictures and his furniture, it almost seemed as if he had left behind him an eerie trail of ghosts, who took to wandering in and out of the deserted rooms and up and down the monumental staircase, scattering an odour of dry-rot and mildew in their wake. And although, after a time, the lower floors were all let as offices to business people, and several families elected to drag out their more or less miserable lives in the apartments up above, that air of emptiness and of decay never ceased to hang about the building, and its walls never lost their musty smell of damp mortar and mildew.

A certain amount of life did, of course, go on inside the house. People came and went about their usual avocations: in one compartment a child was born, a wedding feast was held in another, old women gossiped and young men courted: but they did all this in a silent a furtive manner, as if afraid of rousing dormant echoes; voices were never raised above a whisper, laughter never rang along the corridors, nor did light feet run pattering up and down the stairs.

Far be it from any searcher after truth to suggest that this atmosphere of silence and of gloom was peculiar to the house in the Rue de la Monnaie. Times were getting hard all over France—very hard for most people, and hard times whenever they occur give rise to great silences and engender the desire for solitude. In Paris all the necessities of life—soap, sugar, milk—were not only very dear but difficult to get. Luxuries of the past were unobtainable save to those who, by inflammatory speeches, had fanned the passions of the ignorant and the needy, with promises of happiness and equality for all. Three years of this social upheaval and of the rule of the proletariat had brought throughout the country more misery than happiness. True! the rich—a good many of them—had been dragged down to poverty or exile, but the poor were more needy than they had been before. To see the King dispossessed of his throne, and the nobles and bourgeois either fleeing the country or brought to penury might satisfy a desire for retribution, but it did not warm the body in winter, feed the hungry or clothe the naked. The only equality that this glorious Revolution had brought about was that of wretchedness, and an ever-present dread of denunciation and of death. That is what people murmured in the privacy of their homes, but did not dare to speak of openly. No one dared speak openly these days, for there was always the fear that spies might be lurking about, that accusations of treason would follow, with the inevitable consequences of summary trial and the guillotine.

And so the women and the children suffered in silence, and the men suffered because they could do nothing to alleviate the misery of those they cared for. Some there were lucky enough to have got out of this hell upon earth, who had shaken the dust of their unfortunate country from their shoes in the early days of the Revolution, and had sought—if not happiness, at any rate peace and contentment in other lands. But there were countless others who had ties that bound them indissolubly to France—their profession, their business, or family ties—they could not go away: they were forced to remain in their native land and to watch hunger, penury and disease stalk the countryside, whilst the authors of all this misfortune lived a life of ease in the luxurious homes, sat round their well-filled tables, ate and drank their fill and spent their leisure hours in spouting of class-hatred and of their own patriotism and selflessness. The restaurants of the Rue St. Honoré were thronged with merry-makers night after night. The members of the proletarian government sat in the most expensive seats at the Opéra and the Comédie Française and drove in their barouches to the Bois, while flaunting their democratic ideals by attending the sittings of the National Assembly stockingless and in ragged shirts and breeches. Danton kept open house at d'Arcy-sur-Aube: St. Just and Desmoulins wore jabots of Mechlin lace, and coats of the finest English cloth: Chabot had a sumptuous apartment in the Rue d'Anjou. They say to it, these men, that privations and anxiety did not come nigh them. Privations were for the rabble, who was used to them, and for aristos and bourgeois, who had never known the meaning of want: but for them, who had hoisted the flag of Equality and Fraternity, who had freed the people of France from the tyranny of Kings and nobles, for them luxury had become a right, especially if it could be got at the expense of those who had enjoyed it in the past.

In this year 1792 Maître Bastien de Croissy rented a small set of offices in the three-storied house in the Rue de la Monnaie. He was at this time verging on middle age, with hair just beginning to turn grey, and still an exceptionally handsome man, despite the lines of care and anxiety round his sensitive mouth and the settled look of melancholy in his deep-set, penetrating eyes. Bastien de Croissy had been at one time one of the most successful and most respected members of the Paris bar. He had reckoned royal personages among his clients. Men and women, distinguished in art, politics or literature, had waited on him at his sumptuous office on the Quai de la Mégisserie. Rich, good-looking, well-born, the young advocate had been fêted and courted wherever he went: the King entrusted him with important financial transactions: the duc d'Ayen was his most intimate friend: the Princesse de Lamballe was godmother to his boy, Charles-Léon. His marriage to Louise de Vandeleur, the only daughter of the distinguished general, had been one of the social events of that season in Paris. He had been a great man, a favourite of fortune until the Revolution deprived him of his patrimony and of his income. The proletarian government laid ruthless hands on the former, by forcing him to farm out his lands to tenants who refused to pay him any rent. His income in a couple of years dwindled down to nothing. Most of his former clients had emigrated, all of them were now too poor to need legal or financial advice.

Maître de Croissy was forced presently to give up his magnificent house and sumptuous offices on the Quai. He installed his wife and child in a cheap apartment in the Rue Picpus, and carried on what legal business came his way in a set of rooms which had once been the private apartments of the Austrian banker's valet. Thither he trudged on foot every morning, whatever the weather, and here he interviewed needy bourgeois, groaning under taxation, or out-at-elbows tradesmen on the verge of bankruptcy. He was no longer Maître de Croissy, only plain Citizen Croissy, thankful that men like Chabot or Bazire reposed confidence in him, or that the great Danton deigned to put some legal business in his way. Where six clerks had scarcely been sufficient to aid him in getting through the work of the day, he had only one now—the faithful Reversac—who had obstinately refused to take his congé, when all the others were dismissed.

"You would not throw me out into the street to stave, would you, Maître?" had been the young man's earnest plea.

"But you can find other work, Maurice," de Croissy had argued, not without reason, for Maurice Reversac was a fully qualified lawyer, he was young and active and of a surety he could always have made a living for himself. "And I cannot afford to pay you an adequate salary."

"Give me board and lodging, Maître," Reversac had entreated with obstinacy: "I want nothing else. I have a few louis put by: my clothes will last me three or four years, and by that time..."

"Yes! by that time..." Maître de Croissy sighed. He had been hopeful once that sanity would return presently to the people of France, that this era of chaos and cruelty, of persecution and oppression, could not possibly last. But of late he had become more and more despondent, more and more hopeless. When Frenchmen, after having deposed their anointed king, began to talk of putting him on his trial like a common criminal, it must mean that they had become possessed of the demon of insanity, a tenacious demon who would not easily be exorcised.

But Maurice Reversac got his way. He had board and lodging in the apartment of the Rue Picpus, and in the mornings, whatever the weather, he trudged over to the Rue de la Monnaie and aired, dusted and swept the dingy office of the great advocate. In the evenings the two men would almost invariably walk back together to the Rue Picpus. The cheap, exiguous apartment meant home for both of them, and in it they found what measure of happiness their own hearts helped them to attain. For Bastien de Croissy happiness meant home-life, his love for his wife and child. For Maurice Reversac it meant living under the same roof with Josette, seeing her every day, walking with her in the evenings under the chestnut trees of Cour de la Reine.

A little higher up the narrow Passage des Fèves there stood at this same time a small eating-house, frequented chiefly by the mechanics of the Government workshops close by. It bore the sign: "Aux Trois Singes." Two steps down from the street level gave access to it through a narrow doorway. Food and drink were as cheap here as anywhere, and the landlord, a man named Furet, had the great merit of being rather deaf, and having an impediment in his speech. Added to this was the fact that he had never learned to read or write. These three attributes made of Furet an ideal landlord in a place where men with empty bellies and empty pockets were wont to let themselves go in the matter of grumbling at the present state of affairs, and at the device "Liberté, Fraternité, Égalité" which by order of the revolutionary government was emblazoned outside and in every building to which the public had access.

Furet being deaf could not spy: being mute he could not denounce. Figuratively speaking men loosened their belts when they sat at one of the trestle tables inside the Cabaret des Trois Singes, sipped their sour wine and munched their meal of stale bread and boiled beans. They loosened their belts and talked of the slave-driving that went on in the Government workshops, the tyranny of the overseers, the ever-increasing cost of living, and the paucity of their wages, certain that Furet neither heard what they said nor would be able to repeat the little that he heard.

Inside the cabaret there were two tables that were considered privileged. They were no tables properly speaking, but just empty wine-casks, standing on end, each in a recess to right and left of the narrow doorway. A couple of three-legged stools accommodated two customers and two only in each recess, and those who wished to avail themselves of the privilege of sitting there were expected to order a bottle of Furet's best wine. This was one of those unwritten laws which no frequenter of the Three Monkeys every thought of ignoring. Furet, though an ideal landlord in so many respects, could turn nasty when he chose.

On a sultry evening in the late August of '92, two men were sitting in one of these privileged recesses in the Cabaret des Trois Singes. They had talked earnestly for the past hour, always sinking their voices to a whisper. A bottle of Citizen Furet's best wine stood on the cask between them, but though they had been in the place for over an hour, the bottle was still more than half full. They seemed too deeply engrossed in conversation to waste time in drink.

One of the men was short and thick-set with dark hair and marked Levantine features. He spoke French fluently but with a throaty accent which betrayed his German origin. Whenever he wished to emphasise a point he struck the top of the wine-stained cask with the palm of his fleshy hand.

The other man was Bastien de Croissy. Earlier in the day he had received an anonymous message requesting a private meeting in the Cabaret des Trois Singes. The matter, the message averred, concerned the wellfare of France and the safety of the King. Bastien was no coward, and the wording of the message was a sure passport to his confidence. He sent Maurice Reversac home early and kept the mysterious tryst.

His anonymous correspondent introduced himself as a representative of Baron de Batz, well known to Bastien as they agent of the Austrian Government and confidant of the Emperor, whose intrigues and schemes for the overthrow of the revolutionary government of France had been as daring in conception as they were futile in execution.

"But this time," the man had declared with complete self-assurance, "with your help, cher maître, we are bound to succeed."

And he had elaborated the plan conceived in Vienna by de Batz. A wonderful plan! Neither more nor less than bribing with Austrian gold some of the more venal members of their own party, and the restoration of the monarchy.

Bastien de Croissy was sceptical. He did not believe that any of the more influential Terrorists would risk their necks in so daring an intrigue. Other ways—surer ways—ought to be found, and found quickly for the King's life was indeed in peril: not only the King's but the Queen's and the lives of all the Royal family. But the Austrian agent was obstinate.

"It is from inside the National Convention that M. le Baron wants help. That he must have. If he has the co-operation of half a dozen members of the Executive, he can do the rest, and guarantee success."

Then, as de Croissy still appeared to hesitate, he laid his fleshy hand on the advocate's arm.

"Voyons, cher maître," he said, "you have the overthrow of this abominable Government just as much at heart as M. le Baron, and we none of us question your loyalty to the dynasty."

"It is not want of loyalty," de Croissy retorted hotly, "that makes me hesitate."

"What then?"

"Prudence! lest by a false move we aggravate the peril of our King."

The other shrugged.

"Well! of course," he said, "we reckon that you, cher maître, know the men with whom we wish to deal."

"Yes!" Bastien admitted, "I certainly do."

"They are venal?"

"Yes!"

"Greedy?"

"Yes!"

"Ambitious?"

"For their own pockets, yes."

"Well then?"

There was a pause. A murmur of conversation was going on all round. Some of Furet's customers were munching noisily or drinking with a gurgling sound, others were knocking dominoes about. There was no fear of eavesdropping in this dark and secluded recess where two men were discussing the destinies of France. One was the emissary of a foreign Power, the other an ardent royalist. Both had the same object in view: to save the King and his family from death, and to overthrow a government of assassins, who contemplated adding the crime of regicide to their many malefactions.

"M. le Baron," the foreign agent resumed with increased persuasiveness after a slight pause, "I need not tell you what is their provenance. Our Emperor is not going to see his sister at the mercy of a horde of assassins. M. le Baron is in his council: he will pay twenty thousand louis each to any dozen men who will lend him a hand in this affair."

"A dozen?" de Croissy exclaimed, then added with disheartened sigh: "Where to find them!"

"We are looking to you, cher maître."

"I have no influence. Not now."

"But you know the right men," the agent argued, and added significantly: "You have been watched, you know."

"I guessed."

"We know that you have business relations with members of the Convention who can be very useful to us."

"Which of them had you thought of?"

"Well! there is Chabot, for instance: the unfrocked friar."

"God in Heaven!" de Croissy exclaimed: "what a tool."

"The end will justify the means, my friend," the other retorted drily. Then he added: "And Chabot's brother-in-law Bazire."

"Both these men," de Croissy admitted, "would sell their souls, if they possessed one."

"Then there's Fabre d'Eglantine, Danton's friend."

"You are well informed."

"What about Danton himself?"

The Austrian leaned over the table, eager, excited, conscious that the Frenchman was wavering. Clearly de Croissy's scepticism was on the point of giving way before the other's enthusiasm and certainty of success. It was such a wonderful vista that was being unfolded before him. France free from the tyranny of agitation! the King restored to his throne! the country once more happy and prosperous under a stable government as ordained by God! So thought de Croissy as he lent a more and more willing ear to the projects of de Batz. He himself mentioned several names of men who might prove useful in the scheme; names of men who might be willing to betray their party for Austrian gold. There were a good many of these: agitators who were corrupt and venal, who had incited the needy and the ignorant to all kinds of barbarous deeds, not from any striving after a humanitarian ideal, but for what they themselves could get out of the social upheaval and its attendant chaos.

"If I lend a hand in your scheme," de Croissy said presently with earnest emphasis, "it must be understood that their first aim is the restoration of our King to his throne."

"Of course, cher maître, of course," the other asserted equally forcibly. "Surely you can believe in M. le Baron's disinterested motives."

"What we'll have to do," he continued eagerly, "will be to promise the men whom you will have chosen for the purpose, a certain sum of money, to be paid to them as soon as all the members of the Royal family are safely out of France... we don't want one of the Royal Princesses to be detained as hostage, do we?... Then we can promise them a further and larger sum to be paid when their Majesties make their state re-entry into their capital."

There was no doubt by now that Maître de Croissy's enthusiasm was fully aroused. He was one of those men for whom dynasty and the right of Kings amounted to a religion. For him, all that he had suffered in the past in the way of privations and loss of wealth and prestige was as nothing compared with the horror which he felt at sight of the humiliations which miscreants had imposed upon his King. To save the King! to bring him back triumphant to the throne of his forbears, were thoughts and hopes that filled Bastien de Croissy's soul with intense excitement. It was only with half an ear that he listened to the foreign emissary's further scheme: the ultimate undoing of that herd of assassins. He did not care what happened once the great goal was attained. Let those corrupt knaves of whom the Austrian Emperor stood in need thrive and batten on their own villainy, Bastien de Croissy did not care.

"You see the idea, do you not, cher maître?" the emissary was saying.

"Yes! oh yes!" Bastien murmured vaguely.

"Get as much letter-writing as you can out of the black-guards. Let us have as much written proof of their venality as possible. Then if ever these jackals rear their heads again, we can proclaim their turpitude before the entire world, discredit them before their ignorant dupes, and see them suffer humiliation and die the shameful death which they had planned for their King."

The meeting between the two men lasted well into the night. In the dingy apartment of the Rue Picpus Louise de Croissy sat up, waiting anxiously for her husband. Maurice Reversac, whom she questioned repeatedly, could tell her nothing of Maître de Croissy's whereabouts, beyond the fact that he was keeping a business appointment, made by a new client who desired to remain anonymous. When Bastien finally came home, he looked tired, but singularly excited. Never since the first dark days of the Revolution three years ago had Louise seen him with such flaming eyes, or heard such cheerful, not to say optimistic words from his lips. But he said nothing to her about his interview with the agent of Baron de Batz, he only talked of the brighter outlook in the future. God, he said, would soon tire of the wickedness of men: the present terrible conditions could not possibly last. The King would soon come into his own again.

Louise was quickly infused with some of his enthusiasm, but she did not worry him with questions. Hers was one of those easy-going dispositions that are willing to accept things as they come without probing into the whys and wherefores of events. She had a profound admiration for and deep trust in her clever husband: he appeared hopeful for the future—more hopeful than he had been for a long time, and that was enough for Louise. It was only to the faithful Maurice Reversac that de Croissy spoke of his interview with the Austrian emissary, and the young man tried very hard to show some enthusiasm over the scheme, and to share his employer's optimism and hopes for the future. Maurice Reversac, though painstaking and a very capable lawyer, was not exactly brilliant: against that his love for his employer and his employers family was so genuine and so great that it gave him what amounted to intuition, almost a foreknowledge of any change, good or evil, that destiny had in store for them. And as he listened to Maître de Croissy's earnest talk, he felt a strange foreboding that all would not be well with this scheme: that somehow or other it would lead to disaster, and all the while that he sat at his desk that day copying the letters which the advocate had dictated to him—letters which were in the nature of tentacles, stretched out to catch a set of knaves—he felt an overwhelming temptation to throw himself at his employer's feet and beg him not to sully his hands by contact with this foreign intrigue.

But the temptation had to be resisted. Bastien de Croissy was not the type of man who could be swayed from his purpose by the vapourings of his young clerk, however devoted he might be. And so the letters were written—half a score in all—requests by Citizen Croissy of the Paris bar for private interviews with various influential members of the Convention on matters of urgency to the State.

CHAPTER II

More than a year had gone by since then, and Bastien de Croissy had seen all his fondly cherished hopes turn to despair one by one. There had been no break in the dark clouds of chaos and misery that enveloped the beautiful land of France. Indeed they had gathered, darker and more stormy than before. And now had come what appeared to be the darkest days of all—the autumn of 1793. The King, condemned to death by a majority of 48 in an Assembly of over 700 members, had paid with his life for all the errors, the weaknesses, the misunderstandings of the past: the unfortunate Queen, separated from her children and from all those she cared for, accused of the vilest crimes that distorted minds could invent, was awaiting trial and inevitable death.

The various political parties—the factions and the clubs—were vying with one another in ruthlessness and cruelty. Danton the lion and Robespierre the jackal were at one another's throats; it still meant the mere spin of a coin as to which would succeed in destroying the other. The houses of detention were filled to overflowing, while the guillotine did its grim work day by day, hour by hour, without distinction of rank or sex, or of age. The Law of the Suspect had just been passed, and it was no longer necessary for an unfortunate individual to do or say anything that the Committee of Public Safety might deem counter-revolutionary, it was sufficient to be suspected of such tendencies for denunciation to follow, then arrest and finally death with but the mockery of a trial, without pleading or defence. And while the Terrorists were intent on destroying one another the country was threatened by foes without and within. Famine and disease stalked in the wake of persecution. The countryside was devastated, there were not enough hands left to till the ground and the cities were a prey to epidemics. On the frontier the victorious allied armies were advancing on the sacred soil of France. The English were pouring in from Belgium, the Russians came across the Rhine, the Spaniards crossed the gorges of the Pyrenees, whilst the torch of civil war was blazing anew in La Vendée.

Danton's cry: "To arms!" and "La Patrie is in danger!" resounded from end to end of the land. It echoed through the deserted cities and over the barren fields, while three hundred thousand "Soldiers of Liberty" marched to the frontiers, ill-clothed, ill-shod, ill-fed, to drive back the foreign invader from the gates of France. An epic, what? Worthy of a holier cause.

Those who were left behind, who were old, or weak, or indispensable, had to bear their share in the defence of La Patrie. France was transformed into an immense camp of fighters and workers. The women sewed shirts and knitted socks, salted meat and stitched breeches, and looked after their children and their homes as best they could. France came first, the home was a bad second.

It was then that little Charles-Léon fell ill. That was the beginning of the tragedy. He had always been delicate, which was not to be wondered at, seeing that he was born during the days immediately preceding the Revolution, at the time when the entire world, such as Louise de Croissy had known it, was crumbling to dust at her feet. She never thought he would live, the dear, puny mite, the precious son, whom she and Bastien had longed for, prayed for, by year until this awful winter when food became scarce and poor, and milk was almost unobtainable.

Kind old Doctor Larousse said it was nothing serious, but the child must have change of air. Paris was too unhealthy these days for delicate children. Change of air? Heavens above! how was it to be got? Louise questioned old Citizen Larousse:

"Can you get me a permit, doctor? We still have a small house in the Isère district, not far from Grenoble. I could take my boy there."

"Yes. I can get you a permit for the child—at least, I think so—under the circumstances."

"And one for me?"

"Yes, one for you—to last a week."

"How do you mean to last a week?"

"Well, you can get the diligence to Grenoble. It takes a couple of days. Then you can stay in your house, say, fourty-eight hours to see the child installed. Two days to come back by diligence..."

"But I couldn't come back."

"I'm afraid you'll have to. No one is allowed to be absent from permanent domicile more than seven days. You know that, Citizeness, surely."

"But I couldn't leave Charles-Léon."

"Why not? There is not very much the matter with him. And country air..."

Louise was losing her patience. How obtuse men are, even the best of them!

"But there is no one over there to look after him," she argued.

"Surely a respectable woman from the village would..."

This time she felt her temper rising. "And you suppose that I would leave this sick baby in the care of a stranger?"

"Haven't you a relation who would look after him? Mother? Sister?"

"My mother is dead. I have no sisters. Nor would I leave Charles-Léon in anyone's care but mine."

The doctor shrugged. He was very kind, but he had seen this sort of thing so often lately, and he was powerless to help.

"I am afraid..." he said.

"Citizen Larousse," Louise broke in firmly, "you must give me a certificate that my child is too ill to be separated from his mother."

"Impossible, Citizeness."

"Won't you try?"

"I have tried—for others—often, but it's no use. You know what the decrees of the Convention are these days... no one dares..."

"And I am to see my child perish for want of a scrap of paper?"

Again the old man shrugged. He was a busy man and there were others. Presently he took his leave: there was nothing that he could do, so why should he stay? Louise hardly noticed his going. She stood there like a block of stone, a carved image of despair. The wan cheeks of the sick child seemed less bloodless than hers.

"Louise!"

Josette Gravier had been standing beside the cot all this time. Charles-Léon's tiny hand had fastened round one of her fingers and she didn't like to move, but she had lost nothing of what was going on. Her eyes, those lovely deep blue eyes of hers that seemed to shine, to emit light when she was excited, were fixed on Louise de Croissy. She had loved her and served her ever since Louise's dying mother, Madame de Vadeleur, confided the care of her baby daughter to Madame Gravier, the farmer's wife, Josette's mother, who had just lost her own new-born baby, the same age as Louise. Josette, Ma'me Gravier's first-born, was three years old at the time and, oh! how she took the little new-comer to her heart! She and Louise grew up together like sisters. They shared childish joys and tears. The old farmhouse used to ring with their laughter and the patter of their tiny feet. Papa Gravier taught them to ride and to milk the nanny-goats; they had rabbits of their own, chickens and runner-ducks.

Together they went to the Convent school of the Visitation to learn everything that was desirable for young ladies to know, sewing and embroidery, calligraphy and recitation, a smattering of history and geography, and the art of letter-writing. For there was to be no difference in the education of Louise de Vandeleur, the motherless daughter of the distinguished general, aide-de-camp to His Majesty, and of Josette Gravier, the farmer's daughter.

When, in the course of time, Louise married Bastien de Croissy, the eminent advocate at the Paris bar, Josette nearly broke her heart at parting from her lifelong friend.

Then came the dark days of '89. Papa Gravier was killed during the revolutionary riots in Grenoble; maman died of a broken heart, and Louise begged Josette to come and live with her. The farm was sold, the girl had a small competence; she went up to Paris and continued to love and serve Louise as she had done in the past. She was her comfort and her help during those first terrible days of the Revolution: she was her moral support now that the shadow of the guillotine lay menacing over the household of the once successful lawyer. La Patrie in danger claimed so many hours of her day; she, too, had to sew shirts and stitch breeches for the "Soldiers of Liberty," but her evenings, her nights, her early mornings were her own, and these she devoted to the service of Louise and of Charles-Léon.

She had a tiny room in the apartment of the Rue Picpus, but to her loving little heart that room was paradise, for here, when she was at home, she had Charles-Léon to play with, she had his little clothes to wash and to iron, she saw his great dark eyes, so like his mother's fixed upon her while she told him tales of romance and of chivalry. The boy was only five at this time, but he was strangely precocious where such tales were concerned, he seemed to understand and appreciate the mighty deeds of Hector and Achilles, of Bayard and Joan of Arc, the stories of the Crusades, of Godfrey de Bouillon and Richard of the Lionheart. Perhaps it was because he felt himself to be weak and puny and knew with the unexplainable instinct of childhood that he would never be big enough or strong enough to emulate those deeds of valour, that he loved to hear Josette recount them to him with a wealth of detail supplied by her romantic imagination.

But if Charles-Léon loved to hear these stories of the past, far more eagerly did he listen to those of to-day, and in the recounting of heroic adventures which not only had happened recently, but went on almost every day, Josette's storehouse of hair-raising narratives was well-nigh inexhaustible. Through her impassioned rhetoric he first heard of the heroic deeds of that amazing Englishman who went by the curious name of the Scarlet Pimpernel. Josette told him about a number of gallant gentlemen who had taken such compassion on the sufferings of the innocent that they devoted their lives to rescuing those who were persecuted and oppressed by the tyrannical Government of the day. She told him how women and children, old or feeble men, dragged before a tribunal that knew of no issue save the sentence of death, were spirited away out of prison walls or from the very tumbrils that were taking them to the guillotine, spirited away as if by a miracle, and through the agency of this mysterious hero whose identity had always remained unknown, but whose deeds of self-sacrifice were surely writ large in the book of the Recording Angel.

And while Josette unfolded these tales of valour, and the boy listened to her awed and silent, her eyes would shine with unshed tears, and her lips quiver with enthusiasm. She had made a fetish of the Scarlet Pimpernel: had enshrined him in her heart like a demi-god, and this hero-worship grew all the more fervent within her as she found no response to her enthusiasm in the bosom of her adopted family, only in Charles-Léon. She was too gentle and timid to speak openly of this hero-worship to Maître de Croissy, and Louise, whom she adored, was wont to grow slightly sarcastic at the expense of Josette's imaginary hero. She did not believe in his existence at all, and thought that all the tales of miraculous rescues set down to his agency were either mere coincidence or just the product of a romantic girl's fantasy. As for Maurice Reversac—well! little Josette thought him too dull and unimaginative to appreciate the almost legendary personality of the Scarlet Pimpernel, so, whenever a fresh tale got about the city of how a whole batch of innocent men, women and children had escaped out of France on the very eve of their arrest or condemnation to death, Josette kept the tale to herself, until she and Charles-Léon were alone in her little room, and she found response to her enthusiasm in the boy's glowing eyes and his murmur of passionate admiration.

When Charles-Léon's chronic weakness turned to actual, serious anemia, all the joy seemed to go out of Josette's life. Real joy, that is; for she went about outwardly just as gay as before, singing, crooning to the little invalid, cheering Louise and comforting Bastien, who spoke of her now as the angel in the house. Every minute that she could spare she spent by the side of Charles-Léon's little bed, and when no one was listening she would whisper into his ear some of the old stories which he loved. Then if the ghost of a smile came round the child's pallid lips, Josette would feel almost happy, even though she felt ready to burst into tears.

And now, as soon as the old doctor had gone, Josette disengaged her hand from the sick child's grasp and put her arms around Louise's shoulders.

"We must not lose heart, Louise chérie," she said. "There must be a way out of this impasse."

"A way out?" Louise murmured. "Oh, if I only knew!"

"Sit down here, chérie, and let me talk to you."

There was a measure of comfort even in Josette's voice. It was low and a trifle husky; such a voice as some women have whose mission in life is to comfort and to soothe. She made Louise sit down in the big armchair; then she knelt down in front of her, her little hands clasped together and resting in Louise's lap.

"Listen, Louise chérie," she said with great excitement.

Louise looked down on the beautiful eager face of her friend; the soft red lips were quivering with excitement; the large luminous eyes were aglow with a strange enthusiasm. She felt puzzled, for it was not in Josette's nature to show so much emotion. She was always deemed quiet and sensible. She never spoke at random, and never made a show of her fantastic dreams.

"Well, darling?" Louise said listlessly: "I am listening. What is it?"

Josette looked up, wide-eyed and eager, straight into her friend's face.

"What we must do, chérie," she said with earnest emphasis, "is to get in touch with those wonderful Englishmen. You know who I mean. They have already accomplished miracles on behalf of innocent men, women and children, of people who were in a worse plight than we are now."

Louise frowned. She knew well enough what Josette meant: she had often laughed at the girl's enthusiasm over this imaginary hero, who seemed to haunt her dreams. But just now she felt that there was something flippant and unseemly in talking such fantastic rubbish: dreams seemed out of place when reality was so heart-breaking. She tried to rise to push Josette away, but the girl clung to her and would not let her go.

"I don't know what you are talking about, Josette," Louise said coldly at last. "This is not the time for jest, or for talking of things that only exist in your imagination."

Josette shook her head.

"Why do you say that, Louise chérie? Why should you deliberately close your eyes and ears to facts—hard, sober, solid facts that everybody knows, that everybody admits to be true? I should have thought," the girl went on in her earnest, persuasive way, "that with this terrible thing hanging over you—Charles-Léon getting more and more ill, till there's no hope of his recovery..."

"Josette!! Don't!" Louise cried out in an agony of reproach.

"I must," Josette insisted with quiet force: "it is my duty to make you look straight at facts as they are; and I say, that with this terrible thing hanging over us, you must cast off foolish prejudices and open your mind to what is the truth and will be your salvation."

Louise looked down at the beautiful, eager face turned up to hers. She felt all of a sudden strangely moved. Of course Josette was talking nonsense. Dear, sensible, quiet little Josette! She was simple and not at all clever, but it was funny, to say the least of it, how persuasive she could be when she had set her mind on anything. Even over small things she would sometimes wax so eloquent that there was no resisting her. No! she was not clever, but she was extra-ordinarily shrewd where the welfare of those she loved was in question. And she adored Louise and worshipped Charles-Léon.

Since the doctor's visit Louise had felt herself floundering in such a torrent of grief that she was ready to clutch at any straw that would save her from despair. Josette was talking nonsense, of course. All the family were wont to chaff her over her adoration of the legendary hero, so much so, in fact, that the girl had ceased altogether to talk about him. But now her eyes were positively glowing with enthusiasm, and it seemed to Louise, as she gazed into them, that they radiated hope and trust. And Louise was so longing for a ray of hope.

"I suppose," she said with a wan smile, "that you are harping on your favourite string."

"I am," Josette admitted with fervour.

Then as Louise, still obstinate and unbelieving, gave a slight shrug and a sigh, the girl continued:

"Surely, Louise chérie, you have heard other people besides me—clever, distinguished, important people—talk of the Scarlet Pimpernel."

"I have," Louise admitted: "but only in a vague way."

"And what he did for the Maillys?"

"The general's widow, you mean?"

"Yes. She and her sister and the two children were simply snatched away from under the very noses of the guard who were taking them to execution."

"I did hear something about that," was Louise's dry comment; "but..."

"And of about the de Tournays?" Josette broke in eagerly.

"They are in England now. So I heard."

"They are. And who took them there? The Marquis was in hiding in the woods near his property: Mme. de Tournay and Suzanne were in terror for him and in fear for their lives. It was said openly that their arrest was imminent. And when the National Guard went to arrest them, Mm. de Tournay and Suzanne were gone, and the Marquis was never found. You've said it yourself, they are in England now."

"But Josette darling," Louise argued obstinately, "there's nothing to say in all those stories that any mysterious Englishman had aught to do with the Maillys and the Tournays."

"Who then?"

"It was the intervention of God."

Josette shook her pretty head somewhat sadly.

"God does not intervene directly these days, my darling," she said; "He chooses great and good men to do His bidding."

"And I don't see," Louise concluded with some impatience, "I don't see what the Maillys or the Tournays have to do with me and Charles-Léon."

But at this Josette's angelic temper very nearly forsook her.

"Don't be obtuse, Louise," she cried hotly. "We don't want to get in touch with the Maillys or the Tournays. I never suggested anything so ridiculous. All I mean was that they and hundreds—yes, hundreds—of others owe their life to the Scarlet Pimpernel."

Tears of vexation rose from her loving heart at Louise's obduracy. She it was who tried to rise now, but this time Louise held her down: Poor Louise! She did so long to believe—really believe. Hope is such a precious thing when the heart is full to bursting of anxiety and sorrow. And she longed for hope and for faith: the same hope that made Josette's eyes sparkle and gave a ring of sanguine expectation to her voice.

"Don't run away, Josette," she pleaded. "You don't know how I envy you your hero-worship and your trust. But listen, darling: even if your Scarlet Pimpernel does exist—see, I no longer say that he does not—even if he does, he knows nothing about us. How then can he interfere?"

Josette drew a sigh of relief. For the first time since the hot argument had started she felt that she was gaining ground. Her faith was going to prevail. Louise's scepticism had changed: the look of despair had gone and there was a light in her eyes which suggested that hope had crept at last into her heart. The zealot had vanquished the obstinacy of the sceptic, and Josette having gained her point could speak more calmly now.

She shook her head and smiled.

"Don't you believe it, chérie," she said gently.

"Believe what?"

"That the Scarlet Pimpernel knows nothing about you. He does. I am sure he does. All you have to do is just to invoke him in your heart."

"Nonsense, Josette," Louise protested. "You are not pretending, I suppose, that this Englishman is a supernatural being?"

"I don't know about that," said the young devotee, "but I do know that he is the bravest, finest man that ever lived. And I know also that wherever there is a great misfortune or a great sorrow he appears like a young god, and at once care and anxiety disappear, and grief is turned to joy."

"I wish I could have your faith in miracles, my Josette."

"You need not call it a miracle. The good deeds of the Scarlet Pimpernel are absolutely real."

"But even so, my dear, what can we do? We don't know where to find him. And if we did, what could he do for us—for Charles-Léon?"

"He can get you a permit to go into the country with Charles-Léon, and to remain with him until he is well again."

"I don't believe that. Nothing short of a miracle can accomplish that. You heard what the doctor said."

"Well, I say that the Scarlet Pimpernel can do anything! And I mean to get in touch with him."

"You are stupid, Josette."

"And you are a woman of little faith. Why don't you read your Bible, and see what it says there about faith?"

Louise shrugged. "The Bible," she said coolly, "tells us about moving mountains by faith, but nothing about finding a needle in a haystack or a mysterious Englishman in the streets of Paris."

But Josette was now proof against her friend's sarcasm. She jumped to her feet and put her arms round Louise.

"Well!" she rejoined, "my faith is going to find him, that's all I know. I wish," she went on with a comic little inflection of her voice, "that I had not wasted this past hour in trying to put some of that faith into you. And now I know that I shall have to spend at least another hour driving it into Maurice's wooden head."

Louise smiled. "Why Maurice?" she asked.

"For the same reason," the girl replied, "that I had to wear myself out in order to break your obstinacy. It will take me some time perhaps, as you say, to find the Scarlet Pimpernel in the streets of Paris. I shall have to be out and about a great deal, and if I had said nothing to any of you, you and Maurice and even Bastien would always have been asking me questions: where I had been? why did I go out? why was I late for dinner? And Maurice would have gone about looking like a bear with a sore head, whenever I refused to go for a walk with him. So of course," Josette concluded naïvely, "I shall have to tell him."

Louise said nothing more after that: she sat with clasped hands and eyes fixed into vacancy, thinking, hoping, or perhaps just praying for hope.

But Josette having had her say went across the room to Charles-Léon's little bed. She leaned over him and kissed him. He whispered her name and added feebly: "Tell me some more... about the Scarlet Pimpernel... when will he come... to take me away... to England?"

"Soon," Josette murmured in reply: "very soon. Do not doubt it, my precious. God will send him to you very soon."

Then without another word to Louise she ran quickly out of the room.

CHAPTER III

Josette had picked up her cape and slung it round her shoulders; she pulled the hood over her fair curls and ran swiftly down the stairs and out into the street. Thoughts of the Scarlet Pimpernel had a way of whipping up her blood. When she spoke of him she at once wanted to be up and doing. She wanted to be up and doing something that would emulate the marvellous deeds of that mysterious hero of romance—deeds which she had heard recounted with bated breath by her fellow-workers in the Government workshops where breeches were stitched and stockings knitted by the hundred for the "Soldiers of Liberty," marching against the foreign foe.

Josette on this late afternoon had to put in a couple of hours at the workshop. At six o'clock when the light gave out she would be free; and at six o'clock Maurice Reversac would of a certainty be outside the gates of the workshop waiting to escort her first for a walk along the Quai or the Cour la Reine and then home to cook the family supper.

She came out of the workshop on this late afternoon with glowing eyes and flaming cheeks, and nearly ran past Maurice without seeing him as her mind was so full of other things. She was humming a tune as she ran. Maurice was waiting for her at the gate, and he called to her. He felt very happy all of a sudden because Josette seemed so pleased to see him.

"Maurice!" she cried, "I am so glad you have come."

Maurice, being young and up to his eyes in love, did not think of asking her why she should be so glad. She was glad to see him and that was enough for any lover. He took hold of her by the elbow and led her through the narrow streets as far as the Quai and then over to Cour la Reine, where there were seats under the chestnut trees from which the big prickly burrs were falling fast, and split as they fell, revealing the lovely smooth surface of the chestnuts, in colour like Josette's hair; and as the last glimmer of daylight faded into evening the sparrows in the trees kicked up a great shindy, which was like a paean of joy in complete accord with Maurice's mood.

Nor did Maurice notice that Josette was absorbed; her eyes shone more brightly than usual, and her lips, which were so like ripe fruit, were slightly parted, and Maurice was just aching for a kiss.

He persuaded her to sit down: the air was so soft and balmy—lovely autumn evening with the scent of ripe fruit about; and those sparrows up in the chestnut trees did kick up such a shindy before tucking their little heads under their wings for the night. There were a few passers-by—not many—and this corner of old Paris appeared singularly peaceful, with a whole world of dreams and hope between it and the horrors of the Revolution. Yet this was the hour when the crowds that assembled daily on the Place de la Barrière du Trône to watch the guillotine at its dread work wandered, tired and silent, back to their homes, and when rattling carts bore their gruesome burdens to the public burying-place.

But what are social upheavals, revolutions or cataclysms to a lover absorbed in the contemplation of his beloved? Maurice Reversac sat beside Josette and could see her adorable profile with the small tip-tilted nose and the outline of her cheek so like a ripe peach. Josette sat silent and motionless at first, so Maurice felt emboldened to put out a timid hand and take hold of hers. She made no resistance and he thought of a surety that he would swoon with joy because she allowed that exquisite little hand to rest contented in his great rough palm. It felt just like a bird, soft and warm and fluttering, like those sparrows in up the trees.

"Josette," Maurice ventured to murmur after a little while, "you are glad to see me... you said so... didn't you, Josette?"

She was not looking at him, but he didn't mind that, for though the twilight was fast drawing in he could still see her adorable profile—that delicious tip-tilted nose and the lashes that curled like a fringe of gold over her eyes. The hood had fallen back from her head and the soft evening breeze stirred the tendrils of her chestnut-coloured hair.

"You are so beautiful, Josette," Maurice sighed, "and I am such a clumsy lout, but I would know how to make you happy. Happy! My God! I would make you as happy as the birds—without a care in the world. And all day you would just go about singing—singing—because you would have forgotten by then what sorrow was like."

Encouraged by her silence he ventured to draw a little nearer to her.

"I have seen," he murmured quite close to her ear, "an apartment that would be just the right setting for you, Josette darling: only three rooms and a little kitchen, but the morning sun comes pouring in through the big windows and there is a clump of chestnut trees in front in which the birds will sing in the spring from early dawn while you still lie in bed. I shall have got up by then and will be in the kitchen getting some hot milk for you; then I will bring you the warm milk, and while you drink it I shall sit and watch the sunshine play about in your hair."

Never before had Maurice plucked up sufficient courage to talk at such length, usually when Josette was beside him he was so absorbed in looking at her and longing for her that his tongue refused him service; for these were days when true lovers were timid and la jeune fille was an almost sacred being, whose limpid soul no profane word dared disturb, and Maurice had been brought up by an adoring mother in these rigid principles. This cruel and godless Revolution had, indeed, shattered many ideals and toughened the fibres of men's hearts and women's sensibilities, else Maurice would never have dared thus to approach the object of his dreams—her whom he hoped one day to have for wife.

Josette's silence had emboldened him, and the fact that she had allowed her hand to rest in his all this while. Now he actually dared to put out his arm and encircle her shoulders; he was, in fact, drawing her to him, feeling that he was on the point of stepping across the threshold of Paradise, when slowly she turned her face to him and looked him straight between the eyes. Her own appeared puzzled and there was a frown as of great perplexity between her brows.

"Maurice," she asked, and there was no doubt that she was both puzzled and astonished, "are you, perchance, trying to make love to me?"

Then, as he remained silent and looked, in his turn, both bewildered and hurt, she gave a light laugh, gently disengaged her hand and patted him on the cheek.

"My poor Maurice!" she said, "I wish I had listened sooner, but I was thinking of other things...."

When a man had had the feeling that he has actually reached the gates of Paradise and that a kindly Saint Peter was already rattling his keys so as to let him in—when he has felt this for over half an hour and then, in a few seconds, is hurtled down into an abyss of disappointment, his first sensation is as if he had been stunned by a terrific blow on the head, and he becomes entirely tongue-tied.

Bewildered and dumb, all Maurice could do was to stare at the adorable vision of a golden-haired girl whom he worshipped and who, with a light heart and a gay laugh, had just dealt him the most cruel blow that any man had ever been called upon to endure.

The worst of it was that this adorable golden-haired girl had apparently no notion of how cruel had been the blow, for she prattled on about the other things of which she had been thinking quite oblivious of the subject-matter of poor Maurice's impassioned pleading.

"Maurice dear," she said, "listen to me and do not talk nonsense."

Nonsense!! Ye gods!

"You have got to help me, Maurice, to find the Scarlet Pimpernel."

Her beautiful eyes, which she turned full upon him, were aglow with enthusiasm—enthusiasm for something in which he had no share. Nor did he understand what she was talking about. All he knew was that she had dismissed his pleading as nonsense, and that with a curious smile on her lips she was just turning a knife round and round in his heart.

And, oh, how that hurt!

But she also said that she wanted his help, so he tried very hard to get at her meaning, though she seemed to be prattling on rather inconsequently.

"Charles-Léon," she said, "is very ill, you know, Maurice dear—that is, not so very ill, but the doctor says he must have change of air or he will perish in a decline."

"A doctor can always get a permit for a patient in extremis..." Maurice put in, assuming a judicial manner.

"Don't be stupid, Maurice!" she retorted impatiently. "We all know that the doctor can get a permit for Charles-Léon, but he can't get one for Louise or for me, and where is Charles-Léon to go with neither of us to look after him?"

"Then what's to be done?"

"Try and listen more attentively, Maurice," she retorted. "You are not really listening."

"I am," he protested, "I swear I am!"

"Really—really?"

"Really, Josette—with both ears and all the intelligence I've got."

"Very well, then. You have heard of the Scarlet Pimpernel, haven't you?"

"We all have—in a way."

"What do you mean by 'in a way'?"

"Well, no one is quite sure if he really exists, and..."

"Maurice, don't, in Heaven's name, be stupid! You must have brains or Maître de Croissy could not do with you as his confidential clerk. So do use your brains, Maurice, and tell me if the Scarlet Pimpernel does not exist, then how did the Maillys get away—and the Frontenacs—and the Tournays—and—and...? Oh, Maurice, I hate your being so stupid!"

"You have only got to tell me, Josette, what you wish me to do," poor Maurice put in very humbly, "and I will do it, of course."

"I want you to help me find the Scarlet Pimpernel."

"Gladly will I help you, Josette; but won't it be like looking for a needle in a haystack?"

"Not at all," this intrepid little Joan of Arc asserted. "Listen, Maurice! In our workshop there is a girl, Agnes Minet, who was at one time in service with a Madame Carré, whose son Antoine was in hiding because he was threatened with arrest. His mother didn't dare write to him lest her letters be intercepted. Well, there was a public letter-writer who plied his trade at the corner of the Pont-Neuf—a funny old scarecrow he was—and Agnes, who cannot write, used sometimes to employ him to write to her fiancé who was away with the army. She says she doesn't know exactly how it all happened—s he thinks the old letter-writer must have questioned her very cleverly, or else have followed her home one day—but, anyway, she caught herself telling him all about Antione Carré and took him and his mother safely out of France."

She paused a moment to draw breath, for she had spoken excitedly and all the time scarcely above a whisper, for the subject-matter was not one she would have liked some evil-wisher to hear. There were so many spies about these days eager for blood-money—the forty sous which could be earned for denouncing a "suspect."

Maurice, fully alive to this, made no immediate comment, but after a few seconds he suggested: "Shall we walk?" and took Josette by the elbow. It was getting dark now: the Cour la Reine was only poorly-lighted by a very few street lanterns placed at long intervals. They walked together in silence for a time, looking like young lovers intent on amorous effusions. The few passers-by, furtive and noiseless, took no notice of them.

"Antoine Carré's case is not the only one, Maurice," Josette resumed presently. "I could tell you dozens of others. The girls in the workshop talk about it all the time when the superintendent is out of the room."

Again she paused, and then went on firmly, stressing her command: "You have got to help me, you know, Maurice."

"Of course I will, Josette," Maurice murmured. "But how?"

"You must find the public letter-writer who used to have his pitch at the corner of the Pont-Neuf."

"There isn't one there now. I went past..."

"I know that. He has changed his pitch, that's all."

"How shall I know which is the right man? There are a number of public letter-writers in Paris."

"I shall be with you, Maurice, and I shall know, I am sure I shall know. There is something inside my heart which will make it beat faster as soon as the Scarlet Pimpernel is somewhere nigh. Besides..."

She checked herself, for involuntarily she had raised her voice, and at once Maurice tightened his hold on her arm. In the fast-gathering gloom a shuffling step had slided furtively past them. They could not clearly see the form of this passer-by, only the vague outline of a man stooping under a weight which he carried over his shoulders.

"We must be careful, Josette..." Maurice whispered softly.

"I know—I was carried away. But, Maurice, you will help me?"

"Of course," he said.

And though he did not feel very hopeful he said it fervently, for the prospect of roaming through the streets of Paris in the company of Josette in search of a person who might be mythical and who certainly would take a lot of finding, was of the rosiest. Indeed, Maruice hoped that the same mythical personage would so hide himself that it would be many days before he was ultimately found.

"And when we have found him," Josette continued glibly, once more speaking under her breath, "you shall tell him about Louise and Charles-Léon, and that Louise must have a permit to take the poor sick baby into the country and to remain with him until he is well."

"And you think...?"

"I don't think, Maurice," she said emphatically, "I know that the Scarlet Pimpernel will do the rest."

She was like a young devotee proclaiming the miracles of her patron saint. It was getting very dark now and at home Louise and Charles-Léon would be waiting for Josette, the angel in the house. Mechanically and a little sadly Maurice led the girl's footsteps in the direction of home. They spoke very little together after this: it seemed as if, having made her profession of faith, Josette took her loyal friend's co-operation for granted. She did not even now realise the cruelty of the blow which she had dealt to his fondest hopes. With the image of this heroic Scarlet Pimpernel so firmly fixed in her mind, Josette was not likely to listen to a declaration of love from a humble lawyer's clerk, who had neither deeds of valour nor a handsome presence wherewith to fascinate a young girl so romantically inclined.

Thus they wandered homewards in silence—she indulging in her dreams, and he nursing a sorrow that he felt would be eternal. Up above in the chestnut trees the sparrows had gone to roost. Their paean of joy had ceased, only the many sounds of a great city not yet abed broke in silence of the night. Furtive footsteps still glided well-nigh soundlessly by; now and then there came a twitter, a fluttering of wings from above, or from far away the barking of a dog, the banging of a door, or the rattling of cart-wheels on the cobble-stones. And sometimes the evening breeze would give a great sigh that rose up into the evening air as if coming from hundreds of thousands of prisoners groaning under the tyranny of bloodthirsty oppressors, of a government that proclaimed Liberty and Fraternity from the steps of the guillotine.

And at home in the small apartment of the Rue Picpus, Josette and Maurice found that Louise had cried her eyes out until she had worked herself into a state of hysteria, while Maître de Croissy, silent and thoughtful, sat in dejection by the bedside of his sick child.

CHAPTER IV

The evening was spent—strangely enough—in silence and in gloom. Josette, who a few hours before had thought to have gained her point and to have brought both hope and faith into Louise's heart, found that her friend had fallen back into that state of dejection out of which nothing that Josette said could possibly drag her. Josette put this down to Bastien's influence. Bastien too had always been skeptical about the Scarlet Pimpernel, didn't believe in his existence at all. He somehow confused him in his mind with that Austrian agent Baron de Batz, of whom he had had such bitter experience. De Batz, too, had been full of schemes for rescuing the King, the Royal family, and many a persecuted noble, threatened with death, but months had gone by and nothing had been done. The mint of Austrian money promised by him was never forthcoming. De Batz himself was never on the spot when he wanted. In vain had Bastien de Croissy toiled and striven his hardest to bring negotiations to a head between a certain few members of the revolutionary government who were ready to accept bribes, and the Austrian emissaries who professed themselves ready to pay. Men like Chabot and Bazire, and Fabre d'Eglantine had been willing enough to negotiate, though their demands became more and more exorbitant as time went on and the King's peril more imminent: even Danton had thrown out hints that in these hard times a man must live, so why not on Austrian money, since French gold was so scarce? but somehow, when everything appeared to be ready, and greedy palms were already outstretched to receive the promised bribes, the money was never there, and de Batz, warned of his peril if he remained in France, had fled across the border.

And somehow the recollection of that intriguer was inextricably mixed up in de Croissy's mind with the legendary personality of the Scarlet Pimpernel.

"Josette is quite convinced of his existence," Louise had said to her husband that afternoon, when they stood together in sorrow and tears beside the sick-bed of Charles-Léon, "and that he can and will get me the permit to take our darling away into the country."

But Bastien shook his head, sadly and obstinately.

"Don't lure yourself with false hopes, my dear," he said. "Josette is an angel, but she is also a child. She dreams and persuades herself that her dreams are realities. I have had experience of such dreams myself."

"I know," Louise rejoined with a sigh.

Hers was one of those yielding natures, gentle and affectionate, that can be swayed one way or the other by an event, sometimes by a mere word; and yet at times she would be strangely obstinate, with the obstinacy of the very weak, or of the feather-pillow that seems to yield at the touch only to regain it's own shape the next moment.

A word from Bastien and all the optimism which Josette's ardour had implanted in her heart froze again into scepticism and discouragement.

"If we cannot save Charles-Léon," she said, "I shall die."

Twenty-four hours had gone by since then, and to-day Bastien de Croissy sat alone in the small musty office of the Rue de la Monnaie. He had sent his clerk, Maurice Reversac, off early because he was a kindly man and had not forgotten the days of his own courtship, and knew that the happiest hours of Maurice's day were those when he could meet Josette Gravier outside the gate of the Government workshop and take her out for a walk.

De Croissy had also sent Maurice away early because he wanted to be alone. A crisis had arisen in his life with which he desired to deal thoughtfully and dispassionately. His child was ill, would die, perhaps, unless he, the father, could contrive to send him out of Paris into the country under the care of his mother. The tyranny of this Government of Liberty and Fraternity had made this impossible; no man, woman or child was allowed to be absent from the permanent domicile without a special permit, which was seldom, if ever, granted; not unless some powerful leverage could be found to force those tyrants to grant the permit.

Now Bastien de Croissy was in possession of such a leverage. The question was: had the time come at last to make use of it? He now sat at his desk and a sheaf of letters were laid out before him. These letters, if rightly handled, would, he knew, put so much power into his hands that he could force some of the most influential members of the government to grant him anything he chose to ask.

"Get as much letter-writing as you can out of the black-guards," the Austrian emissary had said to him during that memorable interview in the Cabaret des Trois Singes, and de Croissy had acted on this advice. On one pretext or another he had succeeded in persuading at any rate three influential members of the existing Government to put their demands in writing. Bastien had naturally carefully preserved these letters. De Batz was going to use them for his own ends: as a means wherewith to discredit men who proclaimed their disinterestedness and patriotism from the housetops, and not only to discredit them, "but to make them suffer the same humiliation and the same shameful death which they had planned for their King." These also had been the emissary's words at that fateful interview; and de Croissy had kept the letters up to now, not with a view to using them for his own benefit, or for purposes of blackmail, but with the earnest hope that one day chance would enable him to use them for the overthrow and humiliation of tyrants and regicides.

But now events had suddenly taken a sharp turn. Charles-Léon might die if he was not taken out of the fever-infested city, and Louise, very rightly, would not trust the sick child in a stranger's hands. And if Charles-Léon were to die, Louise would quickly follow the child to his grave.

Bastien de Croissy sat for hours in front of his desk with those letters spread out before him. He picked them up one by one, read and re-read them and put them down again. He rested his weary head against his hand, for thoughts weighed heavily on his mind. To a man of integrity, a high-minded gentleman as he had always been, the alternative was a horrible one. On one side there was that hideous thing, blackmail, which was abhorrent to him, and on the other the life of his wife and child. Honour and conscience ruled one way, and every fibre of his heart the other.

The flickering light of tallow candles threw grotesque shadows on the white-washed walls and cast fantastic gleams of light on the handsome face of the great lawyer, with its massive forehead and nobly sculptured profile, on the well-shaped hands and hair prematurely grey.

The letter which he now held in his hand was signed "François Chabot," once a Capuchin friar, now a member of the National Convention and one of Danton's closest friends, whose uncompromising patriotism had been proclaimed on the house-tops both by himself and his colleagues.

And this is what François Chabot had written not much more than a year ago to Maître de Croissy, advocate:

"My friend, as I told you in our last interview, I am inclined to listen favourably to the proposals of B. If he really disposes of the funds of which he boasts, tell him that I can get C. out of his present impasse and put him once more in possession of the seat which he values. Further, I and the others can keep him in a guarantee that nothing shall happen (say) for five years to disturb him again. But you can also tell B. that his proposals are futile. I shall want twenty thousand on the day that C. enters his house in the park. moreover, your honorarium for carrying this matter through must be paid by B. My friends and I will not incur any expense in connection with it."

Bastien de Croissy now took up his pen and a sheet of paper, and after a moment's reflection he transcribed the somewhat enigmatic letter by substituting names for initials, and intelligible words for those that appeared ununderstandable. The letter so transcribed now began thus:

"My friend, as I told you in our last interview, I am inclined to listen favourably to the proposals of de Batz. If he really disposes of the funds of which he boasts, tell him that I can get the King out of his present impasse and put him once more in possession of his throne..."

The rest of the letter he transcribed in the same way: always substituting the words "the King" for "C." and "de Batz" for "B."; his house in the park Maître de Croissy transcribed as "Versailles."

The whole text would now be clear to anybody. Bastien then took up a number of other letters and transcribed these in the same way as he had done the first: then he made two separate packets of the whole correspondence; one of these contained the original letters, and these he slipped in the inside pocket of his coat, the other he tied loosely together and put it away with other papers in his desk. He then locked the desk and the strong box, turned out the lights in the office and finally went home.

His mind was definitely made up.

The same evening Bastien made a clean breast of all the circumstances to Louise. Maurice was there and Josette of course, and there was little Charles-Léon, who lay like a half-animate bird in his mother's arms.

For Maurice the story was not new. He had known of the first interview between de Croissy and the Austrian emissary, he had watched the intrigue developing step by step, through the good offices of the distinguished advocate. As a matter of fact he had more than once acted as messenger, taking letters to and fro between the dingy offices of the Rue de la Monnaie and the sumptuous apartments of the Representatives of the People. He had spoken to Chabot, the unfrocked friar who lived in unparalleled luxury in the Rue d'Anjou, dressed in town like a Beau Brummel, but attended the sittings of the National Convention in a tattered coat and shoes down at heel, his hair unkempt, his chin unshaven, his hands unwashed, in order to flaunt what he was pleased to call his democratic ideals. He saw Bazire, Chabot's brother-in-law, who hired a mudlark to enact the part of pretended assassin in order that he might raise the cry: "The royalists are murdering the patriots!" (As it happened, the pretended assassin did not turn up at the right moment, and Bazire had been left to wander alone up and down the dark cul-de-sac waiting to receive the stab that was to exalt him before the Convention as the victim of his ardent patriotism.) Maurice had interviewed Fabre d'Eglantine, Danton's most intimate friend, who was only too ready to see his palm greased with foreign gold, and even the ruthless and impeccable Danton had to Maurice's knowledge nibbled at the sweet biscuit held to his nose by the Austrian agent.

All these men Maurice Reversac had known, interviewed and despised. But he had also seen the clouds of bitterness and disappointment gather in Bastien de Croissy's face: he guessed more than he actually knew how one by one all the hopes born of that first interview in the Cabaret des Trois Singes had been laid to dust. The continued captivity of the Royal family, the severance of the Queen from her children had been the first heavy blows dealt to those fond hopes. The King's condemnation and death completely shattered them. Maurice dared not ask what the Austrian was doing, or what final preposterous demands had come from the Representatives of the People, which had caused the negotiations to be finally broken off. For months now the history of those negotiations had almost been forgotten. As far as Maurice was concerned he had ceased to think of them, he only remembered the letters that had passed during that time, as incidents that might have had wonderful consequences, but had since sunk into the limbo of forgetfulness.

To Louise and Josette, on the other hand, the story was entirely new. Each heard it with widely divergent feelings. Obviously to Louise it meant salvation. She listened to her husband with glowing eyes, her lips were parted, her breath came and went with almost feverish rapidity, and every now and then she pressed Charles-Léon closer and closer to her breast. Never for a moment did she appear in doubt that here was complete deliverance from every trouble and every anxiety. Indeed the only thing that seemed to trouble her was the fact that Bastien had withheld this wonderful secret from her for so long.

"We might have been free to leave this hell upon earth long before this," she exclaimed with passionate reproach when Bastien admitted that he had hesitated to use such a weapon for his own benefit.

"It looks so like blackmail," Bastien murmured feebly.

"Blackmail?" Louise retorted vehemently. "Would you call it murder if you killed a mad dog?"

Bastien gave a short, quick sigh. The letters were to have been the magic key wherewith to open the prison door for his King and Queen: the mystic wand that would clear the way for them to their throne.

"Is not Charles-Léon's life more precious than any King's?" Louise protested passionately.

And soon she embarked on plans for the future. She would take the child into the country, and presently, if things didn't get any better, they would join the band loyal émigrés who led a precarious but peaceful existence in Belgium or England; Josette and Maurice would come with them, and together the would all wait for those better times which could not now be very long in coming.

"There is nothing," she declared emphatically, "that these men would dare refuse us. By threatening to send those letters to the Moniteur or any other paper we can force them to grant us permits, passports, anything we choose. Oh, Bastien!" she added impetuously, "why did you not think of all this before?"

Josette alone was silent. She alone had hardly uttered a word the whole evening. In silence she had listened to Bastien's exposition of the case, and to Maurice's comments on the situation, and she remained silent while Louise talked and reproached and planned. She only spoke when Bastien, after he had read aloud some of the more important letters, gathered them all together and tied them once more into a packet. He was about to slip them into his coat pocket when Josette spoke up.

"Don't do that, Bastien," she said impulsively, and stretched out her hand for the packet.

"Don't do what, my dear?" de Croissy asked.

"Let Louise take charge of the letters," the girl pleaded, "until those treacherous devils are ready to give you the permits and safe-conducts in exchange for them. You can show your transcriptions to them at first: but they wouldn't be above sticking a knife into you in the course of conversation, and rifling your pockets if they knew you had the originals on you at the time."

Bastien couldn't help smiling at the girl's eagerness, but he put the packet of letters into her outstretched hand.

"You are right, Josette," he said: "you are always right. The angel in the house! What will you do with them?"

"Sew them into the lining of Louise's corsets," Josette replied.

And she never said another word after that.

CHAPTER V

Louise de Croissy stood by the window and watched her husband's tall massive figure as he strode down the street on his way to the Rue de la Monnaie. When he had finally disappeared out of her sight Louise turned to Josette.

Unconsciously almost, and certainly against her better judgement, Josette felt a strange misgiving about this affair. She hadn't slept all night for thinking about it. And this morning when Bastien had set off so gaily and Louise seemed so full of hope she still felt oppressed and vaguely frightened. There is no doubt that intense love does at times possess psychic powers, the power usually called "second sight." Josette's love for Louise and what she called her "little family" was maternal in its intensity and she always averred that she knew beforehand whenever a great joy was to come to them and also had a premonition of any danger that threatened them.

And somehow this morning she felt unable to shake off a consciousness of impending doom. She, too, had watched at the window while Bastien de Croissy started out in the direction of the Rue de la Monnaie, there to pick up the packet of transcriptions and then to go off on his fateful errand; and when he had turned the angle of the street and she could no longer see him she felt more than ever the approach of calamity.

These were the last days of September: summer had lingered on and it had been wonderfully sunny all along. In the woods the ash, the oak and the chestnut were still heavy with leaf and thrushes and blackbirds still sang gaily their evening melodies, but to-day the weather had turned sultry: there were heavy clouds up above that presaged a coming storm.

"Why, what's the matter, Josette chérie?" Louise asked anxiously, for the girl, as she gazed out into the dull grey light, shivered as if with cold and her pretty face appeared drawn and almost haggard. "Are you disappointed that your mythical Scarlet Pimpernel will not, after all, play his heroic rôle on our stage?"

Louise said this with a light laugh, meaning only to chaff, but Josette winced as if she had been stung, and tears gathered in her eyes.

"Josette!" Louise exclaimed, full of contrition and of tenderness. She felt happy, light-hearted, proud too, of what Bastien could do for them all. Though the morning was grey and dismal, though there were only scanty provisions in the house—aye! even though Charles-Léon lay limp and listless in his little bed, Louise felt that on this wonderful day she could busy herself about her poor dingy home, singing to herself with joy. She, like Bastien himself, had never wished to emigrate, but at times she had yearned passionately for the fields and the woods of the Dauphiné where her husband still owned the family château and where there was a garden in which Charles-Léon could run about, where the air was pure and wholesome so that the colour could once more tinge the poor lamb's wan cheeks.

She could not understand why Josette was not as happy as she was herself. Perhaps she was depressed by the weather, and sure enough soon after Bastien started the first lightning-flash shot across the sky, and after a few seconds there came the distant rumble of thunder. A few heavy drops fell on the cobble-stones and then the rain came down, a veritable cataract, as if the sluices of heaven had suddenly been opened. Within a few minutes the uneven pavements ran with muddy streams and an unfortunate passer-by, caught in the shower, buttoned up their coat collars and bolted for the nearest doorway. The wind howled down the chimneys and rattled the ill-fitting window-panes. No wonder that Josette's spirits were damped by this dismal weather!

Louise drew away from the window, sighing: "Thank God, I made Bastien put on his thick old coat!" Then she sat down and called Josette to her. "You know, chérie," she said, and put loving arms round the girl's shoulders, "I didn't mean anything unkind about your hero: I was only chaffing. I loved your enthusiasm and your belief in miracles; but I am more prosy than you are, chérie, and prefer to pin my faith on the sale of compromising letters rather than on deeds of valour performed by a mythical hero."

To please Louise, Josette made a great effort to appear cheerful; indeed, she chided herself for her ridiculous feeling of depression, which had no reason for its existence and only tended to upset Louise. She pleaded a headache after a sleepless night.

"I lay awake," she said, with an effort to appear light-hearted, "thinking of the happy time we would all have over in the Dauphiné. It is so lovely there in the late autumn when the leaves turn to gold."

The rest of the morning Josette was obliged to spend in the Government workshops sewing shirts for the "Soldiers of Liberty," so presently when the storm began to subside she put on her cloak and hood, gave Charles-Léon a last kiss and hurried off to work. She had hoped to get her allotted task done by twelve o'clock, when Maurice could meet her and they could sally forth together in search of fresh air under the trees of Cour la Reine. Unfortunately, as luck would have it, she was detained in the workshop along with a number of other girls until a special consignment of shirts was ready for packing. When she was finally able to leave the shop it was past one o'clock and Maurice was not waiting at the gate.

She hurried home for her midday meal, only to hear from Louise that Bastien and Maurice had already been and gone. They had snatched a morsel of food and hurried away again, for they had important work to do at the office. Louise was full of enthusiasm and full of hope. Bastien, she said, had seen Fabre d'Eglantine, also Chabot and Bazire, and had already entered into negotiations with them for the exchange of the compromising letters against permits for himself and his family—which would, of course, include Josette and Maurice—to take up permanent domicile on his estate in the Dauphiné. Bastien and Maurice, after they had imparted this joyful news and had their hurried meal, had gone back to the office. It seems that after the three interviews were over and Bastien was back at the Rue de la Monnaie, Françious Chabot had called on him with a ponderous document which he desired put into legal jargon that same afternoon.

"It will take them several hours to get through with the work," Louise went on to explain, "and when it is ready Maurice is to take the document to Citizen Chabot's apartment in Rue d'Anjoy; so I don't suppose we shall see either of them before supper-time. Bastien says he was so amused when Chabot called at the office. His eyes were roaming round the room all the time. I am sure he was wondering in his mind where Bastien kept the letters, and I am so thankful, Josette darling, that we took your advice and have them here in safe-keeping. Do you know, Bastien declares that if those letters were published to-morrow Chabot and the lot of them, not even excepting the great Danton, would find themselves at the bar of the accused, and within the hour their heads would be off their shoulders? And serve them right, the murdering, hypocritical devils!"

After which she unfolded to her darling Josette her plans for leaving this hateful Paris within the next twenty-four hours. Dreams and hopes! Louise was full of them just now: strange that to Josette the whole thing was like a nightmare.

CHAPTER VI

In the late afternoon Josette had again to go back to the workshop to put in a couple of hours' more sewing. She left Louise in the apartment, engrossed in sorting out the necessary clothes required for the journey, and singing merrily like a bird. Bastien and Maurice were not expected home for some hours. Charles-Léon was asleep.

It was past eight o'clock and quite dark when Josette finally returned home to the Rue Picpus for the evening. Under the big port-cochère of the apartment house she nearly fell into the arms of Maurice Reversac, who apparently was waiting for her.

"Oh, Maurice!" she cried, "how you frightened me!" And then, "What are you doing here?"

Instead of replying he took her by the wrist and drew her to the foot of the main staircase, away from the concierge's lodge, where in an angle of the wall they could be secure from prying ears and eyes. Here Maurice halted, but he still clung to her wrist, and leaned against the wall as if exhausted and breathless.

"Maurice, what is it?"

The staircase was in almost total darkness, only a feeble light filtrated down from an oil-lamp fixed on one of the landings above. Josette could not see her friend's face, but she felt the tremor that shook his arm and she heard the stertorous breath that struggled through his lips. The sense of doom, of some calamity that threatened them all, the nameless foreboding that had haunted her all day held her heart in an icy grip.

"Maurice!" she insisted.

At last he spoke; he murmured his employer's name.

"Maître de Croissy..."

Josette could scarcely repress a cry:

"Arrested?"

He shook his head.

"Not...? Dead...? When? How? What is it, Maurice? In God's name, tell me!"

"Murdered!"

"Murd-"

She clapped her hand to her mouth and dug her teeth into it to smother the scream which would have echoed up the well of the stairs. Louise's apartment was only up two flights. She would have heard.

"Tell me!" Josette gasped rather than spoke. She did not really understand. What Maurice had just said was so impossible. Inconceivable! She had expected a cataclysm.... Yes. All day she had felt like the dread hand of Doom hovering over them all. But not this! In Heaven's name, not this! Murdered? Bastien? Why, Maurice must be crazy! And she said it aloud, too.

"You are crazy, Maurice!"

"I thought I was just now."

"You've been dreaming," she insisted. For still she did not believe.

"Murdered, I tell you! Dead!"

"Where?"

"In the office...."

"Then let us go...."

She wanted to run... out... at once, but Maurice got hold of her and held her so that she could not go.

"Wait, Josette! Let me tell you first."

"Let me go, Maurice! I don't believe it. Let me go!"

Maurice had already pulled himself together. He had contrived to steady his voice, and now, with a perfectly firm grip, he pulled Josette's hand under his arm and led her out into the street. There would be no holding her back if she was determined to go. The rain-storm had turned to a nasty drizzle and it was very cold. The few passers-by who hurried along the narrow street had their coat collars buttoned closely round their necks. A very few lights glimmered here and there in the windows of the houses on either side. Street lamps were no longer lighted these days in the side streets for reasons of economy.

Out in the open Maurice put his arm round Josette's shoulder and instinctively she nestled against him. Almost paralysed with horror, she was shivering with cold and her teeth were chattering, but there was a feeling of comfort and of protection in Maurice's arm which seemed to steady her. Also she wanted to hear every word that he said, and he did not dare raise his voice above a whisper. They walked as fast as the unevenness of the cobble-stones allowed, and now and then they broke into a run; and all the while, in short jerky sentences, Maurice tried to tell the girl something of what had happened.

"Maître de Croissy," he said, "had an interview with Citizen Chabot in the morning.... While he was there Chabot sent for Bazire... and after that the three of them went together to Danton's lodgings..."

"You weren't with them?"

"No... I was waiting at the office. Presently Maître de Croissy came back alone. He was full of hope... the interview had gone off very well... better than he expected... Chabot and Bazire were obviously terrified out of their lives... Maître de Croissy had left them with Danton, and come on to the office..."

"Yes! and then?"

"About half an hour later, Chabot called at the office... alone... he brought a document with him... did Madame tell you?"

"Yes! yes!..."

"He stayed a little while talking... talking... explaining the document... a very long one... of which he wanted three copies made... with additions... and so on.... He wanted the papers back by evening..."

Maurice seemed to be gasping for breath. His voice was husky as if his throat were parched. It was difficult to talk coherently while threading one's way through the narrow streets, and once or twice he forced Josette to stand still for a moment or two, to rest against the wall while she listened.

"We went home to dinner after Chabot had gone..." Maurice went on presently. "I can't tell you just how I felt then... a kind of foreboding you know..."

"Yes, I know," she said, "I felt it too... last night..."

"Something in that devil's eyes had frightened me... but you know Maître de Croissy... he won't listen... once he has made up his mind... and he laughed at me when I ventured on a word of warning... you know..."

"Oh, yes!" Josette sighed, "I know!"

"We went back to the office together after dinner. Maître de Croissy worked on the document all afternoon. It was ready just when the light gave out. He gave me the paper and told me to take it to Citizen Chabot. I went. Chabot kept me waiting, an hour or more. It was nearly eight o'clock when I got back to the office. The front door was ajar. I remember thinking this strange. I pushed open the door..."

He paused, and suddenly Josette said quite firmly:

"Don't tell me, Maurice. I can guess."

"What, Josette?'

"Those devils got you out of the way. They meant to filch the letters from Bastien. They killed him in order to get the letters."

"The two rooms," Maurice said, "looked as if they had been shattered by an earthquake."

"They broke everything so as to get the letters, and they killed him first."

They had reached the house in the Rue de la Monnaie. It looked no different than it had always done. Grim, grey, dilapidated. Inside the house there was that smell of damp and of mortar like in a vault. Apparently no one knew anything as yet about what had occurred on the second floor where Citizen Croissy, the lawyer, had his office. No one challenged the young man and the girl as they hurried up the stairs. Josette as she ran was trembling in every limb, but she knew that the time had come for calmness and for courage, and with a mighty effort she regained control over her nerves. She was determined to be a help rather than a hindrance, even though horror had gripped her like some live and savage beast by the throat so that she scarcely could breathe, and turned the dread in her heart to physical nausea.

Maurice had taken the precaution of locking the front door of the office, but he had the key in his pocket. Before inserting it in the keyhole he paused to take another look at Josette. If she had faltered the least bit in the world, if he had perceived the slightest swaying in her young firm body, he would have picked her up in his arms where she stood and carried her away—away from that awful scene behind the door.

He could not see her face, for the stairs were very dark, but through a dim and ghostly light he perceived the outline of her head and saw that she held it erect and her shoulders square. All he said was:

"Shall we go to the Commissariat first?"

But she shook her head. He opened the door and she followed him in. The small vestibule was in darkness, but the door into the office was open, and here the light from the oil-lamp which dangled from the ceiling revealed the prone figure of Bastien de Croissy on the floor, his torn clothing and the convulsive twist of his hands. A heavy crowbar lay close beside the body, and all around there was a litter of broken furniture, wood, glass, a smashed inkstand with the ink still flowing out of it and staining the bit of faded carpet; sand and débris of paper and of string and the smashed drawers of the bureau. The strong-box was also on the floor with its metal door broken open and money and papers scattered around. Indeed, the whole place did look as if it had been shattered by an earthquake.

But Josette did not look at all that. All she saw was Bastien lying there, his body rigid in the last convulsive twitching of death. She prayed to God for the strength to go near him, to kneel beside him and say the prayers for the dead which the Church demanded. Maurice knelt down beside her, and they drew the dead man's hands together over his breast, and Josette took her rosary from her pocket and wound it round the hands; then she and Maurice recited the prayers for the dead: she with eyes closed lest if she continued to look she fell into a swoon. She prayed for Bastien's soul, and she also prayed for guidance as to what she ought to do now that Bastien was gone: for Louise was not strong and after this she would have no one on whom to lean, only on her, Josette.

When she and Maurice had finished their prayers they sought among the débris for the two pewter candlesticks that used to stand on the bureau. Maurice found them presently; they were all twisted, but not broken, and close by there were the pieces of tallow candle that had fallen out of their sconces. He straightened them out, and with a screw of paper held to the lamp he lighted the candles and Josette placed them on the floor, one on each side of the dead man's head.

After which she tiptoed out of the room. Maurice extinguished the hanging lamp; he followed Josette out through the door and locked it behind him.

Then the two of them went silently and quickly down the stairs.

CHAPTER VII

Louise de Croissy lay on the narrow horse-hair sofa like a log. Since Josette had broken the terrible news to her, more than twenty-four hours ago, she had been almost like one dead: unable to speak, unable to eat or sleep. Even Charles-Léon's childish cajoleries could not rouse her from her apathy.

For twenty-four hours she had lain thus, silent and motionless, while Josette did her best to keep Charles-Léon amused and looked after his creature comforts as best she could. She adored Louise, but somehow at this crisis she could not help feeling impatient with the other woman's nervelessness and that devastating inertia. After all, there was Charles-Léon to think of; all the more now as the head of the family had gone. Josette still had her mind set on finding the Scarlet Pimpernel, who of a truth was the only person in the world who could save Louise and Charles-Léon now. Josette had no illusions on the score of the new danger which threatened these two. Bastien had been murdered by Terrorists because he would not give up the letters that compromised them without getting a quid pro quo. They had killed him and ransacked his rooms. They might have ordered his arrest—it was so easy these days to get an enemy arrested—but no doubt feared that he might have a chance of speaking during his trial and revealing what he knew. Only dead men tell no tales.

But the letters had not been found, and at this hour there was a clique of desperate men who knew that their necks were in peril if those letters were ever made public. Josette had no illusions. Sooner or later, within a few hours perhaps, those men would strike at Louise. There would be a perquisition, arrest probably, and possibly another murder. She wanted Louise to destroy the letters, they had been the cause of this awful cataclysm, but at the slightest hint Louise had clutched at her bosom with both hands as if she would guard the letters with her life. The next evening when Josette came home she found Louise already in bed; it was the first time she had moved from that narrow horse-hair sofa since the girl had broken the news to her. She had laid out her clothes on a chair, with her corsets ostentatiously spread out on the top of the other things as if to invite attention. The packet of letters was no longer inside the lining. Josette noticed this at once, also that Louise was feigning sleep and was watching her through half-closed lids.

With well-assumed indifference Josette went about her business in the house, smoothed Louise's pillow, kissed her and Charles-Léon good-night, and then got into bed. But she did not get much sleep, tired to death though she was. She foresaw the complications. Louise had some fixed idea about those letters, the result of shock no doubt, and was clinging to them with the obstinacy of the very weak. She had hidden them and meant to keep their hiding-place a secret, even from Josette. No doubt her nerves had to a certain extent given way, for in spite of her closed eyes as she lay on her bed there was that expression of cunning in her face which is peculiar to those whose minds are deranged.

Josette and Maurice had spent most of that day at the Commissariat of Police. It was a terrible ordeal from the first to last. The airless room that smelt of dirt and humanity, the patient crowd of weary men and women waiting their turn to pass into the presence of the Commissary, the suspense of the present and the horror of the past nearly broke down Josette's fortitude. Nearly, but not quite; for she had Maurice with her, and it was wonderful what comfort she derived from his nearness. She had always been so self-reliant, so accustomed to watch over those she cared for, and cater for their creature comforts, that Maurice Reversac's somewhat diffident ways, his timid speech and dog-like devotion had tempered her genuine affection for him with a slight measure of contempt. She could not help but admire his loyalty to his employer and his disinterestedness and felt bound to admit that he was clever and learned in the law, else Bastien would not have placed reliance on his judgement, as he often did, but all the time she had the feeling that morally and physically he was a weakling, the ivy that clung rather than the oak that supported.

But since this awful trouble had come upon her, how different it all was. Josette felt just as self-reliant as in the past, for Louise and Charles-Léon were more dependent on her than ever before, but there was Maurice now, a different Maurice altogether, and he had become a force.

When their turn came to appear before the Commissary, Josette, having Maurice at her side, did not feel frightened. They both gave their names and address in a clear voice, showed their papers and identity, and gave a plain and sincere account of the terrible events of the day before. Citizen Croissy, the well-known advocate, had been foully murdered in his office in the Rue de la Monnaie. It was their duty as citizens of the Republic to report this terrible fact to the Commissariat of the section.

The Commissary listened, raised his eyebrows, toyed with a paper-knife; his face was a mask of complete incredulity.

"Why should you talk of murder?" he asked.

Maurice mentioned the crowbar, the ransacked room, the scattered papers, the broken strong-box. It was clearly a case of murder for purposes of robbery.

"Any money missing?" the Commissary asked.

"No!"

"Eh bien!" he remarked with a careless shrug. "You see?"

"The murder had a political motive, Citizen Commissary," Josette put in impulsively, "the assassins were not after money, but after certain papers..."

"Now you are talking nonsense," the Commissary broke in curtly. "Murder? What fool do you suppose would resort to murder nowadays?" He checked himself abruptly, for he was on the point of letting his tongue run away with him. What he had very nearly said, and certainly had implied, was that no fool would take the risk and trouble of murder these days when it was so easy to rid oneself of an enemy by denouncing him as "suspect of treason" before the local Committee of Public Safety. Arrest, trial, and the guillotine would then follow as a matter of course, and one got forty sous to boot as a reward for denouncing a traitor. Then why trouble to murder?

No wonder the Commissary checked himself in time before he had said all this: men in office had been degraded before now, if not worse, for daring to criticise the decrees of this paternal Government.

"I'll tell you what I will do, Citizeness," he said, speaking more particularly to Josette because her luminous blue eyes were fixed upon his, and he was a susceptible man; "I don't believe a word of your story, mind! but I will visit the scene of that supposed murder, and listen on the spot to the depositions of witnesses. Then we'll see."

"There were no witnesses to the crime, Citizen Commissary," Josette declared.

Whereupon the Commissary swore loudly, blustered and threatened all false accusers with the utmost penalties the law could impose. Witnesses? There must be witnesses. The concierge of the house... the other lodgers... anyway he would see, and if in the end it was definitely proved that this tale of assassination and political crime was nothing but a cock-and-bull story, well! let all false witnesses look to their own necks... that was all.

"You will appear before me to-morrow," were the parting words with which the Commissary dismissed Maurice and Josette from his presence.

No wonder that after that long and wearisome day, Josette should have lain awake most of the night a-thinkin-g. It was very obvious that nothing would be done to bring the murderers of Bastien to justice. Perhaps she had been wrong after all to speak of "political motives" in connection with the crime: she had only moral proofs for her assertion, and those devils who had perpetrated the abominable deed would be all the more on the alert now, and Louise's peril would be greater even that before.

"Holy Virgin," she murmured naïvely in her prayers, "help me to find the Scarlet Pimpernel!"

On the following morning, Louise, though still listless and apathetic, rose and dressed herself without saying a word. Josette with an aching heart could not help noticing that her face still wore an expression of cunning and obstinacy, and that her eyes were still dry: Louise indeed had not shed a single tear since the awful truth had finally penetrated to her brain, and she had understood that Bastien had been foully murdered because of the letters.

With endearing words and infinite gentleness Josette did her best to soften the poor woman's mood. She drew her to Charles-Léon's bedside and murmured some of the naïve prayers which when they were children together they had learned at the Convent of the Visitation. Her own soulful blue eyes were bathed in tears.

"Don't try and make me cry, Josette," Louise said. These were the first words she had spoken for thirty-six hours, and her voice sounded rasping and harsh. "If I were to shed tears now I would go on crying and crying till my eyes could no longer see and then they would close in death."

"You must not talk of death, Louise," Josette admonished gently, "while you have Charles-Léon to think of."

"It is because I think of him," Louise retorted, "that I don't want to cry."

But of the letters not a word, though Josette, by hint and glance, asked more than one mute question.

"Bastien would rather have seen your tears, Louise," she said with a tone of sad reproach.

"Perhaps he will—from above—when I stand by his graveside... but not now—not yet."

Louise, however, never did stand by her husband's graveside; that morning when Maurice and Josette went to the Commissariat in order to obtain permission for the burial of Citizen Croissy, they were curtly informed that the burial had already taken place, and no amount of questioning, of entreaty and of petitions elected any further information, save that the body had been disposed of by order of what was vaguely designated as "the authorities"; which meant that it had probably been thrown in the fosse commune of the Jardin de Picpus—the old convent garden—the common grave where no cross or stone could mark the last resting-place of the once brilliant and wealthy advocate of the Paris bar. The reason, curtly given, for this summary procedure was that it was the usual one in the case of suicides.

Thus was the foul murder of the distinguished lawyer classed as a case of suicide. It was useless to protest and to argue; only harm would come to Louise and Charles-Léon if either Maurice or Josette entered into any discussion on the subject. As soon as they opened their mouths they were roughly ordered to hold their peace. Maurice Reversac was commanded to accompany the Citizen Substitute to the office of the Rue de la Monnaie, there to complete certain formalities in connection with the goods and chattels belonging to "the suicide," and then officially to give up the keys of the apartment.

CHAPTER VIII

Josette in her naïve little prayers had implored the Holy Virgin to aid her in finding the Scarlet Pimpernel. She was convinced that nothing could save Louise and Charles-Léon from Bastien's awful fate save the intervention of her mysterious hero, but the last two days had been so full of events that it had been quite impossible for her to begin her quest for the one man on whom in this dark hour she could pin her faith. Maurice, on the other hand, had promised that he would do his best, and this was all the more wonderful as he had not the same faith as Josette in the existence of the heroic Englishman. Nevertheless, in order to please and cheer her, and in the intervals of running from pillar to post, from the Rue de la Monnaie to the Commissariat and back again, he did seriously set to work to get on the track of the public letter-writer who was wont to ply his trade at the corner of the Pont-Neuf and who was supposed to be in touch with the Scarlet Pimpernel himself.

Maurice knew all the highways and by-ways of old Paris—the small eating-houses and estaminets where it was possible to enter into casual conversation with simple everyday folk who would suspect no harm in discreet inquiries. Thus he came quite by chance on the track of what he thought might be a clue. There was, it seems, in a distant quarter of the city near the Batignolles, a funny old scarecrow who had set up his tent and carried on his trade of letter-writing for those who were too illiterate or too prudent to put pen to paper themselves. Not that Maurice believed for a moment that the scarecrow in question had anything to do with a band of English aristos, but he thought that the running him to earth, the walk across Paris, even though the weather was at its vilest, would take Josette out of herself for an hour or so, and turn her thoughts into less gloomy channels.

Josette readily agreed, and while Maurice was away on his melancholy errand in the Rue de la Monnaie, she promised that she would wait for him at the Commissariat de Police, and then they could sally forth together in quest of the hero of her dreams.

The waiting-room of the Commissariat was large and square. The walls had at some remote time been white-washed; now they and the ceiling were of a dull grey colour, and all around there was a dado-line of dirt and grease made by the rubbing of innumerable shoulders against the lime. On the wooden benches ranged against the walls, patient, weary-looking women sat, some with shawls over their heads, others shivering in thin bodice and kirtle, and all hugging bundles or babies. One of them made room for Josette, who sat down beside her preparing to wait. There were a number of men, too, mostly in ragged breeches and tattered coats, who hung about in groups whispering and spitting on the floor, or sitting on the table: nearly all of them were either decrepit or maimed. A few children scrambled in the dirt, getting in everybody's way. The place was almost unendurably stuffy, with a mingled odour of boiled cabbage, wet clothes and damp mortar; only from time to time when the outside door was opened for someone to go in or out did a gust of cold air come sweeping through the room. Josette wished she had arranged to meet Maurice somewhere else; she didn't think she could wait much longer in this dank atmosphere. She felt very tired, too, and the want of air made her feel drowsy.

The sound of a familiar voice roused her from the state of semi-torpor into which she had fallen, blinking and rather dazed, she looked about her. Old Doctor Larousse had just come in. He had a bundle of papers in his hand and looked fussy and hurried.

"A dog's life!" he muttered in the face of anyone who listened to him. "All these papers to get signed and more than half an hour to wait, maybe, in this filthy hole!"

Josette at sight of him jumped up and intercepted him at the moment when two or three others tried to get a word with him. All day yesterday she had wished to get in touch with the old doctor, and again this morning, not so much because of

Charles-Léon, but because she was getting seriously anxious about Louise. Citizen Larousse had been away from home for the past twenty-four hours: Josette had called at his rooms two or three times during the day, but always in vain.

Now she pulled the old man by the sleeve, forced him to listen to her.

"Citizen Doctor," she demanded, "at what hour can you come to the Rue Picpus and see Citizeness Croissy, who is seriously ill?"

Larousse shook her hand off his arm with unusual roughness: he was a kindly man, but apparently very harassed this morning.

"At what hour—at what hour?" he muttered petulantly. "Hark at your impudence, Citizeness! At no hour, let me tell you—not to-day, anyhow! I am off to Passy as soon as I can get these cursed papers signed."

"Citizen Doctor, think of the widow! Her mind is nearly deranged. She wants-"

"Many of us want things these days, little Citizeness," the old man said more gently, for Josette's deep blue eyes were fixed upon him and they were irresistible—would have been irresistible, that is, if he, Larousse, had not been quite so worried this morning. "I, for one, want to get to Passy, where my wife is ill with congestion of the lungs, and I shall not leave her bedside until she is well or..."

He shrugged his shoulders. He was a kind-hearted man really, but for two days he had been anxious about his wife. Josette Gravier was pretty, very pretty; she had large blue eyes that looked like a midnight sky in June when she was excited or eager or distressed, and there were delicate golden curls round her ears which always made old Larousse think of the days of his youth, of those summer afternoons when he was wont to wander out in the woods around Fontaine-bleau with his arm round a pretty girl's waist—just such a girl as Josette. But to-day? No, he was not in a mood to think of the days of his youth, and he had no use for pretty girls with large blue reproachable eyes. He was much too worried to be cajoled.

"You will have to find another doctor, little Citizeness," he concluded gruffly, "or else wait a day or two."

"How can I wait a day or two," she retorted, "with Citizeness Croissy nigh to losing her reason? Can't you imagine what she has gone through?"

The old man shrugged. He had seen so much misery, so much sorrow and pain, it was difficult to be compassionate to all. There had never been but One in this world who had compassion for the whole of humanity, and humanity repaid Him by nailing Him to a cross.

"We have to go through a lot these days, Citizeness," the old man said, "and I do not think that your friend will lose her reason. One is apt to let one's anxiety magnify such danger. I'll come as soon as I can."

"How soon?"

"Three or four days—I cannot tell."

"But in the meanwhile, Citizen Doctor, what shall I do?"

"Give her a soothing draught."

"To what purpose? She is calm—too calm-"

"Find another doctor."

"How can I? It takes days to obtain a permit to change one's doctor. You know that well enough, Citizen."

The girl now spoke with bitter dejection and the old man with growing impatience. He had freed himself quickly enough from the subtle spell of the girl's beauty: the weight of care and worry had again descended on him and hardened his heart. A queue had formed against the door which led to the Commissary's private office, and the old doctor feared that he would lose his turn if he did not immediately take his place in the queue. The papers had got to be signed and he was longing to get away to Passy, where his wife lay sick with congestion. He tried to shake off Josette's grip on his arm, but she would not let go.

"Can you get me a permit," she pleaded, "to change our doctor?"

Oh, those permits—those awful, tiresome, cruel permits, without which no citizen of this free Republic could do anything save die! Permit to move, permit for bread, permit for meat or milk, permit to call in a doctor, a midwife or an undertaker! Permits, permits all the time!

The crowd in the room, indifferent at first, had begun to take notice of this pretty girl's importunate demands. They were here, all of them, in quest of some permit or other, the granting of which depended on the mood of the official who sat at his desk the other side of the door. If the official was harassed and tired he would be disobliging, refuse permit after permit: to a sick woman to see a doctor, to an anaemic child to receive more milk, to a man to take work beyond a certain distance from his home. He could be disobliging if he chose, for full powers were vested in him. Such were the ways of the glorious Republic which had for its motto: Liberty and Fraternity. Such was the state of slavery into which the citizens of the free Republic had sunk. And as Josette insisted, still clinging to the doctor's arm, the men shrugged and some of them sneered. They knew that old Larousse could not get the permit for which she craved. It took days to obtain any kind of a permit: there were yards of red tape to measure out before anything of the sort could be obtained, even if the Commissary was in one of his best moods. They were all of them sorry for the girl in a way, chiefly because she was so pretty, but they thought her foolish to be so insistent. The women gazed on her and would have commiserated with her, only that they had so many troubles of their own. And they were all so tired, so tired of hanging about in this stuffy room and waiting their turn in the queue. It was so hard to worry over other people's affairs when one was tired and had countless worries of one's own.

Now someone came out of the inner room and the queue moved on. Josette was suddenly separated from the doctor, who was probably thankful to be rid of her; with a deep sigh of dejection she went back to her seat on the bench. A few glances of pity were still cast on her, but presently the queue was able to move on again and she was soon forgotten. No one took any more notice of her. The men whispered among themselves, the women, fagged and silent, stood waiting for their turn to go in. Only one man seemed to take an interest in Josette: a tall ugly fellow with one leg who was leaning against the wall with his crutches beside him. He was dressed in seedy black with somewhat soiled linen at throat and wrist, and his hair, which was long and lanky, was tied back at the nape of the neck with a frayed-out back ribbon. He wore no hat, his shoes were down at heel and his stockings were in holes. By the look of him he might have been a lawyer's clerk fallen on evil days.

Josette did not at first notice him, until presently she had that peculiar feeling which comes to one at times that a pair of eyes were fixed steadily upon her. She looked up and encountered the man's glance, then she frowned and quickly turned her head away, for the seedy-looking clerk was very ugly, and she did not like the intentness with which he regarded her. Much to her annoyance, however, she presently became conscious that he had gathered up his crutches and hobbled towards her. The crowd made way for him, and a few seconds later he stood before her, leaning upon his crutches.

"Your pardon, Citizeness," he said, and his voice was certainly more pleasing than his looks, "but I could not help hearing just now what you said to Citizen Larousse... about your friend who is sick... and your need of a doctor..."

He paused, and Josette looked up at him. He appeared timid and there certainly was not a suspicion of insolence in the way he addressed her, but he certainly was very ugly to look at. His face was the colour of yellow wax, and on his chin and cheeks there was a three days' growth of beard. His eyebrows were extraordinarily bushy and overshadowed his eyes, which were circled with purple as if from the effects of a blow. So much of his countenance did Josette take in at the first glance, but his voice had certainly sounded kindly, and poor little Josette was so devoured with anxiety just now that any show of kindness went straight to her heart.

"Then you must also have heard, Citizen," she said, "that Doctor Larousse could do nothing for my friend."

"That is why," the man rejoined, "I ventured to address you, Citizeness. I am not a doctor, only a humble apothecary, but I have some knowledge of medicine. Would you like me to see your friend?"

He had gradually dropped his voice until in the end he was hardly speaking above his breath. Josette felt strangely stirred. There was something in the way in which this man spoke which vaguely intrigued her and she couldn't make out why he should have spoken at all. She looked him straight in the eyes; her own were candid, puzzled, inquiring. If only he were less ugly, his skin less like parchment and his chin free from that stubby growth of a beard...

"I could come now," he said again. Then added with a light shrug, "I certainly could do your friend no harm just by seeing her, and I know of a cordial which works wonders on overstrung nerves."

Josette could never have told afterwards what it was that impelled her to rise then and to say:

"Very well, Citizen. Since you are so kind, will you come with me and see my sick friend?"

She made her way to the door and he followed her, working his way through the crowd across the room on his crutches. It was he who, despite his infirmities, opened the door and held it for the girl to pass through. It was close on midday. It had ceased raining and the air was milder, but heavy-laden clouds still hung overhead and the ill-paved streets ran with yellow-coloured mud.

Josette thought of Maurice as she started to walk in the direction of the Rue Picpus. She walked slowly because of the maimed man who hobbled behind her on his crutches, covering the ground in her wake, however, with extraordinary sureness and speed. She thought of Maurice, wondering what he would think of this adventure of hers, and whether he would approve. She was afraid that he would not. Maurice was cautious—more cautious than she was—and that very morning he had warned her to be very circumspect in everything she said and did, for Louise's sake and Charles-Léon's.

"Those devils," he had said to her just before they left home, "are sure to have their eye on Madame de Croissy. They haven't found the letters, but they know that they exist, and will of a surety have another try at getting possession of them."

"We must try and leave Madame alone as seldom as possible," he had said later on. "Unless I am detained over this awful business I will spend most of my day with her while you are at the workshop."

Apparently Maurice had been detained by the authorities, so Josette imagined, for he should have come to meet her at the Commissariat before now, but when he got there presently and found her gone he would probably conclude that she had been tired of waiting and had already gone home—and he would surely follow.

All the while that Josette's thoughts had run on Maurice, she had heard subconsciously the tap-tap of the man's crutches half a dozen paces or so behind her; then her thoughts had gone a-roaming on the terrible past, the dismal present, the hopeless future. What, she thought, would become of Louise and Charles-Léon after this appalling tragedy? Maître de Croissy's property in the Dauphiné brought in nothing: it was administered by a faithful soul who had been bailiff on the estate for close on half a century, and he just contrived to collect a sufficiency of money by the sale of timber and agricultural produce to pay for necessary repairs and stop the buildings and the land from going to rack and ruin, but there was nothing left over to pay as much as the rent of the miserable apartment in the Rue Picpus, let alone clothes and food. Maître de Croissy had been able to make a paltry income by his profession; but now? What was to become of his widow and of his child?

And Josette's thoughts of the future had been so black, so dismal and so absorbing that she was very nearly knocked down by a passing cart. The curses of the driver and the shouts of the passers-by brought her back to present realities, and these included the nearness of her maimed companion. She turned to look for him, but he was nowhere to be seen. She stood by for quite a long time at the angle of the street, thinking perhaps that he had fallen behind and would presently overtake her. But she waited in vain. There was no sign of the strange creature in the seedy black with the one leg and the crutches, the ugly face and gentle voice.

Quite against her will and her better judgement Josette felt vaguely dismayed and disappointed. What could this sudden disappearance mean of a man who had certainly forced his companionship upon her? Why had he gone with her thus far and then vanished so unaccountably? Did he really intend to visit Louise, or was his interest in her only a blind so as to attach himself to Josette? But if so what could be his object? All these thoughts and conjectures were very disturbing. There was always the fear of spies and informers present in every man or woman's mind these days, and Josette remembered Maurice's warning to be very circumspect, and she wished now that she had insisted on waiting at the Commissariat for Maurice's return before she embarked on this adventure with the mysterious stranger.

And then she suddenly remembered that just before coming up to the Pont-Neuf the maimed man had hobbled up close to her and asked:

"But whither are we going, Citizeness?"

And that she had replied:

"To No. 43, in the Rue Picpus, Citizen. My friend has an apartment there on the second floor."

And now she wished she had not given a total stranger such explicit directions.

CHAPTER IX

The rest of the day dragged on in its weary monotony. Josette had spent an hour with Louise at dinner-time, when she had tried again, as she had done in the past ten days, to rouse the unfortunate woman from her apathy. She did not tell her about the seedy apothecary with the one leg, who had thrust himself into her company only to vanish as mysteriously as he had appeared. She was beginning to feel vaguely frightened about that man: his actions had been so very strange that the conviction grew upon her that he must be some sort of Government spy.

Maurice Reversac also came in for a hurried meal at midday, and Josette spoke to him about the man at the Commissariat who had insisted on coming with her to visit Louise and then disappeared as if the cobble-stones of the great city had swallowed him up. Maurice, who was always inclined to prudence, wished that Josette had not been quite so free in her talk with the stranger. He dreaded those Government spies who undoubtedly would be detailed to watch the family of the murdered man; but whatever fears assailed him he kept them buried in his heart and indeed did his best to reassure Josette. But he did beg her to be more than ordinarily cautious. He stayed talking with her for a little while and then went away.

It was too late now to trudge all the way to the Batignolles in search of the public letter-writer, and Maurice, well aware of Josette's impetuosity at the bare mention of the Scarlet Pimpernel, thought it best to say nothing to her to-night on the subject. He was trying to put what order he could in the affairs of the late advocate, and to save what could possibly be saved out of the wreckage of his fortune for the benefit of the widow and the child.

"I have been promised a permit," he said, "to go down into the Dauphiné for a day or two. I can then see the bailiff and perhaps make some arrangement with him by which he can send Madame a small revenue from the estate every month. Then, if they let me carry on the practice..."

"Do you think they will?"

Maurice shrugged.

"One never knows. It all depends if lawyers are scarce now that they have killed so many. There is always some litigation afoot."

Finally he added, with a great show of confidence which he was far from feeling:

"Don't lose heart, Josette chérie. Every moment of my life I will devote to making Madame and the boy comfortable because I know that is the way to make you happy."

But Josette found it difficult not to lose heart. She was convinced in her own mind that danger greater than ever now threatened Louise entirely because of her, Josette's, indiscretion, and that the maimed man of the Commissariat whom she had so foolishly trusted was nothing but a Government spy.

The truth did not dawn upon her, not until many hours later, after she had spent her afternoon as usual at the workshop and then came home in the late afternoon.

As soon as Josette entered the living-room she knew that the miracle had happened—the miracle to which she had pinned her faith, for which she had hoped and prayed and striven. She had left Louise lying like a log on the sofa, silent, dry-eyed, sullen, with Charles-Léon, quietly whimpering in his small bed. She found her a transformed being with eyes bright and colour in her cheeks. But it was not this sudden transformation of her friend, nor yet Louise's cry: "Josette chérie! You were right and I was wrong to doubt." It was something more subtle, more intangible, that revealed to this ardent devotee that the hero of her dreams had filled the air with the radiance of his personality, that he had brought joy where sorrow reigned, and security and happiness where unknown danger threatened. Louise had run up to Josette as soon as she heard the turn of the latch-key in the door. She was laughing and crying, and after she had embraced Josette she ran back into the living-room and picked Charles-Léon up in her arms and hugged him to her breast.

"My baby," she murmured, "my baby! He will get strong and well and we shall be delivered from this hateful country."

Then she put Charles-Léon down, threw herself on the sofa, and burying her face in her arms she burst into tears. She cried and sobbed; her shoulders quivered convulsively. Josette made no movement towards her: it was best that she should cry for a time. The reaction from a state of dull despair had evidently been terrific, and the poor woman's over-wrought nerves would be all the better for this outlet of tears. How could Josette doubt for a moment that the miracle had happened?

As soon as she was a little more calm, Louise dried her eyes, then she drew a much-creased paper from the pocket of her skirt and without a word held it out to Josette. It was a letter written in a bold clear hand and was addressed to Citizeness Croissy at No. 43, Rue Picpus, on the second floor, and this is what it said:

"As soon as you receive this, believe that sincere friends are working for your safety. You must leave Paris and France immediately, not only for the boy's health's sake, but because very serious danger threatens you and him if you remain. This evening at eight o'clock take your boy in your arms and an empty market basket in your hand. Your concierge will probably challenge you; say that you are going to fetch your bread ration which you omitted to get this morning because of the bad weather. If the concierge makes a remark about your having the child with you, say that the Citizen Doctor ordered you to take him out as soon as the rain had ceased. Do not on any account hasten downstairs or through the porte-cochère, just walk quietly as if in truth you were going to the baker's shop. Then walk quietly along the street till you come to the district bakery. There will probably be a queue waiting for rations at the door. Take your place in the queue and go in and get your bread. In the crowd you will see a one-legged man dressed in seedy black. When he walks out of the shop, follow him. Divest yourself of all fear. The League of the Scarlet Pimpernel will see you safely out of Paris and out of France to England or Belgium, whichever you wish. But the first condition for your safety and that of the child is implicit trust in the ability of the League to see you through, and, as a consequence of trust, implicit obedience."

The letter bore no signature, but in the corner there was a small device, a star-shaped flower drawn in red ink. Josette murmured under her breath:

"The Scarlet Pimpernel! I knew that he would come."

Had she been alone she would have raised the paper to her lips, that blessed paper on which her hero's hand had rested. As it was she just held it tight in her hot little palm, and hoped that in her excitement Louise would forget about it and leave it with her as a precious relic.

"And of course you will come with me and Charles-Léon, Josette chérie."

Louise had to reiterate this more than once before the sense of it penetrated to Josette's inner consciousness. Even after the third repetition she still looked vague and ununderstanding.

"Josette chérie, of course you will come."

"But, Louise, no! How can I?" the girl murmured.

"How do you mean, how can you?"

Josette held up the precious letter.

"He does not speak of me in this."

"The English League probably knows nothing about you, Josette."

"But he does."

"How do you know?"

Josette evaded the direct question. She quoted the last few words of the letter:

"As a consequence of trust, implicit obedience."

"That does not mean..."

"It means," Josette broke in firmly, "that you must follow the directions given you in this letter, word for word. It is the least you can do, and you must do it for the sake of Charles-Léon. I am in no danger here, and I would not go if I were. Maurice will be here to look after me."

"You are talking nonsense, chérie. You know I would not go without you."

"You would sacrifice Charles-Léon for me?"

Then as Louise made no reply—how could she?—Josette continued with simple determination and unshaken firmness:

"I assure you, Louise chérie, that I am in no danger. Maurice cannot go away while he has Bastien's affairs to look after. He wouldn't go if he could, and it would be cowardly to leave him all alone here to look after things."

"But, Josette..."

"Don't say anything more about it, Louise. I am in no danger and I am not going. And what's more," she added softly, "I know that the Scarlet Pimpernel will look after me. Don't be afraid, he knows all about me."

And not another word would she say.

Louise, no doubt, knew her of old. Josette was one of those dear, gentle creatures whom nothing in the world could move once she was set on a definite purpose—especially if that purpose had in it the elements of self-sacrifice. The time, too, was getting on. It was already past seven o'clock. Louise busied herself with Charles-Léon, putting on him all the warm bits of garments she still possessed. Josette was equally busy warming up some milk, the little there was over the fire in the tiny kitchen.

At eight o'clock precisely Louise was ready. She prepared to gather the child in her arms. Josette had a big shawl ready to wrap round them both: she thrust the empty market basket over Louise's arm. Her heart ached at thought of this parting. God alone knew when they would meet again. But it all had to be done, it all had to be endured for the sake of Charles-Léon. Louise had declared her intention of going to England rather than to Belgium. She would meet a greater number of friends there.

"I will try and write to you, Josette chérie," she said. "My heart is broken at parting from you, and I shall not know a happy hour until we are together again. But you know, ma chérie, that Bastien was always convinced that this abominable Revolution could not last much longer; and—who knows?—Charlets-Léon and I may be back in Paris before the year is out."

She was, perhaps, too excited to feel the sorrow of parting quite as deeply as did Josette. Indeed, Louise was in a high state of exultation, crying one moment and laughing the next, and the hand with which she clung to Josette was hot and dry as if burning with fever. Just at the last she was suddenly shaken with a fit of violent trembling, her teeth chattered and she sank into a chair, for her knees were giving way under her.

"Josette!" she gasped. "You do not think, perchance...?"

"What, chérie?"

"That this... this letter is all a hoax? And that we—Charles-Léon and I—are walking into a trap?"

But Josette, who still held the letter tightly clasped in her hand, was quite sure that it was not a hoax. She recalled the seedy apothecary at the Commissariat and his gentle voice when he spoke to her, and there had been a moment when his steady gaze had drawn her eyes to him. She had not thought about it much at the time, but since then she had reflected and remembered the brief but very strange spell which seemed to have been cast over her at the moment. No, the letter was not a hoax. Josette would have staked her life on it that it was dictated, or perhaps even written, by the hero of her dreams.

"It is not a trap, Louise," she said firmly, "but the work of the finest man that ever lived. I am as convinced as that I am alive that the one-legged man in seedy black whom you will see in the bakery is the Scarlet Pimpernel himself."

It was Josette who lifted Charles-Léon and placed him in Louise's arms. A final kiss to them both and they were gone. Josette stood in the middle of the room, motionless, hardly breathing, for she tried to catch the last sound of Louise's footsteps going down the stairs. It was only after she had heard the opening and closing of the outside door of the house that she at last gave way to tears.

Just like this Josette had cried when Louise, after her marriage to Bastien de Croissy, left the little farm in the Dauphiné in order to take up her position as a great lady in Paris society. The wedding had taken place in the small village church, and everything had been done very quietly because General de Vandeleur, Louise's father, had only been dead a year and Louise refused to be married from the house of one of her grand relations. Papa and Maman Gravier and Josette were the three people she had cared for most in all the world until Bastien came along, and she had the sentimental feeling that she wished to walk straight out of the one house where her happy girlhood had been passed into the arms of the man to whom she had given her heart.

The wedding had been beautiful and gay, with the whole village hung about with flags and garlands of flowers; and previous to it there had been all the excitement of getting Louise's trousseau together, and of journeys up to Paris in order to try on the wedding gown. And Josette had been determined that no tears or gloomy looks from her should cast a shadow over her friend's happiness. It was when everything was over, when Louise drove away in the barouche en route for Paris, that Josette was suddenly overwhelmed with the sorrow which she had tried to hold in check for so long. Then as now she had thrown herself down on the sofa and cried out her eyes in self-pity for her loneliness. But what was the loneliness of that day in comparison with what it was now? In those days Josette still had her father and mother: there were the many interests of the farm, the dogs, the cows, haymaking, harvesting. Now there was nothing but dreariness ahead. Dreariness and loneliness. No one to look after, no one to fuss over. No Charles-Léon to listen to tales of heroism and adventure. Only the Government workshop, the girls there with their idle chatter and their reiterated complaints: only the getting up in the morning, the munching of stale food, the stitching of shirts, and the going to bed at night!

Josette thought of all this later on when bedtime came along, and she knelt beside Charles-Léon's empty cot and nearly cried her eyes out. Nearly but not quite, for presently Maurice came home. And it was wonderful how his presence put a measure of comfort in Josette's heart. Somehow the moment she heard the turn of his latchkey in the door, and his footsteps across the hall, her life no longer appeared quite so empty. There was someone left in Paris after all, who would need care and attention and fussing over when he was sick; his future would have to be planned, suitable lodgings would have to be found for him, and life generally re-ordained according to the new conditions.

And first of all there was the excitement of telling Maurice all about those new conditions.

Even before he came into the room Josette had jumped to her feet and hastily dried her eyes. But he saw in a moment that she had been crying.

"Josette!" he cried out, "what is it?"

"Take no notice, Maurice," Josette replied, still struggling with her tears, "I am not really crying... it is only because I am so... ever so happy!"

"Why? What has happened?"

"He came, Maurice," she said solemnly, "and they have gone."

Of course Maurice could not make head or tail of that.

"He? They?" he murmured frowning. "Who came, and who has gone?"

She made him sit down on the ugly horse-hair sofa and she sat down beside him and told him about everything. Her dreams had turned to reality, the Scarlet Pimpernel had come to take Louise and Charles-Léon away out of all this danger and all this misery: he had come to take them away to England where Louise would be safe, and Charles-Léon would get quite well and strong.

"And left you here!" Maurice exclaimed involuntarily, when Josette paused, out of breath, after she had imparted the great and glorious news: "gone to safety and left you here to face..."

But Josette with a peremptory gesture put her small hand across his mouth.

"Wait, Maurice," she said, "let me tell you."

She drew the precious letter from under her fichu—Louise, fortunately, had not demanded its return—and she read its contents aloud to Maurice.

"Now you see!" she concluded triumphantly, and fixed her glowing eyes on the young man.

"I only see," he retorted almost roughly, "that they had no right to leave you here... all alone."

"Not alone, Maurice," she replied; "are you not here... to take care of me?"

That, of course, was a heavenly moment in Maurice's life. Never had Josette—Josette who was so independent and self-reliant—spoken like this before, never had she looked quite like she did now, adorable always, but more so with that expression of dependence and appeal in her eyes. The moment was indeed so heavenly that Maurice felt unable to say anything. He was so afraid that the whole thing was not real, that he was only dreaming, and that if he spoke the present rapture would at once be dispelled. He felt alternately hot and cold, his temples throbbed. He tried to express with a glance all that went on in his heart. His silence and his looks did apparently satisfy Josette, for after a moment or two she explained to him just what her feelings were about the letter.

"The Scarlet Pimpernel demands trust and obedience, Maurice," she said with naïve earnestness. "Well! would that have been obedience if Louise had lugged me along with her? He doesn't mention me in the letter. If he had meant me to come, he would have said so."

With this pronouncement Maurice had perforce to be satisfied; but one thing more he wanted to know: what had become of the letters? But Josette couldn't tell him. Ever since Bastien's death, Louise had never spoken of them, or given the slightest hint of what she had done with them.

"Let's hope she has destroyed them," Maurice commented with a sigh.

The next day they spent in hunting for new lodgings for Maurice. Strange! Josette no longer felt lonely. She still grieved after Louise and Charles-Léon, but somehow life no longer seemed as dreary as she thought it would be.

CHAPTER X

Louise, in very truth, was much too excited to feel the pang of parting as keenly as did Josette, and ever since Charles-Léon had fallen sick she had taken a veritable hatred to Paris and her dingy apartment in the Rue Picpus. The horror of her husband's death had increased her abhorrence of the place, and now hatred amounted to loathing.

Therefore it was that she went downstairs with a light heart on that memorable evening of September. She had Charles-Léon in her arms and carried the empty market basket, with her ration card laid ostentatiously in it for anyone to see. The concierge was in the doorway of his lodge and asked her whither she was going. These were not days when one could tell a concierge to mind his own business, so Louise replied meekly:

"To the bakery, Citizen," and she showed the man her ration card.

"Very late," the concierge remarked drily.

"The weather has been so bad all day..."

"Too bad even now to take the child out, I imagine."

"It has left off raining," Louise said still gently, "and the poor cabbage must have some fresh air; the Citizen Doctor insisted on that."

She felt terribly impatient at the delay, but did not dare appear to be in a hurry, whilst the concierge seemed to derive amusement at keeping her standing beside his lodge. He knew her for an aristo, and many there were in these days who found pleasure in irritating or humiliating those who in the past had thought themselves their betters.

However, this ordeal, like so many others, did come to an end after a time; the concierge condescended to open the porte-cochère and Louise was able to slip out into the street. It had certainly left off raining, but it was very cold and damp underfoot. Louise trudged on as fast as she could, her thin shoes squelching through the mud. Fortunately the bakery was not far, and soon she was able to take her place in the queue outside the shop. There was no crowd at this hour: a score of people at the most, chiefly women. Louise's anxious glance swept quickly over them and at once her heart gave a jump, for she had caught sight of a maimed man on crutches, dressed in back as the mysterious letter had described. He was ahead of her in the queue, and she saw him quite distinctly when he entered the shop, and stood for a moment under the lantern which hung above the door. But his face she could not clearly see, for he wore a black hat with a wide brim: a hat as shabby as his clothes. Presently he disappeared inside the shop, and Louise did not see him again until she herself had been to the counter and been served with her ration of bread. Then she saw him just going out of the shop and she followed as soon as she could.

There were still a good many people in the street, and just over the road there were two men of the Republican Guard on duty, set there to watch over the queue outside the licensed bakeries. Some of the people there were still waiting their turn, others were walking away, some in one direction, some in another. But there was no sign anywhere of the one-legged man. Louise stood for a moment in the ill-lighted street, perturbed and anxious, wondering in which direction she ought to go; her heart seemed to sink into her shoes, and she was desperately tired, too, from standing so long with the child in her arms. But with those men of the Republican Guard watching her she did not like to hesitate too long and, thoroughly heart-sick now and nigh unto despair, she began to fear that the letter and all her hopes were only idle dreams. Almost faint with fatigue and disappointment she had just turned her weary footsteps towards home when suddenly she heard the distant tap-tap of crutches on the cobble-stones.

With a deep sigh of relief Louise started at once to walk in the direction whence came the welcome sound. The tap-tap kept on slightly ahead of her, so all she had to do was to follow as closely as she could. With Charles-Léon asleep in her arms she had trudged on thus for about ten minutes, turning out of one street and into another, when suddenly the tap-tap ceased. The maimed man had paused beside an open street door; when Louise came up with him he signed to her to enter.

She hadn't the least idea where she was, but from the direction in which she had gone she conjectured that it was somewhere near the Temple. There were not many people about, and though on the way she had gone past more than one patrol of the National Guard, the men had taken no notice of her; she was just a poor woman with a child in her arms and a ration of bread in her basket; nor had they paid any heed to the maimed, seedy-looking individual hobbling along on crutches.

Now as Louise passed through the open door her guide whispered rapidly to her:

"Go up two flights of stairs and knock at the door on your right."

Strangely enough, Louise had no hesitation in obeying; though she had no idea where she would find herself she felt no fear. Perhaps she was too tired to feel anything but a longing for rest. She went up the two flights of stairs and knocked at the door which her guide had indicated. It was opened by a rough-looking youngish man in ragged clothes, unshaved, unkempt, who blinked his eyes as if he had just been roused out of sleep.

"Is it Madame de Croissy?" he asked, and Louise noted that he spoke French with a foreign accent; also the word "Madame" was unusual these days. This, of course, reassured her. Her thoughts flew back to Josette and the girl's firm belief in the existence of the Scarlet Pimpernel.

The young man led the way through a narrow ill-lit passage to a room where Louise's aching eyes were greeted with the welcome sight of a table spread with a cloth on which were laid a knife and fork, a place and a couple of mugs. There was also a couch in a corner of the room with a pillow on it and a rug. It was rather cold and a solitary tallow candle shed a feeble, vacillating light on the bare whitewashed walls and the blackened ceiling, but Louise thought little of all this; she sank down on a chair by the table, and the young man then said to her in his quaint stilted French:

"In one moment, Madame, I will bring you something to eat, for you must be very hungry; and we also have a little milk for the boy. I hope you won't mind waiting while I get everything ready for you."

He went out of the room before Louise had found sufficient energy to say "Thank you." She just sat there like a log, her purple-rimmed eyes staring into vacancy. Charles-Léon, who, luckily, had been asleep all this time, now woke and began to whimper. Louise hugged him to her bosom until the tousled young ruffian reappeared presently, carrying a tray on which there was a dish and a jug. Louise felt almost like swooning when a delicious smell of hot food and steaming milk tickled her nostrils. The young man had poured out a mugful of milk for Charles-Léon, and while the child drank eagerly Louise made a great effort to murmur an adequate "Thank you."

"It is not to me, Madame," the man retorted, "that you owe thanks. I am here under orders. You, too, I am afraid," he went on with a smile, "will have to submit to the will of my chief."

"Give me the orders, sir," Louise rejoined meekly. "I will obey them."

"The orders are that you eat some supper now and then have a good rest until I call you in the early morning. You will have to leave here a couple of hours before the dawn."

"Charles-Léon and I will be ready, sir. Anything else?"

"Only that you get a good sleep, for to-morrow will be wearisome. Good-night, Madame."

Before Louise could say another word the young man had slipped out of the room.

Charles-Léon slept peacefully all night cuddled up against his mother, but Louise lay awake for hours, thinking of her amazing adventure. She was up betimes, and soon after a distant church clock struck half-past four there was a knock at the door. Her young friend of the evening before had come to fetch her; he looked as if he had been up all night, and certainly he had not taken off his clothes. Louise picked Charles-Léon up, and with him in her arms she followed her friend down the stairs. Outside she found herself in a narrow street: it was quite dark because the street lanterns had already been extinguished and there was not yet a sign of dawn in the sky. Through the darkness Louise perceived the vague silhouette of a covered cart such as the collectors of the city's refuse used for their filthy trade. A small donkey was harnessed to the cart and it was bring driven apparently by a woman.

Neither the woman nor the young man spoke at the moment, but the latter intimated to Louise by a gesture that she must step into the cart. Only for a few seconds did she hesitate. The cart was indeed filthy and reeked of all sorts of horrible odours calculated to make any sensitive person sick. A kindly voice whispered in her ear:

"It cannot be helped, Madame, and you must forgive us: anyway, it is no worse than the inside of one of their prisons."

Her friend now took Charles-Léon from her, and summoning all her courage she stepped into the cart. The child was then handed back to her and she gathered herself and him into a heap under the awning. She wanted to assure her friend that not only was she prepared for anything, but that her heart was full of gratitude for all that was being done for her. But before she could speak a large piece of sacking was thrown right over her, and over the sacking a pile of things the nature of which the poor woman did not venture to guess. As she settled herself down, as comfortably as she could, she came in contact with what appeared to be a number of bottles.

A minute or two later with much creaking of wheels and many a jerk the cart was set in motion. It went jogging along over the cobble-stones of the streets of Paris at foot pace, while under the awning, smothered by a heap of all sorts of vegetable refuse, Louise de Croissy had sunk into a state of semi-consciousness.

CHAPTER XI

She was roused from her torpor by the loud cry of "Halte!" The cart came to a standstill and Louise, with sudden terror gripping her heart, realised that they had come to one of the gates of Paris where detachments of National Guard, officered by men eager for promotion, scrutinised every person who ventured in or out of the city.

The poor woman, crouching under a heap of odds and ends, heard the measured tramp of soldiers and a confused murmur of voices. Through a chink in the awning she could see that the grey light was breaking over this perilous crisis of her life. Presently a gruff commanding voice rose above the shrill croaky tones of a woman, whom Louise guessed to be the drive of the cart. The gruff voice when first it reached Louise's consciousness was demanding to see what there was underneath the awning. She could do nothing but hug the child closer to her breast, for she knew that within the next few seconds her life and his would tremble in the balance. She hardly dared to breathe; her whole body was bathed in a cold sweat. Heavy footsteps, accompanied by short, shuffling ones, came round to the back of the cart, and a few seconds later the end flap of the awning was thrust aside and a wave of cold air swept around inside the cart. Some of it penetrated to poor Louise's nostrils, but she hardly dared to breathe. She knew that her fate and that of Charles-Léon would be decided within the next few minutes perhaps.

The gruff voice was evidently that of one in authority.

"Anyone in there?" it demanded, and to the unfortunate woman it seemed as if the heap of rubbish on the top of her was being prodded with the point of a bayonet.

"No one now, Citizen Officer," a woman's shrill voice responded, obviously the voice of the old hag who was driving the cart: "that's my son there, holding the donkey's head. He can't speak, you know, Citizen... never could since birth... tongued-tied as the saying is. But a good lad... can't gossip, you see. And here's his passport and mine!"

There was some rustle of papers, one or two muttered words and then the woman spoke again:

"I'm picking up my daughter and her boy at Champerret presently," she said: "their passports and permits are all in order too, but I haven't got them here."

"Where are you going then all of you?" the gruff voice asked, and there was more rustle of papers and a tramping of feet. The passports were being taken into the guard-room to be duly stamped.

"Only as far as Clichy, Citizen Officer. It says so on the permit. See here, Citizen. 'Permit for Citizeness Ruffin and her son Pierre to proceed to Clichy for purposes of business!' That's all in order is it not, Citizen Officer?"

"Yes! yes! that's all in order all right. And now let's see what you have got inside the cart."

"All in order... of course it is..." the old woman went on, cackling like an old hen; "you don't catch Mère Ruffin out of order with authorities. Not her. Passports and permits, everything always in order, Citizen Officer. You ask any captain at the gates. They'll tell you. Mother Ruffin is always in order... always... in order..."

And all the while the old hag was shifting and pushing about the heap of rubbish that was lying on the top of the unfortunate Louise.

"It's not a pleasant business, mine, Citizen Officer," she continued with a doleful sigh; "but one must live, what? Citizen Arnould—you know him, don't you, Citizen? Over at the chemical works—he buys all my stuff from me."

"Filthy rubbish, I call it," the officer retorted; "but don't go wasting my time, mother. Just shift that bit of sacking, and you can take your stuff to the devil for aught I care."

Louise, trembling with fear and horror, still half-smothered under the pile of rubbish, was on the point of losing consciousness. Fortunately Charles-Léon was still asleep and she was able to keep her wits sufficiently about her to hold him tightly in her arms. Would the argument between the soldier and the old hag never come to an end?

"I am doing my best, Citizen Officer, but the stuff is heavy," the woman muttered; "and all my papers in order I should have thought... Mother Ruffin's papers always are in order, Citizen Officer.... Ask any captain of the guard... he'll tell you..."

"Nom d'un nom," the soldier broke in with an oath, "are you going to shift that sacking or shall I have to order the men to take you to the guard-room?"

"The guard-room? Me? Mère Ruffin, known all over the country as an honest patriot? You'd get a reprimand, Citizen Officer—that's what you would get for taking Mère Ruffin to the guard-room. Bien! bien! don't lose your temper, Citizen Officer... no harm meant.... Here! can't one of your men give me a hand?... But... I say...."

A click of glass against glass followed: Louise remembered the bottles that were piled up round her. After this ominous click there was a moment's silence. Sounds from the outside reached Louise's consciousness: men talking, the clatter of horses' hoofs, the rattle of wheels, challenge from the guard, cries of "Halte!" distant murmurs of people talking, moving, even laughing, whilst she, hugging Charles-Léon to her breast, marvelled at what precise moment she and her child would be discovered and dragged out of this noisome shelter to some equally noisome prison. The woman had ceased jabbering: the click of glass seemed to have paralysed her tongue; but only for a moment: a minute or so later her shrill voice could be heard again.

"You won't be hard on me will you, Citizen Officer?" she said dolefully.

"Hard?" the soldier retorted. "That'll depend on what you've got under there."

"Nothing to make a fuss over, Citizen Officer: a poor widow has got to live, and..."

There was another click of glass—several clicks, then a thud, the bottles tumbling one against the other, then the officer's harsh voice saying with a laugh:

"So! that's it! is it? Absinthe? What? You old reprobate! No wonder you didn't want me to look under that sacking."

"Citizen Officer, don't be hard on a poor widow..."

"Poor widow indeed? Where did you steal the stuff?"

"I didn't steal it, Citizen Officer... I swear I didn't."

"How many bottles have you got there?"

"Only a dozen, Citizen..."

"Out with them."

"Citizen Officer..."

"Out with them I say..."

"Yes, Citizen," the old woman said meekly with an audible snuffle.

She sprawled over the back of the cart, pushed some of the rubbish aside and Louise was conscious of the bottles being pulled out from round and under her. She heard the soldier say:

"Is that all?"

"One dozen, Citizen Sergeant. You can see for yourself."

The woman dropped down to the ground. Louise could hear her snuffling the other side of the awning. After which there came a terrible moment, almost the worst of this awful and protracted ordeal. The officer appeared to have given an order to one of the soldiers, who used the end of his bayonet for the purpose of ascertaining whether there were any more bottles under the sacking. What he did was to bang away with it on the pile of rubbish that still lay on the top of Louise; some of the bangs hit Louise on the legs: one blow fell heavily on one of her ankles. The courage with which she endured these blows motionless and in silence was truly heroic. Her life and Charles-Léon's depended on her remaining absolutely still. And she did remain quite still, hugging the child to her breast, outwardly just another pile of rubbish on the floor of the cart. The boy was positively wonderful, he seemed to know that he must not move or utter a sound. Though he must have been terrified, he never cried, but just clung to his mother, with eyes tightly closed. Louise in fact came to bless the very noisomeness of the refuse which lay on top of her, for obviously the soldier did not like to touch it with his hands.

"I get most of my stuff from the hospitals," Louise could hear the old hag talking volubly to the officer; "you can see for yourself, Citizen, it is mostly linen which has been used for bandages... sore legs you know and all that... Citizen Arnould over at the chemical works gives me good money for it. It seems they make paper out of the stuff. Paper out of linen I ask you... brown or red paper I should say, for you should see some of it... and all the fever they've got in the wards now... yellow fever if not worse..."

"There! that'll do, Mother Ruffin," the officer broke in roughly: "all your talk won't help you. You've got to pay for taking the stuff though, and you know it... and there'll be a fine for trying to smuggle..."

There followed a loud and long-winded protests on the part of the old hag; but apparently the officer was at the end of his tether and would listen to none of it, although he did seem to have a certain measure of tolerance for the woman's delinquency.

"You come along quietly, Mother," he said in the end, "it will save you trouble in the end."

He called to his men, and snuffling, cackling, protesting, the old woman apparently followed them quietly in the direction of the guard-room. At any rate Louise heard nothing more. For a long, long time she did not hear anything. The reaction after the terror of this past half hour was so great that she fell into a kind of torpor; the noises of the street only came to her ears through a kind of fog. The only feeling she was conscious of was that she must hold Charles-Léon closely to her breast.

How long this state of numbness lasted she did not know. She had lost count of time; and she had lost the use of her limbs. Her ankle where she had been hit with the flat of the soldier's bayonet had ached furiously at first: now she no longer felt the pain. Charles-Léon, she thought, must have gone to sleep, for she could just feel his even breathing against her breast.

Suddenly she was aroused by the sound, still distant, of the woman's shrill voice. It drew gradually nearer.

"Now then, Pierre, let's get on," the old hag was shrieking as she came along.

Pierre, whoever he was, had apparently remained at the donkey's head all this time. Louise from the first had suspected that he was none other than her friend of the tousled head; but who that awful old hag with the snuffle and the cackling voice she could not even conjecture. But she was content to leave it at that. Apparently those wonderful and heroic Englishmen employed strange tools in their work of mercy. At the moment she felt far too tired and too numb even to marvel at the amazing way in which that old woman had hoodwinked the officer of the guard. As Louise returned to consciousness she could hear vaguely in the distance the soldiers laughing and chaffing and the woman muttering and grumbling:

"Making a poor woman pay for an honest trading... a scandal I call it..."

"Ohé, la mère!" the soldiers shouted amidst loud laughter, "bring us some more of that absinthe to-morrow."

"Robbers! thieves! brigands!" the woman ejaculated shrilly, "catch me again coming this way..."

She apparently busied herself with putting the bottles—or some of them at any rate—back into the cart: after which the flap of the awning was again lowered: there was much creaking and shaking of the cart; soon it was once more set in motion; to the accompaniment of more laughter and many ribald jokes on the part of the soldiers, who stood watching the departure of the ramshackle vehicle and its scrubby driver.

Anon the creaking wheels resumed their jolting, axle-deep in mud, over the country roads riddled with ruts. But of this Louise de Croissy now knew little or nothing. She had mercifully once more ceased to think or feel.

CHAPTER XII

Days of strange adventures followed, adventures that never seemed real, only products of a long dream.

There was that halt on the wayside in the afternoon of the first day, with Paris a couple of leagues and more behind. The end flap of the awning was pulled aside and the horrible weight lifted from Louise's inert body. Glad of the relief and of the breath of clean air, she opened her eyes, then closed them again quickly at sight of the hideous old woman whose scarred and grimy face was grinning at her from the rear of the cart. A dream figure in very truth, or a nightmare! But was she not the angel in disguise who, by dint of a comedian's art, had hoodwinked the sergeant at the gate of Paris and passed through the jealously guarded barriers with as much ease as if her passengers in that filthy cart had been provided with the safest of passports?

Yet, strive how she might, Louise could see nothing in that ugly and ungainly figure before her that even remotely suggested a heroine or an angel. She gave up the attempt at fathoming the mystery, and allowed herself and Charles-Léon to be helped out of the cart and, with a great sigh of gladness, she sank down on the mossy bank by the roadside, and ate of the bread and cheese which the hag had placed beside her, together with a bottle of milk for the boy.

When she and Charles-Léon had eaten and drunk and she had taken in as much fresh country air as her lungs would hold, she looked about her, intending to thank that extraordinary old woman for her repeated kindness, but the latter was nowhere to be seen; also the donkey was no longer harnessed to the cart. Somewhere in the near distance there was a group of derelict cottages and, chancing to look that way, Louise saw the woman walking towards it and leading the donkey by the bridle.

She never again set eyes on that old hag. Presently, however, a rough fellow clad in a blue smock, who looked like a farm labourer, appeared upon the scene; he was leading a pony, and as soon as he caught Louise's glance he beckoned to her to get back into the cart. Mechanically she obeyed, and the man lifted Charles-Léon and placed him in his mother's arms. He harnessed the pony to the cart, and once more the tumble-down vehicle went lumbering along the muddy country lanes. Fortunately, though the sky was grey and the wind boisterous, the rain held off most of the time. For three days and nights they were on the road, sleeping when they could, eating whatever was procurable on the way. They never once touched the cities, but avoided them by circuitous ways; always a pony, or sometimes a donkey, was harnessed to the cart, but the same rough-looking farm labourer held the reins the whole time. Two or three times a day he would get down, always in the vicinity of some derelict building or other into which he would disappear, and presently he would emerge once more leading a fresh beast of burden. Once or twice he would be accompanied on those occasions by another man as rough-looking as himself, but for the most part he would attend to the pony or donkey alone.

There were some terrible moments during those days, moments when Louise felt that she must choke with terror. Her heart was in her mouth, for patrols of soldiers would come riding or marching down the road, and now and again there would be a cry of "Halte!" and a brief colloquy would follow between the Sergeant in command and the driver of the cart. But apparently—thank God for that—the cart and its rustic driver appeared too beggarly and insignificant to arouse suspicion or to engage for long the attention of the patrols.

The worst moment of all occurred in the late afternoon of the third day. The driver had turned the cart off the main road into a narrow lane which ran along the edge of a ploughed field. It was uphill work and the pony had done three hours' work already, dragging the rickety vehicle along muddy roads. Its pace got slower and slower. The wind blew straight from the north-east, and Louise felt very sick and cold, nor could she manage to keep Charles-Léon warm: the awning flapped about in the wind and let in gusts of icy draught all round.

When presently the driver pulled up and came round to see how she fared, she ventured to ask him timidly whether it wouldn't be possible to find some sheltered spot where they could all spend the night in comparative warmth for the child. At once the man promised to do his best to find some derelict barn or cottage. He turned into a ploughed field and soon disappeared from view. Louise remained shivering in the cart with Charles-Léon hugged closely to her under her shawl. She had indeed need of all her faith in the wonderful Scarlet Pimpernel to keep her heart warm, while her body was racked with cold.

She had no notion of time, of course; and sundown meant nothing when all day the sky had been just a sheet of heavy, slate-coloured clouds. A dim grey light still hung over the dreary landscape, while slowly the horizon veiled itself in mist. The driver had been gone some time when Louise's sensitive ears caught the distant sound of horses' hoofs splashing in the mud of the road. It was a sound that always terrified her. Up to now nothing serious had happened, but it was impossible to know when some meddlesome or officious Sergeant might with questions and suspicions shatter at one fell swoop all the poor woman's hopes of ultimate safety. The patrol—for such it certainly was—was coming at a fair speed along the main road. Perhaps, thought Louise, the soldiers would ride past the corner of the lane and either not see the cart or think it not worth investigating. Bitterly she reproached herself for her want of endurance. If she had not sent the driver off to go in search of a shelter for the night, he would have driven on at least another half kilometre and then surely the cart would not have been sighted from the road. And, what's more, she would not have been alone to face this awful contingency.

For contingency it certainly was. Anything—the very worst—might happen now, for the man was not there to answer harsh questions with gruff answers, he was not there with his ready response and his amazing knack of averting suspicions. Louise was alone and she heard the squad of soldiers turn into the lane. Her heart seemed to cease beating. A moment or two later the man in command cried "Halte!" and himself drew rein close to the rear of the cart.

"Anyone there?" he queried in a loud voice.

Oh! for an inspiration to know just what to say in reply!

"There's someone under there," the soldier went on peremptorily; "who is it?"

More dead than alive, Louise was unable to speak.

The Sergeant then gave the order! "Allons! just see who is in there; and," he added facetiously, "lets hear where the driver of this elegant barouche has hidden himself."

There was some clatter and jingle of metal: the sound of men dismounting, the pawing and snorting of horses. Through the chinks in the awning Louise could perceive the dim light of a couple of dark lanterns like two yellow eyes staring. Then the awning in the rear of the cart was raised, the lantern lit up the interior and Louise was discovered crouching in the distant corner on a pile of sacking, hugging Charles-Léon.

"Ohé! la petite mère!" the Sergeant called out not unkindly: "come out and lets have a look at you."

Louise crawled out of the darkness, still hugging Charles-Léon. The evening was drawing in. She wondered vaguely if anything in her appearance would betray that she was no rustic, but an unfortunate, fleeing the country. She looked wearied to death, dishevelled and grimy. The Sergeant leaning down from his saddle peered into her face.

"Who is in charge of your barouche, petite mère?" he asked.

"My—my—husband," Louise contrived to stammer through teeth that were chattering.

"Where is he?"

"Gone to the village... to see if we can get... a bed... for the night..."

"Hm!" said the Sergeant. And after a moment or two: "Suppose you let me see your papers."

"Papers?" Louise murmured.

"Yes! Your passports, what?"

"I haven't any papers."

"How do you mean you haven't any papers?" the Sergeant retorted, all the kindliness gone out of his voice.

"My husband..." Louise stammered again.

"Oh! you mean your husband has got your papers?"

Louise, no longer able to utter a sound, merely nodded.

"And he's gone to the village?"

Another nod.

"Where is the village?"

Louise shook her head.

"You mean you don't know?"

The man paused for a moment or two. Clearly there was something unusual in this helpless creature stranded in the open country with a child in her arms, and no man in sight belonging to her.

"Well!" he said after a moment or two, during which he vainly tried to peer more closely in Louise's face, "you'll come along with us now, and when your husband finds the barouche gone he will know where to look for you."

"You get into your carriage, petite mère," he added; "one of the men will drive you."

So shaken and frightened was Louise that she could not move. Her knees were giving way under her. Two men lifted her and Charles-Léon into the cart. They were neither rough nor unkind—family men perhaps with children of their own—or just machines performing their duty. Louise could only wonder what would happen next. Crouching once more in the cart, she felt it give a lurch as one man scrambled into the driver's seat. He took the reins and clicked his tongue, and the pony had just answered to a flick of the whip when from the ploughed field there came loud cries of "Ohé!" coming right out of the evening mist. Louise didn't know if she could feel relief or additional terror when she heard that call. It was her rustic friend coming back at full speed. He was running, and came to a halt in the lane breathless and obviously exhausted.

"Sergeant," he cried, gasping for breath, "give a hand... on your life give a hand... a fortune, Sergeant, if we get him now."

The soldier, taken aback by the sudden appearance of this madman—he thought of him as such—fell to shouting: "What's all this?" and had much ado to hold his horse, which had shied and reared at the strident noise. The other soldiers—there were only four of them—were in a like plight, and for a moment or two there was a good deal of confusion which the quickly gathering darkness helped to intensify.

"What's all this?" the Sergeant queried again as soon as the confusion subsided. "Here! you!" he commanded: "are you the owner of this aristocratic vehicle!"

"I am," the man replied.

"And is that your wife and child inside?"

"They are. But in Satan's name, Sergeant..."

"Never mind about Satan now. You just get into your stylish vehicle and turn your pony's head round; you are coming along with me."

"Where to?"

"To Abbeville, parbleu. And if your papers are not in order..."

"If you go to Abbeville, Sergeant," the man declared, still panting with excitement, "you lose the chance of a lifetime... there's a fortune for you and me and these honest patriots waiting for us in the middle of this ploughed field."

"The man's mad," the Sergeant declared. "Allons, don't let's waste any more time. En evant!"

"But I tell you I saw him, Citizen Sergeant," the man protested.

"Saw whom? The devil?"

"Worse. The English spy."

It was the Sergeant's turn to gasp and to pant.

"The English spy?" he exclaimed.

"Him they call the Scarlet Pimpernel!" the man asserted hotly.

"Where?" the Sergeant cried. And the four men echoed excitedly! "Where?"

The man pointed towards the ploughed field.

"I went to look for a shelter for the night for my wife and child. I came to a barn. I heard voices. I drew near. I peeped in. Aristos I tell you. A dozen of them. All talking gibberish. English, what? And drinking. Drinking. Some of them were asleep on the straw. They mean to spend the night there."

He paused, breathless, and pressed his grimy hands against his chest as if every word he uttered caused him excruciating pain. The words came from his throat in short jerky sentences. Clearly he was on the verge of collapse. But now the Sergeant and his men were as eager, as excited as he was.

"Yes! yes! go on!" they urged.

"They are there still," the man said, trying to speak clearly: "I saw them. Not ten minutes ago. I ran away, for I tell you they looked like devils. And one of them is tall... tall like a giant... and his eyes..."

"Never mind his eyes," the Sergeant broke in gruffly: "I am after those English devils. There's a reward of ten thousand livres for the capture of their chief... and promotion..." he added lustily.

He turned his horse round in the direction of the field, and called loudly "Allons!"

The driver halloed after him.

"But what about me, Citizen Sergeant?"

"You can follow. In what direction did you say?"

"Straight across," the man replied. "See that light over there... keep it on your right... and then follow the track... and there's a gap in the hedge..."

But the Sergeant was no longer listening. No doubt visions of ten thousand livres and fortune rising to giddy heights rose up before him out of the fast-gathering gloom. He was not going to waste time. The men followed him, as eager as the jingle of their accouterments, the creaking of damp leather, the horses snorting and pawing the wet earth. The flap of the awning had been lowered again: she couldn't see anything, but she heard the welcome sounds, and no longer felt the cold.

"My baby, my baby," she murmured, crooning to Charles-Léon, "I do believe that God is on our side."

The cart moved along. She didn't know in which direction. The pony was going at foot-pace: probably the driver was leading it, for the darkness now was intense—the welcome darkness that enveloped the wanderers as in a black shroud. At first Louise could not help thinking of that Sergeant and the soldiers. What would they do when they found that they had been hoodwinked? They would scour the countryside of course to find traces of the cart. Would they succeed in the darkness of the night? She dared not let her thoughts run on farther. All she could do was to press Charles-Léon closer and closer to her heart and to murmur over and over again: "I do believe that God is on our side."

He was indeed, for the night passed by and there was no further sign of the patrol. After a time the cart came to a standstill and the driver came round, and helped her and Charles-Léon to descend. They all sheltered in the angle of a tumble-down wall which had once been part of a cottage. The man wrapped some sacking round Louise and the child and she supposed she slept, for she remembered nothing more until the light of dawn caused her to open her eyes.

The next day they came in sight of Calais. The driver pulled up and bade Louise and the child descend. Louise knew nothing of this part of France. It appeared to her unspeakably dreary and desolate. The earth was of a drab colour, so different to the rich reddish clay of the Dauphiné, and instead of the green pastures and golden cornfields, still scrubby grass grew in irregular tufts here and there. The sky was grey and there was a blustering wind which brought with it a smell of fish and salt water. The stunted trees, with their branches all tending away from the sea, had the mournful appearance of a number of attenuated human beings who were trying to run away and were held back by their fettered feet. Calais lay far away on the right, and there was only one habitation visible in this desolate landscape. This was a forlorn and dilapidated-looking cottage on the top of the cliff to the west: its roof was all crooked on the top like a hat that has been blown aside by the wind. The driver pointed to the cottage and said to Louise:

"That is our objective now, Madame, but I am afraid it has to be reached on foot. Can you do it?"

This was the first time that the man spoke directly to Louise. His voice was serious and kindly, nevertheless she was suddenly conscious of a strange pang of puzzlement and doubt—almost of awe: for the man spoke in perfect French, the language of a highly educated man. Yet he had the appearance of a rough country boor: his clothes were ragged, he wore neither shirt nor stockings: of course his unshaved cheeks and chin added to his look of scrubbiness and his face and hands were far from clean. At first, when he replaced the horrible old hag on the driver's seat of the cart, Louise had concluded that he was one of that heroic band of Englishmen who were leading her and Charles-Léon to safety, but this conclusion was soon dispelled when the man spoke to the several patrols of soldiers who met them on the way. She had heard him talk to them, and also the night before, during those terrible moments in the lane; and he had spoken in the guttural patois peculiar to the peasantry of Northern France.

But now, that pleasant, cultured voice, the elegant diction of a Parisian! Louise did not know what to make of it. Had she detected the slightest trace of a foreign accent she would have understood, and gone back to her first conclusion, that here was one of those heroic Englishmen of whom Josette was wont to talk so ecstatically. But a French gentleman, masquerading in country clothes, what could it mean?

The poor woman's nerves were so terribly on edge that one emotion would chase away another with unaccountable speed. For the past few hours she had felt completely reassured—almost happy—but now, just a few words uttered by this man whom she had learned to trust sent her back into a state of panic, and the vague fears which she had experienced when first she left her apartment in the Rue Picpus once more reared their ugly heads. It was stupid of course! A state bordering on madness! But Louise had not been quite normal since the tragic death of Bastien.

And suddenly she clutched at her skirt, in the inner pocket of which she had stowed the packet of letters which already had cost Bastien de Croissy his life. But the letters were no longer there. She searched and searched, but the packet had indubitably gone. Then she was seized with wild panic. Pressing the child to her bosom she turned as if to fly. Whither she knew not, but to fly before the hideous arms of those vengeful Terrorists were stretched out far enough to get hold of Charles-Léon.

But before she had advanced one step in this wild career a strange sound fell upon her ear, a sound that made her pause and look vaguely about her to find out how it was that le bon Dieu had sent this heaven-born protector to save her and the boy. The sound was just a pleasant mellow laugh, and then the same kindly voice of a moment ago said quietly:

"This is yours, I believe, Madame."

Instinctively she turned like a frightened child, hardly daring to look. Her glance fell first on the packet of letters which she had missed and which was held out to her by a very grimy yet strangely beautiful hand: from the hand her eyes wandered upwards along the tattered sleeve and the bent shoulder to the face of the driver who had been the silent companion of her amazing three days' adventure. And out of that face a pair of lazy deep-set blue eyes regarded her with obvious amusement, whilst the aftermath of that pleasant mellow laugh still lingered round the firm lips.

With her eyes fixed upon that face, which seemed like a mask over a mystical entity, Louise took the packet of letters. Her trembling lips murmured an awed "Who are you?" whereat the strange personage replied lightly, "For the moment your servant, Madame, only anxious to see you safely housed in yonder cottage. Shall we proceed?"

All Louise could do was to nod and then set off as briskly as she could, so as to show this wonderful man how ready she was to follow him in all things. He had already taken the pony out of the cart and set Charles-Léon on its back. The cart he left by the roadside, and he walked beside the pony steadying Charles-Léon with his arm. Thus the little party climbed to the top of the cliff. It was very heavy going, for the ground was soft and Louise's feet sank deeply into the sand; but she dragged herself along bravely, although she felt like a somnambulist, moving in a dream-walk to some unknown, mysterious destination, a heaven peopled by heroic old hags and rough labourers with unshaven cheeks and merry, lazy eyes. The cottage on the cliff was not so dilapidated as it had appeared in the distance. The man brought the pony to a halt and pushed open the door. Louise lifted Charles-Léon down and followed her guide into the cottage. She found herself in a room in which there was a table, two or three chairs and benches, and an iron stove in which a welcome fire was burning. Two men were sitting by the fire and rose as Louise, half-fainting with fatigue, staggered into the room. Together they led her to an inner room where there was a couch, and on this she sank breathless and speechless. Charles-Léon was then laid beside her: the poor child looked ghastly, and Louise, with a pitiable moan, hugged him to her side. One of the men brought her food and milk, whilst the other placed a pillow to her head. Louise, though only half-conscious at this moment, felt that if only she had the strength she would have dragged herself down on her knees and kissed the hands of those rough-looking men in boundless gratitude.

She remained for some time in a state of torpor, lying on the couch holding the boy closely to her. The door between the two rooms was ajar: a welcome warmth from the iron stove penetrated to the tired woman's aching sinews. A vague murmur of voices reached her semi-consciousness. The three men whom she regarded as her saviours were talking together in whispers. They spoke in English, of which Louise understood a few sentences. Now and again that pleasant mellow laugh which she had already heard came to her ears, and somehow it produced in her a sense of comfort and of peace. One of the three men, the one with the mellow laugh, seemed to be in command of the others, for he was giving them directions of what they were to do with reference to a boat, a creek and a path down the side of a cliff, and also to a signal with which the others appeared to be familiar.

But the voices became more and more confused; the gentle murmur, the pleasant roar of the fire acted as a lullaby, and soon Louise fell into a dreamless sleep.

CHAPTER XIII

A pleasant, cultured voice, speaking French with a marked foreign accent, roused Louise out of her sleep. She opened her eyes still feeling dazed and not realising for the moment just where she was. One of the young men whom she had vaguely perceived the night before was standing under the lintel of the door.

"I hope I haven't frightened you, Madame," he now said, "but we ought to be getting on the way."

It was broad daylight, with a grey sky heavy with clouds that threatened rain, and a blustering wind that moaned dismally down the chimney. From the distance came the regular booming of the breakers against the cliffs. It was a sound Louise had never heard in her life before and she could not help feeling alarmed at the prospect of going on the sea with Charles-Léon so weak and ill, even though salvation and hospitable England lay on the other side. But she had made up her mind that however cowardly she felt in her heart of hearts, she would bear herself bravely before her heroic friends. As soon as the young man had gone, she made herself and the boy ready for the journey—the Great Unknown as she called it with a shudder of apprehension.

There was some warm milk and bread for her and Charles-Léon on the table in the other room. She managed to eat and drink and then said bravely: "We are quite ready now, Monsieur."

The young man guided her to the front door of the house. Here she expected to see once more the strange and mysterious man who had driven her all the way from Paris in the ramshackle vehicle and who throughout four long wearisome days and nights had never seemed to tire, and never lost his ready wit and resourcefulness in face of danger from the patrols of the National Guard.

Not seeing him or the cart she turned to her new friend.

"What has happened to our elegant barouche?" she asked with a smile, "and the pony?"

"They wouldn't be much use down the cliff-side, Madame," he replied; "I hope you are not too tired to walk..."

"No, no! of course not, but..."

"And one of us will carry the boy."

"I didn't mean that," she rejoined quickly.

"What then?"

"The... driver who brought us safely here... he was so kind... so... so wonderful... I would love to see him again... if only to thank him..."

The young man remained silent for a minute or two, then when Louise insisted, saying: "Surely I could speak to him before we go?" he said rather curtly, she thought: "I am afraid not, Madame."

She would have liked to have insisted still more urgently, thinking it strange that this young man should speak so curtly of one who deserved all the eulogy and all the recognition that anyone could give for his valour and ingenuity, but somehow she had the feeling that for some obscure reason or other the subject of that wonderful man was distasteful to her new friend, and that she had better not inquire further about him. Anyway, she was so surrounded by mysteries that one more or less did not seem to matter.

Just then she caught sight of another man who was coming up the side of the cliff. He kept his head bent against the force of the wind, which was very boisterous and made going against it very difficult. Soon he reached the top of the cliff. He greeted Louise with a pleasant "Bonjour, Madame," uttered with a marked English accent. Indeed to Louise he looked, just like the other, a fine, upstanding young foreigner, well-groomed despite the inclemency of the weather and the primitiveness of his surroundings. The two men exchanged a few words together which Louise did not understand, after which one of them said, "En route!" and the other added in moderately good French, "I hope you are feeling fit and well, Madame; you have another tiring day before you."

Louise assured him that she was prepared for any amount of fatigue; he then took Charles-Léon in his arms; his friend took hold of Louise by the elbow, and led the way down the cliff, carefully guiding her tottering footsteps.

At the foot of the cliff the little party came to a narrow creek, and Louise perceived a boat hidden in a shallow cave in the rock. Guided by her friends Louise crept into the cave, and stepped into the boat. The young men made her as comfortable as they could and gently laid Charles-Léon in her arms. Except for gentle words of encouragement to the little boy now and then, they spoke very little, and Louise, who by now was in a kind of somnambulistic state, could only nod her thanks when one or the other of them asked if she felt well, or offered her some scanty provisions for herself and Charles-Léon.

The party sat in the boat during the whole of the day, until it was quite dark. In this distance far out at sea Louise's aching eyes perceived from time to time ships riding on the waves. Charles-Léon was frightened at first, and crouched against his mother, and when the waves came tumbling against the rocks and booming loudly he hid his little head under her shawl. But after a time the reassuring voices of the young Englishmen coupled with boyish curiosity induced him to look at the ships; he listened to childish sea-faring yarns told by one or the other of them: soon he became interested and, like his mother, felt no longer afraid.

Poor Louise, was, of course, terribly ignorant of all matters connected with the sea, as she had never been as much as near it in her life. She only knew vaguely the meaning of the word tide, and when the young men spoke of "waiting for the tide" before putting out to sea, she did not know what they meant. She fell to wondering whether they would all presently cross La Manche in the tiny rowing boat which was not much bigger than those in which she and Josette with papa and maman Gravier were wont in the olden days to go out for picnics on the Isère. But she asked no questions. Indeed by now she felt that she had permanently lost the use of her tongue.

Soon the evening began to draw in. A long twilight slowly melted into the darkness of a moonless night. Looking towards the sea it seemed to Louise that she was looking straight at a heavy black curtain—like a solid mass of gloom. The wind continued unabated, and now that she could no longer see the sea, and only heard its continuous roar, Louise once more felt that hideous, cold fear grinding at her heart. Those terrifying waves seemed to come nearer and nearer to the sheltering cave, while the breakers broke on the stony beach with a sound like thunder. As was quite natural, her terror communicated itself to the child. He refused to be comforted, and though the two men did all they could to soothe him, and one of them knelt persistently beside Louise, whispering words of encouragement in the child's ear, poor little Charles-Lèon continued to shiver with terror.

Through the dismal howling of the wind and the booming of the waves no other sound penetrated to Louise's ears. After a while the young men too remained quite silent: they were evidently waiting for the signal of which they had spoken together the night before.

What that signal was Louise did not know. She certainly heard no strange sound, but the men did evidently hear something, for, suddenly and without a word, they seized their oars and pushed the boat off and out of the cave. This was perhaps on the whole the most terrifying moment in Louise's extraordinary adventure. The boat seemed to be plunging straight into a wall of darkness. It rocked incessantly, and poor Louise felt horribly sick. Presently she felt that she was being lifted to her feet and held in a pair of strong arms which carried her upwards through the darkness, whither she knew not at the time, but a little while later it occurred to her that perhaps she had died of fright, and that as of a matter of fact she had not awakened in Paradise. She was lying between snow-white, lavender-scented sheets, her aching head rested on a downy pillow, and a kindly voice was persuading her to sip some hot-spiced wine, which she did. It certainly proved to be delicious.

And there was Charles-Léon sitting opposite to her on the knee of a ruddy-faced, tow-haired sailor who was holding a mug of warm milk to the child's trembling lips. All that and more did indeed confirm Louise's first impression that this was not the cruel, hard world with which she was all too familiar, but rather an outpost of Paradise—if not the blessed heavens themselves.

The movement of the ship, alas! made Louise feel rather sick after a time, and this was an unpleasant and wholly earthly sensation which caused her to doubt her being in the company of angels. But indeed she was so tired that soon she fell asleep, in spite of the many strange noises around and above her, the creaking of wood, the soughing of the wind and the lashing of the water against the side of the ship.

When she woke after several hours' sleep the pale rosy light of dawn came creeping in through the port-hole. It was in very truth a rosy dawn, an augury of the calm and beauty that was now in store for the long-suffering woman. She was in England at last, she and her child: together they were safe from those assassins who had done Bastien to death and would probably have torn Charles-Léon from her breast before they sent her to the guillotine.

Le Bon Dieu had indeed been on their side.

CHAPTER XIV

And while Louise lived through the palpitating events of those fateful days Josette Gravier was quietly taking up the threads of life again. They were not snapped; they had only slipped for a few hours out of her hands, and life, of course, had to go on just the same. She would be alone after this in the apartment of the Rue Picpus: the small rooms, the tiny kitchen seemed vast now that all those whom Josette had cared for had gone. Strangely enough she was not anxious about Louise's fate; her faith was so immense, her belief in the Scarlet Pimpernel so absolute that she was able to go through the days that followed in comparative peace of mind whilst looking forward to Maurice's return.

He had obtained a permit lasting six or seven days to visit the de Croissy estates in the Dauphiné. The permit had been granted before Louise's departure was known to the authorities, or probably she and Charles-Léon, as sole heirs of Bastien de Croissy, would have been classed as émigrés: all their property would then be automatically confiscated and no one but Government officials allowed to administer it. Maurice spent five days of his leave in the diligence between Paris and Grenoble, and one in consultation with the old bailiff on the Croissy estate, trying to extract from him a promise that he would send to Mademoiselle Gravier on behalf of Madame de Croissy a small sum of money every month for rent and the bare necessities of life. Maurice hoped that after Josette had paid the rent out of this money she would contrive to send the remainder over to England as soon as she knew where to find Louise.

Josette had a little money of her own which she kept in her stocking, and she also received a few sous daily pay for the work which she did in the Government shops—stitching, knitting, doing up parcels for the "Soldiers of Liberty" who were fighting on the frontiers against the whole of Europe and keeping the great armies of Prussia and Austria at bay. If the rent of the apartment could be paid with monies sent from the Croissy estate, Josette was quite sure that she could live on her meagre stripend. Penury in the big cities, and especially in Paris, was appalling just now. Sugar and soap were unobtainable, and the scarcity of bread was becoming more and more acute. Queues outside the bakeries began to assemble as early as four o'clock in the morning to wait for the distribution of two ounces of bread, which was all that was allowed per person per day; and the two ounces consisted for the most part of bran and water. The baker favoured Josette because of her pretty face, but she was obliged to go for her ration very early in the morning because she had to be at the workshop by eight o'clock, and if she queued up later in the day Citizen Loquin would sometimes run out of bread before all his customers were served.

When Maurice came back from Grenoble life for Josette became more cheerful. He had found a tiny room for himself under the roof of another house in the Rue Picpus and had at once fallen back into his old habit of calling for Josette in the late afternoon at the Government shop when the day's work was done, and together the two of them would go arm-in-arm for a walk up the Champs Élysées or sometimes as far as the Bois. Maurice would bring what meagre provisions they could afford for their supper, and they would sit under the chestnut trees, now almost shorn of leaves and munch sour bread and dig their young teeth into an apple. Sometimes they would stroll into the town to see the illuminations, for there were illuminations on more than one day every week. What the wretched poverty-stricken, tyrant-ridden citizens of Paris rejoiced for on those evenings heaven alone knew! Certain it is that though tallow and grease were scarce, innumerable candles and lamps were lit, time after time, on some pretext or other, such as the passing of some decree which had a momentary popularity, or the downfall of a particular member of the Convention who had—equally momentarily—become unpopular with the mob. Such occasions were marked, in addition to the brilliant lighting of the city, by a great deal of noise and cheering, as an ill-clad, ill-fed mob thronged the streets, cheering their Robespierre or their Danton, and booing all the poor wretches who had been decreed traitors to the Republic on that day, and whose trial, condemnation and death on the guillotine would—just as night inevitably follows day—follow within twenty-four hours.

Maurice and Josette, jostled by the crowd, neither booed nor cheered: they seldom knew what the rejoicings and illuminations were for, but the movement, the lights and the noise took them out of themselves and caused them to forget for an hour or two the ever-growing problem of how to go on living. Once or twice when Maurice had carried through successfully a bit of legal business, he would buy a couple of tickets for the theatre, and he and Josette would listen enthralled to the sonorous verses of Corneille or Racine as declaimed by Citizen Talma, or laugh their fill over the drolleries of Mascarille or Monsieur Jourdain.

Sunday had been officially abolished by decree of the Convention in the new calendar, but Decadi came once every ten days with a half-holiday for Josette; then, if the day was fine, the two of them would hire a boat and Maurice would row up the river as far as Suresnes, and he and Josette would munch their sour bread and their apples under the trees by the towpath, and watched the boats gliding up and down the Seine and long for the freedom to drift downstream away from the noise and turmoil of the city, and away from the daily horrors of the guillotine and countless deaths of innocents which would for ever remain a stain on the fair fame of the country which they loved.

Maurice had never spoken again of love to Josette. He was not an ordinary lover, for he had intuition, and his love was entirely unselfish. So few lovers have a direct apprehension of the right moment for declaring their feelings; those that have this supreme gift will often succeed where others less sensitive will fail because they have not approached the loved one when she was in a receptive mood. Maurice knew that his hour had not yet come. Josette was still in a dream-state of adoration for a hero whom she had never seen. She was too young and too unsophisticated to analyse her own feelings; too ignorant of men and of life to take Maurice altogether seriously. As a friend or a brother she cared for him more than she had ever cared for another living soul, not excepting Louise; she trusted him, she relied on him: had she not said on that never-to-be-forgotten occasion: "Are you not here to take care of me?" But for the time being her thoughts were too full of that other man's image to add idealism to her affection. And so even though these autumn days were calm and sweet, though the wood-pigeons still cooed in the forests and the black-birds whistled in the chestnut trees, Maurice did not speak of love to Josette; although at times he suffered so acutely from her ingenuousness that tears would well up to his eyes and the words which he forced himself not to utter nearly choked him; yet he did not tell her how he loved her, and how he ached with the longing to take her in his arms, to bury his face in her golden curls, or press his burning lips on her sweet, soft mouth.

He was happy in this, that he was in a measure working for her; all her little pleasure, all the small delicacies which he brought her, and which she munched with the relish of a young animal, came to her through his exertions. He had automatically slipped into his late employer's practice. It did not amount to much, but he was a fully qualified advocate, and as clerk to Citizen Croissy, had become known to the latter's clients. A part of the money which he earned he put by for madame because he considered that it was her due, but there was always a little over which Maurice set aside for the joy of giving Josette some small treat—tickets at the theatre, an excursion into the country, or an intimate little dinner at one of the cheap restaurants. Strange, indeed, that in the midst of the most awful social upheaval the world has ever known, life for many, like Josette Gravier and Maurice Reversac, could go on in such comparative calm.

Three weeks and more went by before Josette had any news of Louise. But one evening when she came home after her walk with Maurice she found that a letter had been thrust under the door of the apartment. It was from Louise.

"My Josette chérie (it said).

"We are in England, Charles-Léon and I, and the man who has wrought this miracle is none other than the mysterious hero of whom you have so often dreamed. I have received word that this letter will reach you. That word was signed with the device which stands for courage and self-sacrifice—a small scarlet flower, my Josette, the Scarlet Pimpernel. I am completely convinced now that I owe my salvation and that of Charles-Léon to your English hero. Here in England no one doubts it. He is the national hero, and people speak of him with bated breath as of a godlike creature, whom only the elect have been privileged to meet in the flesh. It is generally believed that he is a high-born English gentleman who devotes his life to saving the weak and the innocent from the murderous clutches of those awful Terrorists in France. He has a band of followers, nineteen in number, who obey his commands without question, and under his leadership constantly risk their precious lives in the cause of humanity. It is difficult to understand why they do this: some call it the sublimity of self-sacrifice, others the love of sport and adventure, innate in every Englishman. But God alone can judge of motives.

"My darling Josette, you will be happy to know that we are at peace and comfortable now, my poor lamb and I, though my heart is filled with sorrow at being parted from you. Daily do I pray to God that you may come to me some day soon. Remember me to Maurice. He is a brave and loyal soul. I will not tell you of the hopes which I nurse for your future and his. You will have guessed these long ago. I am afraid that he would refuse to come away from Paris just yet, but if you can, Josette, would join me here in England—and you can do that any day with the aid of the Scarlet Pimpernel—we could bide our time quietly until the awful turmoil has subsided, which, by God's will, it soon must, and then return to France, when you and Maurice could be happily united.

"As to my adventures from the moment when I left our apartment with Charles-Léon in my arms until the happy hour when we landed here in England I can tell you nothing. My lips are sealed under a promise of silence, and implicit obedience to the wishes of my heroic rescuers is the only outward token of my boundless gratitude that I can offer them.

"But I can tell you something of our arrival in Dover. I was still very sea-sick, but the feeling of nausea left me soon after I had set food on solid ground. We walked over to a delightful place, a kind of tavern it was, though not a bit like our cafés or restaurants. Later on when I was rested, I made a note of the sign which was painted on a shield outside the door; it was 'The Fisherman's Rest,' and, in English, such places are called inns. I have prayed God ever since I crossed that threshold that you, my Josette chérie might see it one day.

"Here for the first time since I left Paris I came in contact with people of my own sex. The maid who showed me to a room where I could wash and rest was a sight for sore eyes: so clean, so fresh, so happy! So different to our poor girls in France nowadays—underfed, ill-clothed, in constant terror of what the near future might bring. These little maids over here go about their work singing—singing, chéie! Just think of it! Of late I have never heard anyone sing except you!

"We spent the best part of the day at 'The Fisherman's Rest.' In the afternoon we posted to Maidstone, where we now are the guests of some perfectly charming English people. I cannot begin to tell you, chérie, of the kindness and hospitality of these English families who take us in, poor émigrés, feed us and clothe us and look after us until such time as we can get resources of our own. I wish our good Maurice could send me a remittance from time to time, but that, I know, is impossible. But I will try to get some needlework to do; you know how efficient I was always considered, even at the convent, in sewing and embroidery. I do not wish to be a burden longer than I can help to my over-kind hosts.

"How this letter will reach you I know not, but I know that it will reach you, because a day or two ago the post brought me a mysterious communication saying that any letter of mine sent to the Bureau des Émigrés, Fitzroy Square, London, will be delivered to any address in France. This is only one of the many wonderful happenings that have occurred since I left Paris. It seems such a long time ago now, and our little apartment in the Rue Picpus seems so far, so very far away. I have forgotten nothing. Josette chérie, even though my memory has been overclouded by all the strange events which have befallen me. So little have I forgotten that many a time and very bitterly have I reproached myself that I lent such an inattentive ear when you spoke to me about the mysterious English hero who goes by the name of the Scarlet Pimpernel, and of his no less heroic followers. Had I believed in you and them sooner, my Bastien might be beside me even now. The Scarlet Pimpernel, my Josette, is real, very real indeed. He and his nineteen lieutenants have saved the lives of hundreds of innocents: his name here is on everybody's lips, but no one knows who he is. He works in the dark, under that quaint appellation, and those of us who owe our lives to him have, so far as we know, never set eyes on him.

"Well! it is a problem the solution of which I shall probably never know. All I can do is to keep sacred in my heart the memory of all that that man has done for me.

"That is all, my Josette. I hope and pray to Almighty God that some day soon it may be your good fortune to come to me—to come to England under the tender care of the man whom you have almost deified. When that happy day comes you will find your Louise's arms stretched out in loving welcome.

"Your devoted friend.

Louise."

"P.S.—I still have the letters."

Josette could scarcely read the welcome missive to the end. Her eyes were dim with tears. She loved Louise as she had always done, and she adored Charles-Léon, and somehow this letter, coming from far-off England, quickened and accentuated the poignancy of parting: she spent many hours sitting at the table under the lamp with Louise's letter spread out before her. One sentence in it she read over and over again, for it expressed just what she herself felt in her heart for the hero of her dreams: "All I can do," Louise had written, "is to keep sacred the memory of all that that man has done for me."

CHAPTER XV

Josette had read on so late into the night and been so excited over what she read that sleep had quite gone out of her eyes. She could not get to sleep for thinking of Louise and her adventures, of the Scarlet Pimpernel, and also of Maurice Reversac. Poor Maurice! Whatever happened he would have his burden to bear here in Paris. For the sake of the dead, and because of Louise and Charles-Léon, he must carry on his work and trust to God to see him safely through.

That day, for the first time since his return from the Dauphiné, Maurice was not at his usual place outside the gate of the workshop, waiting for Josette to come out. Josette, slightly disappointed, knew, of course, that it must be the exigencies of business that had kept him away. But when the evening hour came and again no Maurice at the gate, Josette was anxious. Before she went home she went over to Maurice's lodgings down the street to inquire from the concierge if, perchance, Maurice was ill. She knew that nothing but illness could possibly have kept him from his evening walk with her, or from sending her a message. But the concierge had seen and heard nothing of Maurice since morning when he started off as usual for the office.

Nothing would do after that but Josette must go off, then and there, to the Rue de la Monnaie. She had not been near the place since that awful day when she saw Maître de Croissy lying dead in his devastated office; and when she turned the angle of the street and saw at a hundred paces farther along the porte-cochère of the house where the terrible tragedy had occurred, she was suddenly overcome with an awful prescience of doom. So powerful was this sense of forewarning that she could no longer stand on her feet, but was obliged to lean against the nearest wall while trying to conquer sheer physical nausea. A horrible, nameless terror assailed her: she was trembling in every limb. However, after a few moments she regained control over herself, chided herself for her weakness, and walked with comparative coolness to the porte-cochère, which had not yet been closed for the night.

Again that awful feeling of giddiness and nausea. The house had always worn that dismal air of desolation and decay with a pervading odour of damp mortar and putrid vegetables. Josette knew its history: she knew that it had once been the fine abode of a rich foreign banker who had fled the country at the first outbreak of the Revolution, that it had stood empty for two or three years, then been appropriated by the State, a concierge put in office, and the house let out in apartments and offices. She had often been to the house and always disliked the sight of it, its air of emptiness despite the fact that most of the apartments were inhabited: the courtyard and stairs looked to her as if they were peopled by ghosts.

Josette went up to the concierge's lodge and asked if Citizen Reversac were still in his office. The concierge eyed her with a quizzical glance. He had seen the pretty girl in the company of Citizen Reversac before now. His sweetheart, no doubt—ah, well! these things were of every-day occurrence these days. Mothers lost their sons, wives their husbands: it was no good grieving over other people's troubles or commiserating over their misfortunes.

"Citizen Reversac was here this morning, little Citizeness," the concierge said in response to Josette's reiterated question, "but... you know..."

"What?"

"He was arrested this morning-"

"Arr-?"

"Easy, easy, little Citizeness," the concierge rejoined quickly, and with outstretched hand steadied Josette, who looked as if she would measure her length outside his lodge. "These things," he added with a shrug, "happen every day. Why, my own sister less than a week ago..."

Josette did not hear what he said. He went rambling on about his sister whose only son had been arrested, and who was breaking her heart this very day because the boy had been guillotined.

"He was not a bad lad either, my nephew; and a good patriot; but there! one never knows."

"One never knows!" Josette murmured mechanically, stupidly, staring at the concierge with great unseeing eyes. The man felt really sorry for the girl. She was so very pretty, that mouth of hers had been fashioned for smiles, those blue eyes made only to shine with merriment, and those chestnut curls to tempt a man to sin. Ah, well, one never knows! These things happened every day!

CHAPTER XVI

How Josette reached home that evening she never knew. She seemed to have spent hours and hours in repeating to herself: "It cannot be true!" and "It must be a mistake."

"He has done nothing!" she murmured from time to time, and then: "In a few days they will set him free again! They must! He has done nothing! Such an innocent!"

But in her heart she knew that innocents suffered these days as often as the guilty. Only a short time ago she had been called on to fill the rôle comforter. She could not help thinking of Louise and of that awful tragedy which was the precursor of the present cataclysm. But now she had to face this trouble alone: there was no one in whom she could confide, no one who could give her a word of advice or comfort. And when she found herself alone at last in the apartment of the Rue Picpus, where every stick of furniture, every door and every wall reminded her of those whom she loved and proclaimed her present loneliness, she realised the immensity of that cataclysm. She felt that with Maurice gone she had nothing more to live for. The dreariness of days without his kindly voice to cheer her, his loving arm to guide her, was inconceivable. It looked before her like a terrifying nightmare. And she pictured to herself Maurice's surprise and indignation at his arrest, his protestations of innocence, his final courage in face of the inevitable. She thought of him in one of the squalid overcrowded prisons, thinking of her, linking his hands tightly together in a proud attempt to appear unconcerned, indifferent to his fate before his fellow-prisoners.

Maurice! Josette never knew till now how she cared for him. Love?... No! She did not know what love was, nor did she believe that the desperate ache which she had in her heart at thought of Maurice had anything to do with the love that poets and authors spoke about. On the contrary, she thought that what she felt for Maurice was far stronger and deeper than the thing people called "love." All she knew was that she suffered intensely at this moment, that his image haunted her in a way it had never done before. She recalled every moment that of late she had spent with him, every trick of his voice, every expression of his face: his kind grey eyes, the gentle smile around his lips, the quaint remarks he would make at times which had often made her laugh. Above all, she was haunted at this hour with the remembrance of a mellow late summer's evening when she chaffed him because he had spoken to her of love. How sad he was that evening, whilst she never thought for a moment that he had been serious.

"Maurice! Maurice!" she cried out in her heart; "if those devils take you from me I shall never know a happy hour again."

But it was not in Josette's nature to sit down and mope. Her instinct was to be up and doing, whatever happened and however undecipherable the riddle set by Fate might be. And so in this instance also. The arrest of Maurice was in truth the knock-down blow: at this juncture Josette could not have imagined a more overwhelming catastrophe. As she was alone in the apartment she indulged in the solace of tears. She cried and cried till her eyes were inflamed and her head ached furiously: she cried because of the intense feeling of loneliness and desolation that gave her such a violent pain in her heart which nothing but a flood of tears seemed able to still. But having had her cry, she pulled herself together, dried her tears, bathed her face, then sat down to think or, rather, to remember. With knitted brows and concentrated force of will she tried to recall all that Bastien de Croissy had said to Louise the evening when first he spoke of the letters and she, Josette suggested stitching the packet in the lining of Louise's corsets. These letters were more precious than any jewels on earth, for they were to be the leverage wherewith to force certain influential members of the Convention to grant Louise a permit to take her child into the country, to remain with him and nurse him back to health and strength. The possession of those letters had been the cause of Bastien de Croissy's terrible death. They were seriously compromising to certain influential representatives of the people, proofs probably of some black-hearted treason to their country. The possession of them was vitally important to their writers, so important that they chose the way of murder rather than risk revelation. A man on trial, a man condemned to death might have the chance of speaking. It is only the dead who cannot speak.

So now for the knowledge of who were the writers of the letters. And Josette, her head buried in her hands, tried to recall every word which Bastien had spoken the night before his death, while she, Josette, sat under the light of the lamp, stitching the precious packet into the lining of Louise's corsets. But unfortunately at one moment during the evening her mind, absorbed in the facts themselves, had been less retentive than usual. Certain it is that at this desperately critical moment she could not recall a single name that Bastien had mentioned, and after his death, Louise, with the obstinacy of the half-demented, had guarded the letters with a kind of fierce jealousy; she had taken them to England with her, with what object God only knew—probably none! Just obstinacy and without definite consciousness.

It was in the small hours of the morning that Josette had an inspiration. It was nothing less, and it so comforted her that she actually fell asleep, and as soon as she was washed and dressed ran out into the street. She ran all the way to the corner of the Pont des Arts, where vendors of old books and newspapers had their booths. She bought a bundle of back numbers of Le Moniteur and, hugging it under her cape, she ran back to the Rue Picpus.

The Moniteur gave the reports of the sittings of the Convention day by day, the debates, the speeches. Josette, whilst sitting by herself the night before with her mind still in a whirl with the terrible news of Maurice's arrest, had not been able to recall a single name mentioned by Bastien in connection with the letters, but with the back numbers of the Moniteur spread out before her, with the names of several members of the Convention staring at her in print, the task of reconstructing the conversation for that night became much easier. For instance, she did remember Louise exclaiming at one moment: "But he is Danton's most intimate friend!" and Bastien saying then: "All three of them are friends of Danton."

And shrewd little Josette concentrated on the Moniteur until she came upon the report of a debate in the Convention over a proposition put forward by Citizen Danton. Who were his friends? Who his supporters? he had a great number, for he was still at the height of his popularity: they agreed and debated and perorated, and Josette while she read, mrumured their names repeatedly to herself: "Desmoulins, Desmoulins, Desmoulins—no! that wasn't it. Hérault, Hérault de Séchelles—no! Delacroix—no, again no! Chabot?... Chabot...?" And slowly memory brought the name back to her mind—Chabot! That was one of the names! Chabot, Danton's friend. "Yes!" Bastien had said at one moment, "an unfrocked Capuchin friar!" and Louise had uttered an exclamation of horror. Chabot! that certainly was one of the names. And Josette read on; taxed her memory, forced it to serve her purpose. More names which meant nothing, and then one that stood out! Fabre d'Eglantine—Danton's most intimate friend! Chabot and Fabre—two names! And then a third one—Bazire! Josette had paid no attention at the time. She had heard Bastien mention those names, but only vaguely, and her brain had only vaguely registered them; but now they came back. Memory had served her a good turn.

Fabre, Chabot, Bazire! Josette had no longer any doubt as to who the men were who had written the letters, letters that were the powerful leverage wherewith to force them to grant whatever might be asked of them: a permit for Louise, freedom for Maurice Reversac.

Josette had not been sufficiently care-free up to now to note that the weather was like, but now, with a sense almost of gladness in her heart, she threw open the window and looked up at the sky. She only had a small glimpse of it because the Rue Picpus was narrow and the houses opposite high, but she did have a glimpse of clear blue, the blue of which Paris among all the great cities of Europe can most justifiably boast, translucent and exhilarating. The air was mild. There was no trace of wintry weather, of rain or of cold. The sun was shining and she, Josette, was going to drag Maurice out of the talons of those revolutionary birds of prey.

From far away came the dismal sound of the bell of St. Germain, booming out the morning hour. Another day had broken over the unfortunate city, another day wherein men waged a war to the death one against the other, wherein they persecuted the innocent, heaped crime upon crime, injustice upon injustice, flouted religion and defied God; another day wherein ruled the devils of hate and dolour, of tribulation and of woe. But Josette did no longer think of devils or of sorrow. She was going to be the means of opening the prison gates for Maurice.

CHAPTER XVII

Since the day when Charlotte Corday forced her way into the apartment of Citizen Marat and plunged a dagger into the heart of that demagogue, the more prominent members of the revolutionary government were wont to take special precautions to guard their valuable lives.

Thus the conventionnel François Chabot in his magnificent apartment in the Rue d'Anjou made it a rule that every person desirous of an interview with him must be thoroughly searched for any possible concealed weapon before being admitted to his august presence. The unfrocked friar proclaimed loudly his patriotism, declared his readiness to die a martyr like Marat, but he was taking no risks. He had married a very rich and very beautiful young wife. Whilst professing in theory the most rigid sans-culottism, he lived in the greatest possible luxury, ate and drank only of the best, wore fine clothes, and surrounded himself with every comfort that his wife's money could buy.

Josette did indeed appear as a humble suppliant when, having mounted the carpeted stairs which led up to the first floor of that fine house in the Rue d'Anjou, she found herself face to face with a stalwart janitor at the door of François Chabot's apartment.

"Your business?" he demanded.

"To speak with Citizen Chabot," Josette replied.

"Does the Citizen expect you?"

"No, but when he knows of the business which has brought me here he will not refuse to see me."

"That is as it may be, but you cannot pass this door without stating your business."

"It is private, and for Citizen Chabot's private ear alone."

The stalwart looked down on the dainty figure before him. Being a man he looked down with considerable pleasure, for Josette in her neat kirtle and well-fitting bodice, her frilled muslin cap perched coquettishly on her chestnut curls, was exceedingly pleasant to look on. Her blue eyes did not so much as demand that her wish to speak with Citizen Chabot should not be peremptorily denied.

The janitor pulled himself up and his waistcoat down, passed his hand over his bristly cheek, hemmed and hawed and cleared his throat, then, unable apparently to resist the command of those shining eyes any longer, he said finally:

"I will see what can be done, Citizeness."

"That is brave of you," Josette said demurely, and then added: "Where shall I wait?" which translated into ordinary language meant: "You would not surely allow me to wait outside the door where any passer-by might behave in an unseemly manner towards me?"

At any rate this was how the janitor interpreted Josette's simple query. He opened the door on the thickly carpeted, richly furnished vestibule and said: "Wait here, Citizeness."

Josette went in. It was years since she had seen such beautiful furniture, such tall mirrors and rich gildings, years since she had trodden on such soft carpets, and these were the days when woman had to go shoeless, and children died for want of nourishment, whilst men like Chabot preached equality and fraternity, and loudly proclaimed the simplicity and abnegation of their lives. Josette's astonishment at all this luxury caused her to open wide her eyes, and when those blue eyes were opened wide, men, even the most stalwart, became like putty.

"Sit down there, Citizeness," the magnificent janitor said, "whilst I go and inquire if the Citizen Representative will see you."

Josette sat down and waited. Two or three minutes later the janitor returned. As soon as he caught sight of Josette he shook his head, then said:

"Not unless you will state your business. And," he added, "you know the rule: no one is admitted to speak with any Representatives of the People without being previously searched."

"Give me pen and paper," Josette rejoined, "that I may state my business in writing."

When the man brought her pen and paper she wrote:

"Dead men tell no tales, but the written words endure."

She folded the paper, then demanded wax and a seal. Presumably the man couldn't read, but one never knew. A seal was safer and Chabot himself would be grateful to her for having thought of it. A few moments later she found herself in a small room, bare of furniture or carpet, into which the janitor had ushered her after he had taken her written message to the Citizen Representative. A middle-aged woman, who was probably the housekeeper, passed her rough hands all over Josette's young body, dived into her shoes, under her muslin fichu, and even under her cap. Satisfied that there was no second Charlotte Corday intent on assassination, she called the janitor back and handed an indignant if silent Josette back to him. The audience could now be granted with safety.

Such were the formalities attendant upon a request for an audience with one of the representatives of the people in this glorious era of Equality and Fraternity.

CHAPTER XVIII

François Chabot was at this time about forty years of age. A small, thin, nervy-looking creature with long nose, thick lips, arched eyebrows above light brown eyes, and a quantity of curly hair which swept the top of his high coat-collar at the back, covering it with grease. He was dressed in the height of fashion, with a very short waist and long tails to his coat. His neck was swathed in a high stock collar, and his somewhat receding chin rested on a voluminous jabot of muslin and lace.

Josette, who had been ushered into his presence with so much ceremony, eyed him with curiosity, for she had heard it said of Representative Chabot that he affected to attend the sittings of the Convention in a tattered shirt, with bare legs and wearing a scarlet cap. In fact, it was said of him that he owed most of his popularity to this display of cynicism: also, that he, like his brother-in-law Bazire, had before now paid a hired assassin to dig a knife between his ribs in order to raise the cry among his friends in the Convention: "See! the counter-revolutionists are murdering the patriots. Marat first, now the incorruptible Chabot. Whose turn will it be next?"

But Josette, though remembering all this, was in no mood to smile. Did not this damnable hypocrite hold Maurice's life in his ugly hands? Those same hands—large, bony, with greyish nails and spatulated fingers—were toying with the written message which Josette had sent in to him. They were perhaps the hands that had dealt the fatal blow to Bastien de Croissy. Josette glanced on them with horror and then quickly drew her eyes away.

The janitor had motioned her to a seat, then he retired, closing the door behind him. Josette was alone with the Citizen Representative. He was sitting at a large desk which was littered with papers, and she sat opposite to him. He now raised his pale, shifty eyes to her, and she returned his searching glance fearlessly. He was obviously nervous; cleared his throat to give himself importance, and shifted his position once or twice. The paper which he held between two fingers and pointed towards Josette rustled audibly.

"Your name?" he asked curtly after a time.

"Josephine Gravier," she replied.

"And occupation?"

"Seamstress in the Government workshops. I was also companion and housekeeper in the household of Maître Croissy..."

"Ah!"

"...until the day of his death."

There was a pause. The man was as nervous as a cat. He made great efforts to appear at ease, and above all to control his voice, which after that first "Ah!" had sounded hoarse and choked.

The handsome Boule clock on the mantelpiece, obviously the spoils of a raid on a confiscated château, struck the hour with deliberate majesty. Chabot shifted his position again, crossed and uncrossed his legs, pushed his chair father away from the bureau, and went on fidgeting with Josette's written message, crushing it between his fingers.

"Advocate Croissy," he said at last with an effort, "committed suicide, I understand."

"It was said so, Citizen."

"What do you mean by that?"

"Nothing beyond what I said."

They were like duellists, these two, measuring their foils in a preliminary passage of arms. Chabot's glance had in it now something malevolent, cruel... the cruelty of a coward who is not sure yet of what it is he has to fear.

Suddenly he said, holding up the crumpled bit of paper:

"Why did you send me this?"

"To warn you, Citizen," Josette replied quite quietly.

"Of what?"

"That certain letters of which you and others are cognisant have not been destroyed."

"Letters?" Chabot demanded roughly. "What letters?"

"Letters written by you, Citizen Representative, to Maître de Croissy, which prove you to be a shameless hypocrite and a traitor to your country."

She had shot this arrow at random, but at once she had the satisfaction of knowing that the shaft had gone home. Chabot's sallow cheeks had become the colour of lead, his thick lips quivered visibly. A slight scum appeared at the corner of his mouth.

"It's all a lie!" he protested, but his voice sounded forced and hollow. "An invention of that traitor Croissy."

"You know best, Citizen Representative," Josette retorted simply.

Chabot tried to put on an air of indifference.

"Croissy," he said as calmly as he could, "told you a deliberate lie if he said that certain letters of mine were anything but perfectly innocent. I personally should not care if anybody read them..."

He paused, then added: "If that is all you wished to tell me, my girl, the interview can end here."

"As you desire, Citizen," Josette said, and made as if to rise.

"Stay a moment," Chabot commanded. "Merely from idle curiosity I would like to know where those famous letters are. Can you perchance tell me?"

"Oh, yes," she replied. "They are in England and out of your reach, Citizen Representative."

"What do you mean by 'in England'?"

"Just what I say. When the widow of Maître de Croissy went to England with her boy she took the packet of letters with her."

"She fled from Paris, I know," Chabot retorted, still trying to control his fury. "I know it. I had the report. That cursed English spy...!" He checked himself; this girl's slightly mocking glance was making a havoc of his nerves.

"The letters, such as they are, are probably destroyed by now," he said as coolly as he could.

"They are not destroyed."

"How do you know?"

Josette shrugged. Would she be here if the letters had been destroyed?

"Why did the woman Croissy run away like a traitor?"

"Her child was sick. It was imperative he should leave Paris for a healthier spot."

"I know. Croissy told me that tale. I didn't then believe a word of it. It was just blackmail, nothing more." Then as Josette was once more silent he reiterated roughly: "Why did the woman Croissy leave Paris in such haste? Why should she have taken the letters with her? You say she did, but I don't believe it."

"Perhaps she was afraid, Citizen."

"Afraid of what? Only traitors need be afraid."

"Afraid of... committing suicide like her husband."

This shaft, too, went straight home. Every drop of blood seemed to ebb from the man's face and left it ashen grey. His pale eyes wandered all round in the room as if in search of a hiding-place from that straight accusing glance. For the next minute or two he affected to busy himself with the papers on his desk, whilst the priceless Boule clock on the mantelshelf ticked away several fateful seconds.

Then he said abruptly, with an attempt at unconcern:

"Ah, bah! little woman. You think yourself very shrewd, what? No doubt you have some nice little project of blackmail in that pretty head of yours. But if you really did know all about the letters you speak of so glibly, you would also be aware that I am the man least concerned in them. There are others whose names apparently are unknown to you and who..."

"Their names are not unknown to me, Citizen Representative," Josette broke in with unruffled calm.

"Then why the hell haven't you been to them! Is it because you know less than you pretend?"

"If you, Citizen, do not choose to bargain with me, I will certainly go to Citizen Bazire and Fabre d'Eglantine, but in that case..."

At mention of the two names Chabot had given a visible start: a nervous twitching of his lips showed how severely he had been hit. He still tried to bluster by reiterating gruffly:

"In that case?"

"I am treating separately with the writers of each individual letter," Josette said firmly. "Those who do not choose to bargain with me must accept the consequences."

"Which are?"

"Publication of the letters in the Moniteur, in Père Duchesne and other newspapers. They will make good reading, Citizen Representative."

"You little devil!"

He had jumped to his feet, and with clenched fists resting upon the bureau he leaned across, staring into her face. His pale brown eyes had glints in them now of cold, calculating cruelty. Had he dared he would have seized this weak woman by the throat and torn the life out of her, slowly, brutally, with hellish cunning until she begged for death.

"You devil!" he reiterated savagely. "You forget that I can make you suffer for this."

Josette gave her habitual shrug.

"You certainly can," she said calmly. "You can do the same to me as you did to Maître de Croissy. But not even a second murder will put you in possession of the letters."

Never for a moment had the girl lost her presence of mind. She knew well enough what she risked when she came to beard this hyena in his lair; but it was the only way to save Maurice. She had thought it all out and had deliberately chosen it.

Throughout the interview she had remained perfectly calm and self-possessed; and now, when for the first time she had the feeling that she was winning the day, she still remained demure and apparently unmoved. But Chabot was pacing up and down the room like a caged beast, kicking savagely at anything that was in his way. At one moment it seemed as if he was on the point of giving way to his fury, of being willing to risk everything, even his own neck, for the satisfaction of his revenge. During that fateful moment Josette's life did indeed hang in the balance, for already the man's hand was on the bell-pull. Another second and he was ready to send for his stalwart and to order him to summon the men of the National Guard who were always on duty in the streets outside the dwellings of the Representatives of the People: to summon the guard and order this woman to be thrown into the most noisome prison of the city, where mental and physical torture would punish her for her presumption.

With his hand on the bell-pull Chabot looked round and encountered the cool, unconcerned glance of a pair of eyes as deeply blue as the midnight sky in June, and other thoughts and desires, more foul than the first, distorted his ugly face. Had he read aught in those eyes but contempt and self-confidence the dark spirits that haunted this house of evil would have had their way with him. But it was the girl's evident complete sell-assurance that made him pause... pause long enough to gauge the depth of the abyss into which he would fall if those compromising letters were by some chance given publicity.

He let go of the bell-pull and came back to his place by the bureau. He sat down and, leaning back in his chair, he allowed a minute or two to go by while he regained control over himself. Knitting his bony hands together he twisted them until all the finger-joints cracked. He took a handkerchief from his pocket and wiped the cold sweat from his brow.

Then at last he spoke:

"You said just now, Citizeness," he rejoined with enforced calm, trying to emulate the girl's sell-assurance and her show of contempt, "that when the widow Croissy ran away to England she took certain letters with her. Is that it?"

"Yes. She did."

"How do you know that?"

"She has told me so... in a letter."

"A letter from England?"

"Yes."

"And that's a lie! How could you get a letter from England? We are at war with that accursed country, and..."

"Do not let us discuss the point, Citizen Representative. Let me assure you that the letters in question are in England: the Citizeness Croissy has not destroyed them—she has told me so. If you agree to my terms I will bring you the letters, otherwise they will be sent to the Moniteur and other newspapers for publication. And that," Josette added firmly, "is my last word."

"What are your terms?"

"First, a safe-conduct to enable me to travel to England without molestation..."

Chabot gave a harsh, ironical laugh.

"To travel to England? Fine idea, in very truth! Go to England and stay in England, what? And from thence make long noses at François Chabot, what? who was fool enough to let you hoodwink him!"

"Had you not best listen to me, Citizen Representative, before you jump to conclusions?"

"I listen. Indeed, I am vastly interested in your naïve project, my engaging young friend."

"My price for placing letters, which you would give your fortune to possess, in your hands, Citizen, is the liberty and life of one, Maurice Reversac, who was clerk to Maître de Croissy."

Chabot sneered. "Your lover, I suppose."

"What you choose to suppose is nothing to me. I have named my price for the letters."

Chabot, his elbow resting on the table, his chin cupped in his hand, was apparently wrapped in thought. He was contemplating that greatly daring woman who had delivered her ultimatum with no apparent consciousness of her danger. He could silence her, of course: send her to the guillotine, her and her lover, Reversac; but she seemed so sure that he would not do this that her assurance became disconcerting. The same reason which had stayed his and his friends' hands when they discussed the advisability of having Bastien de Croissy summarily arrested held good in this girl's case also. There was always the possibility of her getting a word in during her trial—a word which might prove the undoing of them all. How far was she telling the truth at this moment? How far was she lying in order to save her lover? These were the questions which François Chabot was putting to himself while he contemplated the beautiful woman before him.

And whilst he gazed on her she seemed slowly to vanish from his vision, both she and his luxurious surroundings, the costly furniture, the carpets, all the paraphernalia of his sybaritic life. Instead of this there appeared to his mental consciousness the Place de la Barrière du Trône, with the guillotine towering above a sea of faces. He saw himself mounting the fatal steps; he saw the executioner, the glint on the death-dealing knife, the horrible basket into which great and noble heads had often rolled at his, Chabot's, bidding. He heard the roll of drums ordered by Sauterre, the cries of execration of the mob, the strident laugh of those horrible hags who sat knitting and jabbering while the knife worked up and down, up and down.... A hoarse cry nearly escaped him. He passed his bony fingers under his choker for he felt stifled and sick...

The vision vanished. The girl was still sitting opposite to him, demure and silent—curse her!—waiting for him to speak. And looking on her he knew that he must have those letters or he would never know a moment's peace again. Once he had them, once he felt entirely safe, he would have his revenge. Let her look to herself, the miserable trollop! She will have brought her fate upon herself.

He said! "I'll give you the safe-conduct. You can start for England to-day."

"I will start to-morrow," she rejoined coolly. "I still must speak with Citizens Fabre and Bazire."

"I can make that right with them. You need not see them."

"I must have their signatures on the safe-conduct as well as yours, Citizen Chabot."

"You shall have them."

He was searching among the litter on his desk for the paper which he wanted. These men always had forms of safe-conduct made out with blank spaces for the name of a relation or friend who happened to be in trouble and hoped to leave the country before trouble materialised. Chabot found what he wanted. The paper was headed:

"COMMISSARIAT DE POLICE DE LA Villieme

SECTION DE PARIS. "

and

"Laissez passer."

"Your name?" he asked once more.

"Josephine Madeleine Marie Gravier."

And Chabot, with a shaking hand, wrote these names in the blank space left for the purpose.

"Your residence?"

"Forty-three Rue Picpus."

"Your age?"

"Twenty."

"The color of your eyes?"

She looked at him and in the blank space he wrote the word "Blue"; and farther on he made note that the hair was burnished copper, her chin small, her teeth even.

When he had filled in all the blank spaces he stewed the writing with sand; then he said, "You can come and fetch this this evening."

"It will be signed?"

"By myself and by Citizens Fabre and Bazire."

"Then I will start to-morrow."

"You have money?"

"Yes, I thank you."

"When do you return?"

"It will take me a week probably to get to England and a week or more to come back. It will be close on three weeks, Citizen Representative, before your mind is set at rest."

He shrugged and sneered:

"And in the meanwhile, your lover..."

"In the meanwhile, Citizen," Josette broke in firmly, "See to it that Maurice Reversac is safe and well. If on my return he is not there to greet me, if, in fact, you play me false in any way, it is the Moniteur who will have the letters, not you."

Chabot rose slowly from his chair. He stood for a moment quite still beside the desk, his spatulated fingers spread out upon the table-top. All his nervousness, his fury, his excitement seemed suddenly to drop away from him. His ugly face wore an air of cunning, almost of triumph, and there was a hideous leer around his thick lips. He appeared to be watching Josette intently while she rose, shook out her kirtle, smoothed down her fichu and straightened her cap. As she turned towards the door he said slowly:

"We shall see!" he added with mock courtesy, "Au revoir, little Citizeness."

A few minutes later Josette was speeding up the street on her way home.

CHAPTER XIX

Later in the day a meeting took place in the bare white-washed room of the Clud des Cordeliers between three members of the National Convention—François Chabot, Claude Bazire and Fabre d'Eglantine—and an obscure member of the Committee of Public Safety named Armand Chauvelin. This man had at one time been highly influential in the councils of the revolutionary government; before the declaration of war he had been sent to England as secret envoy of the Republic; but conspicuous and repeated failures in various missions which had been entrusted to him had hopelessly ruined his prestige and hurled him down from his high position to one of almost ignoble dependence. Many there were who marvelled how it had come to pass that Armand Chauvelin had kept his head on his shoulders: "The Republic," Danton had thundered more than once from the tribune, "has no use for failures." It is to be supposed, therefore, that the man possessed certain qualities which made him useful to those in power: perhaps he was in possession of secrets which would have made his death undesirable. Be that as it may, Chauvelin, dressed in seedy black, his pale face scored with lines of anxiety, his appearance that of a humble servant of these popular Representatives of the People, sat at one end of the deal table, listening with almost obsequious deference to the words of command from the other three.

He only put in a word now and again, for he had been summoned in order to take orders, not to give advice.

"The girl," Chabot said to him, "lives at No. 43 in the Rue Picpus. She will leave Paris to-morrow. You will shadow her from the moment that she leaves the house: never lose sight of her as you value your life. She is going to England; you will follow her. You have been in England before, Citizen Chauvelin," he added with a sarcastic grin, "so I understand, and are acquainted with the English tongue."

"That is so, Citizen Representative."

Chauvelin's eyes were downcast; not one of the three caught the feline gleam of hate that shot through their pale depths.

"Your safe-conduct is all in order. The wench will probably make for Tréport and take boat there for one of the English ports. It is up to you to board the same ship as she does. You must assume what disguise seems most suitable at the time. Our friend here, Fabre d'Eglantine, has been the means of finding you an English safe-conduct which was taken from one of that accursed nation who was trying to cross over our frontier from Belgium: he was an English spy. Our men caught and shot him; his papers remained in their hands: one of these was a safe-conduct signed by the English Minister of Foreign Affairs. Those stupid English don't usually trouble about passports or safe-conducts. They welcome the émigrés from France, and often among those traitors one or other of our spies have got through. Still, this document will probably serve you well, and you can easily make up to appear like the description of the original holder. Here are the two passports. Examine them carefully first, then I or one of my friends will give you further instructions."

Chabot handed two papers to Chauvelin across the table. Chauvelin took them, and for the next few minutes was absorbed in a minute examination of them. One bore the signature of Fabre d'Eglantine, who was representative for a section of Paris: it was counter-signed by François Chabot (Seine et loire) and by Claud Bazire (Côte d'Or). The second paper bore the seal of the English Foreign Office and was signed by Lord Grenville himself. It was made out in the name of Malcolm Russel Stone, and described the bearer of the safe-conduct as short and slight, with brown hair and a pale face—a description, in fact, which could apply to twenty men out of a hundred. It had the advantage of not being a forgery, but was a genuine passport issued to an unfortunate Secret Service man since dead. As Chabot had said, the English authorities cared little, if anything, about passports; nevertheless, the present one might prove useful.

Chauvelin folded the two papers and put them in the inside pocket of his coat.

"So far, so good," he said drily. "I await your further instructions, Citizen Representative."

Chabot was the spokesman of the party. He was, perhaps, sunk more deeply than the other two in the morass of treachery and veniality which threatened to engulf them all. He it was who had summoned this conference and who had thought of Armand Chauvelin as the man most likely to be useful in this terrible emergency.

"He has a character to redeem," he had said to his friends when first the question was mooted of setting a sleuth-hound on the girl's tracks: "he speaks English, he knows his way about over there..."

"He failed signally," Bazire objected, "over that affair of the English spies."

"You mean the man they call the Scarlet Pimpernel?"

"Yes!"

"Chauvelin has sworn to lay him by the heels."

"But has never succeeded."

"No; but Robespierre tells me that he is the most tenacious tracker of traitors they have on the Committees—a real bloodhound, what!"

Thus it was that Chauvelin had been called in to confer on the best means of circumventing a simple girl in the fateful undertaking she had in view. Four men to defeat one woman in her purpose! What chance would she have to accomplish it?

"It is on the return journey, my friend," Chabot was saying, "that your work will effectually begin. This wench, Josette Gravier, is going to England for the sole purpose of getting hold of a certain packet of letters—seven in all—which are now in the possession of a woman named Croissy, the widow of the lawyer Croissy who—er—committed suicide a month or so ago. You recollect?"

"I do recollect perfectly," Chauvelin remarked blandly.

Chabot cleared his throat, fidgeted in his usual nervous manner, but took good care not to encounter Chauvelin's quizzical glance.

"Those letters," he said after a moment or two, "were written by me and my two friends here in the strictest confidence to Croissy, who was acting as our lawyer at the time. None of us dreamed that he would turn traitor. Well, he did, and no doubt was subsequently stricken either with remorse or fright, for after threatening us all with the betrayal of our confidence he took his own miserable life."

Chabot paused, apparently highly satisfied with his peroration. Chauvelin, silent and with thin white hands folded in front of him, waited calmly for him to continue. But his pale steely eyes were no longer downcast: their glance, bitterly ironical, was fixed on the speaker, and there was no mistaking the question which that glance implied. "Why do you take the trouble to tell me those lies?" those eyes seemed to ask. No wonder that none of the three blackguards dared to look him straight in the face!

"I think," Chabot resumed after a time with added pompousness, "that I have told you enough to make you appreciate the importance of the task which we propose to entrust to you. My friends and I must regain possession of those confidential letters, but we look to you, Citizen Chauvelin, to put us in possession of them and not to the wench Gravier—you understand?"

"Perfectly."

"She is nothing but a trollop and a baggage who has shamelessly resorted to blackmail in order to save her gallant from justice. She has put a dagger at my throat—at the throat of my two friends here—and her dagger is more deadly than the one with which the traitor Charlotte Corday pierced the noble heart of Marat..."

He would have continued in this eloquent strain had not his brother-in-law, Bazire, put a restraining hand on his shoulder. Armand Chauvelin, with his arms tightly clasped over his chest, his thin legs crossed, his pale eyes looking up at the ceiling, presented a perfect picture of irony and contempt. The others dared not resent this attitude. They had need of this man for the furtherance of their schemes. Revenge was what they were looking for now. The wench had indeed put a dagger to their throats, and for this they were determined to make her suffer; and there was no man alive with such a marvellous capacity for tracking an enemy and bringing him to book as Armand Chauvelin, in spite of the fact that he had failed so signally in bringing the greatest enemy of the revolutionary government to the guillotine. In this he certainly had failed. Not one of his colleagues, not one of the three who had need of his services now, knew how the recollection of that failure galled him. He was thankful for this mission which would take him to England once more. He had heart-breaking ill luck over his adventures with the Scarlet Pimpernel, but luck might take a turn at any time, and, anyway, he was the only man in his own country who had definitely identified the mysterious hero with that ballroom exquisite Sir Percy Blakeney. Given a modicum of luck it was still on the cards that he, Chauvelin, might yet be even with his arch-enemy whilst he was engaged in dogging the footsteps of Josette Gravier. That wench was just the type of "persecuted innocent" that would appeal to the chivalrous nature of the elusive Sir Percy.

Yes! on the whole Chauvelin felt satisfied with his immediate prospects, and as soon as Chabot had ceased perorating he put a few curt questions to him.

"When does the girl start?" he asked.

"To-morrow," Chabot replied. "I have told her to call at my house this evening for her safe-conduct."

"It is made out in the name of...?'

"Josephine Gravier."

"Josephine Gravier," Chauvelin iterated slowly; "and the safe-conduct is signed...?"

"By myself, by my friend Fabre and my brother-in-law Claude Bazire."

Chauvelin then rose and said: "That is all I need know for the moment." He paused a moment as if reflecting and then added: "Oh! by the way, I may need a man by me whom I can trust—a man who will give me a hand in an emergency, you understand; who will be discreet and above all obedient."

"I see no objection to that," Chabot said and turned to his colleagues: "do you?"

"No. None," they all agreed.

"Do you know the right sort of man?" one of them asked.

"Yes! Auguste Picard," was Chauvelin's reply: "a sturdy fellow, ready for any adventure. He is attached to the gendarmerie of the VIIIth section at the moment, but he can be spared—Picard would suit me well: he is never troubled with unnecessary scruples," he added with a curl of the lip.

"Auguste Picard. Why not?"

They all agreed as to the suitability of Auguste Picard as a satellite to their friend Chauvelin.

"So long as he is told nothing," one of them remarked.

"Why, of course," Chauvelin hastened to reassure them all. He then concluded with complacency: "You may rest assured, my friends, that in less than a month the letters will be in your hands."

Chabot and the others sighed in unison: "The devil speed you, friend

Chauvelin." One of them said: "Not one of us will know a moment's peace until your return."

On which note of mutual confidence they parted. Chauvelin went his way; the other three stayed talking for a little while at the club; other members strolled in from time to time, Danton among them. The great man himself was none too easy over this affair of the letters which had been recounted to him by his satellite Fabre d'Eglantine. He was not dead sure whether his own name was mentioned or not in the correspondence between de Batz and Croissy. He had at the time been unpleasantly mixed up in those Austrian intrigues, and it was part of de Batz' game to compromise them and thus bring about the downfall of the revolutionary Government and the restoration of the King. Chabot, Fabre and Bazire were in it up to the neck, but the moment mud-slinging began, any of their friends might get spattered with the slime. Robespierre, the wily jackal, was only waiting for an opportunity to be at Danton's throat, to wrest from him that popularity which for the time being made him the master of the Convention. It would indeed be a strange freak of Destiny if the downfall of the great Danton—the lion of the Revolution—were brought about through the intervention of a woman, a chit of a girl more feeble even than Charlotte Corday, whose dagger had put an end to Marat's career.

"But we can leave all that with safety in Armand Chauvelin's hands," was the sum-total of the confabulation between the four men before they bade one another good-night.

CHAPTER XX

The small diligence which had left Les Andelys in the early morning rattled into the courtyard of the Auberge du Cheval Blanc in Rouen soon after seven o'clock in the evening. It had encountered bad weather the whole of the way: torrential rain lashed by gusty north-westerly winds made going difficult for the horses. The roads were fetlock-deep in mud: on the other hand, the load had been light—two passengers in the front compartment and only four in the rear, and very little luggage on top.

In the rear of the coach the four passengers had sat in silence for the greater part of the journey, the grey sky and dreary outlook not being conducive to conversation. The desolation of the country, due to lack of agricultural labour, was apparent even along the fertile stretch of Normandy. The orchard trees were already bare of leaves and bent their boughs to the fury of the blast; their naked branches, weighted with the rain, were stretched out against the wind like the great gaunt arms of skinny old men suffering from rheumatism and doing their best to run away.

Of the two female travellers one looked like the middle-aged wife of some prosperous shopkeeper. She had rings on her fingers and a gold brooch was pinned to her shawl. Her hands were folded above the handle of a wicker basket out of which she extracted, from time to time, miscellaneous provisions with which she regaled herself on the journey. At one moment when the other woman who sat next to her, overcome with sleep, fell up against her shoulder, she drew herself up with obvious disgust and eyed the presumptuous creature up and down with the air of one unaccustomed to any kind of familiarity.

This other woman was Josette Gravier, en route for England, all alone, unprotected, ignorant of the country she was going to, of the districts she would have to traverse, of the sea which she had never seen and of which she had a vague dread; but her courage kept up by the determination to get to England, to wrest the letters from Louise de Croissy and, with them in her hand, to force those influential Terrorists into granting life and liberty to Maurice. It was Josette Gravier who, overcome with sleep, had fallen against the shoulder of her fellow-traveller, but it was a very radically transformed Josette; not disguised, but transformed from the dainty, exquisite apparition she always was into an ugly, dowdy, uncouth-looking girl unlikely to attract the attention of those young gallants who are always ready for an adventure with any pretty woman they might meet on the way. She had dragged her hair out of curl, smeared it with grease till it hung in lankish strands down her cheeks and brows; over it she wore a black cap, frayed and green with age, and this she had tied under her chin with a tired bit of back ribbon. She had rubbed her little nose and held it out to the blast till the tip was blue: she hunched up her shoulders under a tattered shawl, and forced her pretty mouth to wear an expression of boredom and discontent. What she could not hide altogether was the glory of her eyes, but even so she contrived to dim their listre by appearing to be half asleep the whole of the way. Like the other woman she kept her basket of provisions on her lap, and at different times she munched bits of stale bread and cheese and drank thin-looking wine out of a bottle, after which she passed the back of her hand over her mouth and nose and left marks of grease on her chin and cheeks.

Altogether she looked a most unattractive bit of goods, and this, apparently, was the opinion of the two male travellers who sat opposite, for after a quick survey of their fellow-passengers they each settled down in their respective corners and whiled away the dreary hours of the long day by sleep. They did not carry provisions with them, but jumped out of the diligence for refreshments whenever the driver pulled up outside some village hostelry on the way.

At the Auberge du Cheval Blanc in Rouen everyone had to get down. The diligence went no farther, but another would start early the next morning and, in all probability, would reach Tréport in the late afternoon. Josette, like the other travellers, was obliged to go to the Commissariat of the town for the examination of her papers before she could be allowed to hire a bed for the night. Her safe-conduct was in order, which seemed greatly to astonish the Chief Commissary, for he eyed with some curiosity this bedraggled, uncouth female who presented a permit signed by three of the most prominent members of the National Convention.

"Laissez passer la citoyenne Josephine Gravier agée de vingt ans demeurant a

Paris Villieme section Rue Picpus No. 43, etc., etc...."

It was all in order; the Commissary countersigned the safe-conduct, affixed the municipal seal to it and handed it back to Josette. She had been the last of the travellers to present her papers at the desk; she took them now from the Commissary and turned to go out of the narrow stuffy room when a man's voice spoke gently close to her:

"Can I direct you to a respectable hostelry, Citizeness?"

Josette glanced up and encountered a pair of light-coloured eyes that looked kindly and in no way provokingly at her: they were the eyes of one of her fellow-travellers who had entered the diligence at Les Andelys and had sat in the corner opposite to her, half asleep, taking no notice of anything or anybody. He was a small, thin man with pale cheeks and a sad, or perhaps discontented, expression round his thin lips: his hair was lank and plentifully streaked with grey. He was dressed in seedy black and looked quite insignificant and not at all the kind of man to scare a girl who was travelling alone.

Josette thanked him for his kindness:

"I have engaged a bed at the Cheval Blanc," she said, "which I am assured is a model of respectability: I shall be sharing a room with some of the maids at the hostelry, and the charge for this accommodation is not high. All the same," she added politely, "I thank you, sir, for your kind offer."

She was about to turn away when he spoke again:

"I am journeying to England, and if I can be of service there I pray you to command me."

It did not occur to Josette at the moment to wonder how this stranger came to know that she was journeying to England, but she could not help asking him who he was and why he should trouble about her.

"Before the war," he replied, "my business used often to take me to England and I was able to master its difficult language. Now, alas! my business is at an end, but I have friends over the water and, like yourself, I was lucky enough to obtain a permit to visit them."

Once more Josette thanked him: he seemed so very kind; but at the outset of her journey she had made up her mind very firmly not to enter into conversation with anyone, not to trust anyone, least of all one of her own nationality. She had no idea as yet of the difficulties which she might encounter when she landed in a strange country. Indeed, she had undertaken this journey without any thought of possible failure, but wariness and discretion were the rules of conduct which she had imposed on herself and to which she was determined to adhere rigidly. Having thanked her amiable friend, she bade him Good-night and hastened back to the hostelry.

She didn't see him again on the following morning when she took ticket for the diligence that was to take her to Tréport. An altogether different set of people were her fellow-travellers on this stage of her journey: they were a noisy crowd—three men and two women besides herself in the rear compartment of the coach; so they were rather crowded and jammed up against one another. Josette, being small and unobtrusive, was pushed into a corner by the other women, who were large and stout and took up a lot of room. Talk was incessant, chiefly on the recent incidents at Nantes. Carrier, the abominable butcher, had been recalled, but his successors had carried on his infamous work. The war in the Vendée had drawn to its close: those who took part in it fell victims to their loyalty to the throne; their wives and children were murdered wholesale. Travellers who had come from those parts spoke of this with bated breath. Only a few had escaped butchery, and this through the agency of some English spies—so 'twas said—whose activities throughout Brittany had baffled the revolutionary government. One man especially, who went, it seems, by the strange name of a small scarlet flower, had been instrumental in effecting the escape of a number of women and children out of the plague-ridden prisons of Nantes, where such numbers of them died of disease and inanition even while the guillotine was being prepared for them.

Josette, huddled up in the corner of the compartment, listened to these tales with a beating heart. Ever since she had started on this fateful journey she had wondered in her mind whether somewhere or other, in a moment of distress or difficulty, she would suddenly find that unseen hand was there to succour or to help, whether she would hear a comforting voice to cheer her on her way, or catch unexpectedly a glance from eyes that, whilst revealing nothing to the uninitiated, would convey a world of meaning to her.

Now the tales that she heard dispelled any such hope. Women and children in greater distress than herself were claiming the aid and time of the gallant Scarlet Pimpernel. It was sad and terribly disappointing that she would not see him as she had so confidently hoped. Only in her dreams would she see him as she had done hitherto. The rumble of the coach-wheels, the heavy atmosphere made her drowsy: she shrank farther still into her corner and slept and dreamed; she dreamed of the gallant English hero and also of Maurice—Maurice who was so unselfish, so self-effacing, who was suffering somewhere in a dingy prison, pining for his little friend Josette, wondering, perhaps, what had become of her, and eating his heart out with anxiety on her account. And somehow in her dream Josette saw the English hero less clearly than she used to do; his imaginary face and form slowly faded and grew dim and were presently merged in the presentment of Maurice Reversac, who looked sad and ill—so sad and ill that Josette's heart ached for him in her sleep, and that her lips murmured his name "Maurice!" with exquisite longing and tenderness.

CHAPTER XXI

Whenever Josette's thoughts in after years reverted to her memorable journey to England, she never felt that it had been real. It was all so like a dream: her start from

Paris in the early morning; the diligence; the first halt at the barrier; the examination of the passports; and then the incessant rumble of wheels, the rain beating against the windows, the gusts of wind, the atmosphere reeking of stale provisions, of damp cloth and of leather; the murmur of voices; the halts outside village hostelries; the nights in the auberge at Meulan and Les Andelys, at Rouen and Tréport; and her fellow-travellers. They were nothing but dream figures, and it was only when she closed her eyes very tight that Josette could vaguely recall their faces: the prosperous shopman's wife with her rings and her gold brooch and her wicker basket; the crowd in the diligence between Rouen and Tréport who chattered incessantly about the English spy and the horrors of Nantes; her neighbour, who squeezed her into a corner until she could hardly breathe; and then the small, thin man—he, surely, was nothing but a figure in a dream!

Dreams, dreams! they must all have been dreams! All those events, those happenings which memory had never properly recorded, they were surely only dreams; and all the way across the Channel she sat as in a dream: she saw other travellers being very seasick, and there was, indeed, a nasty gale blowing from the south-west, but it was a favourable wind for the packet-boat to Dover and she made excellent going, whilst to Josette the fresh sea air, the excitement of seeing the white cliffs of England looming out of the mist, the sense of contentment that she was nearing the end of her journey and that her efforts on behalf of Maurice would surely be crowned with success were all most welcome after the stuffiness and dreariness of those days passed in the diligence.

And how bright and lovely England seemed to her! It was indeed a dream world into which she had drifted. People looked happy and free! Yes, free! There was no look of furtiveness or terror on their faces; even children had shoes and stockings on their feet, and not one of them had that look of disease and hunger so prevalent—alas!—in revolutionary France. Peace and contentment reigned everywhere; ay! in spite of the war-clouds that hung over the land. And Josette's heart ached when she thought of her own beautiful country, her beloved France, which was all the more dear to all her children for the terrible time she was going through.

Poor little Josette! She felt very forlorn and very much alone when she stood on the quay at Dover with her modest little bundle and her wicker basket which contained all her worldly possessions. For the first time she realised the magnitude of the task which she had imposed on herself when all around her people talked and talked and she could not understand one word that was said. Never before had she been outside France, never before had she heard a language other than her native one. She felt as if she had been dropped down from somewhere into another world and knew not yet what would become of her, a stranger among its denizens. Frightened? Only a little, perhaps, was she frightened, but firm, nevertheless, in her resolve to succeed. But what had seemed like such a simple proposition in Paris looked distinctly complicated now.

She was forlorn and alone—and all round her people bustled and jostled; not that anyone was unkind—far from it—they but were all of them busy coming and going, collecting luggage, meeting friends, asking for information. She, Josette, was the only one who, perforce, was tongue-tied—a pathetic little figure in short kirtle, shawl and frayed-out black cap, with lanky hair and a red nose and a smear across one cheek, for much against her will tears would insist on coming to her eyes and they made the smear when they would roll down her face.

The crowd presently thinned out a bit: Josette could see these or those fellow-passengers hurrying hither or thither, either followed by a porter carrying luggage or shouldering their own valise. They all seemed to know where they were going; she alone was doubtful and ignorant. Indeed, she had never thought it would be as bad as this.

And suddenly a kind voice reached her ear:

"Can I be of service now, Mademoiselle? We all have to report at the constable's office, you know."

Just for the moment it seemed to Josette as if le bon Dieu had just taken pity on her and sent one of His angels to look after her. And yet it was only the thin little man in seedy black who had spoken, and there was nothing angelic about him. He had his papers in his hand and quite instinctively she took hers out from inside her bodice and gave them to him.

"Will you come with me, Mademoiselle," he went on to say, "in case there is a little difficulty about your safe-conduct being entirely made out by the French Government, with which the English are at war! They welcome the émigrés as a matter of course; still, there might be a little trouble. But if you will come with me I feel sure I can see you through."

Josette gave him a look of trust and of gratitude out of her blue eyes. How could she help fancying that here was one of those English heroes of whom she had always dreamed and who were known in the remotest corners of France as angels of rescue to those unfortunates who were forced to flee from their own country and take refuge in hospitable England? Dreams! dreams! Could Josette Gravier be blamed for thinking that here were her dreams coming true? When she felt miserable, helpless and forlorn, a hand was suddenly stretched out to help her over her difficulties. Of course she did not think that this pale-faced little man was the hero of her dreams—she had always thought of the Scarlet Pimpernel as magnificently tall and superbly handsome; but then she had also thought of him as mysterious and endowed with mystic powers that enabled him to assume any kind of personality at will. There was enough talk about him among the girls in the government workshops: how he had driven through the barriers of Paris disguised as an old hag in charge of a refuse-cart in which the Marquis de Tournay and his family lay hidden: and there were other tales more wonderful still. Then why could he not diminish his stature and become a pale-faced little man who spoke both English and French and conducted her, Josette, to an office where he exhibited an English passport which evidently satisfied the official in charge not only as to his own identity, but also as to that of the girl with him?

Who but a hero of romance would have the power so to protect the weak as to smooth out every difficulty that beset Josette Gravier's path after her landing in England, from the finding her a respectably hostelry where she could spend the night to guiding her the next morning to the Bureau des émigrés Français in Dover, where he obtained for her all the information she wanted about her beloved Louise? Louise, indeed, lived and worked not very far from Dover, in a town called Maidstone, to which a public coach plied that very day. And into this coach did Josette Gravier step presently in the company of her new guardian angel, the thin-faced, pale-eyed little man with the soft voice, whose mysterious hints and utterances, now that she fell into more intimate conversation with him, clearly indicated that if he was not actually the Scarlet Pimpernel himself, he was, at any rate, very closely connected with him.

CHAPTER XXII

Louise de Croissy was sitting in the bow-window of the small house in Milsom Street in the city of Maidstone when, looking up from her embroidery frame, she saw Josette Gravier coming down the street in the company of a little man in black who was evidently pointing out the way to her. Louise gave one cry of amazement, jumped up from her chair, and in less than half a minute was out in the street, with arms outstretched and a cry of "Josette! My darling one!" on her lips.

The next moment Josette was in her arms.

"Josette! My little Josette! I am not dreaming, am I? It really is you?"

But Josette, overcome with fatigue and emotion, could not yet speak. She let Louise lead her to the house. She appeared half-dazed; but when they came to the door she turned to look for the guiding angel who had brought her safely within sight of her beloved Louise. All she could see of him was his back in the seedy black coat a hundred yards away, hurrying down the street.

Louise was devoured with curiosity; question after question tumbled out of her mouth.

"Josette chérie, how did you come? And all alone? And who was that funny little man in black? What made you come? Why, why didn't you let me know?"

Josette had sunk into the armchair which Louise had dragged for her beside the fire—a lovely fire glowing with coal, the flames dancing as if with joy and putting life and warmth into the girl's stiffened limbs. And Louise, kneeling beside her, holding her little cold hands, went on excitedly:

"Of course you mustn't talk now, chérie, and you must not heed my silly questions. But imagine my amazement! I thought I was dreaming. I had been thinking of you, too, all these days... and to think of you here and now.... What will Charles-Léon say when he sees you?... He is getting so strong and well and..."

Then she jumped to her feet, struck her forehead with her hand and exclaimed:

"But what a fool I am to keep on chattering when you are so weary and cold, my darling!... Just wait a few minutes and close your eyes and I will get you some lovely hot tea. Everyone here in England drinks tea in the afternoon... At first I couldn't get used to it... I hadn't drunk tea for years, and then not often—only when I had a headache... but I soon got the way of it.... No, no! I won't chatter any more.... Just sit still, chérie, and I'll bring you something you'll like."

She trotted off, eager, excited and longing desperately to hear how Josette had come to travel alone all the way to England; through the instrumentality of that marvellous Scarlet Pimpernel, she decided within herself; and her active brain worked round and round, conjecturing, imagining all sorts of possibilities. "I wonder what has become of poor Maurice Reversac?" she mused at one moment.

She delighted on preparing the tea for Josette and prided herself in the way she made it—one spoonful of tea for each cup and one for the pot—and in the English way of making toast with butter on it. How Josette will love that! Darling, darling Josette! Life from now on would be just perfect; no more loneliness; no more anxiety for Charles-Léon. The angel of the house was present once more.

And in the little sitting-room, ensconced in the big winged chair, Josette Gravier sat with eyes closed, still living in her dream. Was it not marvellous how le bon Dieu had brought her safely to Louise; The events of her journey passed before her mental vision like a kaleidoscope of many shapes and colours. It seemed almost impossible to realise that all these things had truly happened to her, Josette Gravier, and that she was really here in England instead of in the dingy Rue Picpus or stitching away at the Government workshops. And thoughts of the workshop brought back a vision of Maurice, and terror gripped her heart because of what might be happening to him—terror, and then a great feeling of joy because she remembered what she was able to do for him. Maurice to her had become as a child, as Charles-Léon was to Louise, a being dependent on her for love and, in a sense, for protection.

It was a wonderful thing, in very truth, to be sitting in a large, comfortable easy-chair beside a lovely fire here in England, and to be drinking tea and eating pain grillé with delicious butter on it; and, above all, to have Louise sitting beside her and watching her with loving eyes whilst she ate and drank. Tea was lovely! Like Louise, she had not tasted it for years; it was a luxury unknown in France these terrible times, and even in the happy olden days in the farm by the Isère or in the convent school of the Visitation Josette had only been given tea when she had a headache.

After a little while she felt wonderfully comforted; she knew that Louise was consumed with curiosity and, in all conscience, she could not delay satisfying her.

"Can you not guess why I am here, Louise?" she asked abruptly.

"Of course I can, chérie!" Louise replied. "You came to England for the same reason that I did—to get away from those abominable murderers."

But Josette shook her head.

"Should I have run away," she asked, "and left Maurice out there alone?"

"I don't understand, chérie. Where is Maurice?"

"In prison."

"In...?"

"He was arrested two days before I left Paris."

"But on what grounds?"

Josette gave a sigh and a shrug; she stared dreamily into the fire.

"Does one ever know?" she murmured, and then added: "I suppose that Maurice's connection with Bastien disturbed the complacency of some of those devils. They didn't know how much he knew—about those letters."

"The letters?"

"Yes—the letters. You have still got them, Louise?"

"Of course."

A deep sigh of relief came from little Josette's anxious heart. She turned her large, luminous eyes on her friend.

"That is why I came to England, chérie—to fetch those letters."

"Josette!" Louise exclaimed, "what do you mean?"

"Just that. Maurice has been arrested—you know what that means: a week or a fortnight in some dank prison, then the mockery of a trial, and, finally, the guillotine..."

"But..."

"...so le bon Dieu inspired me and gave me courage. I thought of the letters. In order to try and get hold of them, men like Chabot and Fabre went to the length of murder. Fortunately you had taken them away with you. I thought and thought until I remembered the names of those black-guards who had written them and who had murdered Bastien. Then I went to call on them."

"You—my little timid Josette?"

"Yes. I went and I was no longer timid. I went, first of all, to that horrible man Chabot. I told him that those compromising letters of his were still in existence and that I knew where they were. Then I proposed by bargain: complete immunity for Maurice with a safe-conduct to enable him to leave France as soon as I had retrieved the letters and placed them in the hands of their writers."

"You did that, Josette?"

"I did it for Maurice."

"But that was just the bargain which my poor Bastien proposed to those same men, and in consequence of it..."

"...they murdered him in cold blood. I know that."

"Then how could you...?"

"I ran that risk, I know," Josette replied calmly; "but I also knew by then that possession of those letters had become a question of life and death to those assassins. I threatened them with the immediate publication of the letters in the Moniteur if anything happened to Maurice or to me. They didn't know where the letters were; all I told them was that they were in England and that you had kept them. Anyway, they gave me a safe-conduct to go to England and come back. And here I am, my Louise, and if you will give me the letters I will start on my journey back the day after to-morrow."

Louise made no immediate reply: she was staring at her little friend—the frail, modest girl who all alone and sustained only by her own courage had undertaken such a dangerous task for the sake of the man she loved. For, in truth, Louise was forced to the conclusion that Josette's heart, unbeknown to herself, had been touched at last by Maurice Reversac's devotion. Only a woman in love could accomplish what Josette Gravier had done, could so calmly face difficulties and dangers and be ready to face them again without rest or respite. Neither did Josette speak; she was once more staring into the fire, and the dancing flames showed her visions of Maurice suffering in prison and longing for her.

"Josette darling," Louise said after a time, "you cannot possibly start on another long journey just yet."

"Why not?"

"You must have a few days' rest. You are so tired..."

Josette gave a slight shrug.

"Oh!—tired..."

"I cannot imagine how you ever found me—I mean, so quickly. Did you go to London?"

"No, I didn't have to."

"Then, how...?"

"A kind friend helped me."

"A friend? Who was it?"

"I don't know. He was a fellow-passenger first in the diligence and then on board ship."

"A stranger?"

"Why, yes! but you cannot imagine how kind he was. When I landed on the quay at Dover I felt terribly lonely and helpless; indeed, I don't know what was to become of me. Everything was horribly strange, and then I couldn't understand a word anyone said..."

"I know. I felt just like that at first, although, of course, I was in the hands of friends. I told you—in my letter..."

"I thought of you, Louise, and of the wonderful friends who were looking after you. What were they like, darling?"

"It is not easy to describe people, and I was terribly over-wrought at the time, but the two friends whom we met in the cottage on the cliffs and who took us across the sea in that beautiful ship were good-looking young English gentlemen. One was fair, the other had brown hair, and..."

"Was not one of them quite small and thin, with a very pale face and light-coloured eyes...?"

"No, dear, nothing like that."

"That was what my friend looked like. He spoke to me first at Rouen, and then again at Dover when I felt so lost I didn't know what to do. He took me to a nice hostelry where I could hire a bed for the night. Then the next morning he went with me to the Bureau des émigrés, where they spoke French and where they looked up your name and told me where to find you. After that we took the coach for this town. My thin friend with the pale face arranged everything, and when we arrived in this city he walked through the streets with me to show me where you lived; and then—and then, while I ran to embrace you, darling, he hurried away. But I hope and pray that I may meet him again so that I can thank him properly for all the help he gave me."

"Do you think you will?"

"I think so. He told me that he would be in Dover for a couple of days and that a packet-boat would be leaving for Tréport on Thursday at two o'clock in the afternoon. That is the day after to-morrow. He said he would look out for me on the quay. So you see..."

"Josette darling," Louise exclaimed impulsively, "you must be wary of strangers!"

"But of course, Louise, I am wary—very wary. Whenever I spent the night in a hostelry, although I really had enough money to pay for a private room, I always chose to share one with other women or girls. I wouldn't sleep alone in a strange room for anything, although I did so long for privacy sometimes. But if you saw that insignificant little man, Louise, you would know that I had nothing to fear from him."

"I wonder who he is?"

"Sometimes I think..." Josette murmured.

"What, darling?"

"Oh, you will only laugh!"

"Not I. And I know what you were going to say."

"What?"

"That you think he has some connection with the Scarlet Pimpernel."

"Well, don't you?"

"I don't know, dear. You see the members of the League of the Scarlet Pimpernel with whom I came in contact were all English."

"My thin friend with the pale face might be a French member of the League. How otherwise can you explain his kindness to me?"

"I cannot explain it, chérie. Everything that happened to me was so wonderful that I am ready to accept all your theories of the supernatural powers of the mysterious Scarlet Pimpernel. But now, darling, we have chatted quite long enough. You are tired and you must have a rest. After that we'll have supper and you shall go to bed early, if you must leave me again so soon..."

"I must Louise, I must. And you understand, don't you?"

"I suppose I do; but it will break my heart to part from you again."

"I have to think of Maurice," Josette said softly.

"You love him, Josette?"

"I don't know," the girl replied with a sigh. "At one time I thought that my heart and soul belonged to the mysterious hero whom perhaps I would never see; but since Maurice has been in danger I have realised..."

"What, chérie?"

"That he is dear, very dear to me."

CHAPTER XXIII

It seemed so strange to be back in France once more, to hear again one's own tongue spoken and to understand everything that was said.

Josette, standing in the queue outside the Commissariat of Police at Rouen with the same little bundle and the same wicker basket in her hand, waiting to have her safe-conduct examined and stamped, was a very different person to the forlorn young creature who had felt so bewildered and so terribly lonely at Dover.

She had had two very happy days with Louise. Her arrival, her first sight of the beloved friend had been unalloyed joy; sitting by a cosy fire with Louise quite close to her and holding her hand brought back memories of the happiest days of her childhood. Then there was Charles-Léon looking so bright and bonny, with colour in his cheeks and all his pathetic listlessness gone. In a way, Josette had not altogether liked England; the grey clouds, the misty damp atmosphere were so unlike the brilliant blue skies of France and the sparkling clear air of her native Dauphiné that went to the head like wine; but, then, that atmosphere was pure and wholesome, Charles-Léon's bright eyes testified to that: he no longer suffered from the poisonous air of Pairs; and Louise, even in this short time, seemed to have recovered the elasticity of youth.

Yes! it had been a happy, a very happy time, brightened still further by thoughts of what she, Josette, was doing for Maurice. On the very first evening Louise had given her the sealed packet containing the precious letters: the precious, precious packet which would purchase Maurice's life and liberty. Josette turned it over and over in her hands, and gazed down on the seals and on the wrapper as if her eyes could pierce them.

"What are you looking at so intently, darling?" Louise asked with a smile.

"I didn't recognise the seals," Josette replied.

"It must be the one that Bastien used at the office. I never looked closely at the impress before."

"You've never opened the packet?"

"Never. And it never left me since the moment I left our apartment."

"You had it inside your corsets?"

"In the big pocket inside my skirt; and at night I always slipped it under my pillow, or under whatever happened to be my pillow."

"That is what I will do, of course."

"Only once," Louise resumed after a moment or two, "I had a bad scare: one of the last days of our journey. We had reached the desolate region of the Artois and I was terribly, terribly tired. I remembered that the night before I had slipped the letters into my pocket as usual, nevertheless, when we halted the next day and the driver helped me out of the cart, I felt for the packet and imagine my horror when I found it was gone! A wild panic seized me: I don't know why, but I just turned ready to run away. I was suddenly convinced that I had been lured to this lonely spot for the sake of the letters and that Charles-Léon and I would now be murdered. However, I hadn't gone far when the kindest voice imaginable, accompanied by a delicious soft laugh, called me back and, my dear Josette, imagine my joy and surprise when I saw our driver coolly holding the packet out to me!"

"The driver?"

"Yes! I will leave you to guess who he was, just as I did."

They talked by the fire half the day and late into the night, dreaming dreams of happy times to come when that awful revolutionary government would be forced to give way to a spirit of good-will, charity and order—the true birthright of the French nation. Indeed, it had all been a very happy time, and those two days at Maidstone went by like a dream. And now Josette was back, in France on the last stage but one of her journey to Paris. Within three, at most four days, Maurice would be free, and together they would come out to this fair land of England, for it would not be safe to remain in France any longer. Here they would wait for the happy days that were sure to come: Maurice would find work to do, for he was clever and brave, and he would surely earn enough to support himself; then, just as they had always done in Pairs, they would wander together in the English woods, those lovely woods about Maidstone of which Josette had had a passing glimpse. In a few short months spring would come and the birds in England, just like those in France, would all be nesting, and under the trees the ground would be carpeted with snowdrops and anemones just as it was at Fontainebleau. And if Maurice's heart was still unchanged, if the same words of love came to his lips which he had spoken before that awful tragedy had darkened both their lives, then she, Josette, would no longer laugh at him. She would listen silently and reverently to an avowal which she knew now would give her infinite happiness; and she would say "Yes!" to his request that she should become his wife, and together they would steal away in the very early morning to some little English church, and here before God's altar they would swear love and fealty to one another.

Dreams, dreams, which now of a surety would soon become a glowing reality; and all the way since she had left Maidstone in the coach and after she had cried her fill over parting from Louise, Josette had thoughts only of Maurice; and now and then her little hand went up to her bosom, where inside her corsets rested that precious packet; whereupon a look of real joy would gleam out of her eyes, and not even the devices wherewith she had contrived to make her pretty face seem almost ugly could altogether mar its beauty then.

CHAPTER XXIV

The little man with the pale sad face whom Josette looked on as a friend had been most kind and helpful at Dover. He had met Josette on the quay, helped her with her safe-conduct, saw her on the boat for Tréport, and promised that he would meet her again on the journey, probably at Rouen; he himself was bound for Calais, but he would be posting from there to Rouen, and if he was lucky he would get the diligence there for Paris.

Many a time during the next forty-eight hours had Josette longed for his company, not so much because she was lonely, but because the whole way from Dover she had been somewhat worried with the attentions of a stranger, and those attentions had filled her with vague mistrust. She had first caught sight of him on the packet-boat, striding up and down the deck with a swaggering, rolling gait. He was clad like a sailor and ogled all the women as he strode past them—Josette especially—and when he caught a woman's eye a hideous squint further disfigured his ugly face. Somehow she had felt uncomfortable under his glance. Then at Tréport he had seemed to keep an eye on her, and when she boarded the diligence he took a seat in the same compartment and sat opposite to her. He certainly did not molest her in any way, but she felt all the time conscious of his presence. He was very big and fat and entered into conversation with any of the other passengers who were willing to listen to him, telling tall sea yarns and expatiating on his own prowess in various adventures of which, according to his own showing, he was the hero. Oddly enough, he was a native of Nantes—so he informed one of his fellow-travellers—and had been in port there quite recently. Josette, at this, pricked up her ears, and, sure enough, the sailor had something to say about those English spies and their activity in helping aristos and other traitors to evade justice.

"Citizen Carrier," the man had gone on with a dry laugh which revealed some ugly gaps between his teeth, "grows livid with rage at the bare mention of English spies, and lashes about him with a horse-whip like an infuriated tiger with its tail. Only the other day..."

And there followed a long and involved story of how a whole family of aristos—an old man and his grand-children—were spirited away out of the prison of Le Bouffay, how and when nobody ever knew; and Carrier was in such a rage that he had an epileptic fit on the spot. To all this Josette listened eagerly; but all the same she couldn't bear that ugly fat sailor and was vaguely afraid of him.

Josette felt quite happy and relieved when at Rouen she caught sight once more of her pale-faced little friend. She had been lucky enough to fall in on the way with two pleasant women—a mother and daughter—who were ready to share a room with her in the Traverne du Cheval Blanc, and thither the three women repaired after the necessary visit at the Commissariat. It was here that Josette saw her friend again. He was standing in the little hall talking to a rough-looking fellow to whom he appeared to be giving instructions.

When he encountered Josette's glance, he gave her a nod and an encouraging smile.

Josette and the two women went into the public dining-room, where several of the smaller tables were already occupied. In the centre of the room there was one long table, and round it two people were sitting, waiting for supper to be served. They were for the most part a rough-looking crowd of men who were making a good deal of noise. The three women, however, were fortunate enough to find an unoccupied small table in a quiet corner where they could have their meal in comfort.

From where Josette sat she could see the door and watch the people coming in and going out. Two diligences had arrived in Rouen within the hour: the one from Tréport and the other from Paris, and a great number of weary and hungry travellers trooped into the public room, demanding supper. The big fat sailor was among these, and Josette was thankful that there was no seat available at her own table, for already she had seen the glance wherewith he had sought to catch her eye, and she had felt quite a cold wave of dread creep down her spine at sight of that ugly face with the leer and the hideous squint.

However, after that first searching glance round the room the fat sailor took no more notice of her; he lolled up to the centre table and sat down. He ate a hearty supper and continued to regale the rest of the company with his ridiculous tall yarns.

Half-way through supper Josette had the joy of seeing her small, pale-faced friend come into the room. He, too, gave a searching glance all round the room, and when he caught sight of Josette he gave her another of his pleasant smiles. Somehow at sight of him she felt comforted. Later on she could not help noticing with what deference everyone at the Cheval Blanc had welcomed the insignificant-looking little man. The landlord, his wife and daughter all came bustling into the room and, in a trice, had prepared and laid a separate table for him in a corner by the hearth. Though the table d'hôte supper was practically over by then, they brought him steaming hot soup and after that what was obviously a specially prepared dish. Some of the travellers remarked on this and whispered among themselves, but quite unconsciously, no doubt, the deference shown by the landlord and his family communicated itself to them, and the rowdy hilarity of awhile ago gave place to more sober and less noisy conversation.

Only the fat sailor tried for a time to foist his impossible tales on the company, but as no one appeared eager now to listen to him he subsided presently and remained silent and sulky, squinting at the new-coming and moodily picking his teeth. Josette could not help watching him—he was so very ugly and so very large, with his great loose paunch pressed against the table and the hideous black gaps in his mouth; and then those eyes which seemed to be looking both ways at once, one across the other and in no particular direction.

Presently he rose. Josette could not help watching him. She saw him pick up the pepper-pot and toy with it for a moment or two; then, with it in his hand, he lolled across to where Josette's little friend was quietly eating his supper. The latter didn't look up; continued to eat, even while that impudent sailor man stood looking down on him for a moment or two. On the part of a person of consideration this indifference would have seemed strange in the olden days, but now when mudlarks such as this ugly sailor were the virtual rulers of France it was never safe to resent their familiarity or even their impertinence.

The next moment, with slow deliberation, the sailor put the pepper-pot down in front of the stranger, and Josette saw her friend's pale eyes travel upwards from the pepper-pot to the ugly face leering down on him, and she could have sworn that he gave a start and that his thin hands were suddenly clenched convulsively round his knife and fork; also that his pale cheeks took on a kind of grey, ashen hue. No one apparently noticed any of this except Josette, who was watching the two men. She could only see the broad back of the sailor, saw him give a shrug and heard something like a mocking laugh ring across the room.

A second or two later the sailor had lolled out of the door, and Josette might have thought she had imagined the whole scene but for the expression on her little friend's face. It still looked ghastly, and suddenly he put down his knife and fork and strode very quickly out of the room. What happened after that she didn't know, as her friend did not come back to finish his supper, and very soon the two women who were sharing a room with her gave the signal to go upstairs to bed.

The room which the three of them had secured for the night was at the top of the house under the roof. There were two beds in it: a large one in the far corner of the room which the mother and daughter claimed for themselves and a very small truckle bed for Josette which stood across the embrasure of the dormer window between it and the door. Josette, as was her wont, took the precaution of placing the precious packet of letters underneath her pillow; having said her prayers she slid between the coarse sheets and composed herself for sleep. Her room companions, who had the one and only candle by the side of their bed, soon put the light out, and presently their even breathing proclaimed that they had already travelled far in the land of Nod. At first it seemed pitch-dark in the room, for outside the weather was rough and no light whatever came through the dormer window; but presently a tiny gleam became apparent underneath the door. It came from the lamp which was kept alight all night in the vestibule down below for the convenience of belated travellers. Josette welcomed the little gleam; her eyes soon became accustomed to what had become semi-gloom; she felt secure and comforted, and after a few minutes she, too, was fast asleep.

What woke her so suddenly she did not know, but wake she did, and for a while she lay quite still, with eyes wide open, her heart pounding away inside her and her hand seeking the precious packet underneath her pillow. At the far end of the room the two women were obviously asleep: one of them snoring lustily. And suddenly Josette perceived that the narrow streak of light under the door had considerably widened and had become triangular in shape; indeed, it was widening even now; she also perceived that there was now an upright shaft of light which also widened and widened as slowly, very slowly, the door swung open.

Josette in an instant sat straight up in bed and gave a cry which roused her room mates out of their sleep. From where they lay they couldn't see the door, but they called out: "What is it?"

"The door!" Josette gasped in a hoarse whisper, and then, "The light! the light!"

The women had a tinder-box on a chair near their bed: they fumbled for it whilst Josette's wide, terror-filled eyes remained fixed on the door. It was half-open now, but by whose hand? impossible to say, for there was no one to be seen. But it seemed to Josette's terrified senses as if she heard a furtive footstep making its way across the narrow landing and down the rickety stairs.

The older woman from her bed asked rather crossly:

"What is it frightened you, little Citizeness?"

Her daughter was still trying to get a light from the tinder-box, which, as was very usual these days, refused to work.

Josette gave a gasp and murmured under her breath: "The door... someone opened it... I heard..."

"Did you see anyone?"

"I don't know... but the door is open and I heard..."

"The latch didn't go home," the woman said more testily. "That's what it was. I noticed last night it didn't look very safe. The draught blew the door open..."

She settled herself back on her pillow. Her daughter gave up trying to get a light and said as testily as her mother:

"Go and shut it, Citizeness; put a chair to hold it if you are frightened and lets get to sleep again."

For a few moments after that Josette remained silent, sitting up in bed, staring at the door. Some evil-doer, she was sure, had tried it and perhaps, scared by her cry and by the women talking, had slunk away again. Certainly there was no one behind the door now. For a time it remained half-open just as it was and then it swayed gently in the draught and creaked on its rusty hinges. The two women had already turned over and were snoring peaceably once more. What could Josette do but chide herself for her fears? But impossible, of course, to go to sleep again with one's nerves on edge and that door swinging and creaking all the time; so Josette crept out of bed and tiptoed across the floor with the intention of closing the door. She moved about as softly as she could so as not to wake the others again. With her hand on the latch she ventured to peep out on the landing. The feeble glimmer emitted by the lamp down below cast a dim yellowish light up the well of the stairs. The house appeared very still, save for the sounds of the stertorous breathings which came from one or other of the rooms on the various floors where tired travellers were sleeping. Outside a dog barked. Josette listened for a moment or two for that furtive footstep which she had heard before, but everything appeared perfectly peaceful and very still. She closed the door very gently and then she groped for a chair to prop against it, when suddenly there came a loud bang right behind her and a terrific current of air swept across the room; the door was once more torn open, quite wide this time, and continued to rattle and to creak. The chair fell out of Josette's hand and she remained standing in her shift, shivering with cold and fright, with her kirtle flapping about her bare legs and her hair blowing into her eyes. The women woke and grumbled, asked with obvious irritation why the Citizeness didn't go to bed and let others sleep in peace.

Josette's heart was beating so fast that she could neither speak nor move; the weather outside was fairly rough and the draught took her breath away.

"Close the window!" the younger woman shouted to Josette. "The wind has blown it open."

At last Josette was able to get her bearings; she turned to the window and saw that in effect it was wide open and that wind and rain were beating in. She had to climb over her bed in order to get to the window and to secure it.

"I call it sheer robbery," the older woman muttered, half-asleep, "to put honest women in such a ramshackle hole."

But neither she nor her daughter offered to lend a hand to Josette, who, buffeted by the rough weather, had great difficulty in fastening the window. When she had done that she had to climb over her bed again in order to close the door; thus several minutes went by before peace reigned once more in the attic room. Josette crept back to bed. Her first thought was for the precious packet: she slid her hand under the pillow to feel for it, but the packet was no longer there.

With an agonising sinking of the heart, in a state not so much of panic as of despair, she turned and ran just as she was in shift and kirtle without stockings or shoes out of the room and down the stairs, crying: "Thief! thief! thief!" She reached the bottom of the stairs without meeting anyone: she ran across the passage and the vestibule to the front door, tried to open it, but it was locked and bolted. She tore at the handle and at the bolts, still calling wildly: "Thief! thief!" in a voice broken by sobs.

Gradually the whole house was aroused. Doors were heard to open, testy voices wanted to know what all this noise was about. The night watchman came out of the public room, blinking his eyes. Mine host came along from his room down the passage, cursing and swearing at all this disturbance.

"Name of a name! Who is the miscreant who dares to disturb the peace of this highly respectable hostelry?"

Then he caught sight of Josette, who was still fumbling with the door and crying, "Thief! thief!" in a tear-choked voice. Her bare arms and her shoulders were wet, her clothes were wet, her wet hair fell all over her face.

"Name of a dog, wench!" the landlord thundered, and seized the disturber of the peace by the wrist, "what are you doing here? And pray why aren't you in bed where every respectable person should be at this hour?"

It was a blessing in disguise that Josette should be held so firmly by the wrist else she would certainly have measured her length on the floor. Her senses were reeling. Through the gloom she saw angry faces glowering at her. Quite a small crowd had collected in the vestibule: a crowd of angry men roused from their slumbers, clad in whatever garments they happened to have slept in; the women for the most part did not venture beyond the doorway of their rooms, and peeped out thence with eyes heavy with sleep to see what was happening. At sight of Josette most of them murmured:

"A trollop no doubt, caught in some turpitude."

The irate landlord gave Josette's arm a shake: "What were you doing here?" he demanded, "little str-"

He was going to say an ugly word, but just at the moment Josette raised her eyes to his, and Josette's eyes were bathed in tears and they had such an expression of childlike innocence in them that the worthy landlord could think of nothing but of the Madonna whose lovely image had been banished from the village church where he had been baptised and had made his first Communion, and which was now closed because the good curé of the village had refused to conform to the mockery of religion which an impious Government was striving to force upon the people: and looking into Josette's eyes, the landlord's thoughts flew back to the Madonna, before whose picture he had worishipped as a child. How, then, could he speak an ugly word in this innocent angel's ear?

"You have got to tell me, you know," he said somewhat sheepishly, "why you are not in your room and asleep." He paused a moment while Josette made a great effort to collect her scattered senses; ashamed of her bare legs and shoulders she tried to get farther back into the gloom.

Someone in the crowd remarked: "Perhaps she is a sleep-walker and had a nightmare."

But at this suggestion Josette shook her head.

"Did something frighten you, little Citizeness?" the landlord asked quite kindly.

Josette now found her voice again.

"Yes!" she said slowly, swallowing hard, for the last thing she wanted to do was to cry before all these people. "I woke very suddenly. I could see the door. It was being pushed open slowly from outside. I cried out. Then I heard footsteps shuffling down the stairs."

"Impossible!" the landlord said.

"I heard nothing," commented someone.

"Nor I," added another.

"I did hear a bang," remarked a third, "not many minutes ago."

"There was a bang," Josette went on slowly. "While I was closing the door the window flew open behind me. I went to shut it. Then the door flew open, and I went to shut it too. When I crept back to bed I found—oh, mon Dieu! mon Dieu!"

"What is it? What happened?" they all asked.

"A packet of letters," she replied, "more precious to me than life itself..."

"Not stolen?"

"Yes—stolen."

"Where were they?"

"Underneath my pillow."

"And you say that when you went back to bed those letters..."

"Were not there."

"Impossible!" the landlord reiterated obstinately.

One of the men said, "The thief, whoever he was, must still be in the house then, since the front door is bolted on the inside."

"What about the back door?" another suggested.

Several of them, under the lead of the night watchman, went to investigate the back door. It was bolted and barred the same as the front door.

"I knew it was," the night watchman said somewhat illogically. "I pushed all the bolts in myself all over the house and saw to all the windows."

He felt that Josette's story reflected adversely upon his zeal.

"The thief must still be in the house," Josette murmured mechanically.

"Impossible!" the landlord reiterated for the third time.

The glances cast on Josette became anything but kind, and though the landlord and some of the men were under the influence of her innocent blue eyes, the women from their respective doorways had a good deal to say. One of them started the ball rolling by muttering:

"It's all a pack of lies."

After which the others went at it hammer and tongs. Women are like that. Let some vixen give a lead and there is no stopping the flow of evil tongues. Poor Josette felt this hostility growing around her. It added poignancy to her distress over the letters. Indeed, the little crowd had as usual behaved like sheep; after the first doubt had been cast on Josette's story hardly anyone believed her. The theory of her being a sleep-walker was incontinently rejected: she was just a little strumpet roaming through the house at night in search of adventure. In vain did she weep and protest; in vain did she beg that her room mates be questioned as to the truth of her story: those two women refused to leave their bed, where they lay with their heads smothered under the blanket, wishing to God they had never set foot in this abominable hostelry. Josette, overcome with misery and with shame, had shrunk back into a dark angle of the vestibule, trying with all her might to overcome her terror of all these angry faces, and, above all, to swallow her tears. In her heart she prayed as she had never prayed before that le bon Dieu, her patron saint and her guardian angel might guide her with safety out of this awful pass. The landlord stood by, undecided, scratching his head.

"It is a matter for the police, I say." It was a woman who made this suggestion. It was quickly taken up by others, for, indeed, this seemed the easiest solution to the present difficulty; after which everybody would be able to go back to bed and go through the rest of the night in peace.

"I agree," one of the men said. "Let the wench be taken to the nearest Commissariat of Police."

And then a funny thing happened.

The suggestion that the disturber of the peace should be taken to the Commissariat of Police was received with approval, especially by the women. Some of the men were rather doubtful, and there ensued quite a considerable hubbub and a good deal of argument: the women holding to their opinion with loud, shrill voices, the men muttering and cursing.

The landlord stood by scratching his head, not knowing what to do: the casting vote as to Josette's fate would of course rest with him.

And suddenly a quiet vote broke in on the hubbub, saying authoritatively:

"Certainly not. Never shall it be said that a respectable citizeness of the Republic had been put to the indignity of being dragged before the police in the middle of the night."

It was the voice of one accustomed to command and to being obeyed—very quiet and low but peremptory. A small, thin man with pale face and hard penetrating eyes pressed his way through the small crowd. Unlike the rest of them he had slipped on his coat over his shirt, he had stockings on and shoes, and his hair was brushed back tidily. Under his coat and round his waist he wore a tricolour sash. The landlord gave a big sigh of relief: he was truly thankful that decision in this difficult case was taken out of his hands. The girl's story certainly sounded very lame... but, then, she had such lovely blue eyes... and her little mouth—well, well! Anyway, he would not have the unpleasant task of taking her to the police on an ugly charge. The others were all deeply impressed by the little man's authority and by his tricolour sash—badge of service under the Government. As for Josette, she just clasped her tiny hands together and gazed on that insignificant, pale-faced little man as would a devotee upon her favourite saint; her eyes were bathed in tears, her lips already murmured words of gratitude, but actually she was not yet able to speak.

"Where is your wife, landlord?" the little man went on to say in the same peremptory tone.

"At your service, Citizen," the woman replied for herself. She had slipped her bare feet into her shoes and she had on her kirtle and a shawl round her shoulders. Unlike the female guests of the hostelry, she felt that this matter concerned her, and she had dressed herself ready in case of an emergency.

"You will give Citizeness Gravier a bed in your daughter's room, where she will, I hope, spend the rest of the night in peace." So spake the little man with the tricolour sash, and it was marvellous with what alacrity his orders were obeyed. That tricolour sash did indeed work wonders! And now he added curtly: "Remember that the Citizeness is under the special protection of the Central Committee of Public Safety."

Josette could only stare at him with wide-open eyes that looked of a deep luminous blue in this half-light. The little man caught her glance and came over to her. He took her limp, moist hand in his and patted it gently:

"Try and get a little rest now, little woman," he said kindly. "You shall have your letters back, I promise you, even if," he added with a curious smile, "even if we have to set the whole machinery of the law going in order to recover them for you."

He said this so lightly and with so much confidence that Josette felt comforted and almost reassured; indeed, her unsophisticated heart was so full of gratitude that instinctively like a child she raised the thin, clawlike hand which patted her own to her lips. She was on the point of imprinting a kiss upon it when from somewhere in the house there resounded a tremendous crash as of falling furniture. It was immediately followed by loud and prolonged laughter. All the heads were turned towards the stairs as the noise seemed to have come from somewhere above.

"What in the world...?" and other expressions of amazement came to everyone's lips.

"I believe it's that drunken sailor," someone remarked.

"Let me get at him," the landlord said grimly, and pushed his way through the small crowd in the direction of the stairs.

"It can't be him," the night watchman asserted. "I let him out myself by the back door two hours ago and bolted the door after him."

But the little man with the tricolour scarf had snatched his hand out of Josette's grasp. For a moment it seemed as if he was about to join the landlord in his quest after the sailor, but apparently he thought better of it; probably he felt that it would be beneath the dignity of a Government official to chase a mudlark up and down the stairs of a tavern; besides which he well knew in his heart of hearts that no sailor or mudlark would be found inside the house. The laughter had come from outside—there must be an open window somewhere—and its ringing tone was only too familiar to this same Government official with the pale sad face and the badge of office round his waist: it came from a personage that had always proved elusive, whenever the utmost resources of his enemy's intelligence were set to work to run him to earth.

The only thing to do now in this present crisis—for crisis it certainly would prove to be—was to think things over very carefully, to lay plans so secretly and so carefully that no power on earth could counter them. The girl, Josette Gravier, was a magnificent pawn in the game that was to follow the events of this night, just the sort of pawn that would appeal to the so-called chivalry of those damnable English spies: a decoy—what?

So the little man, whose pale face reflected something of the inward rage that tortured him at this moment, turned fiercely on the small crowd of quidnuncs who still stood about quizzing and whispering, and with a peremptory wave of the arm ordered everyone off to bed. They immediately scattered like sheep. The landlord's wife took hold of Josette's hand.

"Come along, little girl," she said; "there is a nice couch in Annette's room:

you'll sleep well on that."

"And remember, both of you," the little man said in the end when Josette meekly allowed herself to be led away, "that you are responsible with your lives—your lives," he iterated emphatically, "for the safety of Citizeness Gravier."

The man and woman both shuddered: their ruddy faces became sallow with terror. They understood the threat well enough, even though the amazing turn which the events of this night had taken was past their comprehension.

Silent and obedient the little crowd had dispersed. They all slunk back to bed, there to exchange surmises, conjectures, gossip with their respective room mates. Josette lay down on the couch in Annette's room. She could not sleep, for her brain was working all the time and her heart still beating with the many emotions to which she had succumbed this night. There were moments when, lying here in the darkness, she doubted and feared. That was because of the tricolour sash and the authority which her friend seemed to wield. Before his appearance in this new guise of authority she had almost persuaded herself that he was intimately connected with the hero of her dreams, but there was no reconciling the badge of officialdom of the Terrorist Government with the personality of the Scarlet Pimpernel. Nevertheless, it was this same little man who had saved her from the ill-will of all those horrid people who said such awful things about her and threatened her with the police. It was he who had given her a solemn promise that the precious letters would be restored to her; so what was an ignorant, unsophisticated girl like Josette Gravier to make of all these mysteries? What she did do was to turn her thoughts to Maurice. Surely le bon Dieu would not be so cruel as to snatch from her the means by which she could demand his life and liberty. Surely not at this hour when she was so near her goal.

And in a private room on the floor above, Citizen Chauvelin was pacing up and down the floor, with hands clasped tightly behind his back, his pale face set, his thin lips murmuring over and over again:

"Now then, à nous deux once more, my gallant Scarlet Pimpernel."

After a time there came a knock at the door. In response to a peremptory "Entrez!" a rough-looking fellow in jersey and breeches undone at the knee came into the room. He had a sealed packet in his large, grimy hands, and this he handed to Chauvelin.

Neither of the men spoke for some time. The man had remained standing in the middle of the room waiting for the other to speak, while Chauvelin sat at the table, his thin delicate hands toying with the packet, his pale eyes hiding their expression of triumph behind their blue-veined lids.

The silence threatened to become oppressive. The newcomer was the first to break it. He pointed a grimy finger at the sealed packet in Chauvelin's hand.

"That is what you wanted," he asked, "was it not, Citizen?"

"Yes," the other replied curtly.

"It was difficult to get. If I had known..."

"Well!" Chauvelin broke in impatiently; "the wind and rain helped you, didn't they?"

"But if I had been caught..."

"You weren't. So why talk about it?"

"And I injured my knee climbing down again from that cursed window," Picard muttered with a surely glance at his employer.

"Your knee will mend," Chauvelin rejoined curtly; "and you have earned good money."

He gave a quiet chuckle at recollection of the night's events. He and Picard. The open door. The open window. The draught. Josette in her shift and kirtle struggling with the door while Picard stole in at the window, and he, Chauvelin, tip—toed noiselessly back down the stairs. Yes! the whole thing had worked wonderfully well, better even than he had hoped. It had been a perfect example of concerted action.

Picard was waiting for his money. Chauvelin gave him the promised two hundred livres—a large sum in these days. The man tried to grumble, but it was no use, and after a few moments he slouched, still grumbling, out of the room.

For close on half an hour after that did Chauvelin remain sitting at the table, toying with the stolen packet. There was a lighted candle on the table, its feeble light flickered in the draught. Chauvelin's pale, expressive eyes were fixed upon the seals. He did not break them, for it was part of the tortuous scheme which he had evolved that these seals should remain intact. He looked at them closely, wondering whose hand had fixed them there: Bastien de Croissy's probably, who had been murdered for his pains, or else the wife's before she entrusted the packet to Josette. The seals told him nothing, and he did not mean to break them: he laid the precious packet down on the table. Then he opened the table drawer. Out of it he took a small lump of soft wax. With the utmost care he took an impression of one of the seals: he examined his work when it was done and was satisfied that it was well done. He then returned the wax impression into the table drawer and locked it.

The stolen packet he slipped into the breast pocket of his coat, and he laid the coat under the mattress in the adjoining room. After which he went to bed.

CHAPTER XXV

The imaginative brain that invented the torment meted out to Damocles could not in very truth have invented torture more unendurable. Poor old Damocles! All he wanted was to taste for a time the splendour and joys of kingship, and Dionysius, the tyrant King of Sicily, thought to gratify his whim and his own sense of humour by giving the ambitious courtier charge of the kingdom for a while.

So good old Damocles ascended the throne which he had coveted and licked his chops in anticipation of all the luxury that was going to be his, until suddenly he perceived that a sword was hanging over his head by nothing but a hair from a horse's tail. Now we must take it, though legend doesn't say so, that this sword followed the poor man about wherever he went, else all he need have done was to wonder through his kingdom and avoid sitting immediately under that blessed sword. As to how the business of the horse's hair was accomplished, say in an open field, is perhaps a little difficult to imagine.

Be that as it may, three worthy Representatives of the People in the autumn of 1793 did in very truth go about their avocations with, figuratively speaking, a sword of doom hanging over their heads.

Three weeks had gone by since Chabot's memorable interview with Josette Gravier, and there was no news of her, no news of Armand Chauvelin, no news, alas! of those compromising letters which were enough to send the whole batch of them to the guillotine.

The Club of the Cordeliers had of late lost a great deal of its prestige, and consequently was not frequented by the most influential members of the Government: it was, therefore, an admirable meeting-place for those who desired to talk things over in the peace and quiet of the club's deserted rooms. Many a time in the past weeks did those three reprobates, quaking in their shoes, hold conclave among themselves, trying to infuse assurance and even hope into one another. Sometimes the great Danton would join them, knowing well that if his three satellites fell, he, too, would be involved in the general débâcle that would ensue. Late into the night they would sit and talk, wondering what had become of the little she-devil who had dared to threaten them, hoping against hope that one of the many accidents attendant on a voyage across France had put an end to her.

Then one day there came a letter from Citizen Chauvelin. It was sent to François Chabot, the unfrocked monk turned traitor, renegade and Terrorist, as being the most deeply involved in the affair of the compromising letters. With trembling fingers Chabot broke the seals of this welcome message, for he had already recognised the thin Italian calligraphy of the writer: he was alone in his luxuriously furnished study. At first he could hardly see what he was doing: the words of the letter danced before his eyes, the blood rushed up to his temples, and the paper rustled in his trembling hands. Then slowly he was able to decipher the writing. The first sentence that he read caused him to utter a gurgle of joy: "I have the girl here..."

That was good news indeed. Chabot closed his eyes so as to savour all the more thoroughly the intense joy produced to him by this message. With the girl in his power Chauvelin could have no possible difficulty in getting hold of the letters as well. Now Chabot came to think of it, it was strange that his colleague chose this enigmatic way of commencing his letter. The girl! Yes! the girl was well enough! But what about the letters? He suddenly felt uncomfortable... vaguely frightened of he knew not what. He blinked his eyes once or twice because they had become blurred, and beads of perspiration stood out at the roots of his hair and trickled down his nose. Then at last he settled down to read, and this is what Citizen Armand Chauvelin had written to him from Rouen:

"Citizen and Dear Colleague. "

"I have the girl here under my eye, and by this you will gather that my mission has been successfully accomplished. I am now in Rouen at the hostelry of the Cheval Blanc, under the same roof as the little blackmailer. So for I have done nothing about the letters. I can get hold of them any moment, but there are other very grave matters that command my attention. Owing to the inclement weather the diligence cannot ply for some days, and this enforced delay suits my purpose admirably, for I do not wish to leave Rouen just now. The wench cannot in any case escape me and, if you will believe me, I have such high quarry close to my hand that I cannot leave this city until I have secured it. This is not a personal matter but one that affects the very safety of the Republic: how, then, could I risk that by deserting my post? You must try and read between the lines, and then explain the matter to all those who are involved in the affair of the Croissy letters. As I have already told you, I can, of course, get hold of the letters at any time, and I suggest that you give me leave in that case to destroy them before any further mischief is wrought. If you agree to this wise course, send me a courier immediately to the hostelry of the Cheval Blanc here in Rouen. But I beg of you not to delay. There are inimical powers at work here of which you can have no conception, and if, as I believe, the safety of the Republic is as dear to you as it is to me, you will be ready to fall in with my views."

François Chabot read and re-read this letter, which did certainly in some of its phrases appear ambiguous. What, for instance, did Chauvelin mean by the closing sentence? To Chabot it seemed to contain a veiled threat, and there were other points, too....

That evening the four men sat in a corner of the club-room in a very different mood to that of the past few weeks. There they were—François Chabot (Loire et Cher), Fabre d'Eglantine (Paris) and Claud Bazire (Côte d'Or), as unprincipled a lot of rascals as ever defamed the country of their birth. The great Danton had joined them at their earnest request—not so much a scoundrel he, as an infuriated wild animal, smarting under many wrongs, lashing out savagely against guilty and innocent alike, and with old ideals long since laid in the dust.

"I would not trust that old fox farther than I could see him," Danton had said as soon as the matter of Chauvelin's letter had been put before him.

"But he can get hold of the letters at any time—there's no doubt about that," one of the others remarked.

"He has probably got them inside his coat pocket by now," the great man retorted, "ready to sell them or use them for his own ends."

"Then what had one better do?"

"Let us send a courier over to Rouen," Fabre d'Eglantine suggested, "with orders to Citizen Chauvelin to come to Paris immediately."

"Suppose he refuses?" Danton said with a shrug.

"He wouldn't dare...."

"And would you dare threaten him if he really has the letters and holds them over you?"

They were silent after that because they knew quite well—in fact had just realised it for the first time—that it was Armand Chauvelin now instead of Bastien de Croissy or Josette Gravier who held the sword of Damocles over their heads.

After a time Chabot murmured, looking to the great Danton for guidance now that the emergency appeared more fateful than before: "What shall we do, then?"

"If you take my advice," Danton said, and strove to appear as if the whole matter did not greatly concern him, "if you take my advice, one of you will go straight to Rouen, see Citizen Chauvelin and get the packet of letters straight from the girl. After that the sooner the wretched things are destroyed the better."

That seemed sound advice, and after discussion it was decided to act upon it, François Chabot declaring his willingness, in spite of the weather, to journey to Rouen by special coach on the morrow.

CHAPTER XXVI

From Meulon, where he spent the night, Chabot sent a courier with a letter over to Rouen to prepare Chauvelin for his arrival.

"Devoured with impatience," (he wrote) "I am coming in person to receive the precious letters from your hands and discuss with you the terms of your reward, which my friends and I are determined shall be as great as your service to our party."

An ironic smile twisted Chauvelin's thin lips when he read this short epistle. The events had not turned out any differently to what he had expected. Those cowardly fools over there were, in fact, playing into his hands.

He had been interrupted by the courier in an important work which had demanded a great deal of time and skill. Five days had gone by since poor little Josette had been robbed of her precious letters, and to-day Chauvelin was sitting at the table in the private room which he still occupied in the hostelry of the Cheval Blanc. Though it was daylight there was a lighted candle on the table, and when the courier arrived, Chauvelin's deft fingers had been busy making up a small parcel which looked like a packet of letters and which he had been engaged in sealing down with red wax and a brand-new seal.

When the courier was announced he blew out the candle and threw the packet into the table-drawer.

Now that he was alone again he took the packet out of the drawer, and then drew another out of the breast-pocket of his coat. The two packets now lay side by side on the table. Chauvelin applied himself sedulously to a final examination of them. To all intents and purposes they were exactly alike. None but a specially trained eye could detect the slightest difference in them. In shape, in size, in the soiled and crumpled appearance of the outside covering, in the disposition of the five seals they were absolutely interchangeable. It was only to Chauvelin's lynx-like eyes that the difference in the seals was apparent. A very minute difference indeed in the sharpness and clearness of the impress.

He gave a deep sigh of satisfaction. All was well. The work of die-sinking had been admirably done from the wax impression of the original, by a skilled workman of Rouen. Chauvelin could indeed be satisfied: his deep-laid scheme was working admirably: he could await the arrival of Chabot with absolute calm and the certainty that his own delicate hands held all the threads of as neat an intrigue as he had ever devised for the ultimate undoing of his own most bitter enemy.

He slipped the two packets inside his coat pockets; the original one stolen from under the pillow of Josette Gravier he thrust against his breast, the other he put into a side pocket. After which he settled his sharp features into an expression of kindliness and went in search of Josette.

He knew just where to find her, sitting on the bench under the chestnut trees—that beautiful avenue which had once formed part of the old convent garden of the Ursulines, driven away by the relentless edicts of the revolutionary government. The mediaeval building, still splendid in its desolation, showed already signs of decay. The garden was untended, the paths overgrown with weeds, the grass rank and covered with a carpet of fallen leaves, the statuary broken, but nothing could mar the beauty of the age-old trees, of the chestnuts already half-denuded of leaves. And the vista over the river was beautiful, with the two islands and the sleepy backwater, and the sight of the ships gliding with such stately majesty down-stream towards the sea. The place was not lonely, for the riverside was a favourite walk of the townsfolk, and on the quay boatmen plied their trade of letting pleasure boats out on hire. The convent itself had been turned into a communal school for the children of Rouennais soldiers who were fighting for their country, and, after school hours or during recreation time, crowds of children trooped out of the building and ran playing up and down the avenue. Indeed, Josette did not come here for solitude: she liked to watch the children and the passers-by and, anyway, it was nicer than sitting in that stuffy public room of the hostelry where prying eyes scanned her none too kindly.

Her pale-faced little friend had insisted that she should continued to share a room with the landlord's daughter: this room had no egress save through the larger one occupied by the landlord himself and his wife, and Josette was quite aware that her friend had made these people responsible for her safety as well as for her comfort. This, of course, had greatly reassured her, and his promise that he would get the letters back for her had cheered her up—especially for the first twenty-four hours. She had such implicit faith not only in his friendship, but also, since that fateful night, in his power; but for that tricolour sash she would have felt happier still, but somehow she didn't like to think of that kind, sad, gentle creature as a member of a government of assassins.

This was the fifth day that Josette had spent in Rouen, waiting and hoping almost against hope. Once or twice she had caught sight of her friend either in the garden or while he wandered along the riverside, with head bent, hands clasped behind his back, evidently wrapped in thought. When he passed by in front of Josette he always looked up and gave her an encouraging smile. And then, again, she saw him in the public room at meal-times, and always he gave her a smile and a nod.

Then yesterday, here in the old garden, he came and sat down beside her under the chestnut tree, and he was so gentle and so kind that she was tempted to confide in him. She told him about the contents of the stolen packet—about the letters, the possession of which had cost brave Bastien de Croissy his life, and about her own journey to England in order to get the letters from Louise. And as he listened with so much attention and sympathy she went so far as to tell him about Maurice, and how it had been the object of her journey—nay! the object of her life—to use the letters as Bastien had intended to use them: as a leverage to obtain what she desired more than anything in the world—the life and liberty of Maurice Reversac.

"I am not afraid of what I mean to do," she concluded. "I have already bearded Citizen Chabot once, and I know that I can get from him everything I want..." She paused and added with a sigh of longing, "if only I have those letters...!"

Her friend had been more than kind after that, and so confident and reassuring that she slept that night more soundly and peacefully than she had done since she arrived in Rouen.

"Have no doubt whatever, little one," he had said in the end. "You shall have your precious letters back very soon."

And then, to-day, even while she sat at her accustomed place under the chestnut tree, and with dreamy glance watched the people coming and going up and down the riverside all intent on affairs of their own, heedless of this poor little waif with the gnawing anxiety in her heart, she suddenly caught sight of the little man coming towards her with a light, springy step. Somehow, directly she saw his face, she knew that he was the bearer of good news. And so it turned out to be. Even before he came close to her he thrust his hand into the side pocket of his coat and she guessed that he had the letters. She could not repress a cry of joy which caused the passers-by to cast astonished glances at the pretty wench, but she paid no heed to them. She was so excited that she jumped up and ran to her friend. He had indeed drawn the sealed packet from the pocket of his coat, and now he actually put it into her hands. It was so wonderful—almost unbelievable. Josette pressed the packet against her cheek and her young palpitating bosom—the precious, precious packet! She was so happy, so marvellously, so completely happy! She didn't care who watched her; just like a child she spread out her arms and would have hugged that kind peerless friend to her breast only that he put up a warning hand, for, in truth, she was attracting too much attention from the quidnuncs on the quay. At once she asked his pardon for her vehemence.

"I am so happy," she murmured 'twixt laughter and tears, "so happy! I was forgetting..."

"I told you I would get the letters for you, didn't I?" he said, and with kindly indulgence patted her trembling little hands.

"And I shall pray God every day of my life," she responded, sinking her voice to a whisper, "to give you due reward."

"So long as you are happy, my child..."

"I could fall at your feet now," she murmured earnestly, "and thank you on my knees."

None but a hardened, stony heart as that which beat in the Terrorist's breast could have resisted the charm, the exquisite sentiment of this beautiful woman's gratitude. To his enduring shame, be it said that Chauvelin felt neither remorse nor pity as he looked on the lovely young face with the glowing eyes and tender mouth quivering with emotion. His tortuous schemes would presently land her on the hideous platform of the guillotine; that beautiful head with the soft chestnut curls would presently fall into the ghoulish basket which already had received so many lovely heads. What cared he? All these people—men, women, young and old—were so many pawns in the game which he had devised; and he, Chauvelin, was still engaged in moving the pieces: he still had his hold on the pawns. Away with them if they proved to be in the way or merely useless. It was more often than not a scramble as to which party would push the other up the steps of the guillotine.

Chauvelin sat himself down quite coolly on the bench and, with a sneer round his lips which he took care the girl should not see, he watched her as she tucked the precious packet away underneath her fichu.

"I have further good news for you, Citizeness," he said as soon as she had sat down beside him.

"More good news!" she exclaimed; then pulled herself together and turned big inquiring eyes on her friend: "I won't hear it," she said resolutely, "until I know your name."

He gave a light shrug and a laugh: "Suppose you call me Armand," he replied, "Citizen Armand."

"Is that your name?"

"Why, yes?"

Josette murmured the name once or twice to herself.

"It will be easier like this for me," she said with naïve seriousness, "when I pray to le bon Dieu for you. And now," she went on gaily, "Citizen Armand, I am ready for your news."

"It is just this: you won't need to go to Paris."

"What do you mean?"

"Just what I say. A courier has just come from Meulon with news that François Chabot, representative of the people, will be in Rouen this evening."

"This—evening?"

"So you see..."

"Yes... I see," she murmured, awed at the prospect of this unexpected event.

"It all becomes so much safer," he hastened to reassure her. "I succeeded in getting that packet back for you this time, but I could not journey all the way to Paris with you, and you might have been robbed again."

"Oh, I see—I do see!" Josette sighed. "Isn't it wonderful?"

She felt rather bewildered. It was all so unexpected and not a little startling. Instinctively her hand sought the packet in the bosom of her gown. She drew it out. The outside wrapper was very soiled and crumpled—it had been through so many hands—but the seals were intact.

"I wouldn't break the seals if I were you, little girl," Chauvelin said. "It will be better for you, I think, also for your friend—what's his name?—Reversac, isn't that it?—if the Citizen Representative is allowed to think that you have not actually read those compromising letters. It will make him less ill-disposed towards you personally. Do you see what I mean?"

"I think I do, but even if I didn't," Josette added naïvely, "I should do as you tell me."

No compunction, no pity for this guileless child who trusted him! Chauvelin patted her on the shoulder:

"That's brave!" was all he said. He appeared ready to go, but Josette put a timid hand on his arm.

"Citizen Armand..."

"Yes? What is it now?"

"Shall I see you before..."

"Before the arrival of François Chabot?"

"Yes."

"I will certainly let you know, and see you if I can.... By the way," he added as if in after-thought, "would it not be wiser for you to leave the packet with me until this evening?... No?" he went on with a smile as Josette quickly crossed her little hands over her bosom as if some powerful instinct had suddenly prompted her not to part again from her precious possession. "No...? Well, just as you like, my child; but take care of them: those spies and thieves are still about, you know."

"Spies?"

"Of course. Surely you guessed that your letters were not stolen by ordinary thieves?'

"No, I did not. I just thought..."

"What?"

"That being a sealed packet a thief would think that it contained money."

"Enough to warrant such an elaborate plot," Chauvelin remarked drily, "and you so obviously not a wealthy traveller?"

"I hadn't thought of that. But, then, of course, Citizen Armand, you must know who stole the packet since..."

"Since I got it back for you? I do know, of course."

"Who was it?" Josette asked and gazed on Chauvelin with wide-open frightened eyes.

"If I were to tell you, you wouldn't understand."

"I think I would," she murmured. "Try me!"

"Well," he replied, sinking his voice to a whisper, "did you happen to notice on the first evening you arrived here a big man dressed as a sailor, who made himself conspicuous in the public room of the Cheval Blanc?"

"Yes, I did—a horrid man, I thought. But surely he...?"

"That man, who I admit wore a clever disguise, is the head of an English organisation whose aim is the destruction of France."

"You don't mean...?" she gasped.

Chauvelin nodded. "I see," he said, "that you have heard of those people. They call themselves the League of the Scarlet Pimpernel and, under the pretence of chivalry and benevolence, are nothing but a pestilential pack of English spies who take money from both sides—their own Governments or ours whichever suits their pocket."

"I'll not believe it!" Josette protested hotly.

"Did you not notice that night as soon as I entered the room that the fat sailor beat a hasty retreat?"

"I noticed," she admitted, "that he did leave the public room soon after you sat down to supper."

"I sent the police after him then, but he had a marvellous faculty for disappearing when he is afraid for his own skin."

"I'll not believe it!" Josette protested again, thinking of Louise's letter and of the hero of her dreams. "Had it not been for the Scarlet Pimpernel..."

"Your friend Louise de Croissy," Chauvelin broke in with a sneer, "would have never reached England—I know that. Did I not tell you just now that pretence of chivalry is one of that man's stock-in-trade? No doubt he wanted to get Citizeness Croissy away, thinking that she would leave the letters with you: when he realised that you hadn't them and that you were journeying to England obviously in order to get them, he followed you. I know he did, and I did my best to circumvent him. I befriended you as far as I could, for he dared not approach you while I was on the watch."

"Oh, I know," Josette sighed, "you have been more than kind."

She felt as if she were floundering in a morass of doubt and misery, tortured by suspicion, wounded in her most cherished ideals. Ignorant, unsophisticated as she was, how could she escape out of this sea of trouble? How could she know whom to trust or in whom to believe? This friend had been so kind, so kind! The precious letters had been stolen from her and he had got them back. Without him where would she be at this hour? Without him she would have nothing wherewith to obtain life and liberty for Maurice. Tears welled up to her eyes; never, perhaps, had she felt quite so unhappy, because never before had she been brought up in such close contact with all that was most hideous in life—treachery and deceit. She turned her head away because she was half-ashamed of her tears. After all, what was the destruction of an illusion in these days when one saw all one's beliefs shattered, all one's ideals crumbled to dust? Josette had almost deified the Scarlet Pimpernel in her mind, and Louise's letter had confirmed her belief in his wonderful personality with the fascinating mystery that surrounded it and the almost legendary acts of bravery and chivalry which characterised it. If any other man had spoken about her hero in the way this pale-faced little friend of hers had done she would have dubbed him a liar and done battle for her ideal; but she owed so much to Citizen Armand, he had been such a wonderful friend, such a help in all her difficulties, and now, but for him, she would have been in the depths of despair.

He was wrong—Josette was certain that he was wrong—in his estimate of the Scarlet Pimpernel, but never for a moment did she doubt his sincerity. She owed him too much to think of doubting him. Whatever he said—and his words had been like cruel darts thrust into her heart—he had said because he was convinced of the truth, and he had spoken only because of his friendship for her. Even now he seemed to divine her thoughts and the reason of her tears.

"It is always sad," he said gently, "to see an illusion shattered; but think of it like this, my child: you have lost a—shall I say friend, though I do not like to misuse the word?—who in very truth had no existence save in your imagination; against that you have found one who, if I may venture to say so, has already proved his worth by restoring to you the magic key which will open the prison doors for the man you love. Am I not right in supposing that Maurice Reversac is that lucky man?"

Josette nodded and smiled up at the hypocrite through her tears.

"I hadn't meant to tell you so much," he said, rising ready to go, "only that I felt compelled to warn you. The man who stole your letters once will try to do so again, and I might not be able to recover them a second time."

It was getting late afternoon now, the shadows were deep under the trees, but on the river twilight lingered still. The girl sat with her head bent, her fingers interlocked and hot tears fell upon her hands. The kind friend who had done so much for her was still standing there about to go, and she could not find it in her heart to look up into his face and to speak the words of gratitude which his marvellous solicitude for her should have brought so readily to her lips. Her thoughts were far away with Louise in her pretty room in England, telling her story of the astounding prowess of the Scarlet Pimpernel, his resourcefulness, his devotion, the glamour that surrounded his mysterious personality in his own country; how could all that be true if this kind and devoted friend over here did not deceive himself and her? And if he did not, then were all the tales she had heard tell of the mystic hero nothing but legends or lies?

A confused hum of sounds was in her ears; the boatmen gossiping on the quay, the shuffling footsteps of passers-by the shrieks and laughter of children up and down the avenue and, suddenly through it all, a stentorian voice chanting the first strains of the Marseillaise completely out of tune. Josette felt rather than saw Citizen Armand give a distinct start: she looked up just in time to see him cross over rapidly to the quay. The ear-splitting song had come from that direction. The boatmen were all laughing and pointing to a boat just putting off the shore, in which a fat sailor in tattered coat and shiny black hat thrust at the back of his head was plying the oars. He it was who was singing so intolerably out of tune; his voice resounded right across the intervening space: even when he reached midstream and headed toward the islands, some of the stentorian notes echoed down the avenue. Josette couldn't help smiling. Was that the man who had stolen the letters from under her pillow—the dangerous spy whom it took all her friend's ingenuity to track? Could, in fact, that ugly uncouth creature, with the lank hair, the tattered clothes and the toothless mouth, be the mysterious and redoubtable Scarlet Pimpernel?

Josette could not help laughing to herself at the very thought. Citizen Armand must indeed be moonstruck to think of connecting that buffoon with the most gallant figure of all times. She glanced anxiously about her to find her friend Armand, for she wanted to speak with him again, to convince him how wrong he was, how utterly mistaken he had been. All at once her big sea of troubles ebbed away. She felt happy and light-hearted once more. Her illusions were not shattered: she could still worship her ideal and yet retain her affection for the sad-faced and kindly man who had befriended her. She was happy—oh, so happy!—and her lips were ready now to speak the words of gratitude.

But look where she might, there was no longer any sign of Citizen Armand.

CHAPTER XXVII

It was now eight o'clock in the evening. An hour ago a post-chaise had driven into the courtyard of the Cheval Blanc and from it descended Citizen François Chabot, Representative of the People for the department of Loire et Cher. He had been received by the landlord of the tavern with all the honours due to his exalted station and to his influence, and had supped in the public room in the company of that pale-faced little man who had already created so much attention in the hostelry and who went by the name of Citizen Armand.

Josette sitting at another table in a dark angle of the room watched the two men with mixed feelings in her heart. She couldn't eat any supper, for inwardly she was terribly excited. The hour had come when all her efforts on behalf of Maurice would come to fruit. Her friend had sent her word that he would summon her when the Citizen Representative was ready to receive her, so she waited as patiently as she could. Watching Chabot she recalled every moment of her first interview with him; she had been perfectly calm and self-possessed then, and she would be calm now when she found herself once more face to face with him. Though ignorant and unsophisticated, Josette was no fool. She knew well what risk she ran by consenting to meet Chabot here in Rouen with the letters actually upon her person. Events had turned out differently from what she had planned. She had meant to meet Chabot in

Paris on neutral ground, conducts for herself and Maurice safely put away. Here it was different.

Danger? There always was danger in coming in conflict with these men who ruled France by terror and the ever-present threat of the guillotine, but there was also that other danger, the risk of the precious letters being stolen again during the final stage of the journey, and no chance of getting them back a second time. Even so, Josette would perhaps have refused to meet Chabot till she could do so in Paris had it not been for Citizen Armand; but it never entered her mind that this faithful and powerful friend would not be there to protect her and to see fair play.

As on that other occasion in the luxurious room of the Rue d'Anjou she was not the least afraid: it was only the waiting that was so trying to her nerves. While she made pretence to eat her supper she tried to catch her friend's eye, but he was deeply absorbed in conversation with Chabot. Once or twice the latter glanced in her direction, then turned back to Armand with a sneer and a shrug.

After supper the two men went out of the room together, and Josette waited quietly for the summons from her friend. At last it came. Looking up, she saw him standing in the doorway: he beckoned to her and she followed him out of the room. She was absolutely calm now, as calm as she had been during the first interview when the precious letters were not yet in her possession. Now she felt the paper crackling against her bosom—the golden key her friend had called the packet, which would open the prison gates for Maurice.

Armand conducted her to a small room at the back of the house, one which had been put at the disposal of the Citizen Representative by the landlord, who probably used it in a general way as a place where he could receive his friends with the privacy which the public room could not offer. It was sparsely furnished with a deal table covered by a faded cloth, on which past libations had left a number of sticky stains: on the table a bottle of ink, a mangy quill pen, a jar of sand and a couple of pewter sconces in which flickered and guttered the tallow candles. There were a few chairs ranged about the place and a wooden bench, all somewhat rickety, covered in grime and innocent of polish. From a small iron stove in an angle of the room a wood fire shed a welcome glow. The only nice bit of furniture in the place was an old Normandy grandfather clock, standing against the wall and ticking away with solemn majesty. There was only one window, and that was shuttered and bolted. The walls had once been whitewashed: they were bare of ornament save for a cap of liberty roughly drawn in red just above the clock and below it the device of the Terrorist Government: "Liberté, Égalité, Fraternité." Recently a zealous hand had chalked up below this the additional words: "Ou la mort."

When Chauvelin ushered Josette into this room Chabot was sitting at the table. The girl came forward and without waiting to be asked she sat down opposite of Chabot and waited for him to speak. She looked him fearlessly in the face, and he returned her glance with an unmistakable sneer. Chauvelin, who had followed Josette into the room, now put the question:

"Shall I go, or would you like me to stay?"

Josette, looking up at him, did not know to whom he had addressed the question, but in case it was to her she hastened to say: "Do please stay, Citizen Armand."

Chauvelin then sat down on the bench against the wall behind Josette, but facing his colleague. For a minute or two no one spoke, and the only sound that broke the fateful silence was the solemn ticking of the old clock. Then Chabot said abruptly:

"Well, little baggage, so you've been in England, I understand."

"Yes, Citizen, I have," Josette replied coolly.

Chabot, his ugly head on one side, was eyeing her quizzically, his thick lips were curled in a sneer. He picked up the pen from the table and toyed with it: stroked his unshaven chin with the quill.

"Let me see," he went on slowly, "what exactly was the object of your journey?"

"To get certain letters, Citizen," she rejoined, unmoved by his attitude of contempt, "which you were anxious to possess."

"H'm!" was Chabot's curt comment. Then he added drily, "Ah! I was anxious to possess those letters, was I?"

"You certainly were, Citizen."

"And it was in order to relieve my anxiety that you travelled all the way to England, what?"

"We'll put it that way if you like, Citizen Representative."

The girl's coolness seemed to exasperate Chabot as it had done in their first interview. Even now at this hour when she was entirely in his power, when his scheme of vengeance against this impudent baggage had matured to such perfection, he could not control that feeling of irritation against his victim, and he envied his colleague over there who sat looking perfectly placid and entirely at his ease. Suddenly he said:

"Where are those letters, Citizeness?"

"I have them here," she answered with disconcerting coldness.

"Let's see them," he commanded.

But she was not to be moved into easy submission.

"You remember, Citizen," she said, "under what conditions I agreed to hand you over the letters?'

"Conditions?" he retorted with a harsh laugh. "Conditions? Say, I have forgotten those conditions. Will you be so gracious as to let me hear them again?"

"I told you, Citizen Representative," Josette proceeded wearily, for she was getting tired of this word play, "I told you at the time; I want a safe-conduct in the name of Maurice Reversac and one in mine to enable us both to quit this country and travel whither we please."

"Is that all?"

"Enough for my purpose. Shall we conclude, Citizen Representative? You must be as tired as I am of all this quibble."

"You are right there, you impudent trollop!" Chabot snapped at her with a short laugh. "Give me those letters!"

Then as she made no answer, only glanced at him with contempt and shrugged, he iterated hoarsely:

"Did you hear me? Give me those letters!"

"Not till I have the safe-conducts written out and signed by your hand."

"So that's it, is it?" Chabot snarled, and leaned right across the table, peering into her face. He looked hideous in the dim, unsteady light of the candles, with his thick lips quivering, a slight scum gathering at the corners of his mouth and his thin face bilious and sallow with rage. Thus he remained for the space of a minute, gloating over his triumph. The wench was in his power—nothing could save her now; the vengeance for which he had thirsted was his at last; but there was exquisite pleasure in the anticipation of it, in looking at that slender neck so soon to be severed by the knife of the guillotine, on that dainty head with its wealth of golden curls soon to fall into the gruesome basket while those luminous eyes were closed in death-agony.

"Ah!" he murmured hoarsely, "you thought you had François Chabot in your power, you little fool, you little idiot! You thought that you could frighten him, torture him with doubts and fears? You triple, triple fool!"

His voice rose to a shriek: he jumped to his feet and, thumping the table with the palm of his hand, he shouted: "Here! Guard! A moi!"

The door flew open: two men of the Republican Guard appeared under the lintel, and there were others standing in the passage. Josette saw it all. While Chabot was raving and spitting venom at her like an angry serpent she had kept hold on herself. She was not frightened because she knew that Armand, her friend, was close by and that Chabot, even though, or perhaps because he was a Representative of the People would not dare to commit a flagrant act of treachery before his colleague: would not dare to provoke her, Josette Gravier, into revealing the existence of letters compromising to himself here and now. But when the door flew open and she caught sight of the soldiers, she jumped to her feet and turned to the friend to whom she looked so confidently for protection. Chabot now was laughing loudly; with head thrown back he laughed as if his sides would split.

"You little fool!" he continued to snarl. "You egregious little idiot!" He paused, and then commanded: "Search her!" The two soldiers advanced. Josette stood quite still and did not utter a single cry. Her great eyes were fixed on her friend—the friend who was playing her false, who had already betrayed her. At first her glance had pleaded to him: "Save me!" Her dark blue eyes, dark as a midsummer's night, had seemed to say: "Are you not my friend?" But gradually entreaty gave place to horror and then to a stony stare; for Citizen Armand, the friend and protector who had wormed himself into her secrets, gained her trust and stolen her gratitude, sat there silent and unmoved, stroking his chin with his talon-like fingers, an enigmatic smile round his thin lips. Slowly Josette averted her gaze: she turned from the treacherous friend to the gloating enemy. The soldiers now stood one on each side of her—she could actually feel their breath upon her neck; the hand of one of them fell upon her shoulder. With a smothered cry of revolt she shook it off and deliberately took the packet of letters from inside her bodice and laid it on the table.

A hoarse sigh of satisfation broke from Chabot's throat. His thick, coarse hand closed over the fateful packet; the soldiers stood by like wooden dummies, one on each side of Josette.

"Can I go now?" the girl asked.

Chabot threw her a mocking glance.

"Go?" he mimicked with a sneer. Then the sarcasm died on his lips, and his ugly face, which he thrust forward within an inch of hers, became distorted with a look of almost bestial rage. "Go? No, you evil-minded young jade—you are not going. Like a born idiot you have placed yourself in my power. For the past month you have been laughing at me and my friends in your sleeve, relishing like a debauched little glutton the torment which you were inflicting upon us. Well, it is our turn to laugh at you now, and laugh we will while you rot in gaol, you and your lover, aye! rot, until the day on which your heads fall under the guillotine will be welcomed by you as the happiest one of your lives."

Except that she recoiled with the feeling of physical disgust when the man's venom-laden breath fanned her cheeks, Josette had not departed for one moment from her attitude of absolute calm. The moment that earthly protection failed her and the friend whom she trusted proved to be a traitor, she knew that she and Maurice were lost. Nothing on earth could save either of them now from whatever fate these assassins chose to mete out to them. She prayed to le bon Dieu to give her courage to bear it all and, above all, she prayed for strength not to let this monster see what she suffered. The name of Maurice thrown at her with such cruelty had made her wince. It was indeed for Maurice's sake that she suffered most acutely. She had built such high hopes—such fond and foolish hopes apparently—on what she could do for him that the disappointment did for the moment seem greater than she could bear.

She no longer looked at the betrayer of her trust: in her innocent mind she thought that he must be overwhelmed with shame at his own cowardice. Le bon Dieu alone would know how to punish him.

At a sign from Chabot the soldiers each placed a hand once more upon the girl's shoulder. They waited for another sign to lead her away. Their officer was standing in the doorway: Chabot spoke to him.

"What accommodation have they got in this city," he asked with a leer at Josette and a refinement of cruelty worthy of the murderer of Bastien de Croissy, "for hardened criminals?"

"There is the town jail, Citizen," the man replied.

"Safe, I suppose?"

"Very well guarded, anyway. It is built underneath the town hall."

"Who is in charge?'

"I am, Citizen, with a score of men."

"And in the town hall?"

"There is a detachment of the National Guard under the command of Captain Favret."

"Quartered there?"

"Yes, Citizen."

Chabot gave another harsh laugh and a shrug.

"That should be enough to guard a wench," he said, "but one never knows—you men are such fools..."

While he spoke Chabot had been idly fingering the packet, breaking the seals one by one. Now the outside wrapper fell apart and disclosed a small bundle of letters—letters...? Letters? Chabot's hand shook as he took up each scrap of paper and unfolded it, and while he did so every drop of blood seemed to be drained from his ugly face and his bilious skin took on a grey ashen hue; for the packet contained only scraps of paper folded to look like letters with not a word on any of them. Chabot's eyes as he looked down on those empty scraps seemed to start out of his head: his face had been distorted before, now it seemed like a mask of death—grey, parchment-like, rigid. He raised his eyes and fixed them on Josette, while one by one the scraps of paper fluttered out of his hand.

But Josette herself was no longer the calm, self-possessed woman of a moment ago. When Chabot fingered the fateful packet and broke the seals one by one, when the outside wrapper fell apart and disclosed what should have been the famous letters, a cruel stab went through her heart at the thought of how different it would all have been if only the man she had trusted had not proved to be a Judas. Then suddenly she saw there here were no letters, only empty scraps of paper: her amazement was as great as that of her tormentor himself. She had received that packet from Louise: she had never parted from it since Louise placed it in her hands—never. But, of course... the last five days... the theft... the miraculous recovery... Oh, mon Dieu! mon Dieu! what did it all mean? Her brain was in a whirl. She could only stare and stare on those scraps of paper which fell out of Chabot's bony hands one by one.

No one spoke: the soldiers stood at attention, waiting for further orders. At the end of the room the old grandfather clock ticked away the minutes with slow and majestic monotony. At last a husky groan came from Chabot's quivering lips. He pointed a finger at Josette and then at the papers on the table.

"So," he murmured in a hoarse whisper, "you thought to fool me again?"

"No, no!" she protested involuntarily.

"You thought," he insisted in the same throaty voice, "to extract a safe-conduct from me and to fool me with these worthless scraps..."

He paused and then his voice rose to a shriek.

"Where are the letters?" he shouted stridently.

"I don't know," Josette protested. "I swear I do not know."

"Bring me those letters now," he iterated, "or by Satan..."

Once more he paused, for the words had died on his lips; indeed, how could he threaten his victim further when already he had promised her all the torments, mental and physical, that it was in his power to inflict. "Or by Satan..." What further threat could he utter? Jail? Death for her and her lover? What else was there?

"Bring me those letters!" he snarled, like a wild cat robbed of its prey, "or I'll have you branded, publicly whipped. I'll have you—I—I thank my stars that we've not given up in France all means of punishing hell-hounds like you."

"I cannot give you what I haven't got, Citizen," Josette declared calmly, "and I swear to you that I believed that the letters were in the packet which I have given you."

"You lie! You..."

Chabot turned to the officer-in-charge. "Take the strumpet away and remember..." He checked himself and for the next few moments swore and blasphemed; then suddenly changing his tone he said to Josette:

"Listen, little Citizeness; I was only trying to frighten you," and the tiger's snarl became a tabby's purr. "I can see that you are a clever wench. You thought you would fool poor old Chabot, did you not? Thought you would have a bit of a game with him, what?"

He tiptoed round the table till he stood close to Josette; he thrust his grimy finger under her chin, forced her to raise her head: "Pretty dear!" he ejaculated, and pursed his thick lips as if to frame a kiss. But it must be supposed that something in the girl's expression of face caused him to spare her this final outrage: or did he really wish to cajole her? Certain it is that he contented himself with leering at her and ogling the sweet pale face which would have stirred compassion in any heart but that of a fiend.

"So now you've had your fun," he resumed with an artful chuckle, "and we are where we were before, eh? You are going to give me the letters which you went all the way to England to fetch, and I will give you a perfectly bee-ee-autiful safe-conduct for yourself and that handsome young lover of yours—lucky dog!—so that you can go and cuddle and kiss each other wherever you like. Now, I suppose you have hidden those naughty letters somewhere in your pretty little bed and we'll just go there together to fetch them, what?"

Josette made no reply and no movement. What could she do or say? She had only listened with half an ear to that abominable hypocrite's cajolries. She had no more idea than he had what had become of the letters, or how it was that a packet in appearance exactly like the one which Louise had given her came to be substituted for the original one. She guessed—but only in a vague way—that Citizen Armand had something to do with the substitution, but she could not imagine what his object could possibly have been. While she stood mute and in an absolute whirl of conjecture and of doubt, Chabot waxed impatient.

"Now then, you little baggage," he said, and already he had dropping his insinuating tone, "don't stand there like a wooden image. Do not force me to send you marching along between two soldiers. Lead the way to your room. My friend and I will follow."

"I have already told you, Citizen," Josette maintained firmly, "I know nothing about any packet except the one which I have given you."

"It's a lie!"

"The truth, so help me God! And," she added solemnly, "I do still believe in God."

"Tshah!"

It was just an ejaculation of baffled rage and disappointment. For the next few seconds Chabot, with his hands behind his back, paced up and down the narrow room like a caged panther. He came to a halt presently in front of his colleague.

"What would you do, friend Chauvelin," he asked him, "if you were in my shoes?"

Chauvelin, during all this time, had remained absolutely quiescent, sitting on the bench immediately behind Josette. It was difficult indeed to conjecture if he had taken in all the phases of the scene which had been enacted in this room in the last quarter of an hour: Chabot's violence, Josette's withering contempt had alike left him unmoved. At one time it almost looked as if he slept: his head was down on his breast, his arms were crossed, his eyes closed. But now when directly interpellated by his colleague he seemed to rouse himself and glanced up at the angry face before him.

"Eh?" he queried vaguely. "What did you say, Citizen Representative?"

"Don't go to sleep, man!" the other retorted furiously. "Your neck and mine are in jeopardy while that baggage is allowed to defy me. What shall I do with her?"

"Keep her under guard and perquisition in her room: 'tis simple enough." And Chauvelin's lips curled in a sarcastic smile.

"Perquisition? Why, yes of course! The simplest thing, is it not?" And Chabot turned to the officer once more. "Sergeant," he commanded, "some of you go find the landlord of this hostelry. Order him to conduct you to the room occupied by the girl Gravier. You will search that room and never leave it until you have found a sealed packet exactly like the one which she laid on the table just now. You understand?"

"Yes, Citizen."

"Then go; and remember," he added significantly, "that packet must be found or there'll be trouble for your for lack of zeal."

"There will be no trouble," the soldier retorted drily.

He turned on his heel and was about to march off with his men when Chauvelin said in a whisper to his friend:

"I would go with them if I were you. You'll want to see that the packet is given to you with the seals unbroken, what?"

"You are right, my friend," the other assented. He signalled to the sergeant, who stood at attention and waited for the distinguished Representative to go out of the room in front of him. In the doorway Chabot turned once more to Chauvelin:

"Look after the hussy while I'm gone," he said, and nodded in the direction of

Josette. "I'm leaving some men outside to guard her."

"Have no fear," Chauvelin responded drily; "she'll not run away."

Chabot strode out of the room; the sergeant followed him, and some of the men fell into step and marched in their wake up the passage.

"You can wait outside, Citizen Soldiers!" Chauvelin said to the two men who were standing beside Josette. He had his tricolour scarf on, so there was no questioning his command: the soldiers fell back, turned and marched out of the room, closing the door behind them. And between those four white-washed walls Josette was now alone with Chauvelin.

CHAPTER XXVIII

"Was I not right, little one, to carry out that small deception?"

If at the moment when Mother Eve was driven out from the Garden of Eden she had suddenly heard the serpent's voice whispering: "Was I not right to suggest your eating that bit of apple?" she would not have been more astonished than was Josette when that gentle, insinuating voice reached her ears.

She woke as from a dream—from a kind of coma into which she had been plunged by despair. She turned and encountered the kindly familiar glance of Citizen Armand, sitting cross-legged, unmoved on the bench, his head propped against the wall. In the feeble light of the guttering candles he appeared if anything paler than usual, and very tired. Josette gazed on him tongue-tied and puzzled, indeed more puzzled than she had ever felt before during these last few days so full of unexplainable events. As she did not attempt to speak he continued after a moment's pause:

"But for the substitution which I thought it best to effect, your precious letters would now be in the hands of that rogue, and nothing in the world could have saved you and your friend Reversac from death." And again he continued: "The situation would be the same as now but we shouldn't have the letters."

He thrust his long thin hand into the inner pocket of his coat and half drew out a packet, wrapped and sealed just as was the other which had contained the pretended letters. Josette gave a gasp, and with her habitual, pathetic gesture pressed her hands against her heart. It had begun to beat furiously. She would have moved only that Armand put a finger quickly to his lips.

"Sh-sh!" he admonished, and slipped the packet back inside his coat.

There was a murmur of voices outside; one of the soldiers cleared his throat, others shuffled their feet. There were sounds of whisperings, of movements and heavy footsteps the other side of the closed door—reminders that watch was being kept there by order of the Citizen Representative. Josette sank her voice to a whisper:

"And you did that...? For me...? Whilst I..."

"Whilst you called me a traitor and a Judas in your heart," he concluded with a wan smile. "Let's say no more about it."

"You may forgive me... I cannot...."

"Don't let's talk of that," he resumed with a show of impatience. "I only wished you to know that the reason why I didn't interfere between Chabot and yourself was because in the existing state of our friend's temper my interference would have been not only useless but harmful to you and your friend. All I could do was to maneuver him into ordering the perquisition in your room and get him to superintend it so as to have the chance of saying these few words to you in private."

"You are right, as you always have been, Citizen Armand," Josette rejoined fervently. "I cannot imagine how I ever came to doubt you."

As if in response to her unspoken request he rose and came across the room to her, gave her the kindest and most gentle of smiles and patted her shoulder.

"Poor little girl!" he murmured softly.

She took hold of his hand and managed to imprint a kiss upon it before he snatched it away.

"You have been such a wonderful friend to me," she sighed. "I shall never doubt you again."

"Even though I were to put your trust to a more severe test than before?" he asked.

"Try me," she rejoined simply.

"Suppose I were to order your arrest... now?... It would only be for a few days," he hastened to assure her.

"I would not doubt you," she declared firmly.

"Only until I can order young Reversac to be brought here."

"Maurice?"

"Yes! For your ultimate release I must have you both here together. You understand?"

"I think I do."

"While one of you is here and the other in Paris, complications can so easily set in, and those fiends might still contrive to play us a trick. But with both of you here, and the letters in my hands, I can negotiate with Chabot for your release and for the necessary safe-conducts. After which you can take the diligence together to Tréport and be in England within three days."

"Yes! yes! I do understand," Josette reiterated, tears of happiness and gratitude welling to her eyes. "And I don't mind prison one little bit, dear Citizen Armand," she added naïvely. "Indeed I don't mind anything that you order me to do. I do trust you absolutely. Absolutely."

"I'll try and make it as easy for you as I can, and with luck I hope to have our friend Reversac here within the week."

Excited and happy, not the least bit frightened, and without the slightest suspicion, Josette saw Chauvelin go to the door, open it and call to the soldiers who were on guard in the passage. She heard him call: "Which of you is in command here?"

She saw one of them step briskly forward; heard his smart reply: "I am, Citizen!" and finally her friend's curt command:

"Corporal, you will take this woman, Josephine Gravier, to the Commissariat of Police. You will give her in charge of the Chief Commissary with orders that she be kept under strict surveillance until further orders." He then came across to the table, took up the quill pen that was lying there and a printed paper out of his pocket, scribbled a few words, signed his name and strewed the writing with sand. The tallow candles had now guttered so low, and emitted such a column of black smoke, that he could hardly see: he tried to re-read what he had written and was apparently satisfied, for he handed the paper to the soldier, saying curtly:

"This will explain to the Chief Commissary that the order for this arrest is issued by a member of the Third Sectional Committee of Public Safety—Armand Chauvelin—and that I hereby denounce Josephine Gravier as suspect of treason against the Republic."

The corporal—a middle-aged man in somewhat shabby uniform—took the paper and stood at attention, while Chauvelin, with a peremptory gesture, beckoned to Josette to fall in with the men. Loyal and trusting until the end, the girl even forbore to throw a glance on the treacherous friend who was playing her this cruel trick: she even went to the length of appearing overcome with terror, indeed she played to perfection the rôle of an unfortunate aristo confronted with treason and preparing for death.

"Now then, young woman," the corporal commanded curtly. Three men were waiting in the passage. With faltering steps and her face buried in her hands, Josette allowed herself to be led out of the room. The corporal was the last to go; the door fell to behind him with a bang. Chauvelin stood for a moment in the centre of the room, listening. He heard the brief word of command, the tramp of heavy feet along the passage in the direction of the front door, the shooting of bolts and rattle of chains. He rubbed his pale, talon-like hands together, and a curious smile played round his thin lips.

"You'll have your work cut out, my gallant Pimpernel," he murmured to himself, "to get the wench away. And even if you do, her lover is still in Paris, and what will you do about him? I think this time..." he added complacently.

Then he paused and once more lent an attentive ear to the sounds that came to him from the other side of the house; to the banging and stamping, the thuds and thunderings, the loud and strident shoutings and medley of angry voices, all gradually merging into a terrific uproar.

And as he listened the enigmatic smile on his lips turned to a contemptuous sneer.

CHAPTER XXIX

It was late in the evening by now and most of the clients of the hostelry had already retired for the night. Awakened by the terrible hubbub some of them had ventured outside their doors, only to find that the corridors and stairs were patrolled by soldiers, who promptly ordered them back into their rooms. On the downstairs floor the landlord and his wife, in the room adjoining the one on which their daughter had shared with Josette Gravier, had been rudely ordered to give up all keys and on peril of their lives not to interfere with the soldiers in the discharge of their duty. The Representative of the People, who had arrived at the hostelry that very evening, appeared to be in a towering rage: he it was who ordered a rigorous search of both the rooms, the landlord vaguely protesting against this outrage put upon his house.

He and his family were, however, soon reduced to silence, as were the guests on the floors above, and the stamping and the banging, the thuds and thunderings, the shouts and imprecations were confined to the two rooms in the house where a squad of soldiers, under the command of their sergeant and egged on by Chabot, carried on a perquisition with ruthless violence.

Within a quarter of an hour there was not a single article of furniture left whole in the place. The men had broken up the flooring, pulled open every drawer, smashed every lock; they had ripped up the mattresses and pillows and pulled the curtains down from their rods. Chabot, stalking about from one room to the other with great strides and arms akimbo, cursed the soldiers loudly for their lack of zeal.

"Did I not say," he bellowed like a raging bull, "that those letters must be found?"

The sergeant was at his wits' ends. The two rooms did, indeed, look in the feeble light of the hanging lamp above as if a Prussian cannon had exploded in their midst. The landlord with his wife and daughter cowered terror-stricken in a corner.

"Never," they protested with sobs, "never has such an indignity been put upon this house."

"You should not have taken in such baggage," Chabot retorted roughly.

"Citizen Chauvelin gave orders..."

"Never mind about Citizen Chauvelin. I am giving you orders, here and now."

He strode across the room and came to a halt in front of the three unfortunates. They struggled to their feet and clung to one another in terror before the fearsome Representative of the People. Indeed, Chabot at this moment, with face twisted into a mask of fury, with hair hanging in fantastic curls over his brow, with eyes bloodshot and curses spluttering out of his quivering lips, looked almost inhuman in his overwhelming rage.

"The hussy who slept here...?" he demanded.

"Yes, Citizen?"

"She had a sealed packet—a small packet about the size of my hand...?"

"Yes, Citizen."

"What did she do with it?"

"It was stolen from her, Citizen Representative, the first night she slept in this house," the landlord explained, his voice quaking with fear.

"So she averred," the woman put in trembling.

"Did any of you see it?"

They all three shook their heads.

"The girl didn't sleep in this room that night, Citizen," the woman explained. "She shared a room with two female travellers who left the next day on the diligence. Citizen Chauvelin then gave orders for her to sleep in my daughter's room and made us responsible for her safety."

Chabot glanced over his shoulder at the sergeant.

"Find out in the morning," he commanded, "at the Commissariat all about the female travellers and whither they went, and report to me." He then turned back to the landlord. "And do you mean to tell me that none of you saw anything of that sealed packet supposed to have been stolen? Think again," he ordered roughly.

"I never set eyes on it, Citizen," the man declared.

"Nor I, I swear it!" both the two women averred.

Chabot kept the wretched family in suspense for a few minutes after that, gloating over their misery and their fear of him, while his bloodshot eyes glared into their faces. Behind him the sergeant now stood at attention, waiting for further orders. There was nothing to be done, since every nook and cranny had been ransacked, and short of pulling down the walls no further search was possible. But Chabot's lust of destruction was not satisfied. He had the feeling at this moment that he wanted to set fire to the house and see it burned to the ground, together with that elusive packet of letters which meant more than life to him.

"Sergeant!" he cried, and was on the point of giving the monstrous order when a quiet, dry voice suddenly broke in:

"There are other ways than fire and brimstone, my friend, of recovering what you desire to possess."

Chabot swung round with an angry snarl and saw Armand Chauvelin standing in the doorway, a placid, slender figure in sober black with inscrutable face and smooth unruffled hair.

"The hussy?" Chabot yelled, his voice husky with choler.

"She is safer than she was when you left her half an hour ago, for I've had her arrested and sent to the Commissary of the district under a denunciation from me. She is safe there for the present, but she certainly won't be for long if you spend your time raving and swearing and pulling the house down about our ears."

"What the devil do you mean—she won't be safe for long? Why not?"

"Because," Chauvelin replied with earnest significance, "there are influences at work about here which will be exerted to their utmost power to get the wench out of your clutches."

"I care nothing about the wench," Chabot muttered under his breath. "It's those accursed letters..."

"Exactly," Chauvelin broke in quietly, "the letters."

Chabot was silent for a moment or two, swallowing the blasphemies that forced themselves to his lips. He glared with mixed feelings of wrath and vague terror into those pale, deep-set eyes that regarded him with unconcealed contempt. Something in their glance seemed to hypnotise him and to weaken his will. After a time his own glance fell; he cleared his throat, tugged at his waistcoat and passed his grimy, moist palm over his curly hair. And in order to gain further control over his nerves he buried his hands in his breeches pockets and started once more to pace up and down the room. The soldiers had lined up the passage outside: their sergeant had stepped back against the doorway and was doing his best not to smile at the Citizen Representative's discomfiture.

"You are right," Chabot said at last to Chauvelin with a semblance of calm. "We must talk the matter of letters over before we can decide what we do with the baggage."

Then he turned to the sergeant.

"Which are the men who took the wench to the Commissariat?" he asked.

"I don't think they are back, Citizen," the sergeant replied.

"Don't think!" Chabot snarled. "Go and find out."

The man moved away and Chabot called after him:

"Report to me in the public room—you'll find me there."

He gave a sign to Chauvelin. "Let's go!" he said curtly. "The sight of this room makes me see red."

He did not throw another glance on the unfortunate landlord and his family, the victims of his unreasoning rage. They stood in the midst of their devastated room looking utterly forlorn, not knowing yet if they had anything more to fear. The house appeared singularly still after the uproar of a while ago, only the measured tread of soldiers patrolling the corridors echoed weirdly through the gloom.

Chabot stalked on ahead of his colleague and made his way to the public room. There he threw himself into a convenient chair and sprawled across the nearest table, ordering the man in charge to bring him a bottle of wine. Then he called loudly to his colleague to come and join him.

But Chauvelin did not respond to the call. He turned into the small private room where the fateful interview had just taken place. He closed the door, locked and bolted it. He then went across to the window and examined its shutter. It was barred as before. There was no fear that he would be interrupted in the task which now lay before him. The candles had burned down almost to their sockets: Chauvelin picked up the snuffers and trimmed the wicks. Then he sat down at the table and drew the original sealed packet out of his breast pocket.

The time had come to break the seals. There was no longer any reason to keep the packet intact. The first act in the drama which he had devised for his own advancement and the destruction of his powerful enemy had been a brilliant success. The wench Josette Gravier and her lover were both in prison—one in Rouen, the other in Paris. Such a situation would of a certainty arouse the sympathy of the Scarlet Pimpernel and induce him to exert that marvellous ingenuity of his for the rescue of the two young people. But this time Chauvelin was more accurately forewarned than he had ever been before. All he need do was keep a close eye on the wench; the English spy, however elusive he might be, must of necessity attempt to get in touch with the girl, and unless he had the power of rendering himself invisible, his capture was bound to follow. It may safely be said that no fear of failure assailed Chauvelin at this hour. He considered his enemy as good as captured already. It would be a triumph for his perseverance, his inventive genius and his patriotism! Once more he would become a power in the land, the master of these men—these venal cowardly fools—who would again fawn at his feet after this and suffer at his hands for all the humiliation they had heaped upon him these past two years.

The compromising letters would be an additional weapon wherewith to chastise these arrogant upstarts—not excluding the powerful Danton himself, perhaps not even Robespierre. Armand Chauvelin saw himself on the very pinnacle of popularity, the veritable ruler of France. To what height of supreme power could not he aspire, who had brought such an inveterate enemy of revolutionary France to death?

And all the while that these pleasant thoughts, these happy anticipations ran through Armand Chauvelin's mind, his delicate hands toyed with the packet of letters—the keystone that held together the edifice of his future. He fingered it lovingly as he had done many a time before. Here it was just as it had been when Picard placed it in his hands: he had never broken the seals, never seen its contents, never set eyes on the letters which caused men like Chabot, Bazire, and Fabre d'Eglantine and even the popular Danton to tremble for their lives. But now that the first act of the little comedy which he had devised had been successfully enacted in this very room, he felt that he could indulge his natural curiosity to probe into the secrets of these men. He felt eager and excited. These letters might reveal secrets that would be a still more powerful leverage than he had hoped for the fulfilment of his ambition.

His fingers shook slightly as they broke the seals. The wrapper fell apart just as that other had done in Chabot's hands, and the contents were revealed to Chauvelin's horror-filled gaze. For here were no letters either; like the wrapper and like the seals the contents were the same as those which had turned Citizen Chabot from a human being into a raging beast: scraps of paper made to appear like letters—nothing more!

Chauvelin stared at them and stared; his pale, deep-set eyes were aflame, his temples throbbed, his whole body shook as with ague. What did the whole thing mean? Where did this monstrous deception begin? What was the initial thread which bound this amazing conspiracy together? Did it have its origin in Bastien de Croissy's tortured brain—in that of his despairing widow? Or did that seemingly guileless girl after all...? But no! this, of course, was nonsense. Chauvelin passed his trembling hand over his burning forehead. He felt as if he had been stunned by a heavy blow on the head. Idly he allowed the scraps of paper to glide in and out between his fingers. There was not a word written on any of them. Mere empty scraps of paper!...

All save one!... Mechanically Chauvelin picked that one up... it was soiled and creased, more so than the others. He passed his hand over it to smooth it out. The candles were guttering and smoking again.. he could hardly see... his eyes, too, were dim—not with tears, of course; just with a kind of film which threw a crimson blur over everything. He was compelled to blink once or twice before he could decipher the words on that one scrap of paper. He did succeed in the end, but only read the first few words:

"We seek him here..."

That maddening doggerel, the sight of which had so often been to him the precursor of some awful disaster! For the first time in his career Chauvelin felt a sense of discouragement. He had been so full of hope only a few minutes ago—so full of certainty. This awful disappointment came like a terrific, physical crash upon his aching head. With arms stretched out upon the table, that one scrap of paper crushed in his hand, he thought of the many failures which had gradually brought him down from his exalted rank to one of humiliation. Calais, Boulogne, Paris, Nantes, and many more—and now this! He had felt it coming when his enemy had so impudently faced him in the public room of this hostelry. The big fat sailor—that unmistakable laugh—the pepper-pot to remind him of his greatest discomfiture over at the Chat Gris in Calais: these and more all seemed to flit past Chauvelin's fevered brain in this moment of bitter disappointment. He had even ceased to think of Josette, communing only with the past. The minutes sped by; the old Normandy clock ticked away, majestic and indifferent.

A few minutes later Chabot's clamorous voice broke in on the lonely man's meditations. He roused himself from his apathy, threw a quick glance around. Then as the familiar voice drew nearer and nearer he gathered the scraps of paper hastily together and thrust them in his pocket out of sight. He went to the door and opened it just in time to meet his colleague, whose walk was not as steady as it had been when rage alone had governed his movements. Since then a bottle of red wine and one of heady Normandy cider had gone to his head; his lips sagged and his eyes were bleary. Lurching forward he nearly fell into Chauvelin's arms.

"I have been waiting for you for half an hour," the latter said with a show of reproach. "What in the world have you been doing?"

"I was in a high fever," Chabot muttered thickly. "A raging thirst I had—must have a drink..."

"Sit down there," Chauvelin commanded, for the man could hardly stand. "We must have more light."

"Yes... more light... I hate this gloom..."

Chabot fell into a chair; he stretched his arms over the table and buried his head in the crook of his elbow, and was soon breathing audibly. Chauvelin looked down on him with bitter contempt. What a partner in this great undertaking which he already had in mind! However, there was nothing for it now... this drunken lout was the only man who could lend him a hand in this juncture. He clapped his hands, and after a moment or two the maid in charge appeared. Chauvelin ordered her to bring more candles and a jug of cold water.

Chabot was snoring. With scant ceremony Chauvelin dashed the water over his head. The maid retired, grinning.

"What in hell...?" Chabot cried out, thus rudely awakened from his slumbers.

The cold water had partially sobered him. He blinked for a time into the fluttering candle-light, the water dripping down the tousled strands of his hair and the furrows of his cheeks.

"We've got to review the situation," Chauvelin began drily.

He sat down opposite Chabot, leaning his elbows on the table, his thin veined hands tightly clasped together.

"The situation?" Chabot iterated dully. "Yes, by Satan!... that hussy... what?"

"Never mind about the hussy now! You are still anxious, I imagine, that certain letters which gravely compromise you and your party do not fall into the hands, say, of the Moniteur or the Pére Duchesne for publication."

Chauvelin spoke slowly and deliberately so as to allow every word to sink into the consciousness of that sot. In this he succeeded, for at mention of those fateful letters the last cloud of drunkenness seemed to vanish from the man's sodden brain. Rage and fear had once more sole possession of him.

"You swore," he countered roughly, "that you would get those letters..."

"And so I will," Chauvelin returned calmly, "but you must do your best to help."

"You have allowed yourself to be hoodwinked by a young baggage—you..."

"If you take up that tone with me, my friend," Chauvelin suddenly said in a sharp, peremptory tone, fixing his colleague with a stern eye, "I will throw up the sponge at once and let the man who now has the letters do his damndest with them."

The threat had the same effect on Chabot as the douche of cold water. He swallowed his choler and said almost humbly:

"What is it you want me to do?"

"I'll tell you. First, about the packet of letters..."

"Yes!... the packet of letters—the real packet.... Who has it—where is it?... I want to know..." And with each phrase he uttered Chabot beat on the table with the palm of his hand, while Chauvelin's quick brain was at work on the last phases of his tortuous scheme.

"I'll tell you," he replied quietly, "who stole the packet of letters from the girl Gravier. It was the English spy who is known under the name of 'The Scarlet Pimpernel.'"

"How do you know?"

"Never mind how I know: I do know. Let that be sufficient! But as true as that you and I are alive at this moment the Scarlet Pimpernel has those letters in his possession..."

"And he can send the lot of us to the guillotine?" Chabot interposed in a raucous whisper.

"He certainly will," Chauvelin retorted drily, "unless..."

"Unless what? Speak, man, unless you wish to see me fall dead at your feet!"

"...unless we can capture him, of course."

"But they say he is as elusive as a ghost. Why, you yourself..."

"I know that. He is not as elusive as you think. I have tried—and failed—that is true. But never before have I had the help of an influential man like you."

Chabot bridled at the implied flattery.

"I'll help you," he said, "of course."

"Then listen, Citizen. Although we have not got the letters, we hold what we might call the trump card in this game..."

"The trump card?"

"Yes, the girl Gravier. I told you I had ordered her arrest..."

"True, but..."

"She is at the present moment at the Commissariat, under strict surveillance..."

Chabot jumped to his feet, glared into his colleague's pale face and brought his heavy fist crashing down upon the table.

"You lie!" he shrieked at the top of his voice. "She is not at the Commissariat."

Chauvelin shrugged.

"Where, then?" he asked coolly.

"The devil knows—I don't!"

It was Chauvelin's turn to stare into his colleague's eyes. Was the man still drunk, or had he gone mad?

"You'd oblige me, Citizen," he said coolly, "by not talking in riddles."

"Riddles?" the other mocked. "Tscha! I tell you that that bit of baggage whom you ordered to be taken to the Commissariat never got there at all."

"Never got there?" Chauvelin queried with a frown. "You are joking, Citizen."

"Joking, am I? Let me tell you this: the sergeant and the soldiers whom I sent to inquire after the wench came back half an hour ago and this is what they reported: neither the soldiers nor the hussy were seen at the Commissariat..."

"But where...?"

"Where the wench is no one knows. The Commissary at once sent out a patrol. They found the four soldiers in the public garden behind the St. Ouen, their legs tied together by their belts, their caps doing duty as gags in their mouths; but not a sign of the girl."

"Well—and?"

"The soldiers were interrogated. They are all under arrest now, the cowardly traitors! They declared that while they crossed the garden on their way to the Commissariat they were suddenly attacked from behind without any warning. They had seen no one and hadn't heard a sound: the place was pitch dark and entirely deserted. It seems that the lights have been abolished in this God-forsaken city every since oil and tallow got so dear, and the townsfolk avoid going through the garden, as it is the haunt of every evil-doer in Rouen. The men swore that they did their best to defend themselves, but that they were outnumbered and outclassed. Anyway, the miscreants, whoever they were, brought them down, bound and gagged them and then made off in the darkness, taking the wench with them."

"But didn't the men see anything? Were they footpads who attacked them, or—or...?"

"The devil only knows! Two of the soldiers declared that they were attacked by men in the same uniform that they wore themselves, and one thought that he recognised a sailor whom he had seen about on the quay the last day or two—a huge, powerful fellow, whose fist would fell an ox."

"Ah?"

"Anyway, the hell-hounds made off in the direction of the river."

"Ah?" Chauvelin remarked again.

"Why do you say 'Ah?' like that?" Chabot queried roughly. "Do you know anything of this affair?"

"No, but it does confirm what I said just now."

"What's that?"

"That those infernal English spies are at work here."

"Why do you say that?"

"Everything points to it: the mode of attack, the disappearance of the girl, the big sailor. Footpads would not have attacked soldiers with empty pockets, nor would they have carried off a girl who has neither friends nor relations to pay ransom for her."

"That's true."

"When did the sergeant tell you all this?"

"Not so long ago—might be a quarter of an hour..."

"Why didn't you let me know at once?"

"It was none of your business. I am here to give orders, not you."

"And what orders did you give? You didn't seem to be in a fit condition to give any orders at all."

"Rage at being baffled again went to my head. If you had not taken it upon yourself to order that girl's arrest..."

"You were about to tell me," Chauvelin broke in harshly, "what orders you gave to the sergeant."

"I ordered them to bring the four delinquents here, as I wish to interrogate them."

"Well—and are they here?"

"Wait, Citizen—all in good time! The sergeant had to go to the Commissariat—then he would have to..."

"I know all that," the other interrupted impatiently. He went to the door and opened it, clapped his hands and waited until the night-watchman came shuffling along the corridor.

"As soon as the sergeant returns," he said to the man, "bring him in here."

Chabot opened his mouth in order to protest; he was jealous of his prerogatives as a Representative of the People, a position of far greater authority than a mere member of the Committee of Public Safety. But there was something in Chauvelin's quiet assumption of command that overawed him and he felt shrunken and insignificant under the other's contemptuous glance. His ugly mouth closed with a snap, and he saw the watchman depart with a glowering look in his eyes. He sat down again by the table and stared stupidly into vacancy; his clumsy fingers toyed with the objects on the table; his thin legs were stretched straight out before him. Now and then he glanced towards the open door and listened to the several sounds which still resounded through the house.

Although the guests had been peremptorily ordered to keep to their rooms they could not be prevented from moving about and whispering among themselves, since sleep had become impossible. The uproar of a while ago, when furniture was being smashed and floors and walls were battered, had awakened them all from their first sleep. Since then vague terror and the ceaseless tramping of soldiers who patrolled the house had kept everyone on the alert. The unfortunate landlord and his family had taken refuge in a vacant room, but for them, more so than for any of their clients, sleep was impossible.

Thus, a constant, if subdued, hubbub reigned throughout the house. Chabot seemed to find a measure of comfort in listening to it all. Like so many persons who profess atheism, he was very superstitious, and all the talk about the mysterious spy, who worked in the dark and was as elusive as a ghost, had exacerbated his nerves. Chauvelin, on the other hand, paced up and down the room; his thin hands were tightly clasped behind his back, his head was down on his chest. His busy mind was ceaselessly at work. Obviously he had lost the first round in this new game which he had engaged in against the Scarlet Pimpernel. And not only that: he had lost what he had so aptly termed the trump card in the game. Josette Gravier was just the type of female in distress who would appeal to the adventurous spirit of Sir Percy Blakeney: while she was a prisoner in Rouen the Scarlet Pimpernel would not vacate the field, and there would have been a good chance of laying him by the heels. There was none now that the girl was in safety, for Chauvelin knew from experience that there was no getting prisoners like her out of the clutches of the Scarlet Pimpernel, once that prince of adventures had them under his guard.

Indeed, the Terrorist would have felt completely baffled but for one fact—yet another trump card which he still held and which if judiciously played...

At this point his reflections were interrupted by the arrival of the sergeant, followed by the four delinquent soldiers. This time Chauvelin made no attempt to interfere. Let Chabot question the men if he wished. He, Chauvelin, knew everything they could possibly say. He listened with half an ear to the interrogatory, only catching a word or a phrase here and there: "We saw nothing... we heard nothing.... They were on us like a lightning flash.... Yes, we had our bayonets... impossible to use them.... It was dark as pitch.... They wore the uniform of the National Guard... the same as ours, at least as far as one could see in the dark.... All except one, and he looked like a boatman... a huge fellow with a powerful fist... I had seen him on the quay before... and here in the public room.... How could we use our bayonets?... They were dressed the same as we were.... They hit about with their fists... the big sailor felled me down... and me too... I saw stars.... So did I.... When I recovered my legs were tied together and my woollen cap was stuffed into my mouth..." and more in the same strain.

The city gates being closed after dark no one could possibly pass them before dawn on the morrow, but there was always the river and no end to the ingenuity and daring of the Scarlet Pimpernel. But there was that last trump card—the ace, Chauvelin fondly hoped.

When Chabot finally dismissed the soldiers the two men once more put their heads together.

"There is not much we can do about the girl Gravier," Chauvelin remarked drily. "Luckily, we hold the man Reversac. It is with him we can deal now."

"The girl's lover?" the other asked.

"Of course."

"I see what you mean."

"Lucky that you do," Chauvelin mocked. "You know where he is, I presume."

"In the Abbaye. I had him taken there myself. A stroke of genius, methinks," he added complacently, "to have the fellow arrested."

"Well, you have had a pretty free hand these last few weeks while that cursed English spy turned his attention to our friend Carrier at Nantes."

"I suppose the death of all those priests and women appealed to him.... As for me..."

"So did Josette Gravier as your victim appeal to him, and so will Maurice Reversac."

"Thank our friend Satan, we've got him safe enough!"

"Yes, he is our trump card," Chauvelin concluded, "and we must play him for all he is worth."

He renewed his pacing up and down the room, while Chabot, quite sober now but with not two ideas in his muddled brain, stared stupidly in front of him.

"Paris will not do," Chauvelin resumed after a little while, mumbling to himself rather than speaking to his colleague. That damned Pimpernel has too many spies and friends there and hidden lairs we know nothing about.

"Eh? What did you say?" Chabot queried tartly.

"I said that we must get Reversac away from Paris."

"Why? We've got him safe enough."

"You have not," Chauvelin asserted forcefully. He came to a halt the other side of the table, and fixing his pale eyes on Chabot asked him: "Have you ever asked Fouquier-Tinville how many prisoners have escaped from Paris alone through the agency of the Scarlet Pimpernel?"

"No, but..."

"Considerably over two hundred since the beginning of this year."

"I don't believe it!"

"It's true, I tell you; and the same number from Nantes. Carrier is at his wits' end."

"Carrier is a fool."

"Perhaps. But you understand now why I want to get Reversac away from Paris. By dint of bribery if nothing else, the Scarlet Pimpernel will drag him out of your clutches."

Chabot reflected for a moment, and Chauvelin, guessing the workings of his mind, added with earnest significance:

"If we lose Reversac we shall have nothing to offer in exchange for the letters."

"The letters..." Chabot murmured vaguely.

"Yes," Chauvelin remarked drily: "you haven't found them, have you?"

By way of a reply Chabot uttered a savage oath.

"Where the girl is, there are the letters," the other went on, "get that into your head, and the letters are in the possession of the English spies. Now remember one thing, my friend: while we hold the girl's lover we can still get the letters, by offering a safe-conduct in exchange for them. And incidentally—don't forget that—we have the chance of laying our hands on the Scarlet Pimpernel, for whose capture there is a reward of ten thousand livres."

As Chabot had exhausted his vocabulary of curses he relieved his feelings this time by blaspheming.

"Ten thousand," he ejaculated.

"Not to mention the glory."

"Damn the glory! But I hate to let the baggage and her lover go."

"You need not."

"How do you mean—I need not? You've just mentioned safe-conducts..."

"So I did. But I can endorse those with a secret sign. It is known to every chief Commissary in France and nullifies every safe-conduct."

"Splendid!" Chabot exclaimed and beat the table with the palm of his hand. "Splendid!" he exclaimed and jumped to his feet. "Now I begin to understand."

The two men exchanged rôles for the moment. It was Chabot now who paced up and down the room, mumbling to himself, while Chauvelin sat down at the table and with idle hands toyed with the quill pen, the snuffers, or anything that was handy. Presently Chabot came to a standstill in front of him.

"You want to get Reversac away from Paris?" he asked.

"Yes."

"And bring him here?"

"Yes."

"The journey down will be dangerous if, as you say, the English spies are on the war-path."

"We must minimise the danger as far as we can."

"How?"

"A strong escort. And there will be the additional chance of capturing the Scarlet Pimpernel."

"You think he will be sure to try and get at Reversac?"

"Absolutely certain."

"And forewarned is forearmed, what?"

"Exactly."

"Splendid!" Chabot reiterated gleefully.

"And if we succeed in capturing one or more of those confounded spies, just think how marvellous our position will be with regard to the letters. We shall have something to bargain with, eh?"

"The Scarlet Pimpernel himself?"

"The whole damned crowd of them, as well as the girl and her lover!"

"You can have the lot," Chabot ejaculated, "so long as I have the accursed letters!"

"If you follow my instructions, point by point," Chauvelin concluded, "I can safely promise you those."

They sat together for another hour after that, elaborating Chauvelin's plan, lingering over every detail, leaving nothing to chance, gloating over the victory which they felt was assured.

It was midnight before they finally went to bed. And at break of day Chabot was already posting for Paris armed with instructions from Chauvelin to the secret agents of the Committee of Public Safety.

CHAPTER XXX

Snow lay thick on the ground; it was heavy going up the hills and slippery coming down. In an ordinary way the diligence between Meulon and Rouen would have ceased to ply in weather as severe as this. Already at Meulon, when an early start was made, the clouds had looked threatening. "We'll have more snow, for sure," everyone had declared, the driver included, who muttered something about its being madness to attempt the journey with those leaden-coloured clouds hanging overhead.

But in spite of these protests and warnings a start was made in the early dawn. Such were the orders of Citizen Representative Chabot (Loire et Cher), who was travelling in the diligence, and his word, of course, was law. Outside the hostelry of the Mouton Blanc a small crowd had gathered despite the early hour, to watch the departure of the diligence. All along people, who stood about at a respectful distance because of the soldiers, declared that this was no ordinary diligence. Though it was one of the small ones with just the coupé and the rotonde, it was drawn by four horses with postilion and all the banquette behind the driver was unoccupied, although the awning was up, and this was odd, declared the gaffers, because the banquette places being the cheapest, three of four passengers usually crowded there, under the lee, too, of the luggage piled upon the top.

In the coupé sat the Citizen Representative himself, and he had that compartment entirely to himself. In the rotonde there was a young man sitting between two soldiers in uniform, and three other men were on the seats opposite. Moreover, and this was the most amazing circumstance of all, what looked at first sight like the usual pile of luggage on the top was no luggage at all, but three men lying huddled up under the tarpaulin, wrapped in greatcoats, for it was bitterly cold up there.

No! It decidedly was on ordinary diligence. And it was under strong escort, too: six mounted men under the command of an officer—a captain, what? So not only was the traveller in the coupé a great personage, but the prisoner must also be one of consequence, for no sooner was he installed with the soldiers in the rotonde than the blinds were at once drawn down, nor was anyone allowed to come nigh the vehicle after that. Naturally all this secrecy and the unusual proceedings created further amazement still, but those quidnucs who came as near as they dared were quickly and peremptorily ordered back by the soldiers: and later in the day, at Vernon outside the Boule d'Or, two boys, who had after the manner of such youngsters succeeded in crawling underneath the coach, were caught when on the point of stepping on the foot-board. The captain in command of the guards seized them both by the ears and ordered them to be soundly flogged then and there, which was done by a couple of soldiers with a will and the buckle end of their belts. The howls that ensued and the sudden report of a pistol-shot, discharged no one could ever tell whence, startled the horses into a panic. The leaders reared, the ostler unable to hold them fell, and fortunately rolled over unhurt in the snow. A more serious catastrophe was just averted through the presence of mind of a passer-by, a poor old vagabond shivering with cold, who did not look as if he had any vitality in him, let alone the pluck to seize the near leader by the bridle as he did and bring the frightened team to a standstill.

The driver and the postilion were having a drink of mulled cider at the moment that all this commotion was going on. They came rushing out of the hostelry just in time to witness the prowess of that miserable old man. The driver was gracious enough to murmur approbation, and even the captain of the guard had something pleasant to say.

It had been so very neatly done.

"I was a stud-groom once," the old man explained with a self-deprecating shrug, "in the house of aristos. 'Tis not much I don't know about horses."

The captain tendered him a few sous.

"This is for your pains, Citizen," he said, and nodded in the direction of the hostelry close by: "you'd better go in there and get a hot drink."

"Thank you kindly, Citizen Captain," the man rejoined as his thin hands, blue with cold, closed over the money. He seemed loth to go away from the horses. They were fine, strong beasts, relays just taken up here and very fresh. The poor man had evidently spoken the truth: there was not much he did not know about horses. One could see that from the way he looked at them and handled them, adjusting a buckle here and there, fondling the beasts' manes, their ears and velvety noses, inspecting their fetlocks and their shoes.

"Good smith's work here," he said approvingly, tapping one shoe after another.

"That's all right, my man," the Captain broke in impatiently. "We must be off now. You go and get your drink."

The vagabond demurred and looked down with a rueful glance on his ragged clothes.

"I can't go in there," he said with a woebegone shake of the head, "not in these rags. The landlord doesn't like it," he went on, "because of other customers...."

The Captain gave a shrug. He didn't really care what happened to that wretched caitiff. Indeed, he was anxious to get away as he had been ordered by the Citizen Representative to make Gaillon before dark. Citizen Chabot was not a man to be lightly disobeyed, and as he had suffered much from cold and discomfort his temper throughout this journey had been of the vilest. So losing no more time the Captain now turned on his heel and went to give orders to his men. The young postilion, more charitably disposed, perhaps, towards the poor wretch, or in less of a hurry to make a start, said:

"I'll bring you out a drink, old gaffer," and he ran back into the hostelry, leaving the driver and the whilom stud-groom to exchange reminiscences of past aristo stablings. He returned after a couple of minutes with a mug of steaming cider in his hand.

"Here you are, Citizen," he said.

The vagabond took the mug but seemed in no hurry to drink. He had a fit of coughing and swayed backwards and forwards on his long legs as if already he had a drop too much. The driver, in the meanwhile, took the opportunity of administering correction to the ostler for failing to hold the horses properly when they shied, and for rolling about in the snow when he should have held on tightly to the bridles.

"Call yourself a stableman," he said contemptuously while the postilion stood by, grinning: "why, look at this poor man here..."

But the "poor man here" seemed in a sorry plight just now. The coughing fit shook him so that the steaming cider squirted out of the mug.

"Let me hold the mug for you, old man," the postilion suggested.

"You drink it, Citizen," the man said between gasps. "I can't. It makes me sick."

Nothing loth, the postilion had a drink, was indeed on the point of draining the mug when the driver with a "Here! I say!" took the mug from him and drank the remainder of the cider down.

Chabot put his head out of the window: "Now then, over there!" he called out with a loud curse. And "En avant!" came in peremptory command from the captain of the guard. The driver made ready to climb up on the box when the old vagabond touched him on the shoulder: "You wouldn't give me a lift," he suggested timidly, "would you, Citizen?"

"Not I," the other retorted gruffly. "I daren't... not without orders." And he nodded in the direction of the captain.

"He wouldn't know," the poor man whispered. "When you move off I'll climb on the step. I'll keep close behind you and hide in the banquette under cover of the luggage. They couldn't see from the back.... My home is in Gaillon and it's three leagues to walk in this damnable weather!"

He looked so sick and so miserable that the driver hesitated. He was possessed of bowels of compassion, even though he was a paid servant of the most cruel, most ruthless government in the world. But despite his feelings of pity for a fellow-creature he would probably have refused point-blank to take up an extra passenger without permission but for the fact that he was not feeling very well just then. That last mugful of steaming cider, coupled with the action of the cold frosty air, had sent the blood up to his head. His temples began to throb furiously and he felt giddy; indeed he had some difficulty in climbing up to his box and never noticed that the vagabond was so close on his heels. Fortunately the Captain at the rear of the coach noticed nothing: he and the soldiers were busy getting to horse. As for Chabot, he had once more curled himself up in the corner of the coupé and was already fast asleep.

Once installed on the box with the reins in his hands the driver felt better, but even so he was comforted by the knowledge that the ex-stud-groom had installed himself behind him. The man was so handy with horses—far more handy than that young postilion—and if that giddy feeling were to return...

It did, about half a league beyond Vernon. That awful sense of giddiness and unconquerable drowsiness! And it was not a moment ago that he had noticed the postilion's strange antics on his horse, his swaying till he nearly fell, and the rolling of his head.

"What the devil can it be?" he muttered to himself when that nasty sick feeling seemed completely to master him. What a comfort it was to feel a pair of strong hands take the reins out of his. Whose those hands were he was too sleepy to guess, and it was so pleasant, so restful, to close one's eyes and to sleep. Daylight was fast drawing in, and with twilight down came the snow: not large, heavy, smooth flakes by nasty thin sleet, which a head wind drove straight into one's face, and which fretted and teased the horses already over-excited by certain judicious touches of the whip. As for the postilion, it was as much as he could do to keep his seat. It was only the instinct of self-preservation that kept him on the horse's back at all.

It was a bad time, too, for the soldiers. They had to keep their heads down against the wind and the driven snow, and to put spur to their horses at the same time, for the diligence, which had lumbered along slowly enough up to now, had taken on sudden speed, and the team galloped up every hill it came to in magnificent style.

Chabot once more thrust his head out of the window and shouted: "Holà!" He had been asleep ever since that halt at Vernon, but this abrupt lurching of the coach had not only wakened him but also frightened him.

"Why the hell are you driving like a fury?" he cried. But the head wind drowned his shouts and his reiterated cries of "Holà!"

The horses did not relax speed. Someone was holding the reins who knew how and when to urge them on, and the sensitive creatures responded with a will to the expert touch. It was as much as the mounted men could do to keep up with the coach.

It was not until the Captain chanced to look that way and caught sight of the Citizen Representative's head out of the coupé window, and of his arms gesticulating wildly, that he called out "Hatle-là!" whereupon the diligence came immediately to a standstill. Instinct caused driver and postilion to pull themselves together, for the Citizen Representative's voice, husky with rage and fear, was raised above the howling of the wind.

"Tell that fool," he yelled, "not to drive like a fury! He will have us in the ditch directly."

"It is getting dark," the driver made effort to retort, "and this infernal snow is fretting the horses. We must make Gaillon soon."

"At least you know your way, Citizen?" the captain asked.

"Know my way?" the other mumbled. "Haven't I been on this road for over fifteen years?"

"En avant, then!" the captain ordered once more.

The horses tossed their heads in the keen, cold air, and forward lurched the clumsy diligence. The driver clicked his tongue and made a feeble attempt at cracking his whip. It was not so much giddy that he felt now but more intolerably sleepy than before.

"Give me back the reins, Citizen," a soothing voice whispered in his ear. The driver thought it might be the devil who had spoken, for who else could it be in this infernal weather and this blinding snow? Who but a devil would want to drive this cursed diligence? But he really didn't care... devil or no he was too infernally sleepy to resist, and the reins were taken out of his hands as before and firmly held above his head. He ventured on a peep round under the awning of the banquette, but all he could see was a pair of legs, set wide apart, with the strong knees that looked as if chiselled in stone, and the powerful hands holding the reins. He remembered the vagabond who climbed up to the banquette behind him and had apparently escaped the officer's notice.

"That old vagabond," he muttered to himself, and then added grudgingly: "He does know how to handle horses."

Another three leagues at galloping speed. But twilight was now sinking into the arms of night. Whoever was holding the reins had the eyes of a cat, for the postilion was mouse. But surely Gaillon would not be far. From Vernon it was only a matter of three leagues altogether, and why was the river on the left and not on the right of the road? And why was it so narrow, more like the Eure than the Seine? Its slender winding ribbon gleamed through the bare branches of the willow trees, its icy surface defying the gloom.

"Where the hell...!" the driver mumbled to himself from time to time as his bleary eyes roamed over the landscape. Some little way ahead a few cottages and a church with a square tower loomed out of the snow, the tiny windows blinking like sleepy eyes through the sparse intervening trees. But this was certainly not Gaillon. The driver rubbed his eyes. He was suddenly very wide awake. He snatched at the reins, held them tight and the team came to a halt, the steam rising like a cloud from their quivering cruppers. The captain swore and called loudly: "En avant!" and then: "Is this Gaillon?" He rode up abreast of the driver. "Is this Gaillon?" he iterated, pointing to the distant village.

"No, it's not," the driver replied. "At least..."

"Then where the devil are we?"

And the driver scratched his head and vowed he was damned if he knew!

"Must have taken the wrong turning," he said ruefully.

"You said you been on this road for over fifteen years."

"But not," the driver growled, "in such confounded weather." He went on muttering about the usual way of diligences... they did not ply in the winter, save in settled weather... sometimes one was caught in a snowstorm, but not often... and it was not fit for horses with all that snow on the ground... it had been madness to start from Mantes this morning and expect to make Gaillon by night-fall. And more to this effect, while the officer with eyes trying to pierce the gloom was evidently debating within himself whether he should beard the irate Representative of the People and rouse him from sleep.

"Where did you miss your road?" he asked roughly. And: "Can't we go back?"

"The only turning I know," the driver muttered, "is close to Vernon. We should have to go back three leagues..."

This time the captain blasphemed. Curses were no longer adequate.

"What's the name of that village?" he queried when he had exhausted most of his vocabulary. "Do you know?"

The driver did not.

"Is there a hostelry where we can commandeer shelter for the night?"

"Sure to be," the other rejoined.

"En avant, then!"

The driver did a good deal more muttering and grumbling and hard swearing when he heard the captain say finally: "The Citizen Representative will have something unpleasant to say to you about this delay."

Something unpleasant! Something unpleasant! He, too, would have something unpleasant to say to that old vagabond who did know all about horses and nothing about the way to Gaillon. Where they were now, the devil knew! He himself had been on the main road for fifteen years. Paris, Mantes, Vernon, Rouen, he knew all about them; and his home was in Paris; how, then could he be supposed to know anything of these country roads and God-forsaken villages? Le Roger it was, probably, in which case he, the driver, had vaguely heard of a dirty hole there where bed and supper might be found. As for stabling for all these horses.... If he dared he would denounce that old vagabond for getting them into this trouble, but he was afraid of the punishment which, of course, he deserved for having taken the man on board without permission.

But the time would come, and very soon too, when the shoulders of the old villain would smart under the whip, so thought the driver as he clutched that whip with special gusto, and then cracked it and clicked his tongue. And the team made another fresh start—in darkness this time and with the wind howling as the lumbering vehicle sped in the teeth of the gale. The snow swirled round the heads of men and beasts and stung their faces as with myraids of tiny whip-lashes. Another ten minutes of this intolerable going through the ever-increasing gloom, with heads bent against the storm and stiffened hands clutching at the sodden reins. Then at last the driver's eyes were gladdened by the sight of a scaffolded pole on which dangled the dismal creakings an iron lantern: its feeble light revealed the sign beneath: Le Bout du Monde.

The End of the World! An appropriate as well as a welcome sign. A desolate conglomeration of isolated cottages, two or three barns grouped at some distance round the tumble-down auberge seemed all there was of the village, with the ice-bound river winding around it and a background of snow-covered fields.

The driver pulled up and looked about him with misgivings and choler. It didn't seem as if a good supper and comfortable beds could be got in this God-forsaken hole. There was only one thing to look forward to with glee, and that was the castigation to be administered to that infernal vagabond. There was any amount of noise and confusion going on to drown the howls of the victim—what with the soldiers dismounting, the horses fretting and stamping, chains rattling, hinges creaking, doors banging, the Representative of the People yelling and cursing and calling for the landlord, a rushing and a running and a swearing as the landlord came racing out of the auberge.

The driver called over his shoulder: "Now then, down you get!"

But there came no sign or movement from the banquette. The driver peered through the darkness and under the awning, but of a certainty the miserable vagabond was not there. Down clambered the driver in double quick time; he paid no heed to the orders shouted at him, to the curses from the irate Representative of the People; he pushed his way through the crowd of soldiers, he jostled the prisoner and the passengers: he even fell up against the sacrosanct person of Citizen Representative Chabot. Like a lunatic he ran hither and thither, peering in every angle, every barn, behind every tree, but there was no sign of that old rogue who had sprung out of the snow at Vernon only to disappear in the darkness around the Bout du Monde.

The End of the World! In very truth, had not such an action been forbidden by decree of the National Convention, the driver, when he finally realised that the man had really and truly vanished, would of a certainty have crossed himself.

The devil couldn't do more, what?

CHAPTER XXXI

There was, of a truth, a great deal of confusion and any amount of cursing and swearing before men and beasts, not to mention the coach and saddlery, were housed under in this poverty-stricken village and wholly inadequate at the hostelry itself. There were close on a score of men all requiring bed and supper and eleven horses to stable and to feed. The resourses of the Bout du Monde were nowhere near equal to such a strain.

The landlord, indeed, was profuse in apologies. Never, never before had his poor house been honoured by such distinguished company. Le Roger was right off the main Paris-Rouen road; seldom did a coach come through the village at all, let alone with so numerous an escort: as for a diligence with a team and postilion, such a thing hadn't been seen here within memory of the oldest inhabitant. Sometimes travellers on horse-back bound for Elboeuf chose this route rather than the longer one by Gaillon, but...

At this point Chabot, fuming with impatience, broke in on the landlord's topographical dissertation and curtly ordered him to prepare the best food the house could muster for himself and the captain of the guard, together with a large jug of mulled cider. As for the rest of the party, they would have to make shift with whatever there was.

The captain and the landlord then worked with a will. There was a large thatched barn at some distance from the Bout du Monde where all the horses were presently jostled in, and such hay and fodder as could be mustered in the village was all commandeered by the soldiers for the poor tired beasts. A couple of men were told off to watch over them. Under the roof of another small barn close by and open to the four winds the coach and saddlery was then stowed. So far, so good. As for the men, they swarmed all over the small hostelry, snatching at what food they could get, raiding the outhouse for wood wherewith to pile up a good fire in the public room, where presently, after their scanty meal of lean pork, hard bread and dry beans, they would finally curl themselves up on the floor in their military cloaks, hoping to get some sleep.

The wretched prisoner was among them. No one had troubled to give him any food or drink. As presumably he was being taken to Rouen in order to be guillotined there was not much object in feeding him. But orders were very strict as to keeping watch over him; and the soldiers of the guard were commanded to take it in turns, two by two, all through the night to keep an eye on him. At the slightest disturbance all the men were to be aroused, the prisoner's safety being a matter of life and death for them all. Having given these orders and uttered these threats, Representative Chabot, in company of the captain, followed the landlord up a flight of rickety stairs to the floor above, where they were served with supper in a private room under the sloping roof. In this room, which was not much more than a loft, there was a truckle bed hastily made up for the Citizen Representative, and in the corner a mattress and pillow for the Citizen Captain. This was the best the landlord could muster for the distinguished personages who were honouring his poor house, and anyway, a good fire was roaring in the iron stove, and the place was away from the noise and confusion of the overcrowded public room.

Chabot's temper was at its worst. Having eaten and drunk his fill, he lay down on the truckle bed and tried to get some sleep; but ne'er a wink did he get. All night he tossed about, furious with everything and everybody. From time to time he tumbled out of bed to throw a log on the fire, for it was very cold: he made as much noise as he could then and tramped heavily once or twice up and down the room so as to wake the captain, who was snoring lustily. During moments of fitful slumber he was haunted by a ghostlike procession of all those who had contributed to his present discomfort: he dreamed of the time, not far distant he hoped, when he would belabour them with tongue and whip-lash to his heart's content. There was the hussy Josette Gravier, who had dared to threaten and then to hoodwink him; there was her lover, Reversac, the wretched prisoner downstairs, who, luckily, could not possibly escape the guillotine; there was, too, that fool of a driver who had landed him, François Chabot, Representative of the People, in this God-forsaken hole, and the captain of the guard, whose persistent snoring chased away even the semblance of sleep. Even his colleague, Chauvelin, were he here, should not escape the trouncing.

The hours of the night went by leaden-footed. At the slightest noise Chabot would rouse himself from his hard pillow and sit up in bed, listening. The prisoner—that valuable hostage for the return of the letters—was well guarded, but the very importance of his safety further exacerbated Chabot's nerves. But nothing happened, and after a while the silence of the night fell on the Bout du Monde.

At last in the distance and through the silence a church clock struck six. It was still quite dark; only the fire in the iron stove shed a modicum of light with its glow into the room. The getting away of the coach with its mounted escort would certainly take some time and, anyway, as he, Chabot, could not sleep there was no reason why anyone else should. He jumped out of bed and roused the captain.

"Why, what's the time?" the latter queried, his eyes still heavy with sleep.

"Damn the time!" Chabot retorted roughly. "'Tis, anyway, late enough for you to stop snoring and begin to see to things."

Very ill-humoured, but not daring to murmur, the captain rose and pulled on his boots. One slept in one's clothes these days, especially on a journey like this; and there was, of course, no question of washing at the Bout du Monde save, perhaps, at the pump outside, and it was much too cold for that. The captain's toilet on this occasion meant slipping on his coat, fastening his belt and smoothing his hair; and it all had to be done in the dark. He peeped out of the window.

"The wind has dropped," he remarked, "but there's a lot more snow to come down."

"Anyway," Chabot rejoined, "we start whatever the weather."

He, too, had pulled on his boots, but was still in his shirt-sleeves, and his coarse curly hair stood out from his head in tufts like an ill-combed poodle dog. He took to marching up and down the room, striding about in the darkness and swearing hard when he barked his shins against a chair. As the captain went out of the room he called to him:

"Tell the landlord to bring candles and a large jug of hot cider with plenty of spice in it."

He resumed his walk up and down the room, varying his oaths with blasphemies, and spat on the floor in the intervals of picking his teeth. He went to the door once or twice and listened to the confused sounds which came from below. A score of men roused from sleep, the inevitable swearing and shouting and tramping up and down the passage. The dormer window in this room gave on the back of the house where it was comparatively quiet; but after a time Chabot heard the men's voices down there, the jingle of their spurs and their heavy footsteps as they went off evidently to see to the horses. The barn where the horses were stabled was at some little distance in the village, and Chabot congratulated himself that he had roused that lazy lout of an officer in good time. He was hungry and cold in spite of the fire in the room, and swore copiously at the landlord when the latter brought him the jug of steaming cider and a couple of lighted candles. The remnants of last night's supper were still on the table; he pushed the dirty plates and dishes impatiently on one side, then poured himself out a mugful of hot drink while the landlord excused himself on the plea that he had such a lot to do with so big a crowd in his small house. Should his daughter come up and attend to the distinguished Representative's commands?

But Chabot was, above all, impatient to get away.

"We must make Rouen before dark," he said tartly, "and the days are so short. I want no attention. You go and speed up the men and give a hand with the horses so that we can make a start within the hour."

He drank the cider and felt a little better, but he could not sit still. After marching up and down the room again once or twice he went to the window and tried to peer out, but the small panes were thick with grime and framed in with snow and it was pitch-dark outside. His nerves were terribly on edge and he cursed Chauvelin for having expected him to undertake this uncomfortable journey alone. Then there was the responsibility about the prisoner and this perpetual talk of English spies. "Bah!" he muttered to himself as if to instill courage into himself: "a score of these louts I've got here can easily grapple with them."

Then why this agonising nervousness, this unconquerable feeling of impending danger? Suddenly he felt hot: the blood had rushed to his head, beads of perspiration gathered on his forehead. He went to the window and unlatched it, but the cold rush of air made him shiver. He feared that he was sickening for a fever. He tried to close the window again, but the latch was stiff with rust and his fingers soon became numb with the cold.

"Curse the blasted thing!" he swore between his teeth as he fumbled with the latch.

"Let me do it for you, Citizen," a pleasant voice said close to his ear.

Chabot swung round on his heel, smothering a cry of terror. A man—tall, broad-shouldered, dressed in sober black that fitted his magnificent figure to perfection—was in the act of closing the window. With firm dexterous fingers he got the latch into position.

"There! that's better now, is it not, my dear Monsieur? I forget your name," he said with a light laugh. Then added: "So now we can talk."

He brushed one slender hand against the other and with a lace-edged handkerchief flicked the dust off from his coat.

"Dirty place, this End of the World, what?" he remarked.

Chabot, tongue-tied and terror stricken, had collapsed upon the truckle bed. He gazed on this tall figure which he could only vaguely distinguish in the gloom. Like the driver of the diligence a while ago, he would have crossed himself if he dared, for this, of a surety, must be Lucifer: tall, slender, in black clothes that melted and merged into the surrounding darkness, allowing the flickering candelight to play upon a touch of white at throat and wrist and on the highly polished leather of the boot.

"Who are you?" he gasped after a time, for the stranger had not moved, and Chabot felt that all the while a pair of eyes, cold and mocking, were fixed upon him from out of the gloom. "Who are you?" he reiterated under his breath.

"The devil you think I am," the other responded lightly, "but won't you come and sit down?"

He motioned towards a chair by the table.

"I haven't much time, I'm afraid; and," he went on lightly, "you'll be more comfortable than on that hard bed."

Then as Chabot made no effort to move, but sat there, one hand resting on the bed, the glow of the firelight upon him, the stranger remarked:

"Why, look at your hand, my dear Monsieur What's-your-name; it looks as if you had dipped it in a sanguinary mess."

Mechanically Chabot looked down on his hand to which the stranger was now pointing. In that crimson glow it certainly looked as if... Hastily he withdrew it and rubbed it against his coat. Then, as if impelled by some unknown force, he rose and made a movement towards the table, but stopped half-way and suddenly made a dash for the door. But the stranger forestalled him, had him by the wrist before he could seize the latch, and with a grip that was irresistible drew him back to the table and forced him down upon a chair. He sat down opposite to him on the other side of the table and reiterated quietly:

"Now we can talk."

Chabot up to this moment was absolutely convinced that this was the devil made manifest. His education, conducted within the narrow limits of a seminary, had in a way prepared him for such a possibility, and during the brief years which he spent as a Capuchin friar he had had every belief implanted into him of demons and evil spirits, and maternal hell and bottomless pit. Cold, terror, discomfort of every sort all helped to unnerve him. Fascinated, he watched that tall dark figure, pouring with white slender hand the mulled cider into a mug and handing it over to him.

"Drink this, man," came the mellow voice out of the darkness, "and pull yourself together. We have no time to lose."

Chabot took the mug, but set it down on the table untasted.

"Well," the stranger said lightly, "as you like; but try and listen to me. I am not a manifestation of your familiar as you suppose, only a plain English gentleman. I happen to have in my possession certain letters which in a moment of carelessness you were rash enough to write to a certain Bastien de Croissy..."

At mention of "letters" Chabot uttered a hoarse cry: his fingers went up to his necktie, for her suddenly felt as if he would choke. "You!" he murmured, "you...?"

"Yes! I, at your service; I know all about those letters, for that is what you were about to say, was it not?"

He held Chabot with his eyes, and Chabot was fascinated by that glance. The eyes held him and he tried to defy them, made a supreme effort to pull himself together. Slowly it dawned upon him that here was no devil made manifest, but rather an enemy who was trying to hit at him to hoodwink him about those letters as that young baggage had tried to do. Another of her lovers probably—yes! that was it: an English lover picked up in England recently: one of those spies, perhaps, of whom his friend Armand Chauvelin was often wont to talk, but certainly another lover, and if he, Chabot, was fool enough to bargain he would be made a fool of once more. This thought had the effect of soothing his nerves: he suddenly felt quite calm. That choking sensation was gone; he took up the mug of cider and drank it down. His hand was perfectly steady; and he was in no hurry. The captain would be back directly and together they would laugh over the discomfiture of this fool when he found himself securely bound with cords in the company of the other prisoner, Maurice Reversac, the hussy's latest lover.

It was all very easy and very amusing. No! there was no hurry. In fact, this hour would have been very dull and very long but for this diversion. The candles were guttering and Chabot took the snuffers and used them very efficiently and deliberately. He pretended not to notice the stranger's nonchalant attitude, sitting there opposite to him, with his arms resting on the table and his very clean white hands interlocked.

"That wick would be all the better for another snick," he remarked; and Chabot tried to imitate his careless manner by saying: "You think so, Citizen?" and carefully trimmed the offending wick.

He really was enjoying every moment of this unexpected interview. How stupid he had been to be so scared! The devil, indeed! Just an English jackanape who had put his head in the lion's jaw previous to laying it under the knife of the guillotine; moreover, a spy could be shot without trial within the hour, in fact, and the captain could see to it that this one didn't talk. He, the captain, would be back directly, and, anyway, there were at least a dozen men in the public room down below, so what was there to fear when all was well and quite amusing?

The stranger had made no movement. Chabot leaned over the table, resting his head in his hand.

"You know, Mr. the Englishman," he said with a well-assumed unconcern, "that you have vastly interested me."

"I am glad," rejoined the other.

"About those letters, I mean."

"Indeed?"

"Now I should be very curious to know just how you came to be in possession of them."

"I will gratify your curiosity with all the pleasure in life," the stranger replied. "I took them out of the pocket of Madame de Croissy while she was asleep."

"Nonsense!" Chabot retorted with an assumption of indifference, although the name de Croissy had grated unpleasantly on his ear. "What in the world had the Widow Croissy got to do with any supposed letters of mine?"

"You forget, my dear sir," the Englishman retorted blandly, "that the letters were written by yourself to that lady's husband; that in order to obtain possession of them you murdered that unfortunate man in a peculiarly cruel and cowardly manner; the lady thereupon was persuaded for obvious reasons to leave for England, taking the letters with her."

"Bah! I've heard that story before."

"Have you now?" the stranger remarked with an engaging smile. "Isn't that funny?"

"Not nearly so funny as your lie that you took those letters—whatever they were—out of the woman's pocket, and that she never noticed the loss."

"How very clever of you to say that, my dear Citizen What's-your-name: a masterpiece, I call it, of skillful cross-examination. You would have made a wonderful advocate at any bar." He gave a short laugh, and Chabot spat like a cat that's being teased. "As a matter of fact," the stranger resumed, quite unperturbed, "the lady certainly might have noticed her loss. You were right there. But, you see, I took the precaution of substituting a sealed packet exactly similar to the one I had stolen and placed it in the lady's pocket."

Then as Chabot made no reply, was obviously thinking over what his next move should be in this singular encounter, the Englishman continued:

"In fact, you will observe, Sir, that my process was identical to the one employed by our mutual friend Chambertin when he stole what he thought was the precious packet of letters from little Josette Gravier and substituted for it another contrived by himself to look exactly similar. I am very fond really of Monsieur Chambertin; for a clever man he is sometimes such a silly fool, what?"

"Chambertin?" Chabot queried, frowning.

"Beg pardon—I should say Chauvelin."

"Do you pretend that it was he?"

"Why, of course. Who else?"

"And that he had those damned letters?"

"No, no, my dear Monsieur What-d'you-call-yourself," the stranger retorted with a light laugh. "I have those blessed—not damned—letters here, as I had the honour of explaining to you just now."

And with his elegant, slender hand he tapped the left breast of his coat. Chabot watched him for a moment or two under beetling brows. The man's coolness, his impudence had irritated him, and while he had thought that he was playing a cat's game with a mouse, somehow the rôles of cat and mouse had come to be reversed. But it had lasted too long already. It was time to put an end to it, and the moment was entirely opportune, for just then Chabot's ears were pleasantly tickled by the sound of the captain's voice down below ordering the landlord to bring him some hot cider. He had evidently returned from the barn, leaving the men to feed and saddle the horses.

Chabot chuckled at thought of the stranger's discomfiture when presently the caption would come tramping up the stairs, and, in anticipation of coming triumph, he fixed his antagonist with what he felt was a searching as well as an ironic glance.

"Suppose," he began slowly, "that before going any further you show me those supposed letters."

"With all the pleasure in life," the Englishman responded blandly. And to Chabot's intense amazement he drew out of his breast-pocket a small sealed packet exactly similarly in appearance to the one which poor little Josette Gravier had so trustingly kept in the bosom of her gown. Chabot chortled at sight of it.

"Will you break the seals, Monsieur the Englishman?" he queried with withering sarcasm, "or shall I?"

But already the stranger's finely shaped hands were busy with the seals. Chabot, his ugly face still wearing a sarcastic expression, drew the candles closer. Soon the seals were broken, the wrapper fell apart and displayed, not scraps of paper this time, but just a few letters, written by diverse hands. Chabot felt as if his eyes would drop out of his head as he gazed. The flickering candles illumined the topmost letter with its unmistakable signature—his own—François Chabot. And there were others:

he remembered every one of them, gazed on the tell-tale signatures—his—Bazire's—Fabre's.

"Name of a dog!" he cried, and made a quick grab for the letters. But the stranger's hands, delicate and slender though they were, were extraordinarily firm and quick. In a moment he had the letters all together, the wrapper round them, a piece of twine, picked out of the devil knew whence, holding the packet once more securely together. Chabot could not take his eyes off him. He watched him as if hypnotised, mute, blind to all else save that calm, high-bred face with the firm lips and the humorous twinkle in the eyes. But when he saw the stranger on the point of putting the packet back inside his coat, he cried, hoarse with passion: "Give me those letters!"

"All in good time, my dear sir. First, as I have already had the honour to remark, we must have a good talk."

Chabot rose slowly to his feet. The captain's voice rising from the public room below, the tramp of the soldiers' feet, his whole surroundings recalled him to himself. Fool that he was to fear anything from this insolent nincompoop!

"I give you one last chance," he said very quietly, even though he could not disguise the tremor of his voice. "Either you give me those letters now—at once—in which case you can go from here a free man and to the devil if you choose; or..."

At this same moment the sound of several voices was wafted upwards. Some of the soldiers had apparently assembled somewhere underneath the window and were talking over some momentous happening. Chabot and the stranger could hear snatches of what they said:

"Luckily the horses were not..."

"The wind unfortunately..."

"The saddles are..."

"So is the coach..."

"What in the world are we going..."

"Better see what the Citizen Captain..."

And so on, until after a time they moved away to the front entrance of the house, which was right the other side. The stranger was smiling while he lent an attentive ear. But Chabot only thought of the fact that now the guard would soon be assembled inside the house. Twenty trained men to cope with this insolent spy. His pale yellow eyes gleamed in the dim light like those of a cat. He was gloating over his coming triumph, licking his chops like a greedy cur in sight of food.

"Or," he concluded between clenched teeth, "I'll call the captain of the guard and have you shot as a spy within the hour."

By way of reply the stranger rose slowly from the table. To Chabot's excited fancy he appeared immensely tall: terrifying in his air of power and physical strength, and instinctively this scrubby worm, this cowardly assassin, this unfrocked friar cowered before the tall, commanding figure of the stranger in abject terror of his own miserable life. He edged round the table, while the Englishman deliberately walked to the window; then he made a dart for the door, expecting every second to feel that steel-like grip once more upon his arm. With his hand already on the latch he looked over his shoulder at his enemy, who was at the moment engaged in opening the window. The gust of wind that ensued was so strong that Chabot could not pull the door open; moreover, his hands were shaking and his knees felt as if they were about to give way under him: only later did he become aware that the door was locked. He heard the stranger give a curious call, like that of sea-mews who are wont to circle about the Pont-Neuf in Paris when the winter is very severe. The call was responded to in the same way from below, whereupon the stranger flung the packet out of the window. Three words were wafted upwards, words with a foreign sound which Chabot could not understand. Subsequently he averred that one of those words sounded something like "Raitt!" and the other like "Fouk's!" but of course that was nonsense.

The stranger then went back to the table and sat down. Once more he reiterated the irritating phrase which so exasperated the Terrorist: "Now we can talk."

Chabot fumbled with the door-knob. He had just heard the men trooping back into the house.

"No use, my friend," the stranger remarked drily. "I locked that door when I came in. And here's the key," he added, and put the rusty old key down on the table.

"Come and sit down," he resumed after a second or two as Chabot had not moved, had in fact seemed glued to that locked door; "or shall I have to come and fetch you?"

"You devil! You hound! You abominable..." Chabot muttered inarticulately. "Get me back those letters or..."

"Come and sit down," the other reiterated coolly. "You have exactly five minutes in which to save your skin. My friend is still outside, just under the window; if within the next five minutes he hears no signal from me he will speed to Paris with those letters, and three days after that they will be published in every newspaper in the city and shouted from every house-top in France."

"It's not true," Chabot muttered huskily. "He cannot do it. He couldn't pass the gates of Paris."

"Would you care to take your chance of that?" the stranger retorted blandly. "If so, here's the key... call your guard... do what you damn well like...."

He laughed, a pleasant infectious laugh, full of the joy of living through this perilous, exciting adventure, full of self-assurance, of arrogance, as you will, a laugh to gladden the hearts of the brave and to strike terror in those of the craven.

"One minute nearly gone," he renewed, and from his breeches pocket drew a jewelled watch attached to a fob, and this he held out for the other man to see.

Birds and rabbits, 'tis averred, are so attracted by the python which is about to gulp them down that they do not attempt to flee from him but become hypnotised, and of themselves draw nearer and nearer to the devouring jaws. In very truth there was nothing snake-like about the tall Englishman with the merry, lazy eyes and the firm mouth so often curled in a pleasant smile, but Chabot was just like a hypnotised rabbit. He crossed the room slowly, very slowly, and presently sat down opposite his tormentor.

"Nearly two minutes gone out of the five," the latter said, "and I verily believe I can hear your friend the captain's footfall in the hall below."

It was then that Chabot had an inspiration. In this moment of crushing humiliation and of real peril he remembered that his friend Chauvelin, saw him as in a vision sitting with him in the small private room of the Cheval Blanc at Rouen. What did he say when there was talk of the prisoner Reversac and his sweetheart Josette? Something about safe-conducts for them to be offered in exchange for the letters. Safe-conducts? And in his quiet, incisive voice Chauvelin had added, "I can endorse those with a secret sign. It is known to every Chief Commissary in France and nullifies every safe-conduct."

Yes, that was it: "Nullifies every safe-conduct." And Chauvelin knew the secret sign as did every Chief Commissary in France. So now to play one's cards carefully, and above all not to show fear; on no account to show that one was afraid.

And Chabot, sitting at the table, stroked his scrubby chin and said:

"I suppose what you want is a safe-conduct for some traitor or other, what?"

But the inspiration proved only to be a mirage and the sense of triumph very short-lived. The very next moment Chabot's fond hopes were rudely dashed to the ground, for the stranger replied, still smiling:

"No, my friend, I want no safe-conduct endorsed by you or your colleague with a secret sign to render them valueless."

And Chabot fell back in his chair; he was sweating at every pore. He marvelled if after all his first impression had not been the true one; since this man appeared to be a reader of thought was he not truly the devil incarnate?

"What is it you do want?" he uttered, choking and gasping.

"That you unlock that door—here's the key—and call to the gallant captain of the guard."

He held the key out to Chabot, who, fascinated, hypnotised, took it from him.

"Go and unlock that door, Monsieur What's-your-name, and call your friend the captain."

Slowly, as if moved by some unseen and compelling power, Chabot tottered towards the door. The stranger spoke to him over his shoulder: "When he comes you will tell him that you desire someone to go over to the village to the house of Citizen Pailleron with a message from you. Pailleron has a nice covered wagonette which he uses for the purpose of his trade as carrier between here and Elboeuf. Your messenger will explain to him that Citizen Representative François Chabot requires the wagonette immediately for his personal use. A sum in compensation will be given to him before a start is made."

Chabot made a final effort to turn on his tormentor: "This is madness!" he cried. "I'll not do it. If I call the captain it will be to have you shot..."

"Another minute gone," quoth the stranger blandly, "and I am sure the captain is coming up the stairs."

"You hellish fiend!"

"My friend down below will be wondering if he should speed for Paris or..."

The key grated in the lock. Chabot's trembling hands were fumbling with the latch.

"Come! that is wise," the Englishman said, "but for you own sake I entreat you to command your nerves. The captain is coming up. You will explain to him about the wagonette, also that you will be leaving here within the hour in the company of two friends, one of them being the young man, Maurice Reversac, at present detained through an unfortunate misunderstanding, and the other your humble servant."

Chabot was like a whipped cur with its tail between its legs. He slunk away from the door and came back across the room, and, like a whipped cur, he made a final effort to bite the hand that smote him.

"You must think me a fool..." he began, trying to swagger.

"I do," the other broke in blandly. "But that is not the point. The point is that I am looking to you to effect the ultimate rescue of two innocent young people out of your murderous clutches. Josette Gravier is in comparative safety for the moment, and Maurice Reversac is close at hand. I propose to convey them to Havre and see them safely on board an English ship en route for our shores, which you must admit are more hospitable than yours. For this expedition your help, my dear Monsieur What's-your-name, will be invaluable, so you are coming with us, my friend, in Citizen Pailleron's wagonette, and I myself will have the honour to drive you. And when we are challenged at the gates of any city, or commune, or at a bridge-head, you will show the guard your pretty face and reveal your identity as Representative of the People in the National Convention and stand upon your rights as such to free passage and no molestation for yourself, your driver and your son—we'll call Maurice Reversac your son for convenience' sake—and at Elboeuf, as well as at Dieppe, on the quay or at any barrier your pleasant countenance and your gentle, authoritative voice will command the obsequiousness they deserve. So I pray you," he concluded with perfect suavity, "call the captain of the guard and explain to him all that is necessary. We ought soon to be getting on the way."

He leaned back in his chair, gave a slight yawn, then rose, and from his magnificent height looked down on the cringing figure of the unfrocked friar. Chabot tried vainly to collect his thoughts, to make some plan, to think, to think, my God! to think of something, and above all to gather courage from the fact that this man, this abominable spy, this arrogant devil, was still in his power: now, at this moment, he could still hand him over to be shot at sight... or else at Rouen; with Chauvelin waiting for him, he could... he could...

But the other, as if divining his thoughts, broke in on them by saying: "You could do nothing at Rouen, my friend, for let me assure you that within twenty-four hours my friend who now has your letters in his possession will be on his way to Paris, there to deliver them at the offices of the Moniteur and of Père Duchnese, unless I myself desire him to hand them over to you."

"And if I yield to your cowardly threats," Chabot hissed between his teeth, "if I lend myself to this dastardly comedy, how shall I know that your associate, as vile a craven as yourself, will give me the letters in the end?"

"You can't know that, my friend," the other retorted simply, "for I cannot expect such as you to know the meaning of a word of honour spoken by an English gentleman."

"How shall I know if I do get the letters that none have been kept back?"

"That's just it: you can't know. But remember, my friend, that there is one thing you do know with absolute certainty, and that is, if my plan to save those two young people fails, if I do not myself request my friend to give up the letters to you, then as sure as we are both alive at this moment those letters will be published in every news-sheet throughout France; your name will become a byword for everything that is most treacherous and most vile, and not even the dirtiest mudrake in the country will care to take you by the hand."

The stranger had spoken with unwonted earnestness, all the more impressive for the flippant way in which he had carried on the conversation before. Chabot, always a bully, was nothing if not a coward. Any danger to himself reduced him to a wriggling worm. That his peril was great he knew well enough, and he had realised at last that there was no threat that he could utter which would shake that cursed English spy from his purpose.

There was a moment of tense silence in the room, whilst the captain's footsteps were heard slowly coming up the stairs. The stranger gave a gay little laugh and sat down once more opposite his writhing victim. He poured out two mugfuls of cider, and the moment that the door was thrown open he was saying with easy familiarity:

"Your good health, my dear François, and to our proposed journey together."

He held the white-livered recreant with his magnetic eyes and made as if to raise the mug to his lips; then he paused and went on lightly:

"By the way, did you happen to see the Moniteur the day before yesterday? It had a scathing attack, inspired of certainty by Couthon, against Danton and some of his methods."

Chabot clenched his teeth. At this moment he would have sold his soul to the devil for the power to slay this over-weening rapscallion.

The captain, seeing the Citizen Representative in conversation with a friend, halted respectfully at the door. He stood at attention, until Chabot looked round at him with tired, bleary eyes.

"What is it, Citizen Captain?" he inquired in a thick, tired voice, while the stranger, as if suddenly aware of the officer's presence, rose courteously from the table.

"I have to report, Citizen Representative," the captain replied, "that during the night certain miscreants found their way to the coach and saddlery, to which they did a good deal of mischief."

"Mischief? What mischief?" Chabot muttered inarticulately, while the stranger gave a polite murmur of sympathy.

"They've cut the saddle-girths, the reins and the stirrup-leathers, and the spokes of two of the coach wheels are broken right across. The damage will take more than a day to repair."

"I hope, Citizen Captain," the stranger said affably, "that you have laid hands on the rascals."

"Alas, no! the mischief was done at night. The barn lies some way back from this house; no one heard anything. The ruffians got clean away."

Chabot was speechless; not only had the quantity of spiced cider got into his head, but rage and despair had made him dumb.

"My dear François," the Englishman commented with good-humoured urbanity, "this is indeed unfortunate for all these fine soldiers who will have to spend a day or two in this God-forsaken hole. I know what that means," he went on, turning once more to the captain, "as I have been through such experience before, travelling on my business in these outlying parts."

"Ah! You know Le Roger then, Citizen?" the captain asked.

"I have been here once before. I am a commercial traveller, you know, and go about the country a good deal. I only arrived last night from St. Pierre half an hour after you did, and was happy to hear that my old friend François Chabot was putting up for the night. Then luckily I happened to bespeak Citizen Pailleron's covered wagonette to take me on to-day to Louviers, but it will be a pleasure as well as an honour for me to drive the Citizen Representative to Rouen if he desires."

"It will be heavy going."

"Perhaps, but my friend Pailleron has excellent horses which he will let me have."

"This is indeed lucky," the captain assented.

Still he seemed to hesitate. As Chabot remained tongue-tied, the stranger touched him lightly on the shoulder.

"It is lucky, is it not, my dear François?" he asked.

Chabot looked up at his tormentor. "Go to hell!" he murmured under his breath.

"The Citizen Captain is waiting for orders, my friend."

"You give them, then."

The stranger gave a light laugh. "I am afraid the cider was rather heady," he explained to the officer. "Will you be so good, captain, as to send round to Citizen Pailleron and let him know that the Representative of the People is ready to start. I believe the snow has left off for the moment; we can make Louviers before noon."

There was nothing in this to rouse the captain's suspicions. The Citizen Representative, though suffering perhaps from an excess of hot, spiced drink, nodded his head as if to confirm the order given by his friend. That this tall stranger was his friend there could be no doubt; the two of them were conversing amicably when he, the captain, first entered the room. And it certainly was the most natural conclusion for any man to come to, that so distinguished a personage as the Representative of the People in the National Convention would not wish to remain snowed up in this desolate village for two days at least, but would gladly avail himself of the means of transit offered to him by a friend. And certainly whatever doubt the officer might have had in his mind was finally dissipated when the stranger spoke again to Citizen Chabot.

"My dear François," he said, once more touching the other on the shoulder, "you have forgotten to speak to our friend the captain about the young man, Reversac."

"The prisoner?" the captain asked.

"Even him."

"He is quite safe at this moment in the public room, and we..."

"That's just the point," the stranger rejoined; and, unseen by the captain, he tightened his grip on Chabot's shoulder. "Do, my dear François, explain to the Citizen Captain..."

Chabot winced under the grip, which seemed like a veritable strangle-hold upon his will-power. He had not an ounce of strength left in him, either moral or physical, to resist. It was as much as he could do to mutter a few words and to gaze with bleared vision on his smiling enemy.

"Do explain, my dear François," the latter insisted.

Chabot brought the palm of his hand down with a crash upon the table.

"Damn explanations!" he snapped savagely. "The prisoner Reversac comes with me. That's enough."

And as the captain, momentarily taken off his balance by this unexpected command, still stood by the door, Chabot shouted at him: "Get out!"

It was the stranger who, with perfect courtesy, went to the door and held it open for the officer to pass out.

"That cider was much too heady," he said, dropping his voice to a whisper, "but the Citizen Representative will be all right when he gets into the cold air." After which he added, "He does not wish to lose sight of the prisoner, and I shall be there to look after them both."

"Well! It is not for me to make comment," the soldier remarked drily, "so long as the Citizen Representative is satisfied..."

"Oh! He is quite satisfied, I do assure you. You are satisfied, are you not, you dear old François?"

But even while he asked this final question he quickly closed the door on the departing soldier, for in very truth the blasphemies which Chabot uttered after that would have polluted even the ears of an old Republican campaigner.

CHAPTER XXXII

Less than half an hour later a covered wagonette to which a couple of sturdy Normandy horses were harnessed drew up outside the front door of the Bout de Monde. The word had soon enough gone round the village and among the men that the Representative of the People was leaving Le Roger in company of a friend, taking the prisoner with him.

He came out of the hostelry wrapped in his big coat. He looked neither to right nor left, nor did he acknowledge the respectful salutes of the landlord and his family assembled at the door to bid him good-bye. The prisoner, hatless, coatless and shivering with cold, was close behind him. But it was the Representative's friend who created most attention. He was very tall and wore the finest of clothes. It was generally whispered among the quidnuncs that he was a commercial traveller who had made much money by smuggling French brandy into England.

While François Chabot and the prisoner stowed themselves away as best they could under the hood of the wagonette, the stranger climbed up on the box and took the reins. He clicked his tongue, tickled the horses with his whip, and the light vehicle bumped along the snow-covered road and was soon lost to sight.

Grey dawn was breaking just then; the sky was clear and gave promise of a fine sunny day. The men who had formed the escort for the diligence and those who had travelled inside in order to guard the prisoner sat around the fire in the public room in the intervals between scanty meals, and discussed the amazing adventures of the past twenty-four hours. They had begun, so it was universally admitted, with the mysterious report of a pistol outside the hostelry at Vernon and the strange appearance of the whilom stud-groom who looked such a miserable tramp. What happened on the road after that no one could aver with any certainty, for the driver, who knew himself to be heavily at fault, never said a word about having taken the tramp aboard on the banquette, and allowing the reins to slip out of his hands into the more capable ones of the stud-groom.

Indeed, while the others talked the driver seemed entrenched in complete dumbness. He drank copiously, and as he was known to become violent in his cups he was left severely alone. The damage done in the night to the coach and saddlery had further aggravated his ill-homour. He put it all down to spite directed against him by some power of evil made manifest in the person of that cursed vagabond. It was supposed that the villagers had set themselves the task to bring the miscreants to book, but the hours sped by and nothing was discovered that would lead to such a happy result. The snow all round the barn where coach and saddlery had been stowed had been trampled down so heavily that it was impossible to determine in which direction the rapscallions had made good their escape.

CHAPTER XXXIII

To François Chabot the journey between Le Roger and the coast was nothing less than a nightmare. He was more virtually the prisoner of that impudent English spy than any aristo had ever been in the hands of Terrorists. And while thoughts and plans and useless desires went hammering through his fevered brain, the wagonette lumbered along on the snow-covered road, and on the driver's seat in front of him sat the man who was the cause of his humiliation and his despair. Oh, for the courage to end it all and plunge a knife into that broad back! But what was the good of wishing, for there was that terrible threat hanging over him of the letters to be published where all who wished could read, and the certainty of disgrace with the inevitable guillotine? Chabot could really thank his stars that he did not happen to have a knife handy. He might surely, in a moment of madness, have killed his tormentor and also the young man who sat squeezed beside him in the interior of the wagonette.

They reached Louvier's at noon. At the entrance to the city they were challenged by the sentry at the gate. The Englishman jumped down from the box. At a mere sign from him Chabot showed his papers of identity:-

"François Chabot, Representative of the People in the National Convention for the department of Loire et Cher..."

He declared the young man sitting next to him to be his son, and the other a friend under his own especial protection. The sentry stood at attention: the officer gave the word:

"Pass on in the name of the Republic!"

A nightmare, what? or else an outpost of hell!

They avoided Rouen, made a circuit of the town and turned into a country lane. Presently the driver pulled up outside a small, somewhat dilapidated house, which lay perdu in the midst of a garden all overgrown with weeds, and surrounded by a wall broken down in many places and with a low iron gate dividing it from the road. He jumped down from the box, fastened the reins to a ring in the wall; then, with his usual impudent glance, peeped underneath the hood of the wagonette. He thrust a parcel and a bottle into Chabot's lap and said curtly:

"Eat and drink, my friend. Monsieur Reversac and I have business inside the house."

The whilom prisoner stepped out of the wagonette and together the two men went inside the house. One or two people passed by while Chabot sat shivering in the draughty vehicle. He ate and drank, for he was hungry and thirsty, but he had entirely ceased to think by now. He no longer felt that he was a real live man, but only an automaton made to move and to speak through the touch of a white slender hand and the glance of a pair of lazy deep-set blue eyes.

Many minutes went by before he heard the rickety door of the old house creak upon its hinges. The two men came down the path towards the wagonette, but they were not alone. There was a girl with them, and Chabot uttered a hoarse cry as he recognised the baggage, Josette Gravier, who had made a fool of him and was now a witness of his humiliation.

This, perhaps, was the most galling experience of all. He, the arrogant bully who had planned the destruction of these innocents, was now the means of their deliverance and their happiness. He closed his eyes so as not to see the triumph which he felt must be gleaming in theirs.

How little he understood human nature! Josette and Maurice had no thought of their enemy, none of the terrible torments which they had endured; their thoughts were of one another, of their happiness in holding each other by the hand; above all, of their love. In the hours of sorrow and peril of death they had realised at last the magnitude of that love, the joy that would be theirs if it pleased God to unite them in the end.

And this happiness they had now attained, and owed it to the brave man who had been the hero of Josette's dreams. When first she discovered his identity, when she knew that she owed her rescue to him, and when to-day he had suddenly walked into the old house where she had been patiently waiting for him under the care of a kindly farmer and his wife, she would gladly, if he had allowed it, have knelt at his feet and kissed his hands in boundless gratitude.

For these two, also, the journey seemed like a dream, but it was a dream of earthly Paradise; hand in hand they sat and hardly were conscious of the presence of that ugly, ungainly creature huddled up, silent and motionless, in a corner of the wagonette.

For them, too, he was just an automaton, moved at will by the mysterious Scarlet Pimpernel. He only bestirred himself when the wagonette was challenged at a bridge-head or the barriers of a commune; then, in answer to a demand from the sentry, he would poke his ugly head, toneless voice recite his name and quality. And Josette and Maurice invariably giggled when they heard themselves described as the son and daughter of that hideous man, and that tall, handsome stranger as his friend.

The sentry then would give the word:

"Pass on in the name of the Republic!" and the wagonette, driven by the mysterious stranger, would once more lumber along on its way.

The journey was broken at a small hostelry, about half a league beyond Elboeuf. The food was scanty and ill-cooked, the beds were hard, the place squalid, the rooms cold; but the idea of sleeping under the same roof with Maurice made Josette in her narrow truckle-bed feel as if she were in heaven.

When they neared the coast of the first tang of the sea coming to Josette's nostrils brought with it recollections of that former journey which she had undertaken all alone for Maurice's sake. And when, presently, they came into Havre, and after the usual formalities at the gates of the city were able to leave the wagonette, these recollections turned to vivid memories. Guided by the tall mysterious stranger, they walked along the quay, whilst the past unrolled itself before Josette's mental vision like an ever-changing kaleidoscope. She remember Citizen Armand, heard again his suave, lying tongue, met his pale eyes with their treacherous, deceptive glance. And she snuggled up close to Maurice, and he put his arm round her to guide her down the bridge to the packet-boat, which was on the point of starting for England.

To follow them thither were a sorry task. Many French men and women there were these days—Louise de Croissy and little Charles-Léon among them—who, fleeing from the terrors of a Government of assassins, found refuge in hospitable England. Helped by friends, made welcome by thousands of kindly hearts, the eked out their precarious existence by working in fields or factories until such time as the return of law and order in their own beautiful country enabled them to go back to their devastated homes.

Heureux la peuple qui n'a pas d'histoire. Of Maurice and Josette Reversac there is nothing further to record, save the fulfulment of their love-dream and their happiness.

CHAPTER XXXIV

"And now we'll go and get those blessed letters."

Sir Percy Blakeney, known to the world as the Scarlet Pimpernel, had stood on the quay watching the packet-boat sailing down the mouth of the river. His arm was linked in that of François Chabot, once a Capuchin friar, now Representative of the People in the National Convention. He held Chabot by the arm, and Chabot stood beside him and also watched the boat gliding out of the range of his vision.

The nightmare was not yet ended, for there was the journey back to Rouen in the wagonette with himself, François Chabot, chained to the chariot wheel of his ruthless conqueror.

A halt was made on the road outside the same old house where they had picked up Josette Gravier. This time Sir Percy bade Chabot follow him into the house. How it all happened Chabot never knew. He never could remember how it came about that presently he found himself fingering those fateful letters: they were all there—three written by himself, two written by his brother-in-law, Bazire, and two by Fabre d'Eglantine—seven letters: mere scraps of paper; but what a price to pay for their possession! An immense wave of despair swept over the recreant. Perhaps at this hour the whole burden of his crimes weighed down his miserable soul and it received its first consciousness of inevitable retribution. The wretch spread his arms out on the table and, laying down his head, he burst into abject tears.

When the paroxysm of weeping was over and he looked about him the tall mysterious stranger was gone.

It was twilight of one of the most dismal days of the year. Looking up at the window, Chabot saw the leaden snow-laden clouds sweeping across the sky. Heavy flakes fell slowly, slowly. All round him absolute silence reigned. The house apparently was quite deserted. He staggered rather than walked to the door. He tramped across the path to the low gate in the wall. Here he stood for a moment looking up and down the narrow road and the heavy snowflakes covered his shoulders and his tufty, ill-kempt hair. There was no sign of the wagonette beyond the ruts made by the wheels in the snow, and for a long time not a soul came by. Presently, however, a couple of men—farm-labourers they were by the look of them—came along and Chabot asked them:

"Where are we?"

The men stopped and in the twilight peered curiously at this hatless man, half-covered with snow.

"What do you mean by 'Where are we?'" one of them asked.

"Just what I am asking," Chabot replied in that same dead tone of voice. "Which is the nearest town or village? I am stranded here and there is no one in this house."

The men seemed surprised.

"No one there?"

"Not a soul."

"Farmer Marron and his wife still live here," one of the men said, "two days ago, and they had a wench with them for a little while."

"They must have gone to Elboeuf where the old grandmother lives," the other suggested. "I know they talked of it."

"Elboeuf?" Chabot queried. "How far is that?"

A league and a quarter, and it was getting dark and snow was falling fast. It was so cold, so cold! and Chabot was very tired.

"Well, good-night, Citizen," the men called out to him. "We are going part of the way to Elboeuf. Would you like to join us?"

A league and a quarter, and Chabot was so tired.

"No, thank you, Citizens," he murmured feebly. "I'll tramp thither to-morrow."

He turned on his heel and went back into the lonely house. The arch-fiend who had brought him hither had seemingly left him some provisions and a bottle of sour wine. There was a fire in the room and upstairs in a room above there was a truckle bed and on it a couple of blankets.

Chabot curled himself up in these and fell into a fitful sleep.

The next day he tramped to Elboeuf and the day after that took coach for Rouen to meet his colleage Armand Chauvelin and give him the trouncing he deserved, for it was because of him, his intrigues and his wild talk of the Scarlet Pimpernel, that he, François Chabot, had been brought to humiliation and despair. The interview between the two men was brief and stormy. They parted deadly enemies.

A week later Chabot was back in his luxurious apartment in the Rue d'Anjou and a month later he perished on the guillotine. He had been denounced as suspect by Armand Chauvelin of the Committee of Public Safety for having on the 15 Frimaire an II de la République connived at the escape of two traitors condemned to death: Josette Gravier and Maurice Reversac, and for having failed to bring to justice the celebrated spy known as the Scarlet Pimpernel.

Mam'zel Guillotine

Book I

CHAPTER I:

1789: The Dawn of the Revolution

"Arms! Arms! Give us arms!"

France to-day is desperate. Her people are starving. Women and children cry for bread; famine, injustice and oppression have made slaves of the men. But the time has come at last when the cry for freedom and for justice has drowned the wails of hungry children. It is Sunday the twelfth of July. Camille Desmoulins the fiery young demagogue is here, standing on a table in the Palais Royal, a pistol in each hand, with a herd of gaunt and hollow-eyed men around him.

"Friends," he demands vehemently, "shall our children die like sheep? Shall we continue to plead for ears that will not hear and appeal to hearts that are made of stone? Shall we labour to feed the welled-filled and see our wives and daughters starve? Frenchmen! The hour has come: the hour of our deliverance. To arms, friends! to arms! Let our oppressors look to themselves. Let them come to grips with us, the oppressed, and see if brutal force can conquer justice."

With burning hearts and quivering lips they listened to him for a while, some in silence, others muttering incoherent words. But soon they took up the echo of the impassioned call: "To arms!" and in a few moments what had been a tentative murmur became a delirious shout: "To arms! To arms!" Throughout the long afternoon, until dusk and nightfall, and thereafter the call to arms like the roar of ocean waves breaking on a rocky shore resounded from one end of Paris to the other. And all night long men in threadbare suits and wooden shoes roamed about the streets, gesticulating, forming groups, talking, arguing, shouting. Shouting always their rallying cry: "To arms!"

By dawn the next day the herd of gaunt, hollowed-eyed men has become a raging multitude. The call for arms has become a vociferous demand: "Give us arms!" Right to-day must be at grips with might. The oppressed shall rise against the oppressor. But the oppressed must have arms wherewith to smite the tyrant, the extortioner, the relentless task-master of the poor. And so they march, these hungry, wan-faced men, at first in their hundreds but soon in their thousands. They march to the Town Hall demanding arms.

"Arms! Arms! Give us arms!"

It is Monday morning but all the shops are shut: neither cobblers, nor weavers, barbers nor venders of miscellaneous goods have taken down their shutters. Labourers and scavengers are idle, for every worker to-day has become a fighter. Alone the bakers and the vinters ply their trade, for fighting men must eat and drink. And the smiths are set to work to forge pikes as fast as they can, and the women up in their attics to sew cockades. Red and blue which are the municipal colours are tacked on to the constitutional white, thus making of the Tricolour the badge of France in revolt.

The rest of Paris continues to roam the streets demanding arms: first at the Hôtel de Ville, the Town Hall where provost and aldermen are forced to admit they have no arms: not in any quantity, only a few antiquated firelocks, which are immediately seized upon. Then they go, those hungry thousands, to the Arsenal, where they only find rubbish and bits of rusty iron which they hurl into the streets, often wounding others who had remained, expectant, outside. Next to the King's warehouse where there are plenty of gewgaws, tapestries, pictures, a gilded sword or two and suits of antiquated armour, also the cannon, silver mounted and coated with grime, which a grateful King of Siam once sent as a present to Louis XIV, but nothing useful, nothing serviceable.

No matter! A Siamese cannon is better than none. It is trundled along the streets of Paris to the Debtors' prison, to the Chatelet, to the House of Correction where prisoners are liberated and made to swell the throng.

News of all this tumult soon wakens the complacent and the luxurious from their slumbers. They tumble out of bed wanting to know what "those brigands" were up to. The "brigands" it seems were in possession of the barriers, had seized the carts which conveyed food into the city for the rich. They were marching through Paris, yelling, and roaring, wearing strange cockades. The tocsin was pealing from every church steeple. Every smith in the town was forging pikes; fifty thousand it was asserted had been forged in twenty-four hours, and still the "brigands" demanded more.

So what were the complacent and the luxurious to do but make haste to depart from this Paris with its strange cockades and its unseemly tumult? There were some quick packings-up and calls for coaches, tumbrils, anything whereon to pile up furniture, silver and provisions and hurry to the nearest barrier. But already Paris in revolt had posted its scrubby hordes at all the gates, with orders to stop every vehicle from going through and to drag every person who attempted to leave the city, willy-nilly to the Town Hall.

And the complacent and the luxurious, driven back into Paris which they wished to quit, desire to know what the commandant of the city, M. le baron Pierre Victor de Besenval is doing about it. They demand to know what is being done for their safety. Well! M. de Besenval has sent courier after courier to Versailles asking for orders, or at least for guidance. But all that he gets in reply to his most urgent messages are a few vague words from His Majesty saying that he has called a Council of his Ministers who will decide what is to be done, and in the meanwhile let M. le baron do his duty as beseems an officer loyal to his King.

Besenval in his turn calls a Council of his Officers. His troops are deserting in their hundreds, taking their arms with them. Two of his Colonels declare that their men will not fight. Later in the afternoon three thousand six hundred Gardes Françaises ordered to march against the insurgents go over to them in a body with their guns and their gunners, their arms and accoutrements. Gardes Françaises no longer, they are re-named Gardes Nationales, and enrolled in the fastgrowing Paris Militia, which is like to number forty—eight thousand soon, and by to-morrow nearer one hundred thousand.

If only it had arms, the Paris Militia would be unconquerable.

And now it is Tuesday, the fourteenth of July, a date destined to remain for all time the most momentous in the annals of France, a date on which century-old institutions shall totter and fall, not only in France, but in the course of time, throughout the civilized world, and archaic systems shall perish that have taken root and gathered power since might became right in the days of cave-dwelling man.

Still no definite orders from Versailles. The Council of Ministers continues to deliberate. Hoary-headed Senators decide to sit in unbroken session, while Commandant Besenval in Paris does his duty as a soldier loyal to his King. But what can Besenval do, even though he be a soldier and loyal to his King? He may be loyal but the men are not. Their Colonels declare that the troops will not fight. Who then can stem that army of National Volunteers, now grown to a hundred and fifty thousand, as they march with their rallying cry "To arms!" and roll like a flood to the Hôtel des Invalides?

"There are arms there. Why had we not thought of that before?"

On they roll, scale the containing wall and demand entrance. The Invalides, old soldiers, veterans of the Seven Years' War stand by; the gates are opened, the Garde Nationale march in, but the veterans still stand by without firing a shot. Their Commandant tries to parley with the insurgents, put they push past him and his bodyguards; they swarm all over the building rummaging through every room and every closet from attic to cellar. And in the cellar the arms are found. Thousands of firelocks soon find their way on the shoulders of the National Guard. What indeed can Commadant Besenval do, even though he be a soldier and loyal to his King?

CHAPTER II

Paris in Revolt

And now to the Bastille, to that monument of arrogance and power, with its drawbridges, its bastions and eight grim towers, which has reared its massive pile of masonry above the "swinish multitude" for over four hundred years. Tyranny frowning down on Impotence. Power holding the weak in bondage. Here it stands on this fourteenth day of July, bloated with pride and, conscious of its impregnability, it seems to mock that chaotic horde which invades its purlieus, swarms round its ditches and its walls, and with a roaring like that of a tempestuous sea, raises the defiant cry: "Surrender!"

A tumult such as Dante in his visions of hell never dreamed of, rises from one hundred and fifty thousand throats. Floods of humanity come pouring into the Place from the outlying suburbs. Paris in revolt has arms now: One hundred thousand muskets, fifty thousand pikes: one hundred and fifty thousand hungry, frenzied men. No longer do these call out with the fury of despair: "Arms! Give us arms!" Rather do they shout : "We'll not yield while stone remains on stone of that cursed fortress."

And the walls of the Bastille are nine feet thick.

Can they be as much as shaken, even by a hurricane of grapeshot and the roaring of a Siamese cannon? Commandant de Launay laughs the very suggestion to scorn. He has less than a hundred and twenty men to defend what is impregnable. Eighty or so veterans, old soldiers who fought in the Seven Years' War, and not more than thirty young Swiss. He has cannons concealed up on the battlements, and piles of missiles and ammunition. Very few victuals, it is true, but that is no matter. As soon as he opens fire on that undisciplined mob, it will scatter as autumn leaves scatter in the wind. And "No Surrender!" has already been his answer to a deputation which came to him from the Town Hall in the early morning, suggesting parley with the men of the National Guard, the disciplined leaders of this riotous mob.

"No surrender!" he reiterates with emphasis; "rather will I hurl myself down from these battlements into the ditch three feet below, or blow up the fortress sky-high and half Paris along with it."

And to show that he will be as good as his word, he takes up a taper and stands for a time within arm's length of the powder magazine. Only for a time, for poor old de Launay never did do what he said he would. All he did just then was to survey the tumulteous crowd below. They have begun the attack. Paris in revolt opens fire on the "accursed stronghold" with volley after volley of musket-fire from every corner of the Place and from every surrounding window. De Launay thrusts the taper away, and turns to his small garrison of veterans and young Swiss. Will they fire on the mob if he gives the order? He has plied them with drink, but feels doubtful of their temper. Anyway, the volley of musket-fire cannot damage walls that are nine feet thick. "We'll wait and see what happens," thinks Commandant de Launay, but he does not rekindle the taper.

Just then a couple of stalwarts down below start an attack on the outer drawbridge. De Launay knows them both for old soldiers, one is a smith, the other a wheelright, both of them resolute and strong as Hercules. They climb on the roof of the guard-room and with heavy axes strike against the chains of the drawbridge, heedles of the rain of grapeshot around them. They strike and strike again, with such force and such persistence that the chain must presently break, seeing which de Launay turns to his veterans and orders fire. The cannon gives one roar from the battlements, and does mighty damage down below. Paris in revolt has shed its first blood and reaches the acme of its frenzy.

The chains of the outer drawbridge yield and break and down comes the bridge with a terrific clatter. This first tangible sign of victory is greeted with a delirious shout, and an umber of insurgents headed by men of the National Guard swarm over the drawbridge and into the outer court. Here they are met by Thuriot, second in command, with a small bodygaurd. He tries to parley with them. No use of course. Paris now is no longer in revolt. It is in revolution.

The insurgents hustle and bustle Thuriot and his bodyguard out of the way. They surge all over the outer court, up to the ditch and the inner drawbridge. De Launay up on the battlements can only guess what is happening down there. His veterans and young Swiss stand by. Shall they fire, or wait till fired on? Indecision is clearly written on their faces. De Launay picks up a taper again, takes up his position once more within arm's length of the powder magazine. Will he, after all, be as good as his word and along with the impregnable stronghold blow half Paris up sky-high? He might have done it. He said he would rather than surrender, but he doesn't do it. Why not? Who shall say? Was it destiny that stayed his arm? destiny which no doubt aeons ago had decreed the downfall of this monument of autocratic sovereignty on his fourteenth day of July, 1789.

All that de Launay does is to order the veterans to fire once more, and the cannons scatter death and mutilation among the aggressors, whilst all kinds of missiles, pavingstones, old iron, granite blocks are hurled down into the ditch, till it too is littered with dead and dying. The wounded in the Place are carried to safety into adjoining streets, but so much blood has let a veritable Bedlam loose. A cartload of straw is trundled over the outer drawbridge into the court. Fire! Conflagaration! Paris in revolution had not thought before of this way of subduing that "cursed fortress", but now fire! Fire everywhere! The Bastille has not surrendered yet.

Soon the guard-room is set ablaze, and the veterans' mess-room. The fire spreads to one of the inner courts. De Launay still hovers on the battlements, still declares that he will blow up half Paris rather than surrender his fortress. But he doesn't do it, and a hundred feet below the conflagaration is threatening his last entrenchments. The flames lick upwards ready to do the work which old de Launay had sworn that he would do.

Inside the dungeons of the Bastille the prisoners, lifewearied and indifferent, dream that a series of earthquakes are shaking Paris, But what do they care? If these walls nine feet thick should totter and fall and bury them under their ruins, it would only mean for them the happy release of death. For hours has this hellish din been going on. In the inner courtyard the big clock continues to tick on; the seconds, the minutes, the hours go by: five hours, perhaps six, and still the Bastille stands.

Up on the battlements the garrison is getting weary. The veterans have been prone on the ground for over four hours making the cannons roar, but now they are tired. They struggle to their feet and stand sullen, with reversed muskets, whilst an old bearded sergeant picks up a a tattered white flag and waves it in the commandant's face. The Swiss down below do better than that. They open a porthole in the inner drawbridge, and one man thrusts out a hand, grasping a paper. It is seized upon by one of the National Guard. "Terms of Surrender," the Swiss cry as with one voice. The insurgents press forward shouting: "What are they?"

"Immunity for all," is the reply. "Will you accept?"

"On the word of an officer we will." It is an officer of the National Guard who says this. Two days ago he was officer in the Gardes Françaises. His word must be believed.

And so the last drawbridge is lowered and Paris in delirious joy rushes into the citadel crying: "Victory! The Bastille is ours!"

CHAPTER III

One of the Derelicts

It is best not to remember what followed. The word of an officer, once of the Gardes Françaises, was not kept. Old veterans and young Swiss fell victims to the fury of frenzied conquerors. Paris in revolution, drunk with its triumph, plunged through the labyrinthine fortress, wreaking vengeance for its dead.

The prisoners were dragged out of their dungeons where some had spent a quarter of a century and more in a living death. They were let loose in a world they knew nothing of, a world that had forgotten them. That miserable old de Launay and his escort of officers were dragged to the Town Hall. But they never got there; hustled by a yelling, hooting throng, the officers fell by the wayside and were trampled to death in the gutters. Seeing which de Launay cried pitiably: "O friends, kill me fast." He had his wish, the poor old weakling, and all of him that reached the Town Hall was his head carried aloft on a pike.

To the credit of the Gardes Nationales, once the Royal Regiment of Gardes Françaises, be it said that they marched back to their barracks in perfect order and discipline; it was this same Garde Nationale who plied hoses on the conflagration inside the fortress and averted an explosion which would have wrecked more than a third of the city.

But no one took any notice of the liberated prisoners. A dozen or so of them were let loose in this World-Bedlam, left to roam about the streets, trying all in vain to gather up threads of life long since turned to dust. The fall of the mighty fortress put to light many of its grim secrets, some horrible, others infinitely pathetic, some carved in the stone of a dank dungeon, others scribbled on scraps of mouldy paper.

"If for my consolation" [was the purport of one of these] "Monseigneur would grant me for the sake of God and the Blessed Trinity, that I could have news of my dear wife: were it only her name on a card to show that she is alive. It were the greatest consolation I could receive, and I would for ever bless the greatness of Monseigneur."

The letter is dated "A la Bastille le 7 Octobre 1752" and signed Quéret-Démery. Thirty-seven years spent in a dark dugeon with no hope of reunion with that dear wife, news of whom would have been a solace to the broken heart. History has no record of one Quéret-Démery who spent close on half a century in the "cursed fortress." What he had done to merit his fate no one will ever know. He was: that is all we know and that he spent a lifetime in agonized longing and ever-shrinking hope.

One can picture him now on this evening of July 14th turned out from that prison which had become his only home, the shelter of his old age, and wandering with mind impaired and memory gone, through the streets of a city he hardly knew again. Wandering with only one fixed aim: to find the old home where he had known youth and happiness, and the love of his dear wife. Dead or Alive? Did he find her? History has no record. Quéret-Démery was just an obscure, forgotten victim of an autocratic rule, sending his humble petition which was never delivered, to "Monseigneur." Monseigneur who? Imagination is lost in conjecture. The profligate Philippe d'Orleans or one of his like? Who can tell?

The attempt to follow the adventures or misadvantures of those thirteen prisoners let loose in the midst of Paris in revolution, would be vain. There were thirteen, it seems. An unlucky number. Again history is silent as to what became to twelve of their number. Only one stands out among the thirteen in subsequent chronicles of the times: a woman. The only woman among the lot. Her name was Gabrielle Damiens. At least that is the name she went by later on, but she never spoke publicly either of her origin or of her parentage. She had forgotten; so she often said. One does forget things when one has spent sixteen years—one's best years—living a life that is so like death. She certainly forgot what she did that night after she had been turned out into the world: she must have wandered through the streets as did the others, trying to find her way to a place somewhere in the city, which had once been her home. But where she slpet then, and for many nights after that she never knew, until the day when she found herself opposite a house in the Boulevard Saint-Germain: a majestic house with an elaborate coronet and coat of arms carved in stone, surmounting the monumental entrance door: and the device also carved in stone: "N'oublie jamais." Seeing which Gabrielle's wanderings came to a sudden halt, and she stood quite still in the gutter opposite the house, staring up at the coronet, the caot of arms and the device. "N'oublie jamais," she murmured. "Jamais!" she reiterated with a curious throaty sound which was neither a cry nor a laugh, but was both in one. "No, Monsieur le Marquis de Saint-Lucque de Tourville," she continued to murmur to herself, "Gabrielle Damiens will see to it that you and your brood never shall forget."

There was a bench opposite the house under the trees of the boulevard and Gabrielle sat down not because she was tired but because she had a good view of the coronet and the device over the front door. Desultory crowds paraded the boulevard laughing and shouting "Victory!" Most of them had been standing for hours in queues outside the bakers' shops, but not everyone had been served with bread. There was not enough to go round, hence the reason why with the cry of "Victory!" there mingled one which sounded like an appeal, and also like a threat:

"Bread! Give us bread!"

Gabrielle watched them unseeing. She too had stood for the past few days in queues, getting what food she could. She had a little money. Where it came from she didn't know. She had a vague recollection of scrubbing floors and washing dishes, so perhaps the money came from that, or a charitable person may have had pity on her: anyway she was neither hungry nor tired, and she was willing to remain here on this bench for an indefinite length of time trying to piece together the fragments of the past from out the confused storehouse of memory.

She saw herself as a child, living almost as a pariah on the charity of relatives who never allowed her to forget her father's crime or his appaling fate. They always spoke of him as "that abominable regicide," which he certainly was not. François Damiens was just a misguided fool, a religious fanatic who saw in the profligate, dissolute monarch, the enemy of France, and struck at him not, he asserted, with a view to murdering his King but just to frighten him and to warn him of the people's growing resentment against his life of immorality. Madness of course. His assertion was obviously true since the weapon which he used was an ordinary pocketknife and did no more than scratch the royal shoulder. But he had struck at the King and royal blood had flown from the scratch, staining the royal shirt. In punishment for this sacrilege, Damiens was hung, drawn and quartered, but to the end, in spite of abominable tortures which he bore stoically, he maintained steadfastly that he had no accomplice and had acted entirely on his own initiative.

François Damiens had left his motherless daughter in the care of a married sister Ursule and her husband Anatole Desèze, a cabinet-maker, who earned a precarious livelihood and begrudged the child every morsel she ate. Gabrielle from earliest childhood had known what hunger meant and the bitter cold of a Paris of winter, often without a fire, always without sufficient clothing. She had relaxation only in sleep and never any kind of childish amusement. The only interests she had in life was to gaze up at an old box fashioned of carved wood, which stood on a shelf in the living-room, high up against the wall, out of her reach. This box for some unknown reason, chiefly because she had never been allowed to touch it, had always fascinated her. It excited her childish curiosity to that extent that on one occasion when her uncle and aunt were out of the house, she managed to drag the table close to the wall, to hoist a chair upon the table, to climb up on the chair and to stretch her little arms out in a vain attempt to reach the tempting box. The attempt was a complete fiasco. The chair slid away from under her on the polished table, and she fell with a clatter and a crash to the floor, bruised all over her body and her head swimming after it had struck against the edge of the table. To make matters worse, she felt so queer and giddy that she had not the strenght at once to put the table and chair back in their accustomed places. Aunt and uncle came back and at once guessed the cause of the catastrophe, with the result that in addition to bruises and an aching head Gabrielle got a sound beating and was threatened with a more severe one still if she ever dared to try and interfere with the mysterious box again. She was ten years old when this disastrous incident occurred. Cowed and fearfull she never made a second attempt to satisfy her curiosity. She drilled herself into avoiding to cast the merest glance up on the shelf. But though she was able to control her eyes, she could not control her mind, and her mind continued to dwell on the mystery of that fatal box.

It was not until she reached the age of sixteen that she lost something of her terror of another beating. She was a strapping girl by then, strong and tall for her age and unusually good-looking inspite of poor food and constant overwork. Her second attempt was entirely succesful. Uncle and aunt were out of the way, table and chair were easily moved and Gabrielle waas now tall enough to reach the shelf and lift down the box. It was locked, but after a brief struggle with the aid of an old kitchen knife the lid fell back and revealed—what? A few old papers tied up in three small bundles. One of these bundles was marked with the name "Saint-Lucque," a name quite unknown to Gabrielle. She turned these papers—they were letters apparently—over and over, conscious of an intense feeling of disappointment. What she had expected to find she didn't know but it certainly wasn't this.

The girl however, was no fool. Soon her wits got to work. They told her that, obviously, if these old letters were of no importance to her, Aunt Ursule would not have kept them all these years out of her reach. As time was getting on and uncle and aunt might be back at any moment, she made haste to replace the box on the shelf, carefully disguising the damamge done by the kitchen knife. Chair and table she put back in their accustomed places and the old letters she tucked away under the folds of her fichu. By this time she had worked herself up into a fever of conjecture, but she had sufficient control over herself to await with apparent calm the moment when she could persue the letters in the privacy of her own room. She had never been allowed to have a candle in the evenings, because there was a street-lamp opposite the window which, as Aunt Ursule said, was quite light enough to go to bed by. Gabrielle hated that street-lamp because as there were no curtains to the window, the glare often prevented her getting to sleep, but on this never-to-be-forgotten night she blessed it. Far into the next morning sitting by the open window, did the daughter of François Damiens read and re-read those old letters by the flickering light of the street-lamp. When the lamp was extinguished she still remained sitting by the window scheming and dreaming until the pale light of dawn enabled her to read and read again. For what did those old letters reveal? They revealed the fact that her unfortunate father who had been sent to his death as a regicide had not been alone in his design against the King. The crime—for so it was called—had been instigated and aided by a body of noble gentlemen who like himself saw in the profligate monarch the true enemy of France. But whilst Damiens bore loyally and in silence the brunt of this conspiracy, whilst he endured torture and went to his death like a hero, those noble gentlemen had remained immune and left their miserable tool to his fate.

All this Gabrielle Damiens learned during those wakeful hours of the night. A great deal of it was of course mere inference; the letters were all addressed to her father apparently by three gentlemen, two of whom with commendable prudence had refrained from appending their signature. But there was one name "Saint-Lucque" which appeared at the foot of some letters more damnatory than most. Before the rising sun had flooded the towers of Notre Dame with gold Gabrielle had committed these to memory.

Yes! Memory was reawakened now, and busy after all these years unravelling the tangled skein of the past. Sitting here on the boulevard opposite the stately mansion with the coat of arms and the device "N'oublie Jamais" carved in stone above its portal, Gabrielle saw herself as she was during the three years following her fateful discovery. Her first task had been to make a copy of the letters in a clean and careful hand, after which there were the days spent in establishing the identity of "Saint-Lucque" and tracing his whereabouts. M. le Marquis de Saint-Lucque turned out to be one of the greatest gentlemen in France, attached to the Court of His Majesty King Louis XV. He lived in a palatial masion on the Boulevard Saint-Germain ans was a widower with one son. His association with François Damiens had seemingly never been found out. Presumably the whole episode was forgotten by now.

Then there came the great day when Gabrielle first called on Monsieur le Marquis. It was not easy for a girl of her class to obtain an interview with so noble a gentlemen, and at once Gabrielle was confronted with a regular barrage of lackeys, all intent apparently on preventing her acces to their master. "No, certainly not," was the final pronouncement of the major-domo, a very great gentleman indeed in this lordly establishment, "you cannot present yourself before Monsieur le Marquis, he will not see you." Gabrielle conscious of her personal charm tried blandishments, but these were of no avail, and undoubtedly she would have failed in her purpose had not Monsieur le Vicomte, son and heir of Monsieur le Marquis, come unexpectedly upon the scene. He was in riding kit. An exceptionally handsome young man, and apparantly more impressionable than the severe major-domo. Here was a lovely girl whose glance was nothing less than a challenge, and she wanted something which was being denied her by a lot of louts. Whatever it was, thought the handsome Vicomte, she must have her wish; preliminary, he added to himself with an appraising look directed at the pretty creature, to his getting what he would want in return for his kind offices. There was an exchange of glances between the two young people and a few moments later Gabrielle was ushered into the presence of Monsieur le Marquis de Saint-Lucque by a humbled and bewildered major-domo. Monsieur le Vicomte had given the order, and there was no disobeying him. "I'll wait for you here," he whispered in the girl's ear, indicating a door on the same landing. She lowered her eyes, put on the airs of a demure country wench, and disappeared within the forbidden precincts.

The first interview with the old aristocrat was distinctly stormy. There was a great deal of shouting at first on his part. A stick was raised. A bell was rung. But Gabrielle held her grounds: very calmly, produced the copy of a damnatory letter, and presently the shouting ceased, the stick was lowered, and the lackey dismissed who came in answer to the bell. The letter doubtless brought up vivid and most unpleasant memories of the past. Presently a bargain was struck, money passed from hand to hand—quite a good deal of money, more than Gabrielle had ever seen in all her life, and the interview ended with a promise on her part to destroy all the original letters. She was to bring them to Monsieur le Marquis the next day and burn them before his eyes. She trotted off with the money safely tucked away in the fold of her fichu. The handsome Vicomte was waiting for her, and she duly paid the tribute which he demanded of her. But she did not call on the old the old Marquis either the next day, or the day after that, or ever again, because a week later Monsieur le Marquis de Saint-Lucque had a paralytic stroke, and thereafter remained bedridden for over four years until the day when he was laid to rest among his ancestors in the family mausoleum in Artois.

In the meantime Gabrielle Damiens's relationship with Vicomte Fernand de Saint-Lucque had become very tender. He was for the time being entirely under the charm of the fascinating blackmailer, unaware of the ugly role she had been playing against his father. He had fitted up what he called a love-nest for her in a rustic chalet in the environs of Versailles and here she lived in the greatest luxury, visited constantly by the Vicomte, who loaded her with money and jewellery to such an extent that she forgot all about her contemplated source of revenue through the medium of the compromising letters.

Everything then was going on very well with the daughter of François Damiens. Her uncle and aunt with the philosophy peculiar to hoc genus omne of their country were only too ready to approve of a situation which contributed largely to their well-being, for Gabrielle, ready to forget the cavalier way in which she had been treated in the past, was not only generous but lavish in her gifts to them. And all went well indeed for nearly three years until the day when Fernand de Saint-Lucque became weary of the tie which bound him to the rather common and exacting beauty and gave her a decisive if somewhat curt congé, together with a goodly sum of money which he considered sufficient as a solace to her wounded vanity. The blow fell so unexpectedly that at first Gabrielle felt absolutely stunned. It came at a moment when, deluded into believing that she had completely enslaved her highborn lover, she saw visions of being herself one day Vicomtesse and subsequently Marquise de Saint-Lucque de Tourville, received at Court, the queen and leader of Paris society.

She certainly did not look upon the Vicomte's partin gift as sufficient solace for her disappointment. It would not do much more than pay her debts to dressmakers, milliners and jewellers. With the prodigality peculiar to her kind she had spent money as freely and easily as she had earned it. She had, of course, some valuable jewellery, but this she would not sell, and the future, as she presently surveyed it, looked anything but cheerful. Soon, however, her sound common sense came to the rescue. She took, as it were, stock of her resources, and in the process remembered the letters on which she had counted three years ago as the foundation of her fortunes. She turned her back without a pang on the rustic chalet, no longer a love-nest now, and returned to her uncle and aunt, in whom she now felt compelled to confide the secret of her disappointment in the present and of her hopes of the future.

She made a fresh attempt to see the old Marquis. Then only did she learn of his sickness and the hopeless state of mind and body in which he now was. But this did not daunt Gabrielle Damiens. Her scheme of blackmail could no longer be succesfully directed against the father, but there was the son, the once enamoured Vicomte, her adoring slave, now nothing but an arrogant aristocrat, treating the humble little bourgeoise as if she were dirt and dismissing her out of his life with nothing but a miserable pittance. Well! He should pay for it, pay so heavily that not only his fortune but also his life would be wrecked in the process. Moreover, she, the daughter of that same François Damiens, who had been dubbed the regicide and died a horrible death, would see her ambition fulfilled and herself paid court to and the hem of germent kissed by obsequious courtiers, when she was Madame la Marquise de Saint-Lucque de Tourville.

She started on her campaign without delay. A humble request for an interview with M. le Vicomte was at first curtly refused, but when it was renewed with certain veiled threats it was conceded. Armed with the copies of the damnatory letters Gabrielle demanded money first and then marriage. Yes! no less a thing than marriage to the hier of one of the greatest names in France, failing which the letters would be sent to the Comte de Meaurevaisre, Chief of the Secret Police of His Majesty the King. Well! When Fernand de Saint-Lucque had dismissed her, Gabrielle, with a curt word of farewell, he had dealt her a blow which had completely knocked her over. But it was her turn now to retaliate. He tried to carry off the affair in his usual high-handed manner. He began with sarcasm, went with bravado, and ended with threats. Gabrielle stood as she had done three years ago before the old Marquis. Already she felt conscious of victory, because she had seen the look almost like a death-mask which had come over Fernand de Saint-Lucque's face when he took in the contents of this the first of the fateful letters. When she held it out to him he had waved her hand aside with disdain. She placed it on the table, and waited until natural curiosity impelled him to pick it up. He did it with a contemptuous shrug, held it as if it were filth.

But the look so like a death-mask soon spread over his face. He did his best to disguise it, but Gabrielle had seen it and felt convinced that victory was already in sight. She left, not taking any money away with her, not exacting any promise at the moment save that her victim—he was her victim already—would see her once more. He had commanded her to bring the letters: "Not the copies remember! The originals!" which the Vicomte declared with all his old arrogance did not exist save in the imagination of a cinderwench.

For days and weeks after that first interview did Gabrielle Damines keep the Vicomte de Saint-Lucque on tednerhooks without going near him. The old Marquis was still alive, slowly sinking, with one foot in the grave, and Gabrielle hugged herself with thoughts of the hier of that great name writhing under the threat of disgrace to the head of the house, disgrace followed by confiscation of all his goods, exile from court and country, his name for ever branded with the stigma of regicide: disgrace which would redound on his heir and on all his family, and migh even be the stepping stone to an ignominious death.

When Gabrielle felt that Fernand had suffered long enough she sent him a harsh command for another interview. Devoured with anxiety, he was only too ready to accede. She came this time in a mood as arrogant as his own, exacting writtenpromise of marriage: the date of the wedding to be fixed here and now. She did not bring the original letters with her. They would, she said curtly, be handed over to him when she, Gabrielle Damines, was incontestably Vicomtesse de Saint-Lucque de Tourville.

Fernand at his wits' end did not know what to do. He tried pretence: a softened manner as if he was prepared to yield. Quite gently and persuasively he explained to her that whatever his ultimate decision might be—and he gave her to understand that it certainly would be favourable—he was compelled at the moment to ask for a few days delay. He had been, he said, paying court to a lady, at His Majesty's express wish, had in fact become officially engaged, and all he needed was a little time for the final breaking off of his obligations. In the meanwhile he was ready, he said, to give her a written promise of marriage duly signed, the wedding to take place within the next three months.

As usual Gabrielle's common sense warned her of a possible trap. The Vicomte had made a very sudden volte-face and had become extraordinarily suave and engaging. He even went to length of assuring her that he never ceased to love her, and that it was only at the King's command that he had become engaged to the lady in question. The breaking off of that engagement, he declared in conclusion, would cause him no heartache. A little doubtful, inclined to mistrust this plausible dissembler, Gabrielle remained impervious to his blandishments, even when she suddenly found herself in his arms, under the once potent spell of his kisses. No longer potent now. She smiled back into his glowing eyes, accepted the written promise of marriage and endured his kisses while keeping her wits about her. When she finally freed herself from his arms she merely assured him that the compromising letters would be returned to him when she had become his lawful wife.

She trotted home that afternoon happy and triumphant with the written promise of marriage duly signed "Fernand de Saint-Lucque de Tourville" safely tucked away in the folds of her fichu. Aunt Ursule and Uncle Desèze congratulated her on her triumph, and the three of them sat up half the night making plans for a golden future. Aunt and uncle would have a farm with cows and horses and pigs, a beautiful garden and plenty of money to give themselves every luxury.

"You need never be afraid of the future," Gabrielle declared proudly. "I'll never be such a fool as to give up the original letters. Even when I am Marquise de Saint-Lucque I will always keep that hold over my husband."

There ensued four days of perfect bliss, unmarred by doubts or fears. They were destined to be the last moments of happiness the blackmailer was ever to know in life. Saint-Lucque, whose engagement to Mademoiselle de Nesle had not only been approved of but actually desired by the King, was nearly crazy with terror at the awful sword of Damocles hanging over his head. Not knowing where to turn or what to do he finally made up his mind to confide the whole of the miserable story to his future mother-in-law, the person most likely to be both discreet abd helpful. Madame de Nesle was just then in high favour with the King, whose daughter Mademoiselle was reputed to be, and she was just as anxious as was His Majesty to see the girl married to the bearer of a great name who would secure for her the entreé to the most exclusive circles of aristocratic France. One could not, Madame declared emphatically, allow a dirty blackmailer to come athwart the royal plans, and at once she suggested a lettre de cachet, one of those abominable sealed orders which consigned any person accused of an offence against the King to lifelong imprisonment, without the formality of a trail. She was confident that she could obtain anything she desired from her adoring Louis, and anyhow incarceration in the Bastille was the only way of silencing that audacious malefactor.

And Madame was as good as her word. Four days later Gabrielle Damiens saw herself cast into a cell in the Bastille. All her possessions were seized by the men who came to arrest her. Pinioned between two of them she watched the other two turning out her table drawers, and pocket everything they found there, including the precious letters, the promise of marriage and the pieces of jewellery which she had saved from the débâcle of the love-nest. Neither tears, nor protest, nor blandishments were of any avail. Her demands for a trail were met with stolid silence, her questions were not answered. She had become a mere chattel cast into a dungeon, there to remain till she was carried out, feet first, to be thrown into an unknown grave. She never knew what had become of her aunt and uncle, nor did she ever hear the name of Saint-Lucque mentioned again while she spent her best years in a living death.

Gabrielle Damiens was nineteen years old when this catastrophe occurred. Sixteen years had gone by since then.

Book Two

CHAPTER IV

London 1794

"Tell me more about that young woman, Blakeney. She interests me."

It was the Prince of Wales who spoke. He was honouring Sir Percy and Lady Blakeney with his presence at dinner in their beautiful home in Richmond. The dinner was over; the ladies had retired leaving the men to enjoy their port and their gossip. It had been a small and intimate dinner-party and after the ladies had gone only half a dozen men were left sitting round the table. In addition to the host and the royal guest, there were present on this occasion four of the more prominent members of that heroic organization known as the League of the Scarlet Pimpernel: Lord Anthony Dewhurst, my Lord Hastings and Sir Philip Glynde, also Sir Andrew Ffoulkes, his chief's right hand and loyal lieutenant, newly wed to Mademoiselle Suzanne de Tournay, one of the fortunate ones whom the League had succeeded in rescuing from the horrors of revolutionary France.

Without waiting for a reply to his command, His Royal Highness went on meditatively:

"I suppose Paris is like hell just now."

"With the lid off, sir," was Blakeney's caustic comment.

"And not only Paris," Sir Andrew added; "Nantes under that fiendish Carrier runs it close."

"As for the province of Artois—" mused my Lord Hastings.

"That is where that interesting young woman takes a hand in the devilish work, isn't that it, Blakeney?" the Prince interposed. "You were about to tell us something more about her. I confess there is something that thrills one in that story in spite of oneself. The idea of a woman—"

His Highness broke off and resumed after a moment or two:

"Is she young and good-looking?"

"Young? No sir," Blakeney answered. "Nearer forty than thirty, I should say."

"And not good-looking?"

"She must have been at one time. But sixteen years in the Bastille has modified all that."

"Sixteen years!" His Highness ejaculated. "What in the world had she done?"

"It has been a little difficult to get to the bottom of her story. But I was interested. So were we all, weren't we, Ffoulkes? As you say, sir, there is something thrilling-horrible really-in the idea of a woman performing the revolting task of a public executioner. For that is Gabrielle Damiens's calling at the moment."

"Damiens?" His Highness mused; "the name sounds vaguely familiar."

"Perhaps you will remember sir, that some twenty-five years ago a kind of religious maniac named François Damiens created a sensation by slashing the late King with a penknife, without doing real harm, of course; but for this so-called crime he was condemned to death, hung, drawn and quartered. He maintained to the end, even under torture, that he had acted entirely on his own and that he never had any accomplice."

"Yes! I remember the story now. And this female executioner is his daughter?"

"His only child. She was only a baby at the time. As far as we have been able to unravel the tangled skein of this extraordinary tragi-comedy, Damiens bequeathed her a packet of old letters which involved the old Marquis de Saint-Lucque-the father of the present man-in that ridiculous conspiracy. Armed with these the girl-she was only sixteen at the time-started a campaign of blackmail, first against the old Marquis and, when he became bedridden, against his son, who, I understand, was deeply in love with her at one time."

"What a complication! But go on, man. Your story is as interesting as a novel by that French fellow Voltaire. Well!" His Highness continued, "and what happened to the blackmailer?"

"The usual thing sir. Saint-Lucque got tired of his liaison, broke it off, became engaged to Mademoiselle de Nesle . . ."

"Good old Louis's daughter, what?"

"Supposed to be," Blakeney replied curtly.

"I remember Madame de Nesle," His Highness mused. A beautiful woman! She even made the du Barry jealous. I was in Paris at the time. And her daughter married Saint-Lucque, of course . . . I remember!"

"Then you can guess the rest of the story, sir. Madame de Nesle wanted her daughter's marriage to take place. She had great influence over the King, and obtained from him one of those damnable lettres de cachet which did effectually silence the blackmailer by keeping her locked up in the Bastille without trial and without a chance of appeal. There she would have ended her days had not the revolutionaries captured the Bastille and liberated the prisoners."

"Most interesting! Most interesting! And how did the blackmailer become the executioner?"

"By easy stages, sir."

"What was she like when she came out, one wonders."

"Like a raging tigress."

"Naturally."

"Vowing before anyone who cared to listen that she would make Saint-Lucque and all his brood pay eye for eye and tooth for tooth."

"That was inevitable, of course," the Prince mused, "and not difficult to accomplish these days. I suppose," he went on, "that this Gabrielle Damiens has already got herself mixed up with the worst of the revolutionary rabble."

"She certainly has. She began by joining in the crowd of ten thousand women who marched to Versailles demanding food. She seized a drum from one of the guard-rooms in the suburb where she lived, and paraded the streets beating the Generale and shouting: 'Bread! we must have bread! . . .' and 'Come, mothers, with your starving children . . .' and so on."

"You weren't there, were you, Blakeney?"

"I was, sir. Tony, Ffoulkes and I were the guests of the King that day at Versailles. We saw it all. It was the queerest crowd, wasn't it, Tony?"

"It certainly was," my Lord Tony agreed lightly; "fat fishwives from the Halles, chambermaids shouldering their brooms, pale-faced milliners and apple-cheeked country wenches. All sorts and conditions."

"And this Damiens woman was among them?"

"She led them, sir," Blakeney replied, "with her drum. The whole thing was really pathetic. Food in Paris was very scarce and very dear and there were many cases of actual starvation. The trouble was, too, that the Queen had chosen to give a huge banquet the day before to the officers of the army of Flanders who came over to take the place of certain disloyal regiments. Three hundred and fifty guests sat down to a Gargantuan feast, ate and drank till the small hours of the morning. It was most injudicious to say the least."

"Wretched woman!" the Prince put in with a sigh; "she always seemed to do the wrong thing even in those days."

"And did so to the end, poor woman," one of the others observed.

"Was that the banquet you told me about, Blakeney, where you first met your adorable wife?"

"It was, sir," Blakeney replied, while a wonderfully soft look came into his lazy blue eyes, as it always did when Marguerite's name was as much as mentioned. It was only a flash, however. The next moment he added casually:

"And where I first saw Mam'zelle Guillotine."

"Such a funny name," His Highness remarked. "As a rule they speak of Madame Guillotine over there."

"Gabrielle deserves the name, sir, odious as it sounds. I have been told that she has guillotined over a hundred men and women and even a number of children with her own hands."

Then as they all remained silent, unable to pass any remark on this horrible statement, Sir Percy went on:

"After the march on Versailles she became more and more prominent in the revolutionary movement. Marat became her close friend and gave her all the publicity she wanted in his paper L'ami du Peuple. I know for a fact that she actually took a hand in the wholesale massacre of prisoners the September before last. Robespierre thinks all the world of her oratory, and she has spoken more than once at the Club des Jacobins and at the Cordeliers. I listened on several occasions to the harangues which she likes to deliver in the Palais Royal Gardens, standing on a table with a pistol in each hand as Camille Desmoulins used to do. They were the most inflammatory speeches I ever heard. And clever, too. The sixteen years she spent in the Bastille did not dull her wits seemingly. Finally," Blakeney concluded, "Robespierre got her appointed last year, at her own request, public executioner in his native province of Artois, and there she has been active ever since."

There was silence round the festive board after that. They were all men here who had seen much of the seamy side of life. Even His Highness had had experiences which do not usually come in the way of royal personages, and he was the only non-member of the League of the Scarlet Pimpernel who knew the identity of its heroic chief. His eyes now rested with an expression of ill-concealed affection and admiration on that chief, whom he honoured with his especial friendship.

He raised his glass of port and sipped it thoughtfully before he spoke again, then he said with an attempt at gaiety:

"I know what you are thinking at this moment, Blakeney."

"Yes, your Highness?" Sir Percy retorted.

"That Mam'zelle Guillotine will soon be . . . what shall we say? . . . lying in the arms of the Scarlet Pimpernel."

This sally made everybody laugh, and conversation presently drifted into other channels.

CHAPTER V

A Social Event

There are many records extant to-day of the wonderful rout offered to the élite of French and English society in London by Her Grace the Duchesse de Roncevaux in her sumptuous house in St. James's Square. The date I believe was somewhere in January, 1794. The decorations, the flowers, the music, the banquet-supper surpassed in magnificence, it is asserted by chroniclers of the time, anything that had ever been seen in the ultra-fashionable world.

The Duchesse, as everybody knows, was English by birth, daughter of Reuben Meyer, the banker, and immensely rich. His Grace the Duc de Roncevaux, first cousin to the royal house of Bourbon, married her not only for her wealth but principally because he was genuinely in love with her. His name and popularity at court secured for his wife a brilliant position in Paris society during the declining years of the monarchy, whilst his charming personality and always deferential love-making brought her a full measure of domestic happiness. He left her an inconsolable widow after five years of married bliss. The revolutionary storm was by then already gathering over France. The English-born Duchesse thought it best to return to her own country, before the cloud-burst which appeared more and more threatening every day. She chose London as her principal home, and here with the aid of her wealth and a heart overflowing with the milk of human kindness she did her best to gather round her those more fortunate French families who had somehow contrived to escape from the murderous clutches of the revolutionary government of France. Thus a delightful set of charming cultured people could always be met with in the Duchesse de Roncevaux's luxurious salons. Here one rubbed shoulders with some of the members of the old French aristocracy now dispossessed of most if not all their wealth, but bringing into the somewhat free-and-easy tone of eighteenth-century London something of their perfect manners, their old-world courtesy and that atmosphere of high-breeding and distinction handed down to them by generations of courtiers. The Comte de Tournay with Madame his wife and their son the young Vicomte were often to be seen at these social gatherings. Mademoiselle de Tournay had recently married Sir Andrew Ffoulkes, the handsome young leader of fashion, who was credited with being a member of the heroic League of the Scarlet Pimpernel. There was Félicien Lézenne, who had been chairman of the Club des Fils du Royaume, his young wife and Monsieur de Lucines, his father-in-law, who were actually known to have been saved from the guillotine by that mysterious and elusive person the Scarlet Pimpernel himself.

There were others, of course, for the list of refugees from revolutionary France waxed longer day by day and all found a welcome in the Duchesse de Roncevaux's hospitable mansion; and not only did they find a welcome but also a measure of gaiety! for the daughter of Reuben Meyer the Jewish banker had understanding as well as social ambition. Her aim was to make her salon the most attractive one in town, and what society could be more attractive than that of those French aristocrats, most of whom had palpitating stories to tell of past horrors, of dangers of death, and, above all, of those almost phenomenal rescues of condemned innocents sometimes under the very shadow of the guillotine, effected by that heroic organization known as the League of the Scarlet Pimpernel and its lion-hearted chief.

To hear one of those deeds of unparalleled courage recounted by one of those who owed their lives to that intriguing personality was voted unanimously to be far more exciting than a melodrama at Drury Lane, and the Duchesse de Roncevaux could always be relied on to provide her guests with one of those soul-stirring narrations which caused every velvet cheek to flush with enthusiasm and every bright eye to glow with hero-worship. There were other entertainments too to be enjoyed in the sumptuous mansion in St. James's Square, there were operas, ballets, comedies, concerts: young musicians often made their first formal bow before a discriminating company which often included the Prince of Wales himself and the élite of English society, and more than one disciple of the late Mr. Garrick first tasted the sweets of success in the Duchesse's salon. But none of these entertainments had the power to excite interest as did the relation of one of those hair-raising exploits of the mysterious Scarlet Pimpernel, told with fervour and a charming French accent by whoever happened to be the honoured guest of the evening.

On this occasion it was the abbé Prud'hon, lately come from France in the company of Monsieur le Marquis de Saint-Lucque and the young Vicomte. The arrival of Monsieur de Saint-Lucque had been a real event in the chronicle of London society. He was known to have been saved from death by the hero of the hour: in fact, he and the abbé had proclaimed this openly, and everybody—the men as well as the ladies—had been on tenterhooks to hear the true version of their amazing rescue. All sorts of rumours had been afloat, as they always were whenever a French family came to join the colony of recent émigrés who had found refuge in hospitable England. Everyone was agog to know how they had been smuggled out of France, for that was what it amounted to. Men, women and children, the old, the infirm, whenever innocent seemed literally to have been snatched from under the very noses of the revolutionary guard, and this led to all sorts of tales, medieval in their superstitious extravagance, of direct interference from the clouds or of a supernatural being, of unearthly appearance and abnormal strength who scattered revolutionary soldiers before him as easily as he would a swarm of flies.

There was a first-class sensation in fashionable circles when Madame la Duchesse de Roncevaux issued invitations for one of her popular routs. The invitation promised a concert by the London String Band, a playlet to be performed by His Majesty's mummers, and a supper prepared by Monsieur Haon formerly cook-in-chief to Madame de Pompadour. But all these attractions paled in interest before the one brief announcement: "Guest of Honour: M. l'Abbé Prud'hon." Everyone in town knew by now that M. l'Abbé Prud'hon was tutor to the young Vicomte de Saint-Lucque and had been summarily arrested along with him and M. le Marquis by the revolutionary government under the usual futile pretext of having plotted against the safety of the Republic.

The salons of Madame la Duchesse de Roncevaux were thronged on this occasion as they had never been before, and there was such a chattering up and down the monumental staircase as the guests filed up to greet their hostess, as in an aviary of love-birds.

"My dear, isn't it too wonderful?"

"I declare I am so excited, I don't know if I am standing on my head or on my heels."

"I know I shall scream if that London String Band goes on too long."

"I call it cruel to put them on before we have heard M. l'Abbé."

"Hush! you mustn't say that. The dear Duchesse had them only in order to bring our blood to boiling point."

"Mine has been over boiling point all day, and I am on the verge of spontaneous combustion."

By ten o'clock all the guests had arrived, and the hostess, wearied after standing for over an hour at the head of the staircase receiving the company, had retired to the rose-coloured boudoir where His Royal Highness the Prince of Wales, Sir Percy and Lady Blakeney, Sir Andrew and Lady Ffoulkes and a small number of the more privileged guests were discussing the coming event somewhat more soberly than did the gaily plumaged birds in the adjoining ball-room. M. l'Abbé was there too, a pathetic figure in his well-worn soutane: his cheeks, once round and full, were pale and wan now, showing signs of the many privations, the lack of food and warmth, which he had suffered recently. He looked ill and very weary. It was only his eyes, tired-looking and red-rimmed though they were, that retained within their depths a merry twinkle which every now and then came to the fore, when his inward glance came to rest on a memory less cruel than most: that merry twinkle was the expression of a keen sense of humour which no amount of sorrow and suffering had the power wholly to eradicate.

At the moment he certainly seemed to have thrown off some of his lassitude; finding himself the centre of interest in a sympathetic crowd, all anxious to make him forget what he had suffered, and to make him feel at home in this land of freedom and of orderly government, his whole being seemed to expand in response. A warm glow came into his eyes and the smiles so freely bestowed on him by the ladies found their reflection round his pale, drooping lips. Everyone was charming to him. The Prince of Wales was most gracious, and his hostess lavish in delicate attentions. He had had an excellent dinner, and a couple of glasses of fine old Burgundy had put heart into him.

"Ah, Monsieur l'Abbé," sighed lovely Lady Lauriston, "you will tell us, won't you, the true, unvarnished facts about your wonderful escape."

"Of course I will, dear lady," the old priest replied; "nothing could make me happier than to let the whole world hear, if it were possible, the story of one of the most valorous deeds ever accomplished on this earth. I have seen men and women, especially recently, show amazing pluck and endurance under the terrible circumstances which alas obtain in my poor country these days, but never did I witness anything like the courage and resourcefulness displayed by that noble gentleman who rescued us from certain death at risk of his life."

The abbé had spoken so earnestly and in a voice quivering with such depth of emotion, that instinctively the chatter around him died down, and for a few moments there was silence in the pretty rose-coloured boudoir, whilst the old priest and several of the ladies surreptitiously wiped away a tear. Everyone felt thrilled, emotional; even the men responded readily to that feeling of pride in the display of courage and endurance, those virtues which make such a strong appeal to the finest of their sex.

It was the hostess who first broke the silence. She asked:

"And you do not know who your rescuer was, M. l'Abbé?"

"Alas, no, Madame la Duchesse. Monsieur de Saint-Lucque, the Vicomte and I were locked up inside the coach which was conveying us to Paris for trial and, of course, execution. It was very dark. To my sorrow I saw nothing, no one. And that is a sorrow I shall take with me to my grave. To touch the hand of the most gallant man on earth would be an infinite joy to me. And I know that Monsieur le Marquis thinks as I do over that."

"How is Monsieur le Marquis, by the way?" His Royal Highness enquired.

The abbé shook his head and drew a deep sigh.

"Sadly, I am afraid. He is heart-broken with anxiety about his wife and the other two children: and he keeps on reproaching himself for being safe and free while they are still in danger."

"Don't let him break his heart over that, M. l'Abbé. Didn't you tell us the other day that the Scarlet Pimpernel had pledged you his word to bring Madame de Saint-Lucque and her two little girls safely to England?"

It was Lady Blakeney who spoke. She was sitting on the sofa near the old priest and while she said those comforting words she put her hand on his arm. She was the most beautiful woman there, easily the queen among this bevy of loveliness. The abbé turned to her and met those wonderful luminous eyes of hers so full of confidence and encouragement. He raised her hand to his old lips.

"Yes," he said; "we did get that marvellous pledge, Monsieur de Saint-Lucque and I. How it came to us is another of the many miracles that occurred during those awful times after we were arrested and incarcerated in the local gaol. There was a funny old fellow, dirty and bedraggled, whom we caught sight of one day through the grated window of our prison-cell. He was stumping up and down the corridor outside singing the Marseillaise very much out of tune. Two days later we saw him again, and this time as he stumped along he recited in a cracked voice that awful blasphemous doggerel: 'Ça ira!' It was then that the miracle occurred, for after he had gone by we saw a crumpled wad of paper on the floor, just beneath the window."

Here the abbé's narration was suddenly broken into by a shrill little cry of distress.

"Sir Percy, I entreat, do hold my hand. I vow I shall swoon if you do not."

The cry broke the tension which was keeping the small company in the boudoir hanging on the words of the old priest. All eyes were turned to the dainty lady who had uttered the pitiful appeal. The Lady Blanche Crewkerne had edged closer and closer to the sofa where sat the abbé; her eyes were glowing, her lips quivered; she was in a regular state of flurry. As soon as she had attracted all the attention she coveted to her engaging personality she raised a perfumed handkerchief to her tip-tilted nose, fluttered her eyelids, closed her eyes and finally tottered backwards as if in very truth she was on the point of losing consciousness. From all around there came an exclamation of concern until a pair of masculine arms was stretched out to receive the swooning beauty, whereupon concern turned to laughter, loud and prolonged laughter while Lady Blanche opened her eyes, thinking to find herself reclining against the magnificent waistcoat of the Prince of Dandies. They encountered the timid glance of old Sir Martin Cheverill, who felt very much embarrassed in the chivalrous role of supporter to a lady in distress thus unexpectedly thrust upon him. Nor did the lady make any effort to conceal her mortification. Already she had recovered her senses, as well as her poise. With nervy movements she plied her fan vigorously and remarked somewhat tartly:

"Methought Sir Percy Blakeney was standing somewhere near."

There was more laughter after this, and old Lady Portarles who never missed an opportunity of putting in a spiteful word where the younger ladies were concerned, interposed mockingly:

"Sir Percy, my dear Blanche? Why, he has been fast asleep this last half-hour."

And picking up her ample train she swept across the room to where a rose-coloured portière was drawn across the archway of a recess. Lady Portarles drew the curtain aside with a dramatic gesture and there of a truth across a satin-covered sofa, his head reclining against a cushion, fast asleep, lay the Prince of Dandies, Sir Percy Blakeney, Bart. An exclamation of horror, amounting to a groan, went round the room. Such disgraceful behaviour surpassed any that that privileged person had ever been guilty of. Had it been anyone else . . .

The groan, the exclamation of horror, had quickly roused the delinquent from his slumbers. He struggled to his feet and looking round on the indignant faces turned on him he had the good grace to look thoroughly embarrassed.

"Ladies, a thousand pardons," he stammered shame-facedly. "His Royal Highness deigned to keep me at hazard the whole afternoon and . . ."

But it was no use appealing to His Highness for protection against the irate ladies. He was sitting back in his chair roaring with laughter.

"Blakeney," he said between his guffaws, "you'll be the death of me one day."

And after a time he added: "It is to Monsieur l'Abbé Prud'hon that you owe an abject apology."

"Monsieur l'Abbé . . ." Sir Percy began in tones of the deepest humility, "to do wrong is human. I have done wrong, I confess. To forgive is divine. Will you exercise your privilege and pronounce absolution on the repentant sinner?"

His manner was so engaging, his diction so suave, and he really did seem so completely ashamed of himself that the kind old priest who had a keen sense of humour was quite ready to forgive the offence.

"On one condition, Sir Percy," he said lightly.

"I am at your mercy, M. l'Abbé."

"That you listen to me—without once going to sleep, mind you—while I narrate to Madame la Duchesse's guests the full story of how Monsieur de Saint-Lucque and his son as well as my own insignificant self were spirited away out of the very jaws of death, and at the risk of his own precious life, by that greatest of living heroes the Scarlet Pimpernel."

"I am at your mercy, M. l'Abbé ," Sir Percy reiterated ruefully.

"And now I pray you, Sir Percy," the Lady Blanche resumed, and gave a playful tap with her fan on Sir Percy's sleeve, "to hold my hand. I am still on the point of swooning, you know," she added archly.

She held out her pretty hand to Blakeney, who raised it to his lips, then turning to the Prince of Wales he pleaded: "Will your Royal Highness pronounce this painful incident closed and command Monsieur l'Abbé to give us the story of what he is pleased to call a miracle."

"Monsieur l'Abbé . . ." His Highness responded, turning to the old priest, "since you have been gracious enough to forgive . . ."

"I will continue, c'est entendu," Monsieur l'Abbé readily agreed. And once more the ladies crowded round him the better to listen to a tale that had their beau ideal for its hero. Nor were the men backward in their desire to hear of the prowess of a man whose identity remained as incomprehensible as were the methods which he employed for getting in touch with those persecuted innocents whom he had pledged himself to save.

"And what was written on that scrap of paper, M. l'Abbé?" His Highness asked.

"Only a few words, your Highness," the priest replied. "It said: We who are working for your safety do pledge you our word of honour that Madame de

Saint-Lucque and her two children will land safely in England before long," and in the corner there was a drawing of a small flower roughly tinted in red chalk."

"The Scarlet Pimpernel!" The three magic words coming from a score of exquisitely rouged lips had the sound of a deep-drawn sigh. It was followed by a tense silence while the abbé mopped his streaming forehead.

"Your pardon, ladies," he murmured. "I always feel overcome with emotion when I think of those horrible and amazing days."

CHAPTER VI

The Prince of Dandies

Thus was the incident closed. The hostess rose somewhat in a flurry.

"In my excitement to hear you, M. l'Abbé," she said, "I am forgetting my guests. Will your Royal Highness deign to excuse me?"

"I'll follow you in a moment, dear lady. Your guests I am sure are dying with impatience. And," he added, turning with a smile to the other ladies, "all the best seats will soon be occupied."

It seemed like a hint, which from royal lips was akin to a command. Lady Lauriston, Lady Portarles and the other ladies followed in the wake of Madame la Duchesse. Only at a sign from His Royal Highness did a privileged few remain in the boudoir: they were Sir Percy and Lady Blakeney, Sir Andrew Ffoulkes and his young wife, Lord Anthony Dewhurst, Monsieur l'Abbé Prud'hon and two or three others.

The Prince turned to the old priest and asked:

"And M. de Saint-Lucque you say, reverend, sir, could find no trace of the whereabouts of his wife and daughters?"

"None, monseigneur," the abbé replied. "When M. de Saint-Lucque did me the honour of seeking shelter under my roof with Monsieur le Vicomte, he entrusted his wife and daughters to the care of a worthy couple named Guidal, who had a small farm a league or so from Rocroi. They had both been in the service of old M. le Marquis, who had loaded them with kindness, and I for one could have sworn that they were loyalty itself. The night before our summary arrest—we already knew that we were under suspicion—the woman Guidal came to my presbytery. She was in tears. I questioned her and through her sobs she contrived to convey to me the terrible news that her husband fearing for his own arrest had talked of denouncing Madame la Marquise to the police; that she herself had entreated and protested in the name of humanity and past loyalty to the family, but terror of the guillotine had got a grip over him and he wouldn't listen. The woman went on to say that Madame la Marquise had unfortunately overheard the discussion and in the early dawn before she and her husband were awake had left the farm with her two little girls going she knew not whither. "Your Highness may well imagine," the old man went on, "how completely heart-broken Monsieur de Saint-Lucque was and has been ever since. At times since then I have even feared for his reason. Had it not been for his son he would I feel sure have done away with himself, but never for one moment would I allow M. le Vicomte to be away from his father. This was not difficult as the guard put over us during our captivity and in the coach that was taking us to Paris kept the three of us forcibly together. The first ray of light that came to us through this abysmal horror," the abbé now concluded, mastering the emotion which had seized him while he told his pitiable story, "were the few lines written on the scrap of paper which a dirty and be-draggled scavenger threw in to us through the grated window of our prison-cell: 'We who are working for your safety do pledge you our word that Madame de Saint-Lucque and her two children will land in England before long.'"

"And you may rest assured, M. l'Abbé, that that pledged word will never be broken."

It was Marguerite Blakeney who said this, breaking the tense silence which had reigned in the gay little boudoir when the old priest had concluded his narrative. She put her hand on his, giving it a comforting pressure and the old man raised it to his lips.

"God bless you!" he murmured. "God bless England and you all who belong to this great country." He rose to his feet and added fervently: "And, above all, God bless the selfless hero of whom you are so justly proud and to whom so many of us owe life and happiness: your mysterious Scarlet Pimpernel."

"God bless him!" they all murmured in unison.

Over in the ball-room the London String Band had finished playing the last item on their programme and the final chords of the Magic Flute followed by a round of applause came floating in on the perfumed air of the rose-coloured boudoir.

"Your Royal Highness," came in meek accents from Sir Percy Blakeney, "will you deign to remember that I am forbidden to go to sleep until Monsieur l'Abbé has told us a lot more about that shadowy Scarlet Pimpernel, and frankly I am dead sick of the demmed fellow already."

The Prince had already regained his habitual insouciance.

"Nor do we wish," he said, and gave the signal for every one to rise and follow him, "to miss another moment of M. le Abbé's interesting talk. But I'll warrant, my friend," he added, with a chuckle, "that you won't get to sleep till after you have completely atoned for your abominable conduct."

He shook an admonishing finger at Sir Percy Blakeney, the darling of society, the pattern of the perfect gentleman, caught in flagrante delicto of bad manners, and finally led the way into the adjoining ball-room. It was crowded with an ultra-fashionable throng. The elite of English society was present in full force as well as a goodly contingent of French émigrés. Lady Lockroy was there with her two pretty daughters. The old Earl of Mainbron had brought his charming young wife, and the Countess of Lauriston, acknowledged to be next to Lady Blakeney the best-dressed woman in town, had donned one of the new-fashioned dresses of clinging material and high waist said to be the latest mode in Vienna. And many others, of course.

When His Highness entered the ball-room and the ladies swept their ceremonial courtesy to him down to the ground, there was such a rustling of silks and satins as if a swarm of bees had suddenly been let loose. His Highness had Lady Blakeney on his arm, and immediately behind him came Sir Percy with young Lady Ffoulkes. The Prince was in the best of humours.

"Ladies! Ladies!" he said gaily; "you have missed such a scandal as London has not witnessed for many a day. Has not our charming hostess told you?"

The select company who had trooped out of the boudoir in the wake of His Highness tittered as the word "scandal" went round the big ball-room in varied tones of horror or suspense.

"Your Highness, I entreat," Sir Percy whispered in the ear of his royal friend.

But the Prince solemnly shook his head and made to look very serious.

"No good your appealing to me, Blakeney," he said with mock severity. "The ladies must hear of your abominable behaviour. Monsieur l'Abbé has been most kind and forbearing, but our royal patience has been sorely tried, and we have decreed that your punishment shall fit your crime, and that you shall be pilloried before all these ladies as the most ill-mannered man in London. What say you, ladies? Lady Blakeney, have I your permission to proceed?"

The ladies with one accord begged His Highness to go on, whilst Lady Blakeney, smiling at her discomfited lord, shrugged her pretty shoulders and said deferentially:

"As your Royal Highness desires."

"Then we will depute Lady Portarles to tell the awful tale." His Highness concluded, and deposited his bulky person in a capacious armchair. He begged his hostess to sit on one side of him and Lady Blakeney on the other. The story of how the Prince of Dandies had gone to sleep while M. l'Abbé Prud'hon was relating one of the miracles accomplished by the heroic Scarlet Pimpernel was told with obvious gusto and a suspicion of malice by Lady Portarles, who, by the way, was known in society as the queen of scandal-mongers. The story lost nothing in the telling and as the horrifying recital of his misdeed progressed, Sir Percy Blakeney became the target of a hundred frowning looks and was forced to listen to a veritable uproar of censure of "Shame on you, Sir Percy!" and "Would you believe it, my dear?" or "Did you ever hear the like?" The whole thing, of course, in a spirit of fun, for there was no more popular man in the whole of England than Sir Percy Blakeney.

Lady Blakeney sat by smiling sweetly whilst His Royal Highness obviously enjoyed the discomfiture of his friend. Protests on Sir Percy's part were of no avail. His Highness had decreed that he should be pilloried—and he was.

"I have often noticed," one of the ladies now remarked, "that Sir Percy makes a point of going to sleep whenever the rest of us are thrilled by one of those marvellous exploits of our beloved Scarlet Pimpernel related here in this very room by those who owe their life to him."

"I seem to have noticed the same thing," mused pretty Lady Blanche, "on more than one occasion."

"My belief," put in Lady Portarles, in a voice that dominated the din of conversation, "my firm belief, I may say, is that our Prince of Dandies is jealous of the Scarlet Pimpernel."

"He is! He is!" came in a loud chorus from everyone around.

"Own to it, Sir Percy, that you are jealous of our wonderful hero."

Sir Percy no longer protested.

"I will own to it at your command, fair ones," he said ruefully. "What can a poor man say when the innermost workings of his heart are read like a book by a whole bevy of lovely ladies. How can I help being jealous of that demmed elusive fellow who monopolises your thoughts and conversations at all hours of the day? That, begad, shadow deprives us mere mortals of your attention when we would desire to lay our homage at your feet."

While this merry interlude went on, the servants had been busy arranging the chairs and putting the room generally in order for the hearing of Monsieur l'Abbé's recital. Now everything was ready. Heavy curtains masked the dais where the String Band had discoursed sweet music, leaving a semicircular alcove in the centre of which the major domo had placed a chair behind a table with a carafe of water and a glass. And gradually chattering and laughter ceased. There was a little whispering here and there, a few discreet ripples of laughter quickly suppressed, when Sir Percy after he had seen Madame la Duchesse to her seat, took up his stand with an air of resignation against the nearest window embrasure. Monsieur l'Abbé Prud'hon now mounted the few steps that led up to the dais whilst the company sat down, the ladies in the front displaying their brocaded gowns to the best advantage, and the men standing in compact groups all round them.

No actor of note or learned lecturer could have boasted of a more attentive audience than had this old Frenchman in the shabby soutane with the wan cheeks and the twinkling eyes. He sat down in the framework of the alcove, and once or twice passed his hand across his brow as if to collect his thoughts.

"Monseigneur," he began, "Mesdames et Messieurs." He spoke in French throughout. Most of the company which consisted exclusively of cultured, well-educated persons, understood every word he said, for his diction was of the clearest, and he spoke his own language with the exquisite purity of the Touraine district. It was Madame Descazes, wife of the eminent advocate at the Paris bar, who being an erudite as well as a meticulous lady, made copious notes of what Monsieur l'Abbé related to the elegant company assembled in the salon of Madame la Duchesse de Roncevaux on that never-to-be-forgotten evening in the winter of 1794; and it is on these notes that all records of the event are based, for Madame Descazes very kindly allowed her intimate friends to study her notes and make a translation of them if they had a mind.

"I am so thankful, my dear, that I learned French at school," the Countess of Mainbron whispered to her neighbour while the abbé paused for breath.

"I wish I had done better with it," the latter responded. "Luckily, the dear old man speaks very slowly, and I shall not miss much."

"I can understand every word he says," the youngest Miss Lockroy put in glibly.

"Hush! Hush over there!" Lady Portarles admonished. "We can't have any chattering or we may miss something."

For Monsieur l'Abbé, after a few preliminaries, had now embarked on the most palpitating point in his narrative.

"The great miracle, for I must call it that," he was saying, "occurred on a steep bit of road which cuts across the forest of Mézières. It was mid-afternoon and very dull and dark. We could see nothing inside the carriage for the windows were veiled by a curtain of misty rain which had fallen in a drizzle ever since early morning. We sat huddled up against one another. Monsieur le Marquis and I had the young Vicomte between us, trying to keep him warm, for as the shades of evening began to draw in, the cold grew intense, and the poor lad had been half starved ever since our arrest eight days before.

"As I say, we could see very little of what went on outside; only the dim outline of horses trotting on each side of the carriage. We were being strongly guarded. You must know, ladies, that Monsieur le Marquis and all his family are the special targets of an insane hatred on the part of the revolutionary government and of a cruel woman, whom may God forgive, who seems to have vast influence with them all."

"You mean the woman they call Mam'zelle Guillotine?" His Royal Highness here put in.

"Your Highness knows?" the hostess asked.

"We heard her life-story a little while ago," the Prince replied. "It is one of the most extraordinary ones we had ever heard."

"What has always remained a puzzle," the abbé continued after this slight interruption, "in the minds of those of us who have had the good fortune of coming in personal contact with the Scarlet Pimpernel is how he comes to be always in close touch with those who presently may have need of his help. I have heard it argued among some of my English friends that on most occasions luck entered largely in the success of his plans. There never was a more false or more unjust suggestion. Let me assure you that certainly as far as we wretched prisoners were concerned it was pluck and pluck only, the courage and resourcefulness of one man, that saved the three of us from death."

From the elegant assembly, from those society ladies peacocking it in their silks and satins, from the men, some of whom spent the best part of their day at the gambling-tables, there came a sound like the intaking of one breath, a deep sigh which proclaimed more eloquently than words could do the admiration amounting almost to reverence laid at the shrine of the bravest of the brave. The sigh died down and a tense silence followed. Nothing was heard for a moment or two, save the faint rustle here and there of stiff brocade, or the flutter of a fan, until suddenly the silence was broken by a pleasant voice saying lightly:

"Surely not one man, Monsieur l'Abbé. I have it from M. de Saint-Lucque himself that there were at least three if not more of the rescuing party . . . and that your Scarlet Pimpernel did no more than . . ."

"Hush! Silence!" came in indignant protest from the ladies at this attempted disparagement of their hero.

"Sir Percy, you are impossible!" one of them declared resolutely, whilst another begged His Royal Highness to intervene.

"Jealousy carried to that point," concluded Lady Portarles, "amounts to a scandal. Your Royal Highness, we entreat . . ."

"Nay, ladies," His Highness responded with his cheery laugh. "Since you ladies have failed in inculcating hero-worship into this flippant courtier of mine, what can I do? . . . a mere man!"

There were few things the Prince enjoyed more than the badgering of his friend over this question of the Scarlet Pimpernel, while he yielded it to none in his admiration for the man's superhuman courage and spirit of self-sacrifice.

"Lady Blakeney," one of the younger ladies pleaded, "have you no influence over Sir Percy? His flippant remarks cut most of us to the quick."

Marguerite Blakeney turned smiling to the speaker.

"I have no influence, my dear, over Sir Percy," she said, "but I am sure that he would sooner remain silent the rest of the evening rather than distress any of you."

"You have heard what her ladyship says, you incorrigible person," His Highness put in. "It amounts to a command which we feel obliged to second."

"What can I do," Blakeney responded humbly, "but bow my diminished head? Lady Blakeney is quite right when she asserts that I would rather remain for ever dumb than bring one tear of distress to so many lovely eyes. It was only a sense of fair play that caused me to say what I did."

"Fair play?"

"Why, yes. Fair play. In your over-estimation of one man's prowess, you, dear ladies, are apt to forget that there are other equally gallant English gentlemen, without whose courage and loyalty your Scarlet Pimpernel would probably by now have fallen into the hands of those murdering devils over in France. Now, I know for a fact, and I am sure that Monsieur l'Abbé will bear my story out, that in this case . . ."

But the mere suggestion that the Scarlet Pimpernel might possibly one day fall into the hands of the Terrorists in France, raised such a storm of indignation from the entire assembly that Sir Percy was unable to proceed. He gave an audible sigh of resignation and thereafter leaned back once more in silence against the window embrasure. His eyes remained fixed on his beautiful wife. She was obviously smiling to herself. It was a mischievous little smile for she, too, like the Prince of Wales, enjoyed the good-humoured chaff to which her husband was invariably exposed when the subject of the Scarlet Pimpernel was on the tapis. She was sitting beside His Royal Highness now and Sir Andrew Ffoulkes sat next to her. There was no more ardent worshipper of his chief than Sir Andrew, the most faithful and loyal lieutenant a leader ever had, and an evening like the present one gave him a measure of happiness almost as great as that experienced by Marguerite Blakeney herself. She was looking radiant and her luminous eyes had a glow in them which had its counterpart in those of her friend. They were made to understand one another, these two, and now, unseen by the rest of the company, he raised her hand to his lips.

CHAPTER VII

A Valorous Deed

After this brief interval the old abbé was allowed to resume his narrative.

"I am quite prepared to admit," he now went on, "that Nature helped our rescuers all she could. It would have been more difficult, of course, had the afternoon been fine and clear. But even so, I am sure that the leader of that gallant league would have found some other means to save us. As it was, the drizzle mixed with sleet and driven by a cutting wind fretted the horses, and the driver had much ado to keep them in hand: a difficult task, as he himself was obliged to keep his head down and his hat pulled well over his eyes. So we went on for what seemed to me an eternity. I had completely lost count of time. We went on and on or rather were being dragged along in the jolting vehicle on the rough, muddy road until we wondered whether body and soul could bear the strain any longer, and would presently disintegrate, be forced to break apart and lose cohesion through the violence of those agonising shocks.

"A slight respite from this torture came presently when the road began to rise sharply, and the horses, sweating and panting, were put at foot-pace while they dragged the heavy coach up the incline, still in squelching mud. As I put it to you just now, I had lost count of time altogether; so, I know, had Monsieur le Marquis. The child was asleep in my arms, his curly head resting against my shoulder. His lips were parted and through them came at regular intervals a gentle, pathetic moan. The shades of evening were drawing in by now, darkness closed in around us; we were prisoners inside that jolting vehicle, aching in every limb, unable to see, unable to move, hearing nothing but the creaking of axles and of damp leather, and the squelching of horses' hoofs in the mud of the road.

"And suddenly out of the gloom there rang the report of a pistol-shot, followed immediately by a loud call: 'Stand and deliver!'"

At which palpitating point in the abbé's narrative one of the ladies gave a shrill cry, another exclaimed, breathless: "Oh, mon Dieu!" and there was a peremptory chorus of "Hush!" in which the men also joined.

"The first pistol-shot was followed by another and then by a third," Monsieur l'Abbé resumed. "The horses must then have reared and plunged wildly, for we were shaken right out of our seats and found ourselves on the floor of the coach in a tumbled heap one on the top of the other. We could hear a great deal of shouting, hoarse words of command from the officer in charge of our escort, and throughout it all a confused jumble of sounds, the jingle of harness, the stamping and plunging of the horses maddened by the noise, the creaking of the carriage wheels, dragged forwards and then backwards by their restless movements, and the constant lashing of wind and sleet beating against the carriage windows. Everything around the coach did, in fact, add to the confusion. We in the meanwhile did our best to extricate ourselves from our unpleasant position and had just succeeded in regaining our seats, when the carriage door was suddenly opened and the figure of a man appeared in the framework. He had a lantern in his hand which he swung about, lighting up the inside of the coach as well as our scared faces. The man wore a mask, and for all the world looked the very picture of a highway-man. The poor little Vicomte huddled up against me and began to whimper. I remember that at the moment my thoughts were busy with conjecture as to what would be preferable under these circumstances: to continue our fateful journey to Paris or to fall into the hands of highway robbers. Before I could make up my mind as to that, the man with the lantern said quite pleasantly: 'As you value your lives, keep as still as you can. There are four of us here working for your safety.'

"And before we had recovered from the shock—the happy shock, I may tell you—which his words had brought to our nerves, the pseudo-highwayman had vanished and closed the carriage door behind him. We were left to marvel at this miracle which the good God had deigned to perform for our salvation. Monsieur le Marquis murmured faintly: 'It is surely that wonderful English gentleman they call the Scarlet Pimpernel who is working for us,' and after a time he sighed and said: 'If only my dear wife and my darling girls could have been here too.' But somehow I felt wonderfully elated. I had said my prayers of thankfulness to God, and after that I was granted the power to comfort our dear little Vicomte, by putting my arms round him and making him rest his head against my shoulder, and also to speak words of encouragement to M. le Marquis. Next to the good God himself, I felt in my very soul complete belief in the Scarlet Pimpernel and trust in his courage and his ability to save us."

The old man paused for a moment or two and mopped his streaming forehead. He had spoken at some length amidst breathless silence on the part of his hearers. Someone poured out a glass of water for him, and he drank this down eagerly. After this he resumed:

"As to what happened subsequently we knew nothing for certain till some days afterwards when we were on board an English ship and saw the shores of France receding from our gaze. Then it was that the details of our amazing rescue were related to me by one of the brave followers of the Scarlet Pimpernel. I believe that it was just boundless enthusiasm for his chief that caused him to speak to me as he did. He was not the Scarlet Pimpernel himself but was, I am sure, the leader's right-hand man. Let me tell you at once that I have pledged my word of honour that I would never reveal his identity under any circumstances whatever. As a matter of fact, he was the pseudo-highwayman who came to comfort us when we were nearly scared to death. What he ultimately told us was in substance this: that the whole surprise attack was the foundation of an ingenious plan devised by his chief. It took no more than a few minutes to carry through. Surprise and swiftness were, as my informant said, the keynote of success. Had there been the slightest slackening of speed, a word of command wrongly interpreted, a mere second of hesitancy and the whole plan would certainly have failed. It was swift action that won the victory, because it brought about a confusion during which—can you believe it?—the Scarlet Pimpernel and his three followers were down on their knees in the squelching mud of the road, engaged in cutting the saddle-girths under the bellies of the troopers' horses. Imagine what pluck, what coolness such an action demanded in view of the fact that our brave rescuers were outnumbered three to one. It is, so I understand, a well-known form of attack practised in the East, fraught with deadly danger even when attackers are numerically stronger than their enemy. In our case I imagine that a kind of superstitious terror on the part of the revolutionary guard must also have played into the hands of those brave English gentlemen. The soldiers had no elbow-room for a good fight. The road was narrow, the afternoon light growing more and more dim. And with it all the constant cracking of pistol-shots, the snorting and terror of their horses, the confusion, the mêlée and the gathering gloom hindered the men from using what arms they had for fear of wounding their comrades or injuring their horses.

"We, of course, kept as quiet as our nerves would allow, marvelling what was happening and repeating our prayers to the good God for mercy and divine help. As a matter of fact, what was happening unbeknown to us remains to my mind the most wonderful act of audacity and contempt of danger I for one have ever heard of. It seems that at a given moment the Scarlet Pimpernel scrambled up the box-seat of the coach, snatched the reins out of the driver's hands and in less time than it takes an old man to tell you of it he had calmed the poor horses down. This, of course, as I say, we did not know at the time, but it thrilled us poor prisoners, I can tell you, when we heard a voice, a wonderful, cheery and yet commanding voice speak the one word: 'Ready.'

"Was it intuition or inspiration, I know not; certain it is that I knew in my innermost soul, that the voice I heard at that moment, was that of the Scarlet Pimpernel. I can't tell you how I knew, but I did know, and I have often talked this over with Monsieur le Marquis and it seems that he too had the same conviction that I had. You must remember that we inside the coach know nothing of what was happening, and yet there we were suddenly convinced that the hour of our deliverance had come. Often since that fateful moment have I been stirred to the soul by the mere recollection of that voice speaking the word: 'Ready!' It was his voice, my friends! I believe I should know it again among thousands, or in the midst of the loudest uproar."

The priest had indeed no cause to complain of a want of attention on the part of his audience. Men and women alike hung upon every word he uttered. They held their breath, their glowing eyes were fixed upon the old man's face.

"But, M. l'Abbé . . ." one lady was heard gasping through the breathless silence that hung on this vast assembly.

"Yes, dear lady?" the abbé responded.

"As you say you would know the voice of the Scarlet Pimpernel again . . ."

"I should . . . anywhere . . ." he assented.

"Then you are the one to identify our mysterious hero . . . to tell us who he is and where, oh where, we are to find him."

This raised a wave of agitation, and a murmur of excitement. But Monsieur l'Abbé only shrugged.

"Alas!" he said. "I have not heard that voice again—only in my dreams."

"If you do not proceed, Monsieur l'Abbé," here interposed Sir Percy Blakeney with a genial laugh, "a number of ladies here will faint on the spot."

"Oh, yes, do go on, we beg of you, Monsieur l'Abbé," the ladies pleaded, and one of them added lightly:

"See, even Sir Percy, the arch scoffer, hangs upon your lips."

"There is not much more to relate," the priest now resumed. "I understand that the word 'Ready' was a command from the chief to his followers to take immediate cover, which they did, whilst he himself with one light click of the tongue whipped up the team, which plunged down the incline at breakneck speed.

"My informant, bless him, cowering with his two friends in the gloom of the thicket, told me that one of the most thrilling moments in the day's adventure was to see the revolutionary soldiers trying to give chase. Had they been circus-riders they might have given a good account of themselves, but never having learned how to sit a horse with their saddle-girths severed, they did not get very far. The three lieutenants of your gallant hero did not stay to see the rest of the fun. They had their orders and made their way to the place assigned to them by their chief. As to the rest of our journey it has always seemed both to Monsieur le Marquis and to me nothing but a dream. I remember—but only vaguely—the dash down the forest road, and subsequently several halts for the night in wayside huts. I remember the three of us being ordered at one time to don the tattered garb of road-menders, and being jolted along interminable roads in a rickety cart driven by an old hunchback who appeared dumb as well as deaf; and I remembering staggering with surprise when I saw that same old mudlark straighten out his back and throw a purse of money to one of his own kind, who after that drove the rickety cart all the way to the coast.

"Many less important events do I remember also. We were I reckoned five days on the way, five days during which I was haunted by a clear, commanding voice calling 'Ready' and by the vision of an out-at-elbows' hunchback whose body presently appeared as tall and as straight as that of a young god, and who threw a purse of gold about as if it were dross.

"And that, your Royal Highness, my lords and ladies," the abbé now concluded, "is all that I can tell you of the great miracle accomplished on our behalf and under the guidance of God by the finest and bravest man that ever walked this earth."

"Marvellous!"

"Prodigious!"

"Incredible!"

"Quite uncanny!"

These were some of the words that flew from mouth to mouth. It had been a glorious story, told with the simplicity of truth. The audience rose soon after that and separate groups were formed, groups in which the palpitating tale of a man's heroism drove from the most flippant minds all desire for frivolous chatter. The Prince of Wales held Monsieur l'Abbé in earnest conversation. There were many here present this evening who vowed that His Royal Highness was deep in the secrets of the League of the Scarlet Pimpernel, and could if he had a mind reveal the identity of the popular hero. Lady Ffoulkes had edged up close to Lady Blakeney and these two beautiful women, wives of two brave English gentlemen, exchanged glances not only of pride but also of anxiety for those precious lives so valiantly and constantly risked in the defence of the helpless and the innocent.

At the other end of the room a group of ladies were trying to remember the famous doggerel which that inimitable dandy, Sir Percy Blakeney, as great a poet as he was a sportsman, had conceived while tying his cravat.

"It went thus," Lady Blanche declared: "They seek him in England, they . . ."

"No! no! no," broke in the eldest Miss Lockroy. "I am sure there was no word about England . . . or France . . ."

"Yes, there was," asserted pretty Miss Norreys; "I remember the word England very distinctly."

"Besides, it stands to reason," argued another fashionable beauty, "they are seeking him in England, aren't they?"

"Wouldn't it be simpler, ladies," one of the men suggested, "to settle the argument by referring it to the author of the deathless rhyme?"

"Yes! Yes! Of course," the ladies agreed.

"Sir Percy! Where is Sir Percy?"

All eyes were turned to the window embrasure against which the darling of society had last been seen reclining with an air of resignation.

"Sir Percy!" the ladies reiterated. "Where is Sir Percy?"

But they looked for him in vain. That Prince of Dandies had, incontinently, it seems, taken his elegant self off to a more congenial atmosphere.

CHAPTER VIII

A Royal Friend

Madame la Duchesse de Roncevaux was preparing to bid good night to her guests. They were all standing in a wide semicircle at one end of the ball-room waiting for His Royal Highness to give the signal for departure before they in their turn took their leave. This he did raising his hostess's hand to his lips.

"We have spent a delightful evening in your charming house, Madame," he said graciously; "one that none of our friends will, I warrant, ever forget."

The frou-frou of brocaded skirts once more swept the parquet floor with a sound like the buzzing of bees; it came as an accompaniment to His Highness's departure. After he had taken final leave of Madame la Duchesse the Prince turned to Sir Percy Blakeney, who with Marguerite on his arm was also ready to take his leave.

"Nay, man," he said jovially. "I won't let you go quite so easily. You are coming with us for we want a turn at hazard."

He gave a gracious nod to Blakeney, who murmured obediently:

"As Your Highness commands."

"I vow," the Prince went on, "I was so thrilled by Monsieur l'Abbé's narration I must do something to take my mind off those horrors that go on continually the other side of the Channel. Come, man, I'll challenge you. The best of five throws, with doubles or quits a time. Lady Blakeney," he went on, addressing Marguerite, "will you honour my poor house by accompanying us? I feel I shall be in luck to-night and win some of that rogue's fortune which is far to great for the needs of any man. The Goddess of Fortune and the Goddess of Love have him under their special care, he cannot expect Dame Chance to favour him also."

Thus chattering with his wonted good humour, His Royal Highness offered his arm to Marguerite who took it and led the way down the monumental staircase closely followed by Sir Percy. After he and his immediate entourage had left, the party broke up. There was a general rush for cloaks and mantles, calls outside for chaises and coaches, endless chattering and shrill little cries as in an aviary of love-birds.

Soon the whole company had dispersed, coaches and calèches rattled over the cobblestones of old London in this or that direction, and the magnificent mansion in St. James's Square was shuttered and presently was wrapped in sleep.

The Prince of Wales who had Sir Percy and Lady Blakeney with him, was being driven round in the royal equipage to Carlton House Terrace. Not a word was spoken during the drive. It was quite a short one. All three occupants of the carriage were absorbed in thought.

Half an hour later the royal host and his two privileged visitors were closeted in the small library adjoining the enfilade of reception-rooms. Attendants and servants had been dismissed and three chairs disposed in front of the mantelpiece in which blazed a cheerful fire of logs. In one of these reclined the rotund form of the future King of England; Lady Blakeney sat beside him, her luminous eyes fixed on the fitful play of the flames. Sir Percy was standing behind these two, close to a table on which was placed a steaming bowl of punch. He was intent on ladling out the hot liquid into a glass which he then placed at the elbow of his royal host. The latter took a long draught, smacked his lips and pronounced the drink to be first-rate.

"There is one thing, Lady Blakeney," he said jovially, "that this scapegrace of a husband of yours can do to perfection and that is to brew a night-cap. This punch is superlatively good."

He had another drink, cleared his throat, and fidgeted with his lace-edged handkerchief. Obviously he had something to say and knew not how to begin.

"You have guessed, gracious lady, I'm sure," he began at last, "the reason why I have asked you to come here to-night knowing well how tired and anxious you must be."

Marguerite murmured: "Yes!" almost inaudibly. She seemed unable to speak.

"I desired your presence while I gave a serious talking to this mauvais sujet."

He then turned to Sir Percy.

"Blakeney," he commanded, "come hither and stand before me while I impart to you our royal behest."

Blakeney smiling and indifferent at once came forward and, leaning against the tall mantelpiece, stood facing His Royal Highness who then resumed:

"While we held converse with M. l'Abbé Prud'hon and afterwards when he gave us such a graphic account of the heroic way in which . . ."

He broke off with a jovial guffaw for Blakeney had made a sign of obvious impatience and put up a hand in protest.

"All right, all right man!" he said good-humouredly, "but don't forget that I who represent the King my father am speaking to you now and I forbid you to interrupt. I was going to say that while our friend the emotional old priest was talking I watched your face, and I may say that this gracious lady here, your wife, did the same, and we both came to the conclusion that you were then and there making up your mind to go back to France in order to effect the rescue of Madame de Saint-Lucque and her children. That is so, is it not?"

He looked up enquiringly at Blakeney, trying to read in his somewhat clumsy way what went on behind those deep-set blue eyes with their far-away look of absorption in one single overwhelming purpose. How could he tell? How could anyone guess the workings of this self-centred mind intent on one thing and one only: the fulfillment of that one purpose? Indeed Blakeney's gaze at this moment, though fixed on his royal friend, was obviously unseeing. It took in nothing of these luxurious surroundings in happy England, the ease, the comfort and the peace. It had come to rest far away over there in France where a helpless woman and two innocent children would soon be facing death unless . . . And at the thought a happy smile came curling round his lips, and a great sigh not only of longing but of resolve rose from out the depths of his heart. The smile lingered until he saw Marguerite's lovely face turned appealingly up to his, saw her sweet mouth a-quiver with silent anguish and her lovely eyes shining with unshed tears. Then the smile faded from his lips, and a kind of grey veil seemed to spread right over his face. For one moment only. Just a few seconds and that look was gone, the grey veil lifted by some ghostly hand. Back came the smile and with it the merry laugh which proclaimed high animal spirits and a carefree heart.

"Blakeney, are you listening?" the Prince demanded sternly.

"At Your Highness's commands."

"My commands are these, man, and note the word 'command.' I am not asking or suggesting. I am ordering you to accompany us to Bath to-morrow where we desire to spend the next month in taking the waters necessary for our health."

A few second's silence and Blakeney put in with seeming irrelevance:

"The thaw has set in, sir. They have resumed hunting in the Shires."

"Well! You may hunt till the frost begins again if you like. But it is Bath or the Shires, understand."

"Your Highness would not forbid me to hunt then?"

"Certainly not."

"Yet you would forbid me to go after a deadlier quarry than the fox. You deign to tell me that I may hunt till the frost begins again. And I will obey you, sir, and run a pack of wolves to earth who are after an unfortunate woman and two defenceless children. I will hunt them down and redeem my solemn word to a man who is breaking his heart at thought of what his wife and little children must endure in the hands of inhuman brutes. You would not forbid me to hunt the fox, sir. He has done nothing more heinous than rob a hen-roost or two. Then why should I run him to earth and let the wolves have their way?"

"Sport, man, sport!" His Highness broke in impatiently; "Fox-hunting is the noblest sport on earth, and methought you were a sportsman."

"And I'll back my favourite sport against any that has ever been invented for whipping up the blood of a man and making him feel akin to the gods. And now in winter with the keen air fanning one's cheeks, with the night wrapping you round with its sable mantle, with woman or child clinging to you, their weak arms holding tightly to your waist, with human wolves behind you, while you ride for dear life through unknown country, riding, riding, not knowing where you may land, out of one death-trap into another, that, Your Highness, is the sport for me. I have tasted of it and so I know. Ask Ffoulkes, ask Tony, ask any of the others, heroes they, every one of them. Fine men all, brave men, and all of them obeying my slightest command. Sport, sir! Had you but tasted it once, you would never ask me to forgo it again!"

Never once did Blakeney raise his voice while he spoke. It never even shook. But the words came tumbling out of his mouth with the rapidity of running water. His voice while it was pitched low and as if muffled, became more sonorous, more vibrant, compelling attention with the overwhelming force of the passion within. He was looking straight out before him, with head thrown back, seeing as it were the vision which he had invoked: the loneliness, the blackness of the night, and those weak arms clinging round his waist. Hearing the thunder of hoofs behind him, scenting the hot breath of wolves in pursuit, and the approach of death which mayhap had marked him for its own. Ride on, thou gay adventurer! Ride on! For dear life, not your own but theirs, the weak, the innocent, the helpless. Ride on! Ride on! while beneficent darkness still lingers and the first grey streak of dawn tinges the east with its light. Ride! gaily ride while the thunder of hoofs behind you grows weaker and slowly dies away, and the breath of human wolves thirsting for blood is lost in the odour of the frosty air. Yes! here was the adventurer born, the reckless gambler, ready to toss his life against any odds of chance, forgetting everything save the thrill of the moment when even love is compelled to yield to the unconquerable spirit of dare-devilment in the name of mercy and the call of the oppressed for self-sacrifice.

Even the Prince, sybarite though he was, was held in thrall by the fascination of this extraordinary personality: courtier, lover, prince of dandies and king of adventurers. Less than an hour ago he had seen him an a ball-room dressed in the latest fashion, with priceless lace at throat and wrists, bandying inanities with brainless women, the butt and darling of society, the maker of merriment and laughter. How difficult it was to imagine this same man in rough and scanty clothing, unwashed, unshorn, dwelling in derelict huts on vermin-infested boards, or cowering in the scrub like some wild animal in its lair.

He, the Prince of Wales, the future King of England, had listened to that man in silence realising how futile his royal commands must sound after the inspired words of this visionary. And when Sir Percy had finished speaking, the silence still persisted. Any comment after this would almost seem like sacrilege. There was a mission here expounded that must surely have its inspiration from the God of Love Himself.

After a time the silence, broken only by the solemn ticking of a monumental clock over the mantelpiece, became strangely oppressive. It seemed as if Fate had taken her stand at the gambler's elbow and defied the two opponents—the wife, the friend—who pitted their weakness against her strength. Blakeney himself was the first to break in with his shy laugh and a quaint ejaculation:

"Good Lord! It must be that demmed punch getting into my head. Will Your Highness forgive me?"

"Forgive you? What have I to forgive?"

"Disobedience to royal commands for one thing, sir. The way I've made a fool of myself for another."

"You are determined to go then?"

"Would Your Highness have an English gentleman break his solemn word?"

"The risks are too great, my friend," the Prince insisted. "You are getting too well known over there. And you will be up against a woman this time, remember."

"Marvellous thought, isn't it, sir?"

"And women have sharper vision than men."

"I hope this one has. If she is as stupid as my old friend Chauvelin she won't give us a good run for our money."

"Percy," the Prince protested, "you are incorrigible."

And thus was the incident closed, the interview at an end. Soon Blakeney begged permission to take his leave. He had ordered his coach to be brought round to Carlton House Terrace for he knew that there was nothing Marguerite loved better than a drive through the night air after ball or rout in a stuffy atmosphere.

The major-domo was summoned to see that the coach was duly at the gate. For a few minutes while Sir Percy went to have a last look at his horses Marguerite was left alone with the Prince of Wales. He took hold of her hand and raised it deferentially to his lips.

"I have done my best, Lady Blakeney," he pleaded.

"I am eternally grateful, Your Highness," she murmured.

He went on with unusual solemnity:

"I am not a religious man, gracious lady, but to-night I will implore the good God on my knees to guard your husband from any kind of danger."

After Blakeney and his wife had left, the Prince of Wales remained for a long time absorbed in a kind of contemplation. He had seldom if ever been so moved as he had been to-night by the stripping naked of a soul—the soul of his friend whom he had never truly understood until now. And he, the voluptuary, the hedonist, felt for the first—perhaps the only time in his life—a vague longing, almost an envy of that spirit which animated the personality of the Scarlet Pimpernel, and gave to him with all the hardships and selflessness necessary for the fulfilment of a self-imposed duty an overflowing cup of happiness and of joy.

"God grant her persuasive eloquence," he murmured to himself, when the time came to retire for the night. He was thinking of Marguerite, and the futile appeal she, poor woman, would also make to keep her beloved from fulfilling that duty which in this case might so easily lead to his death: one mistake, one slight mischance and one of the most precious lives in the land would be sacrificed on the altar of an ideal.

CHAPTER IX

The Bitter Lesson

Marguerite had hardly spoken a word during the interview between her husband and his royal friend. She had sat by gazing into the fitful flames of the log-fire and listening, listening while torturing anxiety went on gnawing at her heart. Nor did she speak during the drive back to their home in Richmond. She loved the drive and to-night the air—which was damp and soft and had brought about the thaw—was sweet and invigorating. The four greys seemed to have the devil in their legs and Percy had another in his sensitive hands. He drove at breakneck speed over the cobblestones of suburban London, and over the squelchy road by the river.

An hour or so later Marguerite, having taken off her brocaded gown, donned a comfortable wrap and dismissed her maids, went to find her husband in the library where she knew he would be sitting now working away and elaborating the plan which he had formed for the rescue of Madame de Saint-Lucque and her children.

The evening in the salon of the Duchesse de Roncevaux had been torture to Marguerite, for while the abbé spoke so eloquently of the Scarlet Pimpernel she had detected every change in Percy's face. Others present only saw in him the fashionable dandy, the fop, the nincompoop who readily allowed himself to be the butt of empty-headed women, but she, his wife, knew just what was going on in his mind: she saw every subtle expression in the eyes, the flicker of the lids, the almost imperceptible set of his firm lips, and clenching of his hand.

But she never questioned him about his plans. She had learned the bitter lesson of waiting. She knew that no power on earth—not even his love for her—could move him once he had heard the call of innocents in distress.

Just when she reached the bottom of the stairs, the library door was thrown open by Percy's confidential valet. She heard Percy's voice from inside the room saying in French: "I will give you further instructions in the morning." A voice, unknown to her, replied: "At your commands, milor."

A small, spare man dressed in sober black came out of the room followed by the valet, who remained at attention whilst Marguerite, in her turn, passed into the library.

Percy was sitting at his desk with a map of Northern France spread out before him. He appeared to be tracing with one finger a route which he had marked out on it. At sight of that map and of Percy's obvious absorption, a pitiful cry was wrung from the poor woman's aching heart. She put her arms round him and murmured in a desperate appeal:

"If you love me, do not go!"

It was useless, of course. She knew that well enough. All he did was to take hold of her hands and press her soft palms against his lips. But his eyes soon wandered back to his desk. He picked up a paper on which were written a few lines in a small foreign-looking hand.

"Listen to this, m'dear," he said softly. "Our loyal friend Chartier of the Comédie Français has sent me the report I asked him for by special courier. You know how well informed he always is. He has such marvellous opportunities in the theatre and out of it. And this is what he says:

"'Chauvelin has been summoned back to Paris. Is not expected to return to Mézières for some time. Has reported to the C. of P.S. on the subject of the St. L's. Committee is sending their most famous spy to track down the woman and her two children. His name is André Renaud. He will arrive in M., so I understand, sometime in February. Up to the hour of writing no trace has been found of the woman and children, but believed to be still in the province not far from M.'"

He read the letter through quite slowly, as if he meant her to weigh every word. He then folded up the paper and slipped it in the inner pocket of his coat, murmuring softly the while:

"A stage coach plies between Barlemont in Belgium over the frontier to Mézières. That will be the best route for us to follow."

"Percy," she entreated, her voice choked with sobs.

Once again he pressed her soft palms to his lips.

"Light of my life," he said in a whisper close to her ear, "pray to God that I may not get there too late."

"Percy," she reiterated with infinite tenderness, "do not go."

She sank down on her knees. His arm rested on the arm of his chair. She laid her head down on it. Her hair fell in soft golden ripples all over her neck and shoulders. She felt his hand gently stroking her hair.

"Have no fear for me, my beloved," he said lightly, "those devils will never get me, I'll swear. But I am sorry," he added with a rueful smile, "that I shall not come to grips with my friend Chauvelin this time. This André Renaud won't be nearly so amusing. As for Mam'zelle Guillotine . . . Well! A nous deux, Mam'zelle."

He paused, gave a light-hearted laugh and then said with sudden earnestness:

"Joy of my heart! Have I not pledged my word to Saint-Lucque?"

Yes! he had pledged his word. Marguerite knew that well enough, also that he had proudly asserted: "The Scarlet Pimpernel never fails."

Nor would he fail, of that Marguerite was convinced. Strange as it may seem she knew within herself even at this hour of torturing anxiety, that Madame de Saint-Lucque and the two little girls would be brought safely to England—and that very soon. But it was his life, his precious life, that was more and more certainly in jeopardy every time he went over to France. His anonymity was no longer absolute. Putting his arch-enemy Chauvelin aside, there must be quite a number of others who would recognise him as the Scarlet Pimpernel directly they saw him. Had he not spent weeks in the Conciergerie prison, when those devils tried to starve him into revealing the whereabouts of the unfortunate Dauphin? His warders and tormentors saw him day after day: any one of them would know him again, would even, perhaps, be able to pierce his cleverest disguise. And there were others! So many, many others and all of them on the look-out for the big reward promised for the capture of the English spy.

Useless? Of course it was useless. To-morrow or perhaps the next day he would steal away in the night, and she, Marguerite, would be left to mourn and to wait. Her arms tightened round him and she murmured in his ear:

"If you go, I go with you."

Before he could move or utter another word she had passed soundlessly out of the room.

And the day after next the social chronicle contained the announcement that Sir Percy and Lady Blakeney had left Richmond on a visit to friends in Leicestershire where they intended staying while the mild weather lasted. For the next twenty-four hours this somewhat sudden departure of these two leaders of fashion gave ample food for gossip over the coffee-cups. But everyone agreed that Sir Percy was eccentric. No one really knew how to take him, or Lady Blakeney for the matter of that.

And then there were other matters to gossip about: the probable marriage of the Prince of Wales in the near future for one thing: the last phase of the trial of Warren Hastings for another.

And of course the Prince of Dandies and his lady would soon be back, for the thaw was not likely to last.

Book Three

CHAPTER X

A Unique Personage

There is actually no authentic portrayal in existence of Gabrielle Damiens, the daughter of the "regicide," who was known during the early days of the revolution throughout the province of Artois as "Mam'zelle Guillotine." The only inkling one has of what she probably looked like comes from a sketch attributed to Louis David, at that time Director of Fine Arts and member of the National Convention. It is without doubt, like all David's work, an idealised representation of that odious, if remarkable woman. Even through the artist's pure and classical treatment of his subject, the woman's coarseness, not to say brutality, is apparent in the low forehead, the wide flat nostrils, the prominent eyes beneath the heavy brows, and above all in the full thick lips slightly parted, displaying a row of teeth sharp and long like the fangs of a wolf.

Nevertheless, one or two intimate chronicles of the time assert that Gabrielle Damiens had une beauté de diable. Thus might a Queen of Darkness be beautiful. Her figure was tall and well-proportioned suggesting great physical strength, and though her dark eyes seldom betrayed any emotion save of fury or hatred, her coarse lips would sometimes part in a smile, not of joy but of sensual pleasure which fascinated when it did not repel. Women, even the most ignoble harpies of this revolutionary period hated and feared her, but men like Marat and Danton looked upon her as the arch-fiend of the revolution and worshipped her as those of their kind worshipped the devil.

It was said of that inhuman monster Marat that he had been passionately in love with her.

Gabrielle Damiens occupied an apartment in what had been until a year ago the episcopal palace in Mézières. The bishop was now deposed. He was in hiding, so it was thought, somewhere in the forest, looked after surreptitiously by a few faithful peasants of the district, who did this act of charity at risk of their lives. The revolutionary government took over the palace, stripped it of everything of value that happened to be in it, desecrated the chapel and converted the fine reception-rooms on the ground floor into offices for the use of the local Committee of Public Safety, which now held its sittings in what had been the bishop's private oratory.

The floor above was assigned to Citizeness Gabrielle Damiens at her special request for her private residence. It was her friend Maximilien Robespierre, one of the most prominent members in the Convention who had obtained for her the position of Public Executioner in his native Province of Artois. The story of how a woman came to be appointed to such an odious post was a curious one. When Gabrielle Damiens was liberated from the Bastille after sixteen years' incarceration, and when full recollection came to her of how and by whose influence she came to be arrested, her one dominating thought was Revenge. Her mind, which had always been active, concentrated on schemes to accomplish that one supreme object. All sorts of different plans presented themselves before her in turn—spying, denunciations, underground work of every sort and kind—she rejected them all. Her diabolic temperament thirsted not for revenge only but for the actual blood of her enemies, of Saint-Lucque, who had engineered her incarceration in the Bastille, a living tomb in which she spent the best sixteen years of her life. And Saint-Lucque, it seems, was married and happy with his wife and young children. At thought of them Gabrielle Damiens became like those legendary vampires thirsting for the life-blood of the entire brood.

But how to attain her heart's desire? Gabrielle thought and thought and gradually a plan formed itself in her mind. A scheme. Only a vision at first but with the possibility of becoming a realisation, more wonderful, more stupendous than anything that had ever been done before. She saw herself like Sanson of Paris or Carrier of Nantes, the promoter and artisan of her own desires. She saw her hands, those large hands of hers with the short spatulate finger-tips dealing out death not vicariously but actually; deaths which she had for years madly longed to witness. The guillotine! Why not?

What a vision! What if it became a reality? She foresaw difficulties, of course. Even in these topsy-turvy times a female wielder of the guillotine had not yet been thought of. But Robespierre was her friend and so was Marat. They were men of influence and both had the same kind of temperament as herself, cruel, vengeful and unscrupulous. It is to them that she turned. They whom she presently consulted, whose prestige she invoked. She was sure of Robespierre's approval. And Marat . . .? Well, Marat would come to heel like a snarling dog whatever she demanded of him. A flash of her eyes, a touch of her hand and he became her slave.

She sent for those two men one day. There was a short recess in the sittings of the Convention at the time and Robespierre had taken the opportunity of going down to his native province of Artois on business of his own, whilst Marat at Gabrielle's summons posted at once from Paris as he would have done from the furthest confines of France if she had called to him.

And so they came to her apartment which had once been a saintly bishop's oratory, and Gabrielle Damiens, "the regicide's daughter," stood before them, tall, spare, admirably poised. She was dressed like a man in crimson shirt and breeches: the sleeves of her shirt were rolled up to display her muscular arms, her bare feet were thrust into sabots.

"Do I not look like a man?" she challenged them. Robespierre nodded assent. Marat measured her with a tigerish glance.

"Mam'zelle Guillotine, what?" he murmured raucously.

"You call me Gabriel Damiens," the woman went on, "and you will present me to your committees as the son, not the daughter of François Damiens who was tortured and put to death by cowardly aristos to conceal their own misdeeds. You will explain that I was imprisoned in the Bastille for sixteen years for being my father's son. A good story eh?" she concluded defiantly.

"Excellent!" was Maximilien Robespierre's curt comment whilst Marat looked her up and down and gave a harsh laugh.

"You'll get found out pretty soon, ma belle," he said.

The woman shrugged: "Would that matter?" she retorted. "If I do my work well, which I certainly will, they will be satisfied and not care whether I am man or woman."

And so it came to pass that the Province of Artois boasted of that unique personage, a female executioner. She did not get found out till after those awful days in September when two hundred helpless prisoners were massacred in the prisons of Paris and in the surging crowd the murderers had their clothes torn off their backs. "Gabriel Damiens," summoned from Artois by Danton to give a hand in the butchery, accomplished, they said, the prodigies of patriotic ardour, by slaying no fewer than twenty women with "his" own hand. The revolutionary government, overruled at the time by the Extremists, desired to reward those who had served it well on that horrible occasion and Gabrielle Damiens had her reward by seeing her appointment confirmed as Public Executioner in the Province of Artois, despite her sex. She had not overestimated her valor when she said to her friends: "I'll do my work well! They will be satisfied with me."

And they were. Gabrielle Damiens, whenever the guillotine in the Province happened to be idle, filled in her time with public speaking. The days were already dawning when the tigers of the revolution were ready to devour one another. Denunciation against one party was eagerly listened to by the other. Extremists were at the throats of the Moderates. Failing them they were at one another's. Not one man who had been foolhardy enough to throw himself into the vortex of public life felt that his head was safe upon his shoulders and the daughter of François Damiens "the regicide" saw to it that those who were avowedly or covertly her enemies became the victims of those who were her friends.

She had a caustic tongue and great power of oratory. Inflamed by her passions of hate and revenge she knew how to sway the populace by fierce attacks on those who had incurred her wrath. She would stand, as Camille Desmoulins had done four years before in Paris, on a table in the public park, holding a pistol in each hand; her harsh voice would ring out above the heads of the crowd gathered round her improvised rostrum. She knew, none better, how to pillory aristos and capitalists in the face of this poor, half-starved multitude, as potential assassins ready to sell the Republic to foreign usurers for gold. They would listen spell-bound, shivering under their miserable rags, a prey to a nameless fear of coming events which would mean death for them, and probably starvation for their wives and children.

And Gabrielle, feeling that she held these people by the magic of her eloquence, would stand there with flashing eyes, her cropped hair standing up on end around her head like a disordered mane, a blood-red flush covering her face like a veil. To the men her fascination soon became irresistible. When she spoke she could do with them what she liked, twist them round her little finger. Her face had in it at times an almost demoniac expression. She was no longer young, and loneliness, semi-starvation for sixteen years in the Bastille had robbed her of any charm she may have had in youth, but there was no denying that she had an extraordinary and compelling personality; and that her very brutishness had a certain attraction for these half-crazed revolutionists.

CHAPTER XI

Baffled

Close upon a year had gone by since Gabrielle Damiens had donned male attire, and exercised the gruesome profession of Public Executioner. A year during which her hatred for an entire caste must—one would have thought—have been appeased to a certain extent, for in the Province of Artois, through its proximity to the capital where the storm of revolution raged more furiously than elsewhere, the guillotine wielded by her hand had been at work day after day, and noble heads, intellectual and saintly heads, had fallen like corn under the harvester's scythe. But Gabrielle's blood-lust knew no appeasement yet. Her desire for vengeance demanded the death of those who had ruined her life and made of it for sixteen years a real hell upon earth. It was Saint-Lucque now Marquis of that name, it was his wife and his children on whom Gabrielle had concentrated the full venom of her wrath. It was for their blood that her very soul had thirsted ever since she had been turned out of the Bastille a free woman, physically free, but an abject slave to her passions. Ever since that day she had worked for their destruction, had put spies on their track when they left their chateau in Artois and became wanderers on the face of France as so many of their kindred had done. At last the spies had run the head of the house to earth, he and his son, a boy of fourteen, who were hiding in the little village of Orcival close to Rocroi, under the protection of the old curé of the parish who had not yet been dispossessed of his benefice owing to the affection in which he was held by the village folk.

The old man had been expecting dispossession, with it arrest and the inevitable guillotine. It was the usual fate of those servants of God who were prepared to give up their lives rather than fail in their spiritual duties to their flock. He had been tutor to the young Vicomte de Saint-Lucque, and had gladly given shelter under his roof to Monsieur le Marquis and the boy, while Madame la Marquise and the two little girls remained in hiding in another corner of the province not far from the Belgian frontier. The blow fell with such suddenness that neither Monsieur le Marquis and his son, nor the priest himself were able to escape arrest: they were incarcerated in the police commissariat of Mézières and the following day found them on the way to Paris for trial on a charge of high treason against the Republic. This was for Gabrielle Damiens the happiest day she had experienced for the past twenty years. Trusting in her powers of persuasion, she had no doubt that she could induce the authorities up in Paris to allow the execution of the three aristos to take place in Mézières. "It would," she argued in a letter which she wrote to the Public Prosecutor, "help to quell certain subversive tendencies in the province, and demonstrate as nothing else could do the power and the determination of the Republic to deal mercilessly with traitors and counter-revolutionists."

Twenty-four hours later the blow came crashing down over her fondest hopes. The coach which conveyed the aristos to Paris was held up by highwaymen in the late afternoon in the forest of Mézières. The brigands had commenced operations by cutting the saddle-girths under the bellies of the soldiers' horses, had held a pistol at the driver's head and driven away the coach under cover of the gathering night. The aristos had vanished. What the brigands had done with them was not yet known. But Gabrielle was not deceived by the story. She knew well enough that the pseudo-highwaymen were none other than the gang of English spies who were the avowed enemies of revolutionary France and spent their time in endeavouring to cheat the Republic of her right to punish the traitors who had conspired against her safety. In that endeavour be it said those abominable spies always succeeded. The escape of the ci-devant aristos and of the priest Prud'hon was a case in point.

Fuming with rage like a wild beast baffled and foiled of its prey, Gabrielle Damiens appeared before the local Committee of Public Safety, in sitting the morning after the outrage, spouting forth invective and abuse, coupled with threats which caused every man there to put his hand up to his cravat. Every member of the august assembly endeavored to fasten the responsibility of the affair on his nearest neighbour, and tempers ran high while Gabrielle raged and stormed like a harpy.

The sergeant who had been in charge of the escort received a full measure of censure and vituperation. He had given a detailed account as far as he was able of the extraordinary event from the moment when the first pistol-shot was fired and the words "Halt and deliver!" rang suddenly out of the gloom. This was immediately followed by a general mêlée, and when a few minutes later the coach was incontinently driven away and he and the troopers were on the point of re-mounting they found that their saddle-girths had been tampered with and they, not being circus-riders were unable to give chase.

"With that infernal din going on," the unfortunate man went on to explain, "with pistols cracking all the time, with hoarse words of command from the unseen foe, with the plunging and rearing of horses and the creaking of coach-wheels, I could not get my men to hear me. They had drawn their sabres but found that in the narrow road, with the thicket on either side and with the fast gathering gloom they could not use their arms without fear of wounding their horses or their comrades. Not one of us had actually seen the attackers, they seemed to have emerged out of the ground, and at once to have vanished again. Rain and sleet were lashed into our faces by the wind. It was hell and pandemonium, I assure you, citizens. You may send me to the guillotine, but all I could say before my judges would be to repeat the story that I have told you now, which is the truth."

The sergeant was not sent to the guillotine for the simple reason that revolutionary France, now at war with half Europe, had need of all the man-power she could muster. High-placed officers might be put to death without compunction for they were aristos and therefore traitors to the Republic, but men like this wretched sergeant were trained soldiers, and they were of the people, nor could they very well be spared. The man, then, was kept in gaol for a week: he was browbeaten and kept in constant fear of death, until the Committee of Public Safety was satisfied that his spirit was sufficiently broken, after which he was sent with written orders to the General commanding the revolutionary troops in the eastern provinces that he be put in the thickest of the fight so that he might have a chance of showing his mettle and redeeming by outstanding bravery his tarnished reputation.

So much for him. It is to be supposed that out there on the Belgian front he spent many a sleepless night brooding over the extraordinary events of that memorable afternoon, and that the story of the mysterious English spies and their legendary chief was told and retold many a time round the bivouac fires, together with several additions and improvements to make it more palpitating than it already was!

CHAPTER XII

Chauvelin Takes a Hand

A few days later in the luxurious apartment on the first floor of the episcopal palace Gabrielle Damiens was pacing up and down the floor like a hungry panther that has been cheated of its prey. Her dark hair, still innocent of grey, stood out all round her head in a crazy tangle, for she had been pulling at it with both hands whenever a fresh access of rage got beyond her control. Hoarse ejaculations found their way from time to time through her quivering lips. She would then pause by the centre table, pick up a bottle and pour some of its contents into a glass. The liquid was clear like water. But it was water only in name: eau de vie, water of life, Gabrielle drank it down at one gulp.

"The fools!" she muttered thickly after she had drunk; "the cowards!"

And then she went on: "If I had my way with them . . ."

"You would deprive the armies of the Republic of a number of good soldiers," a quiet voice here broke in. "Is that it?"

"Bah!" the woman retorted, "the armies have no use for cowards!"

The man who had spoken was sitting by the table, with elbows resting thereon. His long claw-like fingers were interlocked and made a support for his chin. He was a small spare man who would have appeared insignificant but for his pale, sunken eyes, which now and then flashed with a cold, glittering light like those of a cat on the prowl in the night. He was dressed in sober black and wore his dark hair tied at the nape of the neck with a black bow.

"It is not like you, Citizeness Damiens," he went on, with a sarcastic curl of his thin lips, "to brood over the past."

The woman shrugged.

"I would have liked to have the handling of that sergeant's head," she admitted.

"Of course you would," the man responded, with a note of irony in his even voice. He paused for a moment or two, his pale eyes fixed on Gabrielle and then went on coolly:

"But you would rather have the handling of the ci-devant Marquise de Saint-Lucque and her daughters. Am I not right?"

Gabrielle made no immediate response to this. She had come to a halt in the middle of the room with a half-filled glass of eau de vie in her hand, which she was on the point of conveying to her lips. At the name, Saint-Lucque, she suddenly became as if petrified. She stood absolutely still with the glass in her hand half-way up to her lips, rigid as a granite statue. Her face was entirely expressionless, like a death-mask, her eyes were entirely glassy, her lips were pressed tightly together. The man noted all this and smiled. It was a complacent, satisfied kind of smile, and his head nodded up and down once or twice.

"I am right, am I not, citizeness?" he reiterated after a moment or two.

Gabrielle drank down the eau de vie. Life appeared to come back into her eyes. She put the glass down and sank into a chair as if exhausted, passed her outspread fingers through her tousled hair, gave a deep sigh and said finally:

"Chauvelin, if you mention that woman again, I believe I should strangle you."

Chauvelin gave a dry chuckle.

"As bad as that, citizeness?" he queried.

"And worse," she retorted.

"And useless, shall we say?" the man went on flippantly. "My death would serve no purpose as far as you are concerned, and it would be good old Sanson of Paris who would have the handling of your handsome head."

He paused a moment, his pale eyes fixed on the woman as a snake fixes its eyes on the prey it covets. She said nothing either. Her mouth was set in a line of obstinacy and her eyes still glowered with fury. And so there was silence between these two, while up on the wall the old white-faced clock ticked away the seconds of time with irritating monotony. Chauvelin picked up a long quill, held it between two claw-like fingers and toyed with it, tap-tapping it against the table. He never took his eyes off her, noted every quiver of her over-strung nerves, and the power of his own self-control over her unruly temper. As soon as he was satisfied that he had obtained a certain mastery over her he resumed:

"Do not let us quarrel, citizeness," he said, with smooth urbanity, "or bandy empty threats. We have need of one another, you and I, as I will presently show you . . . if you will listen to me."

And as she still remained obstinately silent he added more insistently:

"Will you listen, citizeness?"

Whereupon she replied sullenly:

"I am listening. What is it you want?"

"Nothing but your attention for the moment."

"Well? Go on."

"I am about to give you sound advice, and I know that you do not usually take advice kindly. But will you make an exception in my favour, circumstances being what they are?"

"Well!" she rejoined with a shrug; "I sent for you, didn't I? It wasn't in order to get you to make love to me."

Chauvelin ignored the gibe and went on placidly:

"The escape of the three aristos through the agency of those damnable English spies is a nasty blow, not only for you personally, citizeness, but a blow to the prestige of all the local authorities of this province. That is so, is it not?"

As she gave no reply, he continued in the same suave, urbane tone:

"You will also admit, citizeness, that a repetition of such an incident would gravely compromise the reputation, not to say the lives of all the members of your local government."

He paused for a moment or two, and then added with ironic emphasis:

"Including yours, Mam'zelle Guillotine."

He no longer waited for her to speak. He could read the workings of her mind as he would an open book, knew that she cared for nothing at this moment, except the satisfaction of her vengeful hate, and that he would get nothing out of her until he had finally succeeded in persuading her that her interests and her desires were identical with his. And so he went on:

"That is why, citizeness, you and I must become allies—not enemies. Your one desire in life, now that Saint-Lucque himself has escaped you, is to bring the rest of the family—the wife and the two remaining children—to justice. My one aim so long as I have breath in my body left will be to lay the English spies and their chief, the Scarlet Pimpernel, by the heels."

Gabrielle gave a shrug. "Pshaw!" she muttered contemptuously. What cared she about Chauvelin's grudge against the English spies? Give her the Saint-Lucque woman and her two brats and let Chauvelin deal with that legendary Scarlet Pimpernel as best he could. She for one did not believe in his existence at all.

"I care nothing about your English spies," she said presently. "Give me the Saint-Lucque brood . . ."

"You'll never get them, citizeness," he retorted with firm emphasis, "while the Scarlet Pimpernel is alive."

"Bah!"

"Never!" he reiterated forcibly.

"Well! You have tried often enough to get him, my good man, and you have failed every time, haven't you?"

"I know it. The man is a genius. A devil, if you like. So far he has baffled me. I am willing to admit my many failures. But I'll not fail this time if you, citizeness, will help me."

Gabrielle broke into a loud, prolonged, mirthless laugh.

"So that's it, is it?" she rapped out harshly. "I am to be the tool of your selfish intrigues."

She jumped to her feet, and brought her clenched fist banging down upon the table.

"It is not for me," she went on, hurling vituperation upon vituperation on the silent, smooth-tongued man, who sat quietly by allowing the flood of her wrath to pass unchallenged over his head: "it is not for me and my just cause that your are setting your crooked mind at work. Allies indeed! Friends! You care nothing for the punishment of traitors like that Saint-Lucques brood; all you think of is your petty revenge on the man who has made a fool of you, that creature of your own imagination—the Scarlet Pimpernel."

She sank back into the chair, pausing for want of breath, for she had gradually raised her voice to a strident pitch, screaming at Chauvelin, who for once in his life was completely dumbfounded. He had not expected this outburst, had apparently not read quite deeply enough into the workings of this half-demented woman's mind, a woman whom, by the way, he heartily despised but whom he believed to have so completely mastered that she would be as putty in his hands. In point of fact, she was right when she said that he cared nothing about the Saint-Lucque women, except as a means to his ends. It was the Scarlet Pimpernel he wanted to destroy and he had set his brain to work to devise a trap into which that chivalrous dandy would be fated to fall.

For the moment, however, he allowed the full flood of Gabrielle's vituperations to flow unchecked over his head. He was not the man to be intimidated by the fury of any woman, not even of this one who had the reputation of always getting the better of those who were bold enough to oppose her. He remained silent for the moment, with pale eyes fixed upon the irate harpy, his long, thin fingers drumming a tattoo upon the table-top. Soon, however, a thin, sarcastic smile curled around his lips, and when Gabrielle came to a halt, panting with exhaustion, he put in calmly:

"Are you not rather unjust towards me now, citizeness? You accuse me of scheming for the destruction of the Scarlet Pimpernel rather than for the punishment of three aristos. But let me remind you that while that audacious spy and his accursed league are at large they will never allow the Saint-Lucque women to be tried and condemned either here or in Paris. Never! They will plan their rescue, wherever they may be, and the will succeed in snatching them from under your nose, whatever you may do, even from the very steps of your guillotine."

He paused, letting his words sink into the woman's consciousness, and he had the satisfaction of noting that comprehension of his point of view did gradually filtrate into her mind. The look of rage slowly faded out of her eyes and her breath came and went more slowly through her parted lips. Presently she said with amazing calm:

"Yes! I see what you mean, and I dare say you are right. It would be the death of me if those women slipped through my fingers in the end."

"They won't," Chauvelin rejoined decisively, "once you have those English spies out of the way, and do not forget, citizeness, that the capture and death of the Scarlet Pimpernel will be a political event of the first magnitude and that you will reap as rich a reward as has ever been bestowed on any man or woman before."

He could no longer be in doubt now that he held her attention. Her expressive face showed plainly that she was listening, listening eagerly, and that it rested with him to hold her attention to the end and to force his will upon her. His will! She must bow to it. She must! His plan was so fine, so perfect! So certain of success. But he must have her co-operation. Without it he could not succeed. What a humiliation for this master-sleuth, this incomparable tracker of spies, to see himself dependent on a woman's whim for what meant his whole future, probably his life!

Ah, well! Ends had justified the means in many intrigues before now. Mentally, Chauvelin had counted his cards and could well be satisfied that he held the ace of trumps. Leaning well forward, with forearms resting on the table and hands clasped, he took as it were a final survey of this woman on whom so much depended. She sat opposite to him, lounging in an armchair, one leg crossed over the other, her hands thrust in the pockets of her breeches. She was the first to speak.

"Well!" she said, "what about that wonderful scheme of yours? Your tongue does not seem to be as glib as usual, I am thinking."

"I want to put the matter as briefly as I can before you, citizeness," Chauvelin gave answer; "but first of all, tell me, do you know where the Saint-Lucque women are hiding?"

"No, I don't," she replied curtly.

"Why not?"

"Because I am surrounded by fools and cowards" traitors I call them. . . . The committee and their sleuths are all alike. . . . Dolts, I tell you."

"Obviously then, if your own people cannot track those aristos we have got to find someone who can."

"I won't have a stranger meddling here, you know," Gabrielle snapped out quickly; "I sent for you because it is you I want. Why cannot you . . .?"

Chauvelin gravely shook his head.

"Impossible, citizeness."

"Why?"

"I have been summoned back to Paris, and I must return immediately. It is a matter connected with the arrest of a ci-devant sewing-maid who was intimately acquainted with the Capet family. The Committee of Public Safety fear the intervention of the English spies on her behalf. They have sent for me," he reiterated solemnly, "and I must go."

"I can arrange that," she retorted with her usual arrogance.

He shook his head once again.

"It would be the guillotine for us both," he rejoined, "if owning to any failure on my part or to any interference from you, the ci-devant sewing-maid were spirited away by the Scarlet Pimpernel."

He gave a short dry laugh and added:

"I don't know what you feel about it, citizeness, but there are one or two things I want to do before my unworthy head rolls into old Sanson's basket."

Gabrielle swore under her breath.

"I hate strangers," she reasserted, muttering hoarsely through her teeth: "I will not have a stranger here."

"The man I have in my mind, citizeness, is one of the finest trackers of aristos in the country."

"I hate strangers," she reiterated sullenly.

"Yet, you admit that you cannot trust your own spies to track the Saint-Lucque women to their hiding-place."

Gabrielle gave no reply to that and for a few minutes there was absolute silence in this room where two minds were busy scheming for the death of a helpless woman and her innocent children. Absolute silence, but the white-faced clock ticked on marking the passage of time towards eternity.

"What's the man's name?" Gabrielle queried at last.

"André Renaud, one of the ablest men on the staff of the Chief Commissariat in Paris," was Chauvelin's glib answer.

"And you are sure," she insisted, "that he can run that hateful brood to earth?"

"Quite sure. He will bring his own subordinates with him and within three days you will know where the three women are in hiding."

"And twenty-four hours later we have them under lock and key," she concluded with a sigh of satisfaction.

"Ready for conveyance to Paris. . . ."

But Gabrielle wouldn't have that.

"Don't be a fool, Chauvelin," she snapped out at him; "haven't I told you that I want the handling of those three cursed women myself. Isn't my guillotine good enough for that vermin? I tell you I will not have them sent to Paris."

"And they won't be. Not all the way, at any rate."

"I don't understand what you mean by 'not all the way.' I wish you wouldn't talk in riddles."

"It is quite simple, citizeness. As soon as the aristos are under arrest, let the fact be bruited abroad far and wide. The ci-devant Saint-Lucques are, I understand, very well known in the province and their arrest is sure to cause a sensation. In fact the greater the sensation the better it will suit my . . . our plan. After that let it be also known that the three women will be conveyed to Paris on a given day, for trial and summary condemnation. Surely you can guess what will inevitably follow?"

"You mean that the English spies . . .?"

"Exactly. Flushed with their recent success, they will at once be on the warpath, devising a plan for the rescue of these so-called innocent victims of our wicked revolution."

"Go on, man! Go on! I am getting interested."

"For the journey to Paris—do not interrupt me again I pray you—you must choose just such another day as served the English spies so well in the case of the other Saint-Lucques and the priest—you want a mist or thin drizzle, lashing wind or driven rain. Do not have too big an escort: four to six men will suffice. Having settled on the day you will have a diligence ready in the earliest dawn shuttered so that no one can get so much as a peep into the interior."

"You don't want the crowd to see the prisoners inside the coach?"

"The prisoners will not be in the coach, citizeness."

"What do you mean? . . . not in the coach?"

"In the coach, citizeness, there will be a half a dozen picked men of your own local gendarmerie armed with pistols, ready to meet the surprise attack, which those English spies will of a certainty have engineered for the rescue of the aristos."

Gabrielle now was sitting quite still, with elbows on the table, her head resting against her hand. Her eyes were aglow gazing straight out before her as if she were already seeing a vision of the drama which Chauvelin had so graphically foreshadowed.

"I see it all," she murmured after a minute or two.

"You can rely on the Chief Commissary here, I suppose," Chauvelin added.

"He is my friend," she replied curtly; "he will do what I want."

"That's good, as we must have his co-operation. Will you tell him to order the driver, who had best be a trained soldier, to arrange a breakdown at twilight on the loneliest bit of road in the forest."

"That's simple enough as you say, providing . . ."

"Providing what?" Chauvelin threw a quick anxious glance at Gabrielle. Her manner had suddenly undergone a change. A moment ago her enthusiasm had seemed at fever-pitch. The scheme was grand and certain of success. She saw it all in a series of mental visions. The coach coming to a halt, the spies on the watch. The sudden attack on the diligence filled with stalwarts armed to the teeth. Yes! armed to the teeth. Six to one or more. All very well, providing they had to deal with an ordinary human being, say an eccentric Englishman. Or the usual type of adventurous spy, out for money or promotion. But this man—this legendary creature with his impenetrable anonymity—the Scarlet Pimpernel . . .

Instinctively she shrugged, obviously in doubt, her expressive face showing an inkling almost of fear. Chauvelin was sharp enough to note all this. Her doubts, her fears, and the reason for both. He gave a harsh mocking laugh and said in direct answer to her thoughts:

"Those misgivings which I can see have reared their ugly heads in your mind are unworthy of you, citizeness. I know that people in this country have talked of the Scarlet Pimpernel as if he were some kind of superhuman being bearing a charmed life, and those fools over in England are inclined to foster that belief. Now I know the man. I have seen him and spoken with him and I give you my word that there is nothing unearthly about him except his unfailing luck and . . . well, yes! . . . his physical courage. But let me assure you once more, citizeness, that the aristos whom you hate will never be sent to the guillotine while the Scarlet Pimpernel is alive. Never."

Chauvelin had risen from the table while he gave Gabrielle this assurance. She made no movement while he picked up his hat and cape and made a move towards the door, but he was quite shrewd enough to note that at last his solemn words of warning had their desired effect. His hand had already hold of the latch when she spoke abruptly:

"Where are you going, Chauvelin?"

"To interview the Chief Commissary of your section . . . with your permission that is . . . By the way, what is his name?"

"Lescar."

"Well! I'll go and have a talk with Citizen Lescar. I shan't have the same difficulty with him as I had with you, citizeness," he went on with a wry smile. "There is a reward of ten thousand livres for the capture of the Scarlet Pimpernel, if taken alive. The largest share of that will go to the Chief Commissary of the district in which the capture has taken place. I imagine that our friend Lescar will not be lacking in zeal."

"No," Gabrielle returned with a mocking laugh; "money is the goad which moves you all."

"Perhaps," Chauvelin was willing to admit. After which he asked: "Is there anything else you wish me to do, citizeness?"

"No," she replied at first and then said: "Yes!"

"At your service, citizeness."

"You can tell those dolts up in Paris to send their sleuth down at once. We'll see what he can do."

CHAPTER XIII

The English Spy

The whole Province of Artois was seething by now with the wrath at the audacity of the English spies, and during the long winter evenings, round homely firesides or cabaret tables, that masterstroke accomplished in the forest of Mézières was discussed and commented on in all its aspects.

Just think on it! Three aristos who were being sent to Paris for trial were absolutely spirited away from under the very nose of the highly efficient police administration of the province. Spirited away! There was no other word for it! And the whole thing was obviously the work of those abominable English, who were emissaries of the devil, for no flesh and blood human creature could have engineered so damnable a trick and then disappeared as if the earth had swallowed them up.

No wonder that the good Artesians looked upon this hoodwinking of their Chief Commissary as the work of the devil, and their desire for revenge of the impudent spy was roused to positive fury. The very name of the Scarlet Pimpernel, the leader of that gang of brigands, had but to be mentioned to make the entire population of the province see red.

That barefaced, insolent Englishman and his equally brazen followers must be laid by the heels and handed over to the tender mercies of the citizeness Damiens who would have her quick way with them. Everyone was contemplating with joy the prospect of seeing those blonde heads—they must be blonde since they were English, drop one by one into the basket of Mam'zelle Guillotine. "Not before she had slapped their ugly faces for them," was the express wish formulated by the women, who, as usual, were more rabid than the men.

The intensity of public feeling in Artois against the English spy soon became known in the capital, and Chauvelin, as soon as he arrived in Paris, did his best to magnify every incident that went to prove that the Artesians would be heart and soul in any enterprise directed against the Scarlet Pimpernel. It spite of his many failures in the direction of that elusive personage, he still had the ear of the Committee of Public Safety who did not undervalue his real worth, and though, at the special sitting convened for the purpose, several members were inclined to scoff when Chauvelin expounded his plan for the capture of the spies—seeing the number of times that his masterstrokes had ended in failures—nevertheless when it was put to the vote, the majority decided in favour of the plan being carried through, starting with the arrest of the Saint-Lucque woman and her two daughters. They were to be the bait that must inevitably draw that league of dare-devils into the clever trap laid for them.

Citizen Renaud who had earned his spurs as the most astute sleuth in the service of the Committee, second only to Citizen Chauvelin himself, was the man finally selected for this preliminary work. The three aristos were in hiding somewhere between Mézières and the Belgian frontier, where picked men of the revolutionary guard were on duty night and day as a living barrier against the escape of traitors over the border. Commissioned and non-commissioned officers were one and all ready to swear that no women had crossed the frontier into Belgium since last the aristos took flight from their old home and became wanderers in the land. The ci-devant Marquis and his son, together with a priest, had in due course been arrested, rescued and taken to England, while the three women had disappeared.

CHAPTER XIV

Le Parc Aux Daims

In these days travellers whose calling or business took them through Arras and Mézières to the Belgian frontier could not fail to note the derelict piece of land situated off the main road some two or three leagues before coming to Rocroi. The land still showed signs of having once been an extensive park surrounding a small château. The château in this year of the Republic was falling into ruins. It had been abandoned close on ten years ago, when the then owners, scenting the fast approaching revolutionary storm tried to sell it, failed after repeated efforts, and finally abandoned it, taking themselves and their goods over to their native Flanders and leaving Mother Nature in possession of the house and the park, hoping no doubt to return after the storm had broken or blown over, and to find the château, if not the garden, very much as they had left it.

But Mother Nature is noteworthily the worst care-taker in the world. Civilisation and man's handiwork are needed to fight rust and decay. The park was first to go back to the wild. Flower-beds quickly became weed-beds; shrubs and fruit trees died for lack of pruning and of water, garden statuary split and broke in the course of two severe winters, and lay on the ground, pedestal and all beneath a blanket of fungus and of moss. After three years under Mother Nature's régime le Parc aux Daims prês Rocroi, dans la province d'Artois, was nothing but a piece of derelict land and its château a mere mass of brick and crumbling plaster, broken woodwork and leaky roof, through the cracked tiles of which rain quickly found its devastating way.

Soon the place got the reputation of being haunted. Country folk avoided going near it. At first, when the family had gone, leaving no one to look after the place, enterprising schoolboys would roam through the orchard in quest of apples, and thrifty housewives tried to raise cabbages and spinach on what had once been the vegetable garden. But after a time strange noises were heard to proceed from the château on dark winter nights, while certain mysterious lights were seen through the windows to be moving erratically to and fro, to flicker and presently to die out, only to reappear later or else on the next dark night. The enterprising schoolboys were scared out of their wits one evening in November, when unseen feet trod over the rough ground, making a noise like the crackling of firewood, although there was no firewood lying about; thrifty housewives had seen to that. After this mysterious episode apples hung unheeded on the old trees, and in due course fell to the ground and lay there rotting until the next season, and housewives gave the vegetable garden a wide berth, fearing the bane of cabbage grown on unhallowed soil.

And here in the derelict Parc aux Daims there was enacted in the year three of the Republic—corresponding with our 1794—a quiet little idyll of loyalty on the one hand and of courage on the other.

At the earnest entreaty of his wife, and the advice of devoted friends, Monsieur de Saint-Lucque, taking his young son with him, had sought shelter in Abbé Prud'hon's presbytery, situated in a village in the vicinity of Rocroi; he confided his wife and two little daughters to the care of an old couple on whose loyalty he would have staked his life. The Guidals had been faithful servants of his family for close on half a century. They owned a small farm in the next village and were people to whom the unfortunate Saint-Lucque felt he could entrust with the utmost confidence those three women so dear to him. This occurred in the early autumn of 1793, and for time everything went well both in the presbytery and in the farm near Rocroi. But the trouble was that communication between the two places was fraught with so much danger that it had to be discontinued chiefly at the demand of old man Guidal.

Weeks and months went by while the unfortunate Saint-Lucque nearly broke his heart with anxiety over his beloved wife and daughters and Madame de Saint-Lucque was equally distraught with grief at being parted from her husband and only son. Matters, however, unfortunate though they were, might have gone on a little while longer, had not Christmas come along. The kind hearted abbé determined on that solemn occasion to carry a message through to the farm.

The inevitable happened. The old priest was waylaid by spies of the local Committee of Public Safety and caught in the act of carrying about with him papers of a suspicious nature. The immediate result of his well-meant action was a perquisition in the presbytery, followed by the arrest of Monsieur de Saint-Lucque with his young son, and also of the abbé himself; the latter on a charge of harbouring aristos who were traitors to the Republic.

But the cruel hand of fate had not done with striking at the unhappy Saint-Lucques yet. The law of the Suspect—that most iniquitous of all the edicts passed by the National Convention—had just come into force. By its enactment the very fact that a man or woman or even a child, was as much as suspected of treason, made them liable to summary arrest and more often than not to the sentence of death.

Guidal, a worthy and timorous peasant, was terrified of the guillotine. He flatly refused to allow Madame de Saint-Lucque and her children to remain at the farm any longer. How did he know when he might become suspect of harbouring aristos? He had not the pluck to say this to the unfortunate lady himself, but deputed his wife for this very unpleasant task. The woman, genuinely horrified at what she called the act of an ingrate and a coward, argued and protested, but the old farmer was adamant. There is no worse counsellor or tempter in the world than fear, and Guidal was frightened to death.

At first, no doubt, he had been actuated by loyalty to his former employers, but as times got more and more troublous and the revolutionary waves rose higher and higher, when they broke over the countryside, it became more and more dangerous to aid aristos to escape from justice. To harbour them was reckoned to be a capital offence punishable by death.

And now this awful Law of the Suspect! Guidal was loyal, he was good and honest, but he was not going to risk his neck for anybody. In the end he told his wife, Marianne, that if Madame de Saint-Lucque did not leave the farm within twenty-four hours, he would himself denounce her and her children to the Commissary of Police.

With her heart beating well-nigh to suffocation, Eve de Saint-Lucque overheard the discussion that was going on. Her fate and that of her little girls were being debated by these two poor ignorant rustics. There could be only one issue to the threat uttered by Guidal. She was a pious woman and a loving wife and mother; what could she do but remain on her knees praying to God for protection, while the woman Guidal ran to the next village, to the presbytery and in a flood of tears told the heart-rending tale to the kind old abbé.

Before anything could be done, however, or any decision come to, the Marquis de Saint-Lucque, the little Vicomte and the abbé himself were arrested and dragged to Mézières pending their being taken to Paris for trial and sentence.

And when Marianne returned to the farm, she found that Madame de Saint-Lucque had left the house at dead of night with her two little children.

She had put together a small bundle of primary necessities, had wrapped the children up in all the warm clothing she possessed, and holding each one by the hand, she wandered down the road in the direction of Mézières. Where to go she knew not, only away, away from the danger of denunciation, of arrest and the awful, inevitable guillotine. Her two little girls! Innocent children! To think that there could be such inhuman beasts in the world, in this beautiful France, who would injure them. Who would, Heavens above! put them to death!

Of her husband and her son she had no news whatever. In her heart she cherished the one hope that they were still safe under the care of the Abbé Prud'hon. But of this she could not be sure, and she dared not question people, for fear of compromising those whom she cared for most in all the world.

There followed for the poor woman days of unspeakable misery: days in which she heard her children cry out: "Maman, j'ai faim!" and was unable to give them food. Her children! days, when feeling herself tracked like a wild animal, she became a wanderer on the face of the earth. The weather was cold, but, fortunately, it was dry. With the two little girls clinging to her skirts she roamed down the country roads around Rocroi getting as near the Belgian frontier as she dared, plunging into the woods, hiding in the undergrowth whenever her keen ear detected the slightest sound of approaching footsteps, or the clatter of distant horses' hoofs. And there she would remain crouching sometimes for hours on end, hugging the children as close to her as she could so as to impart some of the warmth inside her to their tender bodies. Then when she felt that immediate danger was past, she would wander out of the wood once more and go along the road, begging for a few sous or something to eat for her hungry little ones from the barefooted passer-by or at the door of the meanest-looking peasant's hut, where news of whole-sale arrests or the iniquitous Law of the Suspect had not yet found its way. For many nights she and the children slept in derelict farm buildings or tumble-down outhouses, and once or twice out in the open. She was almost at the end of her tether when her wanderings brought her to the neighbourhood of the Parc aux Daims. The place was not altogether unknown to her, but while she was still at the Guidals she had heard rumours that the house was visited by ghosts. She had no superstitious fears herself, but came readily to the conclusion that it was soldiers of the Republican Guard or of the military police that haunted the place and had on that account never dared to go near it. But hunger and cold drove her thither one evening, when the children were almost perished with cold, and to add to her misery snow began to fall.

The whole property, garden, orchard and a piece of pasture land, was, as Madame de Saint-Lucque knew, enclosed by a low wall surmounted by iron work, which for the most part was broken down and a prey to rust and decay. The iron gate, too, was off its hinges and lying on the ground in a state of complete dilapidation, obstructing the access to the drive which in its turn led up to the perron of the château. Eve started to skirt the containing wall and presently came to a small postern gate, or rather the remnants of one. Her ears keenly on the alert, could detect no sound breaking through the stillness of the night. She lifted first one little girl and then the other over the broken stonework, and then passed through the gap in the wall. The snow fell in large flakes and was already lying thick on the ground. No light showed anywhere from the direction where the château stood out like a solid block of darkness blacker than the night. Without looking to right or left, but trusting to her instinct to guide her, she made her way through a wilderness of weeds to the house.

Presently she found herself at the foot of a short flight of stone steps leading to the perron. These she mounted and came to the front door, which was wide open. Through this she passed. The place was as dark as pitch. All that Eve could do was to grope her way round. She appeared to be in a square vestibule on which gave several doors, all of which were open. On the left she stumbled against the bottom of a marble staircase with what seemed to the touch like a wrought-iron balustrade.

The little girls, frightened of the dark and shivering with cold, were crying. Eve gathered them to her as a mother-hen does her chicks, and led them through one of the open doors. The room in which she now entered was obviously large and lofty. Vaguely through the gloom she perceived the dim greyish light of three tall windows, the glass of which was broken for the most part. But they were in the lee of the wind and here, at any rate, was shelter against the cold and the snow.

While groping her way about, Eve barked her shins against pieces of furniture that seemed to be lying topsy-turvily about. She set a chair or two up on their legs and lifted her precious children up on these. She had a bit of stale bread and a couple of apples in her pocket which she gave them to munch, and then went on groping. She could have screamed for joy when her hands encountered what was obviously a thick carpet rolled up into a bundle. It is wonderful what the ingenuity of a devoted mother will invent for the well-being of her children. To lay the heavy carpet out on the wooden floor, well away from the night air, to pick up the little girls, lay them down on the carpet and roll it over them, was soon done. The carpet was large and there was warmth in it for Eve also, and though she did not sleep much that night, she had the joy of hearing the even breathing of these two most precious beings on earth.

At daybreak the next morning Eve de Saint-Lucque explored the place where she had found temporary refuge. The room where she and the children had spent the night was one of three in enfilade, with double doors opening one into the other. All three were littered with furniture mostly broken. All three had tall windows with broken glass, oak floors and an air of complete desolation.

Going out to the vestibule, Eve perceived the marble staircase on her right leading to the story above, and, opposite, facing the bottom of the stairs, another tall double door which gave on a very large room with vaulted ceiling and a monumental mantelpiece, obviously a room used in the olden days of luxury and hospitality as a banqueting-hall. Soon after that the children woke. They were warm, but they were hungry. Eve wandered out into what had once been a beautiful garden, but was nothing now but a wilderness of weeds. Beyond it, not far from the house, was the orchard. A few miserable apples still hung upon the trees. Eve gathered the best ones and gave them to the children to eat. Thank God for the good health and sturdy constitution with which they were endowed, or never could they have outlived the privations of the past two weeks.

Eve then wandered out into the road to beg. And this she did the following day also and the day after that, always like some small defenceless animal scenting an enemy in every flutter of a leaf or the crackle of tiny twigs in the woods. On the whole, passers-by were kind. The carriage-way which branches off the main road and winds along in a series of curves to the gateway of the Parc aux Daims was no longer a frequented one these days. No longer did luxurious equipages wend their way to the hospitable château, or gaily bedight cavaliers on prancing horses come cantering down the lane. Only now and then did a market cart go by, taking produce for delivery to the villages around, or an occasional passer-by—farmer or peasant—come stumping along in sabots. They were indigent most of them, the men and the women; but most of them had a sou to spare for the sad-eyed beggar in ragged black clothes in whom it would have been hard to recognise the proud and beautiful Marquise de Saint-Lucque. And when pockets were void of sous, there would be a bit of hard cheese or stale bread, a few apples or a drop of milk, and Eve de Saint-Lucque would murmur in gratitude through her tears: "May le bon Dieu reward you."

On the third day when she had taken her stand in the road at some little distance from the park gates, and stretched out her hand to occasional passers-by, she saw a woman come along who had a good-sized bundle slung over her shoulders. She seemed very weary. As this woman drew near, Eve perceived that she was none other than Marianne Guidal, the farmer's wife.

At sight of Madame de Saint-Lucque she threw her arms up in the air and cried excitedly: "At last! At last!" She seized hold of Eve's hands and covered them with kisses.

"Madame la Marquise! Madame la Marquise!" she continued almost sobbing, and would have fallen on her knees had not Eve restrained her.

"Marianne! My goodness Marianne!" the latter admonished, "in Heaven's name, be careful! there may be prying eyes and ears about!"

Marianne quickly put her hand to her mouth.

"I have been hunting for Madame la—for you everywhere," she resumed, sinking her voice to a whisper. "But I have not dared to question people and I've had to be very careful where I went as I am sure Guidal is watching me. Yesterday he went off to Rocroi Fair. It lasts three days. He won't be back till late to-morrow. So I've been able to get about and keep my ears open for any village gossip. And so I heard casually that a poor woman—your pardon Madame la Mar—,—-had been begging the last day or two in the road near the Parc aux Daims. I guessed it was Madame, so I put a few things together this morning and came along."

She paused a moment, for she was evidently a prey to such deep emotion that she was hardly able to speak. At last she said, her voice shaking with excitement, her tear-dimmed eyes fixed on Eve de Saint-Lucque:

"I had to come. God guided me hither. I came to tell you that Monsieur le Marquis and Monsieur le Vicomte are now safe somewhere in Belgium or in England, people said, and so is our good Abbé Prud'hon."

Eve gave a gasp as much of astonishment as of intense joy.

"Le bon Dieu be praised," she exclaimed fervently, "but what has happened?"

"Monsieur le Marquis, Monsieur le Vicomte and the good abbé were arrested the very night that Madame left the farm. I had run out to the presbytery to let them know what Guidal had threatened to do. A few hours later I heard about the arrests. The news was all over the villages around. I was heart-broken and still more so when I realised that Madame had gone, I knew not whither. Three or four days later it was known in the entire district that the diligence in which Monsieur le Marquis with the young Vicomte and the abbé were being taken to Paris to be tried and put to death by those murdering devils, that the diligence, I say, was waylaid by highwaymen in the forest of Mézières, at dead of night, and driven away no one has ever known what direction. Anyway, it vanished then and there with M. le Marquis, the Vicomte and the abbé inside it. No one ever found a trace of it or of the highwaymen or of the prisoners. It was as if the earth had swallowed the lot of them. But I have heard it said more than once that le bon Dieu himself sent one of his emissaries to save Monsieur le Marquis, who had never harmed any man or woman in all his life, our good abbé, who is such a saintly man, and the dear innocent little Vicomte with them. The whole attack was so mysterious that the highwaymen could not have been quite human. People talk of English spies, but we poor country folk know nothing about that. All I know is that I will pray to le bon Dieu on my knees every night for the rest of my life that He may save Madame and the dear little demoiselles, by any means which He thinks best."

Long after Marianne had ceased talking, which she had done very volubly, Eve remained silent and contemplative savouring, as it were, the joy of knowing that her husband and her son were safe, even though she must continue to suffer, to care for her little girls and to avoid compromising their safety by any careless word or act on her part. Subconsciously she watched Marianne untying the knots which held her bundle together. It fell apart displaying its contents: a bottle of milk, a large piece of cheese, two loaves of bread, half a dozen apples. Also a couple of horse blankets, thick and warm. It was these that had made the bundle so bulky and heavy.

"I've boiled the milk," Marianne said; "it will keep for a day or two, till I can come back."

With innate delicacy she had refrained from intruding by word or look on Madame de Saint-Lucque's absorption, and now she asked with old-world deference:

"Would Madame deign to accept?"

She busied herself with doing up the bundle of provisions again. Eve could only murmur:

"Marianne, my dear, good Marianne!" She put her arms round the old woman's shoulders and kissed her on both cheeks. "How can I ever thank you?" she said, and took the precious bundle from her. "But you must not come again," she went on firmly, "for our sakes as well as your own, you must not come again. It is too dangerous, and much too far for you to walk. If people have already noticed me, I shall have to try and find shelter elsewhere, at any rate for a few days, and then perhaps come back here. But you must not come, Marianne dear. Promise you won't come."

Again she kissed the old woman's wrinkled cheeks and Marianne gave a reluctant promise which obviously she did not mean to keep. After which Eve, carrying the bundle of provisions which meant food for the two children for several days to come, turned back towards the Parc aux Daims, while Marianne, who by now was in a flood of tears, went away in the opposite direction.

There followed three days of comparative relief from hardship, of happiness at the news brought by Marianne, as well as the joy of having sufficient food for the two little girls. Eve only ate what kept body and soul together, but the children ate heartily and were luckily in quite good health.

She saw nothing of Marianne during those three days, but this was not because of the promise the good woman had made, but because the farmer had returned from Rocroi Fair a day earlier than was expected. He said very little to his wife, and appeared sullen and irritable. On the third day following Marianne's first visit to the Parc aux Daims, he pleaded important business in the neighbourhood which, he said, would take up the best part of the morning. Marianne, thinking herself free, made her way with a few more provisions to the park gates, hoping to see Madame de Saint-Lucque again. Her husband suspecting her intention waylaid her: saw her turn into the side-road which leads to the Park aux Daims. He went straight to Mézières and that same afternoon gave information to the Commissary of Police that the ci-devant Saint-Lucque woman with her two children were hiding in the derelict château.

CHAPTER XV

Whatever Happens

Eve de Saint-Lucque knew, of course, nothing during those few days of the terrible danger which threatened her and her children through the rancour of Guidal. The fact that her husband and her son had been rescued in such a mysterious way through an unexplicable agency, had not only given her a great measure of happiness, but also a wonderful feeling of hope. She could not account for that hope, but she certainly felt it. Deep down in her heart she felt it, and for the first time for many weeks and months she went about singing to herself for very joy. Sitting with one little girl on her knee, and the other squatting on the ground at her feet she would recall for them little childish songs of long ago, or tales of three little bears or of the seven dwarfs which enchanted them and caused them to break into the full-throated laughter which she loved to hear.

Only the nights were still terribly trying. They were so long and so cold, and the consequent inactivity so very hard to endure.

Marianne had put tinder and a couple of candles in that first bundle which she brought, but the danger of revealing her presence by allowing a light to filtrate through the windows was far too great to allow of such a luxury. Nor would Eve take the children out with her, even into the garden; their shrill young voices or their laughter might, she feared, attract the attention of a casual passer-by. And any passer-by might be an enemy these days.

Before Marianne's welcome visit she had gone out by day into the road to beg for food, and wandered out at night because of the feeling of peace the deserted garden gave her. Whatever ghosts had been wont to haunt the place had evidently found more congenial headquarters. With ears on the qui vive for the slightest sound that might betoken danger, Eve would then stroll as far as the orchard where a few winter apples still hung half withered on the trees. She never heard as much as a faint rustle among the leaves or the crackling of dry twigs in the undergrowth. Never, until that evening, the third since Marianne's visit. The moon was nearly at its full then, and though she hid her face behind a bank of clouds, the night itself was not very dark. A grey light hovered over the park as far as the surrounding wall, and the air was damp and quite still. Eve wandered as far as the postern gate. Resting her elbows on the broken piece of the wall she glanced up and down the road. It was completely deserted. Not a soul in sight. Not a cat on the prowl.

And chancing to look down on the edge of the road the other side of the wall, she saw something white lying there. Something white which looked like a piece of paper weighted down by a stone. Had it not been for the stone Eve would have thought no more about it. A piece of paper fallen out of the hand of a passer-by probably. But the stone? Someone must have weighted the paper down with a stone. Why? Curiosity impelled Eve first to lean out further over the wall, and then to slip out by the postern, to kneel down by the roadside and timorously to move the stone and extricate that piece of paper. Who put it there? Who put the stone over it, and did it contain a message intended for her? At first she thought it might be a message from Marianne. Dear, kind, thoughtless Marianne! Any passer-by might have picked it up and God only knew what mischief this might cause.

With the paper in her hand Eve quickly slipped back through the broken-down postern and made her way quickly to the château. Groping about in the dark she found one of the candles and the tinder. She had before now explored the house sufficiently to know that there was a large wall-cupboard in one of the rooms in which she could safely venture to light the candle and let it burn for a few minutes, at any rate, while she crouched in its deepest recess just long enough to peruse the contents of the mysterious missive.

She had to read it through two or three times before she took in its full significance. This is what it said:

"Your husband, your son and Abbé Prud'hon are safe in England. You and your little ones will soon join them. Whatever happens do not lose your faith or your trust in those who have pledged their honour to save you and who have never failed to keep their word. Destroy this as soon as read. And remember . . . whatever happens do not lose your faith."

This message was so wonderful, so stupendous that no wonder Eve's poor aching head could not take it all at once.

It was impossible these days to live in France either openly or in hiding, without knowing something about a mysterious agency known as the League of the Scarlet Pimpernel and its activities. In most places throughout the country, villages and small townships situated at some distance from the large cities, the leader of this gang of English spies, as they were called, was believed to be a kind of supernatural being, either an evil or a good spirit, according to taste or political views. To the Terrorists who ruled France, he was the devil incarnate. To the unfortunates whom fear of death compelled to remain in hiding, he was a messenger of God sent to bring into their hearts hope of deliverance and of life.

To Eve de Saint-Lucque he was that and more. She had heard before now of mysterious messages and this was obviously one, for in the right-hand corner, by way of signature, there was a rough drawing in red chalk of a small five-petalled flower. Marianne had already told her that rumour had it that Monsieur le Marquis, the little Vicomte and the good abbé had been rescued by an unknown agency when they were being taken to Paris for trial which could only have one dire issue. And now this wonderful message! This promise! This pledge! This word of honour given! She and her children were soon to join those dear ones in England, in that hospitable land of the free. A promise! A pledge! How could she fail to believe and to trust?

"Whatever happens do not lose your faith." It was so clear, so categorical! such a message of hope and of comfort. No! No! a thousand times No. She would never lose her faith. This she now swore before God, as she knelt by the side of her sleeping children. She buried her face in her hands and sobbed out her heart in an ecstasy of joy and gratitude.

CHAPTER XVI

A Master Sleuth

It was on this same day that Citizen André Renaud, the master sleuth, arrived direct from Paris. He presented his credentials as special envoy of the Committee of Public Safety, first to the Chief Commissary of Police of Mézières, and then asked to be received by Citizeness Damiens, at whose special request he had been sent down from headquarters.

He was ushered into the presence of Mam'zelle Guillotine. She was in a towering rage, turned on the newcomer like a wild cat, showered a volley of abuse and vituperation on the unfortunate man who stood in the doorway mute and obviously flabbergasted at this stormy reception, his credentials, with large seals dangling therefrom, held in his trembling hand, towards the irate harpy. She was marching up and down the long room still muttering curses and generally behaving more like an animal in a rage than a human being.

At last she snatched the paper out of the man's hand. Without as much as glancing down on them, she tore them across and threw them into his face.

"So much for you," she cried hoarsely, and gave him a resounding smack on the cheek, "and so much for your Paris and your Committee. You are nothing but traitors and cowards—traitors, I tell you, and—cowards. But I'll teach you what it costs to fool and cheat Gabrielle Damiens. Mam'zelle Guillotine, they call me. Did you know that? I'll give you and your d—-Committee a taste of my guillotine."

And so she went on yelling and screaming, letting herself go to the full extent of her stupendous rage, while the sleuth, still mute and obviously thrown out of countenance, was picking up the torn pieces of paper, smoothing them out and thrusting them into the pocket of his coat. It was only when the rabid fury paused at last, exhausted and breathless, and, pouring out a mugful of eau de vie drained it at a draught, that he ventured at last to put in a word.

"But what have I done?" he murmured meekly.

Gabrielle put down the empty mug and turned to glance at the sleuth who was ruefully nursing his smarting cheek. She looked him up and down once or twice and gave a contemptuous shrug. Not that she did not like the look of the man. She did. She liked his large face, especially now that one cheek was flaming red, his blonde, tousled hair, his big coarse hands and powerful legs, and after that one shrug of contempt, a tigerish grin spread over her face. This the sleuth was quick to note and all at once he broke into a loud guffaw. And this also appeared to please Mam'zelle Guillotine. He came further into the room, towards her. He had a funny rolling gait, like that of a seaman, and now came to a halt with those big legs of his wide apart, his arms outspread, and coarse hands displaying the hard-skinned palms all disfigured with callosities and warts.

Like to like. Gabrielle Damiens's look, which she gave him now, became quite appreciative. She remained contemplative and silent for a moment or two, and he reiterated with a self-confident smirk this time: "What have I done to anger you, citizeness?"

"You have arrived exactly twenty-four hours too late, my friend," she replied dryly, "and those twenty-four hours will cost you dear, that's all."

"Twenty-four hours too late. What do you mean?" he queried.

"Just what I said."

He said nothing more for the moment, pulled a chair towards him, straddled it, rested his great arms across its back and looked her square in the face.

"What exactly did you say, my pigeon?" he then asked.

"I said that you have come to Mézières twenty-four hours too late."

"How so?"

"The ci-devant Saint-Lucque woman is in hiding with her two brats in a deserted house close by here. We are proceeding with her arrest this very night."

Citizen André Renaud broke into another loud guffaw.

"Oh!" he said, "is that it? I do the work and someone else gets the credit, while I get my face slapped and a torrent of abuse. You are really impayable, my pigeon."

"You do the work?" Gabrielle retorted; "it was Citizen Guidal, the farmer. . . ."

"Of course, it was Citizen Guidal, the farmer, my subordinate, who has been under my orders for the past three days," the sleuth broke in, and brought his large palm with a resounding slap on his thigh. "And he has been clever enough to fool you, my cabbage, into believing that a fool like that could track an aristo to her hiding-place. Why, farmer Guidal has about as much brains as one of his own calves. And what did you give him by way of payment for this information, citizeness? Public money—or a kiss? What?"

And he was roaring with laughter all the time, with that full-throated laughter that Gabrielle loved to hear. But she was feeling completely bewildered now.

"Do you mean to tell me . . ." she began.

And once again he broke in:

"I mean to tell you, my cabbage, that you have been fooled. Do you suppose," he went on with an attempt at seriousness, "that the Committee of Public Safety—not a provincial one, remember, but the Head Committee up in Paris-would have sent me down here to assist you in running to earth the Saint-Lucque women, if any local groundling could do the work for you?"

To this she made no reply, and he drew the torn credentials from his pocket and held them out to Gabrielle.

"Don't tear them up again," he admonished her; "now that my work here is done, I am going back to Paris and I shall want them."

Gabrielle didn't look at the papers again. She felt bewildered and distinctly humiliated.

"I'll send for farmer Guidal," she said.

"Yes, do!" he assented. "I'll comb his hair for him. The master sleuth, eh, what? Why didn't he find the aristos for you before? Why did you have to send to Paris for me? I was here two days ago. It took me twenty-four hours, exactly, to trace the Saint-Lucque aristos to that place—what is it called?"

"The Parc aux Daims."

"And another twenty-four to make sure that the woman and the brats were the traitors you wanted. The Committee in Paris put me on the track of your friend the farmer. He was useful. I have a second subordinate working for me also. He, too, will be coming presently to denounce the ci-devants and to take credit like your friend Guidal, for having tracked them. You have been fooled, my pigeon, fooled. We'll say nothing more about it. But be careful that you do not get fooled again, and give away public money—it was not just a kiss, was it?—to liars and traitors. There might be trouble, you know."

His final outburst of laughter was so hearty that it rang out from attic to cellar of the episcopal mansion. He rubbed his large hands together, banged Gabrielle with easy familiarity on the shoulder, and gave a chuckle of complete self-confidence.

Indeed it was his self-confidence, his self-assurance that had finally subjugated Mam'zelle Guillotine. Like to like. They became the best of friends after this. She allowed him to sit down very close to her, laid her head against his shoulder, and soon was in ecstasy over the wonderful stories he told her of his exploits as a tracker of aristos. He stretched out his spatulate fingers and moved them up and down to demonstrate their vice-like grip round the necks of traitors.

"If you want more work of that sort done," he added complacently, "before I go back to Paris, just command me. I will do it for you, my beauty."

He took hold of her hand and rubbed its palm against the thick stubble of his three-days' beard on his chin and upper lip. He had a way of purring like a wheezy old tom-cat. After which he pinched her ear and said in conclusion:

"Yes! I will do that work for you, citizeness, and for France, and leave you to do the rest, Mam'zelle Guillotine."

Yes! Gabrielle Damiens did like Citizen André Renaud, the master sleuth from Paris, very much.

CHAPTER XVII

Thunder Crash

Eve de Saint-Lucque had not known for months and years so much happiness as she did the whole of this day. With the knowledge that her husband and son were safe, and the certainty that she and the little girls would soon be with them and that they would all be re-united over in England with no daily tales of horror to poison the pure air of heaven, or danger of death hovering over their heads, she went about all day singing softly to herself and kissed her children over and over again for very joy of living. The flames of trust and love were burning brightly in her heart.

And then the blow fell like a thunder crash.

It was six o'clock in the afternoon: a wan, grey light still hovered over the open country. The last two days had been comparatively mild, but when the shades of evening began to draw in, a heavy bank of lead-coloured clouds gathered in the east and gradually spread over the sky. It soon got very cold. There was snow coming, Eve felt sure, shivering in her worn-out black dress. It would soon be bed-time for the children, she thought, and was thankful, because then she could make them snug and warm, rolled up in the old drawing-room carpet. Vaguely she wondered if anything was going to happen and when? She marvelled and tried to conjecture how the mysterious agency, the wonderful Scarlet Pimpernel, would work for her salvation. Would she presently hear the tramp of horses' hoofs and hear the hoarde of heroic rescuers come riding down the drive? Would she see these emissaries from heaven come dashing into the château and hear their rallying calls as one by one they would seize the children and finally herself and carry them off in their arms, away, away from terror and from death, away to happy England.

And suddenly she heard footsteps on the road beyond the gates. Not the tramp of horses' hoofs or the rallying call of heroic rescuers, but heavy, measured steps which came up the drive, approached the perron and then mounted the outside steps to the front door. In a moment Eve de Saint-Lucque's happy exultation was changed to sudden fear, stark agonizing fear. She strained her ears to listen. Two men had just crossed the threshold of the front door. Two men or perhaps a man and a woman. Eve couldn't quite tell but already instinct had told her that here was danger, deadly danger for herself and for her children. She struggled to her feet and tiptoed to the folding doors, which were the sole barriers between her and that enemy, who had come through the darkness as the messenger of death. But there was neither latch nor bolt on the doors. They were rickety and hung loosely on their hinges.

Eve went back to the improvised beds where the little girls were lying. They had been asleep but now they woke and Mariette, the little one, began to cry: "Maman! what is it?"

"Hush, my pigeon," the distraught mother murmured, "say your prayers and ask the good God to protect us."

The footsteps had now got as far as the vestibule. They came to a halt and a man's voice called loudly:

"Open that door!"

Eve could not have moved for very life. She remained crouching by the side of her children, with her protecting arms round them. Her limbs were paralysed and her eyes were fixed on the door, through the chinks of which she perceived the dim light of a lantern.

The next moment the doors were roughly thrown open, and in the framework a man and a woman appeared. He was wrapped in a dark cloak from his neck down to his knees, and wore a felt hat which completely hid the upper part of his face. But it was not on him that Eve de Saint-Lucque fixed her horrified gaze. She was looking on the woman on whose face the light from the lantern drew deep and grotesque shadows. The features coarsened with age, brought back memories of the past, and involuntarily Eve's lips gave a murmur:

"Gabrielle Damiens!"

The woman laughed. It was a harsh and a cruel laugh. Her dark eyes glowed, with a kind of savage triumph. She chuckled and took a step or two into the room.

"Aye, Eve de Nesle!" she said harshly. "It is Gabrielle Damiens right enough. You did not expect to see me again in this world, did you, after your precious mother and your cowardly husband consigned me to a living tomb?"

She stood there in the darkness, her tall gaunt frame silhouetted against the dim light of the lantern. To Eve de Saint-Lucque she appeared as the very incarnation of the spirit of evil, of the power of darkness come to dash her fondest hopes and drag her down into the abyss of despair. The woman went on speaking slowly, as if she had weighed every word before she uttered them.

"For sixteen years did I linger in a dungeon in the Bastille, while you, Eve de Saint-Lucque, lived your life of happiness and luxury with the dastard who had betrayed me and cast me off like a worn-out shoe. Sixteen years! during which my life was at a standstill, and one hope alone compelled death to pass me by. The hope that I should live to see what I see now."

Slowly Eve rose to her feet. The depth of her misery was so immense that in spite of her shorter stature she seemed to tower over the other woman through the very sublimity of her despair. Her slender body appeared as a protective shield between this creature of evil and her innocent children.

"May God forgive you," she murmured. "You tried to do a great wrong sixteen years ago, but I had nothing to do with your punishment."

"That is as it may be," Gabrielle retorted with a shrug, "but let me assure you that I shall have everything to do with your punishment. Your miserable husband has escaped but I'll guarantee that he will be wishing himself dead before I have done with you and your brats."

After which she turned to her companion.

"You can go now, Citizen Renaud," she said curtly. "You have done your work well and I'll do the rest."

"You are satisfied," the man responded, "that these aristos are the women you want?"

"Yes. I am satisfied."

"Sergeant Meridol is just outside with half a dozen troopers. I'll send them along to you." He looked Eve de Saint-Lucque up and down seeming to appraise her weakness; then pointing at her over his shoulder with a grimy thumb he went on with a sneer: "I don't think you need fear trouble from her until they come."

He turned on his heel and strode out of the room and across the vestibule. Eve's sensitive ears caught the sound of his footsteps going down the perron steps and treading the garden path, and after a few minutes she heard his voice calling out: "Citizen sergeant." And another voice answering from a distance: "Present, citizen."

Gabrielle Damiens had remained in the room leaning against the door-jamb, her arms crossed over her sunken bosom. Eve de Saint-Lucque could perceive the vague outline of her silhouetted against the light behind. She closed her eyes trying to shut out this vision of cruelty and of impending doom. Gabrielle never said another word. She seemed just to be gloating in silence at sight of the hopelessness of this woman whom she hated with such brutal intensity.

The measured tread of the sergeant and the guard were heard coming up the path, mounting the perron and presently coming to a halt in the vestibule. The sergeant took one more step forward. Gabrielle, turning to him, demanded gruffly:

"Everything ready, citizen sergeant?"

"Everything, citizeness," the man replied. "I have a couple of good horses harnessed to a covered cart, and as you see the commandant has given me a half a dozen men."

Gabrielle threw one last malevolent look on Eve de Saint-Lucque and the two children, after which she turned and strode out of the room and across the vestibule to the front door without uttering another word. Her footsteps not unlike those of a man resounded down the perron steps and on the frozen ground outside. Then only did Eve open her eyes, and fixed them on the soldiers who had lined up behind their sergeant and were standing at attention the other side of the folding doors. Two of them carried stable lanterns. All were armed with bayonets. They wore the promiscuous shabby uniforms affected by the Republican army: they had red caps on their heads adorned with tricolour cockades. The sergeant now stalked further into the room. He gave a word of command to the men and they followed him in, making straight for Eve and the place where the children lay.

"What do you want?" Eve demanded.

"You and the two brats," the sergeant gave curt reply. "Come quietly," he added sternly, "or there will be trouble."

Two of the men seized hold of her while the others pulled away the old carpet that covered the children.

Eve de Saint-Lucque fought like a lioness, while the two men tried to drag her to the door.

"Leave me alone," she cried while she struggled. "We'll come quietly if you leave us alone."

The men let her go and the sergeant ordered her to put some clothes on the children. The soldiers stood about while Eve collected what warm clothing she had for the little girls and with trembling hands managed to get them dressed. She took the two horse blankets which Marianne had brought her and wrapped these round the children's shoulders. The sergeant said roughly:

"That's enough now. We can't stay here all night." And turning to the men he commanded:

"Pick up these brats and take them outside."

Then, of course, prudence went to the wind. Eve de Saint-Lucque felt her senses going. She became a mad woman, seized hold of a chair, swung it over her head threatening to hurl it at the first man who approached her children, would have done it too the next moment had not one of the soldiers at a word from the sergeant dealt her a blow on the head with the butt-end of his bayonet. She fell in a pathetic heap to the ground, not seriously hurt, only stunned, for the blow had not been a heavy one. To soldiers of the Republic detailed to apprehend fugitive aristos, the general orders were to bring in their prisoners alive.

"Pick up the woman and the brats," the sergeant said reiterating his former order. Eve de Saint-Lucque was unconscious. Mercifully she was spared the sight of seeing her children in the arms of men who were followers of regicides and wholesale murderers. Soon the jolting and creaking of wheels grinding on the axles brought her back to her senses. She and her two little girls had been bundled into a hooded cart, and were lying side by side on its hard wooden flooring. Both the children were crying and calling pitiably for "Maman!" Madame de Saint-Lucque feeling ill and sick from the blow contrived nevertheless to gather the little ones closer to her. Fortunately they were well wrapped up in the thick horse blankets, and their tiny hands felt quite warm. One of these blankets had also been thrown over her, and she did not feel the cold.

The cart went slowly jolting along over the rough roads. Through the canvas hood Eve perceived vague forms stumping along the ground, keeping pace with the cart, and heard the measured footsteps of the troopers each side of her. The children had cried themselves to sleep and both were now cuddled up against their mother. Eve was wide awake. Satisfied that the children were asleep and fairly comfortable, she tried to gather her wits together. As her mind gradually cleared, she became aware of the two words that seemed to stand before her mental vision in letters of fire: "Whatever happens!"

Was it comprehensible? Was it possible that this mysterious behest could apply to the terrible event that had just taken place? "Whatever happens!" the behest had gone on to say, "do not lose your faith or your trust in those who have pledged their honour to save you, and who have never failed to keep their word."

Eve had obeyed the command to destroy the missive as soon as read. But she had committed every word to memory. Until a few hours ago these words had been to her like a profession of faith and of hope. She had sworn before God that she would never lose her faith. But now that faith began to waver, and hope to recede into clouds of despair, she recited them sotto voce over and over again forcing hope to return to her, and faith to revive.

"Whatever happens" was comprehensive, she kept on reiterating to herself, forcing herself with all the will-power she possessed to trust and to believe. Whatever happens! the words at the close of the missive had been underlined. Whatever happens, her arrest and that of her children, the terror, the humiliation, the terrible predicament in which she now was, being driven along, whither she knew not, guarded by a posse of soldiers who of a surety would never allow her to escape—were all these horrors hinted at in the magic word: "Whatever"?

"Oh my God!" she murmured, and hugged her children closer to her, "grant me faith, make me trust those brave men who have sworn to protect me and my innocent little ones."

CHAPTER XVIII

At the Commissariat of Police

The Commissariat of Police, Section City of Mézières, stood, an isolated building, at a corner of the Market Square. It was being guarded day and night by a detachment of the local police which, to make assurance doubly sure, had been reinforced by half a company of troopers with a sergeant and two corporals, all of them trained and experienced men. It had gradually leaked out, though still kept in the deepest secrecy, that an expedition was being set on foot which had for its object nothing less than the apprehension of that gang of English spies and their audacious chief who had set the revolutionary government by the ears for the past three years, by aiding aristos and traitors to escape justice. The reward for the apprehension of the master spy was a matter of ten thousand livres, of which every man who aided in the capture would receive his share, in consequence of which there was no lack of keenness on the part of police and troopers, keenness which amounted to enthusiasm.

On the morning following the arrest of Madame de Saint-Lucque and her children, two men and a woman sat in conference on the upper floor of the Commissariat. The men were the Chief Commissary, Citizen Henri Lescar, and the Citizen André Renaud, the reputed master sleuth, the stranger sent down from Paris to assist the authorities of the province in the difficult task of apprehending the Saint-Lucque family of traitors. The woman was Gabrielle Damiens.

Though the conference was being held at a round table it was pretty evident that the dominating personality among these three officials was the woman.

The Chief Commissary of Police, Citizen Henri Lescar, had a paper covered with writing in his hands and had just completed the reading of it out loud. He then laid the paper down on the table in front of him and said firmly:

"These are my orders. Citizen Chauvelin sent them down to me himself from Paris by special courier. They were drafted by the Head Section of the Committee of Public Safety who sat in special session for the purpose. And these orders," he concluded decisively, "I must obey."

Gabrielle Damiens on the other hand was making no secret of her determination to disobey those orders, wherever they came from. The Saint-Lucque woman and her children were now under arrest, and she had made up her mind as to what she wanted done with the prisoners. Nothing would do but she must have her way, and let the Committee of Public Safety mind its own affairs. In the Province of Artois the will of Mam'zelle Guillotine, in her own estimation at any rate, was law. She spoke in a loud voice and with forceful gestures, bringing her fist down now and again on the table with such a crash that everything on it shook and rattled: the ink spluttered out of the ink-pot, and the grease from the tallow candles flew in all directions.

The men listened to her, dominated by the power of this woman's personality. But at first they had protested.

"I think," Renaud the sleuth had put in tentatively, "that we ought to obey the orders from Paris."

And the Chief Commissary reiterated with a dubious shake of the head:

"They were transmitted to us through Citizen Chauvelin at the bidding of the Committee of Public Safety, who sat in special session in order to discuss the whole question."

This was one of the occasions on which Citizeness Damiens brought her fist down with a bang on the table and the Chief Commissary's immaculate waistcoat was sprinkled with ink and with tallow.

"What do I care," she queried defiantly, "about any Committee of Public Safety and their orders? As for Chauvelin, he is only a fool with one fixed idea—the capture of the English spy. But things here in this province are going to be done my way, let me tell you. If they are not—"

She shrugged, a shrug which implied a threat that neither of the two men dared apparently to disregard. Renaud did put in a feeble: "But . . ."

"There is no but about it," Gabrielle retorted forcibly. "Chauvelin has already used every argument to try and persuade me that the capture of that cursed English spy is of more importance to the government than bringing aristos and traitors to justice. That may be. I dare say he is right, but he has blundered so often that I do not trust his much-vaunted acumen. The capture of that Scarlet Pimpernel may be all very well, but I won't allow the Saint-Lucque brood to slip through my fingers. Let me tell you that. And if you two idiots," she went on with a chuckle and a coarse oath, "go against my will, I can assure you that you will no longer have need of your cravats."

She looked so resolute and so fierce that instinctively the hands of the two men went up to their necks. Chief Commissary Lescar's cheeks had turned a greenish colour, the glance with which he met the woman's savage glare was furtive and terror-stricken. But the sleuth did not allow himself to be intimidated for long. He edged his chair closer to Gabrielle's, put on an amorous air whilst his arm stole round her shoulders.

"You know, my cabbage," he murmured, "that you can always reckon on your little André to do what you want."

Gabrielle coolly shook herself free from his embrace.

"My little André," she retorted dryly, "had better do what I want or . . ."

"Don't let's quarrel, my pigeon," the man went on with fulsome adulation; "give me a kiss. You are my queen, you know, the only love of my life, my beautiful adorable goddess."

And as she turned, half willing to respond to this maudlin flattery, he broke into one of those loud guffaws which experience had taught him always got the better of her irascible moods.

"Did my little cabbage really think," he queried between bursts of immoderate laughter, "that her André would want to thwart her in anything?"

Thus was peace restored between the lovers. What could the unfortunate Commissary do after that but agree to everything that Mam'zelle Guillotine desired? It was, anyway, the safer attitude to take up, for Gabrielle Damiens could be a relentless enemy, and she had power too to enforce her will. So he waited patiently and in silence while a kind of rough bill-ing and coo-ing went on at the other end of the table, whispered endearments, pinching of cheeks and ears, all intermingled with prolonged outbursts of laughter. At last he ventured to interrupt:

"Then what is it you wish to do, Citizeness Damiens?" he asked abruptly.

Gabrielle thrust her ardent lover away from her and turned in her usual resolute way to the Chief Commissary.

"How does the whole affair stand at the present moment?" she countered.

"The women were arrested last evening, as you know, citizeness . . ."

"I know all that," Gabrielle broke in dryly; "that is not what I was asking. Where are the aristos now?"

"In the cells down below," the Commissary replied.

Gabrielle was silent for a moment or two. A deep frown appeared between her brows, giving an almost sinister expression to her face. Her thoughts were concentrated on the one thing that her very soul desired, the death of Eve de Saint-Lucque and the two children. Let that elusive Scarlet Pimpernel do his worst; all that she, Gabrielle Damiens, lived for these days was to see the heads of these three women fall under the knife of the guillotin—her guillotine, hers, wielded by her own hand, and to hear the death-rattle in their throats.

The two men had waited in silence while she appeared buried in thought. At last she spoke.

"The diligence from Rocroi was due in on Wednesday. It does not go back until

Monday. Now I want it brought round here to the back door. I want the Saint-Lucque woman—not the children, mind—to be taken in it to Paris to-morrow, along with a half a dozen fully armed men, who will travel inside the coach with her. And I imagine," she added with a harsh laugh, "that she will not have a very agreeable journey. I propose that we make a start soon after daybreak. I will drive the diligence myself and come to a halt on the crest of the hill in the forest where we shall expect to get in touch with the English spies. The escort shall dismount, we'll eat and drink and pretend to go to sleep."

"Though I am not proposing to obey every command of Citizen Chauvelin," she continued after a slight pause, "I consider him a shrewd man, even though he is in disgrace. He is quite convinced and I am sure he is right that the Scarlet Pimpernel will be at his tricks again and risk everything in an attempt to drag the Saint-Lucque women out of our clutches. Anyway, I shall be ready for him. The trap is set for the English vermin to fall into, and when we have got him and his followers we'll truss them like so many calves, throw them into the diligence and, as I said, I will drive them myself for immediate slaughter to Paris. The men from inside the coach will then march back to Mézières and wait there for further orders. I'll warrant," she concluded with a complacent chuckle, "that no man or superman, spirit of evil or mere audacious spy, will snatch the reins out of these hands."

She spread out her large, coarse hands—hands that had dealt death to many innocent men, women and children. Renaud captured one of them and raised it to his lips.

He broke into the loud guffaw which Gabrielle loved to hear: but it was only a wry smile that curled round the Chief Commissary's lips.

"You are willing, citizeness," he ventured to ask, "to take full responsibility for this direct disobedience to orders?"

"What orders?" Gabrielle questioned with a shrug.

"That the three aristos shall remain here in the cells until after the capture of the English spies has been effected."

Another shrug from Gabrielle and a contemptuous "Pshaw!" After which she said decisively, weighing every word and emphasising it by a tap of her finger on the table-top:

"Did you not hear me say, Citizen Commissary, that I want the Saint-Lucque woman to be taken to Paris in the diligence to-morrow, along with half a dozen fully armed men? I spoke pretty clearly, it seems to me."

"Quite clearly, my sweet dove," André Renaud put in with a smirk.

The Commissary ventured on a final protest, a very weak one this time.

"Orders state categorically that there should be no prisoners in the diligence. Only half a dozen picked men fully armed and . . ."

Gabrielle looked him up and down for a moment or two before she broke in dryly:

"That cravat of yours does not become you, Citizen Lescar. Are you tired of wearing it?"

The threat was obvious. The Commissary swallowed hard. His throat was dry and his cheeks were the colour of ashes.

André Renaud burst into a loud guffaw.

"No use for cravats, Citizen Commissary," he chortled, "if one runs counter to my turtle-dove here."

He then turned to Gabrielle and put his arm round her shoulder, trying to draw her nearer to him.

"And what does my lovely one wish her little André to do in all this?" he asked with an affected simper.

She shook herself roughly free from him.

"You, André," she replied curtly, "will take charge of the cart into which the two Saint-Lucque brats must be thrown sometime during the night, when there are no prying eyes about. The woman, on the other hand, must be taken in the same way from the cells to the diligence, as secretly as possible, and given in charge of the picked men in there. The brats must be securely bound in the cart against possible escape. It will be the Citizen Commissary's business to see that all this is properly done: the diligence brought round here to the back door, half a dozen picked men armed to the teeth settled inside, and the woman thrust in quietly sometime during the night. Everything done, in fact, according to my orders," Gabrielle said finally, and cast an imperious glance on the unfortunate Lescar, now reduced to abject silence.

She waited a moment or two before turning to Renaud.

"Weather permitting, I shall make an early start with the diligence to-morrow," she said to him, "and take what escort I may require. How many men has the citizen captain promised you?"

"Two dozen, my pigeon," he replied.

"Including the six picked men?"

"Yes!"

"Then I'll have twelve troopers with me, and you can have the rest. I shall drive the diligence myself, as I said before, and the picked men will be inside ready for the attack. As soon as we have got the English spies we'll have them bound and gagged and thrown into the coach. We'll drive post-haste to Grécourt and wait for you there."

"For me, my cabbage?"

"You will have made a start half an hour after I have gone. You will drive the cart yourself and go round by Parny and Labat. Make a halt at Grécourt. If I am not there wait for me. If I am there first I'll wait for you. Anyway, it must be at Grécourt that we join forces, and all drive happily to Paris together: the English spies in the diligence, the three women in the cart, two dozen men to escort us and see that the devil himself does not interfere. After that, hey, presto! the tribunal and the guillotine for that lot of vermin, what?"

"And promotion for us all," Renaud put in jovially, turning to the Chief Commissary, "not forgetting the reward of ten thousand livres of which you and I will pocket the largest share, eh, my friend?"

He brought his huge hand down with such force on Lescar's shoulder that the poor little man nearly fell off his chair. A fit of coughing took his breath away. Renaud cast adoring glances on his "little cabbage."

"Isn't she wonderful?" he ejaculated fulsomely, and once more tried to draw her closer to him. But she shook him off as roughly as before.

"Leave off behaving like a maudlin fool," she said harshly.

She turned to the Chief Commissary and queried:

"Have I made everything clear? Are you going to follow my instructions? That is what I want to know." Citizen Lescar was making violent efforts to recover his dignity. Difficult under the circumstances. He had been dominated by this woman, been made to feel abject through sheer terror for his life. He, the chief magistrate in this district, who ought to have it in his power to order her arrest for contempt of the law, for flouting the commands of the Committee of Public Safety; but he couldn't do it. He dared not. He felt humiliated and abject, yet writhing within himself for what he knew was sheer cowardice. That ever-present fear held him down in craven bondage—the fear of the guillotine, of the Committee of Public Safety, of Gabrielle Damiens. He knew not which he feared the most.

At last he said, putting on as pompous an air as he could:

"Since you are taking the lead in this affair, citizeness, everything will be done in accordance with your wishes."

Gabrielle drew a deep sigh of satisfaction.

"I think that is a wise decision, Citizen Commissary," she said dryly. A contemptuous smile curled round her full lips. She had got her way, and knew well enough what had brought this man to heel: but like most dominating women she despised the men who surrendered their will to hers.

While this brief passage of arms went on inside the Commissariat, a tumult in the street below which had been slight at first was growing in volume. A number of people had congregated at the corner of the Market Square, and something, apparently, had annoyed them. A very usual thing these days. Crowds collected in desultory fashion with no known purpose. The women would start grumbling about something or other. There was so much to grumble at. The price of flour, the scarcity of milk, just anything and everything that was very obviously the fault of the government up in Paris. Then the men would take the matter up. Growling and threatening. Drowning the women's shrill voices with their vituperations.

The government? Bah! What are they doing save talking and promising. Promising! always promising! The capture of the English spies, the punishment of all the aristos! The execution of the oppressors of the people! But what came of those promises. Nothing at all. Flour and lard were as dear as ever, and milk more and more unobtainable every day. And what about the English spies? They had been at their tricks again and put the whole of the province to shame. And those aristos, the women whom Mam'zelle Guillotine has sworn to execute with her own hands, what about them? Promises, promises, sacré name of a dog! Why was nothing done?

"Where are the aristos?" came in a strident call from the women.

And the men shouted: "Have the English spies got at them again?"

Loud and ribald laughter greeted this suggestion. Citizen Lescar whose nerves had not yet recovered from repeated shocks, looked at Gabrielle with the eyes of a dog that has been whipped and fears further punishment. Pathetic eyes they were in their avowal of helplessness and reliance on moral support from this strong-willed woman. But all he got from her was another contemptuous shrug and a sneer.

"Hadn't you better reassure them, Citizen Commissary," she said, "before they throw stones at these windows?"

She watched him with that withering glance of hers while he was obviously trying to gain time by collecting papers together, blowing his nose, smoothing his hair, all of it with hands that shook visibly.

"Try not to be such a craven," Gabrielle snapped out at last. "Go out to them like a successful general about to proclaim a smashing victory. You have the aristos under arrest, haven't you? And a trap set for the English spies from which they cannot escape? Tell them so, like a man, and don't look like a whipped cur if you can help it. The revolutionary government has no use for curs, remember."

Thus placed between the devil and the deep sea, the fear of the Committee in Paris and terror of this vitriolic woman, the unfortunate Lescar had no alternative but to obey. He rose in grim silence and tinkled a hand-bell. A subordinate entered to whom he gave orders for the front door of the Commissariat to be thrown open.

"And don't forget to have the diligence sent round to the back door, Citizen Commissary. I expect the driver can still be found at the Ecu d'Or," were Gabrielle's final commands to her victim as, without casting another glance at his tormentor, he followed his subordinate down the stairs.

A few cheers and an equal number of cat-calls greeted him as he stepped out on the perron.

Somehow, now that he no longer felt the eyes of Mam'zelle Guillotine looking down on him with contempt or with fury, he felt more of a man. He looked down on the crowd below, almost unafraid. The cheers had heartened him: the cat-calls he did not hear, or else mistook them for cheers also. Gabrielle's final words had given him his clue. Now that she wasn't there to prod him with her irony he felt proud and sure of himself, and knew just what he meant to say. He would speak like a successful general, and proclaim victory. There he stood now on the top of the perron this winter's morning casting vague and grotesque shadows on his lean face, his long thin nose and pointed chin. He raised his hand demanding silence.

"Citizens," he began in a firm tone of voice, and loudly enough for all to hear, "this is a great day for us all, for we have wiped out the blot from the escutcheon of our beloved province. The impudent English spies got the better of us once, but we have turned the tables on them this time. The three aristos, whom you all know to have been oppressors of the poor, and traitors to the Republic, are under arrest. Citizen Renaud, a stranger to us all, but as great a patriot as ever served his country, came all the way from Paris to track these vermin, these snakes to their lair. Now we have got them safely under lock and key here in the Commissariat and to-morrow we will convey them, under sufficient escort this time, to Paris, where they will be tried on a charge of high treason, judged and condemned to death. Our esteemed citizeness Gabrielle Damiens will have the privilege of presiding over their execution here in Mézières. Long live the Republic!"

All this and more did Citizen Lescar say to the assembled townsfolk, who cheered him to the echoes. And having done this he was conscious of a great sense of relief. He had been given his orders by that irascible and dangerous harpy, whose dictates under the present conditions prevailing in France, no man would ever dare to disobey: these orders ran counter in some respects to those which he had received from Paris, but she didn't care; she had made her own plans for the conveyance of the aristos and for the capture of the Scarlet Pimpernel, and had shouldered full responsibility for her disobedience. In case of failure she must also shoulder the blame and suffer the punishment.

CHAPTER XIX

The Interloper

The news of the arrest of Madame de Saint-Lucque and her daughters created a great stir not only in Mézières itself but throughout the neighbourhood. Madame de Saint-Lucque belonged as it were to the district. Her mother was the daughter of a local estate agent, became for a time King's favourite, was created Comtesse de Nesle and played for some six or eight years a great role in the court life of Paris and Versailles. Her daughter Eve was generally believed to be the daughter of Louis XV, who engineered her marriage with the Vicomte—afterwards Marquis—de Saint-Lucque. The marriage was a very happy one: there were three children—a boy and two girls—and all seemed couleur de rose until the outbreak of the revolution, when persecution followed, flight from the ancestral home, separation, arrest and constant danger of death.

The Marquis de Saint-Lucque and his son had been rescued from the clutches of the Terrorists through the agency of the mysterious Scarlet Pimpernel. This fact had rankled in the midst of all patriotic Artesians, who looked upon this successful feat of the English spies as a disgrace and a direct insult to the whole of their province and their local revolutionary guard. The news that the ci-devant Marquise and her children had at last been run to earth and were now under arrest soothed their wounded pride to a certain extent. Not that the Saint-Lucques were any of them disliked in the district. Monsieur le Marquis—as he was termed in those pre-revolution days—often came to Tourteron, where Madame had inherited the château and demense of that name from her grandfather, the estate agent. He had made himself very popular with the working people round about the neighbourhood. He was good-looking—the women liked him for that—he was genial, open-handed and not proud. Madame was also very much liked. She was a good mother and devoted wife, virtues very much appreciated in provincial France in those olden days, when the King and Court gave a sad example of immorality and loose living, and she took a real and personal interest in the families of the poor, and the hard-working housewives whom she often visited.

But, of course, these things were all of the past. There were no such persons as Monsieur le Marquis and Madame la Marquise now, when all men and all women were equal in the sight of the government of France and an era of Liberty and Fraternity had set in throughout the country. The fact that Fraternity seemed to mean that every man's hand was raised against every other who did not agree with his views did not strike the poor ignorant farmer or charcoal-burner as peculiar. The government had declared that aristos were traitors and avowed enemies of wage-earners whom they had reduced to slavery. They plotted with foreigners for the destruction of France and must be exterminated as vermin, root and crop. And that was that.

Men with stentorian voices and wearing tricolour scarves round their waists toured the country in luxurious chaises and harangued the populace of towns and villages from improvised rostrums set up outside estaminets or public buildings. With impassioned words and gestures they pilloried those who had dared to own land which rightfully belonged to tillers of the soil or houses which were obviously the property of those who had built them with their own hands. The fact that some of those houses, like the château of Labat, had been built two or three hundred years ago, had nothing to do with the principle enunciated by these wine-shop orators and the impecunious Artesians were ready enough to swallow the bait cast to them by these mischief-makers intent on fishing in troubled waters.

Everything then was made ready for the start on the morrow. The ci-devant Marquise was hustled in the small hours of the morning into the diligence which stood outside the back door of the Commissariat of Police.

She was not allowed to bid good-bye to her children who had been incarcerated in a separate cell from hers. The poor woman had been gagged and trussed with cords, and been rendered half unconscious by blows before the men detailed for this abominable work succeeded in getting her locked up in the diligence. Only an hour later was the gag removed from her mouth, and her arms and legs freed from the cords. When she opened her eyes, she found herself propped up in a corner of the vehicle and all around her there were a number of men who stood or sat there in stony silence, filling all the available space inside the coach. It remained at a standstill, and the only light by which Eve was able to take stock of her surroundings came from a small lantern outside. After a time she tried to speak, asked a timid question or two but she received no answer. It would be impossible even to attempt to describe what that poor woman suffered in mind and body during the whole of that awful night. To call her experience a nightmare would be to understate what she went through. For it was no dream. Rather was it hell upon earth. The parting from her children had been the worst of the many ordeals she had had to undergo in these past four years of anxiety and sorrow; and now, when she sat huddled in a corner of the diligence not knowing what had become of them and with those grim and silent men keeping guard over her, she thought that she had at last reached the abysmal depths of misery. In vain did she try and infuse hope into her stricken soul. In vain did she make brave efforts to keep two magic words before her mind: "Whatever happens . . ." She kept on reiterating them, forcing herself to trust and believe but alas! no longer succeeding. Surely when those brave Englishmen planed her rescue they had not anticipated this.

The dawn broke, grey and dim, and very cold. It had snowed all night. The diligence was driven round to the open Market Square in front of the main door of the Commissariat, where a score of troopers from the 61st Regiment of Cavalry were already lined up. Citizeness Damiens was early on the scene, giving orders, seeing to it that every man had his arms and accoutrements in perfect condition, encouraging, admonishing, full of excitement and energy. Once she opened the door of the diligence and peeped in to have a look at the men inside, and also to gloat over her victim. She called out with a strident laugh:

"This is what it felt like, Eve de Nesle, inside a dungeon of the Bastille with nothing to dream of for sixteen years except revenge. I thought you would like to know."

She slammed the door and turned to find herself in the embrace of André Renaud.

"That's right, my cabbage," he said and imprinted a smacking kiss on her neck; "don't spare that vermin. Give it them hot and strong."

He had arrived on the scene with another score of troopers for use as escort if required. A hooded cart into which the two young daughters of Madame de Saint-Lucque had been hustled, as their mother had been, under cover of the grey dawn was drawn up in the narrow street at the side door of the Commissariat.

The military pageant thus formed on the market place was quite imposing. Two score of troopers, the huge diligence and in the forefront an orderly holding the handsome white charger of Citizen André Renaud. The latter was in close conversation with the Chief Commissary. His massive arm was round Gabrielle's neck, and every few moments his loud guffaws would ring out through the frosty air right across the market place.

A huge crowd had assembled by now and cheered the soldiers, the Chief Commissary and Mam'zelle Guillotine with lusty energy. The morning was raw and frosty and it was still snowing. The troopers—ill-clad and ill-shod as were most of the regiments of the Republic—were inclined to grumble. The old clock on the municipal building had just struck seven and there was talk of making a start. The Chief

Commissary was bidding the travellers farewell and wishing them luck: Gabrielle was preparing to climb up to the box-seat of the diligence when there appeared to be some commotion at the further end of the market place. Shrill voices were heard asking hurried questions.

"Where?"

"Art sure they were the English spies?"

"In the Parc aux Daims?"

The crowd round the diligence thinned out a little as several quidnuncs turned to find out what was causing the tumult over there. A young labourer was, it seems, the centre of attraction in a small knot of excited townsfolk. He was being thrust forward by them across the square in the direction of the Commissariat.

"Go and tell the Citizen Commissary."

And above the hubbub three words twice repeated rang out clearly: "The Scarlet Pimpernel!"

It struck Citizen Lescar like a blow on the side of the head.

"What is that?" he thundered. And: "Who is this lad? What does he want?"

"He has news for you, Citizen Commissary," shouted a man from out the crowd.

"Go on, boy," urged one of the women, "tell the Citizen Commissary. Don't be afraid."

The boy was now quite close to the Commissary, but he stood there, looking scared, mute as a carp and scratching his head.

"What is it?" thundered Lescar. "Who is this lad?"

"Jean Bernays," somebody said, "the shepherd."

"What does he want? Name of a dog! Won't anyone speak?"

"He says that there is a gang of foreigners, English he thinks, in hiding in the Parc aux Daims."

"Name of a name!" the Commissary swore hoarsely, and seizing the boy by the shoulder he gave him a vigorous shake. The lad immediately began to cry.

Here Gabrielle intervened. She knew the village lads in the district and that there was nothing ever to be gained by trying to bully them. They at once became scared and dumb.

"Tell me, boy," she said and thrust her tall form between Lescar and the shepherd: "Didst see the foreigners last night or only this morning?"

The boy sniffed and wiped his nose with the back of his hand before he replied:

"I only saw them this morning. I was looking after the farmer's sheep. It was maybe four o'clock. Very dark it was. They weren't there yesterday."

"What were they doing?"

The boy shrugged. "Just moving about," he said.

"How didst know they were foreigners?"

"Well! I didn't understand what they said. And then one man caught sight of me. I was watching them from the gate. He offered me money to run away and to hold my tongue. He spoke like a foreigner."

"Then what didst thou do?"

"I took the money and ran to farmer Matthieu and told him what I had seen."

"What did farmer Matthieu say?"

"Told me to get up behind him on his horse. He was just going off to Charleville market. From Charleville I ran all the way to here."

"Where is the money the foreigners gave thee?" the Commissary demanded.

The boy did not like that, would have run away had he dared. Gabrielle thrust a hand summarily into his breeches' pocket, encountered a screw of paper which she drew out and unfolded. It was crumpled and dirty: inside it there were a few silver coins.

"Something is written here," she said and handed the paper over to Renaud. "Can you read it, citizen? I can't."

Nor could the clever sleuth from Paris. He gazed on the dirty scrap of paper and so did Gabrielle. In the end it was Chief Commissary Lescar who looked over Renaud's shoulder and then pointed with a triumphant finger to the last word of the mysterious writing: and whether you could read the rest or not made no matter, for that one word did stand out clearly and unmistakably and it was scribbled in red chalk: P I M P E R N E L.

The Chief Commissary, the sleuth and Gabrielle Damiens gazed at one another for a moment, open-mouthed, dumbfounded—just long enough for the shepherd to seize his opportunity, snatch his money out of the woman's hand and run away across the square. The Chief commissary was the first to speak.

"I am going after him," he said resolutely.

"After whom?" Gabrielle demanded.

"After that accursed English spy. Citizen sergeant," he commanded, "you and twenty of your men come with me. I am for the Parc aux Daims."

He called to one of the troopers to dismount and bring his horse round to him. In vain did Renaud protest.

"You can't take all these troopers away like that," he said; "Citizeness Damiens and I cannot be left to make a start without sufficient escort."

"You will not need to make a start," Lescar retorted gruffly, "until I come back with my prisoner, that impudent Scarlet Pimpernel."

"But the prisoners . . ." Renaud went on expostulating.

"If you are afraid," the Commissary broke in, "send round to the barracks for reinforcements. I am going to the Parc aux Daims with Sergeant Méridol and twenty men to capture my quarry while I know where I can get it."

A horse was brought round to him and he prepared to mount when Gabrielle's harsh voice once again intervened.

"You are making a fool of yourself, Citizen Lescar," she said roughly. "The purpose of the Scarlet Pimpernel is to get at the aristos. If we get him or when we get him, it will be when he is at one of his tricks either here or in the forest, or in fact anywhere on the road. To run after him when we have set such a fine trap for him is just folly."

But the Chief Commissary had been too long under the domination of this tyrant in petticoats. He refused to listen to her now.

"My duty," he said resolutely, "is to capture the Scarlet Pimpernel. I have had orders to that effect over and over again for the past three years. If I allow this opportunity to slip by I should be a traitor to the Republic. Already I have wasted too much time in talk and recriminations."

He swung himself into the saddle and called again to the sergeant.

"Citizen sergeant," he commanded, "you will accompany me with twenty of these men. The others remain here with Citizeness Damiens, and Citizen Renaud will send to the barracks for as many more as he wants."

In vain did Renaud swear and protest: in vain did Gabrielle growl like an angry tiger: they were both of them powerless in face of the Chief Commissary's superior authority over the soldiers.

"En avant!" he cried, and set off across the square followed by sergeant and troopers.

"En avant!" and the cavalcade rode away with much jingling of harness and clatter of hoofs on the stone pavement and to the accompaniment of loud cheers from the crowd. Young and old, men and women, yelled themselves hoarse with enthusiasm. Admittedly the worthy townsfolk cared nothing about Citizen Renaud who remained standing there looking somewhat sheepish. He was a stranger to them. Nobody knew him. He had certainly been credited with having tracked the female aristos to their hiding-place, but there the matter ended. Many there were who had listened with indignation to the altercation between him and Citizen Lescar. What right, they thought, had this Parisian interloper to interfere with their Chief Commissary in the exercise of his duty. The Chief Commissary was entirely within his rights when he decided to go at once and capture that abominable English spy, who had led the entire province by the nose with his devilish tricks of helping traitors to escape from justice, and it was past any worthy Artesian's comprehension that Citizeness Damiens—herself a god patriot if ever there was one—should have backed up a stranger against one of their own townsfolk. But there! What can one expect from a woman in love? And Mam'zelle Guillotine's infatuation for the Parisian was no longer a mere rumour but a fact known to all who had their wits about them.

Thus had the crowd watched the proceedings with mixed feelings of approbation for their Chief Commissary and a certain measure of hostility towards Renaud, and after the cheering for Lescar and his cavalcade had subsided there was some booing and hissing directed at the stranger.

Two soldiers were standing together on the fringe of the crowd at the junction of the market place with the narrow street on which gave the side door of the Commissariat. They were ill-shod and ill-clothed in the same haphazard uniforms as their comrades of the 61st regiment. Now and then they both looked over their shoulder down the narrow street where the hooded cart was drawn up.

Presently they were joined by a third man, who was dressed as they were, whereupon all three drew back a few steps from the edge of the crowd.

"You have the orders?" one of them asked.

"Yes!"

They spoke in French. Only a keen ear would have detected the foreign accent in their speech, which was scarcely audible through the hubbub and chattering of the crowd.

The newcomer now said:

"When the hubbub is at its height, and the attention of the entire crowd is concentrated on what goes on in the market place, we must work our way unobserved down this narrow street to the cart, garrotte the troopers in charge of it—driver and two troopers—throw them into the cart and drive away like hell, take first turning on the right and drive straight on after that. The chief will meet us soon after on the road."

"Is that all?" one of the others asked.

"Yes! The chief warns us to pay no heed to what goes on in the market place, however startling it may be."

"I wonder what he is thinking of?"

"Something desperate, I take it."

"God protect him!" sighed one of the men.

"To-day and always," the others echoed simultaneously.

Renaud, evidently both furious with things in general and perplexed as to what he had better do in view of the hostility of the crowd, turned for advice to Gabrielle Damiens.

"What shall I do now, my pigeon?" he asked dolefully.

She was standing by the near front wheel of the diligence giving orders to the corporal left in command of her escort.

"Take the reins yourself," she was saying to the soldier, "and drive as far as Grécourt and wait for me there. I will take the reins after that."

Then only did she condescend to notice the somewhat foolish-looking swain.

"What does my little cabbage wish me to do?" he reiterated meekly.

"Stay here," she replied dryly, "and see that the two brats in the cart are not spirited away from under your nose. With half the population of Mézières standing round gaping at you, you would be a fool and worse to let that happen. In the meanwhile send round to the barracks for a score more soldiers. When you have them here you can make a start just as if nothing had happened."

"But you, my love . . ." Renaud ventured to say.

"I shall stay here till that fool Lescar returns either with that English devil in which case I should like to get a squint at the impudent rascal before Paris claims him, or without him which I imagine will be the case. I shall then ride to Grécourt and pick up the diligence there. And everything," she concluded, "will go on just as I have planned."

The corporal had already obeyed orders, climbed to the box-seat of the diligence and taken up the reins. Gabrielle gave the order: "En avant," and the old vehicle giving a great shake like a frowsy dog wakened from sleep, started on its way with much creaking of wheels and grinding of axles. The escort thundered to right and left of it, their horses; hoofs drawing sparks from the stony ground. The crowd forgetting for the moment to boo at the stranger broke into a cheer and the young ones among them ran across the square in the wake of the cavalcade, until it turned into the main road and was lost to view.

The master sleuth remained standing where he was, looking the picture of indecision and bewilderment. He tried to recapture Gabrielle's attention by amorous glances, but she only gave him a contemptuous shrug, and without another word turned on her heel and went up the perron steps into the Commissariat.

CHAPTER XX

The Courier

Chief Commissary Lescar was in the meantime riding hell for leather at the head of his troop of stalwarts on the hard road which winds its tortuous way between Mézières and Rocroi. The Parc aux Daims lay about midway between the two cities, to the right of this main artery; a narrow way, little more than a lane, led up to its front gate. Lescar communicated itself to the soldiers who saw in this expedition the foundation of their future fortune.

"On! On citizens!" the Chief Commissary had cried out lustily at the start; "we'll have that abominable English spy under lock and key, and out share of ten thousand livres in our pockets before the day is out."

So on the rode, twenty of them, a sufficient number surely of well-equipped soldiers of the Republic to put to rout that elusive and dangerous adventurer the Scarlet Pimpernel. On they rode heedless of their empty stomachs and of the inclemency of the weather. An hour or so went by. The weather had turned bright and frosty and the men were hard put to it to prevent their horses from slipping. At a word of command from Lescar they drew rein to give the wearied beasts a breather.

"We'll be at the Parc long before midday," the Commissary said, wishing to put heart into the men. "There will be at least a hundred livres for each of you if we bring back that Scarlet Pimpernel alive."

A quarter of an hour later they turned into the secondary road which led to the Parc aux Daims. Presently they drew rein once more. The château and the park were in sight.

"Now citizen soldiers," Lescar enjoined the men, "attention! Keep your eyes open! Let nothing escape you. The English spies will be on the alert."

He paused a moment, rose in his stirrups and gazed out in the direction of the

Parc.

"They have taken shelter inside the château," he said. "I don't see anything moving in the garden."

"En avant!" he commanded.

The narrow road was bordered with grass. Covered with frozen snow it deadened the clatter of horses' hoofs. Absolute silence reigned around. Lescar proceeded cautiously. He knew the ground well and avoiding what had been the drive and the main gate he made straight for the broken-down postern in the encircling wall. The men passed through behind him, at foot pace, one by one. The château lay at a distance of some two hundred metres to the left. The Commissary gave the order to dismount and to tether the horses to some tall pine trees which formed a spinney close by. While the men obeyed, he stepped out into the open and took a quick survey of the stretch of parkland before him. The quietude all around disconcerted him. Surely those devilish English spies had not slipped through his fingers after all. He was beginning to wish he had listened to Mam'zelle Guillotine's advice and remained with these good troopers on guard round the aristos. As she rightly said the purpose of the Scarlet Pimpernel was the rescue of the aristos. It always was. Perhaps it was foolish to try and run him to earth. The challenge should come from him.

The silence which reigned in park and château was certainly strange. Alone the breeze which had sprung up in the last few moments made a weird sound as it moaned through the leafless twigs of the old trees and the lifeless foliage of evergreen shrubs. Calling to Sergeant Méridol to accompany him Lescar went down on hands and knees and holding his pistol in his right hand, he crept forward cautiously in the direction of the château, closely followed by the sergeant. The broken unshuttered windows seemed to stare at him like giant eyes. Lifeless yet alert. Had the English spies decamped or were they behind those windows, watching him as he moved soundlessly through the tall grass and tangled undergrowth.

Far be it from me to suggest that Chief Commissary Lescar was in any way afraid; rather was he conscious of a feeling of excitement, as if something stupendous was about to happen, something that would prove to be the turning-point of his whole career. Now he came to a halt and beckoned to the sergeant to do the same. They were within a hundred metres of the château. The perron and wide-open front door were clearly visible. Still not a sound from there.

"Go back and tell the men to come along," Lescar murmured under his breath. "I have a feeling that the English spies are in there and are waiting for us."

He didn't wait for the men but crept along under cover of the shrubbery right up to the perron. Pistol in hand, ready for anything he mounted the short flight of steps and peeped through the front door into the vestibule. Not a sound. No sign of any living soul. He passed through the front door taking stock of his surroundings. He had been inside the château before. Long ago when it was inhabited, and before it had fallen into decay. He was familiar with the two smaller rooms in front of him, with the staircase on the left and, on the right, the door which gave on the largest room in the house where receptions and big dinners were wont to be held.

But all the doors were closed now and Lescar did not feel like pushing any of them open while he was alone in case those English devils were on the other side ready to pounce on any intruder. The next moment, however, his straining ears caught the sound of the troopers approaching. Sergeant Méridol was the first to mount the perron and to step over the threshold. The men soon followed. Cocked pistols in hand they filed in through the front door into the vestibule.

The Chief Commissary indicated the door on the right. The soldiers visibly impressed by the silence and by the aspect of this derelict building seemed none too eager to obey, whereupon Lescar, closely followed by the sergeant, strode to the door and kicked it open. It flew back with a loud cracking and banging, disclosing a sight which caused every man there to gasp with astonishment. The room was large and lofty and must at one time have looked imposing, before the paper on the walls had peeled off in strips and the windows were broken. But it was not the aspect of the room itself that roused the men first to surprise and then to excitement, it was the long table which stretched along it from end to end, a table laden with all sorts of good things, most of them unknown to these poor half-starved soldiers of the Republic: meat, bread, cheese, and what's more, three dozen or more bottles of wine, with corks drawn, all ready for a score of hungry, thirsty men who had been in the saddle for three hours and were half perished with cold and fatigue. In vain did Sergeant Méridol attempt to intervene, in vain did Lescar command, threaten, entreat in the name of the Republic; discipline, never very easily enforced in these days of liberty and equality, was thrown to the winter wind that came in gusts through the broken windows. The men, uttering a portentous cheer, pushing and jostling, tumbling over one another, made helter-skelter for the festive board, seized on slabs of meat and hunks of bread and grabbed the thrice-welcome bottles of wine, which in most cases were emptied almost at a draught. The sergeant, of course, was caught in the vortex. In face of such a marvellous spread, he would have been more than human had he allowed duty to interfere with his enjoyment of it.

As for the Chief Commissary, after he had raged and stormed, after he had threatened sergeant and troopers with exemplary punishment, he realised that he was wasting his breath. The scene before him was like the realisation of a human torrent which nothing on earth had the power to stay. He himself remained dumbfounded, unconscious of hunger, thirst or fatigue, conscious only of a weird sensation of something stupendous and fateful to come. No, no! Things were not as they should be. This mysterious repast laid out by unseen hands in a derelict house savoured of witchcraft or the machinations of a devil. The question was: what devil had engineered and brought about this amazing situation and lured twenty good patriots to such a flagrant dereliction of duty. Lescar turned his head away so as not to gaze any longer on this guzzling, already half-besotted, crowd of men whom he had brought hither to help him come to grips with the most audacious adventurer known. In spite of the cold outside, the large room had become hot and stuffy, the atmosphere reeked of the smell of meat, of hot breaths and the fumes of wine: the weird silence which a while ago had reigned in the empty house had given place to sounds of smacking lips and of working jaws.

Disgusted with sight and sound he made his way to the window and stood gazing out on the wintry landscape, the snow-covered ground, the leafless trees. The whole aspect of this deserted parkland seemed like an emblem of the despondency of his soul. He felt lonely and misunderstood, and suddenly gazing out across the park his eyes became aware of something moving over by the broken-down postern gate. The next moment he was able to distinguish that "something" to be a horse picking its way across the overgrown lawn and through the tangled shrubbery. There were two men in the saddle: one of them a soldier in uniform, the other riding behind him had his arm round his companion's waist. His head drooped over the other's shoulder. He appeared half fainting with exhaustion.

Lescar was out on the perron in a trice. The rider had already drawn rein at the foot of the steps.

"Where are you from?" Lescar called out to him.

"From Mézières, citizen," the soldier replied.

"What news?"

"Citizen Renaud sent me to tell you that all was well. The diligence is well on the way and he himself was thinking of making a start with the other aristos. He doesn't want to wait much longer as he wants to make Grécourt before nightfall. He sent to the barracks for more men. They only could spare half a dozen, but citizen Renaud says that these are quite sufficient."

Lescar made no comment on the news. He was wondering in his mind where his own interests lay in this tangled affair. Should he return to his post in Mézières and let the matter of the Scarlet Pimpernel drift? He certainly didn't feel that he would have much chance against the English spies should they return in numbers, and with most of his troop in a state of intoxication. Or should he stand his ground and with the few men who had remained sober, like this newcomer and Sergeant Méridol, effect the wonderful capture which would mean a fortune and his name inscribed on the golden roll of patriots who had rendered signal service to the Republic? It was a difficult problem to solve. The Chief Commissary remained silently brooding for a minute or two and then bethought himself of the man who had ridden behind the soldier.

"Who are you?" he demanded abruptly.

The man appeared almost exhausted, and at Lescar's peremptory question he gave a start and almost rolled out of the saddle. He would have measured his length on the ground had not Lescar run down the perron steps and caught him ere he fell. He was a youngish man decently dressed, save that his clothes were stained with the dirt and mud of the road.

"Your pardon, citizen," he murmured, "but I have ridden all the way from Paris without drawing rein."

"Who are you?" Lescar reiterated, "and what do you want?"

The man drew a sealed letter from the inner pocket of his coat.

"I am courier in the service of the Committee of Public Safety," he said; "I have orders to deliver this to no one but the Chief Commissary of the Mézières Section himself. My credentials are inside," he added and handed the letter to Lescar who at once broke the seal and quickly unfolded the missive.

"I met the courier outside Mézières," the soldier put in. "He was asking for the Chief Commissary. I thought I had best bring him along with me. And as he—"

But he got no further for he was suddenly interrupted by a cry of horror twice repeated from Citizen Lescar, who in his turn appeared as if he was about to measure his length on the ground. "A horse!" the Chief Commissary exclaimed hoarsely. "I must to Mézières at once."

Without waiting to see if the courier or the soldier followed him he ran across the park as fast as the undergrowth and the weedy grass would allow him in the direction of the spinney where his troopers' horses were tethered.

"Follow me," he cried over his shoulder to the soldier, "and let the courier come too."

The two men were inclined to grumble, but Lescar gave them no time to protest.

"It is a matter of life and death," he shouted as he ran, "and all those louts over in the château are either drugged or drunk."

After a moment's hesitation the soldier thought it best to obey, whilst the courier appeared unwilling to be left alone in this derelict spot. At any rate he climbed slowly and rather painfully back into the saddle, and the wearied mount with its double burden picked its way to the spinney where the Chief Commissary was just getting to horse, looking so scared and so death-like pale that the soldier called out instinctively:

"What has happened, citizen? You look scared to death."

But Lescar who had run on the rough ground nearly all the way from the château was hardly able to speak.

"Get fresh horses both of you . . ." he gasped, "and follow me."

CHAPTER XXI

An Outrage

To gather one's thoughts together, to think at all, was quite out of the question. Lescar's brain was at a standstill, all he could do was to ride, ride on, with hope and despair warring in his mind, despair for the most part gaining the upper hand. He had thrust the letter in the inner pocket of his coat and his hand remained there clutching that fateful missive which, undoubtedly, did mean life or death to him.

The wintry sun was past the meridian now and had begun its downward course to the west. Soon the shades of evening would be drawing in and the market cart with the two female aristos would be driven, Satan alone knew whither. And the unfortunate Commissary rode on at breakneck speed, with just enough sense to avoid the frozen puddles on the road, and to take advantage of any patches of mud where a feeble thaw had set in under the midday sun. The two men followed more leisurely. The were, in fact, some little way behind when the town of Mézières at last came in sight.

Ten minutes later Lescar on ahead had reached the first isolated house of the city; another five and his horse's hoofs were drawing sparks from the stones of the main street. The Market Square could already be perceived through the mist-laden atmosphere. Lescar strained his eyes to see what was going on. There was quite a good crowd there still apparently, hanging about in a desultory fashion. And there was a sprinkling of uniforms to be seen among the throng. In the midst of it all there was Citizen Renaud, who held his white charger by the bridle. Gabrielle Damiens ran down the steps of the Commissariat just then and flung herself into his arms.

Lescar gave a cry of jubilation. All was well.

Renaud had just called out:

"One more kiss, my pigeon, and I go."

Gabrielle threw her arms round his neck. The crowd closed in round them, and forgetting its hostility to the stranger, gave the lovers a loud cheer as they exchanged kiss after kiss.

Another minute and Lescar was across the square. He drew rein so abruptly that his horse reared and snorted and the crowd in dismay scattered in all directions. Gabrielle dragged herself out of her lover's embrace.

"What's all this?" she demanded harshly.

"If it is not the Citizen Commissary," ejaculated a woman in the crowd.

Whereupon Renaud, in the act of mounting his white charger, exclaimed with an oath:

"That cursed fool again!"

"What do you want?" Gabrielle demanded as Lescar dismounted in double-quick time and nearly knocked Mam'zelle over, so close to her did he land.

"Have you got the spy? Where is he?" she went on peremptorily, and the men and women in the crowd questioned him eagerly. "Where is the English spy?"

With a dramatic gesture worthy of the finest classical traditions, Lescar pointed to the man on the white charger and spoke the one word at the top of his voice so that all might hear:

"There!"

Gabrielle shrugged and muttered: "The man is drunk." The whole crowd turned to look on Citizen Renaud, who was evidently of the same opinion as Mam'zelle, for he only shrugged and with a click of the tongue urged his horse to start. With a yell that would have shamed a wild beast in a rage, Lescar threw up his arms and with a vigorous working of his elbows forged his way through the crowd to the very side of Renaud and seized the bridle of the prancing white charger.

"I tell you all," he screamed, in a voice hoarse with excitement, "that if you let this man out of your sight you will be the blackest traitors that ever betrayed your country."

Renaud raised his whip and with it struck the Chief Commissary on the head. An outrage against the chief authority of the town. The population resented it. It had appeared dumbfounded for the moment, but now it rose in its wrath and with many murmurings gathered round their Commissary and the man on the white charger, effectually impeding the latter's movements. It was once again a case of animosity against the stranger and loyalty to one of their own kin. Renaud struck out right and left with his whip.

"Let me pass, you dolts," he cried, while Lescar, who had yelled himself hoarse, tried to recover his breath before starting to yell again.

"En avant!" Renaud shouted to the escort of troopers, who had much ado to keep their horses quiet in the midst of all this turmoil. "This man is mad or drunk."

Gabrielle in the meanwhile had also forged her way to the side of her lover. She came to a halt, facing Lescar with flaming eyes.

"What's all this?" she demanded. "Speak, man, ere I denounce you as the traitor you so freely talk about."

"Don't let this man go," Lescar countered, "and I'll tell you."

"Citizen Renaud stays here," Gabrielle responded firmly. And the sleuth accustomed to obey this masterful woman turned to her, holding his horse in check.

"All right, my pigeon," he murmured, "but it's getting late and I can't waste my time with this fool."

"Never mind about your time, citizen," she retorted dryly. "You stay here, understand? I want to hear what the Chief Commissary has to say, and that's enough. Now then, citizen, speak up."

The crowd gathered more closely round the principal actors in this rather puzzling drama, pressing near to one another in an endeavour to get some warmth into their blood, for it was very cold. The women drew their shawls—if they happened to have any—tightly round their shoulders. The men's noses and hands were blue. Their bare feet in their wooden sabots were nearly frozen. But the situation as it now appeared provided excitement enough to make their discomfort seem unimportant. The Chief Commissary looked to be in a fever of agitation. Mam'zelle Guillotine was obviously puzzled, whilst the stranger was in a towering rage. The young corporal in command of the troopers who formed the escort round the cart tried to push his way through the throng, but it had become so dense and the hostility of the people so marked that he ordered three of the men to join him, whilst the others were told to remain with the cart on the fringe of the crowd, one to hold the reins and the others on guard.

"Speak up, Citizen Commissary," the woman shouted to Lescar, and the men echoed the cry. "Speak up!"

Lescar dived into the pocket of his coat. He drew out the papers which the courier from Paris had brought him. He put on a pompous air and forced himself to speak slowly and steadily.

"The Committee of Public Safety sitting in Paris," he began, "sent me a courier this morning with a letter which was to be delivered into no other hands but mine. Here are his credentials."

He unfolded one of the papers and with a grandiose gesture held it out to Gabrielle, who snatched it out of his hand. She had become, as it were, the spokesman of the assembly. The paper bore the signature of two of the principal members of the Committee of Public Safety and also its official seal. It stated that the bearer was an accredited courier to the Committee and had been entrusted with a private letter addressed to the Chief Commissary of the district of Mézières; the letter to be delivered into his own hands.

"Yes, that's in order," Gabrielle declared. "Where's the courier?"

"Not far behind," the Commissary replied. "I rode along full tilt, he followed more slowly. He'll be here in a few minutes."

While he spoke he unfolded the second communication, and, with a flourish more dramatic than before, handed it to Gabrielle. Now there was no one to equal Gabrielle Damiens for shouting, raging and storming when she was roused, and both Citizen Renaud and the rest of the crowd quite expected one of those violent outbursts from Mam'zelle Guillotine while she ran her eyes down the paper which the Citizen Commissary had given her. But the only sound that came through her lips was a growl like that of a wild cat before it starts to spit and to scratch. The crowd remained breathless. Waiting. Wondering. And suddenly the enraged woman's arms shot out, she threw the paper back into the Commissary's face and then with both hands she seized the man on the white charger by the leg, and had dragged him off his horse before he realized what was happening. Thus taken unawares and entirely helpless, he rolled over and over on the ground. The horse reared, plunged, scattering the bystanders, and the unfortunate man had the greatest difficulty in warding off the more dangerous kicks form its hoofs, until the corporal was able to seize the mettlesome beast by the bridle and to bring it to comparative quiescence. But this didn't prove to be the end of the wretched stranger's troubles, for Gabrielle had got hold of his whip and with it was belabouring him on the head, the back, the shoulders with such fury and such strength that he cried and cried again for mercy. Nor did she desist till the whip broke. She threw it from her and stood with arms akimbo, looking down on her half-conscious victim. The man on whom she had lavished her kisses a few short minutes ago. Her face looked positively evil.

True, the good Artesians were not altogether sorry to see the arrogant stranger thus brought to pain and humiliation, for these were days when the sight of physical and mental suffering was an all to familiar one; the tumbrils and the guillotine made it an almost daily spectacle for young and old, and even for children. They looked on it as a part of this life's routine, as a distraction from the monotony of weary, idle hours. But in this case the expression on Mam'zelle's face was almost terrifying.

There was contempt as well as rage in her eyes and the strong vein of cruelty never wholly absent from her mien. They were all of them dumbfounded, even the Chief Commissary had lost his pompous air, and his excitement appeared to have calmed down. He and Gabrielle, the stranger on the ground, the corporal on horseback holding the white charger by the bridle and the three troopers, formed a compact group, round which the throng now stood in a wide circle, eager, expectant, awed into silence. But the silence did not last long. Presently there rose a murmur. It began with the women whispering to one another:

"What has he done?"

"Is he really the English spy?"

"The Scarlet Pimpernel?"

"No, impossible!"

"The Commissary said so."

"He denounced him."

"But how did he know?"

And the murmur was taken up by the men, until there was a hum like a swarm of hornets which filled the market.

"Is he the English spy?"

"How do they know?"

For somehow the stranger, much as they mistrusted him, did not answer to their conception of what the mysterious Scarlet Pimpernel was like. He was tall, but should have been taller still, of Titanic proportions, like the legendary giants: he should have looked less human, more like the supernatural being of the nether world.

"He is not the Scarlet Pimpernel," some of the women asserted boldly.

"I don't believe it," the men said.

Gabrielle turned her glowering eyes on the Chief Commissary.

"Tell them," she commanded, "what is written in that letter."

Lescar smoothed out the crumpled paper which Gabrielle had thrown in his face.

"Attention!" he cried loudly, and then went on:

"This letter comes to me from Citizen Renaud . . ."

"Citizen Renaud?" they exclaimed. "But the letter came by courier from Paris, then how—?"

He then began to read:

"Citizen Chief Commissary of the Section of Mézières in the Province of Artois.

"This is to warn you that there is an English spy known to his followers as the Scarlet Pimpernel, who has been impersonating me these few days past. I have reasons to believe that his latest activities have been directed in your province. So, be on the look-out. I have been detained in Paris, but will be in Mézières within the next twenty-four hours. The Committee of Public Safety here in Paris is sending its special courier to you for me, to bring you this urgent letter.

"And," the Chief Commissary added, "the letter is signed André Renaud, and bears the seal and stamp, as well as two signatures of members of the Committee of Public Safety in Paris."

The unfortunate man, still lying in his semi-unconsciousness on the ground, had made desperate efforts to regain his senses. He struggled and wriggled his bruised body about until he was able to prop himself up on his elbow. Looking up at his tormentor with an expression of hatred at least as intense as her own: "You'll pay for this, Mam'zelle Guillotine," he contrived to murmur between his teeth and then turned his glance on the Chief Commissary, who was in the act of folding up the momentous papers and thrusting them back into his pocket. The expression of hatred in the stricken man's eyes lingered there also for a few seconds, but soon changed to contempt as he broke into a forced, immoderate laughter. But this hilarity was short-lived. The next moment the crowd had suddenly, if somewhat tardily, realised the full significance of the one horrible fact, namely that this man, this intruding, arrogant stranger, was none other than the far-famed Scarlet Pimpernel, the most dangerous enemy of France, who had devised the abominable trick of impersonating a servant of the Republic in order to save a batch of female traitors from the punishment their crimes deserved. The fact that it was this same man who had brought about the arrest of the ci-devant Marquise de Saint-Lucque was lost sight of for the moment. What was remembered was the dramatic gesture of the Chief Commissary pointing to this man when he was asked: "Where is the English spy?" and his voice answering loudly so that all might hear: "There!"

The angry murmurings of the crowd turned to threats of violence.

"The Scarlet Pimpernel! That abominable English spy! That's what this man was all the time, and we never guessed."

"Mam'zelle Guillotine!" one of the women shouted, "you'll know what to do."

The man on the ground realised the danger he was in. Three or four violent kicks had already been dealt to him.

The corporal ordered the troopers to close in round him to protect him from further assaults from the crowd. This audacious English spy was food for the guillotine, not for the mere sadistic entertainment of a lot of provincial louts. They did their best to ward off the kicks and blows that were freely aimed at the prostrate form of the stranger.

Whether it was a sudden inspiration or merely the powerful instinct of self-preservation, who can tell? Certain it is that when matters appeared at their blackest, when the troopers seemed unable to cope any longer with the crowd which had become very violent, the stranger, whoever he was, succeeded in regaining his feet. He looked to right and left of him and over the heads of the multitude and uttered a long-sustained cry of horror and affright.

"The cart," he exclaimed, "where is it?"

Where, indeed? The crowd parted, gazed in direction of the street corner to which the stranger pointed with quaking hand.

"The cart!" the latter reiterated, choking with emotion, whilst men and women vainly tried to switch off their minds from one horrible fact to another, from the personality of one man, his duplicity, his shameless impersonation, their own wrath and desire to punish, to the outrageous trick played upon them by one whose identity could not be in doubt for one moment. For the cart had gone. Vanished with the troopers and their horses. While the attention of the crowd had been drawn to the stranger and his presumed misdeeds, the female aristos had been spirited away from under their nose. The cart had been driven away under cover of the uproar and the gathering mist which enveloped the narrow street. A couple of troopers had been left in charge of it when the others with their corporal were called to protect the stranger from further assaults from the irate and unruly crowd. Their horses had vanished with them, whilst a third trooper who had been holding the reins had also disappeared. When did this outrage happen? Whither had all those men gone? Who could tell? And what in Satan's name had become of the cart and horses?

Both Gabrielle and the Commissary had remained tongue-tied at first, rigid as granite statues; the expression on the Commissary's face was at first one of incredulity, then of bewilderment and finally of horror. But Gabrielle's face remained expressionless, her face became the colour of ashes, it looked like the face of the dead. She never moved, not even when the Commissary gave a loud command to the troopers.

"After them, citizens, they cannot have gone far."

The corporal and the troopers jerked their horses' heads round and set spurs to their flanks, scattering the crowd in all directions. Men and women took up the cry: "They cannot have gone far," and swarmed all over the market place, rushing blindly, aimlessly, hither and thither, shouting confused suggestions to the bewildered soldiers.

"This way, citizen!"

"No, that!"

"This is the short cut to Grécourt."

"They'd avoid that."

"Try the road to Labat."

The way into the side street and that street itself were soon nothing but scenes of the wildest confusion in which men and women effectively obstructed all possibility of pursuit.

"This way, citizen!"

"No, that!"

And so on, while confusion was made more confounded at every moment. There were at least half a dozen ways which led from the centre of the town to anywhere. It was getting late in the afternoon. Evening began to draw in. Soon a misty sleet mixed with snow began to fall and it was difficult to distinguish anything beyond a fraction of a league ahead, past the city lights.

It was all very well to keep on shouting and urging: "They cannot have gone far." That might be true enough but the question was: "In which direction?"

There were only three troopers, besides their corporal, and the Chief Commissary who were mounted, and they might possibly have overtaken the cart even though it was being driven at breakneck speed. The corporal and one of the troopers went in one direction, the others followed the Commissary while the young men in the crowd ran down the various narrow streets which gave all round the Market Square. And with it all there was rush and uproar and enough shouting, clatter of horses' hoofs and of wooden shoes on the pavement stones, as to give any fugitive all the warning required for a good get-away.

CHAPTER XXII

Nightmare

Gabrielle, after those few minutes of stone-like stupefaction, had pulled herself forcefully together. Hers was not a nature to allow herself to be cowed by any man or any event. In spite of the humiliation which she had endured and the many ups and downs of exultation and of horror through which she had passed during this fateful day, she was still Mam'zelle Guillotine, whose commands were law in the Province of Artois, and at whose words the fiercest Terrorists up in Paris were wont to tremble. Renaud, the sleuth, the arrogant stranger on whom she had lavished her kisses a short hour ago, and to whom she had administered such degrading punishment, was standing there, by the white charger, with one hand on the bridle, and was making serious efforts to shake off the feeling of giddiness caused by the heavy blows on his head. They stood isolated now, these two, in front of the Commissariat, the whole crowd having melted away, scattered like leaves before the wind. Gabrielle turned a glance of withering contempt on her former suitor and when she saw that he was preparing to mount, she just seized him by the arm with a grip that was like a vice and thrust him out of her way with such violence that he nearly came down again on his knees. Another contemptuous glance, a shrug, and it was she who had mounted the white charger.

"You stay where you are!" she commanded, "While I try to undo the mischief you have done."

With a click of the tongue she set the horse to walk across the square.

Renaud shouted after her, his voice choked with hatred unspeakable.

"The mischief I have done? You devil incarnate, you shall pay for this. Mark my words."

Whether she heard him or not is difficult to say. Certain it is that she put her horse to the trot without once turning to him. Straight ahead she rode across the square until she turned into the Grécourt road.

It was still snowing, but overhead the clouds were thin and from behind them the wan light of the moon shed a faint, greyish aura over the frozen landscape. Gabrielle knew every inch of the road and with unerring hand and eyes guided her mount. At first she overtook one or two detachments of voluntary search-parties who with much shouting and any amount of voluble talk were still patrolling the road, hopeful of coming up with the cart, which "could not have gone far." They cheered Gabrielle as she went by.

Once past the foremost of these enthusiasts she put her horse to a walk. Her eyes keen as those of a hawk pierced the darkness to right and left of her. She had the feeling that it would be on this road that she would come across some trace of that audacious Scarlet Pimpernel. All around her the stillness could almost be felt. The snow fell in large soft flakes. Not a breath of air stirred the leafless branches of the tall poplars that bordered the road, and Gabrielle's keen ears could not detect the slightest sound of distant wheels or horse's trot. It was only half an hour later that the white charger suddenly shied at a black, shapeless mass which lay by the roadside.

Gabrielle dismounted and holding the horse by the bridle went up to the black mass which had frightened it. Two men, wearing the uniforms of the 61st regiment, were lying half in and half out of the ditch. They were tied to one another with cord, and a woolen scarf was wound round the lower part of their faces. The snow lay over them like a thin, white blanket. As Gabrielle approached them, they made a combined vigorous effort to utter a cry of distress, but it was only a faint gurgle that reached her ears. She threw the reins over her arm and with strong capable hands she released the men of their bonds, and unwound the scarf from round their mouths. Their teeth were chattering and their arms and legs were trembling with the cold. She pulled one man up by his coat collar and then the other, but never uttered a word till she had them both in a sitting posture.

Once this was accomplished her peremptory questions came out sharp and clear.

"What happened?"

"It was while you were hitting out at the English spy," one of the men contrived to reply.

"The English spy?"

"Yes! We thought he was the man sent down here to track the aristos. And he turned out to be that abominable Scarlet Pimpernel."

"Then what happened?"

"We could not help watching," and even through his chattering teeth the soldier gave a chuckle. "It was such a fine sight seeing you belabouring that spy."

"I stood on the front board," added the trooper who had been holding the reins. "The better to see you. Name of a dog, I wouldn't have been in his shoes for a pension."

"And the kisses you had been giving him . . ."

But Gabrielle was not in a mood to listen to any bantering. "Didn't you hear me ask what happened?" she demanded harshly.

"Just this, citizeness," one of the troopers gave reply, the one who was best able to speak; "when the whole crowd in the square was yelling itself hoarse with laughter and when excitement was at its height, my comrade and I were suddenly seized by the leg, dragged off our horses, struck on the head, and rolled over on the ground. We were gagged and bound and thrown into the cart before we could utter a sound."

"The same thing happened to me," said the other. "I held the reins, and I was standing on the front board watching you flourishing that whip, when I was seized by the legs and dragged down from the board. I too was gagged and bound and thrown into the cart, and as I had struck my head heavily against the wheel, I was too dizzy to offer any resistance."

"You were driven away in the cart?"

"Then and there, citizeness."

"Where is the cart now?"

"I don't know, citizeness. But it must be somewhere near here. I just heard it come to a halt and the horses gallop away before I half lost consciousness."

"The horses?"

"Yes! They were taken out of the shafts. I could hear that. It was not far from here."

"Where is your other comrade?"

"I don't know, citizeness. He was with us in the cart. Perhaps he is still there now."

"Anyone else but you three dolts in the cart?"

"Yes! Two brats. And there were others, I think, but I could not see," the soldier gave answer.

"Nor I," echoed the other.

"How many English spies were there?" Gabrielle asked again.

"I couldn't tell exactly, citizeness. There must have been at least a dozen. They fell on us like a swarm of hornets."

"And that's a lie," Gabrielle asserted dryly. "A dozen? I don't believe there were more than two or three—-And perhaps only one," she added slowly.

"I give you my word, citizeness—"

"Hold your tongue. You were nothing but a set of traitors and cowards."

"And that is unfair, citizeness. What could we do? When the cart stopped we were dragged out and thrown down in this ditch and left to perish of cold for all those devils knew. Wasn't that so, comrade?"

There was a grunt of assent, and Gabrielle queried again:

"Where is the cart now?"

"I don't know, citizeness."

To Gabrielle Damiens the whole of this story told jerkily by men whose lips were shaking with cold, was like a nightmare from which she would presently wake and find that nothing of it was real, that all of it was only a hideous phantasmagoria brought before her mind by mischievous emissaries of Satan and sent by him to worry and exasperate her. That she, the strong-minded Amazon, the lion-hearted wielder of the sword of justice, the indomitable scorner of men should thus have been cozened, baffled, bamboozled like any groundling or village dolt was inconceivable. It was maddening and for a time she felt as if her wits had deserted her and she remained crouching there in the ditch beside those two soldiers, with an expression in her face which, but for the darkness, would have been terrifying.

The men never moved. They were sore in limb and their bodies were almost inert. After a time Gabrielle appeared to gather her wits together again. She struggled to her feet, paid no heed to the soldiers, never spoke another word to them. She stood there with the horse's reins swung over her arm, she, more solidly dark than the surrounding darkness, and the white charger beside her like a ghost. Her eyes tried to pierce the veil of snow, searching the gloom for an outline of the cart. The men watched her when presently she mounted and threw herself astride into the saddle. They went on watching as she turned her horse's head back towards Mézières, put him to the trot and was soon engulfed in the night. After which they in their turn struggled to their feet and walked slowly back in the direction of the city.

They walked on in silence at first, stamping their feet and swinging their arms across their chest striving to get the blood back into their frozen limbs. At first and until the sound of the white charger's hoofs died away in the distance down the road.

Had Gabrielle Damiens been endowed with super-human senses, she would have been lost in wonderment, for as soon as the stillness of the night became so absolute that it seemed almost palpable, it was broken by a sound which, in this lonely bit of country, roused the barn-door owl from its nightly contemplation and disturbed the prowling cat in its chase after little birds.

"By George!" a voice suddenly broke forth through the gloom in a language Mam'zelle Guillotine would not have understood, had she heard; "I'm positively frozen stiff."

And another voice then echoed: "I've never been so cold in all my life."

"Got your flask handy, Glynde?"

The other fumbled into his inside pocket and handed a flask to his friend.

"No, you go first," the latter said.

Both had a good pull at the flask.

"I hope we get horses at the Ecu d'Or."

"The chief said we were certain to. It is a posting-inn, you know. Stage-coaches get their relay there."

"Yes, I know. And with all this turmoil going on . . ."

The other man shrugged.

"Well! If we can't get horses we'll have to walk. It is not far and I know the way."

"The walk will do us good," his friend commented with easy philosophy.

"When I think what the chief has put up with . . ."

One of the men who spoke was Sir Philip Glynde, the owner of Glynde Towers, one of the show places in East Anglia, with its famous racing stables, its show gardens and hot-houses. The other was Viscount St. Dennys, one of the richest men in England, who had been equerry to the Prince of Wales till he gave up that position and all the pleasures attached to it, in order to follow his chief in the path of obedience and self-sacrifice. Accustomed to every luxury that the possession of a large fortune can procure, sybarites both, they talked quite gaily of a tramp in the night across country with an icy wind driving snow and sleet into their faces, just as they had endured with equal gaiety and as a matter of course, lying flat on hard frozen ground for over an hour with teeth chattering and limbs growing stiff with cold and the pressure of ropes around their body.

On ahead a bright light glinted through the gloom.

"There's the Ecu d'Or," Glynde remarked.

"Now for a mug of mulled wine," the other rejoined.

"If we get it the Lord be praised."

"If we don't may the devil take the landlord and his ugly wife."

On they tramped after that in silence till they came to the posting-inn into which they turned and made straight for the coffee-room.

There was mulled wine made hot for the asking and the payment thereof, and there were a couple of horses to be had also, old nags but serviceable, anyway. Glynde gave a deep sigh when the obsequious landlord closed his grasping hand over the pieces of gold which St. Dennys had pressed into it.

"I almost wish the brute had not got us everything we wanted," he said ruefully. "The thought of Blakeney at this moment sickens me."

St. Dennys agreed with him, but said more lightly:

"We've obeyed orders. Thank God we were able to do that. I was dreadfully sorry for those kids."

"And there's the poor mother still knocking about somewhere."

"How in Heaven's name will the chief get her away?"

They drank the hot wine while the two nags, which they had been forced to purchase at a preposterous price, were being saddled. Soon they got to horse and rode away, into the night.

"What did they give thee?" the woman asked her husband, while he busied himself putting up the shutters in the house and barring the door.

"Five louis," he replied curtly.

"They are either mad," the wife retorted, "or else English spies; else they wouldn't have parted with all that money."

"It matters not what they are," the man rejoined with a shrug. "Their money is good anyway."

Book Four

CHAPTER XXIII

A Message

All these exciting events just described are put on record in the archives of the city of Mézières: the arrival of the master sleuth from Paris, the arrest of the ci-devant Marquise de Saint-Lucque and her two children, and the preposterous accusation brought against the envoy of the Committee of Public Safety by Citizen Chief Commissary Lescar and the turmoil that ensued in consequence.

It is also on record that three days before this last event the stage-coach which plies fortnightly between Barlemont in Belgium and Paris, came to its habitual halt at the Ecu d'Or, the posting-inn on the outskirts of Mézières. On this occasion it brought its usual complement of travellers who were made to alight in order to have their passports examined and their identity scrutinised. There were not many strangers among the small crowd that tumbled helter-skelter out of the lumbering vehicle which had brought them jogging along the hard frozen road from the other side of the Franco-Belgian frontier, and nearly shaken their souls out of their bodies during four hours of this very trying journey. Half a dozen passengers were allowed to pass immediately through the barrier where the examination took place, and filed into what was still called the coffee-room, though no coffee was ever dispensed there these days. Only mugs of sour wine which was made hot if it was specially paid for, and if the landlord and his wife happened to be in an amiable mood. This privileged half-dozen hungry and thirsty travellers were French citizens, farmers or shopkeepers who traded regularly with Belgium, crossing the frontier backwards and forwards, and personally known to the police. The others, they were Belgians of Dutch for the most part, were kept waiting, standing out in the cold where innumerable questions were put to them, their papers taken away from them and brought back again, and countless other vexations put upon them till one of them, a woman, collapsed, fainting with hunger and cold and had to be carried indoors by her fellow sufferers. These were two men and another woman, all obviously foreigners. One of the men, a stocky little fellow, was described on his passport as of Dutch nationality, native of Batavia, and skipper of the cargo ship Van Tromp of the Netherlands line. He had landed in Antwerp with a load of coffee, part of which was destined for a wholesale house in Paris. His papers were all in order. They had been signed by the Dutch governor of Batavia and countersigned in Antwerp by Citizen Duvernay, representing the revolutionary government of France in the port of Antwerp. Nothing could be more clear or above board, but the police inspector in charge of the revision of foreign passports in the district was inexperienced and officious. He gave himself airs of authority which annoyed the Dutch skipper who became very truculent, heaped curses and abuse on the young officer and was with difficulty restrained from coming to blows with him.

His fellow travellers, a man and a woman, did their best to soothe the ruffled feelings of the irate Dutchman.

"Do, I pray you, intervene," the woman said to her companion, "we shall never get away while this row is going on."

They had each their passports and other papers in one hand, and each carried a small valise. The man thrust the papers without more ado under the young officer's nose.

"If you could get us through quickly, citizen," he said ingratiatingly, "we would be greatly beholden to you. My friend is cold and hungry. We would like to get food and drink and beds for a night or two before we proceed on our way. We are American citizens," he went on, "and our papers are entirely in order."

With this he insinuated a handful of silver coins into the officer's hand, whose manner at once underwent a change: his hand closed over the money and thrust inside his tunic, after which he took the American's papers and made a show of scrutinising them carefully.

Passports and papers were undoubtedly in order. They were signed by Mr. John Adams, the first United States ambassador accredited to England. Possibly, the officer of Mézières knew nothing at all of Mr. John Adams, and very little of the United States of America, but he knew all about Citizen Jean Lambert Tallien and Citizen Barras, two of the most prominent members of the Convention, who had countersigned the passports. The woman was described thereon as Madeleine St. Just and the man as Honoré St. Just her brother, both citizens of the United States, come to Europe in order to visit their cousin Louis St. Just, the friend and intimate of Maximilien Robespierre himself, names indeed to conjure with.

The police officer's manner became almost abject. Completely ignoring the truculent Dutchman and his imperious demands, he stamped passports and papers without further demur, did not order the valises to be opened for examination, and even went to the length of escorting these highly-connected foreigners as far as the inn and recommended them to the special care and attention of the landlord and his ill-favoured wife, with a whispered hint of the financial benefit that would be derived from such attention. The landlord took the hint and forgetting his status of free citizen of the Republic of France, and its laws of Equality for all, became almost servile in his desire to provide his guests with everything they desired.

However, they did not want much seemingly, only a couple of rooms with a clean bed for two or three nights, and for the moment just a quiet corner where they could sit and eat in peace. There was a lot of: "This way, citizeness," from the landlord, and: "The coffee-room is crowded, you will be better here," as he ushered the travellers into a small parlour adjoining the larger room and summoned his wife to lay the table and bring along the best food the Ecu d'Or could muster.

Marguerite Blakeney sank on to the hard horse-hair sofa, and drew a long sigh of relief. She gathered her cape closely round her and gave a little shiver.

"You are cold, Lady Blakeney," her companion said with obvious concern.

There was an iron stove in a corner of the room. A fire of logs was roaring up the chimney. Marguerite held her hands to the blaze.

"And very tired, I am afraid," the man continued; "it has been such a long journey."

"It was not so bad at first," she commented softly, "while Percy was with us."

And her eyes seemed to search the flames as if seeking in them a picture of the face and form she loved. They had only just parted. And no journey, however trying, could be hard to bear while Percy was there with her.

After a moment or two she spoke: "Sir Andrew!"

"Yes?"

"Do you think we shall see Percy again to-day?"

"I don't know, Lady Blakeney . . ." Ffoulkes replied, paused a moment or two and then added: "I am afraid not."

"He only left you the one message, didn't he?"

"That's all. He slipped the note into my hand when he got off the coach at Bouillon and whispered the two words: 'For her.'"

Sir Andrew took a crumpled paper from his pocket, gave it to Marguerite. Her hand closed on it.

"You have seen yours?" she asked.

"Yes!"

"What does it say?"

"Only one word: Wait."

"Not much, is it?" Marguerite commented with a fleeting little smile.

"I suppose Tony has gone by now," she added.

"I'll go and see, shall I?"

"Please do."

"You'll be all right here, won't you?" Sir Andrew asked anxiously.

"Of course I will. Don't worry about me. Our friend the landlord and his grim-faced wife have scented a bribe and are as amiable as you could wish."

He picked up his hat and went out of the room.

After he had gone Marguerite sat for a while with that crumpled paper in her hand. It was early afternoon, but the narrow room with its dingy rep curtains and windows veiled in dust was already wrapped in gloom. Only the red glow from the iron stove shed a warm light on Marguerite's hand and the paper which she held. A confused murmur of voices came from the crowded coffee-room next door. Presently a woman came in carrying a lighted lamp which she set upon the table. She certainly was grim-faced and surly, and looked askance at Marguerite who paid no attention to her.

"I have some soup," she said curtly; "it is hot. Would you like some?"

Marguerite said "Yes!" thinking more of Sir Andrew than of herself.

"There are also potatoes cooked in lard," the woman went on, "and a small piece of pork. You had better have that too as there's nothing else."

She did not wait for a reply, and stumped out of the room.

As soon as she had gone, Marguerite smoothed out the paper which contained

Percy's last message to her. She swallowed the tears which dimmed her eyes and pressed her lips against the paper whereon his dear hand had rested.

And this is what she read:

"On my knees do I beg your forgiveness, my beloved, for the discomfort and suffering you are enduring now. Would I had had the heart not to listen when you said to me: 'If you go, I go with you.' Your eyes, your lips, your lovely arms held me in bonds that no man living should have dared to sever. 'If you love me, do not go,' you entreated, and your exquisite voice broke in an agony of tears. Yet I, like a madman, thought only of two little children who would need a woman's care, and thought more of them and their helpless mother, thought more of an ideal, of my duty and mine honour and of my solemn pledge to Saint-Lucque, more of all that than I did of you. 'If you love me,' you begged, 'do not go.' If I loved you! I love you with my whole soul, with every fibre of my being, more than life and eternity, but I could not love you, dear, so much, loved I not honour more. With the help of my faithful lieutenants I will bring those defenceless women safely to England according to my pledged word, then my arms will close again around you and you will feel my whole soul in a kiss."

His whole soul! his wonderful, self-denying, high-minded soul. That last day in London, how vividly did she recall it now, the rout at the Duchesse de Roncevaux's mansion. The Abbé Prud'hon's tribute to the heroism of her beloved, the intimate talk with the Prince of Wales, and those few brief moments in the library when she made her last desperate appeal to him in the name of love, and felt that appeal was useless and that love stood vanquished before the inner instinct of the sportsman-adventurer, the selfless humanitarian, the knight-errant who had heard the call of the innocent and the weak.

This occurred three days ago. Since then Marguerite Blakeney and Sir Andrew Ffoulkes had obeyed Percy's laconic instructions and waited. Whether they were in danger or not, they neither knew nor cared. Certainly not, declared Marguerite, for Percy was of a surety watching over them. They were objects of special care from the landlord and his wife, who took the money so lavishly poured into their hands and in exchange did their best to secure the privacy of these American guests, and to give them clean beds and as good food as the state of the country allowed. Citizens of the great American Republic for whom the great patriot General Lafayette had fought, were popular in France, and the name of St. Just was also one to conjure with. And they still waited in patience and in fortitude on this third day after their arrival, while the most exciting incidents the city of Mézières had ever known were occurring in the market place, while Mam'zelle Guillotine belaboured her unfortunate swain with his riding-whip, while the hooded cart with the Saint-Lucque children was spirited away and their mother endured soul-racking agony inside the diligence that was taking her off to Paris. Marguerite and Sir Andrew Ffoulkes heard vague rumours that something unusual was going on in the city. Sound of many voices raised in shrill staccato reached their ears, while they were sitting in the parlour waiting for their meagre supper. People seemed to be passing in and out of the front door all the time and the door of the coffee-room kept on banging constantly.

When the woman brought in the supper she appeared less surly than usual. Seemed actually inclined to talk. Her eyes were quite bright and her cheeks flushed. Marguerite ventured to question her.

"Has anything special happened, citizeness? There seems to be such excitement about."

The woman grunted and shrugged.

"Excitement!" she exclaimed. "I should think there was excitement and to spare. They say that the English spy has been captured. The man they have been hunting for for years."

Marguerite's self-control at this moment was super-human. She did not gasp or catch her breath. She never moved. It was Sir Andrew who spoke.

"Oh! I have heard about him. Even in the United States of America people talk about a mystic personage who goes by the name of the Scarlet Pimpernel. I don't know what he is supposed to do. And have they really got him?"

The woman gave another shrug and a short, harsh laugh.

"Not they," she said. "Our people are fools. It seems they collared the wrong man."

"The wrong man?"

"Well, some people said he was the right man and some that he was the wrong one. But what everyone in Mézières knows by now is that the two aristos who should have been taken to Paris to be guillotined—two little traitors, what?—were spirited away under the very nose of Citizeness Damiens, the public executioner. It seems she is mad with rage and the whole town is in a state of terror, wondering on whom she will vent her fury."

Marguerite really was wonderful. How she kept motionless and outwardly calm while she heard the woman actually stating the fact that Percy had been captured is one of the secrets of her intrepid nature. Sir Andrew remained standing close beside her, with one hand on her shoulder. She put up hers and their two hands met in a pressure of reassurance and of comfort.

As soon as the woman had gone Sir Andrew said:

"I don't believe for a moment that anything has happened to Percy. You don't either, do you, Lady Blakeney?"

"No," she replied simply, "I do not."

"But with your permission I'll go and ascertain just what did occur to give rise to the rumour. I might hear something. Shall I go?"

"Do."

"Promise me you won't fret," he urged.

She looked up at him with a wan little smile.

"I promise," she said.

"I won't be long," were his final words before he went out.

He was back half an hour later.

"I've seen Tony," were the first words he spoke as soon as he had closed the door behind him.

"Tony!" Marguerite exclaimed.

She was still sitting by the fire which now was burning low. Ffoulkes put some logs on while he continued.

"I met him a few moments ago. He was coming this way and will meet us on the Grécourt road. He gave me a scribbled note from Percy."

He took the note from his waistcoat pocket and read out its contents by the light of the lamp.

"The Saint-Lucque children are quite safe. I am taking them to a place I know of called Saint Félix. It is a derelict village this side of Grécourt, slightly off the road on the right. You can't miss it. I want you to meet me there. Your landlord at the Ecu d'Or has a cabriolet and a good horse, which you can either hire or purchase outright. Steal it if you must, bring plenty of provisions and drive hell-for-leather."

Ffoulkes thrust the paper into the stove. Marguerite watched it burn.

"Thank God!" she said, "he is safe. And there is at last something for us to do."

"We had better pretend to eat some of this supper," Sir Andrew rejoined, "and then talk about the cabriolet."

They sat down and tried to swallow a morsel. Marguerite asked:

"Did Tony say anything about the Saint-Lucque children?"

"Yes ye did. He was in it all. But he couldn't say much as it would have been dangerous with so many people about."

"But what about Sir Philip Glynde and my Lord St. Dennys?"

Sir Andrew gave a short laugh. Quite a merry one.

"They are having a very hard time, poor devils," he said lightly.

"What do you mean?"

"Tony had been busy trussing them up like a pair of capons and left them lying in a near-by field, getting frozen and cramped like the very devil."

"Great heavens!"

"Oh, they are quite happy, Lady Blakeney. Do not fret about them. The chief's orders, you know. We'd all go to hell for him, if he ordered us to go."

Marguerite made no reply to this. How could she? Ffoulkes, the loyal lieutenant, had spoken and voiced the feelings of eighteen others as true and brave as himself. She could only wonder within the depths of her soul at the marvellous magnetism exercised by the one man who had made her so infinitely proud and happy in his love.

They sat at the table a few minutes longer. The white-faced clock up on the wall struck five. The shades of evening were rapidly drawing it. Ffoulkes rose and went in search of the landlord. The question of hiring a vehicle of some sort was then broached.

"We want to get to Grécourt before nightfall," Ffoulkes explained to the man.

"My aunt, the citizeness St. Just, the mother of the great patriot my cousin, has been expecting us the last two days. We had not intended to stay here so long, but my sister was tired after the journey and we were very comfortable in your house."

A preposterous price was, of course, asked for the purchase, not the hire, of an old-fashioned cabriolet, an equally aged horse and a basket of provisions, such as could be got. The landlord made pretence of being suspicious, talked of police and of taking risks by aiding strangers to wander about the country without special permits. Such risks and suspicious were naturally to be paid for along with the horse and the cabriolet.

In the end the sight of half a dozen louis set all patriotic scruples at rest. The cabriolet was brought round. Sir Andrew Ffoulkes took the reins whilst Marguerite, wrapped in shawl and mantle, snuggled in the corner of the carriage under the hood.

On the road to Saint Félix, they met Lord Anthony Dewhurst, one of the most elegant fops known in the society of London and Bath. He was clothed in the promiscuous bits of uniform, tattered tunic and shoes down at heels, his nose was blue and his fingers stiff. Sir Andrew drew rein and Tony scrambled into the cabriolet by the side of Marguerite.

"What is Percy going to do about Madame de Saint-Lucque," she murmured enquiringly, more to herself than to him.

"God and he alone know," Tony replied, then he added: "It is the devil, the children being separated from their mother. It means two tasks instead of one."

"But he'll do it," murmured Ffoulkes fervently.

"No doubt about that," Tony echoed under his breath.

CHAPTER XXIV

The Cosy Corner

The Parc aux Daims is not by any means the only derelict homestead in Artois. The province, owing to its proximity to the capital, had already suffered much even in the early days of the revolution when inflammatory speeches delivered outside and inside of every cabaret by agents of the government had provoked a half-starved peasantry into acts of brigandage and loot. And not only were these acts directed against landlords and so-called aristos, but more often than not well-to-do farmers and peasant proprietors even in a small way, were faced with the fury of an enraged populace and saw their homesteads invaded and destroyed, even though some of their most virulent attackers had been their equals and friends in the past.

Thus it was with the once prosperous village of Saint Félix, distant a couple of leagues from Mézières and less than half a league off the Grécourt main road. In this year of grace and fraternity—that is 1794—it was nothing but a conglomeration of derelict cottages and a jumble of stones, broken-down walls and charred remains of roofs, doors and window-frames. The tower of the little church had partially collapsed. It was leaning over at an acute angle with great fissures in its sides, its pointed roof with great gaps open to rain and snow, showed glimpses of its cracked bell, now for ever mute. What had been the presbytery beside it had been burnt down to the ground.

Close to the presbytery there had once stood a substantially built wayside inn with stables and outhouses. Its sign was Le bon petit Coin (The Cosy Corner), and had been the property of a worthy Artesian who had drawn home-brewed ale, tapped casks of local wine and led a God-fearing life with his wife and family until a rabble led by paid agitators from Paris had raided his house, set fire to it and destroyed all his belongings till nothing but the crumbling walls remained of what had been a prosperous business place and a happy homestead. The innkeeper and his family drifted away, no one knew or cared whither they went, or what became of them, nor is it the purpose of this chronicle to follow up their traces. Enough that crumbling walls and broken roof of the house withstood the ravages of autumn gales, of winter snow and hail-storms better than the rest of the village had done, and that as a freakish chance would have it, the sign Le bon petit Coin still dangled engagingly on its posts. But no one ever went there. No traveller ever entered its inhospitable doors.

"The Cosy Corner"? It was anything but cosy on this bleak February evening when a hooded cart drawn by a couple of horses came to a halt beneath its creaking signpost. The man who had been driving it threw down the reins and jumped down from the cart. At the back, under the hood, there were two bundles wrapped in thick blankets. Live bundles, through the thick folds of which came the sound of whimpering and little human cries: "Maman?" The man went round to the back of the cart. With infinite precaution he took up the bundles and carried them into the derelict house. Through one room, which had obviously been the public bar once, he carried the two bundles one by one, and thence into an inner room, wherein, as there was no furniture whatever, he deposited them with tender care on the wooden floor. He saw to it that the blankets covered the small human forms efficiently against the cold, and listened for a moment or two to the pathetic cries of "Maman." He then took a bottle out of the pocket of his big coat. It contained milk. Perhaps there was even a tiny, very tiny drop of brandy in the milk.

"That will comfort you, you poor kids," he murmured to himself, and insinuated the bottle into the small human mouths. There was some spluttering, but swallowing also. The man gave a quaint little chuckle. "I ought to have been a nursemaid!" he went on murmuring to himself. He waited for a few moments longer, until gradually the cries of "Maman" became more rare, and the two bundles of blankets no longer betrayed any movement through their folds. He went out of the room and gave himself a good stretch. "Sink me!" he muttered, "but I'm stiff. I never thought a woman could hit so hard."

He went back to the cart and peeped down under the hood. It was still snowing, but the evening had not yet fully drawn in, and he could perceive the forms of three men lying on their sides across the floor of the cart. They were trussed up with cords, and their knees were drawn up to the middle of their chests. Their coats were wrapped round their legs and shoulders, and scarves were wound round their mouths and chins.

"Well," the man muttered again, "you can't come to much harm like that, my friends, and cannot do much mischief either." He tied up the horses to the ring in the wall, picked up an untidy bundle of something soft from the driving-seat of the cart and finally turned into the tap-room of the Cosy Corner.

This was none other than Sir Percy Blakeney, Bart., the prince of dandies, the enfant gâté of London and Bath society, the brilliant sportsman, and always the smartest and gayest man in town. He was anything but that just now when he staggered into the tap-room and let himself go down on the floor. Now that there was nothing imperative left to do, reaction set in, and in spite of indomitable will-power, he was feeling giddy and sick. He ached in every limb. Felt himself all over to see if there were any broken bones to deplore.

"Curse that virago! How she did hit!"

But he was light-hearted for all that. Physical discomfort—that's all this was—had no hold on his spirits. Except for that feeling of giddiness, caused by the blows on his head, he would have burst into song or laughter.

"By George!" he thought, and chuckled inwardly. "How she must have cursed when she learned that the kids had gone. And how she will swear, and threaten and fulminate when—"

He paused abruptly in his reflection, for his keen ear had suddenly detected the sound of wheels in the remote distance. He pulled himself together, struggled to his feet, stretched out his arms, and there he was now, a magnificent specimen of manhood, tall, broad, vigorous, as if he had never known an ache or pain in his life.

Marguerite was nigh! Marguerite was coming! In five minutes she would be here—in his arms. O God! grant a weak man strength to bear up under the fullness of this joy!

A quarter of an hour later the tap-room of the Cosy Corner was giving shelter to the three men who had watched the well-nigh tragic drama enacted by Mam'zelle Guillotine and Chief Commissary Lescar, a drama in which their beloved chief had been the all-too-willing victim.

They crouched on the creviced floor, closely huddled together, for it was very cold. A stable lantern placed in front of them threw a circle of dim light on the floor and on the primitive repast which they were consuming at the moment; they were digging their young teeth into hunks of stale bread and dry cheese and alternately taking pulls at their respective flasks of brandy. They were dressed in the promiscuous clothes that were served out to infantry regiments not required for service in the more important towns. This meant that their breeches were ragged, that they had no tunics or stockings, and that their shoes were down at heels. And here they were, these sybarites, accustomed to silks and satins, perfumes and Mechlin lace, to drinking old Burgundy and feeding on turkeys and Strasburg patties, here they were munching rye bread and drinking raw brandy and enjoying life to the full as they had never done before.

With them at this hour was Sir Andrew Ffoulkes just come over with Lady Blakeney from the neighbourhood of Mézières in a ramshackle cabriolet purchased at a fabulous price from the landlord of the Ecu d'Or. Poor Sir Andrew! He had gone through a bad moment when he entered the tap-room of the Cosy Corner and there was greeted by Sir Philip Glynde and my Lord St. Dennys with a stern demand for something fit to eat.

"Something fit to eat?" Sir Andrew mimicked with biting irony. "You gluttons! Haven't I given you luscious cheese and—-"

"Luscious cheese?" Sir Philip broke in with mock indignation. "St. Dennys, did you hear that? And luscious bread I suppose he would call this jaw-breaking crust."

"Now, listen to me, Ffoulkes," St. Dennys continued sternly. "Either you delve once more into that basket which I saw reposing in the vehicle which brought you here, and bring us along something fit for an English gentleman to eat—-"

"Together with enough good wine to tickle his fastidious palate," the other put in.

Sir Andrew laughed and gave a shrug.

"Well, what is the alternative?" he asked gaily.

"Or you give us a good reason for not doing as we command"

"I'll give you the best of reasons," Ffoulkes retorted. "The provisions were not intended for a set of gluttons like you. They will be kept for the journey which lies ahead of us all. And let me tell you that I will defend them against your predatory fingers to the last drop of my blood."

"You inhuman monster," St. Dennys cried, and with this he flung a lump of cheese at the head of Sir Andrew, who, still laughing, dodged this first missile only to be pelted by others. He was forced ultimately to cry for mercy. A free fight ensued such as all British schoolboys revel in. And they were just schoolboys for the time being, these brave followers of the Scarlet Pimpernel, full of high animal spirits and the very joy of living.

When peace was at last restored, all four of them settled down once more to their repast of dry bread and cheese.

Between the courses of this sumptuous repast they tried to give Ffoulkes some account of what had gone on in Mézières this afternoon.

"Never in all my life," my Lord Tony was saying, "did I see anything so appalling as the chief under the hand of that vixen, and Glynde, St. Dennys and I being obliged to stand by, under strict orders not to interfere and commit a murder. I tell you," he concluded emphatically, "it was hell!"

A hearty, careless laugh broke in on the moodiness which had suddenly fallen on the small company at recollection of the horror they witnessed a few short hours ago. The laughter came from the inner room, where Marguerite at this moment was held closely in her husband's arms, while he whispered in her ear:

"You understand, don't you, my beloved?"

"No, Percy," she said resolutely, and threw her head back so as to look him straight in the eyes. "I do not. What you wish me to do is impossible. Impossible," she reiterated firmly.

A stable lantern was set on a projection in the wall, and by its dim light Marguerite could just see her husband's face. His eyes were looking down into hers and she could see that there was a merry twinkle in them and that the lines round his mouth were set in a gently ironical smile.

It was then that this merry, careless laugh came to the ears of his friend.

"What?" he enquired lightly. "Insubordination?"

"Percy!" she protested.

"I am not wishing you to do anything, my beloved," he said. "You are a member of the League of the Scarlet Pimpernel. The most adored. The most revered amongst all. But you are a member, and I am your chief whom you have sworn to obey in all things. And I am giving you a command."

That was all he said, speaking very softly; his voice was hardly audible it was so low, just a trifle husky, but perfectly firm. Marguerite buried her face against his shoulder. He went on with infinite tenderness:

"Look at me, my beloved. Are we not one, you and I? Have we not gone through endless joy and often bitter sorrow together? This is one of the moments in our life when we must work together—and suffer together—-"

"Why Percy? Why?" she broke in pitiably through her sobs.

"Because somewhere near here, within a stone's throw of this spot which your dear presence has hallowed, there is a helpless, innocent woman who is faced with death, a horrible death which she would have to endure in loneliness and sorrow surpassing in intensity anything you and I have ever known. Also because there are two little children in this very room who will be motherless unless we come to their aid, you and I, and because an English gentleman would stand for ever dishonoured before you and his own conscience if he so shamefully broke his word."

"But if I stayed with you Percy . . ." came as a final entreaty from Marguerite's aching heart. The hood had fallen back from her head. Through the gloom Percy's hand sought the waves of her soft golden hair which rippled gently round her face and neck. With his handkerchief he brushed gently, very gently the tears that were coursing down her cheeks.

"I might fail, my adored one," was his calm reply. "Do you know what that would mean to them and to me?"

She could no longer speak, her heart was so full of sorrow that she thought it must surely break. And suddenly his mood changed. The tender sentiment of a moment ago flew away into the unknown and the adventurous spirit, the spirit of the sportsman, once more gained the mastery over his strange personality.

"You do understand, don't you, my adored, my loyal helpmate," he asked with his habitual light-hearted eagerness, "just what I want you to do?"

Marguerite unable to speak nodded in reply.

"You will take these two innocents with you in the cart. Glynde, St. Dennys and Tony, who are still in their haphazard uniforms, will accompany you. All three will sit on the driving-seat and will look very imposing and official up there in their tattered uniforms. Ffoulkes, of course, will have to remain under the hood with you. Tony will drive you to Perignon, which is on the other side of the French frontier not far from the city of Luxembourg. He knows the way quite well as he has been along there with me more than once. It is one of the loneliest corners in Eastern France. There is no proper road, only a rather wide bridle-path through ploughed fields which skirts a few isolated villages and avoids the approach to any city. Anyway, the news of what has been going on in Mézières has not had time to spread itself in that direction. There are no patrols along the paths and no garrisons anywhere near. If, after the break of dawn, a few labourers going to their work should gape at you, they will be over-awed at sight of three soldiers of the Republic on the driving-seat of a market cart."

He broke off for the sole purpose of gazing anxiously into her tear-filled eyes and to murmur with a short sigh: "How lovely you are, my beloved!" and then went on in the same matter-of-fact tone of voice, giving his direction clearly, succinctly, like a general issuing commands, certain that they would be obeyed. "I have given Tony all the necessary papers in case they are required. They are in perfect order, signed by Tallien, Barras and our faithful friend, Armand Chauvelin. These signatures are the most perfect specimens of forgery I have ever seen in all my life, and I have had some experience in forged safe-conducts, have I not? I need not tell you who did them, nor what I paid for them. The fellow runs great risks every time he serves me, but he must have put by a cosy little fortune by now and he knows that in case of trouble he can always count on us—-"

Once again he paused, his eyes fixed into vacancy, his mind at work on the great problem which he would confront on the morrow. The children were safe, of that he was sure. So sure, in fact, that something of his almost supernal confidence in himself had communicated itself to Marguerite. She had contrived to swallow her tears and it was in a steady voice that she put the all-important question to him:

"What about you, Percy?"

He gave a little chuckle.

"What about me?" he echoed with inimitable merriment. "Why, sweetheart, I will be kissing your lovely hands—let me see—in a sen'night from to-day at the Fisherman's Rest in Dover, while that nice little baggage, Suzan Jellyband, will be seeing to the creature comforts of poor Madame de Saint-Lucque. . . . Hush! my adored one," he added quickly, and placed a finger over her mouth, for she had been on the point of speaking. "If you say one word more I shall be tempted to silence you with a kiss, and then . . . then God help me! for it would be so difficult, so very difficult to slip away. Now you must try and get a couple of hours' rest if not of sleep."

He stooped and picked up the bundle which he had brought with him in the cart. Out of it he took a couple of cushions. One of these he disposed upon the floor in a corner of the room, the other he propped up against the wall. She watched him smiling.

"Promise me you will try and rest," he urged. "The children are asleep and you must not worry about them any more, promise."

She contrived to say firmly "I promise," and did her best to appear comfortably installed on one cushion with her head resting on the other.

He did not look at her again, turned the lantern so as to shade its light from her eyes.

Before he left the room he said earnestly:

"You don't know what your presence here this time has meant to me. God bless you."

In the meanwhile, in the tap-room after that one moment of subdued emotion when their chief's laughter rang so merrily in their ears, Sir Philip Glynde, his eyes fixed on the communicating door, murmured with a quick sigh:

"Poor old Percy!"

"Don't say that!" Sir Andrew Ffoulkes protested earnestly, knowing what was passing in the minds of the three friend. "Percy adores his wife. We all know that. And she worships him. But those two wonderful people would be the first to resent the idea of any of us being sorry for them. They are prepared to sacrifice everything for the cause they have at heart. Their lives, their entire fortune . . ."

"Their love?" put in one of the others.

"Their love, yes," Ffoulkes assented; and then added after a second's hesitation: "He, at any rate. He has proved it more than once. But, of course, with a glamorous woman like Lady Blakeney it is difficult to guess just what she feels."

"What about you, Ffoulkes," St. Dennys put in with a smile. "You ought to know what all that sort of thing feels like. The long separations, the constant 'farewells.'"

None of the others passed a remark on this. They all knew Ffoulkes's love for his young wife and that he, too, like all the others, was ready to follow his chief wherever and whenever he was called. He, too, like Blakeney, was ready for any sacrifice in the cause of suffering humanity. As indeed they all were. But he and Blakeney were the only married men in their ranks, and many a time had some of them like Glynde or Tony or St. Dennys probed their hearts wondering whether if they in their turn would be ready to sacrifice love for the sake of an ideal.

Sir Andrew gave a slight shrug.

"That's quite right, my dear fellow," he said lightly in answer to St. Dennys, and with that reticence in matters of sentiment peculiar to the Anglo-Saxon race. "But you see, Percy means so much to me, and I have such an admiration for him as a man and as our chief, that when I am working with him I seem to become different somehow . . . I feel differently, I mean . . . about everything. . . . I dare say this sounds queer, and I expect you all think me a bounder for saying it . . . but there it is. . . ."

There was no answer to this, for obviously there was nothing that could be said, and silence fell for a few moments on the congenial little company.

But all of a sudden the communicating door was opened and Blakeney came in.

"Well," he queried airily, "you four chatterers, have you had enough of this sumptuous repast, and have you got a last drop of something to drink for a thirsty man?"

Four flasks of brandy were immediately held up to him. He took two and drained them both.

"I know what your were talking about. Your chief under the whip of a virago, what?"

"Don't, Percy," Tony exclaimed, "it was hellish."

Blakeney could not help laughing: the earnestness and the towering rage of his friend filled him with boyish delight.

"I am sure it was," he admitted, "but how else were we going to engage the attention of that huge crowd long enough to give you three fellows time to deal with those poor kids, with the three troopers and with the cart? And you did it splendidly. And that awful time you had lying in the open field, trussed like a brace of chickens, frozen nearly to death. My God! but you were wonderful! weren't they, Ffoulkes? There are no finer men in the whole wide world than you fellows who honour me by your friendship. God bless and reward you! You have been wonderful to-day."

He appeared to be in the highest spirits though to the keen ears of his devoted followers the voice of their valiant leader sounded perhaps a trifle husky, a little less vibrant than usual.

"Thank Heaven!" he added with a short, quick sigh, "Lady Blakeney will know nothing of what happened in Mézières."

"And she never will," Lord Tony declared fervently.

There was a short moment of silence until Blakeney exclaimed:

"Sink me! I never thought a woman could hit quite so hard. I had a good wacking from my friend Chauvelin once. Not himself, but a pair of lusty bullies. It would have made his heart glad to see me this afternoon. Mam'zelle Guillotine hit twice as hard as his myrmidons did that time in Calais. By George!" he concluded, with something approaching admiration, "what a woman!"

"What are you going to do with her, Blakeney," Glynde asked, "when you've got her?"

There arose an animated discussion as to what should be done with the noted fury. Hanging was, of course, too good for her. Lifelong imprisonment to repeat her experiences in the Bastille would be far too merciful. Tony, who felt particularly bloodthirsty, had read something about lynching in America. He would have liked to have seen the harpy who had laid hands on his chief either burned at the stake or beaten to death, something peculiarly painful and lingering, he urged.

Blakeney said nothing while the matter was being discussed. When the arguments were finally silenced he rejoined:

"You sadistic young ruffians! But you won't get your way with Mam'zelle Guillotine, you know."

"Why not?"

As Blakeney made no immediate reply to this, Tony queried anxiously:

"You are not going to let her get away, Percy, are you?"

"No!" Blakeney answered. "I won't do that, I promise you."

The last sight Marguerite had of her husband was when she peeped out under the hood at the back of the cart. His tall form was still vaguely distinguishable through the fast gathering gloom. He stood, a solitary figure, under the portico of the Cosy Corner. Bare-headed. The falling snow made white patches on each of his shoulders. His face she could no longer see. Tony clicked his tongue. The horse's hoofs grated against the frozen road. The cart gave a lurch and moved slowly away into the night. And darkness swallowed the solitary figure of the great leader, who after a moment or two turned and went within.

Book Five

CHAPTER XXV

The Man in Black

Saint Félix is situated half a league, not more, from Grécourt. The latter in itself is not much of a town, all it does is to serve as a stopping-place for one or two diligences that did not halt in Mézières. It also was noted for its fortnightly horse and cattle market which used to be the scene of great activity in the olden days, and of festive gatherings during the spring and summer months when music and dancing went on all day and half the night, on the grass plots of the cabarets around the market place, and copious drinking and jollity in their respective rooms.

But all this merry-making was now a thing of the past. Farmers and cattle-breeders did stroll into the city once a fortnight with their live stock such as it was: poor half-starved animals they were for the most part, because food was dear and scarce now that the brains of the country concentrated on the quickest way to get rid of all landowners who before this era of equality and fraternity had helped nature to produce the necessities of life for man and beast.

It was the eve before market day when Gabrielle Damiens mounted on her whilom swain's white charger rode into Grécourt. She was in an anxious and moody frame of mind. The disappearance of the two Saint-Lucque children, coming on the top of her disappointment over the rescue of the Marquis and the young Vicomte, had dealt a smashing blow not only to her pride, but chiefly to her burning passion of hatred and revenge.

After she had left the three soldiers on the road, she wandered on horseback first into Mézières, then feeling unconquerable restlessness, she prowled about in the fast-gathering darkness along the country roads oblivious of time and place; like an unquiet spirit seeking repose. At one time she almost lost her way. She hardly knew where she was when she came on a deserted village, or rather what had been a village once and was now only a mass of ruins. She gave the charger his head and let him roam around the tumble-down cottages and what had once been the village street.

"This must be Saint Félix," she thought. "And Grécourt must be over that way."

She turned her horse's head in the direction in which she thought the little township lay. The short interlude had caused her to gather her roving thoughts together. But only momentarily. As soon as she found herself on the right road once again, off they went at a tangent. The image of that great, hulking creature, André Renaud, rose out of the darkness confronting her mental vision. The problem of the man's personality, his tempestuous wooing, his exuberant temperament puzzled and harassed her brain, taunted her with its unfathomable mystery. If the man whom she had kissed and trusted and subsequently chastised was not the master sleuth sent to her from Paris, who and what was he? And what had become of him while the crowd dispersed and she herself rode away? She had no recollection of him after she had snatched the reins of the white charger out of his hands and left him lying on the ground muttering threats and imprecations.

She reached Grécourt in this confused state of mind. Even the sight of the diligence which stood in the yard of the Bon Camarade where she intended to spend the night did not rouse her out of her moodiness. She drew rein. The ostler ran along to aid her to dismount. Scorning his help she jumped down from the saddle. The landlord came along quickly. His manner, when in the new arrival he recognised Mam'zelle Guillotine, became almost servile.

"What did the citizeness require?"

"Supper and a room. I leave again early to-morrow." After which she demanded:

"When did the diligence come in?"

"About two hours ago, citizeness."

"Where is the corporal?"

"In the tap-room having supper."

"Many people in the tap-room?"

"A good number. It's market day to-morrow."

"I know that. I want my supper in a quiet corner. By the way, what is your name?"

"Magnol Fernand. At your service, citizeness."

"Get me something hot then, Citizen Magnol, and be quick about it."

She made her way to the tap-room. It was of the usual pattern to be found in varying sizes in every inn and cabaret of eastern France. Drab-coloured walls that had once been white. An iron stove with inside chimney rising to the blackened, raftered ceiling. A long, trestle table in the middle of the room. Benches each side of it, and the inevitable odour of boiled cabbage, garlic, damp clothes and humanity. A score or more of men were sitting at the centre table consuming platefuls of soup with much sound of gustation and smacking of lips. Their steaming contents gave forth the insistent odour of garlic and cabbage.

A girl with tousled hair and dressed in a promiscuous conglomeration of rags, went round the table bearing hunks of bread on a platter. Her name was apparently Philoméne. There was hardly any talking in the room, except for occasional calls for Philoméne and for bread.

When the door was opened and Gabrielle came in a few heads were turned in her direction. Not by any means all. Most of the men knew her by sight as a matter of course, but these were not the days of cheery, friendly greetings, and after a moment or two the smacking of lips and plying of metal spoons went on as before. She strode across the room. The landlord hovered round her and piloted her to a corner of the room where two small tables were seemingly disposed for the reception of privileged guests. One of these tables was occupied by a solitary guest, a man dressed in sober black. Gabrielle bestowed on him a quick appraising glance. She sat down at the other table. Philoméne brought plates, fork, spoon and knife and set a candle on the table.

"What will the citizeness take?" the landlord asked.

"What is there?"

"Cabbage soup . . ."

"I can smell it. Whet else?"

"A piece of pork with beans."

"What else?"

"Potatoes . . ."

"Good. Bring me potatoes, beans and pork, and see that they are hot."

"Any wine?"

"Yes! Red. From the cask."

The landlord shuffled out of the room. Gabrielle sat on, waiting. She tried hard not to appear to be scrutinising her fellow guest too closely. Nevertheless, she took stock of him every time his head was turned away. She could not see him very well because of the flickering candlelight between her and her vision of him. She put him down as an official of some sort. Police probably. His hair was very dark and lanky. He wore it rather long at the back and tied at the nape of the neck with a black ribbon. It was plastered down his forehead in a rigid, straight line, which made it look like a black band just above his bushy eyebrows. He looked well groomed, although his cheeks showed dark blue against his sallow skin and the starched linen stock round his throat. In her present mood Gabrielle felt intrigued. A Marseillais, she thought, and wanted to hear him speak. Anyway, from the South.

She called to Philoméne for salt.

Forestalling the girl, the stranger took the salt box from his own table and placed it in front of Gabrielle. She gave him a curt "Thank you," to which he responded: "At your service, citizeness," stressing the last syllable of citoyen-ne as is the manner of those in the South.

"You are a stranger here, citizen?" Gabrielle asked.

"I am a stranger everywhere, citizeness," he replied, "even in Paris from whence I came yesterday."

"Yes," thought Gabrielle, "you are distinctly of the South, my friend. Your accent is slight but unmistakable."

"So you are from Paris, citizen?" she went on. "Are you making a long stay in our province?

"That depends."

"On what?"

"How soon I can lay hands on a reputed criminal."

"How so?"

"I am of the secret police, Citizeness Damiens," the man replied quietly, and with his left hand he turned back the lapel of his coat, displaying a metal badge surmounted by a tricolour ribbon. It was then that Gabrielle noticed that his right sleeve was pinned empty to his coat.

"You know who I am?" was all she could think of saying at the moment.

"If I did not would I have revealed my mission to you?" he countered dryly.

He spoke all the time in an even, monotonous tone of voice, without the slightest inflexion or emphasis, like one reciting a lesson learned by heart.

"What is that mission, citizen?" Gabrielle queried, this time in her wonted peremptory way.

"As I have told you, citizeness, to hunt after a reputed criminal."

"If he is reputed I must know about him. I know every criminal in the Province of Artois. Who is he?" she demanded, paused for a second or two, and suddenly gave a gasp, exclaiming: "Do you mean the English spy?"

The stranger nodded.

"Do you know him, citizeness?"

"No," she faltered.

"Nevertheless, if rumour does not lie, you had him under your hand a few hours ago. Why did you let him go?"

His voice was still quite even and only just audible, but there was something stern now and rasping in its tone. He did not look at the woman while he spoke, but over her shoulder on the drab-coloured wall on which to the words "Liberté, Fraternité, Egalité," traced thereon in black chalk, had been added the words: "ou la Mort." He looked that way so insistently that Gabrielle, fascinated, turned round to look. But she was not the woman ever to be intimidated by the suggestion of a threat, wherever it came from. She gave a shrug and a harsh, ironic laugh.

"If you have those sort of ideas in your head, citizen," she said dryly, "You won't go far in your career."

"What do you mean?"

"That you are altogether on the wrong track. The man whom I horsewhipped this afternoon is not the celebrated Scarlet Pimpernel."

"What makes you say that?"

"It was he who first called our attention to the disappearance of the cart."

"A clever trick, since he took you in."

"What do you mean by a clever trick?"

"He had to get out of your clutches, citizeness, or you would have killed him."

"I certainly would—" she began, paused a moment or two, then went on: "Do you dare to assert that the man who has been spending the last two days in Mézières, who effected the arrest of the traitor aristos the ci-devant Saint-Lucque and her brats, and who was sent out specially from Paris by Armand Chauvelin to aid me in the capture of the Scarlet Pimpernel, do you dare to tell me that he was . . ."

"The Scarlet Pimpernel himself," the man broke in firmly. "He was not sent out from Paris, citizeness. He only said he was."

"He was André Renaud—I saw his papers. They were sighed by Maximilien Robespierre and two other members of the Committee of Public Safety; André Renaud . . ."

"He was not André Renaud," the other broke in again with increased emphasis.

"How do you know?"

"Because I happen to be André Renaud, citizeness." Gabrielle Damiens gave such a start that the table on which she had leaned her elbows gave a lurch, and the beer bottle which did duty for a candlestick rolled down on the floor. The candle broke, the light went out and the corner where these two sat in close conversation was in greater obscurity than before.

Gabrielle's glowering eyes searched the face of the stranger through this gloom.

"You!" she burst out, gasping for breath.

"Even I," the man responded coolly.

"I don't believe it . . . I don't believe it," she reiterated over and over again, trying to steady her voice, and to stop her teeth from chattering.

"Why shouldn't you believe it, citizeness?" he retorted. "Who do you suppose I am?"

"I don't know," she murmured gruffly.

He gave a short laugh.

"Well, I am not the Scarlet Pimpernel, am I, or I shouldn't be here talking to you?"

That was true enough. Gabrielle passed the back of her hand across her moist forehead. He went on:

"You have been believing and disbelieving so many things here to-day, citizeness, no wonder you are bewildered, and," he added, with, for the first time, the hint of a threat in what he said, "are like now to commit the greatest blunder of your career. And let me tell you, citizeness, that you are not quite so indispensable in the estimation of the government that you can afford to commit blunder after blunder as you have done in the past few days."

She pulled herself together, straightening out her massive shoulders, and retorted defiantly:

"Blunders? I? You forget to whom you are talking, Citizen—"

"André Renaud," he put in with a thin smile.

Whereupon she gave a shrug.

"I don't believe it," she again persisted.

"It makes no matter," he countered coolly, "whether you believe in me or not. I can do my duty without any help from you. I know all the plans that have been made for the capture of the English spy, and I also know that you, Citizeness Gabrielle Damiens, Mam'zelle Guillotine, have run counter to the orders sent to you direct by the Committee of Public Safety . . ."

"How do you know that?" she broke in roughly. "Who was . . ." She paused abruptly, afraid that she was giving herself away.

"It was Citizen Armand Chauvelin who told me what the orders were," he put in quietly.

"I don't believe it," she reiterated with parrot-like insistence.

"Shall I tell you what they were . . . and how you contravened them?"

No reply to that from Gabrielle. She sat there a veritable statue of obstinacy and sullenness, her elbows resting on the table, her chin cupped in her hands. Her mind had got back to that awful state of puzzlement and confusion of a while ago. The very name André Renaud, seemed to be burning inside her brain with letters of fire. She tried to recapture every phase of her association with the man. His arrival at the episcopal palace, her rage against him because he had come when the ci-devant Saint-Lucque woman was already under arrest, on a denunciation from the farmer Guidal. Guidal! She had flung the name in the man's face at the time, whereupon and with consummate self-possession he had erased Guidal's very name from the tablets of her memory. It came back to her now. What a fool she had been not to confront the farmer with the man who called himself André Renaud and claimed to be the master sleuth sent to her from Paris.

Then there was the man's personality, which now obtruded itself with exasperating persistence before her troubled mind. The more she thought of him the more did her brain reject the thought that that huge, hulking male creature with his coarse ways and brutal love-making could possibly be André Renaud the noted sleuth-hound, the tracker of criminals and traitors, a calling requiring suavity of manner, tact, effacement, every quality, in fact, which that rowdy, hoydenish lout did not possess. English—that's what he was. He spoke French, but he was English. He couldn't be anything but English—not with those huge legs and immense shoulders. Frenchmen occasionally were broad and powerful-looking, like this man opposite to her now. Though tall, a Frenchman was graceful and soft of speech, unless he was the spokesman of the government and was obliged to talk forcefully to a crowd of waverers.

Thoughts! Thoughts! Conjectures! There they were going round and round in the whirlpool of Gabrielle's brain. Her dark, glowering eyes remained fixed on the man who had set all this effervescence foaming and boiling inside her, making her temples throb and sending her blood rushing like a fiery torrent through her veins. He was almost sinister-looking in his funereal clothes and that black hair which looked like a mourning band round his forehead, with his measured speech, his sallow skin and that empty sleeve. What a contrast to the burly, noisy boor who had made love to her, to his showy clothes and clumsy boots, his tousled yellow hair and florid skin.

Gabrielle Damiens visualising all this, remembering the other man's fulsome adulation, and his resounding kisses, cursed herself for a fool. Fortune and fame were in her grasp and she let everything go, even the chance of realising a part of her revenge.

The ci-devant Marquis and the boy were gone, the two brats also, probably. And all of this the work of a man who had bamboozled her. Led her by the nose until she became like a despicable noodle, mistrusting her own powers of which she had always been so justly proud.

"If I only could trust you," she burst out, staring like a wild cat at the sober, placid figure of the man before her. "Whom else could you trust, citizeness, if not the man who was sent down for the express purpose of aiding you in the capture of the greatest prize that ever fell to the lot of a patriot like yourself?"

He paused a moment. Looking her full in the face. Returning stare for stare. His eyes looked more sinister than ever overshadowed by those bushy eyebrows and surmounted by that band of straight black hair which seemed to cut off the upper part of his face. It appeared to begin at the eyes and to end just above the chin, where the stock of snow-white linen presented such a crude contrast to his blue-black cheeks and chin. He did look sinister, devilish, for there had crept a look into his eyes that was both malefic and menacing.

"And that prize," he resumed after that short ominous pause, "you actually allowed to slip out of your hands. You held him at your mercy and you let him go."

"I horsewhipped him," she murmured, through clenched teeth.

"Do you think he cared? What you did was to give his followers time to spirit away the two aristos. After that he disappeared. Or am I wrong?" he concluded with biting sarcasm.

Slowly, gradually, step by step, Gabrielle saw her spirit breaking and her will-power crumbling under the vague terror engendered in her by this man's malignant personality. He dominated her. She was half afraid of him, in a way that she had never been afraid of anyone in her life before. She tried to think of him as a minor official, with far less influence with the powers up in Paris than she had. She thought of her own friends, of Robespierre, the virtual dictator of France, and of others in commanding positions who knew and appreciated her patriotic worth. They would stand by her, even if she had committed a blunder or two or contravened a casual order.

Something that went on in her mind at this comforting thought must have shown in her face, for the man broke in on her meditations:

"This is not the time to think of influential friends, citizeness. The dogs of the revolution are at one another's throats. Robespierre is at grips with Danton. Terror is the order of the day. The chase after traitors is swift and hot. Nothing but a spectacular coup can save you from death after the blunder you have committed, Mam'zelle Guillotine."

Having said this he rose.

"This place is insufferably hot," he said dryly. "I shall be at your service in the courtyard, in close proximity to your diligence and in close conversation with your troopers. I must feel assured that they are worthy of the trust which you have placed in them."

He stalked out of the room, leaving Gabrielle Damiens sitting in the gloom with her elbows on the table, her chin resting against her clenched fists, her eyes glowering. Glowering like those of a wild cat. Burning with hatred and with fear. She watched the man walk through the room with a long, rather laboured stride. He was tall, but distinctly round-shouldered, and stooped as he walked. How different, through Gabrielle, to the rolling gait, the straight square shoulders, the heavy tread of her whilom courtier.

Something had to be done about the whole thing. Gabrielle Damiens was no fool. She knew even before this man began to threaten her that if she allowed the English spy to slip through her fingers again it would go ill—very ill—with her. And she would die un-avenged. The hated Saint-Lucque, and the whole brood of them would be spirited away if she blundered again. Well then, what had best be done? This man here with his airs of incorruptible officialdom—imitator of Robespierre what?—in his sober, well-cut clothes, might, after all, be of service. Might have ideas worth considering. He was a blood-hound, a tracker, he might have ideas. Time was getting short. There was the journey to Paris on the morrow, and the certainty that the English spies would work their coup in the forest of Mézières. Everyone thought that. Everyone believed it. Chauvelin had expounded his theory before the Committee of Public Safety, had submitted his plans for the capture of the arch-enemy. The Committee had approved of the theory and agreed to the plan. This man, this Marseillais with the stooping shoulders and blue chin, had knowledge of all that. He seemed to know everything, in fact, like one associated with the high powers in Paris. He knew all about the orders transmitted to her by Chauvelin. He had heard of her defiance and contravention of the orders.

There were calls for the landlord just then. They came from outside. Sharp and peremptory they were, coming from one who was not used to being kept waiting. Gabrielle thought she recognised the voice with its accent from the South. At once there was a commotion. Citizen Magnol ran in and out of the house, backwards and forwards from the tap-room to the kitchen, carrying bottles and tins labelled "cloves" and "nutmeg" or "sugar." After a time he came in carrying a huge bowl of steaming mulled wine. Philoméne was hard on his heels, laden with a number of pewter mugs.

"What's all this?" Gabrielle queried.

"Hot wine, citizeness, for the soldiers," the landlord replied.

"Who ordered it?"

"Citizen Renaud from Paris. He thought the men looked starved with cold. . . . They certainly look it . . . This will do them good."

He took a ladle full of the hot stuff from the bowl, tasted it and smacked his lips. The company at the trestle-table watched the proceedings with covetous eyes. The men laughed. One of them said: "It looks good." Another declared: "I'll have some of that, too, citizen landlord."

"So will I," said a third.

"And I," came lustily all down the length of the table.

"Make haste, citizen landlord," they all shouted at him, as he held up the bowl with both hands and marched with it as with a trophy out of the room. Philoméne ran in his wake, carrying a load of pewter mugs. Their exit was accompanied by lusty cheers, which after a moment or two found their echo in the yard outside.

Gabrielle struggled to her feet, feeling unaccountably weary. Her legs felt heavy like lead. She picked up her mantle and, wrapping it round her, stumped slowly out of the room.

André Renaud—was he really André Renaud?—was out there in the yard. Half a dozen troopers were gathered round him, all laughing and bandying jokes. The landlord had just come out carrying the bowl of mulled wine. Philoméne was close behind him with the pewter mugs. They came to a halt, Magnol holding up the bowl in accordance with the custom of the country, for the customer who paid for the drink to pronounce his approval. This the black-coated stranger did, he took the ladle offered him by the landlord, and pronounced the mixture good.

The landlord assisted by Philoméne now went the round, distributing the hot drink. The soldiers raised their mugs, cheering the black-coated stranger. Nor were the men in the diligence forgotten. From them, after their long confinement in the narrow space, came huzzas and cheers more lustily than the rest.

"Shall we give the prisoner a hot drink, too?" the stranger suggested. "It will put heart into her."

The corporal in charge was quite willing.

"Why shouldn't she get drunk, poor thing?" he said lightly.

He and the men were having a good time. They felt kindly disposed towards that wretched woman, who was being trundled about in a jolting vehicle with nothing short of trial and death at the end of this awful journey. Once or twice during the day she had been jostled out by order of the corporal in charge of the escort. She had been given food on arrival at the Bon Camarade, when she was thrust in and out of the coach as if she had been a bale of goods. But not once during this long day did a word of complaint escape her lips. She sat in a corner of the vehicle, motionless and silent. The soldiers were not cruel men, not all of them by any means. There were some who felt quite sorry for her, especially when Mam'zelle Guillotine came a while ago and had a look at her. Such torrents of abuse as then poured from the lips of the noted patriot, even the troopers had never heard before. But the woman never moved. She scarcely seemed to hear. Yes, the men had been sorry for her then. But, que voulez vous? Duty is duty, and disobedience to orders punishable by death.

The corporal in charge was not averse to allowing the prisoner to take a mug of hot wine at the hands of the stranger who was so generously paying for this treat. There was nothing in his orders against that. Two of the men even got out of the coach to make room for him and helped him up the step because of his one arm, when he handed a mug to the wretched woman and stood by while she drank it down.

Gabrielle had been standing all this while outside the door of the inn gazing at the animated scene. Her glowing eyes followed every movement of André Renaud. He had just come out of the diligence when he caught sight of her. The lanthorn which hung from a rafter under the projecting roof was above his head. The new style sugar-loaf hat which he wore threw an irregular shadow over parts of his face. It also caused him to look taller than she had thought him before, in spite of his decided stoop. Below the hat the funereal looking band of black hair encircled his forehead and the top of his long nose, were the only features visible on his face.

Gabrielle strode across the yard, and he came on to meet her.

"What right had you," she demanded roughly, "to interfere with my men?"

He was profuse in his apologies.

"A thousand pardons, citizeness," he pleaded with unwonted humility; "I did it for the best. The men were getting restive as the cold got into their bones. They will fight better now, being warm inside. I was sure you would approve."

The false air of humility did not last long. Already his voice had become harsh and his tone dictatorial. Gabrielle was up in arms.

"I am not starting before dawn," she declared curtly; "time for them to freeze again before then."

Greatly to her surprise he seemed to acquiesce.

"You must do as you please," he responded dryly, paused a moment, then added with a regretful sigh:

"And so we shall miss that elusive English spy again!"

"Miss him?" she countered. "Why should we, or rather I, miss him?"

"Because, as I said before, the men are already impatient and restive, what with the cold and the delay. If you wait about here all night their enthusiasm will fizzle out before you reach the forest. It is only a fizgig now. You blame me for giving them a warm drink, but they were more tired and dispirited than you think. Make a start soon, citizeness," he urged with great earnestness, "their blood is warm now, don't let it cool down again. You could be in the forest before the dawn and the weather is just perfect for the capture of a gang of marauders like those English spies."

Then, as she remained obstinately silent, he continued with a note in his voice which sounded like a solemn warning:

"Your policy, citizeness, believe me, is to travel by night and to rest by day. The English spies are night birds. They only fly about in the dark."

She was looking straight past him now, across the yard where the bulky diligence with its inside load of picked men loomed out like a huge black mass darker than the darkness around. It held the one thing that to Gabrielle Damiens was more precious than anything on earth, more precious than life itself—her chance of revenge. It was all very well for this man here and for all the Committees in Paris to think only of the capture of the Scarlet Pimpernel; but for her, Gabrielle, who had spent sixteen years in a living tomb to suit the ambitious intrigues of the Saint-Lucque family, the thought of wreaking her revenge on the entire brood outweighed any thought of patriotism or personal advancement. That woman in the diligence meant more to her than a whole army of English spies.

She stood there brooding, unable to make a decision. She felt that in a way this man, André Renaud—was he really André Renaud—was right, whoever he was. The English spies were night birds who flapped their wings only in the night, and they were out to wrest that woman Saint-Lucque out of her clutches. Yes! the man with the maimed arm was probably right, and as for her, Gabrielle, the double capture was the prize to aim for. There had been so much talk, so many intrigues and so much mystery around the personality of the Scarlet Pimpernel, that she herself was caught in the vortex of hatred against the man and in the torrent of this mad longing to see him brought to ruin and to death. The man who had made love to her! The man whom she had kissed! Who had mocked and derided and flouted her! The man whom she had held at her mercy under her whip-lash and whom she had allowed to escape from full retributive justice.

She hated him! By Satan and all his horde, how she did hate him!

"His was not really a clever impersonation," the man in black broke in casually on her thoughts. "I wonder that you, citizeness, who have a great reputation for shrewdness, were so easily taken in. You have met men of the secret police before now, was he at all like any of them? Just think of our mutual friend, Citizen Chauvelin. He is the master of us all. We try to model ourselves on that pattern. Suave. Soft of speech. Gentle of manner. There you have your successful tracker of spies and criminals. Not a great hulking, blundering lout like the man who courted your favours. Look at me, citizeness, and think of him and then say which of us two is the most likely to trap those audacious English spies?"

She did look at him. Suave. Soft of speech. Gentle of manner, he was the very replica of Armand Chauvelin.

She had, however, remained as was her wont, obstinately silent, nor did he say anything more for the moment. He allowed her gaze to travel over his stooping figure, his lean jaw and empty sleeve; a slight, ironical smile hovered round his lips. But this Gabrielle could not see. Then there was silence between them for a time. A distant clock in the city struck ten. The night was going to be very dark. Only a thin film of snow fell intermixed with rain. It no longer spread a mantle of white over the ground, rather did it turn to slush and mud as it fell. The troopers when they had drunk their fill of the good mulled wine, turned into the coach-house for shelter. The doors and windows of the diligence had once again been hermetically closed on the six picked men and their unfortunate prisoner. And gradually all signs of life were stilled in the yard of the Bon Camarade. And darkness became more dense. Almost palpable. The volets throughout the house had been closed one by one, only the door into the inn had remained open, and through it came filtrating a dim shaft of light.

These two, the man and the woman, remained as it were the sole occupants of this dark and noiseless place. They were looking at one another like two swordsmen about to engage. A few moments went by, and then Gabrielle suddenly turned on her heel and went into the house. The man did not follow her. He remained standing almost motionless under the shelter of the projecting roof. He did not seem to feel the cold, nor was he impatient. The distant clock struck the quarter after the hour, and a minute later Gabrielle emerged once more out of the house.

She took no notice of the stranger, strode past him and called loudly for the corporal in charge.

To him she gave the order to make an immediate start.

In a moment the Bon Camarade awoke from its torpor. There was running and shouting. Orders and counter orders. Horses pawing in their stables, the clatter of their hoofs on the cobblestones of the yard. Volets and windows thrown open, heads thrust out to see what was going on. Ostlers and grooms busy. The landlord fussy and obsequious. The team was put to. The carriage lanterns lighted and fixed in position. The escort prepared to mount. A few street urchins ventured into the yard and stood round the diligence gaping at its closed doors and windows, watching the soldiers and the horses, passing criticisms and remarks in their shrill childish voices.

And towering in this vortex of sound and movement the massive form of Mam'zelle Guillotine wrapped in a fur-lined mantle, stood out by the side of the tall, stooping figure clad in black, scarce distinguishable from the darkness around. The master sleuth from Paris.

Gabrielle Damiens prepared to mount to the box-seat of the coach.

"I am driving," she announced briefly, speaking to him. "Are you coming with me?"

"Not with you, citizeness," he replied. "I might hamper you. But there will be a horse to spare for me here. I will start as soon as may be and meet you at the cross-roads just before you come to Falize. Will you wait for me there?"

"Falize itself would be better. We could pull up there."

"As you like, but the cross-roads would suit you best, citizeness. If I am there, and I shall be, we would have command of the two roads and could then decide which would be the safest to take."

"What do you mean by that?" Gabrielle demanded. She had one foot on the axle of the near front wheel, preparing to mount.

"There has been a persistent rumour all day in Grécourt," he said in a whisper, "that the English spies are mustering in this district. They are said to be more numerous than they usually are. Some talk of a dozen, others of two score. Of course, the story may only be a canard. But it is best you should be warned. I shall know more about the rumour when I meet you, and, as I say, we'll take the road that gives the best chance of safety."

"I am not afraid," Gabrielle muttered, and without another word she climbed up to the box-seat and settled herself down, reins in hand, and driving-apron stretched over her massive thighs. The corporal in charge climbed up after her and sat down by her side.

A click of the tongue. A scraping and jolting and lurching. Much pawing and snorting. The iron hoofs drawing sparks from the cobblestones. The damp leather squeaking. The axles grinding. The metal jingling. A shout from Gabrielle:

"The cross-roads then."

A resounding crack of the whip and the lumbering vehicle started on its way.

CHAPTER XXVI

Fortune in Sight

Long after the rumble of wheels had died away in the distance the quidnuncs sat around in the tap-room arguing, talking, discussing they knew not what, and drinking their favourite mulled wine. As a matter of fact nothing very important had happened. Nothing so very unusual. The farmers who had come to Grécourt with their live stock were the first to say that the sight of a coach with closed doors and windows and escorted by a posse of soldiers was not a rare occurrence in the city. A fortnight or so ago-it may have been three weeks, just such a coach had come through Grécourt on its way to Paris. Doors and windows closed. An important detachment of soldiers from one of the local regiments. Great secrecy. Everything, in fact, to arouse the curiosity of patriots who wanted to know what all the mystery was about. In that case it transpired that in the coach were three whilom aristos, one of them none other than the ci-devant Marquis de Saint-Lucque, who was known by all and sundry in the province. With him was his son, a boy who should have been at school. And there was also a caoltin, the abbé Prud'hon. Not at all a bad man, any more than Saint-Lucque and his boy were bad. But it seems that they really were traitors to their country. They wanted to sell the whole of the province of Artois to the Austrians, who were the arch-enemies of France, and who would immediately grind all the Artesians under their iron heel, seize their land, their crops, take their children into bondage and their wives as serving-maids.

And it seems that Saint-Lucque, the abbé Prud'hon and even the boy were all in a huge maleficent plot to do this evil thing. And so they were arrested and were being driven to Paris in the diligence which halted at the Bon Camarade, just as this other one had done this very night. In Paris it seems all three of them were going to be tried for treason. They would be condemned to death and then they were going to be brought back to Mézières where Mam'zelle Guillotine was going to make short work of them.

Yes, the worthy Artesian farmers nodded sagely, that was what happened to traitors who conspired against the Republic and worked against their own country and for the ruin of all the farmers who toiled for the welfare and prosperity of France.

Unfortunately in that case things did not turn out quite in the way that had been anticipated. For while the diligence conveying the traitors to Paris was passing through the forest of Mézières, it was held up by masked highwaymen who attacked the soldiers, killed and wounded most of them, maimed the horses and finally drove the coach away in the darkness, no one knew whither or in which direction. The highwaymen were never apprehended and the traitors vanished as if they had been spirited away by the devil himself.

That was the story that was told in the tap-room of the Bon Camarade on this February night, the eve of market day, by the farmers and breeders gathered in Grécourt for the occasion. Their spirits were not as high as they usually were. Money was scarce these days, in spite of the fact that money-grabbers and aristos had been put to death in hundreds, and the government up in Paris had solemnly promised that when there were no more aristos in France every labourer, every farmer, every toiler and worker would have the fortunes that those traitors had stolen from the people and then squandered like water. Every man in the country would be prosperous and free to do just what he liked and never need do another stroke of work if he had no mind to do it.

Well, promises were all right enough. But as far as agriculture in the Province of Artois was concerned, there was less money to be made out of it now than in the days when the ci-devant Saint-Lucque, the Belforts and others were there to farm the land and pay good wages to those who worked for them.

As for market day, it certainly was not the merry, profitable day it used to be in the past. What about to-morrow? The weather was so bad. Buyers would certainly be scarce and prices would come down to cut-throat level.

"What we each want is money to drop down into our laps without having to toil and moil for it. That is what the government has promised us and nothing less should satisfy us."

The man who spoke was younger than the majority of the guests around the table. This, no doubt, accounted for his lusty speech and full-throated voice. Most of the others approved of what he said and showed their appreciation by banging their half-empty mugs on the table. "Money to drop down into our laps, without having to toil and moil for it." No wonder the prospect appealed to all these harrased, over-taxed, hard-working men.

"The government did promise . . ." somebody remarked.

"And nothing less should satisfy us," another echoed forcefully, while mugs were again banged on the table-top.

Right through the hubbub of voices and the noise of metal against the table, a clear, sharp voice suddenly resounded. It came from near the door, through which the one-armed stranger had just entered the room. He closed the door behind him, stood with his back to it, facing the company, every man of whom had suddenly turned astonished, enquiring eyes upon him. There was silence for a moment or two, while the resonant voice appeared to have raised an echo in the low-raftered room. The pewter mugs were slowly emptied. One old farmer gave a doubtful shrug.

"All very well talking," he said.

"Talking won't feed the stock or manure the ground," objected another grey-beard.

"How are we going to set about it, citizen?" queried a third, with slashing irony.

"About making money drop into to your laps?" he countered.

There was a chorus of "Yes! yes! yes! how is it going to be done?"

"And when?" the youngster added, he who had first brought the question on the tapis.

"When?" the man in black rejoined. "Not later than to-night."

Well, of course, that was something undreamed of. Something so utterly foolish and impossible that the man who suggested it was either a devil or just a mad-man. Roars of mocking laughter greeted him, when he moved away from the door and took his stand at the head of the table. Mocking laughter, jeers, ironical huzzas were hurled at him, and cries of "How? How? How?"

By way of a reply the stranger called loudly for the landlord.

"Our throats are dry," he said; "we'll talk about this over full mugs of mulled wine."

Magnol came in, looking rather scared. He had been on the point of closing his house for the night, not being used to such late hours.

"Citizen landlord," the stranger commanded, turning to him, "a fresh bowl of spiced wine, the best your cellar can procure. Into it you shall pour a bottle of your best brandy. Make it hot and strong, well spiced and as sweet as love. And now be quick about it. We have important business to transact."

This all looked more serious than had at first appeared. The man in black was certainly no devil or he never would have ordered a bowlful of that excellent mulled wine, and all the more excellent with a bottle of good brandy poured into it. He had the welfare of farmers and stockbreeders of Artois at heart. No! No! he was no devil. A madman perhaps, but his next words would settle that question. For the moment he remained standing at the head of the table, obstinately silent, paying no heed to the many questions, some sarcastic, others encouraging and even peremptory, that were hurled at him from one end of the table to the other. Until presently the landlord returned with the bowl of hot wine and received a regular ovation, as he went the round ladling the drink into the mugs.

"This man here," one of the drovers said to him, "tells us that he is going to find a way of throwing money into our laps without our having to do a handstir of work for it."

"More power to his elbow," Magnol assented, "but how is he going to do it?"

"Let's drink his health and see," a farmer suggested who, apparently, had a practical turn of mind.

This was done, with much cheering, and a great deal of laughter mostly sarcastic and sceptical.

"I thank you, friends," responded the man at the end of the table. He scarcely touched the edge of his mug with his lips. "And now," he went on, and allowed his resonant voice to reach every ear and so fill every corner of the room. "Enough of this and let us talk seriously. You want to know how you can earn a substantial sum of money without toiling and moiling for it. You can do it by thwarting the machinations of a grasping harpy who to-morrow will, if you do not put a stop to it, pocket the sum of two thousand louis which by right of justice should be yours."

A gasp went right round the table.

"Two thousand louis!" came bursting out from every mouth.

"Where would two thousand louis be coming from?"

"Can you tell us that?"

"From the government who is paying that sum of money in solid gold to any party of French citizens who between them effect the capture of the noted English spy known as the Scarlet Pimpernel."

It was a loud groan of disappointment that went the round this time when the vibrant voice of the man in black ceased to resound through the room.

"Oh! That!!!" was uttered in tones of withering contempt. Contempt which was expressed in several less salubrious ways. They had all heard of the English spy before, and they had been harangued before now by representatives of the government who came down from Paris and talked, and talked, and made all sorts of promises which where never kept. The English spy! Yes! they knew all about him. A myth, what? An imaginary personage whom no one had ever seen and whose personality was always brought to the fore whenever any aristos who should have been sent to the guillotine managed to evade justice. Whenever that happened there was always a lot of talk. It was at once asserted that the local police officials were not at fault. Of course they were not. The Commissary was invariably spoken of as a man of lofty patriotism and of great acumen. But obviously no man born of woman could grapple with a supernatural creature, with a Titan of immense stature, fiery eyes, hair that bristled and nostrils that emitted crackling flames.

Oh, yes! the good farmers and hard-working drovers and breeders had all heard these stories before. They were not going to listen to them again to-night. They drained their mugs, and grumbled as they drank.

"I am for bed," one of the men said and rose to go.

"So am I," concluded another.

In a moment most of them were on their feet. Moody and disillusioned, they never thought of saying "Thank you!" for the warm drink.

There was quite a stampede in the direction of the door, until that same resonant voice called out: "Stop!" And the call was so compelling that for the space of a minute of two the drive towards the door came to a halt, and twenty pairs of eyes were once more turned in the direction of the stranger.

"Are you fools or madmen?" he cried forcefully. "Are you really going to throw away the one chance you will ever have of bringing ease and comfort to your wives and children? Do you know what two thousand louis means? They mean one hundred louis to each one of you. One hundred louis to put in your pocket this very night. And for doing what? Wresting the English spy from the clutches of a woman, who already has more louis and is richer than any of you can ever hope to be."

"What woman?" someone shouted.

"Mam'zelle Guillotine, of course."

A few of the men gravely shook their heads, others murmured: "That huzzy!" and muttered under their breath: "I wouldn't care to tackle her."

Be it noted that in spite of these grave misgivings on the part of the older men, the younger ones looked eagerly up at the speaker.

Mam'zelle Guillotine had apparently not many friends among this little crowd of country bumpkins. She had certainly become very prominent and very powerful in the province, but many there were who remembered her when in ragged kirtle and torn shift she wandered from one village to another and from an improvised rostrum outside the local inn spouted denunciation against every aristo, and every man who possessed as much as a square bit of land. And when she had finished spouting, she would drag a cap off the head of the man nearest to her and hand it round begging—yes, begging—for a few sous to pay for a bit of supper. And now she wore a fur-lined mantle and lived in Mézières in a palace.

Bah!!

And with riches had come arrogance. She was dictatorial, tyrannical as any aristo. She was feared, but she also was detested.

"Have you never realised," the stranger went on, not loudly but very quietly, leaning slightly forward, his eyes under those beetling brows searching the faces of his hearers, "have you never guessed that all along the arrest of the ci-devant Saint-Lucque family, one after the other, has been connected with the capture of the English spy? He has been at work in your district for some time. Was it not he who dragged the ci-devant Marquis and his son and the calotin Prud'hon out of the clutches of Mam'zelle Guillotine? And now she means to have her revenge on him. She means to capture the Scarlet Pimpernel in the very act of trying to effect the escape of the woman Saint-Lucque, and thus earn the full reward of two thousand louis offered to any patriot who would lay that enemy of France by the heels."

"Lucky Mam'zelle Guillotine," he went on, certain now of holding the attention of his audience. "She has the means of earning twenty times as much money as would keep any one of you in affluence for the rest of your lives. Lucky Mam'zelle Guillotine! And I'll tell you something more, my friends, and that is that she already has the Scarlet Pimpernel gagged and bound in that diligence which you saw standing here in the yard for over two hours. How do you suppose I should know anything of this affair, if it was not already accomplished? No, no, Mam'zelle Guillotine is not one to talk till after a thing is done. And I tell you she talked to me about it all in this very room. And she laughed at me and mocked me and threw my helplessness in my face, knowing that I could do nothing.

"She was right there, citizens. I was alone. What could I do? I had not had the chance of talking to you all, of hearing from you that you would join me in the most glorious expedition ever undertaken by twenty patriots like yourselves."

Indeed, the man had no cause to complain of inattention. Never had an orator so engrossed an audience. Young and old hung upon his words. They exchanged glances, murmuring words of commendation. Eager, excited were they all. Impatient. Expectant. Wanting to hear more about this money, this gold, this fortune that could be theirs for the snatching.

"What must we do?" they asked.

"What must we do to be as lucky as Mam'zelle Guillotine?"

"Just do as I tell you," the speaker replied in stentorian accents, "and the fortune is yours."

"Tell us, then."

"Speak up, citizen."

"We'll go to hell with you."

The man threw back his head and laughed. Laughed immoderately. And the laughter came from the intense joyousness of his heart.

"Not to hell, citizens," he cried exultantly. "Only as far as the cross-roads on this side of Falize."

He dropped his voice and once again spoke in that subdued tone which was more impressive than any shouting could be.

"Some of you, if I mistake not," he said, "have brought in horses for the sale of livestock to-morrow. They could not be put to better use than the purpose which we have in view. If any man has a pistol let him take it, or a sabre if he has one, a goodly knife, a garden tool, a scythe, anything he can fight with. For there may be a bit of fighting, let me tell you. Mam'zelle Guillotine and her myrmidons will not give up their prize-capture without putting up a fight. Mounted on good horses, we'll easily overtake the party at the cross-roads on this side of Falize. I know they mean to call a halt there before deciding which road which they will ultimately take. Both lead to Paris, one through the forest, the other by a round-about way. Well! citizens, what do you say? Shall we decide what their fate is to be? Shall we seize the coach and its occupants, one of which is worth one hundred louis to every one of you? Shall we? Shall we, citizens, who see your wives in ragged kirtles and your children cold and hungry, shall we snatch this rich booty from the hands of an overweening terrorist? What do you say?"

"Yes!" came from a score of sturdy throats, shouting in unison.

"Let's drink to it, then!" And the stranger raised his mug high above his head. He went on once again in his full, vibrant voice. "To the confusion of Mam'zelle Guillotine! To our success in snatching from her the prize that is ours by right! To victory!"

"To victory!"

And the mugs were emptied at one draft.

So compelling was this man's personality, so irresistible his oratory, that these men, some young and eager, others older and sedate, drank and shouted in a way that they never would have dared to do in a more sober mood. To drink to the confusion of Mam'zelle Guillotine would on normal occasions have entailed immediate arrest, prosecution for treason, probably. But this occasion was abnormal. One hundred louis dangling as a golden vision before the eyes of men who had never looked forward to a carefree future, made warriors of these simple country folk. They felt that the blood of heroes was coursing through their veins. Even the grey-beards shouted: "To victory!" as heartily as the youngsters. What would you? Money was so scarce these days! Everyone was so poor. So poor! Starvation was stalking the land. Children cried for bread. Work was grinding and wages small. No wonder that the thought of capturing the mysterious English spy and seeing a hundred louis fall into their laps inflamed the imagination of these ignorant rustics. A hundred louis! And golden louis at that! No dirty scraps of paper, mind you! And with nothing to do for it but an exciting adventure.

So "Hurrah!" for the man who had shown them the way to this marvellous good fortune.

There was only the unfortunate landlord, citizen Magnol, who did not feel as happy as his customers. He had crept back into the tap-room and had been standing in the doorway listening to the harangue of that black-coated, one-armed stranger. He had witnessed the incitement to treason, the appeal to the cupidity of a lot of witless boors, which of a certainty would land the lot of them in gaol. He had heard the shouts and the cheers, and he was terrified. When the cry to "Victory!" echoed from one end of the tap-room to the other, he turned tail and ran helter-skelter up the rickety stairs that led to the loft under the sloping roof, and bolted into the attic where his wife was already in bed. There he joined her, buried his face in the hard pillow and pulled the blanket right over his head so as not to hear anything more of the awful things that were going on down below.

But he was not destined to enjoy tranquillity for long. A few moments during which his wife, roused from her first sleep, tried in vain to get a word out of him. She had just turned over ready to go to sleep again, having made up her mind that her

Fernand had had one of his many drinking bouts, when a heavy step came mounting up the rickety stairs. The sound was followed by repeated hard knocks on the door and a peremptory call for the citizen landlord. The door was thrown open and the black-coated stranger who was making all this pother stalked in. He carried a small lantern, which he flashed into the faces of Magnol and his wife, who sat up straight in bed, shivering and shaking with terror.

"Citizen landlord," he said. And he spoke as one in authority. "A grave injustice is being done to the loyal patriots who are at present under your roof. They are determined that the wrong done to them shall be righted this very night. I have told them how this can best be done, and they are going in a perfectly peaceful frame of mind to put their case before one of the highest authorities in the Province of Artois. I will not mention names, but what the patriots propose to do is in accordance with the laws of the Republic as passed by the National Convention and in strict accordance with the Rights of Man."

He paused a moment, letting his words sink into the feeble minds of these two terrified individuals. Magnol was staring round-eyed not at the stranger, but into the flame of the lantern which appeared to fascinate him and to render him motionless and mute. Only his teeth chattered as if he suffered from ague. The woman had disappeared from view. Her head was buried in the bedclothes.

The stranger continued in the same authoritative voice: "Citizen landlord, two courses are open to you now. Either you side with the patriots in the cause of justice, in which case, if you give them the required help, there will be twenty golden louis for you . . ."

Once more he came to a halt. Magnol's fixed stare seemed suddenly to become galvanised. Cupidity never entirely absent from a peasant's nature gave a spark of vitality to his beady, black eyes. His gaze shifted from the light of the lantern to the hand of the stranger, in whose palm something jingled which sounded uncommonly like precious metal.

"I am a good patriot," he murmured through his chattering teeth.

"I know you are," the stranger rejoined, "that's why I have come to tell you that we count on you to side with us who are fellow patriots and give us what help you can. For," he went on solemnly, emphasising every word, "if you refuse to give us that help, I myself will denounce you as aiding and abetting treason by lending your house to a pack of conspirators and supplying them with food and drink."

Saying this, he turned back the lapel of his coat and allowed the light of the lantern to flash on the metal badge beneath it, which proclaimed him to be a high official of the national police force.

Magnol, scared and bewildered, passed the back of his hand over his humid brow.

"I don't understand," he murmured; "on which side are you, citizen?"

"On your side if you give me the help I need. Dead against you if you refuse."

Once more he allowed the precious metal to jingle in his hand. And Magnol, scared out of his wits, murmured feebly:

"What must I do?"

"Get out of bed," the stranger commanded, "and come with me. You will hand over to the patriots downstairs every gun, every pistol and sabre, every scythe, axe or other tool which you have got stored in your cellars."

"I haven't any stores," Magnol protested.

But he did get out of bed; the jingling metal was a magnet that would have lured him to Gehenna.

"Well, let me see what you have got; and then we will talk."

So far so good. Citizen Magnol, like any landlord of a prosperous country inn, had three or four serviceable guns, a pistol or two and a good number of agricultural implements carefully stored away. He allowed the twenty good patriots to help themselves to what they needed and soon these worthies had laid hands on every available weapon likely to be useful in a fight, if fight there was. And most of them hoped that there would be a good scrap at the very least. Three of them commandeered the guns, two others were quick enough to seize the pistols, while some had to be content with sickles or scythes. One man had a saw, another took a wood-chopper, and there were two or three who had brought their own guns with them, on the chance of getting a pot-shot at a hare.

After that there was a raid on the stables. Most of the men had come into Grécourt on their own horses, and there were a few nags which had been brought in for the sale, for those who had come on foot. There were two fine, mettlesome young horses that had been brought in by a farmer from Tourteron. These were at once appropriated by the stranger without any protest from the owner.

Thus the little cavalcade was formed. They were lined up in the yard, the horses champing and snorting in the cold night air. A pale watery moon had rent the bank of clouds and peeped down on the amazing scene more suggestive of mediæval times than of a winter's night in revolutionary France. The stranger mounted on one young horse held the other by the bridle. He gave the order to start and the cortége filed past him with many a hearty cheer and loud huzzas.

When the last of them had turned out of the yard into the road, he called to the landlord. Magnol had been standing by, gazing on the men, on the horses, on the primitive arms glinting in the blue light of the moon. He was like a man in a trance. He made sure that he was dreaming and would presently wake up to the sound of snoring emitted by his plethoric wife. He was still conscious of an awful feeling of terror, of speeches round him, of Mam'zelle Guillotine wielding her instrument of death, and of a tall, sable-clad figure spouting threats at him. A menacing "either-or."

"Citizen landlord!"

The voice struck his senses as with a whip-lash. He staggered and nearly measured his length on the ground. He blinked his eyes and shielded his head with his arm, for something had been flung at him, something that jingled as it fell at his feet.

The sound of the cavalcade galloping away down the road, the cheers and huzzas were gradually getting fainter. But now there was a fresh clang of hoofs on the cobblestones of the yard. Magnol pulled himself together, tried to collect his scattered senses. He looked about him and perceived a solitary rider wrapped from head to foot in a voluminous mantle. The rider held a second horse by the bridle. In a trice he was across the yard and disappeared round the angle of the house. Magnol could hear the young horses prancing and champing and finally settle down to a swift and fiery gallop.

Then only did Magnol stoop and pick up the missile that had been flung at him. It was a purse and contained twenty golden louis.

CHAPTER XXVII

At the Crossroads

Mam'zelle Guillotine had given the order to halt. It was here, at the cross-roads, that André Renaud had promised to meet her. Falize was distant less than a league away. The road ahead led straight to Paris. There was the secondary road which, as Renaud said, also led by a détour to the capital. Gabrielle was wishing he would soon come. The drive had proved very wearisome, for the roads were heavy and so was the old diligence with its load of armed troopers. And she felt lonely and dispirited. Even the thought of that woman, the last of that family which she hated with such intensity, failed to inflame her blood. The woman was safe enough for the guillotine, but there should have been five of that abominable brood to satisfy Gabrielle Damiens's lust for the blood of the Saint-Lucques.

She gave the order to dismount and the troopers sat by the roadside, or walked up and down the road trying to put warmth into their feet and hands. The moon, peeping through a bank of clouds, made the whole scene appear weird. It did not seem real. Not of this earth. Soon after the start one of the team had gone lame. The corporal in charge was bending over examining the fetlock. Gabrielle, restless and impatient, came down from the box-seat. Wrapped in her warm mantle, with the hood over her head, she looked like a huge furred animal stamping up and down to keep herself warm. Her keen ears were attuned to catch the slightest sound. She felt the tension that kept the men's nerves on edge. They, of course, could do nothing but wait while the time dragged on and there was no sign, as yet, of that mysterious Scarlet Pimpernel whom they were out to capture.

The great lumbering vehicle loomed out of the wan grey light like some grim, spectral monument.

And all at once a sound which caused the men to pause in their pacing, to stand rigid and on the alert, ready to mount the very second that the order was given. Gabrielle too had paused. Her heart seemed to have stopped its beating. Her hot hands gripped the edge of her fur mantle, and with a sharp twist of the head she threw the hood back, away from her ears. The sound which she had heard was of two horses galloping at tip-top speed from the direction of Grécourt. Two horses? Would that be André Renaud? Or was chance really on her side and was it the English spy with one of his followers who were coming this way? She gave a quick appraising glance on the men and gave the order: "Attention!"

The men saw to the priming of their pistols, thrust them back into their belts and drew their sabres. The corporal went round to the door of the diligence, released the lock and to the men cooped up inside he also spoke the one word: "Attention!"

"If that should be the English spies," Gabrielle said aloud, so that the men might hear, "we are ready for them."

The order as far as the escort was concerned was to feign inattention and wait for the attack. The English spies were wily, and should they scent a trap they might scamper away to safety. And the men stood still and waited, their nerves taut, their senses strained. They were like greyhounds held in leash. And now with the Scarlet Pimpernel almost in sight, they were straining the leash to breaking-point.

It was the corporal who first caught sight of the black-coated stranger riding full tilt, from the direction of Grécourt and putting on greater and greater speed as he neared the crossways.

"The stranger with the one arm, citizeness," he said to Gabrielle. She drew a deep sigh of relief. André Renaud—she was sure of him now—had not played her false. With him to give her the weight of his personality with the troopers, she felt more sure of success. Here was a man worthy of her trust. Of late she had felt—oh! so vaguely—a certain weakening of her mettle. Once or twice she had felt conscious of the one thing she had never dreamed of before—Fear. Yes! on two occasions she had actually been afraid. Of whom? Of what? She could not say. It was something indecisively connected with the man with one arm and the fiery eyes under beetling brows. She had not actually been afraid of him or of his threats. He was of the secret police, but she did not fear the police. Her record for militant patriotism was unblemished. At the same time she felt reassured that he was no enemy, and was whole-heartedly on her side.

For Gabrielle Damiens was clever enough to know that her hold on the people of Artois was beginning to slacken. Popular she had never been. But she had been held in awe and that was what she liked. So far there had been no outward sign of waning in the fear which she liked to inspire. Fear? Yes! but no longer that kind of rough admiration which her ruthlessness and free speech was wont to call forth. She had not often indulged in tub-thumping oratory lately, but on the rare occasion when she did, the crowd around her was much thinner than it used to be. She was seldom cheered nowadays, and often she would see her audience diminish in number while she talked. Men on the fringe of the crowd would quietly steal away to the nearest cabaret. Women hardly ever came to hear her.

All these thing were facts which had gradually forced themselves upon her mind. They were the result of her absorption in the one great object of her life, the destruction of the Saint-Lucque family. Thoughts of her revenge obtruded themselves into her oratory until it became dull through the monotony of its theme. The worthy Artesians got tired of listening to vituperations hurled at this one family of aristos, when they wanted to hear all about the doings of the Committee of Public Safety up in Paris, the execution of the Girondins, the quarrels between the Moderates and the Terrorists and other more interesting subjects.

Be that as it may, Gabrielle with her thoughts still centered on the Saint-Lucques and her disappointment in connection with their rescue by the mysterious Scarlet Pimpernel, was inclined after this to allow the man from Paris, whoever he was, to dominate her.

He was out to capture the English spy, she to keep her hold on the prisoner. True he was maimed and, as far as she could judge, past middle-age, in spite of his jet-black hair—which she was sure was dyed with walnut juice—but he had a commanding voice and would keep up the soldiers' morale more easily than she could.

The rider drew rein, arriving at full tilt, and pulled the young horses back on their haunches till they reared and beat the air with their forefeet. In an instant he was out of the saddle and close to Gabrielle. A voluminous dark mantle wrapped him up from head to foot, and the bridle of the two horses were curled round his one arm, leaving the hand free. He took hold of Gabrielle's wrist and drew her to the side of the road out of earshot of the men.

"I don't want to scare them," he said to her in a whisper, "but the rumour has gained ground and what's more it is true."

"What rumour?"

"The English spies have mustered a full force. Some put their numbers down to half a hundred. They were in hiding all day in and about Grécourt. As soon as you had made a start with the diligence they seemed literally to spring out of the ground. So someone told me who saw it all. They were all over the town, swarmed in the market place, in the streets, the cabarets, everywhere. The inhabitants bolted into shelter like rabbits lopping off to their burrows. They were scared out of their wits. Some of them, however, ran to the police and demanded protection. The police duly turned out. The English attacked them with pistols. They killed and wounded a number of them, and then galloped away, hell-for-leather, in this direction."

He still kept a hold on Gabrielle's wrist; but now, when he paused for a moment in order to draw breath, she shook herself free and made for the diligence.

"What are you going to do?" he demanded, and seized hold of her arm again.

"Make an immediate start," she replied curtly.

"How far will you get," he countered, "with that slow-going vehicle? You cannot vanish into the night before the English rabble overtakes you, and they are more numerous than your escort. They are well mounted, too, let me tell you. Now I have two high-mettled horses here. One for you, the other for myself."

"You are crazy!"

"You would be crazy, citizeness, if you tried to flee with that lumbering vehicle, before a pack of well-mounted brigands."

"I would take the secondary road . . ."

"And risk losing the prisoner? The English spies would sight you before you came to the bend of the road. And what chance would your men have, out-numbered four to one?"

"I will not be parted from the prisoner," Gabrielle declared obstinately.

"Why should you be?" he retorted. "Listen to me, citizeness. Name of a dog! can't you understand that the only way to keep the prisoner out of the clutches of the English spies is to leave the coach here standing as a decoy, and to take the woman along with us?"

"Take the woman along with us?" she echoed fiercely. "What in the name of Satan do you mean?"

"You take one horse, citizeness, and I the other. The prisoner can ride pillion behind one of us. They are high-mettled three-year-olds, these horses. We'll be well away before the English horde has discovered that there is no one in the diligence, only the troopers. Order your corporal to wait here and stand his ground. To fight to the last man, and when he has captured the Scarlet Pimpernel, to throw him into the coach and start at once for Falize, where we will meet him as soon as we are satisfied that the storm has blown over and that the coast is clear. Come, citizeness," he urged, "there is no time to lose."

He paused a moment, tensely expectant. Then as she still remained silent and obstinate, he spoke the one word:

"Listen!"

The night was so still that from far, very far away, a confusion of sounds seemed to come floating on the midnight air. Only a murmur at first. Nothing more. A buzzing as from a swarm of bees.

"Listen!" the man said again. And now his voice, though hoarse and toneless, was soul—and spirit-stirring. Gabrielle stood motionless as a statue and listened. She heard the distant murmur like a swarm of bees. The buzzing and the droning. And then, through that confused sound, something like a shout. So vague, so distant, it could scarcely be heard.

"The prisoner, citizeness. It is her they are after."

That compelling voice with its commanding note pierced the armour of Gabrielle's obstinacy.

"Come," she commanded.

She strode to the diligence and he followed her with the horses. With her own hands she opened the door of the coach. The atmosphere inside was suffocating. There was a scramble and a scraping of feet, as the troopers were roused from torpor.

"Present, citizeness," they muttered in unison.

"The prisoner," she commanded again.

"Here, citizeness," one of the soldiers responded.

They pushed and they jostled, each striving to snatch a breath of fresh air at the open door. The unfortunate prisoner was pushed about like a bundle of goods. A feeble moan escaped her lips.

"Hold the horses, citizeness," the stranger broke in curtly.

She obeyed mechanically, moving like an automaton. And like an automaton she called the corporal and gave him what orders the stranger had demanded of her: "Fight to the last man. . . . Throw the English prisoner into the coach. . . . We will meet you at Falize." She watched the man put his foot on the step of the vehicle and with his one arm elbow his way to the woman's side, put that one arm round her and drag her to him. He wrapped his voluminous mantle round her and held her close.

"To horse, citizeness," he urged with desperate intensity. Again she obeyed and was already in the saddle, when the confusion of sounds far away, suddenly became more distinct. A shout arose and then another. Above the buzzing and the humming they arose and seemed to come from many lusty throats. And through the shouting and the buzzing there was a rolling and a drumming and the tramp of many hoofs.

On one high-mettled horse rode Gabrielle Damiens, known throughout the Province of Artois as Mam'zelle Guillotine, on the other a man wrapped in the folds of a black mantle had a woman in his arms.

The moon hid her light behind a bank of clouds.

Darkness fell once more over the land.

The riders galloped on and on into the night.

CHAPTER XXVIII

The Fight

The troopers round and in the diligence were on the alert. They could hear in the distance the sound of horses' hoofs, the shouts and laughter which proclaimed the approach of the English spy and his followers. The English spy! whose capture would mean a goodly sum of money in the pockets of every soldier here present this night. The order to mount was given by the corporal, and in a trice half a dozen stalwarts were in the saddle while six others inside the diligence sat waiting with cocked pistols on their knees.

A few minutes of tense expectation went by, then suddenly round the bend of the road the forms of a dozen or more horsemen galloping, detached themselves from out of the gloom. At sight of the diligence they gave a wild cry of triumph, and brandishing a collection of miscellaneous weapons they rushed to the attack.

"Attention, citizen soldiers," the corporal commanded. "Shoot low. We must have this English horde alive or we'll forfeit half the prize money."

Hardly were the words out of his mouth than with another outburst of frenzied excitement the band of hot-headed farmers and drovers tumbled helter-skelter out of their saddles and rushed to the attack. There was the diligence in front of them looming out of the night like a huge black mass. A fortress to be stormed as the Bastille, that monument of tyranny, had been stormed and reduced four and a half years ago. While some of the party started a hand-to-hand fight with the mounted troopers, others made for the diligence. But before they had come anywhere near it the corporal gave the word of command in a stentorian voice. The carriage door was suddenly thrown open and out came the half-dozen picked men, pistol in hand, eager and ready for the fight. The result of this move was nothing short of disastrous for the unfortunate soldiers.

They were not in the best of trim, after being cooped up in an airless box with only a few short periods of relaxation, for close on twenty-four hours. But apart from that they were from the first at a disadvantage. The attacking party rushed on them as they scrambled out of the coach. Not only were they outnumbered, but as they were forced to come out one by one through the narrow doors, they were fallen on with fists and sickles or axes and soon a number of them were more or less seriously wounded.

It was then that the corporal, who was in the thick of it all, suddenly became aware that the man with whom he was at grips at the moment was not the Scarlet Pimpernel at all or any of the English spies, but farmer Papillon with whom he, Corporal Orgelet, had drunk a mug or two of excellent mulled wine at the Bon Camarade in Grécourt only a few hours ago. He had known Citizen Papillon ever since they had run about together, barefooted ragamuffins in ragged breeches, bent on raiding the nearest apple-orchards.

"What the devil does all this mean?" he thundered, as his friend Papillon raised a powerful, menacing fist high above his head.

"It means that thou art a thief," the farmer fulminated in reply. "Aye! a thief and a liar, and that I'll teach thee not to cheat thy friends another time."

With this, he brought his fist down with a crash on his whilom boon-companion's head.

The fight, such as it was, degenerated into fisticuffs. Farmers and drovers expert enough with a gun when out after a hare or a rabbit had little experience in the use of a pistol or a sabre. Seeing that they were not making any headway with these weapons they cast them incontinently aside and relied on their fists, their sickles and woodchoppers to wreak what mischief they could. And they did wreak any amount of that, for they brought down and wounded a couple of horses, which was an infamous thing to do, and had the effect of turning the wrath of the soldiers into something like execration. They struck at their assailants with their sabres, shouting:

"Take that, thou limb of Satan!"

"'Tis with Mam'zelle Guillotine thou wilt have to reckon."

Indeed, the troopers had already realised that here were no English spies, only a set of drunken jackanapes who in their senseless frenzy were actually daring to lay hands on the soldiers of the Republic. The attack was either an insane hoax, or the result of some ghastly misunderstanding. For the soldiers and the attacking party were all friends together. There was Faret, the drover from Néthon and Constant the washerwoman's son over St. Charles way, and there was Charon the farmer as well as Papillon, and even Antoine, who was own cousin to Corporal Orgelet. What in the devil's name was it all about? It was very mysterious and extremely foolish.

It was also very serious.

These irresponsible fire-eaters would have to be taught a lesson. They would have to learn to their cost that such wanton madness could not remain unpunished and that a man who dares to attack a soldier of the Republic and impede him in the execution of his duty must suffer for his crime. The fight had only lasted a few minutes, but of the thirty-two combatants who took part in it, on one side and the other, there were at least a dozen lying wounded on the ground. And there were the poor horses too. The whole affair might have become even more tragic than it already was. So far the troopers had been unable to use their pistols to good effect. The mounted men were slashing away with their sabres, and the others who had turned out of the diligence, had been at grips each with two or even three assailants who gave them no respite but pounded away at them with their fists. Corporal Orgelet himself was lying on the ground with his friend Papillon holding him down. He had already received from his whilom boon-companion one or two nasty cracks on the head, when with a clever twist of his body he contrived to get hold of his pistol and to discharge it into Papillon's thigh. The latter uttered a loud imprecation and rolled over on his side yelling: "Assassin! Thou hast murdered me!"

The sudden report, however, had the good effect of sobering the aggressors. It also brought the soldiers back to a sense of discipline, and gave them the confidence which this extraordinary surprise attack had so signally shaken. At once the fight between soldiers and civilians assumed its just proportions, and after a few more pistol shots had been discharged, a few more sabre thrusts gone home and a few stalwarts had been sent rolling over on the ground, Orgelet was able to call a "Halt!". The assailants were ready to surrender. He ordered them to be mustered up. Groaning and cursing, for most of them had suffered pretty severely at the hands of the soldiers, they were lined up, guarded by the troopers, some of whom were in as pitiable a state as themselves. The faint, grey gleam of a winter's night revealed some of them standing, others kneeling or crouching, some with their faces smeared with blood, their eyes bunged up and lips bleeding, all with their hair hanging lank and wet over their eyes. They did indeed present a sorry spectacle. Orgelet himself in a sad plight and dizzy with many a crack on the head, passed up and down the short line, eyeing the wretched men with wrath and contempt in his eyes.

"I ought to have the lot of you summarily shot," he said grimly. "Yes! shot here and now. And I will do it, too," he bellowed at them, "Unless you tell me at once what is the meaning of this abominable outrage."

"Thou can'st add murder to thy other crimes, citizen corporal," Papillon retorted loudly, "to thy lying and thy cheating, and joining hands with Mam'zelle Guillotine to rob us of what was our due."

"Joining hands with Mam'zelle Guillotine to rob you?" Orgelet countered, lost in bewilderment. "What the devil do you mean? Of what did I rob you?"

"Of the reward due to us for the capture of the Scarlet Pimpernel."

"The capture of the Scarlet Pimpernel?" Orgelet thundered at them. "You fools! You dolts! That is impossible now after the hellish row you have been making."

"Do not lie to us, Orgelet," one of the wounded men responded. "We know that thou didst capture the English spy in our district and that thou and Mam'zelle Guillotine will share the prize money which is rightly due to us. We came to avenge a wrong . . ."

"What balderdash is this?" Orgelet broke in gruffly. "Who says we captured the English spy?"

"I do," declared Faret, the drover from Néthon.

Orgelet gave a shrug of contempt, a light had suddenly broken in on the confusion of his mind. He was beginning to understand.

"If we captured him," he queried, "what have we done with him?"

"You've got him locked up in there." And with a dramatic gesture Antoine, who was own cousin to Orgelet, pointed to the diligence. "Thief! Liar, thy mother shall hear of this."

This was altogether too much for the corporal's gravity. He burst out laughing and continued to laugh immoderately until feeling faint and giddy with the pain in his head, he nearly measured his length on the road.

"Ah!" he said, his voice still shaking with inward laughter, "is that where that mysterious English spy is? . . . Well," he went on, after a slight pause, "go and get him out, my friends."

Funnily enough, in the heat and excitement of the fight the one object that had induced these madmen to commit the unpardonable folly of attacking troopers of the Republican army had been lost sight of by them. From the moment when they came to close quarters with the soldiers, thoughts of the Scarlet Pimpernel and the English horde vanished from their minds. The only idea that did remain fixed was the question of a hundred louis apiece which these soldiers had filched from them. But now, when Corporal Orgelet himself pointed to the diligence and said: "Go and get him out," there was, in spite of wounds and despite exhaustion, one concerted rush for the coach. Something like a scramble, in fact, which left an unpleasant trail of blood in its wake. The carriage door was still wide open. Farmer Papillon was the first to set foot inside the coach. He groped about the interior with his hands, administered vigorous kicks to supposed and non-existent occupants. Kicks which only reached his unfortunate boon-companions and drew groans and curses from them in response. Some seven or eight of them succeeded in entering the coach and as they tumbled one on the top of the other all they did was to aggravate their woes and the soreness of their wounds.

And all the while Orgelet and the men stood outside whole-heartedly enjoying the joke. For them the whole thing had degenerated into a joke. Whether in the meanwhile the English spies had gone never to return, whether their chance of earning a bit of money had vanished into the night air, on the wings of noise and confusion and hard blows freely dealt and received, they could form no idea as yet. One thing only was certain, and that was that orders must be obeyed. Orders were to fight to the last man and then proceed to Falize where Mam'zelle Guillotine would rejoin the party. Orgelet, who was a good soldier and good disciplinarian, rallied the troopers round him. He ordered the wounded to enter the diligence, and the others to get back to horse. The horses brought hither by the attacking party had wandered away across fields for the most part. A few had stampeded and bolted back to the stables whence they had come. Others again were presently recaptured, after a short difference of opinion 'tween man and beast. Those that were hurt must of necessity be walked along very quietly on the lead. Fortunately their wounds were not serious and Falize was not far.

As for the miserable aggressors, there they were, crestfallen, and dolefully nursing their wounds. It was easy to see that Corporal Orgelet and the soldiers looked upon them with contempt and pity rather than ill-feeling. The whole affair had been inglorious. Victory over such rabble was nothing to be proud of. Orgelet mounted to the box-seat and took the reins. The escort was formed once more. A crack of the whip and a click of the tongue and the team settled into their collars. The cumbrous vehicle once more started on its way, whilst a score of discomfited and bedraggled rustics made their way as best they could afoot or astride a horse, back to Grécourt.

CHAPTER XXIX

Hell-for-Leather

Blakeney held Eve de Saint-Lucque close to him under the folds of his voluminous mantle. Keeping to the edge of the road, where the ground was soft, he gave the mettlesome three-year-old full rein. He seemed indeed to have imbued his mount with all the devilment that was in his own blood, enjoying to the full the noble sport which in an earnest profession of faith he had extolled before his royal friend on that winter's evening more than a sen'night ago, when surrounded by every luxury that wealth and epicurism could devise, he had boldly declared:

"I'll back my favourite sport against any that has ever been invented for making a man feel akin to the gods. . . . With the keen air fanning your cheeks, with the night wrapping you round. With woman or child clinging to you, their weak arms holding tightly to your waist, with human wolves behind you while you ride for dear life through unknown country, riding, galloping, not knowing where you may land, out of one death-trap into another . . . that, Your Highness, is the sport for me . . ."

Gabrielle was doing her best to keep up with him. Something of his wild animal spirits had got into her now. No longer dispirited, no longer doubtful of success, she kept her mind fixed on this wonderful victory which she had achieved over those whom she hated so bitterly. True the other members of the execrated family had escaped her, but she hugged herself with the comforting thought that the Saint-Lucque children would be motherless, and their father a widower, and all of them broken-hearted. And this was thanks to André Renaud—or whoever he was—who had been the deus ex machina, the final instrument of her revenge.

Galloping sometimes behind him, at others some little distance in the rear, all that she could see of him through the gloom was the square mass of his mantle, which enveloped him from the neck to the knees. Yes, there was a devil in the man, she said to herself, while she made vigorous efforts not to lag behind.

After the first ten minutes of this wild gallopade, when the sounds of fighting, way over the cross-roads, had been swallowed up by the night, she had ceased to try to determine whither she was being led. She had lost all sense of direction. All she could do was to follow blindly on. It was only after a long climb over a steep portion of the road, when the man drew rein to give his horse a breather, that she ventured on questioning him.

"What is our first objective?" she asked.

"The unknown," he cried joyously in response.

"The unknown?" she echoed grimly. "You are mad."

"By George! I believe I am," he assented, and peeped down through the closure of his mantle at the burden which lay in his arms.

"We are not heading for Paris," she objected; "I do not even know where we are."

"No more do I, citizeness," he responded with a happy chuckle. "But we'll get somewhere in time. Before dawn if we are lucky. En avant, citizeness, the unknown means victory to two of us over our enemies. They'll never look for us there."

Even before he had finished speaking, he had touched his mount slightly with a spur and off they were again, he with his burden under his mantle, and she, galloping as close to him as she could, with her thoughts once more beginning to whirl about in her brain and her nerves strained to breaking-point.

At one time she thought that they were making tracks for Mézières. It was too dark to see much and Gabrielle Damiens was not a country wench, not a rustic who would know direction by instinct, by the way the wind blew, and by the fleeting clouds. Less than five years ago she was still a captive in the Bastille. Since then she had roamed in and out of cities and knew little of the open country. She had not seen much of her own Province of Artois. Mézières and its immediate neighbourhood she knew, of course. She also knew Grécourt and Falize and the main roads which led to Paris one way and to the Belgian frontier the other. It was not along either of these roads they were speeding now. Then whither were they going? Her tired eyes wandered round striving to pierce the darkness of the night. Now and again, when for a few brief moments the moon peeped through a fissure in the clouds, she thought to perceive somewhere in the distance a half-forgotten landmark: a jutting hillock, a belt of trees or the white church steeple of an isolated village. And when presently the road plunged into a thicket she thought it must be the forest of Mézières. But the forest of Mézières was more dense, the undergrowth thicker, the road in places more steep. It was here that the encounter with the English spies was to have taken place. No, no! This was not the forest of Mézières. Then what was it?

Once outside the belt of trees, her straining ears perceived the sound of running water. Swift and turbulent. Where could this be? They went over a bridge and to right and left she could hear the water rushing and tumbling down from a height over rocky projections. The rider on ahead put his horse to a trot, and she was able to come up to him. Quite close. It seemed to her then as if at a short distance away a few solid masses inky-black and grouped together loomed out of the gloom darker than the night. A village probably.

"The unknown," he called out, with a ring of triumph in his voice, and pointed in that direction. "En avant, citizeness."

And before she was aware of what was happening, he had caught hold of her bridle rein, and thereafter she knew nothing more, for her mount was being carried along with its stable companion, hell-for-leather at breakneck speed.

She made an effort to wrench the bridle out of his hand, but it was held in a grip that was as hard and as unyielding as steel. Half dazed with fatigue and want of breath, she tried to slide down out of the saddle. Her foot had just touched the ground the ground, when with a vigorous jerk he drew rein. Panting and snorting and beating the air with their hoofs, the horses presently came to a dead halt. Gabrielle fell clean out of the saddle and lay in a heap on the ground. She was on the point of swooning. Through a state of semi-consciousness, she heard the man calling repeatedly for the landlord, and later on there was a banging of shutters and creaking of door hinges. She lay quite still for she was bruised all over and inexpressibly weary. Again she heard the man's voice:

"Hey there! citizen landlord."

And she murmured: "Where am I?"

It was shortly before the dawn, a pale grey light in the east picked out with a silvery sheen here and there a sloping roof or the topmost branch of tall cypress trees. It was cold and damp. Gabrielle rolled over on her side. She was lying prone on the mud of the road. Over her head something squeaked with irritating persistency. She glanced up and vaguely discerned a painted sign swinging on its post. She heard one man's voice alternating with another.

"Travellers, citizen landlord. We have lost our way. Can you put us up until daylight?"

There was some demur followed by a jingle of precious metal. After which the other voice put in gruffly:

"I have one room. . . ."

"This purse contains a louis d'or, citizen landlord. If there were two rooms there would be two louis."

Further demur apparently and then:

"It is too late for supper, anyway."

"If you bring us three mugs of hut mulled wine, there will be four louis d'or inside this purse."

After which a shrill voice called from above:

"Don't be a fool, Mathieu. Let the travellers come in and give them mulled wine while I get the rooms ready. It will cost you five louis," she went on after a slight pause, "and no questions asked."

The three of them sat at a table in the tap-room of this wayside inn. The landlord had brought in three large pewter mugs filled to the brim with steaming, spiced wine. There is no better drink in the world than mulled wine concocted by a French countryman. Eve de Saint-Lucque, looking a pitiful rag of femininity, gave a wan smile as Blakeney persuaded her to drink.

"You too, citizeness," he said turning to Gabrielle, who sat there sullen and mute doing her best to fight that intense weariness which took all the life out of her. Blakeney drew a flask out of his pocket.

"The wine is good," he said, "but a drop of good old cognac will improve it."

He poured out the contents of his flask into Gabrielle's pewter mug. She drank it all down at one draught.

A woman's footsteps were heard clattering down the wooden stairs.

"The rooms are ready," she announced curtly.

"And so are the five louis d'or," Blakeney responded gaily and counted out the gold in the woman's wrinkled hand.

"Will you follow our kind hostess, citizeness," he said, lightly touching Gabrielle on the shoulder. She gave no answer, spread out her arms over the table and let her head drop down heavily upon them.

"I'll stay here," she murmured almost inaudibly.

Blakeney stood by for a moment looking down on her with an expression in his face that was partly of contempt and partly of pity. She never moved.

He then went over to the other side of the table where Eve de Saint-Lucque sat fingering the pewter mug, and gazing out before her, at Gabrielle for a time and then at him. Her eyes circled with purple, her quivering lips, her wan and sunken cheeks, showed plainly the extent to which this unfortunate and plucky woman had suffered. But in spite of the pain which she still endured, in spite of intense fatigue, bruised body and aching head, it was a pæan of praise and benediction and reverence that her poor, weary eyes expressed as she looked on the man to whom she owed her life and that of her children.

When she rested in his arms throughout this mad gallopade through the darkness and the frosty air, he had at one moment peeped down at her through the folds of his mantle and murmured just loudly enough for her to hear:

"Your children are safe in the care of my friends. You are safe with me. The Scarlet Pimpernel has kept his word."

She had snuggled up closer to him then, striving to make herself as small, as little burdensome to him as she could. She had never seen him yet, but from the moment that he dragged her out of the diligence, she felt somehow secure in his protecting arms.

Now in this squalid room, with its drab walls and its menacing inscriptions: Liberté, Egalité, Fraternité ou la Mort, with the silence around only broken by the prosaic sound of the other woman's stertorous breathing. Eve looked up and tried to make out something of the mysterious personality of her rescuer. All she saw of him was the top of his head masked by coal-black hair which lay across his forehead like a funereal band. She saw a pair of bushy, black eyebrows, a long thin nose, a chin buried in a white linen stock. The tallow candle set on the table flickered in the draught. The sight which she got of that curious face was fitful and intermittent, but in her own mind she was quite sure that the black hair was a wig and that the nose was a false one, and the beetling brow a final touch to what was obviously a disguise. She gazed at him whilst an expression of puzzlement settled into her eyes. Puzzlement that turned into an appeal. Would she ever look into his face, his real face, she wondered. Would she ever behold the man as he really was, or would he ever remain for her an enigma, a mysterious entity, the hero of her dreams?

"Do you think you can bear it Madame?" he now asked. He had said something else before that, but she had not heard. So she said simply:

"I can bear anything that you impose upon me. What is it?"

"Three, perhaps four days in a rickety, jolting cart with intervals of rest in derelict cottages with a hard floor for a bed and straw for a pillow. Can you bear it?"

"You mock me, sir," she countered with a smile, "by asking me this. When do we start?"

"As soon as I have made arrangements with our rapacious landlord. In the meanwhile try and snatch a couple of hours' sleep. The woman is just outside. She will conduct you to your room."

He went to the door and called to the woman. When he turned back to Eve she was standing beside Gabrielle's inert form. She raised enquiring eyes to his.

"Will she be with us all the time?" she asked.

He gave a short, low laugh. Then he said with a curious sudden change to earnestness.

"No, Madame, whatever the fool or the heathen may say, God is just." He paused a moment, then added:

"We'll leave her here in the care of her master."

"Her master? You mean . . .?"

"I mean the master who has prompted all her actions in the past. He will, I doubt not, looked after her now and in the future."

Eve, wondering what he meant, went thoughtfully to her room.

CHAPTER XXX

The Silent Pool

When Gabrielle roused herself from her drugged sleep, a pale wintry sun was peeping in through the grimy window of the tap-room. It was broad daylight. Half a dozen men were sitting at the table, some of them were drinking wine, others eating some sort of savoury stew which they ladled out for themselves out of a metal tureen. Gabrielle opened her eyes and looked about her. She had no recollection whatever of where she was. She sniffed the air like a hungry dog, the odour of the stew had roused her and she was hungry. Her tongue felt parched and clung to the roof of her mouth.

An elderly woman was busy about the room serving the men who called for this, that and the other. They were all labourers or countrymen of some sort. Gabrielle looked at them with bleared eyes. When her gaze came to rest on the woman, she blinked and then called thickly for food and drink. No one took much notice of her. The woman brought her a mug and a bottle and set them on the table; she also brought a spoon and a metal plate and Gabrielle helped herself to the savoury stew out of the tureen.

"There's a room ready for you upstairs," the woman said to her, "It is paid for. You can go up if you like."

Gabrielle rose, she shook herself like a frowsy cur, for she felt cold and stiff. Wrapping the fur mantle closely round her she strode out of the room. A slaternly wench on the landing showed her up to the attic where a truckle-bed had been made up for her. Gabrielle threw herself down on the palliasse, closed her eyes and went to sleep.

Suddenly she opened her eyes, she was wide awake. It must have been late in the afternoon. The last of a wintry twilight shed its wan light through the cracked window of the squalid attic. Gabrielle rose. She still felt cold and stiff and dizzy from the fatigue of that wild ride through the night. She wandered down the rickety stairs and peeped into the tap-room. The slaternly wench was there doing some perfunctory cleaning of the table and setting down mugs, plates and spoons for supper-guests. The landlord came stumping out form the back premises, his sabots clattering on the tiled floor.

"Your room has been paid for for a week," he said gruffly, as soon as he caught of Gabrielle. "Do you want to stay?"

She said: "Perhaps." And turning on her heel went in the direction of the front door.

"The other two went at crack of dawn," the man went on. "They left a small parcel for you. I'll go and get it."

He stumped back to the kitchen and returned after a moment or two with something soft wrapped in a dirty scrap of paper, held tightly in his hand. Gabrielle took the parcel from him. It was dark in the passage, so she went back to the tap-room, sat down at the table and drew the tallow candle nearer to her. She undid the parcel and spread the contents out on the table. The landlord peered inquisitively over her shoulder.

"Why!" he exclaimed, "what on earth are these things?"

"As you see, citizen," Gabrielle replied. And the landlord declared subsequently that never had he heard a woman's voice sound so strange and inhuman. It was, he said, more like the growling of a wounded beast than the voice of a woman. She fingered the things that were lying on the table: a wig of black hair, a papier-mâché nose, a pair of false eyebrows. She touched each thing with a hand that shook visibly. The man picked them up one by one and quickly dropped them again, as if they scorched his fingers.

"What devil's work is this?" he muttered.

"Devil's work, as you say, citizen landlord," she rejoined dully. "The work of the English spy who was here in this very room a few hours ago. Had you detained him, you would be richer now by a hundred louis. Think of that, citizen landlord. Good night. Pleasant dreams."

She gave a curious, mirthless laugh, as if she were demented, so the landlord said later on. She picked up one by one the miscellaneous contents of the parcel, strode out of the room and went out into the street.

The last of the twilight had faded out of the sky. The village street lay still and dark to right and left of the wayside inn, in the doorway of which stood the lonely woman. She glanced up and down the street, trying to distinguish some landmark or other in the gloom, or perhaps just making up her mind as to which way to turn for her solitary ramble in the night. The sound of running water came faintly to her ear from the left. She turned in that direction, ambling along aimlessly at first. Then as the sound grew more distinct, she quickened her step, walked more resolutely along. Always in the darkness which only revealed vaguely the edge of the road, and always in the direction whence came the sound of running water.

Thus she came to the bridge which spanned the torrent, the bridge over which she had ridden full tilt yesterday, with her bridle rein held in a grip that was like steel, whilst she herself was held in bondage and rendered helpless in the hands of a ruthless and relentless enemy.

"What is our first objective?" she had asked him then.

And he had replied: "The unknown."

And for her the unknown was a torrent that came scurrying and tumbling down over rocky projections. She stood quite still, looking down on the waters which she heard but could not see. On the right a mossy path ran along the edge of the stream. Gabrielle turned her wearied footsteps down that way. On she wandered with the sound of running water falling on her ear like the accusing voice of a relentless Nemesis.

"Thy revenge," it murmured, "where is it now? For it thou didst scheme and murder and commit every crime that disgraced thy womanhood. Where is it now? Those whom thy hatred has pursued are safe and happy out of thy reach. Where art thou at this hour? Whither doest thou go?"

And idly wandering Gabrielle Damiens came to the pool wherein the turbulent eddy found its rest. Here the swirl of the falling waters caused innumerable bubbles to form and to burst again. Beyond the swirl, the pool seemed to be placid and very still. Gabrielle came to a halt, and looking down she tried to gauge the depth of the water, but the night was like ebony and the over-hanging trees threw a further veil of darkness over the silent pool. She stood quite still now, and around her everything was still save for the occasional crackling of dry twigs overhead or the movement of tiny furtive feet in the undergrowth. She still had in her hands that collection of curious objects—the wig, the false eyebrows, the nose made of papier-mâché such as clowns wear at the circus. She fingered them lightly for a while, then laid them down on a flat piece of projecting stone. There was no wind and the things remained all night where she had put them. The were found in the early morning by a couple of labourers on their way to work. They wondered what on earth these things could possibly be, and how they got there. No one ever knew.

Throughout the length and breadth of the Province of Artois no one ever knew what had become of Mam'zelle Guillotine. She had come no one knew whence. She went no one knew whither. Six months later the Reign of Terror in France came to an end. The guillotine in the province was no longer kept busy and an honest butcher of Mézières did all that there was to do.

CHAPTER XXXI

An Interlude

Marguerite Blakeney was in her husband's arms. She was looking pale and wan and her wonderful, luminous eyes still bore the traces of all the tears which she had shed. She had been the first to arrive in Dover at the Fisherman's Rest, in the company of Percy's devoted followers and the two little children for whose sake he had thrown his precious life in the balance of Fate, courting death with joy in his heart and a smile on his lips. For close on a month Marguerite in her weary travelling to Belgium and through Belgium on to England, had known nothing of her adored husband, save that at every hour of the day and night that heroic life was in deadly peril.

Now when his arms were once more round her and she looked into his merry deep-set eyes, the joy of reunion was almost more than she could bear. She tried to make him tell her something of what he had endured and gone through for the sake of an unfortunate woman and two innocent children now happily reunited to husband, father and brother.

"Luck was on my side, light of my life," was all he said, "because you were so near me all the time. And luck was backed by the courage and understanding of brave men like Ffoulkes and Tony, Glynde and St. Dennys, and your adorable self."

"But, Percy," she insisted, "if luck had failed you. If . . ."

"Luck, my beloved," he said, and once more that wonderful look of the born adventurer, the gambler, the fearless sportsman, the look which she dreaded to see more than any other, came back into his eyes; "luck is just an old woman, m'dear, bald save for one hair on her head. It is up to her courtier to seize her by that one hair when perchance she flits by past him at arm's length. But, by George," he concluded with his infectious, merry laugh, "having got hold of that hair, it is up to him not to let it go. And that is all I did, my adored, I did not let go."

ELDORADO

FOREWORD

There has of late years crept so much confusion into the mind of the student as well as of the general reader as to the identity of the Scarlet Pimpernel with that of the Gascon Royalist plotter known to history as the Baron de Batz, that the time seems opportune for setting all doubts on that subject at rest.

The identity of the Scarlet Pimpernel is in no way whatever connected with that of the Baron de Batz, and even superficial reflection will soon bring the mind to the conclusion that great fundamental differences existed in these two men, in their personality, in their character, and, above all, in their aims.

According to one or two enthusiastic historians, the Baron de Batz was the chief agent in a vast network of conspiracy, entirely supported by foreign money—both English and Austrian—and which had for its object the overthrow of the Republican Government and the restoration of the monarchy in France.

In order to attain this political goal, it is averred that he set himself the task of pitting the members of the revolutionary Government one against the other, and bringing hatred and dissensions amongst them, until the cry of "Traitor!" resounded from one end of the Assembly of the Convention to the other, and the Assembly itself became as one vast den of wild beasts wherein wolves and hyenas devoured one another and, still unsatiated, licked their streaming jaws hungering for more prey.

Those same enthusiastic historians, who have a firm belief in the so-called "Foreign Conspiracy," ascribe every important event of the Great Revolution—be that event the downfall of the Girondins, the escape of the Dauphin from the Temple, or the death of Robespierre—to the intrigues of Baron de Batz. He it was, so they say, who egged the Jacobins on against the Mountain, Robespierre against Danton, Hebert against Robespierre. He it was who instigated the massacres of September, the atrocities of Nantes, the horrors of Thermidor, the sacrileges, the noyades: all with the view of causing every section of the National Assembly to vie with the other in excesses and in cruelty, until the makers of the Revolution, satiated with their own lust, turned on one another, and Sardanapalus-like buried themselves and their orgies in the vast hecatomb of a self-consumed anarchy.

Whether the power thus ascribed to Baron de Batz by his historians is real or imaginary it is not the purpose of this preface to investigate. Its sole object is to point out the difference between the career of this plotter and that of the Scarlet Pimpernel.

The Baron de Batz himself was an adventurer without substance, save that which he derived from abroad. He was one of those men who have nothing to lose and everything to gain by throwing themselves headlong in the seething cauldron of internal politics.

Though he made several attempts at rescuing King Louis first, and then the

Queen and Royal Family from prison and from death, he never succeeded, as we know, in any of these undertakings, and he never once so much as attempted the rescue of other equally innocent, if not quite so distinguished, victims of the most bloodthirsty revolution that has ever shaken the foundations of the civilised world.

Nay more; when on the 29th Prairial those unfortunate men and women were condemned and executed for alleged complicity in the so-called "Foreign Conspiracy," de Batz, who is universally admitted to have been the head and prime-mover of that conspiracy—if, indeed, conspiracy there was—never made either the slightest attempt to rescue his confederates from the guillotine, or at least the offer to perish by their side if he could not succeed in saving them.

And when we remember that the martyrs of the 29th Prairial included women like Grandmaison, the devoted friend of de Batz, the beautiful Emilie de St. Amaranthe, little Cecile Renault—a mere child not sixteen years of age—also men like Michonis and Roussell, faithful servants of de Batz, the Baron de Lezardiere, and the Comte de St. Maurice, his friends, we no longer can have the slightest doubt that the Gascon plotter and the English gentleman are indeed two very different persons.

The latter's aims were absolutely non-political. He never intrigued for the restoration of the monarchy, or even for the overthrow of that Republic which he loathed.

His only concern was the rescue of the innocent, the stretching out of a saving hand to those unfortunate creatures who had fallen into the nets spread out for them by their fellow-men; by those who—godless, lawless, penniless themselves—had sworn to exterminate all those who clung to their belongings, to their religion, and to their beliefs.

The Scarlet Pimpernel did not take it upon himself to punish the guilty; his care was solely of the helpless and of the innocent.

For this aim he risked his life every time that he set foot on French soil, for it he sacrificed his fortune, and even his personal happiness, and to it he devoted his entire existence.

Moreover, whereas the French plotter is said to have had confederates even in the Assembly of the Convention, confederates who were sufficiently influential and powerful to secure his own immunity, the Englishman when he was bent on his errands of mercy had the whole of France against him.

The Baron de Batz was a man who never justified either his own ambitions or even his existence; the Scarlet Pimpernel was a personality of whom an entire nation might justly be proud.

PART I

CHAPTER I

In the Theatre National

And yet people found the opportunity to amuse themselves, to dance and to go to the theatre, to enjoy music and open-air cafes and promenades in the Palais Royal.

New fashions in dress made their appearance, milliners produced fresh "creations," and jewellers were not idle. A grim sense of humour, born of the very intensity of ever-present danger, had dubbed the cut of certain tunics "tete tranche," or a favourite ragout was called "a la guillotine."

On three evenings only during the past memorable four and a half years did the theatres close their doors, and these evenings were the ones immediately following that terrible 2nd of September the day of the butchery outside the Abbaye prison, when Paris herself was aghast with horror, and the cries of the massacred might have drowned the calls of the audience whose hands upraised for plaudits would still be dripping with blood.

On all other evenings of these same four and a half years the theatres in the Rue de Richelieu, in the Palais Royal, the Luxembourg, and others, had raised their curtains and taken money at their doors. The same audience that earlier in the day had whiled away the time by witnessing the ever-recurrent dramas of the Place de la Revolution assembled here in the evenings and filled stalls, boxes, and tiers, laughing over the satires of Voltaire or weeping over the sentimental tragedies of persecuted Romeos and innocent Juliets.

Death knocked at so many doors these days! He was so constant a guest in the houses of relatives and friends that those who had merely shaken him by the hand, those on whom he had smiled, and whom he, still smiling, had passed indulgently by, looked on him with that subtle contempt born of familiarity, shrugged their shoulders at his passage, and envisaged his probable visit on the morrow with light-hearted indifference.

Paris—despite the horrors that had stained her walls had remained a city of pleasure, and the knife of the guillotine did scarce descend more often than did the drop-scenes on the stage.

On this bitterly cold evening of the 27th Nivose, in the second year of the Republic—or, as we of the old style still persist in calling it, the 16th of January, 1794—the auditorium of the Theatre National was filled with a very brilliant company.

The appearance of a favourite actress in the part of one of Moliere's volatile heroines had brought pleasure-loving Paris to witness this revival of "Le Misanthrope," with new scenery, dresses, and the aforesaid charming actress to add piquancy to the master's mordant wit.

The Moniteur, which so impartially chronicles the events of those times, tells us under that date that the Assembly of the Convention voted on that same day a new law giving fuller power to its spies, enabling them to effect domiciliary searches at their discretion without previous reference to the Committee of General Security, authorising them to proceed against all enemies of public happiness, to send them to prison at their own discretion, and assuring them the sum of thirty-five livres "for every piece of game thus beaten up for the guillotine." Under that same date the Moniteur also puts it on record that the Theatre National was filled to its utmost capacity for the revival of the late citoyen Moliere's comedy.

The Assembly of the Convention having voted the new law which placed the lives of thousands at the mercy of a few human bloodhounds, adjourned its sitting and proceeded to the Rue de Richelieu.

Already the house was full when the fathers of the people made their way to the seats which had been reserved for them. An awed hush descended on the throng as one by one the men whose very names inspired horror and dread filed in through the narrow gangways of the stalls or took their places in the tiny boxes around.

Citizen Robespierre's neatly bewigged head soon appeared in one of these; his bosom friend St. Just was with him, and also his sister Charlotte. Danton, like a big, shaggy-coated lion, elbowed his way into the stalls, whilst Sauterre, the handsome butcher and idol of the people of Paris, was loudly acclaimed as his huge frame, gorgeously clad in the uniform of the National Guard, was sighted on one of the tiers above.

The public in the parterre and in the galleries whispered excitedly; the awe-inspiring names flew about hither and thither on the wings of the overheated air. Women craned their necks to catch sight of heads which mayhap on the morrow would roll into the gruesome basket at the foot of the guillotine.

In one of the tiny avant-scene boxes two men had taken their seats long before the bulk of the audience had begun to assemble in the house. The inside of the box was in complete darkness, and the narrow opening which allowed but a sorry view of one side of the stage helped to conceal rather than display the occupants.

The younger one of these two men appeared to be something of a stranger in Paris, for as the public men and the well-known members of the Government began to arrive he often turned to his companion for information regarding these notorious personalities.

"Tell me, de Batz," he said, calling the other's attention to a group of men who had just entered the house, "that creature there in the green coat—with his hand up to his face now—who is he?"

"Where? Which do you mean?"

"There! He looks this way now, and he has a playbill in his hand. The man with the protruding chin and the convex forehead, a face like a marmoset, and eyes like a jackal. What?"

The other leaned over the edge of the box, and his small, restless eyes wandered over the now closely-packed auditorium.

"Oh!" he said as soon as he recognised the face which his friend had pointed out to him, "that is citizen Foucquier-Tinville."

"The Public Prosecutor?"

"Himself. And Heron is the man next to him."

"Heron?" said the younger man interrogatively.

"Yes. He is chief agent to the Committee of General Security now."

"What does that mean?"

Both leaned back in their chairs, and their sombrely-clad figures were once more merged in the gloom of the narrow box. Instinctively, since the name of the Public Prosecutor had been mentioned between them, they had allowed their voices to sink to a whisper.

The older man—a stoutish, florid-looking individual, with small, keen eyes, and skin pitted with small-pox—shrugged his shoulders at his friend's question, and then said with an air of contemptuous indifference:

"It means, my good St. Just, that these two men whom you see down there, calmly conning the programme of this evening's entertainment, and preparing to enjoy themselves to-night in the company of the late M. de Moliere, are two hell-hounds as powerful as they are cunning."

"Yes, yes," said St. Just, and much against his will a slight shudder ran through his slim figure as he spoke. "Foucquier-Tinville I know; I know his cunning, and I know his power—but the other?"

"The other?" retorted de Batz lightly. "Heron? Let me tell you, my friend, that even the might and lust of that damned Public Prosecutor pale before the power of Heron!"

"But how? I do not understand."

"Ah! you have been in England so long, you lucky dog, and though no doubt the main plot of our hideous tragedy has reached your ken, you have no cognisance of the actors who play the principal parts on this arena flooded with blood and carpeted with hate. They come and go, these actors, my good St. Just—they come and go. Marat is already the man of yesterday, Robespierre is the man of to-morrow. To-day we still have Danton and Foucquier-Tinville; we still have Pere Duchesne, and your own good cousin Antoine St. Just, but Heron and his like are with us always."

"Spies, of course?"

"Spies," assented the other. "And what spies! Were you present at the sitting of the Assembly to-day?"

"I was. I heard the new decree which already has passed into law. Ah! I tell you, friend, that we do not let the grass grow under our feet these days. Robespierre wakes up one morning with a whim; by the afternoon that whim has become law, passed by a servile body of men too terrified to run counter to his will, fearful lest they be accused of moderation or of humanity—the greatest crimes that can be committed nowadays."

"But Danton?"

"Ah! Danton? He would wish to stem the tide that his own passions have let loose; to muzzle the raging beasts whose fangs he himself has sharpened. I told you that Danton is still the man of to-day; to-morrow he will be accused of moderation. Danton and moderation!—ye gods! Eh? Danton, who thought the guillotine too slow in its work, and armed thirty soldiers with swords, so that thirty heads might fall at one and the same time. Danton, friend, will perish to-morrow accused of treachery against the Revolution, of moderation towards her enemies; and curs like Heron will feast on the blood of lions like Danton and his crowd."

He paused a moment, for he dared not raise his voice, and his whispers were being drowned by the noise in the auditorium. The curtain, timed to be raised at eight o'clock, was still down, though it was close on half-past, and the public was growing impatient. There was loud stamping of feet, and a few shrill whistles of disapproval proceeded from the gallery.

"If Heron gets impatient," said de Batz lightly, when the noise had momentarily subsided, "the manager of this theatre and mayhap his leading actor and actress will spend an unpleasant day to-morrow."

"Always Heron!" said St. Just, with a contemptuous smile.

"Yes, my friend," rejoined the other imperturbably, "always Heron. And he has even obtained a longer lease of existence this afternoon."

"By the new decree?"

"Yes. The new decree. The agents of the Committee of General Security, of whom Heron is the chief, have from to-day powers of domiciliary search; they have full powers to proceed against all enemies of public welfare. Isn't that beautifully vague? And they have absolute discretion; every one may become an enemy of public welfare, either by spending too much money or by spending too little, by laughing to-day or crying to-morrow, by mourning for one dead relative or rejoicing over the execution of another. He may be a bad example to the public by the cleanliness of his person or by the filth upon his clothes, he may offend by walking to-day and by riding in a carriage next week; the agents of the Committee of General Security shall alone decide what constitutes enmity against public welfare. All prisons are to be opened at their bidding to receive those whom they choose to denounce; they have henceforth the right to examine prisoners privately and without witnesses, and to send them to trial without further warrants; their duty is clear—they must 'beat up game for the guillotine.' Thus is the decree worded; they must furnish the Public Prosecutor with work to do, the tribunals with victims to condemn, the Place de la Revolution with death-scenes to amuse the people, and for their work they will be rewarded thirty-five livres for every head that falls under the guillotine Ah! if Heron and his like and his myrmidons work hard and well they can make a comfortable income of four or five thousand livres a week. We are getting on, friend St. Just—we are getting on."

He had not raised his voice while he spoke, nor in the recounting of such inhuman monstrosity, such vile and bloodthirsty conspiracy against the liberty, the dignity, the very life of an entire nation, did he appear to feel the slightest indignation; rather did a tone of amusement and even of triumph strike through his speech; and now he laughed good-humouredly like an indulgent parent who is watching the naturally cruel antics of a spoilt boy.

"Then from this hell let loose upon earth," exclaimed St. Just hotly, "must we rescue those who refuse to ride upon this tide of blood."

His cheeks were glowing, his eyes sparkled with enthusiasm. He looked very young and very eager. Armand St. Just, the brother of Lady Blakeney, had something of the refined beauty of his lovely sister, but the features though manly—had not the latent strength expressed in them which characterised every line of Marguerite's exquisite face. The forehead suggested a dreamer rather than a thinker, the blue-grey eyes were those of an idealist rather than of a man of action.

De Batz's keen piercing eyes had no doubt noted this, even whilst he gazed at his young friend with that same look of good-humoured indulgence which seemed habitual to him.

"We have to think of the future, my good St. Just," he said after a slight pause, and speaking slowly and decisively, like a father rebuking a hot-headed child, "not of the present. What are a few lives worth beside the great principles which we have at stake?"

"The restoration of the monarchy—I know," retorted St. Just, still unsobered, "but, in the meanwhile—"

"In the meanwhile," rejoined de Batz earnestly, "every victim to the lust of these men is a step towards the restoration of law and order—that is to say, of the monarchy. It is only through these violent excesses perpetrated in its name that the nation will realise how it is being fooled by a set of men who have only their own power and their own advancement in view, and who imagine that the only way to that power is over the dead bodies of those who stand in their way. Once the nation is sickened by these orgies of ambition and of hate, it will turn against these savage brutes, and gladly acclaim the restoration of all that they are striving to destroy. This is our only hope for the future, and, believe me, friend, that every head snatched from the guillotine by your romantic hero, the Scarlet Pimpernel, is a stone laid for the consolidation of this infamous Republic."

"I'll not believe it," protested St. Just emphatically.

De Batz, with a gesture of contempt indicative also of complete self-satisfaction and unalterable self-belief, shrugged his broad shoulders. His short fat fingers, covered with rings, beat a tattoo upon the ledge of the box.

Obviously, he was ready with a retort. His young friend's attitude irritated even more than it amused him. But he said nothing for the moment, waiting while the traditional three knocks on the floor of the stage proclaimed the rise of the curtain. The growing impatience of the audience subsided as if by magic at the welcome call; everybody settled down again comfortably in their seats, they gave up the contemplation of the fathers of the people, and turned their full attention to the actors on the boards.

CHAPTER II

This was Armand S. Just's first visit to Paris since that memorable day when first he decided to sever his connection from the Republican party, of which he and his beautiful sister Marguerite had at one time been amongst the most noble, most enthusiastic followers. Already a year and a half ago the excesses of the party had horrified him, and that was long before they had degenerated into the sickening orgies which were culminating to-day in wholesale massacres and bloody hecatombs of innocent victims.

With the death of Mirabeau the moderate Republicans, whose sole and entirely pure aim had been to free the people of France from the autocratic tyranny of the Bourbons, saw the power go from their clean hands to the grimy ones of lustful demagogues, who knew no law save their own passions of bitter hatred against all classes that were not as self-seeking, as ferocious as themselves.

It was no longer a question of a fight for political and religious liberty only, but one of class against class, man against man, and let the weaker look to himself. The weaker had proved himself to be, firstly, the man of property and substance, then the law-abiding citizen, lastly the man of action who had obtained for the people that very same liberty of thought and of belief which soon became so terribly misused.

Armand St. Just, one of the apostles of liberty, fraternity, and equality, soon found that the most savage excesses of tyranny were being perpetrated in the name of those same ideals which he had worshipped.

His sister Marguerite, happily married in England, was the final temptation which caused him to quit the country the destinies of which he no longer could help to control. The spark of enthusiasm which he and the followers of Mirabeau had tried to kindle in the hearts of an oppressed people had turned to raging tongues of unquenchable flames. The taking of the Bastille had been the prelude to the massacres of September, and even the horror of these had since paled beside the holocausts of to-day.

Armand, saved from the swift vengeance of the revolutionaries by the devotion of the Scarlet Pimpernel, crossed over to England and enrolled himself under the banner of the heroic chief. But he had been unable hitherto to be an active member of the League. The chief was loath to allow him to run foolhardy risks. The St. Justs—both Marguerite and Armand—were still very well-known in Paris. Marguerite was not a woman easily forgotten, and her marriage with an English "aristo" did not please those republican circles who had looked upon her as their queen. Armand's secession from his party into the ranks of the emigres had singled him out for special reprisals, if and whenever he could be got hold of, and both brother and sister had an unusually bitter enemy in their cousin Antoine St. Just—once an aspirant to Marguerite's hand, and now a servile adherent and imitator of Robespierre, whose ferocious cruelty he tried to emulate with a view to ingratiating himself with the most powerful man of the day.

Nothing would have pleased Antoine St. Just more than the opportunity of showing his zeal and his patriotism by denouncing his own kith and kin to the Tribunal of the Terror, and the Scarlet Pimpernel, whose own slender fingers were held on the pulse of that reckless revolution, had no wish to sacrifice Armand's life deliberately, or even to expose it to unnecessary dangers.

Thus it was that more than a year had gone by before Armand St. Just—an enthusiastic member of the League of the Scarlet Pimpernel—was able to do aught for its service. He had chafed under the enforced restraint placed upon him by the prudence of his chief, when, indeed, he was longing to risk his life with the comrades whom he loved and beside the leader whom he revered.

At last, in the beginning of '94 he persuaded Blakeney to allow him to join the next expedition to France. What the principal aim of that expedition was the members of the League did not know as yet, but what they did know was that perils—graver even than hitherto—would attend them on their way.

The circumstances had become very different of late. At first the impenetrable mystery which had surrounded the personality of the chief had been a full measure of safety, but now one tiny corner of that veil of mystery had been lifted by two rough pairs of hands at least; Chauvelin, ex-ambassador at the English Court, was no longer in any doubt as to the identity of the Scarlet Pimpernel, whilst Collot d'Herbois had seen him at Boulogne, and had there been effectually foiled by him.

Four months had gone by since that day, and the Scarlet Pimpernel was hardly ever out of France now; the massacres in Paris and in the provinces had multiplied with appalling rapidity, the necessity for the selfless devotion of that small band of heroes had become daily, hourly more pressing. They rallied round their chief with unbounded enthusiasm, and let it be admitted at once that the sporting instinct—inherent in these English gentlemen—made them all the more keen, all the more eager now that the dangers which beset their expeditions were increased tenfold.

At a word from the beloved leader, these young men—the spoilt darlings of society—would leave the gaieties, the pleasures, the luxuries of London or of Bath, and, taking their lives in their hands, they placed them, together with their fortunes, and even their good names, at the service of the innocent and helpless victims of merciless tyranny. The married men—Ffoulkes, my Lord Hastings, Sir Jeremiah Wallescourt—left wife and children at a call from the chief, at the cry of the wretched. Armand—unattached and enthusiastic—had the right to demand that he should no longer be left behind.

He had only been away a little over fifteen months, and yet he found Paris a different city from the one he had left immediately after the terrible massacres of September. An air of grim loneliness seemed to hang over her despite the crowds that thronged her streets; the men whom he was wont to meet in public places fifteen months ago—friends and political allies—were no longer to be seen; strange faces surrounded him on every side—sullen, glowering faces, all wearing a certain air of horrified surprise and of vague, terrified wonder, as if life had become one awful puzzle, the answer to which must be found in the brief interval between the swift passages of death.

Armand St. Just, having settled his few simple belongings in the squalid lodgings which had been assigned to him, had started out after dark to wander somewhat aimlessly through the streets. Instinctively he seemed to be searching for a familiar face, some one who would come to him out of that merry past which he had spent with Marguerite in their pretty apartment in the Rue St. Honore.

For an hour he wandered thus and met no one whom he knew. At times it appeared to him as if he did recognise a face or figure that passed him swiftly by in the gloom, but even before he could fully make up his mind to that, the face or figure had already disappeared, gliding furtively down some narrow unlighted by-street, without turning to look to right or left, as if dreading fuller recognition. Armand felt a total stranger in his own native city.

The terrible hours of the execution on the Place de la Revolution were fortunately over, the tumbrils no longer rattled along the uneven pavements, nor did the death-cry of the unfortunate victims resound through the deserted streets. Armand was, on this first day of his arrival, spared the sight of this degradation of the once lovely city; but her desolation, her general appearance of shamefaced indigence and of cruel aloofness struck a chill in the young man's heart.

It was no wonder, therefore, when anon he was wending his way slowly back to his lodging he was accosted by a pleasant, cheerful voice, that he responded to it with alacrity. The voice, of a smooth, oily timbre, as if the owner kept it well greased for purposes of amiable speech, was like an echo of the past, when jolly, irresponsible Baron de Batz, erst-while officer of the Guard in the service of the late King, and since then known to be the most inveterate conspirator for the restoration of the monarchy, used to amuse Marguerite by his vapid, senseless plans for the overthrow of the newly-risen power of the people.

Armand was quite glad to meet him, and when de Batz suggested that a good talk over old times would be vastly agreeable, the younger man gladly acceded. The two men, though certainly not mistrustful of one another, did not seem to care to reveal to each other the place where they lodged. De Batz at once proposed the avant-scene box of one of the theatres as being the safest place where old friends could talk without fear of spying eyes or ears.

"There is no place so safe or so private nowadays, believe me, my young friend," he said "I have tried every sort of nook and cranny in this accursed town, now riddled with spies, and I have come to the conclusion that a small avant-scene box is the most perfect den of privacy there is in the entire city. The voices of the actors on the stage and the hum among the audience in the house will effectually drown all individual conversation to every ear save the one for whom it is intended."

It is not difficult to persuade a young man who feels lonely and somewhat forlorn in a large city to while away an evening in the companionship of a cheerful talker, and de Batz was essentially good company. His vapourings had always been amusing, but Armand now gave him credit for more seriousness of purpose; and though the chief had warned him against picking up acquaintances in Paris, the young man felt that that restriction would certainly not apply to a man like de Batz, whose hot partisanship of the Royalist cause and hare-brained schemes for its restoration must make him at one with the League of the Scarlet Pimpernel.

Armand accepted the other's cordial invitation. He, too, felt that he would indeed be safer from observation in a crowded theatre than in the streets. Among a closely packed throng bent on amusement the sombrely-clad figure of a young man, with the appearance of a student or of a journalist, would easily pass unperceived.

But somehow, after the first ten minutes spent in de Batz' company within the gloomy shelter of the small avant-scene box, Armand already repented of the impulse which had prompted him to come to the theatre to-night, and to renew acquaintanceship with the ex-officer of the late King's Guard. Though he knew de Batz to be an ardent Royalist, and even an active adherent of the monarchy, he was soon conscious of a vague sense of mistrust of this pompous, self-complacent individual, whose every utterance breathed selfish aims rather than devotion to a forlorn cause.

Therefore, when the curtain rose at last on the first act of Moliere's witty comedy, St. Just turned deliberately towards the stage and tried to interest himself in the wordy quarrel between Philinte and Alceste.

But this attitude on the part of the younger man did not seem to suit his newly-found friend. It was clear that de Batz did not consider the topic of conversation by any means exhausted, and that it had been more with a view to a discussion like the present interrupted one that he had invited St. Just to come to the theatre with him to-night, rather than for the purpose of witnessing Mlle. Lange's debut in the part of Celimene.

The presence of St. Just in Paris had as a matter of fact astonished de Batz not a little, and had set his intriguing brain busy on conjectures. It was in order to turn these conjectures into certainties that he had desired private talk with the young man.

He waited silently now for a moment or two, his keen, small eyes resting with evident anxiety on Armand's averted head, his fingers still beating the impatient tattoo upon the velvet-covered cushion of the box. Then at the first movement of St. Just towards him he was ready in an instant to re-open the subject under discussion.

With a quick nod of his head he called his young friend's attention back to the men in the auditorium.

"Your good cousin Antoine St. Just is hand and glove with Robespierre now," he said. "When you left Paris more than a year ago you could afford to despise him as an empty-headed windbag; now, if you desire to remain in France, you will have to fear him as a power and a menace."

"Yes, I knew that he had taken to herding with the wolves," rejoined Armand lightly. "At one time he was in love with my sister. I thank God that she never cared for him."

"They say that he herds with the wolves because of this disappointment," said de Batz. "The whole pack is made up of men who have been disappointed, and who have nothing more to lose. When all these wolves will have devoured one another, then and then only can we hope for the restoration of the monarchy in France. And they will not turn on one another whilst prey for their greed lies ready to their jaws. Your friend the Scarlet Pimpernel should feed this bloody revolution of ours rather than starve it, if indeed he hates it as he seems to do."

His restless eyes peered with eager interrogation into those of the younger man. He paused as if waiting for a reply; then, as St. Just remained silent, he reiterated slowly, almost in the tones of a challenge:

"If indeed he hates this bloodthirsty revolution of ours as he seems to do."

The reiteration implied a doubt. In a moment St. Just's loyalty was up in arms.

"The Scarlet Pimpernel," he said, "cares naught for your political aims. The work of mercy that he does, he does for justice and for humanity."

"And for sport," said de Batz with a sneer, "so I've been told."

"He is English," assented St. Just, "and as such will never own to sentiment. Whatever be the motive, look at the result!

"Yes! a few lives stolen from the guillotine."

"Women and children—innocent victims—would have perished but for his devotion."

"The more innocent they were, the more helpless, the more pitiable, the louder would their blood have cried for reprisals against the wild beasts who sent them to their death."

St. Just made no reply. It was obviously useless to attempt to argue with this man, whose political aims were as far apart from those of the Scarlet Pimpernel as was the North Pole from the South.

"If any of you have influence over that hot-headed leader of yours," continued de Batz, unabashed by the silence of his friend, "I wish to God you would exert it now."

"In what way?" queried St. Just, smiling in spite of himself at the thought of his or any one else's control over Blakeney and his plans.

It was de Batz' turn to be silent. He paused for a moment or two, then he asked abruptly:

"Your Scarlet Pimpernel is in Paris now, is he not?"

"I cannot tell you," replied Armand.

"Bah! there is no necessity to fence with me, my friend. The moment I set eyes on you this afternoon I knew that you had not come to Paris alone."

"You are mistaken, my good de Batz," rejoined the young man earnestly; "I came to Paris alone."

"Clever parrying, on my word—but wholly wasted on my unbelieving ears. Did I not note at once that you did not seem overpleased to-day when I accosted you?"

"Again you are mistaken. I was very pleased to meet you, for I had felt singularly lonely all day, and was glad to shake a friend by the hand. What you took for displeasure was only surprise."

"Surprise? Ah, yes! I don't wonder that you were surprised to see me walking unmolested and openly in the streets of Paris—whereas you had heard of me as a dangerous conspirator, eh?—and as a man who has the entire police of his country at his heels—on whose head there is a price—what?"

"I knew that you had made several noble efforts to rescue the unfortunate King and Queen from the hands of these brutes."

"All of which efforts were unsuccessful," assented de Batz imperturbably, "every one of them having been either betrayed by some d——d confederate or ferreted out by some astute spy eager for gain. Yes, my friend, I made several efforts to rescue King Louis and Queen Marie Antoinette from the scaffold, and every time I was foiled, and yet here I am, you see, unscathed and free. I walk about the streets boldly, and talk to my friends as I meet them."

"You are lucky," said St. Just, not without a tinge of sarcasm.

"I have been prudent," retorted de Batz. "I have taken the trouble to make friends there where I thought I needed them most—the mammon of unrighteousness, you know-what?"

And he laughed a broad, thick laugh of perfect self-satisfaction.

"Yes, I know," rejoined St. Just, with the tone of sarcasm still more apparent in his voice now. "You have Austrian money at your disposal."

"Any amount," said the other complacently, "and a great deal of it sticks to the grimy fingers of these patriotic makers of revolutions. Thus do I ensure my own safety. I buy it with the Emperor's money, and thus am I able to work for the restoration of the monarchy in France."

Again St. Just was silent. What could he say? Instinctively now, as the fleshy personality of the Gascon Royalist seemed to spread itself out and to fill the tiny box with his ambitious schemes and his far-reaching plans, Armand's thoughts flew back to that other plotter, the man with the pure and simple aims, the man whose slender fingers had never handled alien gold, but were ever there ready stretched out to the helpless and the weak, whilst his thoughts were only of the help that he might give them, but never of his own safety.

De Batz, however, seemed blandly unconscious of any such disparaging thoughts in the mind of his young friend, for he continued quite amiably, even though a note of anxiety seemed to make itself felt now in his smooth voice:

"We advance slowly, but step by step, my good St. Just," he said. "I have not been able to save the monarchy in the person of the King or the Queen, but I may yet do it in the person of the Dauphin."

"The Dauphin," murmured St. Just involuntarily.

That involuntary murmur, scarcely audible, so soft was it, seemed in some way to satisfy de Batz, for the keenness of his gaze relaxed, and his fat fingers ceased their nervous, intermittent tattoo on the ledge of the box.

"Yes! the Dauphin," he said, nodding his head as if in answer to his own thoughts, "or rather, let me say, the reigning King of France—Louis XVII, by the grace of God—the most precious life at present upon the whole of this earth."

"You are right there, friend de Batz," assented Armand fervently, "the most precious life, as you say, and one that must be saved at all costs."

"Yes," said de Batz calmly, "but not by your friend the Scarlet Pimpernel."

"Why not?"

Scarce were those two little words out of St. Just's mouth than he repented of them. He bit his lip, and with a dark frown upon his face he turned almost defiantly towards his friend.

But de Batz smiled with easy bonhomie.

"Ah, friend Armand," he said, "you were not cut out for diplomacy, nor yet for intrigue. So then," he added more seriously, "that gallant hero, the Scarlet Pimpernel, has hopes of rescuing our young King from the clutches of Simon the cobbler and of the herd of hyenas on the watch for his attenuated little corpse, eh?"

"I did not say that," retorted St. Just sullenly.

"No. But I say it. Nay! nay! do not blame yourself, my over-loyal young friend. Could I, or any one else, doubt for a moment that sooner or later your romantic hero would turn his attention to the most pathetic sight in the whole of Europe—the child-martyr in the Temple prison? The wonder were to me if the Scarlet Pimpernel ignored our little King altogether for the sake of his subjects. No, no; do not think for a moment that you have betrayed your friend's secret to me. When I met you so luckily today I guessed at once that you were here under the banner of the enigmatical little red flower, and, thus guessing, I even went a step further in my conjecture. The Scarlet Pimpernel is in Paris now in the hope of rescuing Louis XVII from the Temple prison."

"If that is so, you must not only rejoice but should be able to help."

"And yet, my friend, I do neither the one now nor mean to do the other in the future," said de Batz placidly. "I happen to be a Frenchman, you see."

"What has that to do with such a question?"

"Everything; though you, Armand, despite that you are a Frenchman too, do not look through my spectacles. Louis XVII is King of France, my good St. Just; he must owe his freedom and his life to us Frenchmen, and to no one else."

"That is sheer madness, man," retorted Armand. "Would you have the child perish for the sake of your own selfish ideas?"

"You may call them selfish if you will; all patriotism is in a measure selfish. What does the rest of the world care if we are a republic or a monarchy, an oligarchy or hopeless anarchy? We work for ourselves and to please ourselves, and I for one will not brook foreign interference."

"Yet you work with foreign money!"

"That is another matter. I cannot get money in France, so I get it where I can; but

I can arrange for the escape of Louis XVII is King of France, my good St. Just; he must of France should belong the honour and glory of having saved our King."

For the third time now St. Just allowed the conversation to drop; he was gazing wide-eyed, almost appalled at this impudent display of well-nigh ferocious selfishness and vanity. De Batz, smiling and complacent, was leaning back in his chair, looking at his young friend with perfect contentment expressed in every line of his pock-marked face and in the very attitude of his well-fed body. It was easy enough now to understand the remarkable immunity which this man was enjoying, despite the many foolhardy plots which he hatched, and which had up to now invariably come to naught.

A regular braggart and empty windbag, he had taken but one good care, and that was of his own skin. Unlike other less fortunate Royalists of France, he neither fought in the country nor braved dangers in town. He played a safer game—crossed the frontier and constituted himself agent of Austria; he succeeded in gaining the Emperor's money for the good of the Royalist cause, and for his own most especial benefit.

Even a less astute man of the world than was Armand St. Just would easily have guessed that de Batz' desire to be the only instrument in the rescue of the poor little Dauphin from the Temple was not actuated by patriotism, but solely by greed. Obviously there was a rich reward waiting for him in Vienna the day that he brought Louis XVII safely into Austrian territory; that reward he would miss if a meddlesome Englishman interfered in this affair. Whether in this wrangle he risked the life of the child-King or not mattered to him not at all. It was de Batz who was to get the reward, and whose welfare and prosperity mattered more than the most precious life in Europe.

CHAPTER III

The Demon Chance

St. Just would have given much to be back in his lonely squalid lodgings now. Too late did he realise how wise had been the dictum which had warned him against making or renewing friendships in France.

Men had changed with the times. How terribly they had changed! Personal safety had become a fetish with most—a goal so difficult to attain that it had to be fought for and striven for, even at the expense of humanity and of self-respect.

Selfishness—the mere, cold-blooded insistence for self-advancement—ruled supreme. De Batz, surfeited with foreign money, used it firstly to ensure his own immunity, scattering it to right and left to still the ambition of the Public Prosecutor or to satisfy the greed of innumerable spies.

What was left over he used for the purpose of pitting the bloodthirsty demagogues one against the other, making of the National Assembly a gigantic bear-den, wherein wild beasts could rend one another limb from limb.

In the meanwhile, what cared he—he said it himself—whether hundreds of innocent martyrs perished miserably and uselessly? They were the necessary food whereby the Revolution was to be satiated and de Batz' schemes enabled to mature. The most precious life in Europe even was only to be saved if its price went to swell the pockets of de Batz, or to further his future ambitions.

Times had indeed changed an entire nation. St. Just felt as sickened with this self-seeking Royalist as he did with the savage brutes who struck to right or left for their own delectation. He was meditating immediate flight back to his lodgings, with a hope of finding there a word for him from the chief—a word to remind him that men did live nowadays who had other aims besides their own advancement—other ideals besides the deification of self.

The curtain had descended on the first act, and traditionally, as the works of M. de Moliere demanded it, the three knocks were heard again without any interval. St. Just rose ready with a pretext for parting with his friend. The curtain was being slowly drawn up on the second act, and disclosed Alceste in wrathful conversation with Celimene.

Alceste's opening speech is short. Whilst the actor spoke it Armand had his back to the stage; with hand outstretched, he was murmuring what he hoped would prove a polite excuse for thus leaving his amiable host while the entertainment had only just begun.

De Batz—vexed and impatient—had not by any means finished with his friend yet. He thought that his specious arguments—delivered with boundless conviction—had made some impression on the mind of the young man. That impression, however, he desired to deepen, and whilst Armand was worrying his brain to find a plausible excuse for going away, de Batz was racking his to find one for keeping him here.

Then it was that the wayward demon Chance intervened. Had St. Just risen but two minutes earlier, had his active mind suggested the desired excuse more readily, who knows what unspeakable sorrow, what heartrending misery, what terrible shame might have been spared both him and those for whom he cared? Those two minutes—did he but know it—decided the whole course of his future life. The excuse hovered on his lips, de Batz reluctantly was preparing to bid him good-bye, when Celimene, speaking common-place words enough in answer to her quarrelsome lover, caused him to drop the hand which he was holding out to his friend and to turn back towards the stage.

It was an exquisite voice that had spoken—a voice mellow and tender, with deep tones in it that betrayed latent power. The voice had caused Armand to look, the lips that spoke forged the first tiny link of that chain which riveted him forever after to the speaker.

It is difficult to say if such a thing really exists as love at first sight. Poets and romancists will have us believe that it does; idealists swear by it as being the only true love worthy of the name.

I do not know if I am prepared to admit their theory with regard to Armand St. Just. Mlle. Lange's exquisite voice certainly had charmed him to the extent of making him forget his mistrust of de Batz and his desire to get away. Mechanically almost he sat down again, and leaning both elbows on the edge of the box, he rested his chin in his hand, and listened. The words which the late M. de Moliere puts into the mouth of Celimene are trite and flippant enough, yet every time that Mlle. Lange's lips moved Armand watched her, entranced.

There, no doubt, the matter would have ended: a young man fascinated by a pretty woman on the stage—'tis a small matter, and one from which there doth not often spring a weary trail of tragic circumstances. Armand, who had a passion for music, would have worshipped at the shrine of Mlle. Lange's perfect voice until the curtain came down on the last act, had not his friend de Batz seen the keen enchantment which the actress had produced on the young enthusiast.

Now de Batz was a man who never allowed an opportunity to slip by, if that opportunity led towards the furtherance of his own desires. He did not want to lose sight of Armand just yet, and here the good demon Chance had given him an opportunity for obtaining what he wanted.

He waited quietly until the fall of the curtain at the end of Act II.; then, as Armand, with a sigh of delight, leaned back in his chair, and closing his eyes appeared to be living the last half-hour all over again, de Batz remarked with well-assumed indifference:

"Mlle. Lange is a promising young actress. Do you not think so, my friend?"

"She has a perfect voice—it was exquisite melody to the ear," replied Armand. "I was conscious of little else."

"She is a beautiful woman, nevertheless," continued de Batz with a smile. "During the next act, my good St. Just, I would suggest that you open your eyes as well as your ears."

Armand did as he was bidden. The whole appearance of Mlle. Lange seemed in harmony with her voice. She was not very tall, but eminently graceful, with a small, oval face and slender, almost childlike figure, which appeared still more so above the wide hoops and draped panniers of the fashions of Moliere's time.

Whether she was beautiful or not the young man hardly knew. Measured by certain standards, she certainly was not so, for her mouth was not small, and her nose anything but classical in outline. But the eyes were brown, and they had that half-veiled look in them—shaded with long lashes that seemed to make a perpetual tender appeal to the masculine heart: the lips, too, were full and moist, and the teeth dazzling white. Yes!—on the whole we might easily say that she was exquisite, even though we did not admit that she was beautiful.

Painter David has made a sketch of her; we have all seen it at the Musee Carnavalet, and all wondered why that charming, if irregular, little face made such an impression of sadness.

There are five acts in "Le Misanthrope," during which Celimene is almost constantly on the stage. At the end of the fourth act de Batz said casually to his friend:

"I have the honour of personal acquaintanceship with Mlle. Lange. An you care for an introduction to her, we can go round to the green room after the play."

Did prudence then whisper, "Desist"? Did loyalty to the leader murmur, "Obey"? It were indeed difficult to say. Armand St. Just was not five-and-twenty, and Mlle. Lange's melodious voice spoke louder than the whisperings of prudence or even than the call of duty.

He thanked de Batz warmly, and during the last half-hour, while the misanthropical lover spurned repentant Celimene, he was conscious of a curious sensation of impatience, a tingling of his nerves, a wild, mad longing to hear those full moist lips pronounce his name, and have those large brown eyes throw their half-veiled look into his own.

CHAPTER IV

Mademoiselle Lange

The green-room was crowded when de Batz and St. Just arrived there after the performance. The older man cast a hasty glance through the open door. The crowd did not suit his purpose, and he dragged his companion hurriedly away from the contemplation of Mlle. Lange, sitting in a far corner of the room, surrounded by an admiring throng, and by innumerable floral tributes offered to her beauty and to her success.

De Batz without a word led the way back towards the stage. Here, by the dim light of tallow candles fixed in sconces against the surrounding walls, the scene-shifters were busy moving drop-scenes, back cloths and wings, and paid no heed to the two men who strolled slowly up and down silently, each wrapped in his own thoughts.

Armand walked with his hands buried in his breeches pockets, his head bent forward on his chest; but every now and again he threw quick, apprehensive glances round him whenever a firm step echoed along the empty stage or a voice rang clearly through the now deserted theatre.

"Are we wise to wait here?" he asked, speaking to himself rather than to his companion.

He was not anxious about his own safety; but the words of de Batz had impressed themselves upon his mind: "Heron and his spies we have always with us."

From the green-room a separate foyer and exit led directly out into the street. Gradually the sound of many voices, the loud laughter and occasional snatches of song which for the past half-hour had proceeded from that part of the house, became more subdued and more rare. One by one the friends of the artists were leaving the theatre, after having paid the usual banal compliments to those whom they favoured, or presented the accustomed offering of flowers to the brightest star of the night.

The actors were the first to retire, then the older actresses, the ones who could no longer command a court of admirers round them. They all filed out of the greenroom and crossed the stage to where, at the back, a narrow, rickety wooden stairs led to their so-called dressing-rooms—tiny, dark cubicles, ill-lighted, unventilated, where some half-dozen of the lesser stars tumbled over one another while removing wigs and grease-paint.

Armand and de Batz watched this exodus, both with equal impatience. Mlle. Lange was the last to leave the green-room. For some time, since the crowd had become thinner round her, Armand had contrived to catch glimpses of her slight, elegant figure. A short passage led from the stage to the green-room door, which was wide open, and at the corner of this passage the young man had paused from time to time in his walk, gazing with earnest admiration at the dainty outline of the young girl's head, with its wig of powdered curls that seemed scarcely whiter than the creamy brilliance of her skin.

De Batz did not watch Mlle. Lange beyond casting impatient looks in the direction of the crowd that prevented her leaving the green-room. He did watch Armand, however—noted his eager look, his brisk and alert movements, the obvious glances of admiration which he cast in the direction of the young actress, and this seemed to afford him a considerable amount of contentment.

The best part of an hour had gone by since the fall of the curtain before Mlle. Lange finally dismissed her many admirers, and de Batz had the satisfaction of seeing her running down the passage, turning back occasionally in order to bid gay "good-nights" to the loiterers who were loath to part from her. She was a child in all her movements, quite unconscious of self or of her own charms, but frankly delighted with her success. She was still dressed in the ridiculous hoops and panniers pertaining to her part, and the powdered peruke hid the charm of her own hair; the costume gave a certain stilted air to her unaffected personality, which, by this very sense of contrast, was essentially fascinating.

In her arms she held a huge sheaf of sweet-scented narcissi, the spoils of some favoured spot far away in the South. Armand thought that never in his life had he seen anything so winsome or so charming.

Having at last said the positively final adieu, Mlle. Lange with a happy little sigh turned to run down the passage.

She came face to face with Armand, and gave a sudden little gasp of terror. It was not good these days to come on any loiterer unawares.

But already de Batz had quickly joined his friend, and his smooth, pleasant voice, and podgy, beringed hand extended towards Mlle. Lange, were sufficient to reassure her.

"You were so surrounded in the green-room, mademoiselle," he said courteously, "I did not venture to press in among the crowd of your admirers. Yet I had the great wish to present my respectful congratulations in person."

"Ah! c'est ce cher de Batz!" exclaimed mademoiselle gaily, in that exquisitely rippling voice of hers. "And where in the world do you spring from, my friend?

"Hush-sh-sh!" he whispered, holding her small bemittened hand in his, and putting one finger to his lips with an urgent entreaty for discretion; "not my name, I beg of you, fair one."

"Bah!" she retorted lightly, even though her full lips trembled now as she spoke and belied her very words. "You need have no fear whilst you are in this part of the house. It is an understood thing that the Committee of General Security does not send its spies behind the curtain of a theatre. Why, if all of us actors and actresses were sent to the guillotine there would be no play on the morrow. Artistes are not replaceable in a few hours; those that are in existence must perforce be spared, or the citizens who govern us now would not know where to spend their evenings."

But though she spoke so airily and with her accustomed gaiety, it was easily perceived that even on this childish mind the dangers which beset every one these days had already imprinted their mark of suspicion and of caution.

"Come into my dressing-room," she said. "I must not tarry here any longer, for they will be putting out the lights. But I have a room to myself, and we can talk there quite agreeably."

She led the way across the stage towards the wooden stairs. Armand, who during this brief colloquy between his friend and the young girl had kept discreetly in the background, felt undecided what to do. But at a peremptory sign from de Batz he, too, turned in the wake of the gay little lady, who ran swiftly up the rickety steps, humming snatches of popular songs the while, and not turning to see if indeed the two men were following her.

She had the sheaf of narcissi still in her arms, and the door of her tiny dressing-room being open, she ran straight in and threw the flowers down in a confused, sweet-scented mass upon the small table that stood at one end of the room, littered with pots and bottles, letters, mirrors, powder-puffs, silk stockings, and cambric handkerchiefs.

Then she turned and faced the two men, a merry look of unalterable gaiety dancing in her eyes.

"Shut the door, mon ami," she said to de Batz, "and after that sit down where you can, so long as it is not on my most precious pot of unguent or a box of costliest powder."

While de Batz did as he was told, she turned to Armand and said with a pretty tone of interrogation in her melodious voice:

"Monsieur?"

"St. Just, at your service, mademoiselle," said Armand, bowing very low in the most approved style obtaining at the English Court.

"St. Just?" she repeated, a look of puzzlement in her brown eyes. "Surely—"

"A kinsman of citizen St. Just, whom no doubt you know, mademoiselle," he exclaimed.

"My friend Armand St. Just," interposed de Batz, "is practically a new-comer in Paris. He lives in England habitually."

"In England?" she exclaimed. "Oh! do tell me all about England. I would love to go there. Perhaps I may have to go some day. Oh! do sit down, de Batz," she continued, talking rather volubly, even as a delicate blush heightened the colour in her cheeks under the look of obvious admiration from Armand St. Just's expressive eyes.

She swept a handful of delicate cambric and silk from off a chair, making room for de Batz' portly figure. Then she sat upon the sofa, and with an inviting gesture and a call from the eyes she bade Armand sit down next to her. She leaned back against the cushions, and the table being close by, she stretched out a hand and once more took up the bunch of narcissi, and while she talked to Armand she held the snow-white blooms quite close to her face—so close, in fact, that he could not see her mouth and chin, only her dark eyes shone across at him over the heads of the blossoms.

"Tell me all about England," she reiterated, settling herself down among the cushions like a spoilt child who is about to listen to an oft-told favourite story.

Armand was vexed that de Batz was sitting there. He felt he could have told this dainty little lady quite a good deal about England if only his pompous, fat friend would have had the good sense to go away.

As it was, he felt unusually timid and gauche, not quite knowing what to say, a fact which seemed to amuse Mlle. Lange not a little.

"I am very fond of England," he said lamely; "my sister is married to an Englishman, and I myself have taken up my permanent residence there."

"Among the society of emigres?" she queried.

Then, as Armand made no reply, de Batz interposed quickly:

"Oh! you need not fear to admit it, my good Armand; Mademoiselle Lange, has many friends among the emigres—have you not, mademoiselle?"

"Yes, of course," she replied lightly; "I have friends everywhere. Their political views have nothing to do with me. Artistes, I think, should have naught to do with politics. You see, citizen St. Just, I never inquired of you what were your views. Your name and kinship would proclaim you a partisan of citizen Robespierre, yet I find you in the company of M. de Batz; and you tell me that you live in England."

"He is no partisan of citizen Robespierre," again interposed de Batz; "in fact, mademoiselle, I may safely tell you, I think, that my friend has but one ideal on this earth, whom he has set up in a shrine, and whom he worships with all the ardour of a Christian for his God."

"How romantic!" she said, and she looked straight at Armand. "Tell me, monsieur, is your ideal a woman or a man?"

His look answered her, even before he boldly spoke the two words:

"A woman."

She took a deep draught of sweet, intoxicating scent from the narcissi, and his gaze once more brought blushes to her cheeks. De Batz' good-humoured laugh helped her to hide this unwonted access of confusion.

"That was well turned, friend Armand," he said lightly; "but I assure you, mademoiselle, that before I brought him here to-night his ideal was a man."

"A man!" she exclaimed, with a contemptuous little pout. "Who was it?"

"I know no other name for him but that of a small, insignificant flower—the Scarlet Pimpernel," replied de Batz.

"The Scarlet Pimpernel!" she ejaculated, dropping the flowers suddenly, and gazing on Armand with wide, wondering eyes. "And do you know him, monsieur?"

He was frowning despite himself, despite the delight which he felt at sitting so close to this charming little lady, and feeling that in a measure his presence and his personality interested her. But he felt irritated with de Batz, and angered at what he considered the latter's indiscretion. To him the very name of his leader was almost a sacred one; he was one of those enthusiastic devotees who only care to name the idol of their dreams with bated breath, and only in the ears of those who would understand and sympathise.

Again he felt that if only he could have been alone with mademoiselle he could have told her all about the Scarlet Pimpernel, knowing that in her he would find a ready listener, a helping and a loving heart; but as it was he merely replied tamely enough:

"Yes, mademoiselle, I do know him."

"You have seen him?" she queried eagerly; "spoken to him?"

"Yes."

"Oh! do tell me all about him. You know quite a number of us in France have the greatest possible admiration for your national hero. We know, of course, that he is an enemy of our Government—but, oh! we feel that he is not an enemy of France because of that. We are a nation of heroes, too, monsieur," she added with a pretty, proud toss of the head; "we can appreciate bravery and resource, and we love the mystery that surrounds the personality of your Scarlet Pimpernel. But since you know him, monsieur, tell me what is he like?"

Armand was smiling again. He was yielding himself up wholly to the charm which emanated from this young girl's entire being, from her gaiety and her unaffectedness, her enthusiasm, and that obvious artistic temperament which caused her to feel every sensation with superlative keenness and thoroughness.

"What is he like?" she insisted.

"That, mademoiselle," he replied, "I am not at liberty to tell you."

"Not at liberty to tell me!" she exclaimed; "but monsieur, if I command you—"

"At risk of falling forever under the ban of your displeasure, mademoiselle, I would still remain silent on that subject."

She gazed on him with obvious astonishment. It was quite an unusual thing for this spoilt darling of an admiring public to be thus openly thwarted in her whims.

"How tiresome and pedantic!" she said, with a shrug of her pretty shoulders and a moue of discontent. "And, oh! how ungallant! You have learnt ugly, English ways, monsieur; for there, I am told, men hold their womenkind in very scant esteem. There!" she added, turning with a mock air of hopelessness towards de Batz, "am I not a most unlucky woman? For the past two years I have used my best endeavours to catch sight of that interesting Scarlet Pimpernel; here do I meet monsieur, who actually knows him (so he says), and he is so ungallant that he even refuses to satisfy the first cravings of my just curiosity."

"Citizen St. Just will tell you nothing now, mademoiselle," rejoined de Batz with his good-humoured laugh; "it is my presence, I assure you, which is setting a seal upon his lips. He is, believe me, aching to confide in you, to share in your enthusiasm, and to see your beautiful eyes glowing in response to his ardour when he describes to you the exploits of that prince of heroes. En tete-a-tete one day, you will, I know, worm every secret out of my discreet friend Armand."

Mademoiselle made no comment on this—that is to say, no audible comment—but she buried the whole of her face for a few seconds among the flowers, and Armand from amongst those flowers caught sight of a pair of very bright brown eyes which shone on him with a puzzled look.

She said nothing more about the Scarlet Pimpernel or about England just then, but after awhile she began talking of more indifferent subjects: the state of the weather, the price of food, the discomforts of her own house, now that the servants had been put on perfect equality with their masters.

Armand soon gathered that the burning questions of the day, the horrors of massacres, the raging turmoil of politics, had not affected her very deeply as yet. She had not troubled her pretty head very much about the social and humanitarian aspect of the present seething revolution. She did not really wish to think about it at all. An artiste to her finger-tips, she was spending her young life in earnest work, striving to attain perfection in her art, absorbed in study during the day, and in the expression of what she had learnt in the evenings.

The terrors of the guillotine affected her a little, but somewhat vaguely still. She had not realised that any dangers could assail her whilst she worked for the artistic delectation of the public.

It was not that she did not understand what went on around her, but that her artistic temperament and her environment had kept her aloof from it all. The horrors of the Place de la Revolution made her shudder, but only in the same way as the tragedies of M. Racine or of Sophocles which she had studied caused her to shudder, and she had exactly the same sympathy for poor Queen Marie Antoinette as she had for Mary Stuart, and shed as many tears for King Louis as she did for Polyeucte.

Once de Batz mentioned the Dauphin, but mademoiselle put up her hand quickly and said in a trembling voice, whilst the tears gathered in her eyes:

"Do not speak of the child to me, de Batz. What can I, a lonely, hard-working woman, do to help him? I try not to think of him, for if I did, knowing my own helplessness, I feel that I could hate my countrymen, and speak my bitter hatred of them across the footlights; which would be more than foolish," she added naively, "for it would not help the child, and I should be sent to the guillotine. But oh sometimes I feel that I would gladly die if only that poor little child-martyr were restored to those who love him and given back once more to joy and happiness. But they would not take my life for his, I am afraid," she concluded, smiling through her tears. "My life is of no value in comparison with his."

Soon after this she dismissed her two visitors. De Batz, well content with the result of this evening's entertainment, wore an urbane, bland smile on his rubicund face. Armand, somewhat serious and not a little in love, made the hand-kiss with which he took his leave last as long as he could.

"You will come and see me again, citizen St. Just?" she asked after that preliminary leave-taking.

"At your service, mademoiselle," he replied with alacrity.

"How long do you stay in Paris?"

"I may be called away at any time."

"Well, then, come to-morrow. I shall be free towards four o'clock. Square du Roule. You cannot miss the house. Any one there will tell you where lives citizeness Lange."

"At your service, mademoiselle," he replied.

The words sounded empty and meaningless, but his eyes, as they took final leave of her, spoke the gratitude and the joy which he felt.

CHAPTER V

The Temple Prison

It was close on midnight when the two friends finally parted company outside the doors of the theatre. The night air struck with biting keenness against them when they emerged from the stuffy, overheated building, and both wrapped their caped cloaks tightly round their shoulders. Armand—more than ever now—was anxious to rid himself of de Batz. The Gascon's platitudes irritated him beyond the bounds of forbearance, and he wanted to be alone, so that he might think over the events of this night, the chief event being a little lady with an enchanting voice and the most fascinating brown eyes he had ever seen.

Self-reproach, too, was fighting a fairly even fight with the excitement that had been called up by that same pair of brown eyes. Armand for the past four or five hours had acted in direct opposition to the earnest advice given to him by his chief; he had renewed one friendship which had been far better left in oblivion, and he had made an acquaintance which already was leading him along a path that he felt sure his comrade would disapprove. But the path was so profusely strewn with scented narcissi that Armand's sensitive conscience was quickly lulled to rest by the intoxicating fragrance.

Looking neither to right nor left, he made his way very quickly up the Rue Richelieu towards the Montmartre quarter, where he lodged.

De Batz stood and watched him for as long as the dim lights of the street lamps illumined his slim, soberly-clad figure; then he turned on his heel and walked off in the opposite direction.

His florid, pock-marked face wore an air of contentment not altogether unmixed with a kind of spiteful triumph.

"So, my pretty Scarlet Pimpernel," he muttered between his closed lips, "you wish to meddle in my affairs, to have for yourself and your friends the credit and glory of snatching the golden prize from the clutches of these murderous brutes. Well, we shall see! We shall see which is the wiliest—the French ferret or the English fox."

He walked deliberately away from the busy part of the town, turning his back on the river, stepping out briskly straight before him, and swinging his gold-beaded cane as he walked.

The streets which he had to traverse were silent and deserted, save occasionally where a drinking or an eating house had its swing-doors still invitingly open. From these places, as de Batz strode rapidly by, came sounds of loud voices, rendered raucous by outdoor oratory; volleys of oaths hurled irreverently in the midst of impassioned speeches; interruptions from rowdy audiences that vied with the speaker in invectives and blasphemies; wordy war-fares that ended in noisy vituperations; accusations hurled through the air heavy with tobacco smoke and the fumes of cheap wines and of raw spirits.

De Batz took no heed of these as he passed, anxious only that the crowd of eating-house politicians did not, as often was its wont, turn out pele-mele into the street, and settle its quarrel by the weight of fists. He did not wish to be embroiled in a street fight, which invariably ended in denunciations and arrests, and was glad when presently he had left the purlieus of the Palais Royal behind him, and could strike on his left toward the lonely Faubourg du Temple.

From the dim distance far away came at intervals the mournful sound of a roll of muffled drums, half veiled by the intervening hubbub of the busy night life of the great city. It proceeded from the Place de la Revolution, where a company of the National Guard were on night watch round the guillotine. The dull, intermittent notes of the drum came as a reminder to the free people of France that the watchdog of a vengeful revolution was alert night and day, never sleeping, ever wakeful, "beating up game for the guillotine," as the new decree framed to-day by the Government of the people had ordered that it should do.

From time to time now the silence of this lonely street was broken by a sudden cry of terror, followed by the clash of arms, the inevitable volley of oaths, the call for help, the final moan of anguish. They were the ever-recurring brief tragedies which told of denunciations, of domiciliary search, of sudden arrests, of an agonising desire for life and for freedom—for life under these same horrible conditions of brutality and of servitude, for freedom to breathe, if only a day or two longer, this air, polluted by filth and by blood.

De Batz, hardened to these scenes, paid no heed to them. He had heard it so often, that cry in the night, followed by death-like silence; it came from comfortable bourgeois houses, from squalid lodgings, or lonely cul-de-sac, wherever some hunted quarry was run to earth by the newly-organised spies of the Committee of General Security.

Five and thirty livres for every head that falls trunkless into the basket at the foot of the guillotine! Five and thirty pieces of silver, now as then, the price of innocent blood. Every cry in the night, every call for help, meant game for the guillotine, and five and thirty livres in the hands of a Judas.

And de Batz walked on unmoved by what he saw and heard, swinging his cane and looking satisfied. Now he struck into the Place de la Victoire, and looked on one of the open-air camps that had recently been established where men, women, and children were working to provide arms and accoutrements for the Republican army that was fighting the whole of Europe.

The people of France were up in arms against tyranny; and on the open places of their mighty city they were encamped day and night forging those arms which were destined to make them free, and in the meantime were bending under a yoke of tyranny more complete, more grinding and absolute than any that the most despotic kings had ever dared to inflict.

Here by the light of resin torches, at this late hour of the night, raw lads were being drilled into soldiers, half-naked under the cutting blast of the north wind, their knees shaking under them, their arms and legs blue with cold, their stomachs empty, and their teeth chattering with fear; women were sewing shirts for the great improvised army, with eyes straining to see the stitches by the flickering light of the torches, their throats parched with the continual inhaling of smoke-laden air; even children, with weak, clumsy little fingers, were picking rags to be woven into cloth again all, all these slaves were working far into the night, tired, hungry, and cold, but working unceasingly, as the country had demanded it: "the people of France in arms against tyranny!" The people of France had to set to work to make arms, to clothe the soldiers, the defenders of the people's liberty.

And from this crowd of people—men, women, and children—there came scarcely a sound, save raucous whispers, a moan or a sigh quickly suppressed. A grim silence reigned in this thickly-peopled camp; only the crackling of the torches broke that silence now and then, or the flapping of canvas in the wintry gale. They worked on sullen, desperate, and starving, with no hope of payment save the miserable rations wrung from poor tradespeople or miserable farmers, as wretched, as oppressed as themselves; no hope of payment, only fear of punishment, for that was ever present.

The people of France in arms against tyranny were not allowed to forget that grim taskmaster with the two great hands stretched upwards, holding the knife which descended mercilessly, indiscriminately on necks that did not bend willingly to the task.

A grim look of gratified desire had spread over de Batz' face as he skirted the open-air camp. Let them toil, let them groan, let them starve! The more these clouts suffer, the more brutal the heel that grinds them down, the sooner will the Emperor's money accomplish its work, the sooner will these wretches be clamoring for the monarchy, which would mean a rich reward in de Batz' pockets.

To him everything now was for the best: the tyranny, the brutality, the massacres. He gloated in the holocausts with as much satisfaction as did the most bloodthirsty Jacobin in the Convention. He would with his own hands have wielded the guillotine that worked too slowly for his ends. Let that end justify the means, was his motto. What matter if the future King of France walked up to his throne over steps made of headless corpses and rendered slippery with the blood of martyrs?

The ground beneath de Batz' feet was hard and white with the frost. Overhead the pale, wintry moon looked down serene and placid on this giant city wallowing in an ocean of misery.

There, had been but little snow as yet this year, and the cold was intense. On his right now the Cimetiere des SS. Innocents lay peaceful and still beneath the wan light of the moon. A thin covering of snow lay evenly alike on grass mounds and smooth stones. Here and there a broken cross with chipped arms still held pathetically outstretched, as if in a final appeal for human love, bore mute testimony to senseless excesses and spiteful desire for destruction.

But here within the precincts of the dwelling of the eternal Master a solemn silence reigned; only the cold north wind shook the branches of the yew, causing them to send forth a melancholy sigh into the night, and to shed a shower of tiny crystals of snow like the frozen tears of the dead.

And round the precincts of the lonely graveyard, and down narrow streets or open places, the night watchmen went their rounds, lanthorn in hand, and every five minutes their monotonous call rang clearly out in the night:

"Sleep, citizens! everything is quiet and at peace!"

We may take it that de Batz did not philosophise over-much on what went on around him. He had walked swiftly up the Rue St. Martin, then turning sharply to his right he found himself beneath the tall, frowning walls of the Temple prison, the grim guardian of so many secrets, such terrible despair, such unspeakable tragedies.

Here, too, as in the Place de la Revolution, an intermittent roll of muffled drums proclaimed the ever-watchful presence of the National Guard. But with that exception not a sound stirred round the grim and stately edifice; there were no cries, no calls, no appeals around its walls. All the crying and wailing was shut in by the massive stone that told no tales.

Dim and flickering lights shone behind several of the small windows in the facade of the huge labyrinthine building. Without any hesitation de Batz turned down the Rue du Temple, and soon found himself in front of the main gates which gave on the courtyard beyond. The sentinel challenged him, but he had the pass-word, and explained that he desired to have speech with citizen Heron.

With a surly gesture the guard pointed to the heavy bell-pull up against the gate, and de Batz pulled it with all his might. The long clang of the brazen bell echoed and re-echoed round the solid stone walls. Anon a tiny judas in the gate was cautiously pushed open, and a peremptory voice once again challenged the midnight intruder.

De Batz, more peremptorily this time, asked for citizen Heron, with whom he had immediate and important business, and a glimmer of a piece of silver which he held up close to the judas secured him the necessary admittance.

The massive gates slowly swung open on their creaking hinges, and as de Batz passed beneath the archway they closed again behind him.

The concierge's lodge was immediately on his left. Again he was challenged, and again gave the pass-word. But his face was apparently known here, for no serious hindrance to proceed was put in his way.

A man, whose wide, lean frame was but ill-covered by a threadbare coat and ragged breeches, and with soleless shoes on his feet, was told off to direct the citoyen to citizen Heron's rooms. The man walked slowly along with bent knees and arched spine, and shuffled his feet as he walked; the bunch of keys which he carried rattled ominously in his long, grimy hands; the passages were badly lighted, and he also carried a lanthorn to guide himself on the way.

Closely followed by de Batz, he soon turned into the central corridor, which is open to the sky above, and was spectrally alight now with flag-stones and walls gleaming beneath the silvery sheen of the moon, and throwing back the fantastic elongated shadows of the two men as they walked.

On the left, heavily barred windows gave on the corridor, as did here and there the massive oaken doors, with their gigantic hinges and bolts, on the steps of which squatted groups of soldiers wrapped in their cloaks, with wild, suspicious eyes beneath their capotes, peering at the midnight visitor as he passed.

There was no thought of silence here. The very walls seemed alive with sounds, groans and tears, loud wails and murmured prayers; they exuded from the stones and trembled on the frost-laden air.

Occasionally at one of the windows a pair of white hands would appear, grasping the heavy iron bar, trying to shake it in its socket, and mayhap, above the hands, the dim vision of a haggard face, a man's or a woman's, trying to get a glimpse of the outside world, a final look at the sky, before the last journey to the place of death to-morrow. Then one of the soldiers, with a loud, angry oath, would struggle to his feet, and with the butt-end of his gun strike at the thin, wan fingers till their hold on the iron bar relaxed, and the pallid face beyond would sink back into the darkness with a desperate cry of pain.

A quick, impatient sigh escaped de Batz' lips. He had skirted the wide courtyard in the wake of his guide, and from where he was he could see the great central tower, with its tiny windows lighted from within, the grim walls behind which the descendant of the world's conquerors, the bearer of the proudest name in Europe, and wearer of its most ancient crown, had spent the last days of his brilliant life in abject shame, sorrow, and degradation. The memory had swiftly surged up before him of that night when he all but rescued King Louis and his family from this same miserable prison: the guard had been bribed, the keeper corrupted, everything had been prepared, save the reckoning with the one irresponsible factor—chance!

He had failed then and had tried again, and again had failed; a fortune had been his reward if he had succeeded. He had failed, but even now, when his footsteps echoed along the flagged courtyard, over which an unfortunate King and Queen had walked on their way to their last ignominious Calvary, he hugged himself with the satisfying thought that where he had failed at least no one else had succeeded.

Whether that meddlesome English adventurer, who called himself the Scarlet Pimpernel, had planned the rescue of King Louis or of Queen Marie Antoinette at any time or not—that he did not know; but on one point at least he was more than ever determined, and that was that no power on earth should snatch from him the golden prize offered by Austria for the rescue of the little Dauphin.

"I would sooner see the child perish, if I cannot save him myself," was the burning thought in this man's tortuous brain. "And let that accursed Englishman look to himself and to his d——d confederates," he added, muttering a fierce oath beneath his breath.

A winding, narrow stone stair, another length or two of corridor, and his guide's shuffling footsteps paused beside a low iron-studded door let into the solid stone. De Batz dismissed his ill-clothed guide and pulled the iron bell-handle which hung beside the door.

The bell gave forth a dull and broken clang, which seemed like an echo of the wails of sorrow that peopled the huge building with their weird and monotonous sounds.

De Batz—a thoroughly unimaginative person—waited patiently beside the door until it was opened from within, and he was confronted by a tall stooping figure, wearing a greasy coat of snuff-brown cloth, and holding high above his head a lanthorn that threw its feeble light on de Batz' jovial face and form.

"It is even I, citizen Heron," he said, breaking in swiftly on the other's ejaculation of astonishment, which threatened to send his name echoing the whole length of corridors and passages, until round every corner of the labyrinthine house of sorrow the murmur would be borne on the wings of the cold night breeze: "Citizen Heron is in parley with ci-devant Baron de Batz!"

A fact which would have been equally unpleasant for both these worthies.

"Enter!" said Heron curtly.

He banged the heavy door to behind his visitor; and de Batz, who seemed to know his way about the place, walked straight across the narrow landing to where a smaller door stood invitingly open.

He stepped boldly in, the while citizen Heron put the lanthorn down on the floor of the couloir, and then followed his nocturnal visitor into the room.

CHAPTER VI

The Committee's Agent

It was a narrow, ill-ventilated place, with but one barred window that gave on the courtyard. An evil-smelling lamp hung by a chain from the grimy ceiling, and in a corner of the room a tiny iron stove shed more unpleasant vapour than warm glow around.

There was but little furniture: two or three chairs, a table which was littered with papers, and a corner-cupboard—the open doors of which revealed a miscellaneous collection—bundles of papers, a tin saucepan, a piece of cold sausage, and a couple of pistols. The fumes of stale tobacco-smoke hovered in the air, and mingled most unpleasantly with those of the lamp above, and of the mildew that penetrated through the walls just below the roof.

Heron pointed to one of the chairs, and then sat down on the other, close to the table, on which he rested his elbow. He picked up a short-stemmed pipe, which he had evidently laid aside at the sound of the bell, and having taken several deliberate long-drawn puffs from it, he said abruptly:

"Well, what is it now?"

In the meanwhile de Batz had made himself as much at home in this uncomfortable room as he possibly could. He had deposited his hat and cloak on one rickety rush-bottomed chair, and drawn another close to the fire. He sat down with one leg crossed over the other, his podgy be-ringed hand wandering with loving gentleness down the length of his shapely calf.

He was nothing if not complacent, and his complacency seemed highly to irritate his friend Heron.

"Well, what is it?" reiterated the latter, drawing his visitor's attention roughly to himself by banging his fist on the table. "Out with it! What do you want? Why have you come at this hour of the night to compromise me, I suppose—bring your own d—d neck and mine into the same noose—what?"

"Easy, easy, my friend," responded de Batz imperturbably; "waste not so much time in idle talk. Why do I usually come to see you? Surely you have had no cause to complain hitherto of the unprofitableness of my visits to you?"

"They will have to be still more profitable to me in the future," growled the other across the table. "I have more power now."

"I know you have," said de Batz suavely. "The new decree? What? You may denounce whom you please, search whom you please, arrest whom you please, and send whom you please to the Supreme Tribunal without giving them the slightest chance of escape."

"Is it in order to tell me all this that you have come to see me at this hour of the night?" queried Heron with a sneer.

"No; I came at this hour of the night because I surmised that in the future you and your hell-hounds would be so busy all day 'beating up game for the guillotine' that the only time you would have at the disposal of your friends would be the late hours of the night. I saw you at the theatre a couple of hours ago, friend Heron; I didn't think to find you yet abed."

"Well, what do you want?"

"Rather," retorted de Batz blandly, "shall we say, what do YOU want, citizen Heron?"

"For what?

"For my continued immunity at the hands of yourself and your pack?"

Heron pushed his chair brusquely aside and strode across the narrow room deliberately facing the portly figure of de Batz, who with head slightly inclined on one side, his small eyes narrowed till they appeared mere slits in his pockmarked face, was steadily and quite placidly contemplating this inhuman monster who had this very day been given uncontrolled power over hundreds of thousands of human lives.

Heron was one of those tall men who look mean in spite of their height. His head was small and narrow, and his hair, which was sparse and lank, fell in untidy strands across his forehead. He stooped slightly from the neck, and his chest, though wide, was hollow between the shoulders. But his legs were big and bony, slightly bent at the knees, like those of an ill-conditioned horse.

The face was thin and the cheeks sunken; the eyes, very large and prominent, had a look in them of cold and ferocious cruelty, a look which contrasted strangely with the weakness and petty greed apparent in the mouth, which was flabby, with full, very red lips, and chin that sloped away to the long thin neck.

Even at this moment as he gazed on de Batz the greed and the cruelty in him were fighting one of those battles the issue of which is always uncertain in men of his stamp.

"I don't know," he said slowly, "that I am prepared to treat with you any longer. You are an intolerable bit of vermin that has annoyed the Committee of General Security for over two years now. It would be excessively pleasant to crush you once and for all, as one would a buzzing fly."

"Pleasant, perhaps, but immeasurably foolish," rejoined de Batz coolly; "you would only get thirty-five livres for my head, and I offer you ten times that amount for the self-same commodity."

"I know, I know; but the whole thing has become too dangerous."

"Why? I am very modest. I don't ask a great deal. Let your hounds keep off my scent."

"You have too many d—d confederates."

"Oh! Never mind about the others. I am not bargaining about them. Let them look after themselves."

"Every time we get a batch of them, one or the other denounces you."

"Under torture, I know," rejoined de Batz placidly, holding his podgy hands to the warm glow of the fire. "For you have started torture in your house of Justice now, eh, friend Heron? You and your friend the Public Prosecutor have gone the whole gamut of devilry—eh?"

"What's that to you?" retorted the other gruffly.

"Oh, nothing, nothing! I was even proposing to pay you three thousand five hundred livres for the privilege of taking no further interest in what goes on inside this prison!"

"Three thousand five hundred!" ejaculated Heron involuntarily, and this time even his eyes lost their cruelty; they joined issue with the mouth in an expression of hungering avarice.

"Two little zeros added to the thirty-five, which is all you would get for handing me over to your accursed Tribunal," said de Batz, and, as if thoughtlessly, his hand wandered to the inner pocket of his coat, and a slight rustle as of thin crisp paper brought drops of moisture to the lips of Heron.

"Leave me alone for three weeks and the money is yours," concluded de Batz pleasantly.

There was silence in the room now. Through the narrow barred window the steely rays of the moon fought with the dim yellow light of the oil lamp, and lit up the pale face of the Committee's agent with its lines of cruelty in sharp conflict with those of greed.

"Well! is it a bargain?" asked de Batz at last in his usual smooth, oily voice, as he half drew from out his pocket that tempting little bundle of crisp printed paper. "You have only to give me the usual receipt for the money and it is yours."

Heron gave a vicious snarl.

"It is dangerous, I tell you. That receipt, if it falls into some cursed meddler's hands, would send me straight to the guillotine."

"The receipt could only fall into alien hands," rejoined de Batz blandly, "if I happened to be arrested, and even in that case they could but fall into those of the chief agent of the Committee of General Security, and he hath name Heron. You must take some risks, my friend. I take them too. We are each in the other's hands. The bargain is quite fair."

For a moment or two longer Heron appeared to be hesitating whilst de Batz watched him with keen intentness. He had no doubt himself as to the issue. He had tried most of these patriots in his own golden crucible, and had weighed their patriotism against Austrian money, and had never found the latter wanting.

He had not been here to-night if he were not quite sure. This inveterate conspirator in the Royalist cause never took personal risks. He looked on Heron now, smiling to himself the while with perfect satisfaction.

"Very well," said the Committee's agent with sudden decision, "I'll take the money. But on one condition."

"What is it?"

"That you leave little Capet alone."

"The Dauphin!"

"Call him what you like," said Heron, taking a step nearer to de Batz, and from his great height glowering down in fierce hatred and rage upon his accomplice; "call the young devil what you like, but leave us to deal with him."

"To kill him, you mean? Well, how can I prevent it, my friend?"

"You and your like are always plotting to get him out of here. I won't have it. I tell you I won't have it. If the brat disappears I am a dead man. Robespierre and his gang have told me as much. So you leave him alone, or I'll not raise a finger to help you, but will lay my own hands on your accursed neck."

He looked so ferocious and so merciless then, that despite himself, the selfish adventurer, the careless self-seeking intriguer, shuddered with a quick wave of unreasoning terror. He turned away from Heron's piercing gaze, the gaze of a hyena whose prey is being snatched from beneath its nails. For a moment he stared thoughtfully into the fire.

He heard the other man's heavy footsteps cross and re-cross the narrow room, and was conscious of the long curved shadow creeping up the mildewed wall or retreating down upon the carpetless floor.

Suddenly, without any warning he felt a grip upon his shoulder. He gave a start and almost uttered a cry of alarm which caused Heron to laugh. The Committee's agent was vastly amused at his friend's obvious access of fear. There was nothing that he liked better than that he should inspire dread in the hearts of all those with whom he came in contact.

"I am just going on my usual nocturnal round," he said abruptly. "Come with me, citizen de Batz."

A certain grim humour was apparent in his face as he proffered this invitation, which sounded like a rough command. As de Batz seemed to hesitate he nodded peremptorily to him to follow. Already he had gone into the hall and picked up his lanthorn. From beneath his waistcoat he drew forth a bunch of keys, which he rattled impatiently, calling to his friend to come.

"Come, citizen," he said roughly. "I wish to show you the one treasure in this house which your d—d fingers must not touch."

Mechanically de Batz rose at last. He tried to be master of the terror which was invading his very bones. He would not own to himself even that he was afraid, and almost audibly he kept murmuring to himself that he had no cause for fear.

Heron would never touch him. The spy's avarice, his greed of money were a perfect safeguard for any man who had the control of millions, and Heron knew, of course, that he could make of this inveterate plotter a comfortable source of revenue for himself. Three weeks would soon be over, and fresh bargains could be made time and again, while de Batz was alive and free.

Heron was still waiting at the door, even whilst de Batz wondered what this nocturnal visitation would reveal to him of atrocity and of outrage. He made a final effort to master his nervousness, wrapped his cloak tightly around him, and followed his host out of the room.

CHAPTER VII

The Most Precious Life in Europe

Once more he was being led through the interminable corridors of the gigantic building. Once more from the narrow, barred windows close by him he heard the heart-breaking sighs, the moans, the curses which spoke of tragedies that he could only guess.

Heron was walking on ahead of him, preceding him by some fifty metres or so, his long legs covering the distances more rapidly than de Batz could follow them. The latter knew his way well about the old prison. Few men in Paris possessed that accurate knowledge of its intricate passages and its network of cells and halls which de Batz had acquired after close and persevering study.

He himself could have led Heron to the doors of the tower where the little Dauphin was being kept imprisoned, but unfortunately he did not possess the keys that would open all the doors which led to it. There were sentinels at every gate, groups of soldiers at each end of every corridor, the great—now empty—courtyards, thronged with prisoners in the daytime, were alive with soldiery even now. Some walked up and down with fixed bayonet on shoulder, others sat in groups on the stone copings or squatted on the ground, smoking or playing cards, but all of them were alert and watchful.

Heron was recognised everywhere the moment he appeared, and though in these days of equality no one presented arms, nevertheless every guard stood aside to let him pass, or when necessary opened a gate for the powerful chief agent of the Committee of General Security.

Indeed, de Batz had no keys such as these to open the way for him to the presence of the martyred little King.

Thus the two men wended their way on in silence, one preceding the other. De Batz walked leisurely, thought-fully, taking stock of everything he saw—the gates, the barriers, the positions of sentinels and warders, of everything in fact that might prove a help or a hindrance presently, when the great enterprise would be hazarded. At last—still in the wake of Heron—he found himself once more behind the main entrance gate, underneath the archway on which gave the guichet of the concierge.

Here, too, there seemed to be an unnecessary number of soldiers: two were doing sentinel outside the guichet, but there were others in a file against the wall.

Heron rapped with his keys against the door of the concierge's lodge, then, as it was not immediately opened from within, he pushed it open with his foot.

"The concierge?" he queried peremptorily.

From a corner of the small panelled room there came a grunt and a reply:

"Gone to bed, quoi!"

The man who previously had guided de Batz to Heron's door slowly struggled to his feet. He had been squatting somewhere in the gloom, and had been roused by Heron's rough command. He slouched forward now still carrying a boot in one hand and a blacking brush in the other.

"Take this lanthorn, then," said the chief agent with a snarl directed at the sleeping concierge, "and come along. Why are you still here?" he added, as if in after-thought.

"The citizen concierge was not satisfied with the way I had done his boots," muttered the man, with an evil leer as he spat contemptuously on the floor; "an aristo, quoi? A hell of a place this... twenty cells to sweep out every day... and boots to clean for every aristo of a concierge or warder who demands it.... Is that work for a free born patriot, I ask?"

"Well, if you are not satisfied, citoyen Dupont," retorted Heron dryly, "you may go when you like, you know there are plenty of others ready to do your work..."

"Nineteen hours a day, and nineteen sous by way of payment.... I have had fourteen days of this convict work..."

He continued to mutter under his breath, whilst Heron, paying no further heed to him, turned abruptly towards a group of soldiers stationed outside.

"En avant, corporal!" he said; "bring four men with you... we go up to the tower."

The small procession was formed. On ahead the lanthorn-bearer, with arched spine and shaking knees, dragging shuffling footsteps along the corridor, then the corporal with two of his soldiers, then Heron closely followed by de Batz, and finally two more soldiers bringing up the rear.

Heron had given the bunch of keys to the man Dupont. The latter, on ahead, holding the lanthorn aloft, opened one gate after another. At each gate he waited for the little procession to file through, then he re-locked the gate and passed on.

Up two or three flights of winding stairs set in the solid stone, and the final heavy door was reached.

De Batz was meditating. Heron's precautions for the safe-guarding of the most precious life in Europe were more complete than he had anticipated. What lavish liberality would be required! what superhuman ingenuity and boundless courage in order to break down all the barriers that had been set up round that young life that flickered inside this grim tower!

Of these three requisites the corpulent, complacent intriguer possessed only the first in a considerable degree. He could be exceedingly liberal with the foreign money which he had at his disposal. As for courage and ingenuity, he believed that he possessed both, but these qualities had not served him in very good stead in the attempts which he had made at different times to rescue the unfortunate members of the Royal Family from prison. His overwhelming egotism would not admit for a moment that in ingenuity and pluck the Scarlet Pimpernel and his English followers could outdo him, but he did wish to make quite sure that they would not interfere with him in the highly remunerative work of saving the Dauphin.

Heron's impatient call roused him from these meditations. The little party had come to a halt outside a massive iron-studded door.

At a sign from the chief agent the soldiers stood at attention. He then called de Batz and the lanthorn-bearer to him.

He took a key from his breeches pocket, and with his own hand unlocked the massive door. He curtly ordered the lanthorn-bearer and de Batz to go through, then he himself went in, and finally once more re-locked the door behind him, the soldiers remaining on guard on the landing outside.

Now the three men were standing in a square antechamber, dank and dark, devoid of furniture save for a large cupboard that filled the whole of one wall; the others, mildewed and stained, were covered with a greyish paper, which here and there hung away in strips.

Heron crossed this ante-chamber, and with his knuckles rapped against a small door opposite.

"Hola!" he shouted, "Simon, mon vieux, tu es la?"

From the inner room came the sound of voices, a man's and a woman's, and now, as if in response to Heron's call, the shrill tones of a child. There was some shuffling, too, of footsteps, and some pushing about of furniture, then the door was opened, and a gruff voice invited the belated visitors to enter.

The atmosphere in this further room was so thick that at first de Batz was only conscious of the evil smells that pervaded it; smells which were made up of the fumes of tobacco, of burning coke, of a smoky lamp, and of stale food, and mingling through it all the pungent odour of raw spirits.

Heron had stepped briskly in, closely followed by de Batz. The man Dupont with a mutter of satisfaction put down his lanthorn and curled himself up in a corner of the antechamber. His interest in the spectacle so favoured by citizen Heron had apparently been exhausted by constant repetition.

De Batz looked round him with keen curiosity with which disgust was ready enough to mingle.

The room itself might have been a large one; it was almost impossible to judge of its size, so crammed was it with heavy and light furniture of every conceivable shape and type. There was a monumental wooden bedstead in one corner, a huge sofa covered in black horsehair in another. A large table stood in the centre of the room, and there were at least four capacious armchairs round it. There were wardrobes and cabinets, a diminutive washstand and a huge pier-glass, there were innumerable boxes and packing-cases, cane-bottomed chairs and what-nots every-where. The place looked like a depot for second-hand furniture.

In the midst of all the litter de Batz at last became conscious of two people who stood staring at him and at Heron. He saw a man before him, somewhat fleshy of build, with smooth, mouse-coloured hair brushed away from a central parting, and ending in a heavy curl above each ear; the eyes were wide open and pale in colour, the lips unusually thick and with a marked downward droop. Close beside him stood a youngish-looking woman, whose unwieldy bulk, however, and pallid skin revealed the sedentary life and the ravages of ill-health.

Both appeared to regard Heron with a certain amount of awe, and de Batz with a vast measure of curiosity.

Suddenly the woman stood aside, and in the far corner of the room there was displayed to the Gascon Royalist's cold, calculating gaze the pathetic figure of the uncrowned King of France.

"How is it Capet is not yet in bed?" queried Heron as soon as he caught sight of the child.

"He wouldn't say his prayers this evening," replied Simon with a coarse laugh, "and wouldn't drink his medicine. Bah!" he added with a snarl, "this is a place for dogs and not for human folk."

"If you are not satisfied, mon vieux," retorted Heron curtly, "you can send in your resignation when you like. There are plenty who will be glad of the place."

The ex-cobbler gave another surly growl and expectorated on the floor in the direction where stood the child.

"Little vermin," he said, "he is more trouble than man or woman can bear."

The boy in the meanwhile seemed to take but little notice of the vulgar insults put upon him by his guardian. He stood, a quaint, impassive little figure, more interested apparently in de Batz, who was a stranger to him, than in the three others whom he knew. De Batz noted that the child looked well nourished, and that he was warmly clad in a rough woollen shirt and cloth breeches, with coarse grey stockings and thick shoes; but he also saw that the clothes were indescribably filthy, as were the child's hands and face. The golden curls, among which a young and queenly mother had once loved to pass her slender perfumed fingers, now hung bedraggled, greasy, and lank round the little face, from the lines of which every trace of dignity and of simplicity had long since been erased.

There was no look of the martyr about this child now, even though, mayhap, his small back had often smarted under his vulgar tutor's rough blows; rather did the pale young face wear the air of sullen indifference, and an abject desire to please, which would have appeared heart-breaking to any spectator less self-seeking and egotistic than was this Gascon conspirator.

Madame Simon had called him to her while her man and the citizen Heron were talking, and the child went readily enough, without any sign of fear. She took the corner of her coarse dirty apron in her hand, and wiped the boy's mouth and face with it.

"I can't keep him clean," she said with an apologetic shrug of the shoulders and a look at de Batz. "There now," she added, speaking once more to the child, "drink like a good boy, and say your lesson to please maman, and then you shall go to bed."

She took a glass from the table, which was filled with a clear liquid that de Batz at first took to be water, and held it to the boy's lips. He turned his head away and began to whimper.

"Is the medicine very nasty?" queried de Batz.

"Mon Dieu! but no, citizen," exclaimed the woman, "it is good strong eau de vie, the best that can be procured. Capet likes it really—don't you, Capet? It makes you happy and cheerful, and sleep well of nights. Why, you had a glassful yesterday and enjoyed it. Take it now," she added in a quick whisper, seeing that Simon and Heron were in close conversation together; "you know it makes papa angry if you don't have at least half a glass now and then."

The child wavered for a moment longer, making a quaint little grimace of distaste. But at last he seemed to make up his mind that it was wisest to yield over so small a matter, and he took the glass from Madame Simon.

And thus did de Batz see the descendant of St. Louis quaffing a glass of raw spirit at the bidding of a rough cobbler's wife, whom he called by the fond and foolish name sacred to childhood, maman!

Selfish egoist though he was, de Batz turned away in loathing.

Simon had watched the little scene with obvious satisfaction. He chuckled audibly when the child drank the spirit, and called Heron's attention to him, whilst a look of triumph lit up his wide, pale eyes.

"And now, mon petit," he said jovially, "let the citizen hear you say your prayers!"

He winked toward de Batz, evidently anticipating a good deal of enjoyment for the visitor from what was coming. From a heap of litter in a corner of the room he fetched out a greasy red bonnet adorned with a tricolour cockade, and a soiled and tattered flag, which had once been white, and had golden fleur-de-lys embroidered upon it.

The cap he set on the child's head, and the flag he threw upon the floor.

"Now, Capet—your prayers!" he said with another chuckle of amusement.

All his movements were rough, and his speech almost ostentatiously coarse. He banged against the furniture as he moved about the room, kicking a footstool out of the way or knocking over a chair. De Batz instinctively thought of the perfumed stillness of the rooms at Versailles, of the army of elegant high-born ladies who had ministered to the wants of this child, who stood there now before him, a cap on his yellow hair, and his shoulder held up to his ear with that gesture of careless indifference peculiar to children when they are sullen or uncared for.

Obediently, quite mechanically it seemed, the boy trod on the flag which Henri IV had borne before him at Ivry, and le Roi Soleil had flaunted in the face of the armies of Europe. The son of the Bourbons was spitting on their flag, and wiping his shoes upon its tattered folds. With shrill cracked voice he sang the Carmagnole, "Ca ira! ca ira! les aristos a la lanterne!" until de Batz himself felt inclined to stop his ears and to rush from the place in horror.

Louis XVII, whom the hearts of many had proclaimed King of France by the grace of God, the child of the Bourbons, the eldest son of the Church, was stepping a vulgar dance over the flag of St. Louis, which he had been taught to defile. His pale cheeks glowed as he danced, his eyes shone with the unnatural light kindled in them by the intoxicating liquor; with one slender hand he waved the red cap with the tricolour cockade, and shouted "Vive la Republique!"

Madame Simon was clapping her hands, looking on the child with obvious pride, and a kind of rough maternal affection. Simon was gazing on Heron for approval, and the latter nodded his head, murmuring words of encouragement and of praise.

"Thy catechism now, Capet—thy catechism," shouted Simon in a hoarse voice.

The boy stood at attention, cap on head, hands on his hips, legs wide apart, and feet firmly planted on the fleur-de-lys, the glory of his forefathers.

"Thy name?" queried Simon.

"Louis Capet," replied the child in a clear, high-pitched voice.

"What art thou?"

"A citizen of the Republic of France."

"What was thy father?"

"Louis Capet, ci-devant king, a tyrant who perished by the will of the people!"

"What was thy mother?"

"A ——"

De Batz involuntarily uttered a cry of horror. Whatever the man's private character was, he had been born a gentleman, and his every instinct revolted against what he saw and heard. The scene had positively sickened him. He turned precipitately towards the door.

"How now, citizen?" queried the Committee's agent with a sneer. "Are you not satisfied with what you see?"

"Mayhap the citizen would like to see Capet sitting in a golden chair," interposed Simon the cobbler with a sneer, "and me and my wife kneeling and kissing his hand—what?"

"'Tis the heat of the room," stammered de Batz, who was fumbling with the lock of the door; "my head began to swim."

"Spit on their accursed flag, then, like a good patriot, like Capet," retorted Simon gruffly. "Here, Capet, my son," he added, pulling the boy by the arm with a rough gesture, "get thee to bed; thou art quite drunk enough to satisfy any good Republican."

By way of a caress he tweaked the boy's ear and gave him a prod in the back with his bent knee. He was not wilfully unkind, for just now he was not angry with the lad; rather was he vastly amused with the effect Capet's prayer and Capet's recital of his catechism had had on the visitor.

As to the lad, the intensity of excitement in him was immediately followed by an overwhelming desire for sleep. Without any preliminary of undressing or of washing, he tumbled, just as he was, on to the sofa. Madame Simon, with quite pleasing solicitude, arranged a pillow under his head, and the very next moment the child was fast asleep.

"'Tis well, citoyen Simon," said Heron in his turn, going towards the door. "I'll report favourably on you to the Committee of Public Security. As for the citoyenne, she had best be more careful," he added, turning to the woman Simon with a snarl on his evil face. "There was no cause to arrange a pillow under the head of that vermin's spawn. Many good patriots have no pillows to put under their heads. Take that pillow away; and I don't like the shoes on the brat's feet; sabots are quite good enough."

Citoyenne Simon made no reply. Some sort of retort had apparently hovered on her lips, but had been checked, even before it was uttered, by a peremptory look from her husband. Simon the cobbler, snarling in speech but obsequious in manner, prepared to accompany the citizen agent to the door.

De Batz was taking a last look at the sleeping child; the uncrowned King of France was wrapped in a drunken sleep, with the last spoken insult upon his dead mother still hovering on his childish lips.

CHAPTER VIII

Arcades Ambo

"That is the way we conduct our affairs, citizen," said Heron gruffly, as he once more led his guest back into his office.

It was his turn to be complacent now. De Batz, for once in his life cowed by what he had seen, still wore a look of horror and disgust upon his florid face.

"What devils you all are!" he said at last.

"We are good patriots," retorted Heron, "and the tyrant's spawn leads but the life that hundreds of thousands of children led whilst his father oppressed the people. Nay! what am I saying? He leads a far better, far happier life. He gets plenty to eat and plenty of warm clothes. Thousands of innocent children, who have not the crimes of a despot father upon their conscience, have to starve whilst he grows fat."

The leer in his face was so evil that once more de Batz felt that eerie feeling of terror creeping into his bones. Here were cruelty and bloodthirsty ferocity personified to their utmost extent. At thought of the Bourbons, or of all those whom he considered had been in the past the oppressors of the people, Heron was nothing but a wild and ravenous beast, hungering for revenge, longing to bury his talons and his fangs into the body of those whose heels had once pressed on his own neck.

And de Batz knew that even with millions or countless money at his command he could not purchase from this carnivorous brute the life and liberty of the son of King Louis. No amount of bribery would accomplish that; it would have to be ingenuity pitted against animal force, the wiliness of the fox against the power of the wolf.

Even now Heron was darting savagely suspicious looks upon him.

"I shall get rid of the Simons," he said; "there's something in that woman's face which I don't trust. They shall go within the next few hours, or as soon as I can lay my hands upon a better patriot than that mealy-mouthed cobbler. And it will be better not to have a woman about the place. Let me see—to-day is Thursday, or else Friday morning. By Sunday I'll get those Simons out of the place. Methought I saw you ogling that woman," he added, bringing his bony fist crashing down on the table so that papers, pen, and inkhorn rattled loudly; "and if I thought that you—"

De Batz thought it well at this point to finger once more nonchalantly the bundle of crisp paper in the pocket of his coat.

"Only on that one condition," reiterated Heron in a hoarse voice; "if you try to get at Capet, I'll drag you to the Tribunal with my own hands."

"Always presuming that you can get me, my friend," murmured de Batz, who was gradually regaining his accustomed composure.

Already his active mind was busily at work. One or two things which he had noted in connection with his visit to the Dauphin's prison had struck him as possibly useful in his schemes. But he was disappointed that Heron was getting rid of the Simons. The woman might have been very useful and more easily got at than a man. The avarice of the French bourgeoise would have proved a promising factor. But this, of course, would now be out of the question. At the same time it was not because Heron raved and stormed and uttered cries like a hyena that he, de Batz, meant to give up an enterprise which, if successful, would place millions into his own pocket.

As for that meddling Englishman, the Scarlet Pimpernel, and his crack-brained followers, they must be effectually swept out of the way first of all. De Batz felt that they were the real, the most likely hindrance to his schemes. He himself would have to go very cautiously to work, since apparently Heron would not allow him to purchase immunity for himself in that one matter, and whilst he was laying his plans with necessary deliberation so as to ensure his own safety, that accursed Scarlet Pimpernel would mayhap snatch the golden prize from the Temple prison right under his very nose.

When he thought of that the Gascon Royalist felt just as vindictive as did the chief agent of the Committee of General Security.

While these thoughts were coursing through de Batz' head, Heron had been indulging in a volley of vituperation.

"If that little vermin escapes," he said, "my life will not be worth an hour's purchase. In twenty-four hours I am a dead man, thrown to the guillotine like those dogs of aristocrats! You say I am a night-bird, citizen. I tell you that I do not sleep night or day thinking of that brat and the means to keep him safely under my hand. I have never trusted those Simons—"

"Not trusted them!" exclaimed de Batz; "surely you could not find anywhere more inhuman monsters!"

"Inhuman monsters?" snarled Heron. "Bah! they don't do their business thoroughly; we want the tyrant's spawn to become a true Republican and a patriot—aye! to make of him such a one that even if you and your cursed confederates got him by some hellish chance, he would be no use to you as a king, a tyrant to set above the people, to set up in your Versailles, your Louvre, to eat off golden plates and wear satin clothes. You have seen the brat! By the time he is a man he should forget how to eat save with his fingers, and get roaring drunk every night. That's what we want!—to make him so that he shall be no use to you, even if you did get him away; but you shall not! You shall not, not if I have to strangle him with my own hands."

He picked up his short-stemmed pipe and pulled savagely at it for awhile. De Batz was meditating.

"My friend," he said after a little while, "you are agitating yourself quite unnecessarily, and gravely jeopardising your prospects of getting a comfortable little income through keeping your fingers off my person. Who said I wanted to meddle with the child?"

"You had best not," growled Heron.

"Exactly. You have said that before. But do you not think that you would be far wiser, instead of directing your undivided attention to my unworthy self, to turn your thoughts a little to one whom, believe me, you have far greater cause to fear?"

"Who is that?"

"The Englishman."

"You mean the man they call the Scarlet Pimpernel?"

"Himself. Have you not suffered from his activity, friend Heron? I fancy that citizen Chauvelin and citizen Collot would have quite a tale to tell about him."

"They ought both to have been guillotined for that blunder last autumn at Boulogne."

"Take care that the same accusation be not laid at your door this year, my friend," commented de Batz placidly.

"Bah!"

"The Scarlet Pimpernel is in Paris even now."

"The devil he is!"

"And on what errand, think you?"

There was a moment's silence, and then de Batz continued with slow and dramatic emphasis:

"That of rescuing your most precious prisoner from the Temple."

"How do you know?" Heron queried savagely.

"I guessed."

"How?"

"I saw a man in the Theatre National to-day..."

"Well?"

"Who is a member of the League of the Scarlet Pimpernel."

"D—— him! Where can I find him?"

"Will you sign a receipt for the three thousand five hundred livres, which I am pining to hand over to you, my friend, and I will tell you?"

"Where's the money?"

"In my pocket."

Without further words Heron dragged the inkhorn and a sheet of paper towards him, took up a pen, and wrote a few words rapidly in a loose, scrawly hand. He strewed sand over the writing, then handed it across the table to de Batz.

"Will that do?" he asked briefly.

The other was reading the note through carefully.

"I see you only grant me a fortnight," he remarked casually.

"For that amount of money it is sufficient. If you want an extension you must pay more."

"So be it," assented de Batz coolly, as he folded the paper across. "On the whole a fortnight's immunity in France these days is quite a pleasant respite. And I prefer to keep in touch with you, friend Heron. I'll call on you again this day fortnight."

He took out a letter-case from his pocket. Out of this he drew a packet of bank-notes, which he laid on the table in front of Heron, then he placed the receipt carefully into the letter-case, and this back into his pocket.

Heron in the meanwhile was counting over the banknotes. The light of ferocity had entirely gone from his eyes; momentarily the whole expression of the face was one of satisfied greed.

"Well!" he said at last when he had assured himself that the number of notes was quite correct, and he had transferred the bundle of crisp papers into an inner pocket of his coat—"well, what about your friend?"

"I knew him years ago," rejoined de Batz coolly; "he is a kinsman of citizen St. Just. I know that he is one of the confederates of the Scarlet Pimpernel."

"Where does he lodge?"

"That is for you to find out. I saw him at the theatre, and afterwards in the green-room; he was making himself agreeable to the citizeness Lange. I heard him ask for leave to call on her to-morrow at four o'clock. You know where she lodges, of course!"

He watched Heron while the latter scribbled a few words on a scrap of paper, then he quietly rose to go. He took up his cloak and once again wrapped it round his shoulders. There was nothing more to be said, and he was anxious to go.

The leave-taking between the two men was neither cordial nor more than barely courteous. De Batz nodded to Heron, who escorted him to the outside door of his lodging, and there called loudly to a soldier who was doing sentinel at the further end of the corridor.

"Show this citizen the way to the guichet," he said curtly. "Good-night, citizen," he added finally, nodding to de Batz.

Ten minutes later the Gascon once more found himself in the Rue du Temple between the great outer walls of the prison and the silent little church and convent of

St. Elizabeth. He looked up to where in the central tower a small grated window lighted from within showed the place where the last of the Bourbons was being taught to desecrate the traditions of his race, at the bidding of a mender of shoes—a naval officer cashiered for misconduct and fraud.

Such is human nature in its self-satisfied complacency that de Batz, calmly ignoring the vile part which he himself had played in the last quarter of an hour of his interview with the Committee's agent, found it in him to think of Heron with loathing, and even of the cobbler Simon with disgust.

Then with a self-righteous sense of duty performed, and an indifferent shrug of the shoulders, he dismissed Heron from his mind.

"That meddlesome Scarlet Pimpernel will find his hands over-full to-morrow, and mayhap will not interfere in my affairs for some time to come," he mused; "meseems that that will be the first time that a member of his precious League has come within the clutches of such unpleasant people as the sleuth-hounds of my friend Heron!"

CHAPTER IX

What Love Can Do

"Yesterday you were unkind and ungallant. How could I smile when you seemed so stern?"

"Yesterday I was not alone with you. How could I say what lay next my heart, when indifferent ears could catch the words that were meant only for you?"

"Ah, monsieur, do they teach you in England how to make pretty speeches?"

"No, mademoiselle, that is an instinct that comes into birth by the fire of a woman's eyes."

Mademoiselle Lange was sitting upon a small sofa of antique design, with cushions covered in faded silks heaped round her pretty head. Armand thought that she looked like that carved cameo which his sister Marguerite possessed.

He himself sat on a low chair at some distance from her. He had brought her a large bunch of early violets, for he knew that she was fond of flowers, and these lay upon her lap, against the opalescent grey of her gown.

She seemed a little nervous and agitated, his obvious admiration bringing a ready blush to her cheeks.

The room itself appeared to Armand to be a perfect frame for the charming picture which she presented. The furniture in it was small and old; tiny tables of antique Vernis-Martin, softly faded tapestries, a pale-toned Aubusson carpet. Everything mellow and in a measure pathetic. Mademoiselle Lange, who was an orphan, lived alone under the duennaship of a middle-aged relative, a penniless hanger-on of the successful young actress, who acted as her chaperone, housekeeper, and maid, and kept unseemly or over-bold gallants at bay.

She told Armand all about her early life, her childhood in the backshop of Maitre Meziere, the jeweller, who was a relative of her mother's; of her desire for an artistic career, her struggles with the middle-class prejudices of her relations, her bold defiance of them, and final independence.

She made no secret of her humble origin, her want of education in those days; on the contrary, she was proud of what she had accomplished for herself. She was only twenty years of age, and already held a leading place in the artistic world of Paris.

Armand listened to her chatter, interested in everything she said, questioning her with sympathy and discretion. She asked him a good deal about himself, and about his beautiful sister Marguerite, who, of course, had been the most brilliant star in that most brilliant constellation, the Comedie Francaise. She had never seen Marguerite St. Just act, but, of course, Paris still rang with her praises, and all art-lovers regretted that she should have married and left them to mourn for her.

Thus the conversation drifted naturally back to England. Mademoiselle professed a vast interest in the citizen's country of adoption.

"I had always," she said, "thought it an ugly country, with the noise and bustle of industrial life going on everywhere, and smoke and fog to cover the landscape and to stunt the trees."

"Then, in future, mademoiselle," he replied, "must you think of it as one carpeted with verdure, where in the spring the orchard trees covered with delicate blossom would speak to you of fairyland, where the dewy grass stretches its velvety surface in the shadow of ancient monumental oaks, and ivy-covered towers rear their stately crowns to the sky."

"And the Scarlet Pimpernel? Tell me about him, monsieur."

"Ah, mademoiselle, what can I tell you that you do not already know? The Scarlet Pimpernel is a man who has devoted his entire existence to the benefit of suffering mankind. He has but one thought, and that is for those who need him; he hears but one sound the cry of the oppressed."

"But they do say, monsieur, that philanthropy plays but a sorry part in your hero's schemes. They aver that he looks on his own efforts and the adventures through which he goes only in the light of sport."

"Like all Englishmen, mademoiselle, the Scarlet Pimpernel is a little ashamed of sentiment. He would deny its very existence with his lips, even whilst his noble heart brimmed over with it. Sport? Well! mayhap the sporting instinct is as keen as that of charity—the race for lives, the tussle for the rescue of human creatures, the throwing of a life on the hazard of a die."

"They fear him in France, monsieur. He has saved so many whose death had been decreed by the Committee of Public Safety."

"Please God, he will save many yet."

"Ah, monsieur, the poor little boy in the Temple prison!"

"He has your sympathy, mademoiselle?"

"Of every right-minded woman in France, monsieur. Oh!" she added with a pretty gesture of enthusiasm, clasping her hands together, and looking at Armand with large eyes filled with tears, "if your noble Scarlet Pimpernel will do aught to save that poor innocent lamb, I would indeed bless him in my heart, and help him with all my humble might if I could."

"May God's saints bless you for those words, mademoiselle," he said, whilst, carried away by her beauty, her charm, her perfect femininity, he stooped towards her until his knee touched the carpet at her feet. "I had begun to lose my belief in my poor misguided country, to think all men in France vile, and all women base. I could thank you on my knees for your sweet words of sympathy, for the expression of tender motherliness that came into your eyes when you spoke of the poor forsaken Dauphin in the Temple."

She did not restrain her tears; with her they came very easily, just as with a child, and as they gathered in her eyes and rolled down her fresh cheeks they in no way marred the charm of her face. One hand lay in her lap fingering a diminutive bit of cambric, which from time to time she pressed to her eyes. The other she had almost unconsciously yielded to Armand.

The scent of the violets filled the room. It seemed to emanate from her, a fitting attribute of her young, wholly unsophisticated girlhood. The citizen was goodly to look at; he was kneeling at her feet, and his lips were pressed against her hand.

Armand was young and he was an idealist. I do not for a moment imagine that just at this moment he was deeply in love. The stronger feeling had not yet risen up in him; it came later when tragedy encompassed him and brought passion to sudden maturity. Just now he was merely yielding himself up to the intoxicating moment, with all the abandonment, all the enthusiasm of the Latin race. There was no reason why he should not bend the knee before this exquisite little cameo, that by its very presence was giving him an hour of perfect pleasure and of aesthetic joy.

Outside the world continued its hideous, relentless way; men butchered one another, fought and hated. Here in this small old-world salon, with its faded satins and bits of ivory-tinted lace, the outer universe had never really penetrated. It was a tiny world—quite apart from the rest of mankind, perfectly peaceful and absolutely beautiful.

If Armand had been allowed to depart from here now, without having been the cause as well as the chief actor in the events that followed, no doubt that Mademoiselle Lange would always have remained a charming memory with him, an exquisite bouquet of violets pressed reverently between the leaves of a favourite book of poems, and the scent of spring flowers would in after years have ever brought her dainty picture to his mind.

He was murmuring pretty words of endearment; carried away by emotion, his arm stole round her waist; he felt that if another tear came like a dewdrop rolling down her cheek he must kiss it away at its very source. Passion was not sweeping them off their feet—not yet, for they were very young, and life had not as yet presented to them its most unsolvable problem.

But they yielded to one another, to the springtime of their life, calling for Love, which would come presently hand in hand with his grim attendant, Sorrow.

Even as Armand's glowing face was at last lifted up to hers asking with mute lips for that first kiss which she already was prepared to give, there came the loud noise of men's heavy footsteps tramping up the old oak stairs, then some shouting, a woman's cry, and the next moment Madame Belhomme, trembling, wide-eyed, and in obvious terror, came rushing into the room.

"Jeanne! Jeanne! My child! It is awful! It is awful! Mon Dieu—mon Dieu! What is to become of us?"

She was moaning and lamenting even as she ran in, and now she threw her apron over her face and sank into a chair, continuing her moaning and her lamentations.

Neither Mademoiselle nor Armand had stirred. They remained like graven images, he on one knee, she with large eyes fixed upon his face. They had neither of them looked on the old woman; they seemed even now unconscious of her presence. But their ears had caught the sound of that measured tramp of feet up the stairs of the old house, and the halt upon the landing; they had heard the brief words of command:

"Open, in the name of the people!"

They knew quite well what it all meant; they had not wandered so far in the realms of romance that reality—the grim, horrible reality of the moment—had not the power to bring them back to earth.

That peremptory call to open in the name of the people was the prologue these days to a drama which had but two concluding acts: arrest, which was a certainty; the guillotine, which was more than probable. Jeanne and Armand, these two young people who but a moment ago had tentatively lifted the veil of life, looked straight into each other's eyes and saw the hand of death interposed between them: they looked straight into each other's eyes and knew that nothing but the hand of death would part them now. Love had come with its attendant, Sorrow; but he had come with no uncertain footsteps. Jeanne looked on the man before her, and he bent his head to imprint a glowing kiss upon her hand.

"Aunt Marie!"

It was Jeanne Lange who spoke, but her voice was no longer that of an irresponsible child; it was firm, steady and hard. Though she spoke to the old woman, she did not look at her; her luminous brown eyes rested on the bowed head of Armand St. Just.

"Aunt Marie!" she repeated more peremptorily, for the old woman, with her apron over her head, was still moaning, and unconscious of all save an overmastering fear.

"Open, in the name of the people!" came in a loud harsh voice once more from the other side of the front door.

"Aunt Marie, as you value your life and mine, pull yourself together," said Jeanne firmly.

"What shall we do? Oh! what shall we do?" moaned Madame Belhomme. But she had dragged the apron away from her face, and was looking with some puzzlement at meek, gentle little Jeanne, who had suddenly become so strange, so dictatorial, all unlike her habitual somewhat diffident self.

"You need not have the slightest fear, Aunt Marie, if you will only do as I tell you," resumed Jeanne quietly; "if you give way to fear, we are all of us undone. As you value your life and mine," she now repeated authoritatively, "pull yourself together, and do as I tell you."

The girl's firmness, her perfect quietude had the desired effect. Madame Belhomme, though still shaken up with sobs of terror, made a great effort to master herself; she stood up, smoothed down her apron, passed her hand over her ruffled hair, and said in a quaking voice:

"What do you think we had better do?"

"Go quietly to the door and open it."

"But—the soldiers—"

"If you do not open quietly they will force the door open within the next two minutes," interposed Jeanne calmly. "Go quietly and open the door. Try and hide your fears, grumble in an audible voice at being interrupted in your cooking, and tell the soldiers at once that they will find mademoiselle in the boudoir. Go, for God's sake!" she added, whilst suppressed emotion suddenly made her young voice vibrate; "go, before they break open that door!"

Madame Belhomme, impressed and cowed, obeyed like an automaton. She turned and marched fairly straight out of the room. It was not a minute too soon. From outside had already come the third and final summons:

"Open, in the name of the people!"

After that a crowbar would break open the door.

Madame Belhomme's heavy footsteps were heard crossing the ante-chamber. Armand still knelt at Jeanne's feet, holding her trembling little hand in his.

"A love-scene," she whispered rapidly, "a love-scene—quick—do you know one?"

And even as he had tried to rise she held him back, down on his knees.

He thought that fear was making her distracted.

"Mademoiselle—" he murmured, trying to soothe her.

"Try and understand," she said with wonderful calm, "and do as I tell you. Aunt Marie has obeyed. Will you do likewise?"

"To the death!" he whispered eagerly.

"Then a love-scene," she entreated. "Surely you know one. Rodrigue and Chimene! Surely—surely," she urged, even as tears of anguish rose into her eyes, "you must—you must, or, if not that, something else. Quick! The very seconds are precious!"

They were indeed! Madame Belhomme, obedient as a frightened dog, had gone to the door and opened it; even her well-feigned grumblings could now be heard and the rough interrogations from the soldiery.

"Citizeness Lange!" said a gruff voice.

"In her boudoir, quoi!"

Madame Belhomme, braced up apparently by fear, was playing her part remarkably well.

"Bothering good citizens! On baking day, too!" she went on grumbling and muttering.

"Oh, think—think!" murmured Jeanne now in an agonised whisper, her hot little hand grasping his so tightly that her nails were driven into his flesh. "You must know something, that will do—anything—for dear life's sake.... Armand!"

His name—in the tense excitement of this terrible moment—had escaped her lips.

All in a flash of sudden intuition he understood what she wanted, and even as the door of the boudoir was thrown violently open Armand—still on his knees, but with one hand pressed to his heart, the other stretched upwards to the ceiling in the most approved dramatic style, was loudly declaiming:

"Pour venger son honneur il perdit son amour,
Pour venger sa maitresse il a quitte le jour!"

Whereupon Mademoiselle Lange feigned the most perfect impatience.

"No, no, my good cousin," she said with a pretty moue of disdain, "that will never do! You must not thus emphasise the end of every line; the verses should flow more evenly, as thus...."

Heron had paused at the door. It was he who had thrown it open—he who, followed by a couple of his sleuth-hounds, had thought to find here the man denounced by de Batz as being one of the followers of that irrepressible Scarlet Pimpernel. The obviously Parisian intonation of the man kneeling in front of citizeness Lange in an attitude no ways suggestive of personal admiration, and coolly reciting verses out of a play, had somewhat taken him aback.

"What does this mean?" he asked gruffly, striding forward into the room and glaring first at mademoiselle, then at Armand.

Mademoiselle gave a little cry of surprise.

"Why, if it isn't citizen Heron!" she cried, jumping up with a dainty movement of coquetry and embarrassment. "Why did not Aunt Marie announce you?... It is indeed remiss of her, but she is so ill-tempered on baking days I dare not even rebuke her. Won't you sit down, citizen Heron? And you, cousin," she added, looking down airily on Armand, "I pray you maintain no longer that foolish attitude."

The febrileness of her manner, the glow in her cheeks were easily attributable to natural shyness in face of this unexpected visit. Heron, completely bewildered by this little scene, which was so unlike what he expected, and so unlike those to which he was accustomed in the exercise of his horrible duties, was practically speechless before the little lady who continued to prattle along in a simple, unaffected manner.

"Cousin," she said to Armand, who in the meanwhile had risen to his knees, "this is citizen Heron, of whom you have heard me speak. My cousin Belhomme," she continued, once more turning to Heron, "is fresh from the country, citizen. He hails from Orleans, where he has played leading parts in the tragedies of the late citizen Corneille. But, ah me! I fear that he will find Paris audiences vastly more critical than the good Orleanese. Did you hear him, citizen, declaiming those beautiful verses just now? He was murdering them, say I—yes, murdering them—the gaby!"

Then only did it seem as if she realised that there was something amiss, that citizen Heron had come to visit her, not as an admirer of her talent who would wish to pay his respects to a successful actress, but as a person to be looked on with dread.

She gave a quaint, nervous little laugh, and murmured in the tones of a frightened child:

"La, citizen, how glum you look! I thought you had come to compliment me on my latest success. I saw you at the theatre last night, though you did not afterwards come to see me in the green-room. Why! I had a regular ovation! Look at my flowers!" she added more gaily, pointing to several bouquets in vases about the room. "Citizen Danton brought me the violets himself, and citizen Santerre the narcissi, and that laurel wreath—is it not charming?—that was a tribute from citizen Robespierre himself."

She was so artless, so simple, and so natural that Heron was completely taken off his usual mental balance. He had expected to find the usual setting to the dramatic episodes which he was wont to conduct—screaming women, a man either at bay, sword in hand, or hiding in a linen cupboard or up a chimney.

Now everything puzzled him. De Batz—he was quite sure—had spoken of an Englishman, a follower of the Scarlet Pimpernel; every thinking French patriot knew that all the followers of the Scarlet Pimpernel were Englishmen with red hair and prominent teeth, whereas this man....

Armand—who deadly danger had primed in his improvised role—was striding up and down the room declaiming with ever-varying intonations:

> "Joignez tous vos efforts contre un espoir si doux
> Pour en venir a bout, c'est trop peu que de vous."

"No! no!" said mademoiselle impatiently; "you must not make that ugly pause midway in the last line: 'pour en venir a bout, c'est trop peu que de vous!'"

She mimicked Armand's diction so quaintly, imitating his stride, his awkward gesture, and his faulty phraseology with such funny exaggeration that Heron laughed in spite of himself.

"So that is a cousin from Orleans, is it?" he asked, throwing his lanky body into an armchair, which creaked dismally under his weight.

"Yes! a regular gaby—what?" she said archly. "Now, citizen Heron, you must stay and take coffee with me. Aunt Marie will be bringing it in directly. Hector," she added, turning to Armand, "come down from the clouds and ask Aunt Marie to be quick."

This certainly was the first time in the whole of his experience that Heron had been asked to stay and drink coffee with the quarry he was hunting down. Mademoiselle's innocent little ways, her desire for the prolongation of his visit, further addled his brain. De Batz had undoubtedly spoken of an Englishman, and the cousin from Orleans was certainly a Frenchman every inch of him.

Perhaps had the denunciation come from any one else but de Batz, Heron might have acted and thought more circumspectly; but, of course, the chief agent of the Committee of General Security was more suspicious of the man from whom he took a heavy bribe than of any one else in France. The thought had suddenly crossed his mind that mayhap de Batz had sent him on a fool's errand in order to get him safely out of the way of the Temple prison at a given hour of the day.

The thought took shape, crystallised, caused him to see a rapid vision of de Batz sneaking into his lodgings and stealing his keys, the guard being slack, careless, inattentive, allowing the adventurer to pass barriers that should have been closed against all comers.

Now Heron was sure of it; it was all a conspiracy invented by de Batz. He had forgotten all about his theories that a man under arrest is always safer than a man that is free. Had his brain been quite normal, and not obsessed, as it always was now by thoughts of the Dauphin's escape from prison, no doubt he would have been more suspicious of Armand, but all his worst suspicions were directed against de Batz. Armand seemed to him just a fool, an actor quoi? and so obviously not an Englishman.

He jumped to his feet, curtly declining mademoiselle's offers of hospitality. He wanted to get away at once. Actors and actresses were always, by tacit consent of the authorities, more immune than the rest of the community. They provided the only amusement in the intervals of the horrible scenes around the scaffolds; they were irresponsible, harmless creatures who did not meddle in politics.

Jeanne the while was gaily prattling on, her luminous eyes fixed upon the all-powerful enemy, striving to read his thoughts, to understand what went on behind those cruel, prominent eyes, the chances that Armand had of safety and of life.

She knew, of course, that the visit was directed against Armand—some one had betrayed him, that odious de Batz mayhap—and she was fighting for Armand's safety, for his life. Her armoury consisted of her presence of mind, her cool courage, her self-control; she used all these weapons for his sake, though at times she felt as if the strain on her nerves would snap the thread of life in her. The effort seemed more than she could bear.

But she kept up her part, rallying Heron for the shortness of his visit, begging him to tarry for another five minutes at least, throwing out—with subtle feminine intuition—just those very hints anent little Capet's safety that were most calculated to send him flying back towards the Temple.

"I felt so honoured last night, citizen," she said coquettishly, "that you even forgot little Capet in order to come and watch my debut as Celimene."

"Forget him!" retorted Heron, smothering a curse, "I never forget the vermin. I must go back to him; there are too many cats nosing round my mouse. Good day to you, citizeness. I ought to have brought flowers, I know; but I am a busy man—a harassed man."

"Je te crois," she said with a grave nod of the head; "but do come to the theatre to-night. I am playing Camille—such a fine part! one of my greatest successes."

"Yes, yes, I'll come—mayhap, mayhap—but I'll go now—glad to have seen you, citizeness. Where does your cousin lodge?" he asked abruptly.

"Here," she replied boldly, on the spur of the moment.

"Good. Let him report himself to-morrow morning at the Conciergerie, and get his certificate of safety. It is a new decree, and you should have one, too."

"Very well, then. Hector and I will come together, and perhaps Aunt Marie will come too. Don't send us to maman guillotine yet awhile, citizen," she said lightly; "you will never get such another Camille, nor yet so good a Celimene."

She was gay, artless to the last. She accompanied Heron to the door herself, chaffing him about his escort.

"You are an aristo, citizen," she said, gazing with well-feigned admiration on the two sleuth-hounds who stood in wait in the anteroom; "it makes me proud to see so many citizens at my door. Come and see me play Camille—come to-night, and don't forget the green-room door—it will always be kept invitingly open for you."

She bobbed him a curtsey, and he walked out, closely followed by his two men; then at last she closed the door behind them. She stood there for a while, her ear glued against the massive panels, listening for their measured tread down the oak staircase. At last it rang more sharply against the flagstones of the courtyard below; then she was satisfied that they had gone, and went slowly back to the boudoir.

CHAPTER X

Shadows

The tension on her nerves relaxed; there was the inevitable reaction. Her knees were shaking under her, and she literally staggered into the room.

But Armand was already near her, down on both his knees this time, his arms clasping the delicate form that swayed like the slender stems of narcissi in the breeze.

"Oh! you must go out of Paris at once—at once," she said through sobs which no longer would be kept back.

"He'll return—I know that he will return—and you will not be safe until you are back in England."

But he could not think of himself or of anything in the future. He had forgotten Heron, Paris, the world; he could only think of her.

"I owe my life to you!" he murmured. "Oh, how beautiful you are—how brave!

How I love you!"

It seemed that he had always loved her, from the moment that first in his boyish heart he had set up an ideal to worship, and then, last night, in the box of the theatre—he had his back turned toward the stage, and was ready to go—her voice had called him back; it had held him spellbound; her voice, and also her eyes.... He did not know then that it was Love which then and there had enchained him. Oh, how foolish he had been! for now he knew that he had loved her with all his might, with all his soul, from the very instant that his eyes had rested upon her.

He babbled along—incoherently—in the intervals of covering her hands and the hem of her gown with kisses. He stooped right down to the ground and kissed the arch of her instep; he had become a devotee worshipping at the shrine of his saint, who had performed a great and a wonderful miracle.

Armand the idealist had found his ideal in a woman. That was the great miracle which the woman herself had performed for him. He found in her all that he had admired most, all that he had admired in the leader who hitherto had been the only personification of his ideal. But Jeanne possessed all those qualities which had roused his enthusiasm in the noble hero whom he revered. Her pluck, her ingenuity, her calm devotion which had averted the threatened danger from him!

What had he done that she should have risked her own sweet life for his sake?

But Jeanne did not know. She could not tell. Her nerves now were somewhat unstrung, and the tears that always came so readily to her eyes flowed quite unchecked. She could not very well move, for he held her knees imprisoned in his arms, but she was quite content to remain like this, and to yield her hands to him so that he might cover them with kisses.

Indeed, she did not know at what precise moment love for him had been born in her heart. Last night, perhaps... she could not say ... but when they parted she felt that she must see him again... and then today... perhaps it was the scent of the violets... they were so exquisitely sweet... perhaps it was his enthusiasm and his talk about England... but when Heron came she knew that she must save Armand's life at all cost... that she would die if they dragged him away to prison.

Thus these two children philosophised, trying to understand the mystery of the birth of Love. But they were only children; they did not really understand. Passion was sweeping them off their feet, because a common danger had bound them irrevocably to one another. The womanly instinct to save and to protect had given the young girl strength to bear a difficult part, and now she loved him for the dangers from which she had rescued him, and he loved her because she had risked her life for him.

The hours sped on; there was so much to say, so much that was exquisite to listen to. The shades of evening were gathering fast; the room, with its pale-toned hangings and faded tapestries, was sinking into the arms of gloom. Aunt Marie was no doubt too terrified to stir out of her kitchen; she did not bring the lamps, but the darkness suited Armand's mood, and Jeanne was glad that the gloaming effectually hid the perpetual blush in her cheeks.

In the evening air the dying flowers sent their heady fragrance around. Armand was intoxicated with the perfume of violets that clung to Jeanne's fingers, with the touch of her satin gown that brushed his cheek, with the murmur of her voice that quivered through her tears.

No noise from the ugly outer world reached this secluded spot. In the tiny square outside a street lamp had been lighted, and its feeble rays came peeping in through the lace curtains at the window. They caught the dainty silhouette of the young girl, playing with the loose tendrils of her hair around her forehead, and outlining with a thin band of light the contour of neck and shoulder, making the satin of her gown shimmer with an opalescent glow.

Armand rose from his knees. Her eyes were calling to him, her lips were ready to yield.

"Tu m'aimes?" he whispered.

And like a tired child she sank upon his breast.

He kissed her hair, her eyes, her lips; her skin was fragrant as the flowers of spring, the tears on her cheeks glistened like morning dew.

Aunt Marie came in at last, carrying the lamp. She found them sitting side by side, like two children, hand in hand, mute with the eloquence which comes from boundless love. They were under a spell, forgetting even that they lived, knowing nothing except that they loved.

The lamp broke the spell, and Aunt Marie's still trembling voice:

"Oh, my dear! how did you manage to rid yourself of those brutes?"

But she asked no other question, even when the lamp showed up quite clearly the glowing cheeks of Jeanne and the ardent eyes of Armand. In her heart, long since atrophied, there were a few memories, carefully put away in a secret cell, and those memories caused the old woman to understand.

Neither Jeanne nor Armand noticed what she did; the spell had been broken, but the dream lingered on; they did not see Aunt Marie putting the room tidy, and then quietly tiptoeing out by the door.

But through the dream, reality was struggling for recognition. After Armand had asked for the hundredth time: "Tu m'aimes?" and Jeanne for the hundredth time had replied mutely with her eyes, her fears for him suddenly returned.

Something had awakened her from her trance—a heavy footstep, mayhap, in the street below, the distant roll of a drum, or only the clash of steel saucepans in Aunt Marie's kitchen. But suddenly Jeanne was alert, and with her alertness came terror for the beloved.

"Your life," she said—for he had called her his life just then, "your life—and I was forgetting that it is still in danger... your dear, your precious life!"

"Doubly dear now," he replied, "since I owe it to you."

"Then I pray you, I entreat you, guard it well for my sake—make all haste to leave Paris... oh, this I beg of you!" she continued more earnestly, seeing the look of demur in his eyes; "every hour you spend in it brings danger nearer to your door."

"I could not leave Paris while you are here."

"But I am safe here," she urged; "quite, quite safe, I assure you. I am only a poor actress, and the Government takes no heed of us mimes. Men must be amused, even between the intervals of killing one another. Indeed, indeed, I should be far safer here now, waiting quietly for awhile, while you make preparations to go... My hasty departure at this moment would bring disaster on us both."

There was logic in what she said. And yet how could he leave her? now that he had found this perfect woman—this realisation of his highest ideals, how could he go and leave her in this awful Paris, with brutes like Heron forcing their hideous personality into her sacred presence, threatening that very life he would gladly give his own to keep inviolate?

"Listen, sweetheart," he said after awhile, when presently reason struggled back for first place in his mind. "Will you allow me to consult with my chief, with the Scarlet Pimpernel, who is in Paris at the present moment? I am under his orders; I could not leave France just now. My life, my entire person are at his disposal. I and my comrades are here under his orders, for a great undertaking which he has not yet unfolded to us, but which I firmly believe is framed for the rescue of the Dauphin from the Temple."

She gave an involuntary exclamation of horror.

"No, no!" she said quickly and earnestly; "as far as you are concerned, Armand, that has now become an impossibility. Some one has betrayed you, and you are henceforth a marked man. I think that odious de Batz had a hand in Heron's visit of this afternoon. We succeeded in putting these spies off the scent, but only for a moment... within a few hours—less perhaps—Heron will repent him of his carelessness; he'll come back—I know that he will come back. He may leave me, personally, alone; but he will be on your track; he'll drag you to the Conciergerie to report yourself, and there your true name and history are bound to come to light. If you succeed in evading him, he will still be on your track. If the Scarlet Pimpernel keeps you in Paris now, your death will be at his door."

Her voice had become quite hard and trenchant as she said these last words; womanlike, she was already prepared to hate the man whose mysterious personality she had hitherto admired, now that the life and safety of Armand appeared to depend on the will of that elusive hero.

"You must not be afraid for me, Jeanne," he urged. "The Scarlet Pimpernel cares for all his followers; he would never allow me to run unnecessary risks."

She was unconvinced, almost jealous now of his enthusiasm for that unknown man. Already she had taken full possession of Armand; she had purchased his life, and he had given her his love. She would share neither treasure with that nameless leader who held Armand's allegiance.

"It is only for a little while, sweetheart," he reiterated again and again. "I could not, anyhow, leave Paris whilst I feel that you are here, maybe in danger. The thought would be horrible. I should go mad if I had to leave you."

Then he talked again of England, of his life there, of the happiness and peace that were in store for them both.

"We will go to England together," he whispered, "and there we will be happy together, you and I. We will have a tiny house among the Kentish hills, and its walls will be covered with honeysuckle and roses. At the back of the house there will be an orchard, and in May, when the fruit-blossom is fading and soft spring breezes blow among the trees, showers of sweet-scented petals will envelop us as we walk along, falling on us like fragrant snow. You will come, sweetheart, will you not?"

"If you still wish it, Armand," she murmured.

Still wish it! He would gladly go to-morrow if she would come with him. But, of course, that could not be arranged. She had her contract to fulfil at the theatre, then there would be her house and furniture to dispose of, and there was Aunt Marie.... But, of course, Aunt Marie would come too.... She thought that she could get away some time before the spring; and he swore that he could not leave Paris until she came with him.

It seemed a terrible deadlock, for she could not bear to think of him alone in those awful Paris streets, where she knew that spies would always be tracking him. She had no illusions as to the impression which she had made on Heron; she knew that it could only be a momentary one, and that Armand would henceforth be in daily, hourly danger.

At last she promised him that she would take the advice of his chief; they would both be guided by what he said. Armand would confide in him to-night, and if it could be arranged she would hurry on her preparations and, mayhap, be ready to join him in a week.

"In the meanwhile, that cruel man must not risk your dear life," she said. "Remember, Armand, your life belongs to me. Oh, I could hate him for the love you bear him!"

"Sh—sh—sh!" he said earnestly. "Dear heart, you must not speak like that of the man whom, next to your perfect self, I love most upon earth."

"You think of him more than of me. I shall scarce live until I know that you are safely out of Paris."

Though it was horrible to part, yet it was best, perhaps, that he should go back to his lodgings now, in case Heron sent his spies back to her door, and since he meant to consult with his chief. She had a vague hope that if the mysterious hero was indeed the noble-hearted man whom Armand represented him to be, surely he would take compassion on the anxiety of a sorrowing woman, and release the man she loved from bondage.

This thought pleased her and gave her hope. She even urged Armand now to go.

"When may I see you to-morrow?" he asked.

"But it will be so dangerous to meet," she argued.

"I must see you. I could not live through the day without seeing you."

"The theatre is the safest place."

"I could not wait till the evening. May I not come here?"

"No, no. Heron's spies may be about."

"Where then?"

She thought it over for a moment.

"At the stage-door of the theatre at one o'clock," she said at last. "We shall have finished rehearsal. Slip into the guichet of the concierge. I will tell him to admit you, and send my dresser to meet you there; she will bring you along to my room, where we shall be undisturbed for at least half an hour."

He had perforce to be content with that, though he would so much rather have seen her here again, where the faded tapestries and soft-toned hangings made such a perfect background for her delicate charm. He had every intention of confiding in Blakeney, and of asking his help for getting Jeanne out of Paris as quickly as may be.

Thus this perfect hour was past; the most pure, the fullest of joy that these two young people were ever destined to know. Perhaps they felt within themselves the consciousness that their great love would rise anon to yet greater, fuller perfection when Fate had crowned it with his halo of sorrow. Perhaps, too, it was that consciousness that gave to their kisses now the solemnity of a last farewell.

CHAPTER XI

The League of the Scarlet Pimpernel

Armand never could say definitely afterwards whither he went when he left the Square du Roule that evening. No doubt he wandered about the streets for some time in an absent, mechanical way, paying no heed to the passers-by, none to the direction in which he was going.

His mind was full of Jeanne, her beauty, her courage, her attitude in face of the hideous bloodhound who had come to pollute that charming old-world boudoir by his loathsome presence. He recalled every word she uttered, every gesture she made.

He was a man in love for the first time—wholly, irremediably in love.

I suppose that it was the pangs of hunger that first recalled him to himself. It was close on eight o'clock now, and he had fed on his imaginings—first on anticipation, then on realisation, and lastly on memory—during the best part of the day. Now he awoke from his day-dream to find himself tired and hungry, but fortunately not very far from that quarter of Paris where food is easily obtainable.

He was somewhere near the Madeleine—a quarter he knew well. Soon he saw in front of him a small eating-house which looked fairly clean and orderly. He pushed open its swing-door, and seeing an empty table in a secluded part of the room, he sat down and ordered some supper.

The place made no impression upon his memory. He could not have told you an hour later where it was situated, who had served him, what he had eaten, or what other persons were present in the dining-room at the time that he himself entered it.

Having eaten, however, he felt more like his normal self—more conscious of his actions. When he finally left the eating-house, he realised, for instance, that it was very cold—a fact of which he had for the past few hours been totally unaware. The snow was falling in thin close flakes, and a biting north-easterly wind was blowing those flakes into his face and down his collar. He wrapped his cloak tightly around him. It was a good step yet to Blakeney's lodgings, where he knew that he was expected.

He struck quickly into the Rue St. Honore, avoiding the great open places where the grim horrors of this magnificent city in revolt against civilisation were displayed in all their grim nakedness—on the Place de la Revolution the guillotine, on the Carrousel the open-air camps of workers under the lash of slave-drivers more cruel than the uncivilised brutes of the Far West.

And Armand had to think of Jeanne in the midst of all these horrors. She was still a petted actress to-day, but who could tell if on the morrow the terrible law of the "suspect" would not reach her in order to drag her before a tribunal that knew no mercy, and whose sole justice was a condemnation?

The young man hurried on; he was anxious to be among his own comrades, to hear his chief's pleasant voice, to feel assured that by all the sacred laws of friendship Jeanne henceforth would become the special care of the Scarlet Pimpernel and his league.

Blakeney lodged in a small house situated on the Quai de l'Ecole, at the back of St. Germain l'Auxerrois, from whence he had a clear and uninterrupted view across the river, as far as the irregular block of buildings of the Chatelet prison and the house of Justice.

The same tower-clock that two centuries ago had tolled the signal for the massacre of the Huguenots was even now striking nine. Armand slipped through the half-open porte cochere, crossed the narrow dark courtyard, and ran up two flights of winding stone stairs. At the top of these, a door on his right allowed a thin streak of light to filtrate between its two folds. An iron bell handle hung beside it; Armand gave it a pull.

Two minutes later he was amongst his friends. He heaved a great sigh of content and relief. The very atmosphere here seemed to be different. As far as the lodging itself was concerned, it was as bare, as devoid of comfort as those sort of places—so-called chambres garnies—usually were in these days. The chairs looked rickety and uninviting, the sofa was of black horsehair, the carpet was threadbare, and in places in actual holes; but there was a certain something in the air which revealed, in the midst of all this squalor, the presence of a man of fastidious taste.

To begin with, the place was spotlessly clean; the stove, highly polished, gave forth a pleasing warm glow, even whilst the window, slightly open, allowed a modicum of fresh air to enter the room. In a rough earthenware jug on the table stood a large bunch of Christmas roses, and to the educated nostril the slight scent of perfumes that hovered in the air was doubly pleasing after the fetid air of the narrow streets.

Sir Andrew Ffoulkes was there, also my Lord Tony, and Lord Hastings. They greeted Armand with whole-hearted cheeriness.

"Where is Blakeney?" asked the young man as soon as he had shaken his friends by the hand.

"Present!" came in loud, pleasant accents from the door of an inner room on the right.

And there he stood under the lintel of the door, the man against whom was raised the giant hand of an entire nation—the man for whose head the revolutionary government of France would gladly pay out all the savings of its Treasury—the man whom human bloodhounds were tracking, hot on the scent—for whom the nets of a bitter revenge and relentless reprisals were constantly being spread.

Was he unconscious of it, or merely careless? His closest friend, Sir Andrew Ffoulkes, could not say. Certain it is that, as he now appeared before Armand, picturesque as ever in perfectly tailored clothes, with priceless lace at throat and wrists, his slender fingers holding an enamelled snuff-box and a handkerchief of delicate cambric, his whole personality that of a dandy rather than a man of action, it seemed impossible to connect him with the foolhardy escapades which had set one nation glowing with enthusiasm and another clamouring for revenge.

But it was the magnetism that emanated from him that could not be denied; the light that now and then, swift as summer lightning, flashed out from the depths of the blue eyes usually veiled by heavy, lazy lids, the sudden tightening of firm lips, the setting of the square jaw, which in a moment—but only for the space of a second—transformed the entire face, and revealed the born leader of men.

Just now there was none of that in the debonnair, easy-going man of the world who advanced to meet his friend. Armand went quickly up to him, glad to grasp his hand, slightly troubled with remorse, no doubt, at the recollection of his adventure of to-day. It almost seemed to him that from beneath his half-closed lids Blakeney had shot a quick inquiring glance upon him. The quick flash seemed to light up the young man's soul from within, and to reveal it, naked, to his friend.

It was all over in a moment, and Armand thought that mayhap his conscience had played him a trick: there was nothing apparent in him—of this he was sure—that could possibly divulge his secret just yet.

"I am rather late, I fear," he said. "I wandered about the streets in the late afternoon and lost my way in the dark. I hope I have not kept you all waiting."

They all pulled chairs closely round the fire, except Blakeney, who preferred to stand. He waited awhile until they were all comfortably settled, and all ready to listen, then:

"It is about the Dauphin," he said abruptly without further preamble.

They understood. All of them had guessed it, almost before the summons came that had brought them to Paris two days ago. Sir Andrew Ffoulkes had left his young wife because of that, and Armand had demanded it as a right to join hands in this noble work. Blakeney had not left France for over three months now. Backwards and forwards between Paris, or Nantes, or Orleans to the coast, where his friends would meet him to receive those unfortunates whom one man's whole-hearted devotion had rescued from death; backwards and forwards into the very hearts of those cities wherein an army of sleuth-hounds were on his track, and the guillotine was stretching out her arms to catch the foolhardy adventurer.

Now it was about the Dauphin. They all waited, breathless and eager, the fire of a noble enthusiasm burning in their hearts. They waited in silence, their eyes fixed on the leader, lest one single word from him should fail to reach their ears.

The full magnetism of the man was apparent now. As he held these four men at this moment, he could have held a crowd. The man of the world—the fastidious dandy—had shed his mask; there stood the leader, calm, serene in the very face of the most deadly danger that had ever encompassed any man, looking that danger fully in the face, not striving to belittle it or to exaggerate it, but weighing it in the balance with what there was to accomplish: the rescue of a martyred, innocent child from the hands of fiends who were destroying his very soul even more completely than his body.

"Everything, I think, is prepared," resumed Sir Percy after a slight pause. "The Simons have been summarily dismissed; I learned that to-day. They remove from the Temple on Sunday next, the nineteenth. Obviously that is the one day most likely to help us in our operations. As far as I am concerned, I cannot make any hard-and-fast plans. Chance at the last moment will have to dictate. But from every one of you I must have co-operation, and it can only be by your following my directions implicitly that we can even remotely hope to succeed."

He crossed and recrossed the room once or twice before he spoke again, pausing now and again in his walk in front of a large map of Paris and its environs that hung upon the wall, his tall figure erect, his hands behind his back, his eyes fixed before him as if he saw right through the walls of this squalid room, and across the darkness that overhung the city, through the grim bastions of the mighty building far away, where the descendant of an hundred kings lived at the mercy of human fiends who worked for his abasement.

The man's face now was that of a seer and a visionary; the firm lines were set and rigid as those of an image carved in stone—the statue of heart-whole devotion, with the self-imposed task beckoning sternly to follow, there where lurked danger and death.

"The way, I think, in which we could best succeed would be this," he resumed after a while, sitting now on the edge of the table and directly facing his four friends. The light from the lamp which stood upon the table behind him fell full upon those four glowing faces fixed eagerly upon him, but he himself was in shadow, a massive silhouette broadly cut out against the light-coloured map on the wall beyond.

"I remain here, of course, until Sunday," he said, "and will closely watch my opportunity, when I can with the greatest amount of safety enter the Temple building and take possession of the child. I shall, of course choose the moment when the Simons are actually on the move, with their successors probably coming in at about the same time. God alone knows," he added earnestly, "how I shall contrive to get possession of the child; at the moment I am just as much in the dark about that as you are."

He paused a moment, and suddenly his grave face seemed flooded with sunshine, a kind of lazy merriment danced in his eyes, effacing all trace of solemnity within them.

"La!" he said lightly, "on one point I am not at all in the dark, and that is that His Majesty King Louis XVII will come out of that ugly house in my company next Sunday, the nineteenth day of January in this year of grace seventeen hundred and ninety-four; and this, too, do I know—that those murderous blackguards shall not lay hands on me whilst that precious burden is in my keeping. So I pray you, my good Armand, do not look so glum," he added with his pleasant, merry laugh; "you'll need all your wits about you to help us in our undertaking."

"What do you wish me to do, Percy?" said the young man simply.

"In one moment I will tell you. I want you all to understand the situation first. The child will be out of the Temple on Sunday, but at what hour I know not. The later it will be the better would it suit my purpose, for I cannot get him out of Paris before evening with any chance of safety. Here we must risk nothing; the child is far better off as he is now than he would be if he were dragged back after an abortive attempt at rescue. But at this hour of the night, between nine and ten o'clock, I can arrange to get him out of Paris by the Villette gate, and that is where I want you, Ffoulkes, and you, Tony, to be, with some kind of covered cart, yourselves in any disguise your ingenuity will suggest. Here are a few certificates of safety; I have been making a collection of them for some time, as they are always useful."

He dived into the wide pocket of his coat and drew forth a number of cards, greasy, much-fingered documents of the usual pattern which the Committee of General Security delivered to the free citizens of the new republic, and without which no one could enter or leave any town or country commune without being detained as "suspect." He glanced at them and handed them over to Ffoulkes.

"Choose your own identity for the occasion, my good friend," he said lightly; "and you too, Tony. You may be stonemasons or coal-carriers, chimney-sweeps or farm-labourers, I care not which so long as you look sufficiently grimy and wretched to be unrecognisable, and so long as you can procure a cart without arousing suspicions, and can wait for me punctually at the appointed spot."

Ffoulkes turned over the cards, and with a laugh handed them over to Lord Tony. The two fastidious gentlemen discussed for awhile the respective merits of a chimney-sweep's uniform as against that of a coal-carrier.

"You can carry more grime if you are a sweep," suggested Blakeney; "and if the soot gets into your eyes it does not make them smart like coal does."

"But soot adheres more closely," argued Tony solemnly, "and I know that we shan't get a bath for at least a week afterwards."

"Certainly you won't, you sybarite!" asserted Sir Percy with a laugh.

"After a week soot might become permanent," mused Sir Andrew, wondering what, under the circumstance, my lady would say to him.

"If you are both so fastidious," retorted Blakeney, shrugging his broad shoulders, "I'll turn one of you into a reddleman, and the other into a dyer. Then one of you will be bright scarlet to the end of his days, as the reddle never comes off the skin at all, and the other will have to soak in turpentine before the dye will consent to move.... In either case... oh, my dear Tony!... the smell...."

He laughed like a schoolboy in anticipation of a prank, and held his scented handkerchief to his nose. My Lord Hastings chuckled audibly, and Tony punched him for this unseemly display of mirth.

Armand watched the little scene in utter amazement. He had been in England over a year, and yet he could not understand these Englishmen. Surely they were the queerest, most inconsequent people in the world. Here were these men, who were engaged at this very moment in an enterprise which for cool-headed courage and foolhardy daring had probably no parallel in history. They were literally taking their lives in their hands, in all probability facing certain death; and yet they now sat chaffing and fighting like a crowd of third-form schoolboys, talking utter, silly nonsense, and making foolish jokes that would have shamed a Frenchman in his teens. Vaguely he wondered what fat, pompous de Batz would think of this discussion if he could overhear it. His contempt, no doubt, for the Scarlet Pimpernel and his followers would be increased tenfold.

Then at last the question of the disguise was effectually dismissed. Sir Andrew Ffoulkes and Lord Anthony Dewhurst had settled their differences of opinion by solemnly agreeing to represent two over-grimy and overheated coal-heavers. They chose two certificates of safety that were made out in the names of Jean Lepetit and Achille Grospierre, labourers.

"Though you don't look at all like an Achille, Tony," was Blakeney's parting shot to his friend.

Then without any transition from this schoolboy nonsense to the serious business of the moment, Sir Andrew Ffoulkes said abruptly:

"Tell us exactly, Blakeney, where you will want the cart to stand on Sunday."

Blakeney rose and turned to the map against the wall, Ffoulkes and Tony following him. They stood close to his elbow whilst his slender, nervy hand wandered along the shiny surface of the varnished paper. At last he placed his finger on one spot.

"Here you see," he said, "is the Villette gate. Just outside it a narrow street on the right leads down in the direction of the canal. It is just at the bottom of that narrow street at its junction with the tow-path there that I want you two and the cart to be. It had better be a coal-car by the way; they will be unloading coal close by there to-morrow," he added with one of his sudden irrepressible outbursts of merriment. "You and Tony can exercise your muscles coal-heaving, and incidentally make yourselves known in the neighbourhood as good if somewhat grimy patriots."

"We had better take up our parts at once then," said Tony. "I'll take a fond farewell of my clean shirt to-night."

"Yes, you will not see one again for some time, my good Tony. After your hard day's work to-morrow you will have to sleep either inside your cart, if you have already secured one, or under the arches of the canal bridge, if you have not."

"I hope you have an equally pleasant prospect for Hastings," was my Lord Tony's grim comment.

It was easy to see that he was as happy as a schoolboy about to start for a holiday. Lord Tony was a true sportsman. Perhaps there was in him less sentiment for the heroic work which he did under the guidance of his chief than an inherent passion for dangerous adventures. Sir Andrew Ffoulkes, on the other hand, thought perhaps a little less of the adventure, but a great deal of the martyred child in the Temple. He was just as buoyant, just as keen as his friend, but the leaven of sentiment raised his sporting instincts to perhaps a higher plane of self-devotion.

"Well, now, to recapitulate," he said, in turn following with his finger the indicated route on the map. "Tony and I and the coal-cart will await you on this spot, at the corner of the towpath on Sunday evening at nine o'clock."

"And your signal, Blakeney?" asked Tony.

"The usual one," replied Sir Percy, "the seamew's cry thrice repeated at brief intervals. But now," he continued, turning to Armand and Hastings, who had taken no part in the discussion hitherto, "I want your help a little further afield."

"I thought so," nodded Hastings.

"The coal-cart, with its usual miserable nag, will carry us a distance of fifteen or sixteen kilometres, but no more. My purpose is to cut along the north of the city, and to reach St. Germain, the nearest point where we can secure good mounts. There is a farmer just outside the commune; his name is Achard. He has excellent horses, which I have borrowed before now; we shall want five, of course, and he has one powerful beast that will do for me, as I shall have, in addition to my own weight, which is considerable, to take the child with me on the pillion. Now you, Hastings and Armand, will have to start early to-morrow morning, leave Paris by the Neuilly gate, and from there make your way to St. Germain by any conveyance you can contrive to obtain. At St. Germain you must at once find Achard's farm; disguised as labourers you will not arouse suspicion by so doing. You will find the farmer quite amenable to money, and you must secure the best horses you can get for our own use, and, if possible, the powerful mount I spoke of just now. You are both excellent horse-men, therefore I selected you amongst the others for this special errand, for you two, with the five horses, will have to come and meet our coal-cart some seventeen kilometres out of St. Germain, to where the first sign-post indicates the road to Courbevoie. Some two hundred metres down this road on the right there is a small spinney, which will afford splendid shelter for yourselves and your horses. We hope to be there at about one o'clock after midnight of Monday morning. Now, is all that quite clear, and are you both satisfied?"

"It is quite clear," exclaimed Hastings placidly; "but I, for one, am not at all satisfied."

"And why not?"

"Because it is all too easy. We get none of the danger."

"Oho! I thought that you would bring that argument forward, you incorrigible grumbler," laughed Sir Percy good-humouredly. "Let me tell you that if you start to-morrow from Paris in that spirit you will run your head and Armand's into a noose long before you reach the gate of Neuilly. I cannot allow either of you to cover your faces with too much grime; an honest farm labourer should not look over-dirty, and your chances of being discovered and detained are, at the outset, far greater than those which Ffoulkes and Tony will run—"

Armand had said nothing during this time. While Blakeney was unfolding his plan for him and for Lord Hastings—a plan which practically was a command—he had sat with his arms folded across his chest, his head sunk upon his breast. When Blakeney had asked if they were satisfied, he had taken no part in Hastings' protest nor responded to his leader's good-humoured banter.

Though he did not look up even now, yet he felt that Percy's eyes were fixed upon him, and they seemed to scorch into his soul. He made a great effort to appear eager like the others, and yet from the first a chill had struck at his heart. He could not leave Paris before he had seen Jeanne.

He looked up suddenly, trying to seem unconcerned; he even looked his chief fully in the face.

"When ought we to leave Paris?" he asked calmly.

"You MUST leave at daybreak," replied Blakeney with a slight, almost imperceptible emphasis on the word of command. "When the gates are first opened, and the work-people go to and fro at their work, that is the safest hour. And you must be at St. Germain as soon as may be, or the farmer may not have a sufficiency of horses available at a moment's notice. I want you to be spokesman with Achard, so that Hastings' British accent should not betray you both. Also you might not get a conveyance for St. Germain immediately. We must think of every eventuality, Armand. There is so much at stake."

Armand made no further comment just then. But the others looked astonished. Armand had but asked a simple question, and Blakeney's reply seemed almost like a rebuke—so circumstantial too, and so explanatory. He was so used to being obeyed at a word, so accustomed that the merest wish, the slightest hint from him was understood by his band of devoted followers, that the long explanation of his orders which he gave to Armand struck them all with a strange sense of unpleasant surprise.

Hastings was the first to break the spell that seemed to have fallen over the party.

"We leave at daybreak, of course," he said, "as soon as the gates are open. We can, I know, get one of the carriers to give us a lift as far as St. Germain. There, how do we find Achard?"

"He is a well-known farmer," replied Blakeney. "You have but to ask."

"Good. Then we bespeak five horses for the next day, find lodgings in the village that night, and make a fresh start back towards Paris in the evening of Sunday. Is that right?"

"Yes. One of you will have two horses on the lead, the other one. Pack some fodder on the empty saddles and start at about ten o'clock. Ride straight along the main road, as if you were making back for Paris, until you come to four cross-roads with a sign-post pointing to Courbevoie. Turn down there and go along the road until you meet a close spinney of fir-trees on your right. Make for the interior of that. It gives splendid shelter, and you can dismount there and give the horses a feed. We'll join you one hour after midnight. The night will be dark, I hope, and the moon anyhow will be on the wane."

"I think I understand. Anyhow, it's not difficult, and we'll be as careful as may be."

"You will have to keep your heads clear, both of you," concluded Blakeney.

He was looking at Armand as he said this; but the young man had not made a movement during this brief colloquy between Hastings and the chief. He still sat with arms folded, his head falling on his breast.

Silence had fallen on them all. They all sat round the fire buried in thought. Through the open window there came from the quay beyond the hum of life in the open-air camp; the tramp of the sentinels around it, the words of command from the drill-sergeant, and through it all the moaning of the wind and the beating of the sleet against the window-panes.

A whole world of wretchedness was expressed by those sounds! Blakeney gave a quick, impatient sigh, and going to the window he pushed it further open, and just then there came from afar the muffled roll of drums, and from below the watchman's cry that seemed such dire mockery:

"Sleep, citizens! Everything is safe and peaceful."

"Sound advice," said Blakeney lightly. "Shall we also go to sleep? What say you all—eh?"

He had with that sudden rapidity characteristic of his every action, already thrown off the serious air which he had worn a moment ago when giving instructions to Hastings. His usual debonnair manner was on him once again, his laziness, his careless insouciance. He was even at this moment deeply engaged in flicking off a grain of dust from the immaculate Mechlin ruff at his wrist. The heavy lids had fallen over the tell-tale eyes as if weighted with fatigue, the mouth appeared ready for the laugh which never was absent from it very long.

It was only Ffoulkes's devoted eyes that were sharp enough to pierce the mask of light-hearted gaiety which enveloped the soul of his leader at the present moment. He saw—for the first time in all the years that he had known Blakeney—a frown across the habitually smooth brow, and though the lips were parted for a laugh, the lines round mouth and chin were hard and set.

With that intuition born of whole-hearted friendship Sir Andrew guessed what troubled Percy. He had caught the look which the latter had thrown on Armand, and knew that some explanation would have to pass between the two men before they parted to-night. Therefore he gave the signal for the breaking up of the meeting.

"There is nothing more to say, is there, Blakeney?" he asked.

"No, my good fellow, nothing," replied Sir Percy. "I do not know how you all feel, but I am demmed fatigued."

"What about the rags for to-morrow?" queried Hastings.

"You know where to find them. In the room below. Ffoulkes has the key. Wigs and all are there. But don't use false hair if you can help it—it is apt to shift in a scrimmage."

He spoke jerkily, more curtly than was his wont. Hastings and Tony thought that he was tired. They rose to say good night. Then the three men went away together, Armand remaining behind.

CHAPTER XII

What Love Is

"Well, now, Armand, what is it?" asked Blakeney, the moment the footsteps of his friends had died away down the stone stairs, and their voices had ceased to echo in the distance.

"You guessed, then, that there was... something?" said the younger man, after a slight hesitation.

"Of course."

Armand rose, pushing the chair away from him with an impatient nervy gesture. Burying his hands in the pockets of his breeches, he began striding up and down the room, a dark, troubled expression in his face, a deep frown between his eyes.

Blakeney had once more taken up his favourite position, sitting on the corner of the table, his broad shoulders interposed between the lamp and the rest of the room. He was apparently taking no notice of Armand, but only intent on the delicate operation of polishing his nails.

Suddenly the young man paused in his restless walk and stood in front of his friend—an earnest, solemn, determined figure.

"Blakeney," he said, "I cannot leave Paris to-morrow."

Sir Percy made no reply. He was contemplating the polish which he had just succeeded in producing on his thumbnail.

"I must stay here for a while longer," continued Armand firmly. "I may not be able to return to England for some weeks. You have the three others here to help you in your enterprise outside Paris. I am entirely at your service within the compass of its walls."

Still no comment from Blakeney, not a look from beneath the fallen lids. Armand continued, with a slight tone of impatience apparent in his voice:

"You must want some one to help you here on Sunday. I am entirely at your service... here or anywhere in Paris... but I cannot leave this city... at any rate, not just yet...."

Blakeney was apparently satisfied at last with the result of his polishing operations. He rose, gave a slight yawn, and turned toward the door.

"Good night, my dear fellow," he said pleasantly; "it is time we were all abed. I am so demmed fatigued."

"Percy!" exclaimed the young man hotly.

"Eh? What is it?" queried the other lazily.

"You are not going to leave me like this—without a word?"

"I have said a great many words, my good fellow. I have said 'good night,' and remarked that I was demmed fatigued."

He was standing beside the door which led to his bedroom, and now he pushed it open with his hand.

"Percy, you cannot go and leave me like this!" reiterated Armand with rapidly growing irritation.

"Like what, my dear fellow?" queried Sir Percy with good-humoured impatience.

"Without a word—without a sign. What have I done that you should treat me like a child, unworthy even of attention?"

Blakeney had turned back and was now facing him, towering above the slight figure of the younger man. His face had lost none of its gracious air, and beneath their heavy lids his eyes looked down not unkindly on his friend.

"Would you have preferred it, Armand," he said quietly, "if I had said the word that your ears have heard even though my lips have not uttered it?"

"I don't understand," murmured Armand defiantly.

"What sign would you have had me make?" continued Sir Percy, his pleasant voice falling calm and mellow on the younger man's supersensitive consciousness: "That of branding you, Marguerite's brother, as a liar and a cheat?"

"Blakeney!" retorted the other, as with flaming cheeks and wrathful eyes he took a menacing step toward his friend; "had any man but you dared to speak such words to me—"

"I pray to God, Armand, that no man but I has the right to speak them."

"You have no right."

"Every right, my friend. Do I not hold your oath?... Are you not prepared to break it?"

"I'll not break my oath to you. I'll serve and help you in every way you can command... my life I'll give to the cause... give me the most dangerous—the most difficult task to perform.... I'll do it—I'll do it gladly."

"I have given you an over-difficult and dangerous task."

"Bah! To leave Paris in order to engage horses, while you and the others do all the work. That is neither difficult nor dangerous."

"It will be difficult for you, Armand, because your head is not sufficiently cool to foresee serious eventualities and to prepare against them. It is dangerous, because you are a man in love, and a man in love is apt to run his head—and that of his friends—blindly into a noose."

"Who told you that I was in love?"

"You yourself, my good fellow. Had you not told me so at the outset," he continued, still speaking very quietly and deliberately and never raising his voice, "I would even now be standing over you, dog-whip in hand, to thrash you as a defaulting coward and a perjurer .... Bah!" he added with a return to his habitual bonhomie, "I would no doubt even have lost my temper with you. Which would have been purposeless and excessively bad form. Eh?"

A violent retort had sprung to Armand's lips. But fortunately at that very moment his eyes, glowing with anger, caught those of Blakeney fixed with lazy good-nature upon his. Something of that irresistible dignity which pervaded the whole personality of the man checked Armand's hotheaded words on his lips.

"I cannot leave Paris to-morrow," he reiterated more calmly.

"Because you have arranged to see her again?"

"Because she saved my life to-day, and is herself in danger."

"She is in no danger," said Blakeney simply, "since she saved the life of my friend."

"Percy!"

The cry was wrung from Armand St. Just's very soul. Despite the tumult of passion which was raging in his heart, he was conscious again of the magnetic power which bound so many to this man's service. The words he had said—simple though they were—had sent a thrill through Armand's veins. He felt himself disarmed. His resistance fell before the subtle strength of an unbendable will; nothing remained in his heart but an overwhelming sense of shame and of impotence.

He sank into a chair and rested his elbows on the table, burying his face in his hands. Blakeney went up to him and placed a kindly hand upon his shoulder.

"The difficult task, Armand," he said gently.

"Percy, cannot you release me? She saved my life. I have not thanked her yet."

"There will be time for thanks later, Armand. Just now over yonder the son of kings is being done to death by savage brutes."

"I would not hinder you if I stayed."

"God knows you have hindered us enough already."

"How?"

"You say she saved your life... then you were in danger... Heron and his spies have been on your track; your track leads to mine, and I have sworn to save the Dauphin from the hands of thieves.... A man in love, Armand, is a deadly danger among us.... Therefore at daybreak you must leave Paris with Hastings on your difficult and dangerous task."

"And if I refuse?" retorted Armand.

"My good fellow," said Blakeney earnestly, "in that admirable lexicon which the League of the Scarlet Pimpernel has compiled for itself there is no such word as refuse."

"But if I do refuse?" persisted the other.

"You would be offering a tainted name and tarnished honour to the woman you pretend to love."

"And you insist upon my obedience?"

"By the oath which I hold from you."

"But this is cruel—inhuman!"

"Honour, my good Armand, is often cruel and seldom human. He is a godlike taskmaster, and we who call ourselves men are all of us his slaves."

"The tyranny comes from you alone. You could release me an you would."

"And to gratify the selfish desire of immature passion, you would wish to see me jeopardise the life of those who place infinite trust in me."

"God knows how you have gained their allegiance, Blakeney. To me now you are selfish and callous."

"There is the difficult task you craved for, Armand," was all the answer that Blakeney made to the taunt—"to obey a leader whom you no longer trust."

But this Armand could not brook. He had spoken hotly, impetuously, smarting under the discipline which thwarted his desire, but his heart was loyal to the chief whom he had reverenced for so long.

"Forgive me, Percy," he said humbly; "I am distracted. I don't think I quite realised what I was saying. I trust you, of course ... implicitly... and you need not even fear... I shall not break my oath, though your orders now seem to me needlessly callous and selfish.... I will obey... you need not be afraid."

"I was not afraid of that, my good fellow."

"Of course, you do not understand... you cannot. To you, your honour, the task which you have set yourself, has been your only fetish.... Love in its true sense does not exist for you.... I see it now... you do not know what it is to love."

Blakeney made no reply for the moment. He stood in the centre of the room, with the yellow light of the lamp falling full now upon his tall powerful frame, immaculately dressed in perfectly-tailored clothes, upon his long, slender hands half hidden by filmy lace, and upon his face, across which at this moment a heavy strand of curly hair threw a curious shadow. At Armand's words his lips had imperceptibly tightened, his eyes had narrowed as if they tried to see something that was beyond the range of their focus.

Across the smooth brow the strange shadow made by the hair seemed to find a reflex from within. Perhaps the reckless adventurer, the careless gambler with life and liberty, saw through the walls of this squalid room, across the wide, ice-bound river, and beyond even the gloomy pile of buildings opposite, a cool, shady garden at Richmond, a velvety lawn sweeping down to the river's edge, a bower of clematis and roses, with a carved stone seat half covered with moss. There sat an exquisitely beautiful woman with great sad eyes fixed on the far-distant horizon. The setting sun was throwing a halo of gold all round her hair, her white hands were clasped idly on her lap.

She gazed out beyond the river, beyond the sunset, toward an unseen bourne of peace and happiness, and her lovely face had in it a look of utter hopelessness and of sublime self-abnegation. The air was still. It was late autumn, and all around her the russet leaves of beech and chestnut fell with a melancholy hush-sh-sh about her feet.

She was alone, and from time to time heavy tears gathered in her eyes and rolled slowly down her cheeks.

Suddenly a sigh escaped the man's tightly-pressed lips. With a strange gesture, wholly unusual to him, he passed his hand right across his eyes.

"Mayhap you are right, Armand," he said quietly; "mayhap I do not know what it is to love."

Armand turned to go. There was nothing more to be said. He knew Percy well enough by now to realise the finality of his pronouncements. His heart felt sore, but he was too proud to show his hurt again to a man who did not understand. All thoughts of disobedience he had put resolutely aside; he had never meant to break his oath. All that he had hoped to do was to persuade Percy to release him from it for awhile.

That by leaving Paris he risked to lose Jeanne he was quite convinced, but it is nevertheless a true fact that in spite of this he did not withdraw his love and trust from his chief. He was under the influence of that same magnetism which enchained all his comrades to the will of this man; and though his enthusiasm for the great cause had somewhat waned, his allegiance to its leader was no longer tottering.

But he would not trust himself to speak again on the subject.

"I will find the others downstairs," was all he said, "and will arrange with Hastings for to-morrow. Good night, Percy."

"Good night, my dear fellow. By the way, you have not told me yet who she is."

"Her name is Jeanne Lange," said St. Just half reluctantly. He had not meant to divulge his secret quite so fully as yet.

"The young actress at the Theatre National?"

"Yes. Do you know her?"

"Only by name."

"She is beautiful, Percy, and she is an angel.... Think of my sister Marguerite... she, too, was an actress.... Good night, Percy."

"Good night."

The two men grasped one another by the hand. Armand's eyes proffered a last desperate appeal. But Blakeney's eyes were impassive and unrelenting, and Armand with a quick sigh finally took his leave.

For a long while after he had gone Blakeney stood silent and motionless in the middle of the room. Armand's last words lingered in his ear:

"Think of Marguerite!"

The walls had fallen away from around him—the window, the river below, the Temple prison had all faded away, merged in the chaos of his thoughts.

Now he was no longer in Paris; he heard nothing of the horrors that even at this hour of the night were raging around him; he did not hear the call of murdered victims, of innocent women and children crying for help; he did not see the descendant of St. Louis, with a red cap on his baby head, stamping on the fleur-de-lys, and heaping insults on the memory of his mother. All that had faded into nothingness.

He was in the garden at Richmond, and Marguerite was sitting on the stone seat, with branches of the rambler roses twining themselves in her hair.

He was sitting on the ground at her feet, his head pillowed in her lap, lazily dreaming whilst at his feet the river wound its graceful curves beneath overhanging willows and tall stately elms.

A swan came sailing majestically down the stream, and Marguerite, with idle, delicate hands, threw some crumbs of bread into the water. Then she laughed, for she was quite happy, and anon she stooped, and he felt the fragrance of her lips as she bent over him and savoured the perfect sweetness of her caress. She was happy because her husband was by her side. He had done with adventures, with risking his life for others' sake. He was living only for her.

The man, the dreamer, the idealist that lurked behind the adventurous soul, lived an exquisite dream as he gazed upon that vision. He closed his eyes so that it might last all the longer, so that through the open window opposite he should not see the great gloomy walls of the labyrinthine building packed to overflowing with innocent men, women, and children waiting patiently and with a smile on their lips for a cruel and unmerited death; so that he should not see even through the vista of houses and of streets that grim Temple prison far away, and the light in one of the tower windows, which illumined the final martyrdom of a boy-king.

Thus he stood for fully five minutes, with eyes deliberately closed and lips tightly set. Then the neighbouring tower-clock of St. Germain l'Auxerrois slowly tolled the hour of midnight. Blakeney woke from his dream. The walls of his lodging were once more around him, and through the window the ruddy light of some torch in the street below fought with that of the lamp.

He went deliberately up to the window and looked out into the night. On the quay, a little to the left, the outdoor camp was just breaking up for the night. The people of France in arms against tyranny were allowed to put away their work for the day and to go to their miserable homes to gather rest in sleep for the morrow. A band of soldiers, rough and brutal in their movements, were hustling the women and children. The little ones, weary, sleepy, and cold, seemed too dazed to move. One woman had two little children clinging to her skirts; a soldier suddenly seized one of them by the shoulders and pushed it along roughly in front of him to get it out of the way. The woman struck at the soldier in a stupid, senseless, useless way, and then gathered her trembling chicks under her wing, trying to look defiant.

In a moment she was surrounded. Two soldiers seized her, and two more dragged the children away from her. She screamed and the children cried, the soldiers swore and struck out right and left with their bayonets. There was a general melee, calls of agony rent the air, rough oaths drowned the shouts of the helpless. Some women, panic-stricken, started to run.

And Blakeney from his window looked down upon the scene. He no longer saw the garden at Richmond, the lazily-flowing river, the bowers of roses; even the sweet face of Marguerite, sad and lonely, appeared dim and far away.

He looked across the ice-bound river, past the quay where rough soldiers were brutalising a number of wretched defenceless women, to that grim Chatelet prison, where tiny lights shining here and there behind barred windows told the sad tale of weary vigils, of watches through the night, when dawn would bring martyrdom and death.

And it was not Marguerite's blue eyes that beckoned to him now, it was not her lips that called, but the wan face of a child with matted curls hanging above a greasy forehead, and small hands covered in grime that had once been fondled by a Queen.

The adventurer in him had chased away the dream.

"While there is life in me I'll cheat those brutes of prey," he murmured.

CHAPTER XIII

Then Everything Was Dark

The night that Armand St. Just spent tossing about on a hard, narrow bed was the most miserable, agonising one he had ever passed in his life. A kind of fever ran through him, causing his teeth to chatter and the veins in his temples to throb until he thought that they must burst.

Physically he certainly was ill; the mental strain caused by two great conflicting passions had attacked his bodily strength, and whilst his brain and heart fought their battles together, his aching limbs found no repose.

His love for Jeanne! His loyalty to the man to whom he owed his life, and to whom he had sworn allegiance and implicit obedience!

These superacute feelings seemed to be tearing at his very heartstrings, until he felt that he could no longer lie on the miserable palliasse which in these squalid lodgings did duty for a bed.

He rose long before daybreak, with tired back and burning eyes, but unconscious of any pain save that which tore at his heart.

The weather, fortunately, was not quite so cold—a sudden and very rapid thaw had set in; and when after a hurried toilet Armand, carrying a bundle under his arm, emerged into the street, the mild south wind struck pleasantly on his face.

It was then pitch dark. The street lamps had been extinguished long ago, and the feeble January sun had not yet tinged with pale colour the heavy clouds that hung over the sky.

The streets of the great city were absolutely deserted at this hour. It lay, peaceful and still, wrapped in its mantle of gloom. A thin rain was falling, and Armand's feet, as he began to descend the heights of Montmartre, sank ankle deep in the mud of the road. There was but scanty attempt at pavements in this outlying quarter of the town, and Armand had much ado to keep his footing on the uneven and intermittent stones that did duty for roads in these parts. But this discomfort did not trouble him just now. One thought—and one alone—was clear in his mind: he must see Jeanne before he left Paris.

He did not pause to think how he could accomplish that at this hour of the day. All he knew was that he must obey his chief, and that he must see Jeanne. He would see her, explain to her that he must leave Paris immediately, and beg her to make her preparations quickly, so that she might meet him as soon as maybe, and accompany him to England straight away.

He did not feel that he was being disloyal by trying to see Jeanne. He had thrown prudence to the winds, not realising that his imprudence would and did jeopardise, not only the success of his chief's plans, but also his life and that of his friends. He had before parting from Hastings last night arranged to meet him in the neighbourhood of the Neuilly Gate at seven o'clock; it was only six now. There was plenty of time for him to rouse the concierge at the house of the Square du Roule, to see Jeanne for a few moments, to slip into Madame Belhomme's kitchen, and there into the labourer's clothes which he was carrying in the bundle under his arm, and to be at the gate at the appointed hour.

The Square du Roule is shut off from the Rue St. Honore, on which it abuts, by tall iron gates, which a few years ago, when the secluded little square was a fashionable quarter of the city, used to be kept closed at night, with a watchman in uniform to intercept midnight prowlers. Now these gates had been rudely torn away from their sockets, the iron had been sold for the benefit of the ever-empty Treasury, and no one cared if the homeless, the starving, or the evil-doer found shelter under the porticoes of the houses, from whence wealthy or aristocratic owners had long since thought it wise to flee.

No one challenged Armand when he turned into the square, and though the darkness was intense, he made his way fairly straight for the house where lodged Mademoiselle Lange.

So far he had been wonderfully lucky. The foolhardiness with which he had exposed his life and that of his friends by wandering about the streets of Paris at this hour without any attempt at disguise, though carrying one under his arm, had not met with the untoward fate which it undoubtedly deserved. The darkness of the night and the thin sheet of rain as it fell had effectually wrapped his progress through the lonely streets in their beneficent mantle of gloom; the soft mud below had drowned the echo of his footsteps. If spies were on his track, as Jeanne had feared and Blakeney prophesied, he had certainly succeeded in evading them.

He pulled the concierge's bell, and the latch of the outer door, manipulated from within, duly sprang open in response. He entered, and from the lodge the concierge's voice emerging, muffled from the depths of pillows and blankets, challenged him with an oath directed at the unseemliness of the hour.

"Mademoiselle Lange," said Armand boldly, as without hesitation he walked quickly past the lodge making straight for the stairs.

It seemed to him that from the concierge's room loud vituperations followed him, but he took no notice of these; only a short flight of stairs and one more door separated him from Jeanne.

He did not pause to think that she would in all probability be still in bed, that he might have some difficulty in rousing Madame Belhomme, that the latter might not even care to admit him; nor did he reflect on the glaring imprudence of his actions. He wanted to see Jeanne, and she was the other side of that wall.

"He, citizen! Hola! Here! Curse you! Where are you?" came in a gruff voice to him from below.

He had mounted the stairs, and was now on the landing just outside Jeanne's door. He pulled the bell-handle, and heard the pleasing echo of the bell that would presently wake Madame Belhomme and bring her to the door.

"Citizen! Hola! Curse you for an aristo! What are you doing there?"

The concierge, a stout, elderly man, wrapped in a blanket, his feet thrust in slippers, and carrying a guttering tallow candle, had appeared upon the landing.

He held the candle up so that its feeble flickering rays fell on Armand's pale face, and on the damp cloak which fell away from his shoulders.

"What are you doing there?" reiterated the concierge with another oath from his prolific vocabulary.

"As you see, citizen," replied Armand politely, "I am ringing Mademoiselle Lange's front door bell."

"At this hour of the morning?" queried the man with a sneer.

"I desire to see her."

"Then you have come to the wrong house, citizen," said the concierge with a rude laugh.

"The wrong house? What do you mean?" stammered Armand, a little bewildered.

"She is not here—quoi!" retorted the concierge, who now turned deliberately on his heel. "Go and look for her, citizen; it'll take you some time to find her."

He shuffled off in the direction of the stairs. Armand was vainly trying to shake himself free from a sudden, an awful sense of horror.

He gave another vigorous pull at the hell, then with one bound he overtook the concierge, who was preparing to descend the stairs, and gripped him peremptorily by the arm.

"Where is Mademoiselle Lange?" he asked.

His voice sounded quite strange in his own ear; his throat felt parched, and he had to moisten his lips with his tongue before he was able to speak.

"Arrested," replied the man.

"Arrested? When? Where? How?"

"When—late yesterday evening. Where?—here in her room. How?—by the agents of the Committee of General Security. She and the old woman! Basta! that's all I know. Now I am going back to bed, and you clear out of the house. You are making a disturbance, and I shall be reprimanded. I ask you, is this a decent time for rousing honest patriots out of their morning sleep?"

He shook his arm free from Armand's grasp and once more began to descend.

Armand stood on the landing like a man who has been stunned by a blow on the head. His limbs were paralysed. He could not for the moment have moved or spoken if his life had depended on a sign or on a word. His brain was reeling, and he had to steady himself with his hand against the wall or he would have fallen headlong on the floor. He had lived in a whirl of excitement for the past twenty-four hours; his nerves during that time had been kept at straining point. Passion, joy, happiness, deadly danger, and moral fights had worn his mental endurance threadbare; want of proper food and a sleepless night had almost thrown his physical balance out of gear. This blow came at a moment when he was least able to bear it.

Jeanne had been arrested! Jeanne was in the hands of those brutes, whom he, Armand, had regarded yesterday with insurmountable loathing! Jeanne was in prison—she was arrested—she would be tried, condemned, and all because of him!

The thought was so awful that it brought him to the verge of mania. He watched as in a dream the form of the concierge shuffling his way down the oak staircase; his portly figure assumed Gargantuan proportions, the candle which he carried looked like the dancing flames of hell, through which grinning faces, hideous and contortioned, mocked at him and leered.

Then suddenly everything was dark. The light had disappeared round the bend of the stairs; grinning faces and ghoulish visions vanished; he only saw Jeanne, his dainty, exquisite Jeanne, in the hands of those brutes. He saw her as he had seen a year and a half ago the victims of those bloodthirsty wretches being dragged before a tribunal that was but a mockery of justice; he heard the quick interrogatory, and the responses from her perfect lips, that exquisite voice of hers veiled by tones of anguish. He heard the condemnation, the rattle of the tumbril on the ill-paved streets—saw her there with hands clasped together, her eyes—

Great God! he was really going mad!

Like a wild creature driven forth he started to run down the stairs, past the concierge, who was just entering his lodge, and who now turned in surly anger to watch this man running away like a lunatic or a fool, out by the front door and into the street. In a moment he was out of the little square; then like a hunted hare he still ran down the Rue St. Honore, along its narrow, interminable length. His hat had fallen from his head, his hair was wild all round his face, the rain weighted the cloak upon his shoulders; but still he ran.

His feet made no noise on the muddy pavement. He ran on and on, his elbows pressed to his sides, panting, quivering, intent but upon one thing—the goal which he had set himself to reach.

Jeanne was arrested. He did not know where to look for her, but he did know whither he wanted to go now as swiftly as his legs would carry him.

It was still dark, but Armand St. Just was a born Parisian, and he knew every inch of this quarter, where he and Marguerite had years ago lived. Down the Rue St. Honore, he had reached the bottom of the interminably long street at last. He had kept just a sufficiency of reason—or was it merely blind instinct?—to avoid the places where the night patrols of the National Guard might be on the watch. He avoided the Place du Carrousel, also the quay, and struck sharply to his right until he reached the facade of St. Germain l'Auxerrois.

Another effort; round the corner, and there was the house at last. He was like the hunted creature now that has run to earth. Up the two flights of stone stairs, and then the pull at the bell; a moment of tense anxiety, whilst panting, gasping, almost choked with the sustained effort and the strain of the past half-hour, he leaned against the wall, striving not to fall.

Then the well-known firm step across the rooms beyond, the open door, the hand upon his shoulder.

After that he remembered nothing more.

CHAPTER XIV

The Chief

He had not actually fainted, but the exertion of that long run had rendered him partially unconscious. He knew now that he was safe, that he was sitting in Blakeney's room, and that something hot and vivifying was being poured down his throat.

"Percy, they have arrested her!" he said, panting, as soon as speech returned to his paralysed tongue.

"All right. Don't talk now. Wait till you are better."

With infinite care and gentleness Blakeney arranged some cushions under Armand's head, turned the sofa towards the fire, and anon brought his friend a cup of hot coffee, which the latter drank with avidity.

He was really too exhausted to speak. He had contrived to tell Blakeney, and now Blakeney knew, so everything would be all right. The inevitable reaction was asserting itself; the muscles had relaxed, the nerves were numbed, and Armand lay back on the sofa with eyes half closed, unable to move, yet feeling his strength gradually returning to him, his vitality asserting itself, all the feverish excitement of the past twenty-four hours yielding at last to a calmer mood.

Through his half-closed eyes he could see his brother-in-law moving about the room. Blakeney was fully dressed. In a sleepy kind of way Armand wondered if he had been to bed at all; certainly his clothes set on him with their usual well-tailored perfection, and there was no suggestion in his brisk step and alert movements that he had passed a sleepless night.

Now he was standing by the open window. Armand, from where he lay, could see his broad shoulders sharply outlined against the grey background of the hazy winter dawn. A wan light was just creeping up from the east over the city; the noises of the streets below came distinctly to Armand's ear.

He roused himself with one vigorous effort from his lethargy, feeling quite ashamed of himself and of this breakdown of his nervous system. He looked with frank admiration on Sir Percy, who stood immovable and silent by the window—a perfect tower of strength, serene and impassive, yet kindly in distress.

"Percy," said the young man, "I ran all the way from the top of the Rue St. Honore. I was only breathless. I am quite all right. May I tell you all about it?"

Without a word Blakeney closed the window and came across to the sofa; he sat down beside Armand, and to all outward appearances he was nothing now but a kind and sympathetic listener to a friend's tale of woe. Not a line in his face or a look in his eyes betrayed the thoughts of the leader who had been thwarted at the outset of a dangerous enterprise, or of the man, accustomed to command, who had been so flagrantly disobeyed.

Armand, unconscious of all save of Jeanne and of her immediate need, put an eager hand on Percy's arm.

"Heron and his hell-hounds went back to her lodgings last night," he said, speaking as if he were still a little out of breath. "They hoped to get me, no doubt; not finding me there, they took her. Oh, my God!"

It was the first time that he had put the whole terrible circumstance into words, and it seemed to gain in reality by the recounting. The agony of mind which he endured was almost unbearable; he hid his face in his hands lest Percy should see how terribly he suffered.

"I knew that," said Blakeney quietly. Armand looked up in surprise.

"How? When did you know it?" he stammered.

"Last night when you left me. I went down to the Square du Roule. I arrived there just too late."

"Percy!" exclaimed Armand, whose pale face had suddenly flushed scarlet, "you did that?—last night you—"

"Of course," interposed the other calmly; "had I not promised you to keep watch over her? When I heard the news it was already too late to make further inquiries, but when you arrived just now I was on the point of starting out, in order to find out in what prison Mademoiselle Lange is being detained. I shall have to go soon, Armand, before the guard is changed at the Temple and the Tuileries. This is the safest time, and God knows we are all of us sufficiently compromised already."

The flush of shame deepened in St. Just's cheek. There had not been a hint of reproach in the voice of his chief, and the eyes which regarded him now from beneath the half-closed lids showed nothing but lazy bonhomie.

In a moment now Armand realised all the harm which his recklessness had done, was still doing to the work of the League. Every one of his actions since his arrival in Paris two days ago had jeopardised a plan or endangered a life: his friendship with de Batz, his connection with Mademoiselle Lange, his visit to her yesterday afternoon, the repetition of it this morning, culminating in that wild run through the streets of Paris, when at any moment a spy lurking round a corner might either have barred his way, or, worse still, have followed him to Blakeney's door. Armand, without a thought of any one save of his beloved, might easily this morning have brought an agent of the Committee of General Security face to face with his chief.

"Percy," he murmured, "can you ever forgive me?"

"Pshaw, man!" retorted Blakeney lightly; "there is naught to forgive, only a great deal that should no longer be forgotten; your duty to the others, for instance, your obedience, and your honour."

"I was mad, Percy. Oh! if you only could understand what she means to me!"

Blakeney laughed, his own light-hearted careless laugh, which so often before now had helped to hide what he really felt from the eyes of the indifferent, and even from those of his friends.

"No! no!" he said lightly, "we agreed last night, did we not? that in matters of sentiment I am a cold-blooded fish. But will you at any rate concede that I am a man of my word? Did I not pledge it last night that Mademoiselle Lange would be safe? I foresaw her arrest the moment I heard your story. I hoped that I might reach her before that brute Heron's return; unfortunately he forestalled me by less than half an hour. Mademoiselle Lange has been arrested, Armand; but why should you not trust me on that account? Have we not succeeded, I and the others, in worse cases than this one? They mean no harm to Jeanne Lange," he added emphatically; "I give you my word on that. They only want her as a decoy. It is you they want. You through her, and me through you. I pledge you my honour that she will be safe. You must try and trust me, Armand. It is much to ask, I know, for you will have to trust me with what is most precious in the world to you; and you will have to obey me blindly, or I shall not be able to keep my word."

"What do you wish me to do?"

"Firstly, you must be outside Paris within the hour. Every minute that you spend inside the city now is full of danger—oh, no! not for you," added Blakeney, checking with a good-humoured gesture Armand's words of protestation, "danger for the others—and for our scheme tomorrow."

"How can I go to St. Germain, Percy, knowing that she—"

"Is under my charge?" interposed the other calmly. "That should not be so very difficult. Come," he added, placing a kindly hand on the other's shoulder, "you shall not find me such an inhuman monster after all. But I must think of the others, you see, and of the child whom I have sworn to save. But I won't send you as far as St. Germain. Go down to the room below and find a good bundle of rough clothes that will serve you as a disguise, for I imagine that you have lost those which you had on the landing or the stairs of the house in the Square du Roule. In a tin box with the clothes downstairs you will find the packet of miscellaneous certificates of safety. Take an appropriate one, and then start out immediately for Villette. You understand?"

"Yes, yes!" said Armand eagerly. "You want me to join Ffoulkes and Tony."

"Yes! You'll find them probably unloading coal by the canal. Try and get private speech with them as early as may be, and tell Tony to set out at once for St. Germain, and to join Hastings there, instead of you, whilst you take his place with Ffoulkes."

"Yes, I understand; but how will Tony reach St. Germain?"

"La, my good fellow," said Blakeney gaily, "you may safely trust Tony to go where I send him. Do you but do as I tell you, and leave him to look after himself. And now," he added, speaking more earnestly, "the sooner you get out of Paris the better it will be for us all. As you see, I am only sending you to La Villette, because it is not so far, but that I can keep in personal touch with you. Remain close to the gates for an hour after nightfall. I will contrive before they close to bring you news of Mademoiselle Lange."

Armand said no more. The sense of shame in him deepened with every word spoken by his chief. He felt how untrustworthy he had been, how undeserving of the selfless devotion which Percy was showing him even now. The words of gratitude died on his lips; he knew that they would be unwelcome. These Englishmen were so devoid of sentiment, he thought, and his brother-in-law, with all his unselfish and heroic deeds, was, he felt, absolutely callous in matters of the heart.

But Armand was a noble-minded man, and with the true sporting instinct in him, despite the fact that he was a creature of nerves, highly strung and imaginative. He could give ungrudging admiration to his chief, even whilst giving himself up entirely to the sentiment for Jeanne.

He tried to imbue himself with the same spirit that actuated my Lord Tony and the other members of the League. How gladly would he have chaffed and made senseless schoolboy jokes like those which—in face of their hazardous enterprise and the dangers which they all ran—had horrified him so much last night.

But somehow he knew that jokes from him would not ring true. How could he smile when his heart was brimming over with his love for Jeanne, and with solicitude on her account? He felt that Percy was regarding him with a kind of indulgent amusement; there was a look of suppressed merriment in the depths of those lazy blue eyes.

So he braced up his nerves, trying his best to look cool and unconcerned, but he could not altogether hide from his friend the burning anxiety which was threatening to break his heart.

"I have given you my word, Armand," said Blakeney in answer to the unspoken prayer; "cannot you try and trust me—as the others do? Then with sudden transition he pointed to the map behind him.

"Remember the gate of Villette, and the corner by the towpath. Join Ffoulkes as soon as may be and send Tony on his way, and wait for news of Mademoiselle Lange some time to-night."

"God bless you, Percy!" said Armand involuntarily. "Good-bye!"

"Good-bye, my dear fellow. Slip on your disguise as quickly as you can, and be out of the house in a quarter of an hour."

He accompanied Armand through the ante-room, and finally closed the door on him. Then he went back to his room and walked up to the window, which he threw open to the humid morning air. Now that he was alone the look of trouble on his face deepened to a dark, anxious frown, and as he looked out across the river a sigh of bitter impatience and disappointment escaped his lips.

CHAPTER XV

The Gate of la Villette

And now the shades of evening had long since yielded to those of night. The gate of La Villette, at the northeast corner of the city, was about to close. Armand, dressed in the rough clothes of a labouring man, was leaning against a low wall at the angle of the narrow street which abuts on the canal at its further end; from this point of vantage he could command a view of the gate and of the life and bustle around it.

He was dog-tired. After the emotions of the past twenty-four hours, a day's hard manual toil to which he was unaccustomed had caused him to ache in every limb. As soon as he had arrived at the canal wharf in the early morning he had obtained the kind of casual work that ruled about here, and soon was told off to unload a cargo of coal which had arrived by barge overnight. He had set-to with a will, half hoping to kill his anxiety by dint of heavy bodily exertion. During the course of the morning he had suddenly become aware of Sir Andrew Ffoulkes and of Lord Anthony Dewhurst working not far away from him, and as fine a pair of coalheavers as any shipper could desire.

It was not very difficult in the midst of the noise and activity that reigned all about the wharf for the three men to exchange a few words together, and Armand soon communicated the chief's new instructions to my Lord Tony, who effectually slipped away from his work some time during the day. Armand did not even see him go, it had all been so neatly done.

Just before five o'clock in the afternoon the labourers were paid off. It was then too dark to continue work. Armand would have liked to talk to Sir Andrew, if only for a moment. He felt lonely and desperately anxious. He had hoped to tire out his nerves as well as his body, but in this he had not succeeded. As soon as he had given up his tools, his brain began to work again more busily than ever. It followed Percy in his peregrinations through the city, trying to discover where those brutes were keeping Jeanne.

That task had suddenly loomed up before Armand's mind with all its terrible difficulties. How could Percy—a marked man if ever there was one—go from prison to prison to inquire about Jeanne? The very idea seemed preposterous. Armand ought never to have consented to such an insensate plan. The more he thought of it, the more impossible did it seem that Blakeney could find anything out.

Sir Andrew Ffoulkes was nowhere to be seen. St. Just wandered about in the dark, lonely streets of this outlying quarter vainly trying to find the friend in whom he could confide, who, no doubt, would reassure him as to Blakeney's probable movements in Paris. Then as the hour approached for the closing of the city gates Armand took up his stand at an angle of the street from whence he could see both the gate on one side of him and the thin line of the canal intersecting the street at its further end.

Unless Percy came within the next five minutes the gates would be closed and the difficulties of crossing the barrier would be increased a hundredfold. The market gardeners with their covered carts filed out of the gate one by one; the labourers on foot were returning to their homes; there was a group of stonemasons, a few road-makers, also a number of beggars, ragged and filthy, who herded somewhere in the neighbourhood of the canal.

In every form, under every disguise, Armand hoped to discover Percy. He could not stand still for very long, but strode up and down the road that skirts the fortifications at this point.

There were a good many idlers about at this hour; some men who had finished their work, and meant to spend an hour or so in one of the drinking shops that abounded in the neighbourhood of the wharf; others who liked to gather a small knot of listeners around them, whilst they discoursed on the politics of the day, or rather raged against the Convention, which was all made up of traitors to the people's welfare.

Armand, trying manfully to play his part, joined one of the groups that stood gaping round a street orator. He shouted with the best of them, waved his cap in the air, and applauded or hissed in unison with the majority. But his eyes never wandered for long away from the gate whence Percy must come now at any moment—now or not at all.

At what precise moment the awful doubt took birth in his mind the young man could not afterwards have said. Perhaps it was when he heard the roll of drums proclaiming the closing of the gates, and witnessed the changing of the guard.

Percy had not come. He could not come now, and he (Armand) would have the night to face without news of Jeanne. Something, of course, had detained Percy; perhaps he had been unable to get definite information about Jeanne; perhaps the information which he had obtained was too terrible to communicate.

If only Sir Andrew Ffoulkes had been there, and Armand had had some one to talk to, perhaps then he would have found sufficient strength of mind to wait with outward patience, even though his nerves were on the rack.

Darkness closed in around him, and with the darkness came the full return of the phantoms that had assailed him in the house of the Square du Roule when first he had heard of Jeanne's arrest. The open place facing the gate had transformed itself into the Place de la Revolution, the tall rough post that held a flickering oil lamp had become the gaunt arm of the guillotine, the feeble light of the lamp was the knife that gleamed with the reflection of a crimson light.

And Armand saw himself, as in a vision, one of a vast and noisy throng—they were all pressing round him so that he could not move; they were brandishing caps and tricolour flags, also pitchforks and scythes. He had seen such a crowd four years ago rushing towards the Bastille. Now they were all assembled here around him and around the guillotine.

Suddenly a distant rattle caught his subconscious ear: the rattle of wheels on rough cobble-stones. Immediately the crowd began to cheer and to shout; some sang the "Ca ira!" and others screamed:

"Les aristos! a la lanterne! a mort! a mort! les aristos!"

He saw it all quite plainly, for the darkness had vanished, and the vision was more vivid than even reality could have been. The rattle of wheels grew louder, and presently the cart debouched on the open place.

Men and women sat huddled up in the cart; but in the midst of them a woman stood, and her eyes were fixed upon Armand. She wore her pale-grey satin gown, and a white kerchief was folded across her bosom. Her brown hair fell in loose soft curls all round her head. She looked exactly like the exquisite cameo which Marguerite used to wear. Her hands were tied with cords behind her back, but between her fingers she held a small bunch of violets.

Armand saw it all. It was, of course, a vision, and he knew that it was one, but he believed that the vision was prophetic. No thought of the chief whom he had sworn to trust and to obey came to chase away these imaginings of his fevered fancy. He saw Jeanne, and only Jeanne, standing on the tumbril and being led to the guillotine. Sir Andrew was not there, and Percy had not come. Armand believed that a direct message had come to him from heaven to save his beloved.

Therefore he forgot his promise—his oath; he forgot those very things which the leader had entreated him to remember—his duty to the others, his loyalty, his obedience. Jeanne had first claim on him. It were the act of a coward to remain in safety whilst she was in such deadly danger.

Now he blamed himself severely for having quitted Paris. Even Percy must have thought him a coward for obeying quite so readily. Maybe the command had been but a test of his courage, of the strength of his love for Jeanne.

A hundred conjectures flashed through his brain; a hundred plans presented themselves to his mind. It was not for Percy, who did not know her, to save Jeanne or to guard her. That task was Armand's, who worshipped her, and who would gladly die beside her if he failed to rescue her from threatened death.

Resolution was not slow in coming. A tower clock inside the city struck the hour of six, and still no sign of Percy.

Armand, his certificate of safety in his hand, walked boldly up to the gate.

The guard challenged him, but he presented the certificate. There was an agonising moment when the card was taken from him, and he was detained in the guard-room while it was being examined by the sergeant in command.

But the certificate was in good order, and Armand, covered in coal-dust, with the perspiration streaming down his face, did certainly not look like an aristocrat in disguise. It was never very difficult to enter the great city; if one wished to put one's head in the lion's mouth, one was welcome to do so; the difficulty came when the lion thought fit to close his jaws.

Armand, after five minutes of tense anxiety, was allowed to cross the barrier, but his certificate of safety was detained. He would have to get another from the Committee of General Security before he would be allowed to leave Paris again.

The lion had thought fit to close his jaws.

CHAPTER XVI

The Weary Search

Blakeney was not at his lodgings when Armand arrived there that evening, nor did he return, whilst the young man haunted the precincts of St. Germain l'Auxerrois and wandered along the quays hours and hours at a stretch, until he nearly dropped under the portico of a house, and realised that if he loitered longer he might lose consciousness completely, and be unable on the morrow to be of service to Jeanne.

He dragged his weary footsteps back to his own lodgings on the heights of Montmartre. He had not found Percy, he had no news of Jeanne; it seemed as if hell itself could hold no worse tortures than this intolerable suspense.

He threw himself down on the narrow palliasse and, tired nature asserting herself, at last fell into a heavy, dreamless torpor, like the sleep of a drunkard, deep but without the beneficent aid of rest.

It was broad daylight when he awoke. The pale light of a damp, wintry morning filtered through the grimy panes of the window. Armand jumped out of bed, aching of limb but resolute of mind. There was no doubt that Percy had failed in discovering Jeanne's whereabouts; but where a mere friend had failed a lover was more likely to succeed.

The rough clothes which he had worn yesterday were the only ones he had.

They would, of course, serve his purpose better than his own, which he had left at Blakeney's lodgings yesterday. In half an hour he was dressed, looking a fairly good imitation of a labourer out of work.

He went to a humble eating house of which he knew, and there, having ordered some hot coffee with a hunk of bread, he set himself to think.

It was quite a usual thing these days for relatives and friends of prisoners to go wandering about from prison to prison to find out where the loved ones happened to be detained. The prisons were over full just now; convents, monasteries, and public institutions had all been requisitioned by the Government for the housing of the hundreds of so-called traitors who had been arrested on the barest suspicion, or at the mere denunciation of an evil-wisher.

There were the Abbaye and the Luxembourg, the erstwhile convents of the Visitation and the Sacre-Coeur, the cloister of the Oratorians, the Salpetriere, and the St. Lazare hospitals, and there was, of course, the Temple, and, lastly, the Conciergerie, to which those prisoners were brought whose trial would take place within the next few days, and whose condemnation was practically assured.

Persons under arrest at some of the other prisons did sometimes come out of them alive, but the Conciergerie was only the ante-chamber of the guillotine.

Therefore Armand's idea was to visit the Conciergerie first. The sooner he could reassure himself that Jeanne was not in immediate danger the better would he be able to endure the agony of that heart-breaking search, that knocking at every door in the hope of finding his beloved.

If Jeanne was not in the Conciergerie, then there might be some hope that she was only being temporarily detained, and through Armand's excited brain there had already flashed the thought that mayhap the Committee of General Security would release her if he gave himself up.

These thoughts, and the making of plans, fortified him mentally and physically; he even made a great effort to eat and drink, knowing that his bodily strength must endure if it was going to be of service to Jeanne.

He reached the Quai de l'Horloge soon after nine. The grim, irregular walls of the Chatelet and the house of Justice loomed from out the mantle of mist that lay on the river banks. Armand skirted the square clock-tower, and passed through the monumental gateways of the house of Justice.

He knew that his best way to the prison would be through the halls and corridors of the Tribunal, to which the public had access whenever the court was sitting. The sittings began at ten, and already the usual crowd of idlers were assembling—men and women who apparently had no other occupation save to come day after day to this theatre of horrors and watch the different acts of the heartrending dramas that were enacted here with a kind of awful monotony.

Armand mingled with the crowd that stood about the courtyard, and anon moved slowly up the gigantic flight of stone steps, talking lightly on indifferent subjects. There was quite a goodly sprinkling of workingmen amongst this crowd, and

Armand in his toil-stained clothes attracted no attention.

Suddenly a word reached his ear—just a name flippantly spoken by spiteful lips—and it changed the whole trend of his thoughts. Since he had risen that morning he had thought of nothing but of Jeanne, and—in connection with her—of Percy and his vain quest of her. Now that name spoken by some one unknown brought his mind back to more definite thoughts of his chief.

"Capet!" the name—intended as an insult, but actually merely irrelevant—whereby the uncrowned little King of France was designated by the revolutionary party.

Armand suddenly recollected that to-day was Sunday, the 19th of January. He had lost count of days and of dates lately, but the name, "Capet," had brought everything back: the child in the Temple; the conference in Blakeney's lodgings; the plans for the rescue of the boy. That was to take place to-day—Sunday, the 19th. The Simons would be moving from the Temple, at what hour Blakeney did not know, but it would be today, and he would be watching his opportunity.

Now Armand understood everything; a great wave of bitterness swept over his soul. Percy had forgotten Jeanne! He was busy thinking of the child in the Temple, and whilst Armand had been eating out his heart with anxiety, the Scarlet Pimpernel, true only to his mission, and impatient of all sentiment that interfered with his schemes, had left Jeanne to pay with her life for the safety of the uncrowned King.

But the bitterness did not last long; on the contrary, a kind of wild exultation took its place. If Percy had forgotten, then Armand could stand by Jeanne alone. It was better so! He would save the loved one; it was his duty and his right to work for her sake. Never for a moment did he doubt that he could save her, that his life would be readily accepted in exchange for hers.

The crowd around him was moving up the monumental steps, and Armand went with the crowd. It lacked but a few minutes to ten now; soon the court would begin to sit. In the olden days, when he was studying for the law, Armand had often wandered about at will along the corridors of the house of Justice. He knew exactly where the different prisons were situated about the buildings, and how to reach the courtyards where the prisoners took their daily exercise.

To watch those aristos who were awaiting trial and death taking their recreation in these courtyards had become one of the sights of Paris. Country cousins on a visit to the city were brought hither for entertainment. Tall iron gates stood between the public and the prisoners, and a row of sentinels guarded these gates; but if one was enterprising and eager to see, one could glue one's nose against the ironwork and watch the ci-devant aristocrats in threadbare clothes trying to cheat their horror of death by acting a farce of light-heartedness which their wan faces and tear-dimmed eyes effectually belied.

All this Armand knew, and on this he counted. For a little while he joined the crowd in the Salle des Pas Perdus, and wandered idly up and down the majestic colonnaded hall. He even at one time formed part of the throng that watched one of those quick tragedies that were enacted within the great chamber of the court. A number of prisoners brought in, in a batch; hurried interrogations, interrupted answers, a quick indictment, monstrous in its flaring injustice, spoken by Fouc-quier-Tinville, the public prosecutor, and listened to in all seriousness by men who dared to call themselves judges of their fellows.

The accused had walked down the Champs Elysees without wearing a tricolour cockade; the other had invested some savings in an English industrial enterprise; yet another had sold public funds, causing them to depreciate rather suddenly in the market!

Sometimes from one of these unfortunates led thus wantonly to butchery there would come an excited protest, or from a woman screams of agonised entreaty. But these were quickly silenced by rough blows from the butt-ends of muskets, and condemnations—wholesale sentences of death—were quickly passed amidst the cheers of the spectators and the howls of derision from infamous jury and judge.

Oh! the mockery of it all—the awful, the hideous ignominy, the blot of shame that would forever sully the historic name of France. Armand, sickened with horror, could not bear more than a few minutes of this monstrous spectacle. The same fate might even now be awaiting Jeanne. Among the next batch of victims to this sacrilegious butchery he might suddenly spy his beloved with her pale face and cheeks stained with her tears.

He fled from the great chamber, keeping just a sufficiency of presence of mind to join a knot of idlers who were drifting leisurely towards the corridors. He followed in their wake and soon found himself in the long Galerie des Prisonniers, along the flagstones of which two days ago de Batz had followed his guide towards the lodgings of Heron.

On his left now were the arcades shut off from the courtyard beyond by heavy iron gates. Through the ironwork Armand caught sight of a number of women walking or sitting in the courtyard. He heard a man next to him explaining to his friend that these were the female prisoners who would be brought to trial that day, and he felt that his heart must burst at the thought that mayhap Jeanne would be among them.

He elbowed his way cautiously to the front rank. Soon he found himself beside a sentinel who, with a good-humoured jest, made way for him that he might watch the aristos. Armand leaned against the grating, and his every sense was concentrated in that of sight.

At first he could scarcely distinguish one woman from another amongst the crowd that thronged the courtyard, and the close ironwork hindered his view considerably. The women looked almost like phantoms in the grey misty air, gliding slowly along with noiseless tread on the flag-stones.

Presently, however, his eyes, which mayhap were somewhat dim with tears, became more accustomed to the hazy grey light and the moving figures that looked so like shadows. He could distinguish isolated groups now, women and girls sitting together under the colonnaded arcades, some reading, others busy, with trembling fingers, patching and darning a poor, torn gown. Then there were others who were actually chatting and laughing together, and—oh, the pity of it! the pity and the shame!—a few children, shrieking with delight, were playing hide and seek in and out amongst the columns.

And, between them all, in and out like the children at play, unseen, yet familiar to all, the spectre of Death, scythe and hour-glass in hand, wandered, majestic and sure.

Armand's very soul was in his eyes. So far he had not yet caught sight of his beloved, and slowly—very slowly—a ray of hope was filtering through the darkness of his despair.

The sentinel, who had stood aside for him, chaffed him for his intentness.

"Have you a sweetheart among these aristos, citizen?" he asked. "You seem to be devouring them with your eyes."

Armand, with his rough clothes soiled with coal-dust, his face grimy and streaked with sweat, certainly looked to have but little in common with the ci-devant aristos who formed the hulk of the groups in the courtyard. He looked up; the soldier was regarding him with obvious amusement, and at sight of Armand's wild, anxious eyes he gave vent to a coarse jest.

"Have I made a shrewd guess, citizen?" he said. "Is she among that lot?"

"I do not know where she is," said Armand almost involuntarily.

"Then why don't you find out?" queried the soldier.

The man was not speaking altogether unkindly. Armand, devoured with the maddening desire to know, threw the last fragment of prudence to the wind. He assumed a more careless air, trying to look as like a country bumpkin in love as he could.

"I would like to find out," he said, "but I don't know where to inquire. My sweetheart has certainly left her home," he added lightly; "some say that she has been false to me, but I think that, mayhap, she has been arrested."

"Well, then, you gaby," said the soldier good-humouredly, "go straight to La Tournelle; you know where it is?"

Armand knew well enough, but thought it more prudent to keep up the air of the ignorant lout.

"Straight down that first corridor on your right," explained the other, pointing in the direction which he had indicated, "you will find the guichet of La Tournelle exactly opposite to you. Ask the concierge for the register of female prisoners—every freeborn citizen of the Republic has the right to inspect prison registers. It is a new decree framed for safeguarding the liberty of the people. But if you do not press half a livre in the hand of the concierge," he added, speaking confidentially, "you will find that the register will not be quite ready for your inspection."

"Half a livre!" exclaimed Armand, striving to play his part to the end. "How can a poor devil of a labourer have half a livre to give away?"

"Well! a few sous will do in that case; a few sous are always welcome these hard times."

Armand took the hint, and as the crowd had drifted away momentarily to a further portion of the corridor, he contrived to press a few copper coins into the hand of the obliging soldier.

Of course, he knew his way to La Tournelle, and he would have covered the distance that separated him from the guichet there with steps flying like the wind, but, commending himself for his own prudence, he walked as slowly as he could along the interminable corridor, past the several minor courts of justice, and skirting the courtyard where the male prisoners took their exercise.

At last, having struck sharply to his left and ascended a short flight of stairs, he found himself in front of the guichet—a narrow wooden box, wherein the clerk in charge of the prison registers sat nominally at the disposal of the citizens of this free republic.

But to Armand's almost overwhelming chagrin he found the place entirely deserted. The guichet was closed down; there was not a soul in sight. The disappointment was doubly keen, coming as it did in the wake of hope that had refused to be gainsaid. Armand himself did not realise how sanguine he had been until he discovered that he must wait and wait again—wait for hours, all day mayhap, before he could get definite news of Jeanne.

He wandered aimlessly in the vicinity of that silent, deserted, cruel spot, where a closed trapdoor seemed to shut off all his hopes of a speedy sight of Jeanne. He inquired of the first sentinels whom he came across at what hour the clerk of the registers would be back at his post; the soldiers shrugged their shoulders and could give no information. Then began Armand's aimless wanderings round La Tournelle, his fruitless inquiries, his wild, excited search for the hide-bound official who was keeping from him the knowledge of Jeanne.

He went back to his sentinel well-wisher by the women's courtyard, but found neither consolation nor encouragement there.

"It is not the hour—quoi?" the soldier remarked with laconic philosophy.

It apparently was not the hour when the prison registers were placed at the disposal of the public. After much fruitless inquiry, Armand at last was informed by a bon bourgeois, who was wandering about the house of Justice and who seemed to know its multifarious rules, that the prison registers all over Paris could only be consulted by the public between the hours of six and seven in the evening.

There was nothing for it but to wait. Armand, whose temples were throbbing, who was footsore, hungry, and wretched, could gain nothing by continuing his aimless wanderings through the labyrinthine building. For close upon another hour he stood with his face glued against the ironwork which separated him from the female prisoners' courtyard. Once it seemed to him as if from its further end he caught the sound of that exquisitely melodious voice which had rung forever in his ear since that memorable evening when Jeanne's dainty footsteps had first crossed the path of his destiny. He strained his eyes to look in the direction whence the voice had come, but the centre of the courtyard was planted with a small garden of shrubs, and Armand could not see across it. At last, driven forth like a wandering and lost soul, he turned back and out into the streets. The air was mild and damp. The sharp thaw had persisted through the day, and a thin, misty rain was falling and converting the ill-paved roads into seas of mud.

But of this Armand was wholly unconscious. He walked along the quay holding his cap in his hand, so that the mild south wind should cool his burning forehead.

How he contrived to kill those long, weary hours he could not afterwards have said. Once he felt very hungry, and turned almost mechanically into an eating-house, and tried to eat and drink. But most of the day he wandered through the streets, restlessly, unceasingly, feeling neither chill nor fatigue. The hour before six o'clock found him on the Quai de l'Horloge in the shadow of the great towers of the Hall of Justice, listening for the clang of the clock that would sound the hour of his deliverance from this agonising torture of suspense.

He found his way to La Tournelle without any hesitation. There before him was the wooden box, with its guichet open at last, and two stands upon its ledge, on which were placed two huge leather-bound books.

Though Armand was nearly an hour before the appointed time, he saw when he arrived a number of people standing round the guichet. Two soldiers were there keeping guard and forcing the patient, long-suffering inquirers to stand in a queue, each waiting his or her turn at the books.

It was a curious crowd that stood there, in single file, as if waiting at the door of the cheaper part of a theatre; men in substantial cloth clothes, and others in ragged blouse and breeches; there were a few women, too, with black shawls on their shoulders and kerchiefs round their wan, tear-stained faces.

They were all silent and absorbed, submissive under the rough handling of the soldiery, humble and deferential when anon the clerk of the registers entered his box, and prepared to place those fateful books at the disposal of those who had lost a loved one—father, brother, mother, or wife—and had come to search through those cruel pages.

From inside his box the clerk disputed every inquirer's right to consult the books; he made as many difficulties as he could, demanding the production of certificates of safety, or permits from the section. He was as insolent as he dared, and Armand from where he stood could see that a continuous if somewhat thin stream of coppers flowed from the hands of the inquirers into those of the official.

It was quite dark in the passage where the long queue continued to swell with amazing rapidity. Only on the ledge in front of the guichet there was a guttering tallow candle at the disposal of the inquirers.

Now it was Armand's turn at last. By this time his heart was beating so strongly and so rapidly that he could not have trusted himself to speak. He fumbled in his pocket, and without unnecessary preliminaries he produced a small piece of silver, and pushed it towards the clerk, then he seized on the register marked "Femmes" with voracious avidity.

The clerk had with stolid indifference pocketed the half-livre; he looked on Armand over a pair of large bone-rimmed spectacles, with the air of an old hawk that sees a helpless bird and yet is too satiated to eat. He was apparently vastly amused at Armand's trembling hands, and the clumsy, aimless way with which he fingered the book and held up the tallow candle.

"What date?" he asked curtly in a piping voice.

"What date?" reiterated Armand vaguely.

"What day and hour was she arrested?" said the man, thrusting his beak-like nose closer to Armand's face. Evidently the piece of silver had done its work well; he meant to be helpful to this country lout.

"On Friday evening," murmured the young man.

The clerk's hands did not in character gainsay the rest of his appearance; they were long and thin, with nails that resembled the talons of a hawk. Armand watched them fascinated as from above they turned over rapidly the pages of the book; then one long, grimy finger pointed to a row of names down a column.

"If she is here," said the man curtly, "her name should be amongst these."

Armand's vision was blurred. He could scarcely see. The row of names was dancing a wild dance in front of his eyes; perspiration stood out on his forehead, and his breath came in quick, stertorous gasps.

He never knew afterwards whether he actually saw Jeanne's name there in the book, or whether his fevered brain was playing his aching senses a cruel and mocking trick. Certain it is that suddenly amongst a row of indifferent names hers suddenly stood clearly on the page, and to him it seemed as if the letters were writ out in blood.

582. Belhomme, Louise, aged sixty. Discharged.

And just below, the other entry:

583. Lange, Jeanne, aged twenty, actress. Square du Roule
No.5. Suspected of harbouring traitors and ci-devants.
Transferred 29th Nivose to the Temple, cell 29.

He saw nothing more, for suddenly it seemed to him as if some one held a vivid scarlet veil in front of his eyes, whilst a hundred claw-like hands were tearing at his heart and at his throat.

"Clear out now! it is my turn—what? Are you going to stand there all night?"

A rough voice seemed to be speaking these words; rough hands apparently were pushing him out of the way, and some one snatched the candle out of his hand; but nothing was real. He stumbled over a corner of a loose flagstone, and would have fallen, but something seemed to catch bold of him and to lead him away for a little distance, until a breath of cold air blew upon his face.

This brought him back to his senses.

Jeanne was a prisoner in the Temple; then his place was in the prison of the

Temple, too. It could not be very difficult to run one's head into the noose that caught so many necks these days. A few cries of "Vive le roi!" or "A bas la republique!" and more than one prison door would gape invitingly to receive another guest.

The hot blood had rushed into Armand's head. He did not see clearly before him, nor did he hear distinctly. There was a buzzing in his ears as of myriads of mocking birds' wings, and there was a veil in front of his eyes—a veil through which he saw faces and forms flitting ghost-like in the gloom, men and women jostling or being jostled, soldiers, sentinels; then long, interminable corridors, more crowd and more soldiers, winding stairs, courtyards and gates; finally the open street, the quay, and the river beyond.

An incessant hammering went on in his temples, and that veil never lifted from before his eyes. Now it was lurid and red, as if stained with blood; anon it was white like a shroud but it was always there.

Through it he saw the Pont-au-Change, which he crossed, then far down on the Quai de l'Ecole to the left the corner house behind St. Germain l'Auxerrois, where Blakeney lodged—Blakeney, who for the sake of a stranger had forgotten all about his comrade and Jeanne.

Through it he saw the network of streets which separated him from the neighbourhood of the Temple, the gardens of ruined habitations, the closely-shuttered and barred windows of ducal houses, then the mean streets, the crowded drinking bars, the tumble-down shops with their dilapidated awnings.

He saw with eyes that did not see, heard the tumult of daily life round him with ears that did not hear. Jeanne was in the Temple prison, and when its grim gates closed finally for the night, he—Armand, her chevalier, her lover, her defender—would be within its walls as near to cell No. 29 as bribery, entreaty, promises would help him to attain.

Ah! there at last loomed the great building, the pointed bastions cut through the surrounding gloom as with a sable knife.

Armand reached the gate; the sentinels challenged him; he replied:

"Vive le roi!" shouting wildly like one who is drunk.

He was hatless, and his clothes were saturated with moisture. He tried to pass, but crossed bayonets barred the way. Still he shouted:

"Vive le roi!" and "A bas la republique!"

"Allons! the fellow is drunk!" said one of the soldiers.

Armand fought like a madman; he wanted to reach that gate. He shouted, he laughed, and he cried, until one of the soldiers in a fit of rage struck him heavily on the head.

Armand fell backwards, stunned by the blow; his foot slipped on the wet pavement. Was he indeed drunk, or was he dreaming? He put his hand up to his forehead; it was wet, but whether with the rain or with blood he did not know; but for the space of one second he tried to collect his scattered wits.

"Citizen St. Just!" said a quiet voice at his elbow.

Then, as he looked round dazed, feeling a firm, pleasant grip on his arm, the same quiet voice continued calmly:

"Perhaps you do not remember me, citizen St. Just. I had not the honour of the same close friendship with you as I had with your charming sister. My name is Chauvelin. Can I be of any service to you?"

CHAPTER XVII

Chauvelin

Chauvelin! The presence of this man here at this moment made the events of the past few days seem more absolutely like a dream. Chauvelin!—the most deadly enemy he, Armand, and his sister Marguerite had in the world. Chauvelin!—the evil genius that presided over the Secret Service of the Republic. Chauvelin—the aristocrat turned revolutionary, the diplomat turned spy, the baffled enemy of the Scarlet Pimpernel.

He stood there vaguely outlined in the gloom by the feeble rays of an oil lamp fixed into the wall just above. The moisture on his sable clothes glistened in the flickering light like a thin veil of crystal; it clung to the rim of his hat, to the folds of his cloak; the ruffles at his throat and wrist hung limp and soiled.

He had released Armand's arm, and held his hands now underneath his cloak; his pale, deep-set eyes rested gravely on the younger man's face.

"I had an idea, somehow," continued Chauvelin calmly, "that you and I would meet during your sojourn in Paris. I heard from my friend Heron that you had been in the city; he, unfortunately, lost your track almost as soon as he had found it, and I, too, had begun to fear that our mutual and ever enigmatical friend, the Scarlet Pimpernel, had spirited you away, which would have been a great disappointment to me."

Now he once more took hold of Armand by the elbow, but quite gently, more like a comrade who is glad to have met another, and is preparing to enjoy a pleasant conversation for a while. He led the way back to the gate, the sentinel saluting at sight of the tricolour scarf which was visible underneath his cloak. Under the stone rampart Chauvelin paused.

It was quiet and private here. The group of soldiers stood at the further end of the archway, but they were out of hearing, and their forms were only vaguely discernible in the surrounding darkness.

Armand had followed his enemy mechanically like one bewitched and irresponsible for his actions. When Chauvelin paused he too stood still, not because of the grip on his arm, but because of that curious numbing of his will.

Vague, confused thoughts were floating through his brain, the most dominant one among them being that Fate had effectually ordained everything for the best.

Here was Chauvelin, a man who hated him, who, of course, would wish to see him dead. Well, surely it must be an easier matter now to barter his own life for that of Jeanne; she had only been arrested on suspicion of harbouring him, who was a known traitor to the Republic; then, with his capture and speedy death, her supposed guilt would, he hoped, be forgiven. These people could have no ill-will against her, and actors and actresses were always leniently dealt with when possible. Then surely, surely, he could serve Jeanne best by his own arrest and condemnation, than by working to rescue her from prison.

In the meanwhile Chauvelin shook the damp from off his cloak, talking all the time in his own peculiar, gently ironical manner.

"Lady Blakeney?" he was saying—"I hope that she is well!"

"I thank you, sir," murmured Armand mechanically.

"And my dear friend, Sir Percy Blakeney? I had hoped to meet him in Paris. Ah! but no doubt he has been busy very busy; but I live in hopes—I live in hopes. See how kindly Chance has treated me," he continued in the same bland and mocking tones. "I was taking a stroll in these parts, scarce hoping to meet a friend, when, passing the postern-gate of this charming hostelry, whom should I see but my amiable friend St. Just striving to gain admission. But, la! here am I talking of myself, and I am not re-assured as to your state of health. You felt faint just now, did you not? The air about this building is very dank and close. I hope you feel better now. Command me, pray, if I can be of service to you in any way."

Whilst Chauvelin talked he had drawn Armand after him into the lodge of the concierge. The young man now made a great effort to pull himself vigorously together and to steady his nerves.

He had his wish. He was inside the Temple prison now, not far from Jeanne, and though his enemy was older and less vigorous than himself, and the door of the concierge's lodge stood wide open, he knew that he was in-deed as effectually a prisoner already as if the door of one of the numerous cells in this gigantic building had been bolted and barred upon him.

This knowledge helped him to recover his complete presence of mind. No thought of fighting or trying to escape his fate entered his head for a moment. It had been useless probably, and undoubtedly it was better so. If he only could see Jeanne, and assure himself that she would be safe in consequence of his own arrest, then, indeed, life could hold no greater happiness for him.

Above all now he wanted to be cool and calculating, to curb the excitement which the Latin blood in him called forth at every mention of the loved one's name. He tried to think of Percy, of his calmness, his easy banter with an enemy; he resolved to act as Percy would act under these circumstances.

Firstly, he steadied his voice, and drew his well-knit, slim figure upright. He called to mind all his friends in England, with their rigid manners, their impassiveness in the face of trying situations. There was Lord Tony, for instance, always ready with some boyish joke, with boyish impertinence always hovering on his tongue.

Armand tried to emulate Lord Tony's manner, and to borrow something of Percy's calm impudence.

"Citizen Chauvelin," he said, as soon as he felt quite sure of the steadiness of his voice and the calmness of his manner, "I wonder if you are quite certain that that light grip which you have on my arm is sufficient to keep me here walking quietly by your side instead of knocking you down, as I certainly feel inclined to do, for I am a younger, more vigorous man than you."

"H'm!" said Chauvelin, who made pretence to ponder over this difficult problem; "like you, citizen St. Just, I wonder—"

"It could easily be done, you know."

"Fairly easily," rejoined the other; "but there is the guard; it is numerous and strong in this building, and—"

"The gloom would help me; it is dark in the corridors, and a desperate man takes risks, remember—"

"Quite so! And you, citizen St. Just, are a desperate man just now."

"My sister Marguerite is not here, citizen Chauvelin. You cannot barter my life for that of your enemy."

"No! no! no!" rejoined Chauvelin blandly; "not for that of my enemy, I know, but—"

Armand caught at his words like a drowning man at a reed.

"For hers!" he exclaimed.

"For hers?" queried the other with obvious puzzlement.

"Mademoiselle Lange," continued Armand with all the egoistic ardour of the lover who believes that the attention of the entire world is concentrated upon his beloved.

"Mademoiselle Lange! You will set her free now that I am in your power."

Chauvelin smiled, his usual suave, enigmatical smile.

"Ah, yes!" he said. "Mademoiselle Lange. I had forgotten."

"Forgotten, man?—forgotten that those murderous dogs have arrested her?—the best, the purest, this vile, degraded country has ever produced. She sheltered me one day just for an hour. I am a traitor to the Republic—I own it. I'll make full confession; but she knew nothing of this. I deceived her; she is quite innocent, you understand? I'll make full confession, but you must set her free."

He had gradually worked himself up again to a state of feverish excitement. Through the darkness which hung about in this small room he tried to peer in Chauvelin's impassive face.

"Easy, easy, my young friend," said the other placidly; "you seem to imagine that I have something to do with the arrest of the lady in whom you take so deep an interest. You forget that now I am but a discredited servant of the Republic whom I failed to serve in her need. My life is only granted me out of pity for my efforts, which were genuine if not successful. I have no power to set any one free."

"Nor to arrest me now, in that case!" retorted Armand.

Chauvelin paused a moment before he replied with a deprecating smile:

"Only to denounce you, perhaps. I am still an agent of the Committee of General Security."

"Then all is for the best!" exclaimed St. Just eagerly. "You shall denounce me to the Committee. They will be glad of my arrest, I assure you. I have been a marked man for some time. I had intended to evade arrest and to work for the rescue of Mademoiselle Lange; but I will give up all thought of that—I will deliver myself into your hands absolutely; nay, more, I will give you my most solemn word of honour that not only will I make no attempt at escape, but that I will not allow any one to help me to do so. I will be a passive and willing prisoner if you, on the other hand, will effect Mademoiselle Lange's release."

"H'm!" mused Chauvelin again, "it sounds feasible."

"It does! it does!" rejoined Armand, whose excitement was at fever-pitch. "My arrest, my condemnation, my death, will be of vast deal more importance to you than that of a young and innocent girl against whom unlikely charges would have to be tricked up, and whose acquittal mayhap public feeling might demand. As for me, I shall be an easy prey; my known counter-revolutionary principles, my sister's marriage with a foreigner—"

"Your connection with the Scarlet Pimpernel," suggested Chauvelin blandly.

"Quite so. I should not defend myself—"

"And your enigmatical friend would not attempt your rescue. C'est entendu," said Chauvelin with his wonted blandness. "Then, my dear, enthusiastic young friend, shall we adjourn to the office of my colleague, citizen Heron, who is chief agent of the Committee of General Security, and will receive your—did you say confession?—and note the conditions under which you place yourself absolutely in the hands of the Public Prosecutor and subsequently of the executioner. Is that it?"

Armand was too full of schemes, too full of thoughts of Jeanne to note the tone of quiet irony with which Chauvelin had been speaking all along. With the unreasoning egoism of youth he was quite convinced that his own arrest, his own affairs were as important to this entire nation in revolution as they were to himself. At moments like these it is difficult to envisage a desperate situation clearly, and to a young man in love the fate of the beloved never seems desperate whilst he himself is alive and ready for every sacrifice for her sake. "My life for hers" is the sublime if often foolish battle-cry that has so often resulted in whole-sale destruction. Armand at this moment, when he fondly believed that he was making a bargain with the most astute, most unscrupulous spy this revolutionary Government had in its pay—Armand just then had absolutely forgotten his chief, his friends, the league of mercy and help to which he belonged.

Enthusiasm and the spirit of self-sacrifice were carrying him away. He watched his enemy with glowing eyes as one who looks on the arbiter of his fate.

Chauvelin, without another word, beckoned to him to follow. He led the way out of the lodge, then, turning sharply to his left, he reached the wide quadrangle with the covered passage running right round it, the same which de Batz had traversed two evenings ago when he went to visit Heron.

Armand, with a light heart and springy step, followed him as if he were going to a feast where he would meet Jeanne, where he would kneel at her feet, kiss her hands, and lead her triumphantly to freedom and to happiness.

CHAPTER XVIII

The Removal

Chauvelin no longer made any pretence to hold Armand by the arm. By temperament as well as by profession a spy, there was one subject at least which he had mastered thoroughly: that was the study of human nature. Though occasionally an exceptionally complex mental organisation baffled him—as in the case of Sir Percy Blakeney—he prided himself, and justly, too, on reading natures like that of Armand St. Just as he would an open book.

The excitable disposition of the Latin races he knew out and out; he knew exactly how far a sentimental situation would lead a young Frenchman like Armand, who was by disposition chivalrous, and by temperament essentially passionate. Above all things, he knew when and how far he could trust a man to do either a sublime action or an essentially foolish one.

Therefore he walked along contentedly now, not even looking back to see whether St. Just was following him. He knew that he did.

His thoughts only dwelt on the young enthusiast—in his mind he called him the young fool—in order to weigh in the balance the mighty possibilities that would accrue from the present sequence of events. The fixed idea ever working in the man's scheming brain had already transformed a vague belief into a certainty. That the Scarlet Pimpernel was in Paris at the present moment Chauvelin had now become convinced. How far he could turn the capture of Armand St. Just to the triumph of his own ends remained to be seen.

But this he did know: the Scarlet Pimpernel—the man whom he had learned to know, to dread, and even in a grudging manner to admire—was not like to leave one of his followers in the lurch. Marguerite's brother in the Temple would be the surest decoy for the elusive meddler who still, and in spite of all care and precaution, continued to baffle the army of spies set upon his track.

Chauvelin could hear Armand's light, elastic footsteps resounding behind him on the flagstones. A world of intoxicating possibilities surged up before him. Ambition, which two successive dire failures had atrophied in his breast, once more rose up buoyant and hopeful. Once he had sworn to lay the Scarlet Pimpernel by the heels, and that oath was not yet wholly forgotten; it had lain dormant after the catastrophe of Boulogne, but with the sight of Armand St. Just it had re-awakened and confronted him again with the strength of a likely fulfilment.

The courtyard looked gloomy and deserted. The thin drizzle which still fell from a persistently leaden sky effectually held every outline of masonry, of column, or of gate hidden as beneath a shroud. The corridor which skirted it all round was ill-lighted save by an occasional oil-lamp fixed in the wall.

But Chauvelin knew his way well. Heron's lodgings gave on the second courtyard, the Square du Nazaret, and the way thither led past the main square tower, in the top floor of which the uncrowned King of France eked out his miserable existence as the plaything of a rough cobbler and his wife.

Just beneath its frowning bastions Chauvelin turned back towards Armand. He pointed with a careless hand up-wards to the central tower.

"We have got little Capet in there," he said dryly. "Your chivalrous Scarlet Pimpernel has not ventured in these precincts yet, you see."

Armand was silent. He had no difficulty in looking unconcerned; his thoughts were so full of Jeanne that he cared but little at this moment for any Bourbon king or for the destinies of France.

Now the two men reached the postern gate. A couple of sentinels were standing by, but the gate itself was open, and from within there came the sound of bustle and of noise, of a good deal of swearing, and also of loud laughter.

The guard-room gave on the left of the gate, and the laughter came from there. It was brilliantly lighted, and Armand, peering in, in the wake of Chauvelin, could see groups of soldiers sitting and standing about. There was a table in the centre of the room, and on it a number of jugs and pewter mugs, packets of cards, and overturned boxes of dice.

But the bustle did not come from the guard-room; it came from the landing and the stone stairs beyond.

Chauvelin, apparently curious, had passed through the gate, and Armand followed him. The light from the open door of the guard-room cut sharply across the landing, making the gloom beyond appear more dense and almost solid. From out the darkness, fitfully intersected by a lanthorn apparently carried to and fro, moving figures loomed out ghost-like and weirdly gigantic. Soon Armand distinguished a number of large objects that encumbered the landing, and as he and Chauvelin left the sharp light of the guard-room 'behind them, he could see that the large objects were pieces of furniture of every shape and size; a wooden bedstead—dismantled—leaned against the wall, a black horsehair sofa blocked the way to the tower stairs, and there were numberless chairs and several tables piled one on the top of the other.

In the midst of this litter a stout, flabby-cheeked man stood, apparently giving directions as to its removal to persons at present unseen.

"Hola, Papa Simon!" exclaimed Chauvelin jovially; "moving out to-day? What?"

"Yes, thank the Lord!—if there be a Lord!" retorted the other curtly. "Is that you, citizen Chauvelin?"

"In person, citizen. I did not know you were leaving quite so soon. Is citizen

Heron anywhere about?"

"Just left," replied Simon. "He had a last look at Capet just before my wife locked the brat up in the inner room. Now he's gone back to his lodgings."

A man carrying a chest, empty of its drawers, on his back now came stumbling down the tower staircase. Madame Simon followed close on his heels, steadying the chest with one hand.

"We had better begin to load up the cart," she called to her husband in a high-pitched querulous voice; "the corridor is getting too much encumbered."

She looked suspiciously at Chauvelin and at Armand, and when she encountered the former's bland, unconcerned gaze she suddenly shivered and drew her black shawl closer round her shoulders.

"Bah!" she said, "I shall be glad to get out of this God-forsaken hole. I hate the very sight of these walls."

"Indeed, the citizeness does not look over robust in health," said Chauvelin with studied politeness. "The stay in the tower did not, mayhap, bring forth all the fruits of prosperity which she had anticipated."

The woman eyed him with dark suspicion lurking in her hollow eyes.

"I don't know what you mean, citizen," she said with a shrug of her wide shoulders.

"Oh! I meant nothing," rejoined Chauvelin, smiling. "I am so interested in your removal; busy man as I am, it has amused me to watch you. Whom have you got to help you with the furniture?"

"Dupont, the man-of-all-work, from the concierge," said Simon curtly. "Citizen Heron would not allow any one to come in from the outside."

"Rightly too. Have the new commissaries come yet?

"Only citizen Cochefer. He is waiting upstairs for the others."

"And Capet?"

"He is all safe. Citizen Heron came to see him, and then he told me to lock the little vermin up in the inner room. Citizen Cochefer had just arrived by that time, and he has remained in charge."

During all this while the man with the chest on his back was waiting for orders. Bent nearly double, he was grumbling audibly at his uncomfortable position.

"Does the citizen want to break my back?" he muttered.

"We had best get along—quoi?"

He asked if he should begin to carry the furniture out into the street.

"Two sous have I got to pay every ten minutes to the lad who holds my nag," he said, muttering under his breath; "we shall be all night at this rate."

"Begin to load then," commanded Simon gruffly. "Here!—begin with this sofa."

"You'll have to give me a hand with that," said the man. "Wait a bit; I'll just see that everything is all right in the cart. I'll be back directly."

"Take something with you then as you are going down," said Madame Simon in her querulous voice.

The man picked up a basket of linen that stood in the angle by the door. He hoisted it on his back and shuffled away with it across the landing and out through the gate.

"How did Capet like parting from his papa and maman?" asked Chauvelin with a laugh.

"H'm!" growled Simon laconically. "He will find out soon enough how well off he was under our care."

"Have the other commissaries come yet?"

"No. But they will be here directly. Citizen Cochefer is upstairs mounting guard over Capet."

"Well, good-bye, Papa Simon," concluded Chauvelin jovially. "Citizeness, your servant!"

He bowed with unconcealed irony to the cobbler's wife, and nodded to Simon, who expressed by a volley of motley oaths his exact feelings with regard to all the agents of the Committee of General Security.

"Six months of this penal servitude have we had," he said roughly, "and no thanks or pension. I would as soon serve a ci-devant aristo as your accursed Committee."

The man Dupont had returned. Stolidly, after the fashion of his kind, he commenced the removal of citizen Simon's goods. He seemed a clumsy enough creature, and Simon and his wife had to do most of the work themselves.

Chauvelin watched the moving forms for a while, then he shrugged his shoulders with a laugh of indifference, and turned on his heel.

CHAPTER XIX

It is About the Dauphin

Heron was not at his lodgings when, at last, after vigorous pulls at the bell, a great deal of waiting and much cursing, Chauvelin, closely followed by Armand, was introduced in the chief agent's office.

The soldier who acted as servant said that citizen Heron had gone out to sup, but would surely be home again by eight o'clock. Armand by this time was so dazed with fatigue that he sank on a chair like a log, and remained there staring into the fire, unconscious of the flight of time.

Anon Heron came home. He nodded to Chauvelin, and threw but a cursory glance on Armand.

"Five minutes, citizen," he said, with a rough attempt at an apology. "I am sorry to keep you waiting, but the new commissaries have arrived who are to take charge of Capet. The Simons have just gone, and I want to assure myself that everything is all right in the Tower. Cochefer has been in charge, but I like to cast an eye over the brat every day myself."

He went out again, slamming the door behind him. His heavy footsteps were heard treading the flagstones of the corridor, and gradually dying away in the distance. Armand had paid no heed either to his entrance or to his exit. He was only conscious of an intense weariness, and would at this moment gladly have laid his head on the scaffold if on it he could find rest.

A white-faced clock on the wall ticked off the seconds one by one. From the street below came the muffled sounds of wheeled traffic on the soft mud of the road; it was raining more heavily now, and from time to time a gust of wind rattled the small windows in their dilapidated frames, or hurled a shower of heavy drops against the panes.

The heat from the stove had made Armand drowsy; his head fell forward on his chest. Chauvelin, with his hands held behind his back, paced ceaselessly up and down the narrow room.

Suddenly Armand started—wide awake now. Hurried footsteps on the flagstones outside, a hoarse shout, a banging of heavy doors, and the next moment Heron stood once more on the threshold of the room. Armand, with wide-opened eyes, gazed on him in wonder. The whole appearance of the man had changed. He looked ten years older, with lank, dishevelled hair hanging matted over a moist forehead, the cheeks ashen-white, the full lips bloodless and hanging, flabby and parted, displaying both rows of yellow teeth that shook against each other. The whole figure looked bowed, as if shrunk within itself.

Chauvelin had paused in his restless walk. He gazed on his colleague, a frown of puzzlement on his pale, set face.

"Capet!" he exclaimed, as soon as he had taken in every detail of Heron's altered appearance, and seen the look of wild terror that literally distorted his face.

Heron could not speak; his teeth were chattering in his mouth, and his tongue seemed paralysed. Chauvelin went up to him. He was several inches shorter than his colleague, but at this moment he seemed to be towering over him like an avenging spirit. He placed a firm hand on the other's bowed shoulders.

"Capet has gone—is that it?" he queried peremptorily.

The look of terror increased in Heron's eyes, giving its mute reply.

"How? When?"

But for the moment the man was speechless. An almost maniacal fear seemed to hold him in its grip. With an impatient oath Chauvelin turned away from him.

"Brandy!" he said curtly, speaking to Armand.

A bottle and glass were found in the cupboard. It was St. Just who poured out the brandy and held it to Heron's lips. Chauvelin was once more pacing up and down the room in angry impatience.

"Pull yourself together, man," he said roughly after a while, "and try and tell me what has occurred."

Heron had sunk into a chair. He passed a trembling hand once or twice over his forehead.

"Capet has disappeared," he murmured; "he must have been spirited away while the Simons were moving their furniture. That accursed Cochefer was completely taken in."

Heron spoke in a toneless voice, hardly above a whisper, and like one whose throat is dry and mouth parched. But the brandy had revived him somewhat, and his eyes lost their former glassy look.

"How?" asked Chauvelin curtly.

"I was just leaving the Tower when he arrived. I spoke to him at the door. I had seen Capet safely installed in the room, and gave orders to the woman Simon to let citizen Cochefer have a look at him, too, and then to lock up the brat in the inner room and install Cochefer in the antechamber on guard. I stood talking to Cochefer for a few moments in the antechamber. The woman Simon and the man-of-all-work, Dupont—whom I know well—were busy with the furniture. There could not have been any one else concealed about the place—that I'll swear. Cochefer, after he took leave of me, went straight into the room; he found the woman Simon in the act of turning the key in the door of the inner chamber. I have locked Capet in there,' she said, giving the key to Cochefer; 'he will be quite safe until to-night; when the other commissaries come.'

"Didn't Cochefer go into the room and ascertain whether the woman was lying?"

"Yes, he did! He made the woman re-open the door and peeped in over her shoulder. She said the child was asleep. He vows that he saw the child lying fully dressed on a rug in the further corner of the room. The room, of course, was quite empty of furniture and only lighted by one candle, but there was the rug and the child asleep on it. Cochefer swears he saw him, and now—when I went up—"

"Well?"

"The commissaries were all there—Cochefer and Lasniere, Lorinet and Legrand. We went into the inner room, and I had a candle in my hand. We saw the child lying on the rug, just as Cochefer had seen him, and for a while we took no notice of it. Then some one—I think it was Lorinet—went to have a closer look at the brat. He took up the candle and went up to the rug. Then he gave a cry, and we all gathered round him. The sleeping child was only a bundle of hair and of clothes, a dummy—what?"

There was silence now in the narrow room, while the white-faced clock continued to tick off each succeeding second of time. Heron had once more buried his head in his hands; a trembling—like an attack of ague—shook his wide, bony shoulders. Armand had listened to the narrative with glowing eyes and a beating heart. The details which the two Terrorists here could not probably understand he had already added to the picture which his mind had conjured up.

He was back in thought now in the small lodging in the rear of St. Germain l'Auxerrois; Sir Andrew Ffoulkes was there, and my Lord Tony and Hastings, and a man was striding up and down the room, looking out into the great space beyond the river with the eyes of a seer, and a firm voice said abruptly:

"It is about the Dauphin!"

"Have you any suspicions?" asked Chauvelin now, pausing in his walk beside Heron, and once more placing a firm, peremptory hand on his colleague's shoulder.

"Suspicions!" exclaimed the chief agent with a loud oath. "Suspicions! Certainties, you mean. The man sat here but two days ago, in that very chair, and bragged of what he would do. I told him then that if he interfered with Capet I would wring his neck with my own hands."

And his long, talon-like fingers, with their sharp, grimy nails, closed and unclosed like those of feline creatures when they hold the coveted prey.

"Of whom do you speak?" queried Chauvelin curtly.

"Of whom? Of whom but that accursed de Batz? His pockets are bulging with Austrian money, with which, no doubt, he has bribed the Simons and Cochefer and the sentinels—"

"And Lorinet and Lasniere and you," interposed Chauvelin dryly.

"It is false!" roared Heron, who already at the suggestion was foaming at the mouth, and had jumped up from his chair, standing at bay as if prepared to fight for his life.

"False, is it?" retorted Chauvelin calmly; "then be not so quick, friend Heron, in slashing out with senseless denunciations right and left. You'll gain nothing by denouncing any one just now. This is too intricate a matter to be dealt with a sledge-hammer. Is any one up in the Tower at this moment?" he asked in quiet, business-like tones.

"Yes. Cochefer and the others are still there. They are making wild schemes to cover their treachery. Cochefer is aware of his own danger, and Lasniere and the others know that they arrived at the Tower several hours too late. They are all at fault, and they know it. As for that de Batz," he continued with a voice rendered raucous with bitter passion, "I swore to him two days ago that he should not escape me if he meddled with Capet. I'm on his track already. I'll have him before the hour of midnight, and I'll torture him—yes! I'll torture him—the Tribunal shall give me leave. We have a dark cell down below here where my men know how to apply tortures worse than the rack—where they know just how to prolong life long enough to make it unendurable. I'll torture him! I'll torture him!"

But Chauvelin abruptly silenced the wretch with a curt command; then, without another word, he walked straight out of the room.

In thought Armand followed him. The wild desire was suddenly born in him to run away at this moment, while Heron, wrapped in his own meditations, was paying no heed to him. Chauvelin's footsteps had long ago died away in the distance; it was a long way to the upper floor of the Tower, and some time would be spent, too, in interrogating the commissaries. This was Armand's opportunity. After all, if he were free himself he might more effectually help to rescue Jeanne. He knew, too, now where to join his leader. The corner of the street by the canal, where Sir Andrew

Ffoulkes would be waiting with the coal-cart; then there was the spinney on the road to St. Germain. Armand hoped that, with good luck, he might yet overtake his comrades, tell them of Jeanne's plight, and entreat them to work for her rescue.

He had forgotten that now he had no certificate of safety, that undoubtedly he would be stopped at the gates at this hour of the night; that his conduct proving suspect he would in all probability he detained, and, mayhap, be brought back to this self-same place within an hour. He had forgotten all that, for the primeval instinct for freedom had suddenly been aroused. He rose softly from his chair and crossed the room. Heron paid no attention to him. Now he had traversed the antechamber and unlatched the outer door.

Immediately a couple of bayonets were crossed in front of him, two more further on ahead scintillated feebly in the flickering light. Chauvelin had taken his precautions. There was no doubt that Armand St. Just was effectually a prisoner now.

With a sigh of disappointment he went back to his place beside the fire. Heron had not even moved whilst he had made this futile attempt at escape. Five minutes later Chauvelin re-entered the room.

CHAPTER XX

The Certificate of Safety

"You can leave de Batz and his gang alone, citizen Heron," said Chauvelin, as soon as he had closed the door behind him; "he had nothing to do with the escape of the Dauphin."

Heron growled out a few words of incredulity. But Chauvelin shrugged his shoulders and looked with unutterable contempt on his colleague. Armand, who was watching him closely, saw that in his hand he held a small piece of paper, which he had crushed into a shapeless mass.

"Do not waste your time, citizen," he said, "in raging against an empty wind-bag. Arrest de Batz if you like, or leave him alone an you please—we have nothing to fear from that braggart."

With nervous, slightly shaking fingers he set to work to smooth out the scrap of paper which he held. His hot hands had soiled it and pounded it until it was a mere rag and the writing on it illegible. But, such as it was, he threw it down with a blasphemous oath on the desk in front of Heron's eyes.

"It is that accursed Englishman who has been at work again," he said more calmly; "I guessed it the moment I heard your story. Set your whole army of sleuth-hounds on his track, citizen; you'll need them all."

Heron picked up the scrap of torn paper and tried to decipher the writing on it by the light from the lamp. He seemed almost dazed now with the awful catastrophe that had befallen him, and the fear that his own wretched life would have to pay the penalty for the disappearance of the child.

As for Armand—even in the midst of his own troubles, and of his own anxiety for Jeanne, he felt a proud exultation in his heart. The Scarlet Pimpernel had succeeded; Percy had not failed in his self-imposed undertaking. Chauvelin, whose piercing eyes were fixed on him at that moment, smiled with contemptuous irony.

"As you will find your hands overfull for the next few hours, citizen Heron," he said, speaking to his colleague and nodding in the direction of Armand, "I'll not trouble you with the voluntary confession this young citizen desired to make to you. All I need tell you is that he is an adherent of the Scarlet Pimpernel—I believe one of his most faithful, most trusted officers."

Heron roused himself from the maze of gloomy thoughts that were again paralysing his tongue. He turned bleary, wild eyes on Armand.

"We have got one of them, then?" he murmured incoherently, babbling like a drunken man.

"M'yes!" replied Chauvelin lightly; "but it is too late now for a formal denunciation and arrest. He cannot leave Paris anyhow, and all that your men need to do is to keep a close look-out on him. But I should send him home to-night if I were you."

Heron muttered something more, which, however, Armand did not understand. Chauvelin's words were still ringing in his ear. Was he, then, to be set free to-night? Free in a measure, of course, since spies were to be set to watch him—but free, nevertheless? He could not understand Chauvelin's attitude, and his own self-love was not a little wounded at the thought that he was of such little account that these men could afford to give him even this provisional freedom. And, of course, there was still Jeanne.

"I must, therefore, bid you good-night, citizen," Chauvelin was saying in his bland, gently ironical manner. "You will be glad to return to your lodgings. As you see, the chief agent of the Committee of General Security is too much occupied just now to accept the sacrifice of your life which you were prepared so generously to offer him."

"I do not understand you, citizen," retorted Armand coldly, "nor do I desire indulgence at your hands. You have arrested an innocent woman on the trumped-up charge that she was harbouring me. I came here to-night to give myself up to justice so that she might be set free."

"But the hour is somewhat late, citizen," rejoined Chauvelin urbanely. "The lady in whom you take so fervent an interest is no doubt asleep in her cell at this hour. It would not be fitting to disturb her now. She might not find shelter before morning, and the weather is quite exceptionally unpropitious."

"Then, sir," said Armand, a little bewildered, "am I to understand that if I hold myself at your disposition Mademoiselle Lange will be set free as early to-morrow morning as may be?"

"No doubt, sir—no doubt," replied Chauvelin with more than his accustomed blandness; "if you will hold yourself entirely at our disposition, Mademoiselle Lange will be set free to-morrow. I think that we can safely promise that, citizen Heron, can we not?" he added, turning to his colleague.

But Heron, overcome with the stress of emotions, could only murmur vague, unintelligible words.

"Your word on that, citizen Chauvelin?" asked Armand.

"My word on it an you will accept it."

"No, I will not do that. Give me an unconditional certificate of safety and I will believe you."

"Of what use were that to you?" asked Chauvelin.

"I believe my capture to be of more importance to you than that of Mademoiselle Lange," said Armand quietly.

"I will use the certificate of safety for myself or one of my friends if you break your word to me anent Mademoiselle Lange."

"H'm! the reasoning is not illogical, citizen," said Chauvelin, whilst a curious smile played round the corners of his thin lips. "You are quite right. You are a more valuable asset to us than the charming lady who, I hope, will for many a day and year to come delight pleasure-loving Paris with her talent and her grace."

"Amen to that, citizen," said Armand fervently.

"Well, it will all depend on you, sir! Here," he added, coolly running over some papers on Heron's desk until he found what he wanted, "is an absolutely unconditional certificate of safety. The Committee of General Security issue very few of these. It is worth the cost of a human life. At no barrier or gate of any city can such a certificate be disregarded, nor even can it be detained. Allow me to hand it to you, citizen, as a pledge of my own good faith."

Smiling, urbane, with a curious look that almost expressed amusement lurking in his shrewd, pale eyes, Chauvelin handed the momentous document to Armand.

The young man studied it very carefully before he slipped it into the inner pocket of his coat.

"How soon shall I have news of Mademoiselle Lange?" he asked finally.

"In the course of to-morrow. I myself will call on you and redeem that precious document in person. You, on the other hand, will hold yourself at my disposition. That's understood, is it not?"

"I shall not fail you. My lodgings are—"

"Oh! do not trouble," interposed Chauvelin, with a polite bow; "we can find that out for ourselves."

Heron had taken no part in this colloquy. Now that Armand prepared to go he made no attempt to detain him, or to question his colleague's actions. He sat by the table like a log; his mind was obviously a blank to all else save to his own terrors engendered by the events of this night.

With bleary, half-veiled eyes he followed Armand's progress through the room, and seemed unaware of the loud slamming of the outside door. Chauvelin had escorted the young man past the first line of sentry, then he took cordial leave of him.

"Your certificate will, you will find, open every gate to you. Good-night, citizen.

A demain."

"Good-night."

Armand's slim figure disappeared in the gloom. Chauvelin watched him for a few moments until even his footsteps had died away in the distance; then he turned back towards Heron's lodgings.

"A nous deux," he muttered between tightly clenched teeth; "a nous deux once more, my enigmatical Scarlet Pimpernel."

CHAPTER XXI

Back to Paris

It was an exceptionally dark night, and the rain was falling in torrents. Sir Andrew Ffoulkes, wrapped in a piece of sacking, had taken shelter right underneath the coal-cart; even then he was getting wet through to the skin.

He had worked hard for two days coal-heaving, and the night before he had found a cheap, squalid lodging where at any rate he was protected from the inclemencies of the weather; but to-night he was expecting Blakeney at the appointed hour and place. He had secured a cart of the ordinary ramshackle pattern used for carrying coal. Unfortunately there were no covered ones to be obtained in the neighbourhood, and equally unfortunately the thaw had set in with a blustering wind and diving rain, which made waiting in the open air for hours at a stretch and in complete darkness excessively unpleasant.

But for all these discomforts Sir Andrew Ffoulkes cared not one jot. In England, in his magnificent Suffolk home, he was a confirmed sybarite, in whose service every description of comfort and luxury had to be enrolled. Here tonight in the rough and tattered clothes of a coal-heaver, drenched to the skin, and crouching under the body of a cart that hardly sheltered him from the rain, he was as happy as a schoolboy out for a holiday.

Happy, but vaguely anxious.

He had no means of ascertaining the time. So many of the church-bells and clock towers had been silenced recently that not one of those welcome sounds penetrated to the dreary desolation of this canal wharf, with its abandoned carts standing ghost-like in a row. Darkness had set in very early in the afternoon, and the heavers had given up work soon after four o'clock.

For about an hour after that a certain animation had still reigned round the wharf, men crossing and going, one or two of the barges moving in or out alongside the quay. But for some time now darkness and silence had been the masters in this desolate spot, and that time had seemed to Sir Andrew an eternity. He had hobbled and tethered his horse, and stretched himself out at full length under the cart. Now and again he had crawled out from under this uncomfortable shelter and walked up and down in ankle-deep mud, trying to restore circulation in his stiffened limbs; now and again a kind of torpor had come over him, and he had fallen into a brief and restless sleep. He would at this moment have given half his fortune for knowledge of the exact time.

But through all this weary waiting he was never for a moment in doubt. Unlike Armand St. Just, he had the simplest, most perfect faith in his chief. He had been Blakeney's constant companion in all these adventures for close upon four years now; the thought of failure, however vague, never once entered his mind.

He was only anxious for his chief's welfare. He knew that he would succeed, but he would have liked to have spared him much of the physical fatigue and the nerve-racking strain of these hours that lay between the daring deed and the hope of safety. Therefore he was conscious of an acute tingling of his nerves, which went on even during the brief patches of fitful sleep, and through the numbness that invaded his whole body while the hours dragged wearily and slowly along.

Then, quite suddenly, he felt wakeful and alert; quite a while—even before he heard the welcome signal—he knew, with a curious, subtle sense of magnetism, that the hour had come, and that his chief was somewhere near by, not very far.

Then he heard the cry—a seamew's call—repeated thrice at intervals, and five minutes later something loomed out of the darkness quite close to the hind wheels of the cart.

"Hist! Ffoulkes!" came in a soft whisper, scarce louder than the wind.

"Present!" came in quick response.

"Here, help me to lift the child into the cart. He is asleep, and has been a dead weight on my arm for close on an hour now. Have you a dry bit of sacking or something to lay him on?"

"Not very dry, I am afraid."

With tender care the two men lifted the sleeping little King of France into the rickety cart. Blakeney laid his cloak over him, and listened for awhile to the slow regular breathing of the child.

"St. Just is not here—you know that?" said Sir Andrew after a while.

"Yes, I knew it," replied Blakeney curtly.

It was characteristic of these two men that not a word about the adventure itself, about the terrible risks and dangers of the past few hours, was exchanged between them. The child was here and was safe, and Blakeney knew the whereabouts of St. Just—that was enough for Sir Andrew Ffoulkes, the most devoted follower, the most perfect friend the Scarlet Pimpernel would ever know.

Ffoulkes now went to the horse, detached the nose-bag, and undid the nooses of the hobble and of the tether.

"Will you get in now, Blakeney?" he said; "we are ready."

And in unbroken silence they both got into the cart; Blakeney sitting on its floor beside the child, and Ffoulkes gathering the reins in his hands.

The wheels of the cart and the slow jog-trot of the horse made scarcely any noise in the mud of the roads, what noise they did make was effectually drowned by the soughing of the wind in the bare branches of the stunted acacia trees that edged the towpath along the line of the canal.

Sir Andrew had studied the topography of this desolate neighbourhood well during the past twenty-four hours; he knew of a detour that would enable him to avoid the La Villette gate and the neighbourhood of the fortifications, and yet bring him out soon on the road leading to St. Germain.

Once he turned to ask Blakeney the time.

"It must be close on ten now," replied Sir Percy. "Push your nag along, old man. Tony and Hastings will be waiting for us."

It was very difficult to see clearly even a metre or two ahead, but the road was a straight one, and the old nag seemed to know it almost as well and better than her driver. She shambled along at her own pace, covering the ground very slowly for Ffoulkes's burning impatience. Once or twice he had to get down and lead her over a rough piece of ground. They passed several groups of dismal, squalid houses, in some of which a dim light still burned, and as they skirted St. Ouen the church clock slowly tolled the hour of midnight.

But for the greater part of the way derelict, uncultivated spaces of terrains vagues, and a few isolated houses lay between the road and the fortifications of the city. The darkness of the night, the late hour, the soughing of the wind, were all in favour of the adventurers; and a coal-cart slowly trudging along in this neighbourhood, with two labourers sitting in it, was the least likely of any vehicle to attract attention.

Past Clichy, they had to cross the river by the rickety wooden bridge that was unsafe even in broad daylight. They were not far from their destination now. Half a dozen kilometres further on they would be leaving Courbevoie on their left, and then the sign-post would come in sight. After that the spinney just off the road, and the welcome presence of Tony, Hastings, and the horses. Ffoulkes got down in order to make sure of the way. He walked at the horse's head now, fearful lest he missed the cross-roads and the sign-post.

The horse was getting over-tired; it had covered fifteen kilometres, and it was close on three o'clock of Monday morning.

Another hour went by in absolute silence. Ffoulkes and Blakeney took turns at the horse's head. Then at last they reached the cross-roads; even through the darkness the sign-post showed white against the surrounding gloom.

"This looks like it," murmured Sir Andrew. He turned the horse's head sharply towards the left, down a narrower road, and leaving the sign-post behind him. He walked slowly along for another quarter of an hour, then Blakeney called a halt.

"The spinney must be sharp on our right now," he said.

He got down from the cart, and while Ffoulkes remained beside the horse, he plunged into the gloom. A moment later the cry of the seamew rang out three times into the air. It was answered almost immediately.

The spinney lay on the right of the road. Soon the soft sounds that to a trained ear invariably betray the presence of a number of horses reached Ffoulkes' straining senses. He took his old nag out of the shafts, and the shabby harness from off her, then he turned her out on the piece of waste land that faced the spinney. Some one would find her in the morning, her and the cart with the shabby harness laid in it, and, having wondered if all these things had perchance dropped down from heaven, would quietly appropriate them, and mayhap thank much-maligned heaven for its gift.

Blakeney in the meanwhile had lifted the sleeping child out of the cart. Then he called to Sir Andrew and led the way across the road and into the spinney.

Five minutes later Hastings received the uncrowned King of France in his arms.

Unlike Ffoulkes, my Lord Tony wanted to hear all about the adventure of this afternoon. A thorough sportsman, he loved a good story of hairbreadth escapes, of dangers cleverly avoided, risks taken and conquered.

"Just in ten words, Blakeney," he urged entreatingly; "how did you actually get the boy away?"

Sir Percy laughed—despite himself—at the young man's eagerness.

"Next time we meet, Tony," he begged; "I am so demmed fatigued, and there's this beastly rain—"

"No, no—now! while Hastings sees to the horses. I could not exist long without knowing, and we are well sheltered from the rain under this tree."

"Well, then, since you will have it," he began with a laugh, which despite the weariness and anxiety of the past twenty-four hours had forced itself to his lips, "I have been sweeper and man-of-all-work at the Temple for the past few weeks, you must know—"

"No!" ejaculated my Lord Tony lustily. "By gum!"

"Indeed, you old sybarite, whilst you were enjoying yourself heaving coal on the canal wharf, I was scrubbing floors, lighting fires, and doing a number of odd jobs for a lot of demmed murdering villains, and"—he added under his breath—"incidentally, too, for our league. Whenever I had an hour or two off duty I spent them in my lodgings, and asked you all to come and meet me there."

"By Gad, Blakeney! Then the day before yesterday?—when we all met—"

"I had just had a bath—sorely needed, I can tell you. I had been cleaning boots half the day, but I had heard that the Simons were removing from the Temple on the Sunday, and had obtained an order from them to help them shift their furniture."

"Cleaning boots!" murmured my Lord Tony with a chuckle. "Well! and then?"

"Well, then everything worked out splendidly. You see by that time I was a well-known figure in the Temple. Heron knew me well. I used to be his lanthorn-bearer when at nights he visited that poor mite in his prison. It was 'Dupont, here! Dupont there!' all day long. 'Light the fire in the office, Dupont! Dupont, brush my coat! Dupont, fetch me a light!' When the Simons wanted to move their household goods they called loudly for Dupont. I got a covered laundry cart, and I brought a dummy with me to substitute for the child. Simon himself knew nothing of this, but Madame was in my pay. The dummy was just splendid, with real hair on its head; Madame helped me to substitute it for the child; we laid it on the sofa and covered it over with a rug, even while those brutes Heron and Cochefer were on the landing outside, and we stuffed His Majesty the King of France into a linen basket. The room was badly lighted, and any one would have been deceived. No one was suspicious of that type of trickery, so it went off splendidly. I moved the furniture of the Simons out of the Tower. His Majesty King Louis XVII was still concealed in the linen basket. I drove the Simons to their new lodgings—the man still suspects nothing—and there I helped them to unload the furniture—with the exception of the linen basket, of course. After that I drove my laundry cart to a house I knew of and collected a number of linen baskets, which I had arranged should be in readiness for me. Thus loaded up I left Paris by the Vincennes gate, and drove as far as Bagnolet, where there is no road except past the octroi, where the officials might have proved unpleasant. So I lifted His Majesty out of the basket and we walked on hand in hand in the darkness and the rain until the poor little feet gave out. Then the little fellow—who has been wonderfully plucky throughout, indeed, more a Capet than a Bourbon—snuggled up in my arms and went fast asleep, and—and—well, I think that's all, for here we are, you see."

"But if Madame Simon had not been amenable to bribery?" suggested Lord Tony after a moment's silence.

"Then I should have had to think of something else."

"If during the removal of the furniture Heron had remained resolutely in the room?"

"Then, again, I should have had to think of something else; but remember that in life there is always one supreme moment when Chance—who is credited to have but one hair on her head—stands by you for a brief space of time; sometimes that space is infinitesimal—one minute, a few seconds—just the time to seize Chance by that one hair. So I pray you all give me no credit in this or any other matter in which we all work together, but the quickness of seizing Chance by the hair during the brief moment when she stands by my side. If Madame Simon had been un-amenable, if Heron had remained in the room all the time, if Cochefer had had two looks at the dummy instead of one—well, then, something else would have helped me, something would have occurred; something—I know not what—but surely something which Chance meant to be on our side, if only we were quick enough to seize it—and so you see how simple it all is."

So simple, in fact, that it was sublime. The daring, the pluck, the ingenuity and, above all, the super-human heroism and endurance which rendered the hearers of this simple narrative, simply told, dumb with admiration.

Their thoughts now were beyond verbal expression.

"How soon was the hue and cry for the child about the streets?" asked Tony, after a moment's silence.

"It was not out when I left the gates of Paris," said Blakeney meditatively; "so quietly has the news of the escape been kept, that I am wondering what devilry that brute Heron can be after. And now no more chattering," he continued lightly; "all to horse, and you, Hastings, have a care. The destinies of France, mayhap, will be lying asleep in your arms."

"But you, Blakeney?" exclaimed the three men almost simultaneously.

"I am not going with you. I entrust the child to you. For God's sake guard him well! Ride with him to Mantes. You should arrive there at about ten o'clock. One of you then go straight to No.9 Rue la Tour. Ring the bell; an old man will answer it. Say the one word to him, 'Enfant'; he will reply, 'De roi!' Give him the child, and may Heaven bless you all for the help you have given me this night!"

"But you, Blakeney?" reiterated Tony with a note of deep anxiety in his fresh young voice.

"I am straight for Paris," he said quietly.

"Impossible!"

"Therefore feasible."

"But why? Percy, in the name of Heaven, do you realise what you are doing?"

"Perfectly."

"They'll not leave a stone unturned to find you—they know by now, believe me, that your hand did this trick."

"I know that."

"And yet you mean to go back?"

"And yet I am going back."

"Blakeney!"

"It's no use, Tony. Armand is in Paris. I saw him in the corridor of the Temple prison in the company of Chauvelin."

"Great God!" exclaimed Lord Hastings.

The others were silent. What was the use of arguing? One of themselves was in danger. Armand St. Just, the brother of Marguerite Blakeney! Was it likely that Percy would leave him in the lurch.

"One of us will stay with you, of course?" asked Sir Andrew after awhile.

"Yes! I want Hastings and Tony to take the child to Mantes, then to make all possible haste for Calais, and there to keep in close touch with the Day-Dream; the skipper will contrive to open communication. Tell him to remain in Calais waters. I hope I may have need of him soon.

"And now to horse, both of you," he added gaily. "Hastings, when you are ready, I will hand up the child to you. He will be quite safe on the pillion with a strap round him and you."

Nothing more was said after that. The orders were given, there was nothing to do but to obey; and the uncrowned King of France was not yet out of danger. Hastings and Tony led two of the horses out of the spinney; at the roadside they mounted, and then the little lad for whose sake so much heroism, such selfless devotion had been expended, was hoisted up, still half asleep, on the pillion in front of my

Lord Hastings.

"Keep your arm round him," admonished Blakeney; "your horse looks quiet enough. But put on speed as far as Mantes, and may Heaven guard you both!"

The two men pressed their heels to their horses' flanks, the beasts snorted and pawed the ground anxious to start. There were a few whispered farewells, two loyal hands were stretched out at the last, eager to grasp the leader's hand.

Then horses and riders disappeared in the utter darkness which comes before the dawn.

Blakeney and Ffoulkes stood side by side in silence for as long as the pawing of hoofs in the mud could reach their ears, then Ffoulkes asked abruptly:

"What do you want me to do, Blakeney?"

"Well, for the present, my dear fellow, I want you to take one of the three horses we have left in the spinney, and put him into the shafts of our old friend the coal-cart; then I am afraid that you must go back the way we came."

"Yes?"

"Continue to heave coal on the canal wharf by La Villette; it is the best way to avoid attention. After your day's work keep your cart and horse in readiness against my arrival, at the same spot where you were last night. If after having waited for me like this for three consecutive nights you neither see nor hear anything from me, go back to England and tell Marguerite that in giving my life for her brother I gave it for her!"

"Blakeney—!"

"I spoke differently to what I usually do, is that it?" he interposed, placing his firm hand on his friend's shoulder. "I am degenerating, Ffoulkes—that's what it is. Pay no heed to it. I suppose that carrying that sleeping child in my arms last night softened some nerves in my body. I was so infinitely sorry for the poor mite, and vaguely wondered if I had not saved it from one misery only to plunge it in another. There was such a fateful look on that wan little face, as if destiny had already writ its veto there against happiness. It came on me then how futile were our actions, if God chooses to interpose His will between us and our desires."

Almost as he left off speaking the rain ceased to patter down against the puddles in the road. Overhead the clouds flew by at terrific speed, driven along by the blustering wind. It was less dark now, and Sir Andrew, peering through the gloom, could see his leader's face. It was singularly pale and hard, and the deep-set lazy eyes had in them just that fateful look which he himself had spoken of just now.

"You are anxious about Armand, Percy?" asked Ffoulkes softly.

"Yes. He should have trusted me, as I had trusted him. He missed me at the Villette gate on Friday, and without a thought left me—left us all in the lurch; he threw himself into the lion's jaws, thinking that he could help the girl he loved. I knew that I could save her. She is in comparative safety even now. The old woman, Madame Belhomme, had been freely released the day after her arrest, but Jeanne Lange is still in the house in the Rue de Charonne. You know it, Ffoulkes. I got her there early this morning. It was easy for me, of course: 'Hola, Dupont! my boots, Dupont!' 'One moment, citizen, my daughter—' 'Curse thy daughter, bring me my boots!' and Jeanne Lange walked out of the Temple prison her hand in that of that lout Dupont."

"But Armand does not know that she is in the Rue de Charonne?"

"No. I have not seen him since that early morning on Saturday when he came to tell me that she had been arrested. Having sworn that he would obey me, he went to meet you and Tony at La Villette, but returned to Paris a few hours later, and drew the undivided attention of all the committees on Jeanne Lange by his senseless, foolish inquiries. But for his action throughout the whole of yesterday I could have smuggled Jeanne out of Paris, got her to join you at Villette, or Hastings in St. Germain. But the barriers were being closely watched for her, and I had the Dauphin to think of. She is in comparative safety; the people in the Rue de Charonne are friendly for the moment; but for how long? Who knows? I must look after her of course. And Armand! Poor old Armand! The lion's jaws have snapped over him, and they hold him tight. Chauvelin and his gang are using him as a decoy to trap me, of course. All that had not happened if Armand had trusted me."

He sighed a quick sigh of impatience, almost of regret. Ffoulkes was the one man who could guess the bitter disappointment that this had meant. Percy had longed to be back in England soon, back to Marguerite, to a few days of unalloyed happiness and a few days of peace.

Now Armand's actions had retarded all that; they were a deliberate bar to the future as it had been mapped out by a man who foresaw everything, who was prepared for every eventuality.

In this case, too, he had been prepared, but not for the want of trust which had brought on disobedience akin to disloyalty. That absolutely unforeseen eventuality had changed Blakeney's usual irresponsible gaiety into a consciousness of the inevitable, of the inexorable decrees of Fate.

With an anxious sigh, Sir Andrew turned away from his chief and went back to the spinney to select for his own purpose one of the three horses which Hastings and Tony had unavoidably left behind.

"And you, Blakeney—how will you go back to that awful Paris?" he said, when he had made his choice and was once more back beside Percy.

"I don't know yet," replied Blakeney, "but it would not be safe to ride. I'll reach one of the gates on this side of the city and contrive to slip in somehow. I have a certificate of safety in my pocket in case I need it.

"We'll leave the horses here," he said presently, whilst he was helping Sir Andrew to put the horse in the shafts of the coal-cart; "they cannot come to much harm. Some poor devil might steal them, in order to escape from those vile brutes in the city. If so, God speed him, say I. I'll compensate my friend the farmer of St. Germain for their loss at an early opportunity. And now, good-bye, my dear fellow! Some time to-night, if possible, you shall hear direct news of me—if not, then to-morrow or the day after that. Good-bye, and Heaven guard you!"

"God guard you, Blakeney!" said Sir Andrew fervently.

He jumped into the cart and gathered up the reins. His heart was heavy as lead, and a strange mist had gathered in his eyes, blurring the last dim vision which he had of his chief standing all alone in the gloom, his broad, magnificent figure looking almost weirdly erect and defiant, his head thrown back, and his kind, lazy eyes watching the final departure of his most faithful comrade and friend.

CHAPTER XXII

Of That There Could Be No Question

Blakeney had more than one pied-a-terre in Paris, and never stayed longer than two or three days in any of these. It was not difficult for a single man, be he labourer or bourgeois, to obtain a night's lodging, even in these most troublous times, and in any quarter of Paris, provided the rent—out of all proportion to the comfort and accommodation given—was paid ungrudgingly and in advance.

Emigration and, above all, the enormous death-roll of the past eighteen months, had emptied the apartment houses of the great city, and those who had rooms to let were only too glad of a lodger, always providing they were not in danger of being worried by the committees of their section.

The laws framed by these same committees now demanded that all keepers of lodging or apartment houses should within twenty-four hours give notice at the bureau of their individual sections of the advent of new lodgers, together with a description of the personal appearance of such lodgers, and an indication of their presumed civil status and occupation. But there was a margin of twenty-four hours, which could on pressure be extended to forty-eight, and, therefore, any one could obtain shelter for forty-eight hours, and have no questions asked, provided he or she was willing to pay the exorbitant sum usually asked under the circumstances.

Thus Blakeney had no difficulty in securing what lodgings he wanted when he once more found himself inside Paris at somewhere about noon of that same Monday.

The thought of Hastings and Tony speeding on towards Mantes with the royal child safely held in Hastings' arms had kept his spirits buoyant and caused him for a while to forget the terrible peril in which Armand St. Just's thoughtless egoism had placed them both.

Blakeney was a man of abnormal physique and iron nerve, else he could never have endured the fatigues of the past twenty-four hours, from the moment when on the Sunday afternoon he began to play his part of furniture-remover at the Temple, to that when at last on Monday at noon he succeeded in persuading the sergeant at the Maillot gate that he was an honest stonemason residing at Neuilly, who was come to Paris in search of work.

After that matters became more simple. Terribly foot-sore, though he would never have admitted it, hungry and weary, he turned into an unpretentious eating-house and ordered some dinner. The place when he entered was occupied mostly by labourers and workmen, dressed very much as he was himself, and quite as grimy as he had become after having driven about for hours in a laundry-cart and in a coal-cart, and having walked twelve kilometres, some of which he had covered whilst carrying a sleeping child in his arms.

Thus, Sir Percy Blakeney, Bart., the friend and companion of the Prince of Wales, the most fastidious fop the salons of London and Bath had ever seen, was in no way distinguishable outwardly from the tattered, half-starved, dirty, and out-at-elbows products of this fraternising and equalising Republic.

He was so hungry that the ill-cooked, badly-served meal tempted him to eat; and he ate on in silence, seemingly more interested in boiled beef than in the conversation that went on around him. But he would not have been the keen and daring adventurer that he was if he did not all the while keep his ears open for any fragment of news that the desultory talk of his fellow-diners was likely to yield to him.

Politics were, of course, discussed; the tyranny of the sections, the slavery that this free Republic had brought on its citizens. The names of the chief personages of the day were all mentioned in turns Focquier-Tinville, Santerre, Danton, Robespierre. Heron and his sleuth-hounds were spoken of with execrations quickly suppressed, but of little Capet not one word.

Blakeney could not help but infer that Chauvelin, Heron and the commissaries in charge were keeping the escape of the child a secret for as long as they could.

He could hear nothing of Armand's fate, of course. The arrest—if arrest there had been—was not like to be bruited abroad just now. Blakeney having last seen Armand in Chauvelin's company, whilst he himself was moving the Simons' furniture, could not for a moment doubt that the young man was imprisoned,—unless, indeed, he was being allowed a certain measure of freedom, whilst his every step was being spied on, so that he might act as a decoy for his chief.

At thought of that all weariness seemed to vanish from Blakeney's powerful frame. He set his lips firmly together, and once again the light of irresponsible gaiety danced in his eyes.

He had been in as tight a corner as this before now; at Boulogne his beautiful Marguerite had been used as a decoy, and twenty-four hours later he had held her in his arms on board his yacht the Day-Dream. As he would have put it in his own forcible language:

"Those d—d murderers have not got me yet."

The battle mayhap would this time be against greater odds than before, but Blakeney had no fear that they would prove overwhelming.

There was in life but one odd that was overwhelming, and that was treachery.

But of that there could be no question.

In the afternoon Blakeney started off in search of lodgings for the night. He found what would suit him in the Rue de l'Arcade, which was equally far from the

House of Justice as it was from his former lodgings. Here he would be safe for at least twenty-four hours, after which he might have to shift again. But for the moment the landlord of the miserable apartment was over-willing to make no fuss and ask no questions, for the sake of the money which this aristo in disguise dispensed with a lavish hand.

Having taken possession of his new quarters and snatched a few hours of sound, well-deserved rest, until the time when the shades of evening and the darkness of the streets would make progress through the city somewhat more safe, Blakeney sallied forth at about six o'clock having a threefold object in view.

Primarily, of course, the threefold object was concentrated on Armand. There was the possibility of finding out at the young man's lodgings in Montmartre what had become of him; then there were the usual inquiries that could be made from the registers of the various prisons; and, thirdly, there was the chance that Armand had succeeded in sending some kind of message to Blakeney's former lodgings in the Rue St. Germain l'Auxerrois.

On the whole, Sir Percy decided to leave the prison registers alone for the present. If Armand had been actually arrested, he would almost certainly be confined in the Chatelet prison, where he would be closer to hand for all the interrogatories to which, no doubt, he would be subjected.

Blakeney set his teeth and murmured a good, sound, British oath when he thought of those interrogatories. Armand St. Just, highly strung, a dreamer and a bundle of nerves—how he would suffer under the mental rack of questions and cross-questions, cleverly-laid traps to catch information from him unawares!

His next objective, then, was Armand's former lodging, and from six o'clock until close upon eight Sir Percy haunted the slopes of Montmartre, and more especially the neighbourhood of the Rue de la Croix Blanche, where Armand had lodged these former days. At the house itself he could not inquire as yet; obviously it would not have been safe; tomorrow, perhaps, when he knew more, but not tonight. His keen eyes had already spied at least two figures clothed in the rags of out-of-work labourers like himself, who had hung with suspicious persistence in this same neighbourhood, and who during the two hours that he had been in observation had never strayed out of sight of the house in the Rue de la Croix Blanche.

That these were two spies on the watch was, of course, obvious; but whether they were on the watch for St. Just or for some other unfortunate wretch it was at this stage impossible to conjecture.

Then, as from the Tour des Dames close by the clock solemnly struck the hour of eight, and Blakeney prepared to wend his way back to another part of the city, he suddenly saw Armand walking slowly up the street.

The young man did not look either to right or left; he held his head forward on his chest, and his hands were hidden underneath his cloak. When he passed immediately under one of the street lamps Blakeney caught sight of his face; it was pale and drawn. Then he turned his head, and for the space of two seconds his eyes across the narrow street encountered those of his chief. He had the presence of mind not to make a sign or to utter a sound; he was obviously being followed, but in that brief moment Sir Percy had seen in the young man's eyes a look that reminded him of a hunted creature.

"What have those brutes been up to with him, I wonder?" he muttered between clenched teeth.

Armand soon disappeared under the doorway of the same house where he had been lodging all along. Even as he did so Blakeney saw the two spies gather together like a pair of slimy lizards, and whisper excitedly one to another. A third man, who obviously had been dogging Armand's footsteps, came up and joined them after a while.

Blakeney could have sworn loudly and lustily, had it been possible to do so without attracting attention. The whole of Armand's history in the past twenty-four hours was perfectly clear to him. The young man had been made free that he might prove a decoy for more important game.

His every step was being watched, and he still thought Jeanne Lange in immediate danger of death. The look of despair in his face proclaimed these two facts, and Blakeney's heart ached for the mental torture which his friend was enduring. He longed to let Armand know that the woman he loved was in comparative safety.

Jeanne Lange first, and then Armand himself; and the odds would be very heavy against the Scarlet Pimpernel! But that Marguerite should not have to mourn an only brother, of that Sir Percy made oath.

He now turned his steps towards his own former lodgings by St. Germain l'Auxerrois. It was just possible that Armand had succeeded in leaving a message there for him. It was, of course, equally possible that when he did so Heron's men had watched his movements, and that spies would be stationed there, too, on the watch.

But that risk must, of course, be run. Blakeney's former lodging was the one place that Armand would know of to which he could send a message to his chief, if he wanted to do so. Of course, the unfortunate young man could not have known until just now that Percy would come back to Paris, but he might guess it, or wish it, or only vaguely hope for it; he might want to send a message, he might long to communicate with his brother-in-law, and, perhaps, feel sure that the latter would not leave him in the lurch.

With that thought in his mind, Sir Percy was not likely to give up the attempt to ascertain for himself whether Armand had tried to communicate with him or not. As for spies—well, he had dodged some of them often enough in his time—the risks that he ran to-night were no worse than the ones to which he had so successfully run counter in the Temple yesterday.

Still keeping up the slouchy gait peculiar to the out-at-elbows working man of the day, hugging the houses as he walked along the streets, Blakeney made slow progress across the city. But at last he reached the facade of St. Germain l'Auxerrois, and turning sharply to his right he soon came in sight of the house which he had only quitted twenty-four hours ago.

We all know that house—all of us who are familiar with the Paris of those terrible days. It stands quite detached—a vast quadrangle, facing the Quai de l'Ecole and the river, backing on the Rue St. Germain l'Auxerrois, and shouldering the Carrefour des Trois Manes. The porte-cochere, so-called, is but a narrow doorway, and is actually situated in the Rue St. Germain l'Auxerrois.

Blakeney made his way cautiously right round the house; he peered up and down the quay, and his keen eyes tried to pierce the dense gloom that hung at the corners of the Pont Neuf immediately opposite. Soon he assured himself that for the present, at any rate, the house was not being watched.

Armand presumably had not yet left a message for him here; but he might do so at any time now that he knew that his chief was in Paris and on the look-out for him.

Blakeney made up his mind to keep this house in sight. This art of watching he had acquired to a masterly extent, and could have taught Heron's watch-dogs a remarkable lesson in it. At night, of course, it was a comparatively easy task. There were a good many unlighted doorways along the quay, whilst a street lamp was fixed on a bracket in the wall of the very house which he kept in observation.

Finding temporary shelter under various doorways, or against the dank walls of the houses, Blakeney set himself resolutely to a few hours' weary waiting. A thin, drizzly rain fell with unpleasant persistence, like a damp mist, and the thin blouse which he wore soon became wet through and clung hard and chilly to his shoulders.

It was close on midnight when at last he thought it best to give up his watch and to go back to his lodgings for a few hours' sleep; but at seven o'clock the next morning he was back again at his post.

The porte-cochere of his former lodging-house was not yet open; he took up his stand close beside it. His woollen cap pulled well over his forehead, the grime cleverly plastered on his hair and face, his lower jaw thrust forward, his eyes looking lifeless and bleary, all gave him an expression of sly villainy, whilst the short clay pipe struck at a sharp angle in his mouth, his hands thrust into the pockets of his ragged breeches, and his bare feet in the mud of the road, gave the final touch to his representation of an out-of-work, ill-conditioned, and supremely discontented loafer.

He had not very long to wait. Soon the porte-cochere of the house was opened, and the concierge came out with his broom, making a show of cleaning the pavement in front of the door. Five minutes later a lad, whose clothes consisted entirely of rags, and whose feet and head were bare, came rapidly up the street from the quay, and walked along looking at the houses as he went, as if trying to decipher their number. The cold grey dawn was just breaking, dreary and damp, as all the past days had been. Blakeney watched the lad as he approached, the small, naked feet falling noiselessly on the cobblestones of the road. When the boy was quite close to him and to the house, Blakeney shifted his position and took the pipe out of his mouth.

"Up early, my son!" he said gruffly.

"Yes," said the pale-faced little creature; "I have a message to deliver at No. 9 Rue St. Germain l'Auxerrois. It must be somewhere near here."

"It is. You can give me the message."

"Oh, no, citizen!" said the lad, into whose pale, circled eyes a look of terror had quickly appeared. "It is for one of the lodgers in No. 9. I must give it to him."

With an instinct which he somehow felt could not err at this moment, Blakeney knew that the message was one from Armand to himself; a written message, too, since—instinctively when he spoke—the boy clutched at his thin shirt, as if trying to guard something precious that had been entrusted to him.

"I will deliver the message myself, sonny," said Blakeney gruffly. "I know the citizen for whom it is intended. He would not like the concierge to see it."

"Oh! I would not give it to the concierge," said the boy. "I would take it upstairs myself."

"My son," retorted Blakeney, "let me tell you this. You are going to give that message up to me and I will put five whole livres into your hand."

Blakeney, with all his sympathy aroused for this poor pale-faced lad, put on the airs of a ruffianly bully. He did not wish that message to be taken indoors by the lad, for the concierge might get hold of it, despite the boy's protests and tears, and after that Blakeney would perforce have to disclose himself before it would be given up to him. During the past week the concierge had been very amenable to bribery. Whatever suspicions he had had about his lodger he had kept to himself for the sake of the money which he received; but it was impossible to gauge any man's trend of thought these days from one hour to the next. Something—for aught Blakeney knew—might have occurred in the past twenty-four hours to change an amiable and accommodating lodging-house keeper into a surly or dangerous spy.

Fortunately, the concierge had once more gone within; there was no one abroad, and if there were, no one probably would take any notice of a burly ruffian brow-beating a child.

"Allons!" he said gruffly, "give me the letter, or that five livres goes back into my pocket."

"Five livres!" exclaimed the child with pathetic eagerness. "Oh, citizen!"

The thin little hand fumbled under the rags, but it reappeared again empty, whilst a faint blush spread over the hollow cheeks.

"The other citizen also gave me five livres," he said humbly. "He lodges in the house where my mother is concierge. It is in the Rue de la Croix Blanche. He has been very kind to my mother. I would rather do as he bade me."

"Bless the lad," murmured Blakeney under his breath; "his loyalty redeems many a crime of this God-forsaken city. Now I suppose I shall have to bully him, after all."

He took his hand out of his breeches pocket; between two very dirty fingers he held a piece of gold. The other hand he placed quite roughly on the lad's chest.

"Give me the letter," he said harshly, "or—"

He pulled at the ragged blouse, and a scrap of soiled paper soon fell into his hand. The lad began to cry.

"Here," said Blakeney, thrusting the piece of gold into the thin small palm, "take this home to your mother, and tell your lodger that a big, rough man took the letter away from you by force. Now run, before I kick you out of the way."

The lad, terrified out of his poor wits, did not wait for further commands; he took to his heels and ran, his small hand clutching the piece of gold. Soon he had disappeared round the corner of the street.

Blakeney did not at once read the paper; he thrust it quickly into his breeches pocket and slouched away slowly down the street, and thence across the Place du Carrousel, in the direction of his new lodgings in the Rue de l'Arcade.

It was only when he found himself alone in the narrow, squalid room which he was occupying that he took the scrap of paper from his pocket and read it slowly through. It said:

Percy, you cannot forgive me, nor can I ever forgive myself, but if you only knew what I have suffered for the past two days you would, I think, try and forgive. I am free and yet a prisoner; my every footstep is dogged. What they ultimately mean to do with me I do not know. And when I think of Jeanne I long for the power to end mine own miserable existence. Percy! she is still in the hands of those fiends.... I saw the prison register; her name written there has been like a burning brand on my heart ever since. She was still in prison the day that you left Paris; to-morrow, to-night mayhap, they will try her, condemn her, torture her, and I dare not go to see you, for I would only be bringing spies to your door. But will you come to me, Percy? It should be safe in the hours of the night, and the concierge is devoted to me. To-night at ten o'clock she will leave the porte-cochere unlatched. If you find it so, and if on the ledge of the window immediately on your left as you enter you find a candle alight, and beside it a scrap of paper with your initials S. P. traced on it, then it will be quite safe for you to come up to my room. It is on the second landing—a door on your right—that too I will leave on the latch. But in the name of the woman you love best in all the world come at once to me then, and bear in mind, Percy, that the woman I love is threatened with immediate death, and that I am powerless to save her. Indeed, believe me, I would gladly die even now but for the thought of Jeanne, whom I should be leaving in the hands of those fiends. For God's sake, Percy, remember that Jeanne is all the world to me.

"Poor old Armand," murmured Blakeney with a kindly smile directed at the absent friend, "he won't trust me even now. He won't trust his Jeanne in my hands. Well," he added after a while, "after all, I would not entrust Marguerite to anybody else either."

CHAPTER XXIII

The Overwhelming Odds

At half-past ten that same evening, Blakeney, still clad in a workman's tattered clothes, his feet bare so that he could tread the streets unheard, turned into the Rue de la Croix Blanche.

The porte-cochere of the house where Armand lodged had been left on the latch; not a soul was in sight. Peering cautiously round, he slipped into the house. On the ledge of the window, immediately on his left when he entered, a candle was left burning, and beside it there was a scrap of paper with the initials S. P. roughly traced in pencil. No one challenged him as he noiselessly glided past it, and up the narrow stairs that led to the upper floor. Here, too, on the second landing the door on the right had been left on the latch. He pushed it open and entered.

As is usual even in the meanest lodgings in Paris houses, a small antechamber gave between the front door and the main room. When Percy entered the antechamber was unlighted, but the door into the inner room beyond was ajar. Blakeney approached it with noiseless tread, and gently pushed it open.

That very instant he knew that the game was up; he heard the footsteps closing up behind him, saw Armand, deathly pale, leaning against the wall in the room in front of him, and Chauvelin and Heron standing guard over him.

The next moment the room and the antechamber were literally alive with soldiers—twenty of them to arrest one man.

It was characteristic of that man that when hands were laid on him from every side he threw back his head and laughed—laughed mirthfully, light-heartedly, and the first words that escaped his lips were:

"Well, I am d—d!"

"The odds are against you, Sir Percy," said Chauvelin to him in English, whilst Heron at the further end of the room was growling like a contented beast.

"By the Lord, sir," said Percy with perfect sang-froid, "I do believe that for the moment they are."

"Have done, my men—have done!" he added, turning good-humouredly to the soldiers round him. "I never fight against overwhelming odds. Twenty to one, eh? I could lay four of you out easily enough, perhaps even six, but what then?"

But a kind of savage lust seemed to have rendered these men temporarily mad, and they were being egged on by Heron. The mysterious Englishman, about whom so many eerie tales were told! Well, he had supernatural powers, and twenty to one might be nothing to him if the devil was on his side. Therefore a blow on his forearm with the butt-end of a bayonet was useful for disabling his right hand, and soon the left arm with a dislocated shoulder hung limp by his side. Then he was bound with cords.

The vein of luck had given out. The gambler had staked more than usual and had lost; but he knew how to lose, just as he had always known how to win.

"Those d—d brutes are trussing me like a fowl," he murmured with irrepressible gaiety at the last.

Then the wrench on his bruised arms as they were pulled roughly back by the cords caused the veil of unconsciousness to gather over his eyes.

"And Jeanne was safe, Armand," he shouted with a last desperate effort; "those devils have lied to you and tricked you into this ... Since yesterday she is out of prison... in the house... you know...."

After that he lost consciousness.

And this occurred on Tuesday, January 21st, in the year 1794, or, in accordance with the new calendar, on the 2nd Pluviose, year II of the Republic.

It is chronicled in the Moniteur of the 3rd Pluviose that, "on the previous evening, at half-past ten of the clock, the Englishman known as the Scarlet Pimpernel, who for three years has conspired against the safety of the Republic, was arrested through the patriotic exertions of citizen Chauvelin, and conveyed to the Conciergerie, where he now lies—sick, but closely guarded. Long live the Republic!"

PART II.

CHAPTER XXIV

The News

The grey January day was falling, drowsy, and dull into the arms of night.

Marguerite, sitting in the dusk beside the fire in her small boudoir, shivered a little as she drew her scarf closer round her shoulders.

Edwards, the butler, entered with the lamp. The room looked peculiarly cheery now, with the delicate white panelling of the wall glowing under the soft kiss of the flickering firelight and the steadier glow of the rose-shaded lamp.

"Has the courier not arrived yet, Edwards?" asked Marguerite, fixing the impassive face of the well-drilled servant with her large purple-rimmed eyes.

"Not yet, m'lady," he replied placidly.

"It is his day, is it not?"

"Yes, m'lady. And the forenoon is his time. But there have been heavy rains, and the roads must be rare muddy. He must have been delayed, m'lady."

"Yes, I suppose so," she said listlessly. "That will do, Edwards. No, don't close the shutters. I'll ring presently."

The man went out of the room as automatically as he had come. He closed the door behind him, and Marguerite was once more alone.

She picked up the book which she had fingered idly before the light gave out. She tried once more to fix her attention on this tale of love and adventure written by Mr. Fielding; but she had lost the thread of the story, and there was a mist between her eyes and the printed pages.

With an impatient gesture she threw down the book and passed her hand across her eyes, then seemed astonished to find that her hand was wet.

She rose and went to the window. The air outside had been singularly mild all day; the thaw was persisting, and a south wind came across the Channel—from France.

Marguerite threw open the casement and sat down on the wide sill, leaning her head against the window-frame, and gazing out into the fast gathering gloom. From far away, at the foot of the gently sloping lawns, the river murmured softly in the night; in the borders to the right and left a few snowdrops still showed like tiny white specks through the surrounding darkness. Winter had begun the process of slowly shedding its mantle, coquetting with Spring, who still lingered in the land of Infinity. Gradually the shadows drew closer and closer; the reeds and rushes on the river bank were the first to sink into their embrace, then the big cedars on the lawn, majestic and defiant, but yielding still unconquered to the power of night.

The tiny stars of snowdrop blossoms vanished one by one, and at last the cool, grey ribbon of the river surface was wrapped under the mantle of evening.

Only the south wind lingered on, soughing gently in the drowsy reeds, whispering among the branches of the cedars, and gently stirring the tender corollas of the sleeping snowdrops.

Marguerite seemed to open out her lungs to its breath. It had come all the way from France, and on its wings had brought something of Percy—a murmur as if he had spoken—a memory that was as intangible as a dream.

She shivered again, though of a truth it was not cold. The courier's delay had completely unsettled her nerves. Twice a week he came especially from Dover, and always he brought some message, some token which Percy had contrived to send from Paris. They were like tiny scraps of dry bread thrown to a starving woman, but they did just help to keep her heart alive—that poor, aching, disappointed heart that so longed for enduring happiness which it could never get.

The man whom she loved with all her soul, her mind and her body, did not belong to her; he belonged to suffering humanity over there in terror-stricken France, where the cries of the innocent, the persecuted, the wretched called louder to him than she in her love could do.

He had been away three months now, during which time her starving heart had fed on its memories, and the happiness of a brief visit from him six weeks ago, when—quite unexpectedly—he had appeared before her... home between two desperate adventures that had given life and freedom to a number of innocent people, and nearly cost him his—and she had lain in his arms in a swoon of perfect happiness.

But he had gone away again as suddenly as he had come, and for six weeks now she had lived partly in anticipation of the courier with messages from him, and partly on the fitful joy engendered by these messages. To-day she had not even that, and the disappointment seemed just now more than she could bear.

She felt unaccountably restless, and could she but have analysed her feelings—had she dared so to do—she would have realised that the weight which oppressed her heart so that she could hardly breathe, was one of vague yet dark foreboding.

She closed the window and returned to her seat by the fire, taking up her hook with the strong resolution not to allow her nerves to get the better of her. But it was difficult to pin one's attention down to the adventures of Master Tom Jones when one's mind was fully engrossed with those of Sir Percy Blakeney.

The sound of carriage wheels on the gravelled forecourt in the front of the house suddenly awakened her drowsy senses. She threw down the book, and with trembling hands clutched the arms of her chair, straining her ears to listen. A carriage at this hour—and on this damp winter's evening! She racked her mind wondering who it could be.

Lady Ffoulkes was in London, she knew. Sir Andrew, of course, was in Paris. His Royal Highness, ever a faithful visitor, would surely not venture out to Richmond in this inclement weather—and the courier always came on horseback.

There was a murmur of voices; that of Edwards, mechanical and placid, could be heard quite distinctly saying:

"I'm sure that her ladyship will be at home for you, m'lady. But I'll go and ascertain."

Marguerite ran to the door and with joyful eagerness tore it open.

"Suzanne!" she called "my little Suzanne! I thought you were in London. Come up quickly! In the boudoir—yes. Oh! what good fortune hath brought you?"

Suzanne flew into her arms, holding the friend whom she loved so well close and closer to her heart, trying to hide her face, which was wet with tears, in the folds of Marguerite's kerchief.

"Come inside, my darling," said Marguerite. "Why, how cold your little hands are!"

She was on the point of turning back to her boudoir, drawing Lady Ffoulkes by the hand, when suddenly she caught sight of Sir Andrew, who stood at a little distance from her, at the top of the stairs.

"Sir Andrew!" she exclaimed with unstinted gladness.

Then she paused. The cry of welcome died on her lips, leaving them dry and parted. She suddenly felt as if some fearful talons had gripped her heart and were tearing at it with sharp, long nails; the blood flew from her cheeks and from her limbs, leaving her with a sense of icy numbness.

She backed into the room, still holding Suzanne's hand, and drawing her in with her. Sir Andrew followed them, then closed the door behind him. At last the word escaped Marguerite's parched lips:

"Percy! Something has happened to him! He is dead?"

"No, no!" exclaimed Sir Andrew quickly.

Suzanne put her loving arms round her friend and drew her down into the chair by the fire. She knelt at her feet on the hearthrug, and pressed her own burning lips on Marguerite's icy-cold hands. Sir Andrew stood silently by, a world of loving friendship, of heart-broken sorrow, in his eyes.

There was silence in the pretty white-panelled room for a while. Marguerite sat with her eyes closed, bringing the whole armoury of her will power to bear her up outwardly now.

"Tell me!" she said at last, and her voice was toneless and dull, like one that came from the depths of a grave—"tell me—exactly—everything. Don't be afraid. I can bear it. Don't be afraid."

Sir Andrew remained standing, with bowed head and one hand resting on the table. In a firm, clear voice he told her the events of the past few days as they were known to him. All that he tried to hide was Armand's disobedience, which, in his heart, he felt was the primary cause of the catastrophe. He told of the rescue of the Dauphin from the Temple, the midnight drive in the coal-cart, the meeting with Hastings and Tony in the spinney. He only gave vague explanations of Armand's stay in Paris which caused Percy to go back to the city, even at the moment when his most daring plan had been so successfully carried through.

"Armand, I understand, has fallen in love with a beautiful woman in Paris, Lady Blakeney," he said, seeing that a strange, puzzled look had appeared in Marguerite's pale face. "She was arrested the day before the rescue of the Dauphin from the Temple. Armand could not join us. He felt that he could not leave her. I am sure that you will understand."

Then as she made no comment, he resumed his narrative:

"I had been ordered to go back to La Villette, and there to resume my duties as a labourer in the day-time, and to wait for Percy during the night. The fact that I had received no message from him for two days had made me somewhat worried, but I have such faith in him, such belief in his good luck and his ingenuity, that I would not allow myself to be really anxious. Then on the third day I heard the news."

"What news?" asked Marguerite mechanically.

"That the Englishman who was known as the Scarlet Pimpernel had been captured in a house in the Rue de la Croix Blanche, and had been imprisoned in the Conciergerie."

"The Rue de la Croix Blanche? Where is that?"

"In the Montmartre quarter. Armand lodged there. Percy, I imagine, was working to get him away; and those brutes captured him."

"Having heard the news, Sir Andrew, what did you do?"

"I went into Paris and ascertained its truth."

"And there is no doubt of it?"

"Alas, none! I went to the house in the Rue de la Croix Blanche. Armand had disappeared. I succeeded in inducing the concierge to talk. She seems to have been devoted to her lodger. Amidst tears she told me some of the details of the capture. Can you bear to hear them, Lady Blakeney?"

"Yes—tell me everything—don't be afraid," she reiterated with the same dull monotony.

"It appears that early on the Tuesday morning the son of the concierge—a lad about fifteen—was sent off by her lodger with a message to No. 9 Rue St. Germain l'Auxerrois. That was the house where Percy was staying all last week, where he kept disguises and so on for us all, and where some of our meetings were held. Percy evidently expected that Armand would try and communicate with him at that address, for when the lad arrived in front of the house he was accosted—so he says—by a big, rough workman, who browbeat him into giving up the lodger's letter, and finally pressed a piece of gold into his hand. The workman was Blakeney, of course. I imagine that Armand, at the time that he wrote the letter, must have been under the belief that Mademoiselle Lange was still in prison; he could not know then that Blakeney had already got her into comparative safety. In the letter he must have spoken of the terrible plight in which he stood, and also of his fears for the woman whom he loved. Percy was not the man to leave a comrade in the lurch! He would not be the man whom we all love and admire, whose word we all obey, for whose sake we would gladly all of us give our life—he would not be that man if he did not brave even certain dangers in order to be of help to those who call on him. Armand called and Percy went to him. He must have known that Armand was being spied upon, for Armand, alas! was already a marked man, and the watch-dogs of those infernal committees were already on his heels. Whether these sleuth-hounds had followed the son of the concierge and seen him give the letter to the workman in the Rue St. Germain l'Auxerrois, or whether the concierge in the Rue de la Croix Blanche was nothing but a spy of Heron's, or, again whether the Committee of General Security kept a company of soldiers in constant alert in that house, we shall, of course, never know. All that I do know is that Percy entered that fatal house at half-past ten, and that a quarter of an hour later the concierge saw some of the soldiers descending the stairs, carrying a heavy burden. She peeped out of her lodge, and by the light in the corridor she saw that the heavy burden was the body of a man bound closely with ropes: his eyes were closed, his clothes were stained with blood. He was seemingly unconscious. The next day the official organ of the Government proclaimed the capture of the Scarlet Pimpernel, and there was a public holiday in honour of the event."

Marguerite had listened to this terrible narrative dry-eyed and silent. Now she still sat there, hardly conscious of what went on around her—of Suzanne's tears, that fell unceasingly upon her fingers—of Sir Andrew, who had sunk into a chair, and buried his head in his hands. She was hardly conscious that she lived; the universe seemed to have stood still before this awful, monstrous cataclysm.

But, nevertheless, she was the first to return to the active realities of the present.

"Sir Andrew," she said after a while, "tell me, where are my Lords Tony and Hastings?"

"At Calais, madam," he replied. "I saw them there on my way hither. They had delivered the Dauphin safely into the hands of his adherents at Mantes, and were awaiting Blakeney's further orders, as he had commanded them to do."

"Will they wait for us there, think you?"

"For us, Lady Blakeney?" he exclaimed in puzzlement.

"Yes, for us, Sir Andrew," she replied, whilst the ghost of a smile flitted across her drawn face; "you had thought of accompanying me to Paris, had you not?"

"But Lady Blakeney—"

"Ah! I know what you would say, Sir Andrew. You will speak of dangers, of risks, of death, mayhap; you will tell me that I as a woman can do nothing to help my husband—that I could be but a hindrance to him, just as I was in Boulogne. But everything is so different now. Whilst those brutes planned his capture he was clever enough to outwit them, but now they have actually got him, think you they'll let him escape? They'll watch him night and day, my friend, just as they watched the unfortunate Queen; but they'll not keep him months, weeks, or even days in prison—even Chauvelin now will no longer attempt to play with the Scarlet Pimpernel. They have him, and they will hold him until such time as they take him to the guillotine."

Her voice broke in a sob; her self-control was threatening to leave her. She was but a woman, young and passionately in love with the man who was about to die an ignominious death, far away from his country, his kindred, his friends.

"I cannot let him die alone, Sir Andrew; he will be longing for me, and—and, after all, there is you, and my Lord Tony, and Lord Hastings and the others; surely—surely we are not going to let him die, not like that, and not alone."

"You are right, Lady Blakeney," said Sir Andrew earnestly; "we are not going to let him die, if human agency can do aught to save him. Already Tony, Hastings and I have agreed to return to Paris. There are one or two hidden places in and around the city known only to Percy and to the members of the League where he must find one or more of us if he succeeds in getting away. All the way between Paris and Calais we have places of refuge, places where any of us can hide at a given moment; where we can find disguises when we want them, or horses in an emergency. No! no! we are not going to despair, Lady Blakeney; there are nineteen of us prepared to lay down our lives for the Scarlet Pimpernel. Already I, as his lieutenant, have been selected as the leader of as determined a gang as has ever entered on a work of rescue before. We leave for Paris to-morrow, and if human pluck and devotion can destroy mountains then we'll destroy them. Our watchword is: 'God save the Scarlet Pimpernel.'"

He knelt beside her chair and kissed the cold fingers which, with a sad little smile, she held out to him.

"And God bless you all!" she murmured.

Suzanne had risen to her feet when her husband knelt; now he stood up beside her. The dainty young woman hardly more than a child—was doing her best to restrain her tears.

"See how selfish I am," said Marguerite. "I talk calmly of taking your husband from you, when I myself know the bitterness of such partings."

"My husband will go where his duty calls him," said Suzanne with charming and simple dignity. "I love him with all my heart, because he is brave and good. He could not leave his comrade, who is also his chief, in the lurch. God will protect him, I know. I would not ask him to play the part of a coward."

Her brown eyes glowed with pride. She was the true wife of a soldier, and with all her dainty ways and childlike manners she was a splendid woman and a staunch friend. Sir Percy Blakeney bad saved her entire family from death, the Comte and Comtesse de Tournai, the Vicomte, her brother, and she herself all owed their lives to the Scarlet Pimpernel.

This she was not like to forget.

"There is but little danger for us, I fear me," said Sir Andrew lightly; "the revolutionary Government only wants to strike at a head, it cares nothing for the limbs. Perhaps it feels that without our leader we are enemies not worthy of persecution. If there are any dangers, so much the better," he added; "but I don't anticipate any, unless we succeed in freeing our chief; and having freed him, we fear nothing more."

"The same applies to me, Sir Andrew," rejoined Marguerite earnestly. "Now that they have captured Percy, those human fiends will care naught for me. If you succeed in freeing Percy I, like you, will have nothing more to fear, and if you fail—"

She paused and put her small, white hand on Sir Andrew's arm.

"Take me with you, Sir Andrew," she entreated; "do not condemn me to the awful torture of weary waiting, day after day, wondering, guessing, never daring to hope, lest hope deferred be more hard to bear than dreary hopelessness."

Then as Sir Andrew, very undecided, yet half inclined to yield, stood silent and irresolute, she pressed her point, gently but firmly insistent.

"I would not be in the way, Sir Andrew; I would know how to efface myself so as not to interfere with your plans. But, oh!" she added, while a quivering note of passion trembled in her voice, "can't you see that I must breathe the air that he breathes else I shall stifle or mayhap go mad?"

Sir Andrew turned to his wife, a mute query in his eyes.

"You would do an inhuman and a cruel act," said Suzanne with seriousness that sat quaintly on her baby face, "if you did not afford your protection to Marguerite, for I do believe that if you did not take her with you to-morrow she would go to Paris alone."

Marguerite thanked her friend with her eyes. Suzanne was a child in nature, but she had a woman's heart. She loved her husband, and, therefore, knew and understood what Marguerite must be suffering now.

Sir Andrew no longer could resist the unfortunate woman's earnest pleading. Frankly, he thought that if she remained in England while Percy was in such deadly peril she ran the grave risk of losing her reason before the terrible strain of suspense. He knew her to be a woman of courage, and one capable of great physical endurance; and really he was quite honest when he said that he did not believe there would be much danger for the headless League of the Scarlet Pimpernel unless they succeeded in freeing their chief. And if they did succeed, then indeed there would be nothing to fear, for the brave and loving wife who, like every true woman does, and has done in like circumstances since the beginning of time, was only demanding with passionate insistence the right to share the fate, good or ill, of the man whom she loved.

CHAPTER XXV

Paris Once More

Sir Andrew had just come in. He was trying to get a little warmth into his half-frozen limbs, for the cold had set in again, and this time with renewed vigour, and Marguerite was pouring out a cup of hot coffee which she had been brewing for him. She had not asked for news. She knew that he had none to give her, else he had not worn that wearied, despondent look in his kind face.

"I'll just try one more place this evening," he said as soon as he had swallowed some of the hot coffee—"a restaurant in the Rue de la Harpe; the members of the Cordeliers' Club often go there for supper, and they are usually well informed. I might glean something definite there."

"It seems very strange that they are so slow in bringing him to trial," said Marguerite in that dull, toneless voice which had become habitual to her. "When you first brought me the awful news that... I made sure that they would bring him to trial at once, and was in terror lest we arrived here too late to—to see him."

She checked herself quickly, bravely trying to still the quiver of her voice.

"And of Armand?" she asked.

He shook his head sadly.

"With regard to him I am at a still greater loss," he said: "I cannot find his name on any of the prison registers, and I know that he is not in the Conciergerie. They have cleared out all the prisoners from there; there is only Percy—"

"Poor Armand!" she sighed; "it must be almost worse for him than for any of us; it was his first act of thoughtless disobedience that brought all this misery upon our heads."

She spoke sadly but quietly. Sir Andrew noted that there was no bitterness in her tone. But her very quietude was heart-breaking; there was such an infinity of despair in the calm of her eyes.

"Well! though we cannot understand it all, Lady Blakeney," he said with forced cheerfulness, "we must remember one thing—that whilst there is life there is hope."

"Hope!" she exclaimed with a world of pathos in her sigh, her large eyes dry and circled, fixed with indescribable sorrow on her friend's face.

Ffoulkes turned his head away, pretending to busy himself with the coffee-making utensils. He could not bear to see that look of hopelessness in her face, for in his heart he could not find the wherewithal to cheer her. Despair was beginning to seize on him too, and this he would not let her see.

They had been in Paris three days now, and it was six days since Blakeney had been arrested. Sir Andrew and Marguerite had found temporary lodgings inside Paris, Tony and Hastings were just outside the gates, and all along the route between Paris and Calais, at St. Germain, at Mantes, in the villages between Beauvais and Amiens, wherever money could obtain friendly help, members of the devoted League of the Scarlet Pimpernel lay in hiding, waiting to aid their chief.

Ffoulkes had ascertained that Percy was kept a close prisoner in the Conciergerie, in the very rooms occupied by Marie Antoinette during the last months of her life. He left poor Marguerite to guess how closely that elusive Scarlet Pimpernel was being guarded, the precautions surrounding him being even more minute than those which bad made the unfortunate Queen's closing days a martyrdom for her.

But of Armand he could glean no satisfactory news, only the negative probability that he was not detained in any of the larger prisons of Paris, as no register which he, Ffoulkes, so laboriously consulted bore record of the name of St. Just.

Haunting the restaurants and drinking booths where the most advanced Jacobins and Terrorists were wont to meet, he had learned one or two details of Blakeney's incarceration which he could not possibly impart to Marguerite. The capture of the mysterious Englishman known as the Scarlet Pimpernel had created a great deal of popular satisfaction; but it was obvious that not only was the public mind not allowed to associate that capture with the escape of little Capet from the Temple, but it soon became clear to Ffoulkes that the news of that escape was still being kept a profound secret.

On one occasion he had succeeded in spying on the Chief Agent of the Committee of General Security, whom he knew by sight, while the latter was sitting at dinner in the company of a stout, florid man with pock-marked face and podgy hands covered with rings.

Sir Andrew marvelled who this man might be. Heron spoke to him in ambiguous phrases that would have been unintelligible to any one who did not know the circumstances of the Dauphin's escape and the part that the League of the Scarlet Pimpernel had played in it. But to Sir Andrew Ffoulkes, who—cleverly disguised as a farrier, grimy after his day's work—was straining his ears to listen whilst apparently consuming huge slabs of boiled beef, it soon became clear that the chief agent and his fat friend were talking of the Dauphin and of Blakeney.

"He won't hold out much longer, citizen," the chief agent was saying in a confident voice; "our men are absolutely unremitting in their task. Two of them watch him night and day; they look after him well, and practically never lose sight of him, but the moment he tries to get any sleep one of them rushes into the cell with a loud banging of bayonet and sabre, and noisy tread on the flagstones, and shouts at the top of his voice: 'Now then, aristo, where's the brat? Tell us now, and you shall be down and go to sleep.' I have done it myself all through one day just for the pleasure of it. It's a little tiring for you to have to shout a good deal now, and sometimes give the cursed Englishman a good shake-up. He has had five days of it, and not one wink of sleep during that time—not one single minute of rest—and he only gets enough food to keep him alive. I tell you he can't last. Citizen Chauvelin had a splendid idea there. It will all come right in a day or two."

"H'm!" grunted the other sulkily; "those Englishmen are tough."

"Yes!" retorted Heron with a grim laugh and a leer of savagery that made his gaunt face look positively hideous—"you would have given out after three days, friend de Batz, would you not? And I warned you, didn't I? I told you if you tampered with the brat I would make you cry in mercy to me for death."

"And I warned you," said the other imperturbably, "not to worry so much about me, but to keep your eyes open for those cursed Englishmen."

"I am keeping my eyes open for you, nevertheless, my friend. If I thought you knew where the vermin's spawn was at this moment I would—"

"You would put me on the same rack that you or your precious friend, Chauvelin, have devised for the Englishman. But I don't know where the lad is. If I did I would not be in Paris."

"I know that," assented Heron with a sneer; "you would soon be after the reward—over in Austria, what?—but I have your movements tracked day and night, my friend. I dare say you are as anxious as we are as to the whereabouts of the child. Had he been taken over the frontier you would have been the first to hear of it, eh? No," he added confidently, and as if anxious to reassure himself, "my firm belief is that the original idea of these confounded Englishmen was to try and get the child over to England, and that they alone know where he is. I tell you it won't be many days before that very withered Scarlet Pimpernel will order his followers to give little Capet up to us. Oh! they are hanging about Paris some of them, I know that; citizen Chauvelin is convinced that the wife isn't very far away. Give her a sight of her husband now, say I, and she'll make the others give the child up soon enough."

The man laughed like some hyena gloating over its prey. Sir Andrew nearly betrayed himself then. He had to dig his nails into his own flesh to prevent himself from springing then and there at the throat of that wretch whose monstrous ingenuity had invented torture for the fallen enemy far worse than any that the cruelties of medieval Inquisitions had devised.

So they would not let him sleep! A simple idea born in the brain of a fiend. Heron had spoken of Chauvelin as the originator of the devilry; a man weakened deliberately day by day by insufficient food, and the horrible process of denying him rest. It seemed inconceivable that human, sentient beings should have thought of such a thing. Perspiration stood up in beads on Sir Andrew's brow when he thought of his friend, brought down by want of sleep to—what? His physique was splendidly powerful, but could it stand against such racking torment for long? And the clear, the alert mind, the scheming brain, the reckless daring—how soon would these become enfeebled by the slow, steady torture of an utter want of rest?

Ffoulkes had to smother a cry of horror, which surely must have drawn the attention of that fiend on himself had he not been so engrossed in the enjoyment of his own devilry. As it is, he ran out of the stuffy eating-house, for he felt as if its fetid air must choke him.

For an hour after that he wandered about the streets, not daring to face Marguerite, lest his eyes betrayed some of the horror which was shaking his very soul.

That was twenty-four hours ago. To-day he had learnt little else. It was generally known that the Englishman was in the Conciergerie prison, that he was being closely watched, and that his trial would come on within the next few days; but no one seemed to know exactly when. The public was getting restive, demanding that trial and execution to which every one seemed to look forward as to a holiday. In the meanwhile the escape of the Dauphin had been kept from the knowledge of the public; Heron and his gang, fearing for their lives, had still hopes of extracting from the Englishman the secret of the lad's hiding-place, and the means they employed for arriving at this end was worthy of Lucifer and his host of devils in hell.

From other fragments of conversation which Sir Andrew Ffoulkes had gleaned that same evening, it seemed to him that in order to hide their defalcations Heron and the four commissaries in charge of little Capet had substituted a deaf and dumb child for the escaped little prisoner. This miserable small wreck of humanity was reputed to be sick and kept in a darkened room, in bed, and was in that condition exhibited to any member of the Convention who had the right to see him. A partition had been very hastily erected in the inner room once occupied by the Simons, and the child was kept behind that partition, and no one was allowed to come too near to him. Thus the fraud was succeeding fairly well. Heron and his accomplices only cared to save their skins, and the wretched little substitute being really ill, they firmly hoped that he would soon die, when no doubt they would bruit abroad the news of the death of Capet, which would relieve them of further responsibility.

That such ideas, such thoughts, such schemes should have engendered in human minds it is almost impossible to conceive, and yet we know from no less important a witness than Madame Simon herself that the child who died in the Temple a few weeks later was a poor little imbecile, a deaf and dumb child brought hither from one of the asylums and left to die in peace. There was nobody but kindly Death to take him out of his misery, for the giant intellect that had planned and carried out the rescue of the uncrowned King of France, and which alone might have had the power to save him too, was being broken on the rack of enforced sleeplessness.

CHAPTER XXVI

The Bitterest Foe

That same evening Sir Andrew Ffoulkes, having announced his intention of gleaning further news of Armand, if possible, went out shortly after seven o'clock, promising to be home again about nine.

Marguerite, on the other hand, had to make her friend a solemn promise that she would try and eat some supper which the landlady of these miserable apartments had agreed to prepare for her. So far they had been left in peaceful occupation of these squalid lodgings in a tumble-down house on the Quai de la Ferraille, facing the house of Justice, the grim walls of which Marguerite would watch with wide-open dry eyes for as long as the grey wintry light lingered over them.

Even now, though the darkness had set in, and snow, falling in close, small flakes, threw a thick white veil over the landscape, she sat at the open window long after Sir Andrew had gone out, watching the few small flicks of light that blinked across from the other side of the river, and which came from the windows of the Chatelet towers. The windows of the Conciergerie she could not see, for these gave on one of the inner courtyards; but there was a melancholy consolation even in the gazing on those walls that held in their cruel, grim embrace all that she loved in the world.

It seemed so impossible to think of Percy—the laughter-loving, irresponsible, light-hearted adventurer—as the prey of those fiends who would revel in their triumph, who would crush him, humiliate him, insult him—ye gods alive! even torture him, perhaps—that they might break the indomitable spirit that would mock them even on the threshold of death.

Surely, surely God would never allow such monstrous infamy as the deliverance of the noble soaring eagle into the hands of those preying jackals! Marguerite—though her heart ached beyond what human nature could endure, though her anguish on her husband's account was doubled by that which she felt for her brother—could not bring herself to give up all hope. Sir Andrew said it rightly; while there was life there was hope. While there was life in those vigorous limbs, spirit in that daring mind, how could puny, rampant beasts gain the better of the immortal soul? As for Armand—why, if Percy were free she would have no cause to fear for Armand.

She sighed a sigh of deep, of passionate regret and longing. If she could only see her husband; if she could only look for one second into those laughing, lazy eyes, wherein she alone knew how to fathom the infinity of passion that lay within their depths; if she could but once feel his—ardent kiss on her lips, she could more easily endure this agonising suspense, and wait confidently and courageously for the issue.

She turned away from the window, for the night was getting bitterly cold. From the tower of St. Germain l'Auxerrois the clock slowly struck eight. Even as the last sound of the historic bell died away in the distance she heard a timid knocking at the door.

"Enter!" she called unthinkingly.

She thought it was her landlady, come up with more wood, mayhap, for the fire, so she did not turn to the door when she heard it being slowly opened, then closed again, and presently a soft tread on the threadbare carpet.

"May I crave your kind attention, Lady Blakeney?" said a harsh voice, subdued to tones of ordinary courtesy.

She quickly repressed a cry of terror. How well she knew that voice! When last she heard it it was at Boulogne, dictating that infamous letter—the weapon wherewith Percy had so effectually foiled his enemy. She turned and faced the man who was her bitterest foe—hers in the person of the man she loved.

"Chauvelin!" she gasped.

"Himself at your service, dear lady," he said simply.

He stood in the full light of the lamp, his trim, small figure boldly cut out against the dark wall beyond. He wore the usual sable-coloured clothes which he affected, with the primly-folded jabot and cuffs edged with narrow lace.

Without waiting for permission from her he quietly and deliberately placed his hat and cloak on a chair. Then he turned once more toward her, and made a movement as if to advance into the room; but instinctively she put up a hand as if to ward off the calamity of his approach.

He shrugged his shoulders, and the shadow of a smile, that had neither mirth nor kindliness in it, hovered round the corners of his thin lips.

"Have I your permission to sit?" he asked.

"As you will," she replied slowly, keeping her wide-open eyes fixed upon him as does a frightened bird upon the serpent whom it loathes and fears.

"And may I crave a few moments of your undivided attention, Lady Blakeney?" he continued, taking a chair, and so placing it beside the table that the light of the lamp when he sat remained behind him and his face was left in shadow.

"Is it necessary?" asked Marguerite.

"It is," he replied curtly, "if you desire to see and speak with your husband—to be of use to him before it is too late."

"Then, I pray you, speak, citizen, and I will listen."

She sank into a chair, not heeding whether the light of the lamp fell on her face or not, whether the lines in her haggard cheeks, or her tear-dimmed eyes showed plainly the sorrow and despair that had traced them. She had nothing to hide from this man, the cause of all the tortures which she endured. She knew that neither courage nor sorrow would move him, and that hatred for Percy—personal deadly hatred for the man who had twice foiled him—had long crushed the last spark of humanity in his heart.

"Perhaps, Lady Blakeney," he began after a slight pause and in his smooth, even voice, "it would interest you to hear how I succeeded in procuring for myself this pleasure of an interview with you?"

"Your spies did their usual work, I suppose," she said coldly.

"Exactly. We have been on your track for three days, and yesterday evening an unguarded movement on the part of Sir Andrew Ffoulkes gave us the final clue to your whereabouts."

"Of Sir Andrew Ffoulkes?" she asked, greatly puzzled.

"He was in an eating-house, cleverly disguised, I own, trying to glean information, no doubt as to the probable fate of Sir Percy Blakeney. As chance would have it, my friend Heron, of the Committee of General Security, chanced to be discussing with reprehensible openness—er—certain—what shall I say?—certain measures which, at my advice, the Committee of Public Safety have been forced to adopt with a view to—"

"A truce on your smooth-tongued speeches, citizen Chauvelin," she interposed firmly. "Sir Andrew Ffoulkes has told me naught of this—so I pray you speak plainly and to the point, if you can."

He bowed with marked irony.

"As you please," he said. "Sir Andrew Ffoulkes, hearing certain matters of which I will tell you anon, made a movement which betrayed him to one of our spies. At a word from citizen Heron this man followed on the heels of the young farrier who had shown such interest in the conversation of the Chief Agent. Sir Andrew, I imagine, burning with indignation at what he had heard, was perhaps not quite so cautious as he usually is. Anyway, the man on his track followed him to this door. It was quite simple, as you see. As for me, I had guessed a week ago that we would see the beautiful Lady Blakeney in Paris before long. When I knew where Sir Andrew Ffoulkes lodged, I had no difficulty in guessing that Lady Blakeney would not be far off."

"And what was there in citizen Heron's conversation last night," she asked quietly, "that so aroused Sir Andrew's indignation?"

"He has not told you?" "Oh! it is very simple. Let me tell you, Lady Blakeney, exactly how matters stand. Sir Percy Blakeney—before lucky chance at last delivered him into our hands—thought fit, as no doubt you know, to meddle with our most important prisoner of State."

"A child. I know it, sir—the son of a murdered father whom you and your friends were slowly doing to death."

"That is as it may be, Lady Blakeney," rejoined Chauvelin calmly; "but it was none of Sir Percy Blakeney's business. This, however, he chose to disregard. He succeeded in carrying little Capet from the Temple, and two days later we had him under lock, and key."

"Through some infamous and treacherous trick, sir," she retorted.

Chauvelin made no immediate reply; his pale, inscrutable eyes were fixed upon her face, and the smile of irony round his mouth appeared more strongly marked than before.

"That, again, is as it may be," he said suavely; "but anyhow for the moment we have the upper hand. Sir Percy is in the Conciergerie, guarded day and night, more closely than Marie Antoinette even was guarded."

"And he laughs at your bolts and bars, sir," she rejoined proudly. "Remember Calais, remember Boulogne. His laugh at your discomfiture, then, must resound in your ear even to-day."

"Yes; but for the moment laughter is on our side. Still we are willing to forego even that pleasure, if Sir Percy will but move a finger towards his own freedom."

"Again some infamous letter?" she asked with bitter contempt; "some attempt against his honour?"

"No, no, Lady Blakeney," he interposed with perfect blandness. "Matters are so much simpler now, you see. We hold Sir Percy at our mercy. We could send him to the guillotine to-morrow, but we might be willing—remember, I only say we might—to exercise our prerogative of mercy if Sir Percy Blakeney will on his side accede to a request from us."

"And that request?"

"Is a very natural one. He took Capet away from us, and it is but credible that he knows at the present moment exactly where the child is. Let him instruct his followers—and I mistake not, Lady Blakeney, there are several of them not very far from Paris just now—let him, I say, instruct these followers of his to return the person of young Capet to us, and not only will we undertake to give these same gentlemen a safe conduct back to England, but we even might be inclined to deal somewhat less harshly with the gallant Scarlet Pimpernel himself."

She laughed a harsh, mirthless, contemptuous laugh.

"I don't think that I quite understand," she said after a moment or two, whilst he waited calmly until her out-break of hysterical mirth had subsided. "You want my husband—the Scarlet Pimpernel, citizen—to deliver the little King of France to you after he has risked his life to save the child out of your clutches? Is that what you are trying to say?"

"It is," rejoined Chauvelin complacently, "just what we have been saying to Sir Percy Blakeney for the past six days, madame."

"Well! then you have had your answer, have you not?"

"Yes," he replied slowly; "but the answer has become weaker day by day."

"Weaker? I don't understand."

"Let me explain, Lady Blakeney," said Chauvelin, now with measured emphasis. He put both elbows on the table and leaned well forward, peering into her face, lest one of its varied expressions escaped him. "Just now you taunted me with my failure in Calais, and again at Boulogne, with a proud toss of the head, which I own is excessive becoming; you threw the name of the Scarlet Pimpernel in my face like a challenge which I no longer dare to accept. 'The Scarlet Pimpernel,' you would say to me, 'stands for loyalty, for honour, and for indomitable courage. Think you he would sacrifice his honour to obtain your mercy? Remember Boulogne and your discomfiture!' All of which, dear lady, is perfectly charming and womanly and enthusiastic, and I, bowing my humble head, must own that I was fooled in Calais and baffled in Boulogne. But in Boulogne I made a grave mistake, and one from which I learned a lesson, which I am putting into practice now."

He paused a while as if waiting for her reply. His pale, keen eyes had already noted that with every phrase he uttered the lines in her beautiful face became more hard and set. A look of horror was gradually spreading over it, as if the icy-cold hand of death had passed over her eyes and cheeks, leaving them rigid like stone.

"In Boulogne," resumed Chauvelin quietly, satisfied that his words were hitting steadily at her heart—"in Boulogne Sir Percy and I did not fight an equal fight. Fresh from a pleasant sojourn in his own magnificent home, full of the spirit of adventure which puts the essence of life into a man's veins, Sir Percy Blakeney's splendid physique was pitted against my feeble powers. Of course I lost the battle. I made the mistake of trying to subdue a man who was in the zenith of his strength, whereas now—"

"Yes, citizen Chauvelin," she said, "whereas now—"

"Sir Percy Blakeney has been in the prison of the Conciergerie for exactly one week, Lady Blakeney," he replied, speaking very slowly, and letting every one of his words sink individually into her mind. "Even before he had time to take the bearings of his cell or to plan on his own behalf one of those remarkable escapes for which he is so justly famous, our men began to work on a scheme which I am proud to say originated with myself. A week has gone by since then, Lady Blakeney, and during that time a special company of prison guard, acting under the orders of the Committee of General Security and of Public Safety, have questioned the prisoner unremittingly—unremittingly, remember—day and night. Two by two these men take it in turns to enter the prisoner's cell every quarter of an hour—lately it has had to be more often—and ask him the one question, 'Where is little Capet?' Up to now we have received no satisfactory reply, although we have explained to Sir Percy that many of his followers are honouring the neighbourhood of Paris with their visit, and that all we ask for from him are instructions to those gallant gentlemen to bring young Capet back to us. It is all very simple, unfortunately the prisoner is somewhat obstinate. At first, even, the idea seemed to amuse him; he used to laugh and say that he always had the faculty of sleeping with his eyes open. But our soldiers are untiring in their efforts, and the want of sleep as well as of a sufficiency of food and of fresh air is certainly beginning to tell on Sir Percy Blakeney's magnificent physique. I don't think that it will be very long before he gives way to our gentle persuasions; and in any case now, I assure you, dear lady, that we need not fear any attempt on his part to escape. I doubt if he could walk very steadily across this room—"

Marguerite had sat quite silent and apparently impassive all the while that Chauvelin had been speaking; even now she scarcely stirred. Her face expressed absolutely nothing but deep puzzlement. There was a frown between her brows, and her eyes, which were always of such liquid blue, now looked almost black. She was trying to visualise that which Chauvelin had put before her: a man harassed day and night, unceasingly, unremittingly, with one question allowed neither respite nor sleep—his brain, soul, and body fagged out at every hour, every moment of the day and night, until mind and body and soul must inevitably give way under anguish ten thousand times more unendurable than any physical torment invented by monsters in barbaric times.

That man thus harassed, thus fagged out, thus martyrised at all hours of the day and night, was her husband, whom she loved with every fibre of her being, with every throb of her heart.

Torture? Oh, no! these were advanced and civilised times that could afford to look with horror on the excesses of medieval days. This was a revolution that made for progress, and challenged the opinion of the world. The cells of the Temple of La Force or the Conciergerie held no secret inquisition with iron maidens and racks and thumbscrews; but a few men had put their tortuous brains together, and had said one to another: "We want to find out from that man where we can lay our hands on little Capet, so we won't let him sleep until he has told us. It is not torture—oh, no! Who would dare to say that we torture our prisoners? It is only a little horseplay, worrying to the prisoner, no doubt; but, after all, he can end the unpleasantness at any moment. He need but to answer our question, and he can go to sleep as comfortably as a little child. The want of sleep is very trying, the want of proper food and of fresh air is very weakening; the prisoner must give way sooner or later—"

So these fiends had decided it between them, and they had put their idea into execution for one whole week. Marguerite looked at Chauvelin as she would on some monstrous, inscrutable Sphinx, marveling if God—even in His anger—could really have created such a fiendish brain, or, having created it, could allow it to wreak such devilry unpunished.

Even now she felt that he was enjoying the mental anguish which he had put upon her, and she saw his thin, evil lips curled into a smile.

"So you came to-night to tell me all this?" she asked as soon as she could trust herself to speak. Her impulse was to shriek out her indignation, her horror of him, into his face. She longed to call down God's eternal curse upon this fiend; but instinctively she held herself in check. Her indignation, her words of loathing would only have added to his delight.

"You have had your wish," she added coldly; "now, I pray you, go."

"Your pardon, Lady Blakeney," he said with all his habitual blandness; "my object in coming to see you tonight was twofold. Methought that I was acting as your friend in giving you authentic news of Sir Percy, and in suggesting the possibility of your adding your persuasion to ours."

"My persuasion? You mean that I—"

"You would wish to see your husband, would you not, Lady Blakeney?"

"Yes."

"Then I pray you command me. I will grant you the permission whenever you wish to go."

"You are in the hope, citizen," she said, "that I will do my best to break my husband's spirit by my tears or my prayers—is that it?"

"Not necessarily," he replied pleasantly. "I assure you that we can manage to do that ourselves, in time."

"You devil!" The cry of pain and of horror was involuntarily wrung from the depths of her soul. "Are you not afraid that God's hand will strike you where you stand?"

"No," he said lightly; "I am not afraid, Lady Blakeney. You see, I do not happen to believe in God. Come!" he added more seriously, "have I not proved to you that my offer is disinterested? Yet I repeat it even now. If you desire to see Sir Percy in prison, command me, and the doors shall be open to you."

She waited a moment, looking him straight and quite dispassionately in the face; then she said coldly:

"Very well! I will go."

"When?" he asked.

"This evening."

"Just as you wish. I would have to go and see my friend Heron first, and arrange with him for your visit."

"Then go. I will follow in half an hour."

"C'est entendu. Will you be at the main entrance of the Conciergerie at half-past nine? You know it, perhaps—no? It is in the Rue de la Barillerie, immediately on the right at the foot of the great staircase of the house of Justice."

"Of the house of Justice!" she exclaimed involuntarily, a world of bitter contempt in her cry. Then she added in her former matter-of-fact tones:

"Very good, citizen. At half-past nine I will be at the entrance you name."

"And I will be at the door prepared to escort you."

He took up his hat and coat and bowed ceremoniously to her. Then he turned to go. At the door a cry from her—involuntarily enough, God knows!—made him pause.

"My interview with the prisoner," she said, vainly trying, poor soul! to repress that quiver of anxiety in her voice, "it will be private?"

"Oh, yes! Of course," he replied with a reassuring smile. "Au revoir, Lady Blakeney! Half-past nine, remember—"

She could no longer trust herself to look on him as he finally took his departure. She was afraid—yes, absolutely afraid that her fortitude would give way—meanly, despicably, uselessly give way; that she would suddenly fling herself at the feet of that sneering, inhuman wretch, that she would pray, implore—Heaven above! what might she not do in the face of this awful reality, if the last lingering shred of vanishing reason, of pride, and of courage did not hold her in check?

Therefore she forced herself not to look on that departing, sable-clad figure, on that evil face, and those hands that held Percy's fate in their cruel grip; but her ears caught the welcome sound of his departure—the opening and shutting of the door, his light footstep echoing down the stone stairs.

When at last she felt that she was really alone she uttered a loud cry like a wounded doe, and falling on her knees she buried her face in her hands in a passionate fit of weeping. Violent sobs shook her entire frame; it seemed as if an overwhelming anguish was tearing at her heart—the physical pain of it was almost unendurable. And yet even through this paroxysm of tears her mind clung to one root idea: when she saw Percy she must be brave and calm, be able to help him if he wanted her, to do his bidding if there was anything that she could do, or any message that she could take to the others. Of hope she had none. The last lingering ray of it had been extinguished by that fiend when he said, "We need not fear that he will escape. I doubt if he could walk very steadily across this room now."

CHAPTER XXVII

In the Conciergerie

Marguerite, accompanied by Sir Andrew Ffoulkes, walked rapidly along the quay. It lacked ten minutes to the half hour; the night was dark and bitterly cold. Snow was still falling in sparse, thin flakes, and lay like a crisp and glittering mantle over the parapets of the bridges and the grim towers of the Chatelet prison.

They walked on silently now. All that they had wanted to say to one another had been said inside the squalid room of their lodgings when Sir Andrew Ffoulkes had come home and learned that Chauvelin had been.

"They are killing him by inches, Sir Andrew," had been the heartrending cry which burst from Marguerite's oppressed heart as soon as her hands rested in the kindly ones of her best friend. "Is there aught that we can do?"

There was, of course, very little that could be done. One or two fine steel files which Sir Andrew gave her to conceal beneath the folds of her kerchief; also a tiny dagger with sharp, poisoned blade, which for a moment she held in her hand hesitating, her eyes filling with tears, her heart throbbing with unspeakable sorrow.

Then slowly—very slowly—she raised the small, death-dealing instrument to her lips, and reverently kissed the narrow blade.

"If it must be!" she murmured, "God in His mercy will forgive!"

She sheathed the dagger, and this, too, she hid in the folds of her gown.

"Can you think of anything else, Sir Andrew, that he might want?" she asked. "I have money in plenty, in case those soldiers—"

Sir Andrew sighed, and turned away from her so as to hide the hopelessness which he felt. Since three days now he had been exhausting every conceivable means of getting at the prison guard with bribery and corruption. But Chauvelin and his friends had taken excellent precautions. The prison of the Conciergerie, situated as it was in the very heart of the labyrinthine and complicated structure of the Chatelet and the house of Justice, and isolated from every other group of cells in the building, was inaccessible save from one narrow doorway which gave on the guard-room first, and thence on the inner cell beyond. Just as all attempts to rescue the late unfortunate Queen from that prison had failed, so now every attempt to reach the imprisoned Scarlet Pimpernel was equally doomed to bitter disappointment.

The guard-room was filled with soldiers day and night; the windows of the inner cell, heavily barred, were too small to admit of the passage of a human body, and they were raised twenty feet from the corridor below. Sir Andrew had stood in the corridor two days ago, he had looked on the window behind which he knew that his friend must be eating out his noble heart in a longing for liberty, and he had realised then that every effort at help from the outside was foredoomed to failure.

"Courage, Lady Blakeney," he said to Marguerite, when anon they had crossed the Pont au Change, and were wending their way slowly along the Rue de la Barillerie; "remember our proud dictum: the Scarlet Pimpernel never fails! and also this, that whatever messages Blakeney gives you for us, whatever he wishes us to do, we are to a man ready to do it, and to give our lives for our chief. Courage! Something tells me that a man like Percy is not going to die at the hands of such vermin as Chauvelin and his friends."

They had reached the great iron gates of the house of Justice. Marguerite, trying to smile, extended her trembling band to this faithful, loyal comrade.

"I'll not be far," he said. "When you come out do not look to the right or left, but make straight for home; I'll not lose sight of you for a moment, and as soon as possible will overtake you. God bless you both."

He pressed his lips on her cold little hand, and watched her tall, elegant figure as she passed through the great gates until the veil of falling snow hid her from his gaze. Then with a deep sigh of bitter anguish and sorrow he turned away and was soon lost in the gloom.

Marguerite found the gate at the bottom of the monumental stairs open when she arrived. Chauvelin was standing immediately inside the building waiting for her.

"We are prepared for your visit, Lady Blakeney," he said, "and the prisoner knows that you are coming."

He led the way down one of the numerous and interminable corridors of the building, and she followed briskly, pressing her hand against her bosom there where the folds of her kerchief hid the steel files and the precious dagger.

Even in the gloom of these ill-lighted passages she realised that she was surrounded by guards. There were soldiers everywhere; two had stood behind the door when first she entered, and had immediately closed it with a loud clang behind her; and all the way down the corridors, through the half-light engendered by feebly flickering lamps, she caught glimpses of the white facings on the uniforms of the town guard, or occasionally the glint of steel of a bayonet. Presently Chauvelin paused beside a door, which he had just reached. His hand was on the latch, for it did not appear to be locked, and he turned toward Marguerite.

"I am very sorry, Lady Blakeney," he said in simple, deferential tones, "that the prison authorities, who at my request are granting you this interview at such an unusual hour, have made a slight condition to your visit."

"A condition?" she asked. "What is it?"

"You must forgive me," he said, as if purposely evading her question, "for I give you my word that I had nothing to do with a regulation that you might justly feel was derogatory to your dignity. If you will kindly step in here a wardress in charge will explain to you what is required."

He pushed open the door, and stood aside ceremoniously in order to allow her to pass in. She looked on him with deep puzzlement and a look of dark suspicion in her eyes. But her mind was too much engrossed with the thought of her meeting with Percy to worry over any trifle that might—as her enemy had inferred—offend her womanly dignity.

She walked into the room, past Chauvelin, who whispered as she went by:

"I will wait for you here. And, I pray you, if you have aught to complain of summon me at once."

Then he closed the door behind her. The room in which Marguerite now found herself was a small unventilated quadrangle, dimly lighted by a hanging lamp. A woman in a soiled cotton gown and lank grey hair brushed away from a parchment-like forehead rose from the chair in which she had been sitting when Marguerite entered, and put away some knitting on which she had apparently been engaged.

"I was to tell you, citizeness," she said the moment the door had been closed and she was alone with Marguerite, "that the prison authorities have given orders that I should search you before you visit the prisoner."

She repeated this phrase mechanically like a child who has been taught to say a lesson by heart. She was a stoutish middle-aged woman, with that pasty, flabby skin peculiar to those who live in want of fresh air; but her small, dark eyes were not unkindly, although they shifted restlessly from one object to another as if she were trying to avoid looking the other woman straight in the face.

"That you should search me!" reiterated Marguerite slowly, trying to understand.

"Yes," replied the woman. "I was to tell you to take off your clothes, so that I might look them through and through. I have often had to do this before when visitors have been allowed inside the prison, so it is no use your trying to deceive me in any way. I am very sharp at finding out if any one has papers, or files or ropes concealed in an underpetticoat. Come," she added more roughly, seeing that Marguerite had remained motionless in the middle of the room; "the quicker you are about it the sooner you will be taken to see the prisoner."

These words had their desired effect. The proud Lady Blakeney, inwardly revolting at the outrage, knew that resistance would be worse than useless. Chauvelin was the other side of the door. A call from the woman would bring him to her assistance, and Marguerite was only longing to hasten the moment when she could be with her husband.

She took off her kerchief and her gown and calmly submitted to the woman's rough hands as they wandered with sureness and accuracy to the various pockets and folds that might conceal prohibited articles. The woman did her work with peculiar stolidity; she did not utter a word when she found the tiny steel files and placed them on a table beside her. In equal silence she laid the little dagger beside them, and the purse which contained twenty gold pieces. These she counted in front of Marguerite and then replaced them in the purse. Her face expressed neither surprise, nor greed nor pity. She was obviously beyond the reach of bribery—just a machine paid by the prison authorities to do this unpleasant work, and no doubt terrorised into doing it conscientiously.

When she had satisfied herself that Marguerite had nothing further concealed about her person, she allowed her to put her dress on once more. She even offered to help her on with it. When Marguerite was fully dressed she opened the door for her. Chauvelin was standing in the passage waiting patiently. At sight of Marguerite, whose pale, set face betrayed nothing of the indignation which she felt, he turned quick, inquiring eyes on the woman.

"Two files, a dagger and a purse with twenty louis," said the latter curtly.

Chauvelin made no comment. He received the information quite placidly, as if it had no special interest for him. Then he said quietly:

"This way, citizeness!"

Marguerite followed him, and two minutes later he stood beside a heavy nail-studded door that had a small square grating let into one of the panels, and said simply:

"This is it."

Two soldiers of the National Guard were on sentry at the door, two more were pacing up and down outside it, and had halted when citizen Chauvelin gave his name and showed his tricolour scarf of office. From behind the small grating in the door a pair of eyes peered at the newcomers.

"Qui va la?" came the quick challenge from the guard-room within.

"Citizen Chauvelin of the Committee of Public Safety," was the prompt reply.

There was the sound of grounding of arms, of the drawing of bolts and the turning of a key in a complicated lock. The prison was kept locked from within, and very heavy bars had to be moved ere the ponderous door slowly swung open on its hinges.

Two steps led up into the guard-room. Marguerite mounted them with the same feeling of awe and almost of reverence as she would have mounted the steps of a sacrificial altar.

The guard-room itself was more brilliantly lighted than the corridor outside. The sudden glare of two or three lamps placed about the room caused her momentarily to close her eyes that were aching with many shed and unshed tears. The air was rank and heavy with the fumes of tobacco, of wine and stale food. A large barred window gave on the corridor immediately above the door.

When Marguerite felt strong enough to look around her, she saw that the room was filled with soldiers. Some were sitting, others standing, others lay on rugs against the wall, apparently asleep. There was one who appeared to be in command, for with a word he checked the noise that was going on in the room when she entered, and then he said curtly:

"This way, citizeness!"

He turned to an opening in the wall on the left, the stone-lintel of a door, from which the door itself had been removed; an iron bar ran across the opening, and this the sergeant now lifted, nodding to Marguerite to go within.

Instinctively she looked round for Chauvelin.

But he was nowhere to be seen.

CHAPTER XXVIII

The Caged Lion

Was there some instinct of humanity left in the soldier who allowed Marguerite through the barrier into the prisoner's cell? Had the wan face of this beautiful woman stirred within his heart the last chord of gentleness that was not wholly atrophied by the constant cruelties, the excesses, the mercilessness which his service under this fraternising republic constantly demanded of him?

Perhaps some recollection of former years, when first he served his King and country, recollection of wife or sister or mother pleaded within him in favour of this sorely-stricken woman with the look of unspeakable sorrow in her large blue eyes.

Certain it is that as soon as Marguerite passed the barrier he put himself on guard against it with his back to the interior of the cell and to her.

Marguerite had paused on the threshold.

After the glaring light of the guard-room the cell seemed dark, and at first she could hardly see. The whole length of the long, narrow cubicle lay to her left, with a slight recess at its further end, so that from the threshold of the doorway she could not see into the distant corner. Swift as a lightning flash the remembrance came back to her of proud Marie Antoinette narrowing her life to that dark corner where the insolent eyes of the rabble soldiery could not spy her every movement.

Marguerite stepped further into the room. Gradually by the dim light of an oil lamp placed upon a table in the recess she began to distinguish various objects: one or two chairs, another table, and a small but very comfortable-looking camp bedstead.

Just for a few seconds she only saw these inanimate things, then she became conscious of Percy's presence.

He sat on a chair, with his left arm half-stretched out upon the table, his head hidden in the bend of the elbow.

Marguerite did not utter a cry; she did not even tremble. Just for one brief instant she closed her eyes, so as to gather up all her courage before she dared to look again. Then with a steady and noiseless step she came quite close to him. She knelt on the flagstones at his feet and raised reverently to her lips the hand that hung nerveless and limp by his side.

He gave a start; a shiver seemed to go right through him; he half raised his head and murmured in a hoarse whisper:

"I tell you that I do not know, and if I did—"

She put her arms round him and pillowed her head upon his breast. He turned his head slowly toward her, and now his eyes—hollowed and rimmed with purple—looked straight into hers.

"My beloved," he said, "I knew that you would come." His arms closed round her. There was nothing of lifelessness or of weariness in the passion of that embrace; and when she looked up again it seemed to her as if that first vision which she had had of him with weary head bent, and wan, haggard face was not reality, only a dream born of her own anxiety for him, for now the hot, ardent blood coursed just as swiftly as ever through his veins, as if life—strong, tenacious, pulsating life—throbbed with unabated vigour in those massive limbs, and behind that square, clear brow as though the body, but half subdued, had transferred its vanishing strength to the kind and noble heart that was beating with the fervour of self-sacrifice.

"Percy," she said gently, "they will only give us a few moments together. They thought that my tears would break your spirit where their devilry had failed."

He held her glance with his own, with that close, intent look which binds soul to soul, and in his deep blue eyes there danced the restless flames of his own undying mirth:

"La! little woman," he said with enforced lightness, even whilst his voice quivered with the intensity of passion engendered by her presence, her nearness, the perfume of her hair, "how little they know you, eh? Your brave, beautiful, exquisite soul, shining now through your glorious eyes, would defy the machinations of Satan himself and his horde. Close your dear eyes, my love. I shall go mad with joy if I drink their beauty in any longer."

He held her face between his two hands, and indeed it seemed as if he could not satiate his soul with looking into her eyes. In the midst of so much sorrow, such misery and such deadly fear, never had Marguerite felt quite so happy, never had she felt him so completely her own. The inevitable bodily weakness, which of necessity had invaded even his splendid physique after a whole week's privations, had made a severe breach in the invincible barrier of self-control with which the soul of the inner man was kept perpetually hidden behind a mask of indifference and of irresponsibility.

And yet the agony of seeing the lines of sorrow so plainly writ on the beautiful face of the woman he worshipped must have been the keenest that the bold adventurer had ever experienced in the whole course of his reckless life. It was he—and he alone—who was making her suffer; her for whose sake he would gladly have shed every drop of his blood, endured every torment, every misery and every humiliation; her whom he worshipped only one degree less than he worshipped his honour and the cause which he had made his own.

Yet, in spite of that agony, in spite of the heartrending pathos of her pale wan face, and through the anguish of seeing her tears, the ruling passion—strong in death—the spirit of adventure, the mad, wild, devil-may-care irresponsibility was never wholly absent.

"Dear heart," he said with a quaint sigh, whilst he buried his face in the soft masses of her hair, "until you came I was so d—d fatigued."

He was laughing, and the old look of boyish love of mischief illumined his haggard face.

"Is it not lucky, dear heart," he said a moment or two later, "that those brutes do not leave me unshaved? I could not have faced you with a week's growth of beard round my chin. By dint of promises and bribery I have persuaded one of that rabble to come and shave me every morning. They will not allow me to handle a razor my-self. They are afraid I should cut my throat—or one of theirs. But mostly I am too d—d sleepy to think of such a thing."

"Percy!" she exclaimed with tender and passionate reproach.

"I know—I know, dear," he murmured, "what a brute I am! Ah, God did a cruel thing the day that He threw me in your path. To think that once—not so very long ago—we were drifting apart, you and I. You would have suffered less, dear heart, if we had continued to drift."

Then as he saw that his bantering tone pained her, he covered her hands with kisses, entreating her forgiveness.

"Dear heart," he said merrily, "I deserve that you should leave me to rot in this abominable cage. They haven't got me yet, little woman, you know; I am not yet dead—only d—d sleepy at times. But I'll cheat them even now, never fear."

"How, Percy—how?" she moaned, for her heart was aching with intolerable pain; she knew better than he did the precautions which were being taken against his escape, and she saw more clearly than he realised it himself the terrible barrier set up against that escape by ever encroaching physical weakness.

"Well, dear," he said simply, "to tell you the truth I have not yet thought of that all-important 'how.' I had to wait, you see, until you came. I was so sure that you would come! I have succeeded in putting on paper all my instructions for Ffoulkes and the others. I will give them to you anon. I knew that you would come, and that I could give them to you; until then I had but to think of one thing, and that was of keeping body and soul together. My chance of seeing you was to let them have their will with me. Those brutes were sure, sooner or later, to bring you to me, that you might see the caged fox worn down to imbecility, eh? That you might add your tears to their persuasion, and succeed where they have failed."

He laughed lightly with an unstrained note of gaiety, only Marguerite's sensitive ears caught the faint tone of bitterness which rang through the laugh.

"Once I know that the little King of France is safe," he said, "I can think of how best to rob those d—d murderers of my skin."

Then suddenly his manner changed. He still held her with one arm closely to, him, but the other now lay across the table, and the slender, emaciated hand was tightly clutched. He did not look at her, but straight ahead; the eyes, unnaturally large now, with their deep purple rims, looked far ahead beyond the stone walls of this grim, cruel prison.

The passionate lover, hungering for his beloved, had vanished; there sat the man with a purpose, the man whose firm hand had snatched men and women and children from death, the reckless enthusiast who tossed his life against an ideal.

For a while he sat thus, while in his drawn and haggard face she could trace every line formed by his thoughts—the frown of anxiety, the resolute setting of the lips, the obstinate look of will around the firm jaw. Then he turned again to her.

"My beautiful one," he said softly, "the moments are very precious. God knows I could spend eternity thus with your dear form nestling against my heart. But those d—d murderers will only give us half an hour, and I want your help, my beloved, now that I am a helpless cur caught in their trap. Will you listen attentively, dear heart, to what I am going to say?

"Yes, Percy, I will listen," she replied.

"And have you the courage to do just what I tell you, dear?"

"I would not have courage to do aught else," she said simply.

"It means going from hence to-day, dear heart, and perhaps not meeting again. Hush-sh-sh, my beloved," he said, tenderly placing his thin hand over her mouth, from which a sharp cry of pain had well-nigh escaped; "your exquisite soul will be with me always. Try—try not to give way to despair. Why! your love alone, which I see shining from your dear eyes, is enough to make a man cling to life with all his might. Tell me! will you do as I ask you?"

And she replied firmly and courageously:

"I will do just what you ask, Percy."

"God bless you for your courage, dear. You will have need of it."

CHAPTER XXIX

For the Sake of that Helpless Innocent

The next instant he was kneeling on the floor and his hands were wandering over the small, irregular flagstones immediately underneath the table. Marguerite had risen to her feet; she watched her husband with intent and puzzled eyes; she saw him suddenly pass his slender fingers along a crevice between two flagstones, then raise one of these slightly and from beneath it extract a small bundle of papers, each carefully folded and sealed. Then he replaced the stone and once more rose to his knees.

He gave a quick glance toward the doorway. That corner of his cell, the recess wherein stood the table, was invisible to any one who had not actually crossed the threshold. Reassured that his movements could not have been and were not watched, he drew Marguerite closer to him.

"Dear heart," he whispered, "I want to place these papers in your care. Look upon them as my last will and testament. I succeeded in fooling those brutes one day by pretending to be willing to accede to their will. They gave me pen and ink and paper and wax, and I was to write out an order to my followers to bring the Dauphin hither. They left me in peace for one quarter of an hour, which gave me time to write three letters—one for Armand and the other two for Ffoulkes, and to hide them under the flooring of my cell. You see, dear, I knew that you would come and that I could give them to you then."

He paused, and that, ghost of a smile once more hovered round his lips. He was thinking of that day when he had fooled Heron and Chauvelin into the belief that their devilry had succeeded, and that they had brought the reckless adventurer to his knees. He smiled at the recollection of their wrath when they knew that they had been tricked, and after a quarter of an hour's anxious waiting found a few sheets of paper scribbled over with incoherent words or satirical verse, and the prisoner having apparently snatched ten minutes' sleep, which seemingly had restored to him quite a modicum of his strength.

But of this he told Marguerite nothing, nor of the insults and the humiliation which he had had to bear in consequence of that trick. He did not tell her that directly afterwards the order went forth that the prisoner was to be kept on bread and water in the future, nor that Chauvelin had stood by laughing and jeering while...

No! he did not tell her all that; the recollection of it all had still the power to make him laugh; was it not all a part and parcel of that great gamble for human lives wherein he had held the winning cards himself for so long?

"It is your turn now," he had said even then to his bitter enemy.

"Yes!" Chauvelin had replied, "our turn at last. And you will not bend my fine English gentleman, we'll break you yet, never fear."

It was the thought of it all, of that hand to hand, will to will, spirit to spirit struggle that lighted up his haggard face even now, gave him a fresh zest for life, a desire to combat and to conquer in spite of all, in spite of the odds that had martyred his body but left the mind, the will, the power still unconquered.

He was pressing one of the papers into her hand, holding her fingers tightly in his, and compelling her gaze with the ardent excitement of his own.

"This first letter is for Ffoulkes," he said. "It relates to the final measures for the safety of the Dauphin. They are my instructions to those members of the League who are in or near Paris at the present moment. Ffoulkes, I know, must be with you—he was not likely, God bless his loyalty, to let you come to Paris alone. Then give this letter to him, dear heart, at once, to-night, and tell him that it is my express command that he and the others shall act in minute accordance with my instructions."

"But the Dauphin surely is safe now," she urged. "Ffoulkes and the others are here in order to help you."

"To help me, dear heart?" he interposed earnestly. "God alone can do that now, and such of my poor wits as these devils do not succeed in crushing out of me within the next ten days."

Ten days!

"I have waited a week, until this hour when I could place this packet in your hands; another ten days should see the Dauphin out of France—after that, we shall see."

"Percy," she exclaimed in an agony of horror, "you cannot endure this another day—and live!"

"Nay!" he said in a tone that was almost insolent in its proud defiance, "there is but little that a man cannot do an he sets his mind to it. For the rest, 'tis in God's hands!" he added more gently. "Dear heart! you swore that you would be brave. The Dauphin is still in France, and until he is out of it he will not really be safe; his friends wanted to keep him inside the country. God only knows what they still hope; had I been free I should not have allowed him to remain so long; now those good people at Mantes will yield to my letter and to Ffoulkes' earnest appeal—they will allow one of our League to convey the child safely out of France, and I'll wait here until I know that he is safe. If I tried to get away now, and succeeded—why, Heaven help us! the hue and cry might turn against the child, and he might be captured before I could get to him. Dear heart! dear, dear heart! try to understand. The safety of that child is bound with mine honour, but I swear to you, my sweet love, that the day on which I feel that that safety is assured I will save mine own skin—what there is left of it—if I can!"

"Percy!" she cried with a sudden outburst of passionate revolt, "you speak as if the safety of that child were of more moment than your own. Ten days!—but, God in Heaven! have you thought how I shall live these ten days, whilst slowly, inch by inch, you give your dear, your precious life for a forlorn cause?

"I am very tough, m'dear," he said lightly; "'tis not a question of life. I shall only be spending a few more very uncomfortable days in this d—d hole; but what of that?"

Her eyes spoke the reply; her eyes veiled with tears, that wandered with heart-breaking anxiety from the hollow circles round his own to the lines of weariness about the firm lips and jaw. He laughed at her solicitude.

"I can last out longer than these brutes have any idea of," he said gaily.

"You cheat yourself, Percy," she rejoined with quiet earnestness. "Every day that you spend immured between these walls, with that ceaseless nerve-racking torment of sleeplessness which these devils have devised for the breaking of your will—every day thus spent diminishes your power of ultimately saving yourself. You see, I speak calmly—dispassionately—I do not even urge my claims upon your life. But what you must weigh in the balance is the claim of all those for whom in the past you have already staked your life, whose lives you have purchased by risking your own. What, in comparison with your noble life, is that of the puny descendant of a line of decadent kings? Why should it be sacrificed—ruthlessly, hopelessly sacrificed that a boy might live who is as nothing to the world, to his country—even to his own people?"

She had tried to speak calmly, never raising her voice beyond a whisper. Her hands still clutched that paper, which seemed to sear her fingers, the paper which she felt held writ upon its smooth surface the death-sentence of the man she loved.

But his look did not answer her firm appeal; it was fixed far away beyond the prison walls, on a lonely country road outside Paris, with the rain falling in a thin drizzle, and leaden clouds overhead chasing one another, driven by the gale.

"Poor mite," he murmured softly; "he walked so bravely by my side, until the little feet grew weary; then he nestled in my arms and slept until we met Ffoulkes waiting with the cart. He was no King of France just then, only a helpless innocent whom Heaven aided me to save."

Marguerite bowed her head in silence. There was nothing more that she could say, no plea that she could urge. Indeed, she had understood, as he had begged her to understand. She understood that long ago he had mapped out the course of his life, and now that that course happened to lead up a Calvary of humiliation and of suffering he was not likely to turn back, even though, on the summit, death already was waiting and beckoning with no uncertain hand; not until he could murmur, in the wake of the great and divine sacrifice itself, the sublime words:

"It is accomplished."

"But the Dauphin is safe enough now," was all that she said, after that one moment's silence when her heart, too, had offered up to God the supreme abnegation of self, and calmly faced a sorrow which threatened to break it at last.

"Yes!" he rejoined quietly, "safe enough for the moment. But he would be safer still if he were out of France. I had hoped to take him one day with me to England. But in this plan damnable Fate has interfered. His adherents wanted to get him to Vienna, and their wish had best be fulfilled now. In my instructions to Ffoulkes I have mapped out a simple way for accomplishing the journey. Tony will be the one best suited to lead the expedition, and I want him to make straight for Holland; the Northern frontiers are not so closely watched as are the Austrian ones. There is a faithful adherent of the Bourbon cause who lives at Delft, and who will give the shelter of his name and home to the fugitive King of France until he can be conveyed to Vienna. He is named Nauudorff. Once I feel that the child is safe in his hands I will look after myself, never fear."

He paused, for his strength, which was only factitious, born of the excitement that Marguerite's presence had called forth, was threatening to give way. His voice, though he had spoken in a whisper all along, was very hoarse, and his temples were throbbing with the sustained effort to speak.

"If those friends had only thought of denying me food instead of sleep," he murmured involuntarily, "I could have held out until—"

Then with characteristic swiftness his mood changed in a moment. His arms closed round Marguerite once more with a passion of self-reproach.

"Heaven forgive me for a selfish brute," he said, whilst the ghost of a smile once more lit up the whole of his face. "Dear soul, I must have forgotten your sweet presence, thus brooding over my own troubles, whilst your loving heart has a graver burden—God help me!—than it can possibly bear. Listen, my beloved, for I don't know how many minutes longer they intend to give us, and I have not yet spoken to you about Armand—"

"Armand!" she cried.

A twinge of remorse had gripped her. For fully ten minutes now she had relegated all thoughts of her brother to a distant cell of her memory.

"We have no news of Armand," she said. "Sir Andrew has searched all the prison registers. Oh! were not my heart atrophied by all that it has endured this past sennight it would feel a final throb of agonising pain at every thought of Armand."

A curious look, which even her loving eyes failed to interpret, passed like a shadow over her husband's face. But the shadow lifted in a moment, and it was with a reassuring smile that he said to her:

"Dear heart! Armand is comparatively safe for the moment. Tell Ffoulkes not to search the prison registers for him, rather to seek out Mademoiselle Lange. She will know where to find Armand."

"Jeanne Lange!" she exclaimed with a world of bitterness in the tone of her voice, "the girl whom Armand loved, it seems, with a passion greater than his loyalty. Oh! Sir Andrew tried to disguise my brother's folly, but I guessed what he did not choose to tell me. It was his disobedience, his want of trust, that brought this unspeakable misery on us all."

"Do not blame him overmuch, dear heart. Armand was in love, and love excuses every sin committed in its name. Jeanne Lange was arrested and Armand lost his reason temporarily. The very day on which I rescued the Dauphin from the Temple I had the good fortune to drag the little lady out of prison. I had given my promise to Armand that she should be safe, and I kept my word. But this Armand did not know—or else—"

He checked himself abruptly, and once more that strange, enigmatical look crept into his eyes.

"I took Jeanne Lange to a place of comparative safety," he said after a slight pause, "but since then she has been set entirely free."

"Free?"

"Yes. Chauvelin himself brought me the news," he replied with a quick, mirthless laugh, wholly unlike his usual light-hearted gaiety. "He had to ask me where to find Jeanne, for I alone knew where she was. As for Armand, they'll not worry about him whilst I am here. Another reason why I must bide a while longer. But in the meanwhile, dear, I pray you find Mademoiselle Lange; she lives at No. 5 Square du Roule. Through her I know that you can get to see Armand. This second letter," he added, pressing a smaller packet into her hand, "is for him. Give it to him, dear heart; it will, I hope, tend to cheer him. I fear me the poor lad frets; yet he only sinned because he loved, and to me he will always be your brother—the man who held your affection for all the years before I came into your life. Give him this letter, dear; they are my instructions to him, as the others are for Ffoulkes; but tell him to read them when he is all alone. You will do that, dear heart, will you not?"

"Yes, Percy," she said simply. "I promise."

Great joy, and the expression of intense relief, lit up his face, whilst his eyes spoke the gratitude which he felt.

"Then there is one thing more," he said. "There are others in this cruel city, dear heart, who have trusted me, and whom I must not fail—Marie de Marmontel and her brother, faithful servants of the late queen; they were on the eve of arrest when I succeeded in getting them to a place of comparative safety; and there are others there, too all of these poor victims have trusted me implicitly. They are waiting for me there, trusting in my promise to convey them safely to England. Sweetheart, you must redeem my promise to them. You will?—you will? Promise me that you will—"

"I promise, Percy," she said once more.

"Then go, dear, to-morrow, in the late afternoon, to No. 98, Rue de Charonne. It is a narrow house at the extreme end of that long street which abuts on the fortifications. The lower part of the house is occupied by a dealer in rags and old clothes. He and his wife and family are wretchedly poor, but they are kind, good souls, and for a consideration and a minimum of risk to themselves they will always render service to the English milors, whom they believe to be a band of inveterate smugglers. Ffoulkes and all the others know these people and know the house; Armand by the same token knows it too. Marie de Marmontel and her brother are there, and several others; the old Comte de Lezardiere, the Abbe de Firmont; their names spell suffering, loyalty, and hopelessness. I was lucky enough to convey them safely to that hidden shelter. They trust me implicitly, dear heart. They are waiting for me there, trusting in my promise to them. Dear heart, you will go, will you not?"

"Yes, Percy," she replied. "I will go; I have promised."

"Ffoulkes has some certificates of safety by him, and the old clothes dealer will supply the necessary disguises; he has a covered cart which he uses for his business, and which you can borrow from him. Ffoulkes will drive the little party to Achard's farm in St. Germain, where other members of the League should be in waiting for the final journey to England. Ffoulkes will know how to arrange for everything; he was always my most able lieutenant. Once everything is organised he can appoint Hastings to lead the party. But you, dear heart, must do as you wish. Achard's farm would be a safe retreat for you and for Ffoulkes: if... I know—I know, dear," he added with infinite tenderness. "See I do not even suggest that you should leave me. Ffoulkes will be with you, and I know that neither he nor you would go even if I commanded. Either Achard's farm, or even the house in the Rue de Charonne, would be quite safe for you, dear, under Ffoulkes's protection, until the time when I myself can carry you back—you, my precious burden—to England in mine own arms, or until... Hush-sh-sh, dear heart," he entreated, smothering with a passionate kiss the low moan of pain which had escaped her lips; "it is all in God's hands now; I am in a tight corner—tighter than ever I have been before; but I am not dead yet, and those brutes have not yet paid the full price for my life. Tell me, dear heart, that you have understood—that you will do all that I asked. Tell me again, my dear, dear love; it is the very essence of life to hear your sweet lips murmur this promise now."

And for the third time she reiterated firmly:

"I have understood every word that you said to me, Percy, and I promise on your precious life to do what you ask."

He sighed a deep sigh of satisfaction, and even at that moment there came from the guard-room beyond the sound of a harsh voice, saying peremptorily:

"That half-hour is nearly over, sergeant; 'tis time you interfered."

"Three minutes more, citizen," was the curt reply.

"Three minutes, you devils," murmured Blakeney between set teeth, whilst a sudden light which even Marguerite's keen gaze failed to interpret leapt into his eyes. Then he pressed the third letter into her hand.

Once more his close, intent gaze compelled hers; their faces were close one to the other, so near to him did he draw her, so tightly did he hold her to him. The paper was in her hand and his fingers were pressed firmly on hers.

"Put this in your kerchief, my beloved," he whispered. "Let it rest on your exquisite bosom where I so love to pillow my head. Keep it there until the last hour when it seems to you that nothing more can come between me and shame.... Hush-sh-sh, dear," he added with passionate tenderness, checking the hot protest that at the word "shame" had sprung to her lips, "I cannot explain more fully now. I do not know what may happen. I am only a man, and who knows what subtle devilry those brutes might not devise for bringing the untamed adventurer to his knees. For the next ten days the Dauphin will be on the high roads of France, on his way to safety. Every stage of his journey will be known to me. I can from between these four walls follow him and his escort step by step. Well, dear, I am but a man, already brought to shameful weakness by mere physical discomfort—the want of sleep—such a trifle after all; but in case my reason tottered—God knows what I might do—then give this packet to Ffoulkes—it contains my final instructions—and he will know how to act. Promise me, dear heart, that you will not open the packet unless—unless mine own dishonour seems to you imminent—unless I have yielded to these brutes in this prison, and sent Ffoulkes or one of the others orders to exchange the Dauphin's life for mine; then, when mine own handwriting hath proclaimed me a coward, then and then only, give this packet to Ffoulkes. Promise me that, and also that when you and he have mastered its contents you will act exactly as I have commanded. Promise me that, dear, in your own sweet name, which may God bless, and in that of Ffoulkes, our loyal friend."

Through the sobs that well-nigh choked her she murmured the promise he desired.

His voice had grown hoarser and more spent with the inevitable reaction after the long and sustained effort, but the vigour of the spirit was untouched, the fervour, the enthusiasm.

"Dear heart," he murmured, "do not look on me with those dear, scared eyes of yours. If there is aught that puzzles you in what I said, try and trust me a while longer. Remember, I must save the Dauphin at all costs; mine honour is bound with his safety. What happens to me after that matters but little, yet I wish to live for your dear sake."

He drew a long breath which had naught of weariness in it. The haggard look had completely vanished from his face, the eyes were lighted up from within, the very soul of reckless daring and immortal gaiety illumined his whole personality.

"Do not look so sad, little woman," he said with a strange and sudden recrudescence of power; "those d—d murderers have not got me yet—even now."

Then he went down like a log.

The effort had been too prolonged—weakened nature reasserted her rights and he lost consciousness. Marguerite, helpless and almost distraught with grief, had yet the strength of mind not to call for assistance. She pillowed the loved one's head upon her breast, she kissed the dear, tired eyes, the poor throbbing temples. The unutterable pathos of seeing this man, who was always the personification of extreme vitality, energy, and boundless endurance and pluck, lying thus helpless, like a tired child, in her arms, was perhaps the saddest moment of this day of sorrow. But in her trust she never wavered for one instant. Much that he had said had puzzled her; but the word "shame" coming from his own lips as a comment on himself never caused her the slightest pang of fear. She had quickly hidden the tiny packet in her kerchief. She would act point by point exactly as he had ordered her to do, and she knew that Ffoulkes would never waver either.

Her heart ached well-nigh to breaking point. That which she could not understand had increased her anguish tenfold. If she could only have given way to tears she could have borne this final agony more easily. But the solace of tears was not for her; when those loved eyes once more opened to consciousness they should see hers glowing with courage and determination.

There had been silence for a few minutes in the little cell. The soldiery outside, inured to their hideous duty, thought no doubt that the time had come for them to interfere. The iron bar was raised and thrown back with a loud crash, the butt-ends of muskets were grounded against the floor, and two soldiers made noisy irruption into the cell.

"Hola, citizen! Wake up," shouted one of the men; "you have not told us yet what you have done with Capet!"

Marguerite uttered a cry of horror. Instinctively her arms were interposed between the unconscious man and these inhuman creatures, with a beautiful gesture of protecting motherhood.

"He has fainted," she said, her voice quivering with indignation. "My God! are you devils that you have not one spark of manhood in you?"

The men shrugged their shoulders, and both laughed brutally. They had seen worse sights than these, since they served a Republic that ruled by bloodshed and by terror. They were own brothers in callousness and cruelty to those men who on this self-same spot a few months ago had watched the daily agony of a martyred Queen, or to those who had rushed into the Abbaye prison on that awful day in September, and at a word from their infamous leaders had put eighty defenceless prisoners—men, women, and children—to the sword.

"Tell him to say what he has done with Capet," said one of the soldiers now, and this rough command was accompanied with a coarse jest that sent the blood flaring up into Marguerite's pale cheeks.

The brutal laugh, the coarse words which accompanied it, the insult flung at Marguerite, had penetrated to Blakeney's slowly returning consciousness. With sudden strength, that appeared almost supernatural, he jumped to his feet, and before any of the others could interfere he had with clenched fist struck the soldier a full blow on the mouth.

The man staggered back with a curse, the other shouted for help; in a moment the narrow place swarmed with soldiers; Marguerite was roughly torn away from the prisoner's side, and thrust into the far corner of the cell, from where she only saw a confused mass of blue coats and white belts, and—towering for one brief moment above what seemed to her fevered fancy like a veritable sea of heads—the pale face of her husband, with wide dilated eyes searching the gloom for hers.

"Remember!" he shouted, and his voice for that brief moment rang out clear and sharp above the din.

Then he disappeared behind the wall of glistening bayonets, of blue coats and uplifted arms; mercifully for her she remembered nothing more very clearly. She felt herself being dragged out of the cell, the iron bar being thrust down behind her with a loud clang. Then in a vague, dreamy state of semi-unconsciousness she saw the heavy bolts being drawn back from the outer door, heard the grating of the key in the monumental lock, and the next moment a breath of fresh air brought the sensation of renewed life into her.

CHAPTER XXX

Afterwards

"I am sorry, Lady Blakeney," said a harsh, dry voice close to her; "the incident at the end of your visit was none of our making, remember."

She turned away, sickened with horror at thought of contact with this wretch. She had heard the heavy oaken door swing to behind her on its ponderous hinges, and the key once again turn in the lock. She felt as if she had suddenly been thrust into a coffin, and that clods of earth were being thrown upon her breast, oppressing her heart so that she could not breathe.

Had she looked for the last time on the man whom she loved beyond everything else on earth, whom she worshipped more ardently day by day? Was she even now carrying within the folds of her kerchief a message from a dying man to his comrades?

Mechanically she followed Chauvelin down the corridor and along the passages which she had traversed a brief half-hour ago. From some distant church tower a clock tolled the hour of ten. It had then really only been little more than thirty brief minutes since first she had entered this grim building, which seemed less stony than the monsters who held authority within it; to her it seemed that centuries had gone over her head during that time. She felt like an old woman, unable to straighten her back or to steady her limbs; she could only dimly see some few paces ahead the trim figure of Chauvelin walking with measured steps, his hands held behind his back, his head thrown up with what looked like triumphant defiance.

At the door of the cubicle where she had been forced to submit to the indignity of being searched by a wardress, the latter was now standing, waiting with characteristic stolidity. In her hand she held the steel files, the dagger and the purse which, as Marguerite passed, she held out to her.

"Your property, citizeness," she said placidly.

She emptied the purse into her own hand, and solemnly counted out the twenty pieces of gold. She was about to replace them all into the purse, when Marguerite pressed one of them back into her wrinkled hand.

"Nineteen will be enough, citizeness," she said; "keep one for yourself, not only for me, but for all the poor women who come here with their heart full of hope, and go hence with it full of despair."

The woman turned calm, lack-lustre eyes on her, and silently pocketed the gold piece with a grudgingly muttered word of thanks.

Chauvelin during this brief interlude, had walked thoughtlessly on ahead. Marguerite, peering down the length of the narrow corridor, spied his sable-clad figure some hundred metres further on as it crossed the dim circle of light thrown by one of the lamps.

She was about to follow, when it seemed to her as if some one was moving in the darkness close beside her. The wardress was even now in the act of closing the door of her cubicle, and there were a couple of soldiers who were disappearing from view round one end of the passage, whilst Chauvelin's retreating form was lost in the gloom at the other.

There was no light close to where she herself was standing, and the blackness around her was as impenetrable as a veil; the sound of a human creature moving and breathing close to her in this intense darkness acted weirdly on her overwrought nerves.

"Qui va la?" she called.

There was a more distinct movement among the shadows this time, as of a swift tread on the flagstones of the corridor. All else was silent round, and now she could plainly hear those footsteps running rapidly down the passage away from her. She strained her eyes to see more clearly, and anon in one of the dim circles of light on ahead she spied a man's figure—slender and darkly clad—walking quickly yet furtively like one pursued. As he crossed the light the man turned to look back. It was her brother Armand.

Her first instinct was to call to him; the second checked that call upon her lips.

Percy had said that Armand was in no danger; then why should he be sneaking along the dark corridors of this awful house of Justice if he was free and safe?

Certainly, even at a distance, her brother's movements suggested to Marguerite that he was in danger of being seen. He cowered in the darkness, tried to avoid the circles of light thrown by the lamps in the passage. At all costs Marguerite felt that she must warn him that the way he was going now would lead him straight into Chauvelin's arms, and she longed to let him know that she was close by.

Feeling sure that he would recognise her voice, she made pretence to turn back to the cubicle through the door of which the wardress had already disappeared, and called out as loudly as she dared:

"Good-night, citizeness!"

But Armand—who surely must have heard—did not pause at the sound. Rather was he walking on now more rapidly than before. In less than a minute he would be reaching the spot where Chauvelin stood waiting for Marguerite. That end of the corridor, however, received no light from any of the lamps; strive how she might, Marguerite could see nothing now either of Chauvelin or of Armand.

Blindly, instinctively, she ran forward, thinking only to reach Armand, and to warn him to turn back before it was too late; before he found himself face to face with the most bitter enemy he and his nearest and dearest had ever had. But as she at last came to a halt at the end of the corridor, panting with the exertion of running and the fear for Armand, she almost fell up against Chauvelin, who was standing there alone and imperturbable, seemingly having waited patiently for her. She could only dimly distinguish his face, the sharp features and thin cruel mouth, but she felt—more than she actually saw—his cold steely eyes fixed with a strange expression of mockery upon her.

But of Armand there was no sign, and she—poor soul!—had difficulty in not betraying the anxiety which she felt for her brother. Had the flagstones swallowed him up? A door on the right was the only one that gave on the corridor at this point; it led to the concierge's lodge, and thence out into the courtyard. Had Chauvelin been dreaming, sleeping with his eyes open, whilst he stood waiting for her, and had Armand succeeded in slipping past him under cover of the darkness and through that door to safety that lay beyond these prison walls?

Marguerite, miserably agitated, not knowing what to think, looked somewhat wild-eyed on Chauvelin; he smiled, that inscrutable, mirthless smile of his, and said blandly:

"Is there aught else that I can do for you, citizeness? This is your nearest way out. No doubt Sir Andrew will be waiting to escort you home."

Then as she—not daring either to reply or to question—walked straight up to the door, he hurried forward, prepared to open it for her. But before he did so he turned to her once again:

"I trust that your visit has pleased you, Lady Blakeney," he said suavely. "At what hour do you desire to repeat it to-morrow?"

"To-morrow?" she reiterated in a vague, absent manner, for she was still dazed with the strange incident of Armand's appearance and his flight.

"Yes. You would like to see Sir Percy again to-morrow, would you not? I myself would gladly pay him a visit from time to time, but he does not care for my company. My colleague, citizen Heron, on the other hand, calls on him four times in every twenty-four hours; he does so a few moments before the changing of the guard, and stays chatting with Sir Percy until after the guard is changed, when he inspects the men and satisfies himself that no traitor has crept in among them. All the men are personally known to him, you see. These hours are at five in the morning and again at eleven, and then again at five and eleven in the evening. My friend Heron, as you see, is zealous and assiduous, and, strangely enough, Sir Percy does not seem to view his visit with any displeasure. Now at any other hour of the day, Lady Blakeney, I pray you command me and I will arrange that citizen Heron grant you a second interview with the prisoner."

Marguerite had only listened to Chauvelin's lengthy speech with half an ear; her thoughts still dwelt on the past half-hour with its bitter joy and its agonising pain; and fighting through her thoughts of Percy there was the recollection of Armand which so disquieted her. But though she had only vaguely listened to what Chauvelin was saying, she caught the drift of it.

Madly she longed to accept his suggestion. The very thought of seeing Percy on the morrow was solace to her aching heart; it could feed on hope to-night instead of on its own bitter pain. But even during this brief moment of hesitancy, and while her whole being cried out for this joy that her enemy was holding out to her, even then in the gloom ahead of her she seemed to see a vision of a pale face raised above a crowd of swaying heads, and of the eyes of the dreamer searching for her own, whilst the last sublime cry of perfect self-devotion once more echoed in her ear:

"Remember!"

The promise which she had given him, that would she fulfil. The burden which he had laid on her shoulders she would try to bear as heroically as he was bearing his own. Aye, even at the cost of the supreme sorrow of never resting again in the haven of his arms.

But in spite of sorrow, in spite of anguish so terrible that she could not imagine Death itself to have a more cruel sting, she wished above all to safeguard that final, attenuated thread of hope which was wound round the packet that lay hidden on her breast.

She wanted, above all, not to arouse Chauvelin's suspicions by markedly refusing to visit the prisoner again—suspicions that might lead to her being searched once more and the precious packet filched from her. Therefore she said to him earnestly now:

"I thank you, citizen, for your solicitude on my behalf, but you will understand, I think, that my visit to the prisoner has been almost more than I could bear. I cannot tell you at this moment whether to-morrow I should be in a fit state to repeat it."

"As you please," he replied urbanely. "But I pray you to remember one thing, and that is—"

He paused a moment while his restless eyes wandered rapidly over her face, trying, as it were, to get at the soul of this woman, at her innermost thoughts, which he felt were hidden from him.

"Yes, citizen," she said quietly; "what is it that I am to remember?"

"That it rests with you, Lady Blakeney, to put an end to the present situation."

"How?"

"Surely you can persuade Sir Percy's friends not to leave their chief in durance vile. They themselves could put an end to his troubles to-morrow."

"By giving up the Dauphin to you, you mean?" she retorted coldly.

"Precisely."

"And you hoped—you still hope that by placing before me the picture of your own fiendish cruelty against my husband you will induce me to act the part of a traitor towards him and a coward before his followers?"

"Oh!" he said deprecatingly, "the cruelty now is no longer mine. Sir Percy's release is in your hands, Lady Blakeney—in that of his followers. I should only be too willing to end the present intolerable situation. You and your friends are applying the last turn of the thumbscrew, not I—"

She smothered the cry of horror that had risen to her lips. The man's cold-blooded sophistry was threatening to make a breach in her armour of self-control.

She would no longer trust herself to speak, but made a quick movement towards the door.

He shrugged his shoulders as if the matter were now entirely out of his control. Then he opened the door for her to pass out, and as her skirts brushed against him he bowed with studied deference, murmuring a cordial "Good-night!"

"And remember, Lady Blakeney," he added politely, "that should you at any time desire to communicate with me at my rooms, 19, Rue Dupuy, I hold myself entirely at your service."

Then as her tall, graceful figure disappeared in the outside gloom he passed his thin hand over his mouth as if to wipe away the last lingering signs of triumphant irony:

"The second visit will work wonders, I think, my fine lady," he murmured under his breath.

CHAPTER XXXI

An Interlude

It was close on midnight now, and still they sat opposite one another, he the friend and she the wife, talking over that brief half-hour that had meant an eternity to her.

Marguerite had tried to tell Sir Andrew everything; bitter as it was to put into actual words the pathos and misery which she had witnessed, yet she would hide nothing from the devoted comrade whom she knew Percy would trust absolutely. To him she repeated every word that Percy had uttered, described every inflection of his voice, those enigmatical phrases which she had not understood, and together they cheated one another into the belief that hope lingered somewhere hidden in those words.

"I am not going to despair, Lady Blakeney," said Sir Andrew firmly; "and, moreover, we are not going to disobey. I would stake my life that even now Blakeney has some scheme in his mind which is embodied in the various letters which he has given you, and which—Heaven help us in that case!—we might thwart by disobedience. Tomorrow in the late afternoon I will escort you to the Rue de Charonne. It is a house that we all know well, and which Armand, of course, knows too. I had already inquired there two days ago to ascertain whether by chance St. Just was not in hiding there, but Lucas, the landlord and old-clothes dealer, knew nothing about him."

Marguerite told him about her swift vision of Armand in the dark corridor of the house of Justice.

"Can you understand it, Sir Andrew?" she asked, fixing her deep, luminous eyes inquiringly upon him.

"No, I cannot," he said, after an almost imperceptible moment of hesitancy; "but we shall see him to-morrow. I have no doubt that Mademoiselle Lange will know where to find him; and now that we know where she is, all our anxiety about him, at any rate, should soon be at an end."

He rose and made some allusion to the lateness of the hour. Somehow it seemed to her that her devoted friend was trying to hide his innermost thoughts from her. She watched him with an anxious, intent gaze.

"Can you understand it all, Sir Andrew?" she reiterated with a pathetic note of appeal.

"No, no!" he said firmly. "On my soul, Lady Blakeney, I know no more of Armand than you do yourself. But I am sure that Percy is right. The boy frets because remorse must have assailed him by now. Had he but obeyed implicitly that day, as we all did—"

But he could not frame the whole terrible proposition in words. Bitterly as he himself felt on the subject of Armand, he would not add yet another burden to this devoted woman's heavy load of misery.

"It was Fate, Lady Blakeney," he said after a while. "Fate! a damnable fate which did it all. Great God! to think of Blakeney in the hands of those brutes seems so horrible that at times I feel as if the whole thing were a nightmare, and that the next moment we shall both wake hearing his merry voice echoing through this room."

He tried to cheer her with words of hope that he knew were but chimeras. A heavy weight of despondency lay on his heart. The letter from his chief was hidden against his breast; he would study it anon in the privacy of his own apartment so as to commit every word to memory that related to the measures for the ultimate safety of the child-King. After that it would have to be destroyed, lest it fell into inimical hands.

Soon he bade Marguerite good-night. She was tired out, body and soul, and he—her faithful friend—vaguely wondered how long she would be able to withstand the strain of so much sorrow, such unspeakable misery.

When at last she was alone Marguerite made brave efforts to compose her nerves so as to obtain a certain modicum of sleep this night. But, strive how she might, sleep would not come. How could it, when before her wearied brain there rose constantly that awful vision of Percy in the long, narrow cell, with weary head bent over his arm, and those friends shouting persistently in his ear:

"Wake up, citizen! Tell us, where is Capet?"

The fear obsessed her that his mind might give way; for the mental agony of such intense weariness must be well-nigh impossible to bear. In the dark, as she sat hour after hour at the open window, looking out in the direction where through the veil of snow the grey walls of the Chatelet prison towered silent and grim, she seemed to see his pale, drawn face with almost appalling reality; she could see every line of it, and could study it with the intensity born of a terrible fear.

How long would the ghostly glimmer of merriment still linger in the eyes? When would the hoarse, mirthless laugh rise to the lips, that awful laugh that proclaims madness? Oh! she could have screamed now with the awfulness of this haunting terror. Ghouls seemed to be mocking her out of the darkness, every flake of snow that fell silently on the window-sill became a grinning face that taunted and derided; every cry in the silence of the night, every footstep on the quay below turned to hideous jeers hurled at her by tormenting fiends.

She closed the window quickly, for she feared that she would go mad. For an hour after that she walked up and down the room making violent efforts to control her nerves, to find a glimmer of that courage which she promised Percy that she would have.

CHAPTER XXXII

Sisters

The morning found her fagged out, but more calm. Later on she managed to drink some coffee, and having washed and dressed, she prepared to go out.

Sir Andrew appeared in time to ascertain her wishes.

"I promised Percy to go to the Rue de Charonne in the late afternoon," she said. "I have some hours to spare, and mean to employ them in trying to find speech with Mademoiselle Lange."

"Blakeney has told you where she lives?"

"Yes. In the Square du Roule. I know it well. I can be there in half an hour."

He, of course, begged to be allowed to accompany her, and anon they were walking together quickly up toward the Faubourg St. Honore. The snow had ceased falling, but it was still very cold, but neither Marguerite nor Sir Andrew were conscious of the temperature or of any outward signs around them. They walked on silently until they reached the torn-down gates of the Square du Roule; there Sir Andrew parted from Marguerite after having appointed to meet her an hour later at a small eating-house he knew of where they could have some food together, before starting on their long expedition to the Rue de Charonne.

Five minutes later Marguerite Blakeney was shown in by worthy Madame Belhomme, into the quaint and pretty drawing-room with its soft-toned hangings and old-world air of faded grace. Mademoiselle Lange was sitting there, in a capacious armchair, which encircled her delicate figure with its frame-work of dull old gold.

She was ostensibly reading when Marguerite was announced, for an open book lay on a table beside her; but it seemed to the visitor that mayhap the young girl's thoughts had played truant from her work, for her pose was listless and apathetic, and there was a look of grave trouble upon the childlike face.

She rose when Marguerite entered, obviously puzzled at the unexpected visit, and somewhat awed at the appearance of this beautiful woman with the sad look in her eyes.

"I must crave your pardon, mademoiselle," said Lady Blakeney as soon as the door had once more closed on Madame Belhomme, and she found herself alone with the young girl. "This visit at such an early hour must seem to you an intrusion. But I am Marguerite St. Just, and—"

Her smile and outstretched hand completed the sentence.

"St. Just!" exclaimed Jeanne.

"Yes. Armand's sister!"

A swift blush rushed to the girl's pale cheeks; her brown eyes expressed unadulterated joy. Marguerite, who was studying her closely, was conscious that her poor aching heart went out to this exquisite child, the far-off innocent cause of so much misery.

Jeanne, a little shy, a little confused and nervous in her movements, was pulling a chair close to the fire, begging Marguerite to sit. Her words came out all the while in short jerky sentences, and from time to time she stole swift shy glances at Armand's sister.

"You will forgive me, mademoiselle," said Marguerite, whose simple and calm manner quickly tended to soothe Jeanne Lange's confusion; "but I was so anxious about my brother—I do not know where to find him."

"And so you came to me, madame?"

"Was I wrong?"

"Oh, no! But what made you think that—that I would know?"

"I guessed," said Marguerite with a smile. "You had heard about me then?"

"Oh, yes!"

"Through whom? Did Armand tell you about me?"

"No, alas! I have not seen him this past fortnight, since you, mademoiselle, came into his life; but many of Armand's friends are in Paris just now; one of them knew, and he told me."

The soft blush had now overspread the whole of the girl's face, even down to her graceful neck. She waited to see Marguerite comfortably installed in an armchair, then she resumed shyly:

"And it was Armand who told me all about you. He loves you so dearly."

"Armand and I were very young children when we lost our parents," said Marguerite softly, "and we were all in all to each other then. And until I married he was the man I loved best in all the world."

"He told me you were married—to an Englishman."

"Yes?"

"He loves England too. At first he always talked of my going there with him as his wife, and of the happiness we should find there together."

"Why do you say 'at first'?"

"He talks less about England now."

"Perhaps he feels that now you know all about it, and that you understand each other with regard to the future."

"Perhaps."

Jeanne sat opposite to Marguerite on a low stool by the fire. Her elbows were resting on her knees, and her face just now was half-hidden by the wealth of her brown curls. She looked exquisitely pretty sitting like this, with just the suggestion of sadness in the listless pose. Marguerite had come here to-day prepared to hate this young girl, who in a few brief days had stolen not only Armand's heart, but his allegiance to his chief, and his trust in him. Since last night, when she had seen her brother sneak silently past her like a thief in the night, she had nurtured thoughts of ill-will and anger against Jeanne.

But hatred and anger had melted at the sight of this child. Marguerite, with the perfect understanding born of love itself, had soon realised the charm which a woman like Mademoiselle Lange must of necessity exercise over a chivalrous, enthusiastic nature like Armand's. The sense of protection—the strongest perhaps that exists in a good man's heart—would draw him irresistibly to this beautiful child, with the great, appealing eyes, and the look of pathos that pervaded the entire face. Marguerite, looking in silence on the—dainty picture before her, found it in her heart to forgive Armand for disobeying his chief when those eyes beckoned to him in a contrary direction.

How could he, how could any chivalrous man endure the thought of this delicate, fresh flower lying crushed and drooping in the hands of monsters who respected neither courage nor purity? And Armand had been more than human, or mayhap less, if he had indeed consented to leave the fate of the girl whom he had sworn to love and protect in other hands than his own.

It seemed almost as if Jeanne was conscious of the fixity of Marguerite's gaze, for though she did not turn to look at her, the flush gradually deepened in her cheeks.

"Mademoiselle Lange," said Marguerite gently, "do you not feel that you can trust me?"

She held out her two hands to the girl, and Jeanne slowly turned to her. The next moment she was kneeling at Marguerite's feet, and kissing the beautiful kind hands that had been stretched out to her with such sisterly love.

"Indeed, indeed, I do trust you," she said, and looked with tear-dimmed eyes in the pale face above her. "I have longed for some one in whom I could confide. I have been so lonely lately, and Armand—"

With an impatient little gesture she brushed away the tears which had gathered in her eyes.

"What has Armand been doing?" asked Marguerite with an encouraging smile.

"Oh, nothing to grieve me!" replied the young girl eagerly, "for he is kind and good, and chivalrous and noble. Oh, I love him with all my heart! I loved him from the moment that I set eyes on him, and then he came to see me—perhaps you know! And he talked so beautiful about England, and so nobly about his leader the Scarlet Pimpernel—have you heard of him?"

"Yes," said Marguerite, smiling. "I have heard of him."

"It was that day that citizen Heron came with his soldiers! Oh! you do not know citizen Heron. He is the most cruel man in France. In Paris he is hated by every one, and no one is safe from his spies. He came to arrest Armand, but I was able to fool him and to save Armand. And after that," she added with charming naivete, "I felt as if, having saved Armand's life, he belonged to me—and his love for me had made me his."

"Then I was arrested," she continued after a slight pause, and at the recollection of what she had endured then her fresh voice still trembled with horror.

"They dragged me to prison, and I spent two days in a dark cell, where—"

She hid her face in her hands, whilst a few sobs shook her whole frame; then she resumed more calmly:

"I had seen nothing of Armand. I wondered where he was, and I knew that he would be eating out his heart with anxiety for me. But God was watching over me. At first I was transferred to the Temple prison, and there a kind creature—a sort of man-of-all work in the prison took compassion on me. I do not know how he contrived it, but one morning very early he brought me some filthy old rags which he told me to put on quickly, and when I had done that he bade me follow him. Oh! he was a very dirty, wretched man himself, but he must have had a kind heart. He took me by the hand and made me carry his broom and brushes. Nobody took much notice of us, the dawn was only just breaking, and the passages were very dark and deserted; only once some soldiers began to chaff him about me: 'C'est ma fille—quoi?' he said roughly. I very nearly laughed then, only I had the good sense to restrain myself, for I knew that my freedom, and perhaps my life, depended on my not betraying myself. My grimy, tattered guide took me with him right through the interminable corridors of that awful building, whilst I prayed fervently to God for him and for myself. We got out by one of the service stairs and exit, and then he dragged me through some narrow streets until we came to a corner where a covered cart stood waiting. My kind friend told me to get into the cart, and then he bade the driver on the box take me straight to a house in the Rue St. Germain l'Auxerrois. Oh! I was infinitely grateful to the poor creature who had helped me to get out of that awful prison, and I would gladly have given him some money, for I am sure he was very poor; but I had none by me. He told me that I should be quite safe in the house in the Rue St. Germain l'Auxerrois, and begged me to wait there patiently for a few days until I heard from one who had my welfare at heart, and who would further arrange for my safety."

Marguerite had listened silently to this narrative so naively told by this child, who obviously had no idea to whom she owed her freedom and her life. While the girl talked, her mind could follow with unspeakable pride and happiness every phase of that scene in the early dawn, when that mysterious, ragged man-of-all-work, unbeknown even to the woman whom he was saving, risked his own noble life for the sake of her whom his friend and comrade loved.

"And did you never see again the kind man to whom you owe your life?" she asked.

"No!" replied Jeanne. "I never saw him since; but when I arrived at the Rue St. Germain l'Auxerrois I was told by the good people who took charge of me that the ragged man-of-all-work had been none other than the mysterious Englishman whom Armand reveres, he whom they call the Scarlet Pimpernel."

"But you did not stay very long in the Rue St. Germain l'Auxerrois, did you?"

"No. Only three days. The third day I received a communique from the Committee of General Security, together with an unconditional certificate of safety. It meant that I was free—quite free. Oh! I could scarcely believe it. I laughed and I cried until the people in the house thought that I had gone mad. The past few days had been such a horrible nightmare."

"And then you saw Armand again?"

"Yes. They told him that I was free. And he came here to see me. He often comes; he will be here anon."

"But are you not afraid on his account and your own? He is—he must be still—'suspect'; a well-known adherent of the Scarlet Pimpernel, he would be safer out of Paris."

"No! oh, no! Armand is in no danger. He, too, has an unconditional certificate of safety."

"An unconditional certificate of safety?" asked Marguerite, whilst a deep frown of grave puzzlement appeared between her brows. "What does that mean?

"It means that he is free to come and go as he likes; that neither he nor I have anything to fear from Heron and his awful spies. Oh! but for that sad and careworn look on Armand's face we could be so happy; but he is so unlike himself. He is Armand and yet another; his look at times quite frightens me."

"Yet you know why he is so sad," said Marguerite in a strange, toneless voice which she seemed quite unable to control, for that tonelessness came from a terrible sense of suffocation, of a feeling as if her heart-strings were being gripped by huge, hard hands.

"Yes, I know," said Jeanne half hesitatingly, as if knowing, she was still unconvinced.

"His chief, his comrade, the friend of whom you speak, the Scarlet Pimpernel, who risked his life in order to save yours, mademoiselle, is a prisoner in the hands of those that hate him."

Marguerite had spoken with sudden vehemence. There was almost an appeal in her voice now, as if she were trying not to convince Jeanne only, but also herself, of something that was quite simple, quite straightforward, and yet which appeared to be receding from her, an intangible something, a spirit that was gradually yielding to a force as yet unborn, to a phantom that had not yet emerged from out chaos.

But Jeanne seemed unconscious of all this. Her mind was absorbed in Armand, the man whom she loved in her simple, whole-hearted way, and who had seemed so different of late.

"Oh, yes!" she said with a deep, sad sigh, whilst the ever-ready tears once more gathered in her eyes, "Armand is very unhappy because of him. The Scarlet Pimpernel was his friend; Armand loved and revered him. Did you know," added the girl, turning large, horror-filled eyes on Marguerite, "that they want some information from him about the Dauphin, and to force him to give it they—they—"

"Yes, I know," said Marguerite.

"Can you wonder, then, that Armand is unhappy. Oh! last night, after he went from me, I cried for hours, just because he had looked so sad. He no longer talks of happy England, of the cottage we were to have, and of the Kentish orchards in May. He has not ceased to love me, for at times his love seems so great that I tremble with a delicious sense of fear. But oh! his love for me no longer makes him happy."

Her head had gradually sunk lower and lower on her breast, her voice died down in a murmur broken by heartrending sighs. Every generous impulse in Marguerite's noble nature prompted her to take that sorrowing child in her arms, to comfort her if she could, to reassure her if she had the power. But a strange icy feeling had gradually invaded her heart, even whilst she listened to the simple unsophisticated talk of Jeanne Lange. Her hands felt numb and clammy, and instinctively she withdrew away from the near vicinity of the girl. She felt as if the room, the furniture in it, even the window before her were dancing a wild and curious dance, and that from everywhere around strange whistling sounds reached her ears, which caused her head to whirl and her brain to reel.

Jeanne had buried her head in her hands. She was crying—softly, almost humbly at first, as if half ashamed of her grief; then, suddenly it seemed, as if she could not contain herself any longer, a heavy sob escaped her throat and shook her whole delicate frame with its violence. Sorrow no longer would be gainsaid, it insisted on physical expression—that awful tearing of the heart-strings which leaves the body numb and panting with pain.

In a moment Marguerite had forgotten; the dark and shapeless phantom that had knocked at the gate of her soul was relegated back into chaos. It ceased to be, it was made to shrivel and to burn in the great seething cauldron of womanly sympathy. What part this child had played in the vast cataclysm of misery which had dragged a noble-hearted enthusiast into the dark torture-chamber, whence the only outlet led to the guillotine, she—Marguerite Blakeney—did not know; what part Armand, her brother, had played in it, that she would not dare to guess; all that she knew was that here was a loving heart that was filled with pain—a young, inexperienced soul that was having its first tussle with the grim realities of life—and every motherly instinct in Marguerite was aroused.

She rose and gently drew the young girl up from her knees, and then closer to her; she pillowed the grief-stricken head against her shoulder, and murmured gentle, comforting words into the tiny ear.

"I have news for Armand," she whispered, "that will comfort him, a message—a letter from his friend. You will see, dear, that when Armand reads it he will become a changed man; you see, Armand acted a little foolishly a few days ago. His chief had given him orders which he disregarded—he was so anxious about you—he should have obeyed; and now, mayhap, he feels that his disobedience may have been the—the innocent cause of much misery to others; that is, no doubt, the reason why he is so sad. The letter from his friend will cheer him, you will see."

"Do you really think so, madame?" murmured Jeanne, in whose tear-stained eyes the indomitable hopefulness of youth was already striving to shine.

"I am sure of it," assented Marguerite.

And for the moment she was absolutely sincere. The phantom had entirely vanished. She would even, had he dared to re-appear, have mocked and derided him for his futile attempt at turning the sorrow in her heart to a veritable hell of bitterness.

CHAPTER XXXIII

Little Mother

The two women, both so young still, but each of them with a mark of sorrow already indelibly graven in her heart, were clinging to one another, bound together by the strong bond of sympathy. And but for the sadness of it all it were difficult to conjure up a more beautiful picture than that which they presented as they stood side by side; Marguerite, tall and stately as an exquisite lily, with the crown of her ardent hair and the glory of her deep blue eyes, and Jeanne Lange, dainty and delicate, with the brown curls and the child-like droop of the soft, moist lips.

Thus Armand saw them when, a moment or two later, entered unannounced. He had pushed open the door and looked on the two women silently for a second or two; on the girl whom he loved so dearly, for whose sake he had committed the great, the unpardonable sin which would send him forever henceforth, Cain-like, a wanderer on the face of the earth; and the other, his sister, her whom a Judas act would condemn to lonely sorrow and widowhood.

He could have cried out in an agony of remorse, and it was the groan of acute soul anguish which escaped his lips that drew Marguerite's attention to his presence.

Even though many things that Jeanne Lange had said had prepared her for a change in her brother, she was immeasurably shocked by his appearance. He had always been slim and rather below the average in height, but now his usually upright and trim figure seemed to have shrunken within itself; his clothes hung baggy on his shoulders, his hands appeared waxen and emaciated, but the greatest change was in his face, in the wide circles round the eyes, that spoke of wakeful nights, in the hollow cheeks, and the mouth that had wholly forgotten how to smile.

Percy after a week's misery immured in a dark and miserable prison, deprived of food and rest, did not look such a physical wreck as did Armand St. Just, who was free.

Marguerite's heart reproached her for what she felt had been neglect, callousness on her part. Mutely, within herself, she craved his forgiveness for the appearance of that phantom which should never have come forth from out that chaotic hell which had engendered it.

"Armand!" she cried.

And the loving arms that had guided his baby footsteps long ago, the tender hands that had wiped his boyish tears, were stretched out with unalterable love toward him.

"I have a message for you, dear," she said gently—"a letter from him. Mademoiselle Jeanne allowed me to wait here for you until you came."

Silently, like a little shy mouse, Jeanne had slipped out of the room. Her pure love for Armand had ennobled every one of her thoughts, and her innate kindliness and refinement had already suggested that brother and sister would wish to be alone. At the door she had turned and met Armand's look. That look had satisfied her; she felt that in it she had read the expression of his love, and to it she had responded with a glance that spoke of hope for a future meeting.

As soon as the door had closed on Jeanne Lange, Armand, with an impulse that refused to be checked, threw himself into his sister's arms. The present, with all its sorrows, its remorse and its shame, had sunk away; only the past remained—the unforgettable past, when Marguerite was "little mother"—the soother, the comforter, the healer, the ever-willing receptacle wherein he had been wont to pour the burden of his childish griefs, of his boyish escapades.

Conscious that she could not know everything—not yet, at any rate—he gave himself over to the rapture of this pure embrace, the last time, mayhap, that those fond arms would close round him in unmixed tenderness, the last time that those fond lips would murmur words of affection and of comfort.

To-morrow those same lips would, perhaps, curse the traitor, and the small hand be raised in wrath, pointing an avenging finger on the Judas.

"Little mother," he whispered, babbling like a child, "it is good to see you again."

"And I have brought you a message from Percy," she said, "a letter which he begged me to give you as soon as may be."

"You have seen him?" he asked.

She nodded silently, unable to speak. Not now, not when her nerves were strung to breaking pitch, would she trust herself to speak of that awful yesterday. She groped in the folds of her gown and took the packet which Percy had given her for Armand. It felt quite bulky in her hand.

"There is quite a good deal there for you to read, dear," she said. "Percy begged me to give you this, and then to let you read it when you were alone."

She pressed the packet into his hand. Armand's face was ashen pale. He clung to her with strange, nervous tenacity; the paper which he held in one hand seemed to sear his fingers as with a branding-iron.

"I will slip away now," she said, for strangely enough since Percy's message had been in Armand's hands she was once again conscious of that awful feeling of iciness round her heart, a sense of numbness that paralysed her very thoughts.

"You will make my excuses to Mademoiselle Lange," she said, trying to smile. "When you have read, you will wish to see her alone."

Gently she disengaged herself from Armand's grasp and made for the door. He appeared dazed, staring down at that paper which was scorching his fingers. Only when her hand was on the latch did he seem to realise that she was going.

"Little mother," came involuntarily to his lips.

She came straight back to him and took both his wrists in her small hands. She was taller than he, and his head was slightly bent forward. Thus she towered over him, loving but strong, her great, earnest eyes searching his soul.

"When shall I see you again, little mother?" he asked.

"Read your letter, dear," she replied, "and when you have read it, if you care to impart its contents to me, come to-night to my lodgings, Quai de la Ferraille, above the saddler's shop. But if there is aught in it that you do not wish me to know, then do not come; I shall understand. Good-bye, dear."

She took his head between her two cold hands, and as it was still bowed she placed a tender kiss, as of a long farewell, upon his hair.

Then she went out of the room.

CHAPTER XXXIV

The Letter

Armand sat in the armchair in front of the fire. His head rested against one hand; in the other he held the letter written by the friend whom he had betrayed.

Twice he had read it now, and already was every word of that minute, clear writing graven upon the innermost fibres of his body, upon the most secret cells of his brain.

Armand, I know. I knew even before Chauvelin came to me, and stood there hoping to gloat over the soul-agony a man who finds that he has been betrayed by his dearest friend. But that d—d reprobate did not get that satisfaction, for I was prepared. Not only do I know, Armand, but I UNDERSTAND. I, who do not know what love is, have realised how small a thing is honour, loyalty, or friendship when weighed in the balance of a loved one's need.

To save Jeanne you sold me to Heron and his crowd. We are men, Armand, and the word forgiveness has only been spoken once these past two thousand years, and then it was spoken by Divine lips. But Marguerite loves you, and mayhap soon you will be all that is left her to love on this earth. Because of this she must never know.... As for you, Armand—well, God help you! But meseems that the hell which you are enduring now is ten thousand times worse than mine. I have heard your furtive footsteps in the corridor outside the grated window of this cell, and would not then have exchanged my hell for yours. Therefore, Armand, and because Marguerite loves you, I would wish to turn to you in the hour that I need help. I am in a tight corner, but the hour may come when a comrade's hand might mean life to me. I have thought of you, Armand partly because having taken more than my life, your own belongs to me, and partly because the plan which I have in my mind will carry with it grave risks for the man who stands by me.

I swore once that never would I risk a comrade's life to save mine own; but matters are so different now... we are both in hell, Armand, and I in striving to get out of mine will be showing you a way out of yours.

Will you retake possession of your lodgings in the Rue de la Croix Blanche? I should always know then where to find you in an emergency. But if at any time you receive another letter from me, be its contents what they may, act in accordance with the letter, and send a copy of it at once to Ffoulkes or to Marguerite. Keep in close touch with them both. Tell her I so far forgave your disobedience (there was nothing more) that I may yet trust my life and mine honour in your hands.

I shall have no means of ascertaining definitely whether you will do all that I ask; but somehow, Armand, I know that you will.

For the third time Armand read the letter through.

"But, Armand," he repeated, murmuring the words softly under his breath, "I know that you will."

Prompted by some indefinable instinct, moved by a force that compelled, he allowed himself to glide from the chair on to the floor, on to his knees.

All the pent-up bitterness, the humiliation, the shame of the past few days, surged up from his heart to his lips in one great cry of pain.

"My God!" he whispered, "give me the chance of giving my life for him."

Alone and unwatched, he gave himself over for a few moments to the almost voluptuous delight of giving free rein to his grief. The hot Latin blood in him, tempestuous in all its passions, was firing his heart and brain now with the glow of devotion and of self-sacrifice.

The calm, self-centred Anglo-Saxon temperament—the almost fatalistic acceptance of failure without reproach yet without despair, which Percy's letter to him had evidenced in so marked a manner—was, mayhap, somewhat beyond the comprehension of this young enthusiast, with pure Gallic blood in his veins, who was ever wont to allow his most elemental passions to sway his actions. But though he did not altogether understand, Armand St. Just could fully appreciate. All that was noble and loyal in him rose triumphant from beneath the devastating ashes of his own shame.

Soon his mood calmed down, his look grew less wan and haggard. Hearing Jeanne's discreet and mouselike steps in the next room, he rose quickly and hid the letter in the pocket of his coat.

She came in and inquired anxiously about Marguerite; a hurriedly expressed excuse from him, however, satisfied her easily enough. She wanted to be alone with Armand, happy to see that he held his head more erect to-day, and that the look as of a hunted creature had entirely gone from his eyes.

She ascribed this happy change to Marguerite, finding it in her heart to be grateful to the sister for having accomplished what the fiancee had failed to do.

For awhile they remained together, sitting side by side, speaking at times, but mostly silent, seeming to savour the return of truant happiness. Armand felt like a sick man who has obtained a sudden surcease from pain. He looked round him with a kind of melancholy delight on this room which he had entered for the first time less than a fortnight ago, and which already was so full of memories.

Those first hours spent at the feet of Jeanne Lange, how exquisite they had been, how fleeting in the perfection of their happiness! Now they seemed to belong to a far distant past, evanescent like the perfume of violets, swift in their flight like the winged steps of youth. Blakeney's letter had effectually taken the bitter sting from out his remorse, but it had increased his already over-heavy load of inconsolable sorrow.

Later in the day he turned his footsteps in the direction of the river, to the house in the Quai de la Ferraille above the saddler's shop. Marguerite had returned alone from the expedition to the Rue de Charonne. Whilst Sir Andrew took charge of the little party of fugitives and escorted them out of Paris, she came back to her lodgings in order to collect her belongings, preparatory to taking up her quarters in the house of Lucas, the old-clothes dealer. She returned also because she hoped to see Armand.

"If you care to impart the contents of the letter to me, come to my lodgings to-night," she had said.

All day a phantom had haunted her, the phantom of an agonising suspicion.

But now the phantom had vanished never to return. Armand was sitting close beside her, and he told her that the chief had selected him amongst all the others to stand by him inside the walls of Paris until the last.

"I shall mayhap," thus closed that precious document, "have no means of ascertaining definitely whether you will act in accordance with this letter. But somehow, Armand, I know that you will."

"I know that you will, Armand," reiterated Marguerite fervently.

She had only been too eager to be convinced; the dread and dark suspicion which had been like a hideous poisoned sting had only vaguely touched her soul; it had not gone in very deeply. How could it, when in its death-dealing passage it encountered the rampart of tender, almost motherly love?

Armand, trying to read his sister's thoughts in the depths of her blue eyes, found the look in them limpid and clear. Percy's message to Armand had reassured her just as he had intended that it should do. Fate had dealt over harshly with her as it was, and Blakeney's remorse for the sorrow which he had already caused her, was scarcely less keen than Armand's. He did not wish her to bear the intolerable burden of hatred against her brother; and by binding St. Just close to him at the supreme hour of danger he hoped to prove to the woman whom he loved so passionately that Armand was worthy of trust.

PART III

CHAPTER XXXV

The Last Phase

"Well? How is it now?"

"The last phase, I think."

"He will yield?"

"He must."

"Bah! you have said it yourself often enough; those English are tough."

"It takes time to hack them to pieces, perhaps. In this case even you, citizen

Chauvelin, said that it would take time. Well, it has taken just seventeen days, and now the end is in sight."

It was close on midnight in the guard-room which gave on the innermost cell of the Conciergerie. Heron had just visited the prisoner as was his wont at this hour of the night. He had watched the changing of the guard, inspected the night-watch, questioned the sergeant in charge, and finally he had been on the point of retiring to his own new quarters in the house of Justice, in the near vicinity of the Conciergerie, when citizen Chauvelin entered the guard-room unexpectedly and detained his colleague with the peremptory question:

"How is it now?"

"If you are so near the end, citizen Heron," he now said, sinking his voice to a whisper, "why not make a final effort and end it to-night?"

"I wish I could; the anxiety is wearing me out more'n him," added with a jerky movement of the head in direction of the inner cell.

"Shall I try?" rejoined Chauvelin grimly.

"Yes, an you wish."

Citizen Heron's long limbs were sprawling on a guard-room chair. In this low narrow room he looked like some giant whose body had been carelessly and loosely put together by a 'prentice hand in the art of manufacture. His broad shoulders were bent, probably under the weight of anxiety to which he had referred, and his head, with the lank, shaggy hair overshadowing the brow, was sunk deep down on his chest.

Chauvelin looked on his friend and associate with no small measure of contempt. He would no doubt have preferred to conclude the present difficult transaction entirely in his own way and alone; but equally there was no doubt that the Committee of Public Safety did not trust him quite so fully as it used to do before the fiasco at Calais and the blunders of Boulogne. Heron, on the other hand, enjoyed to its outermost the confidence of his colleagues; his ferocious cruelty and his callousness were well known, whilst physically, owing to his great height and bulky if loosely knit frame, he had a decided advantage over his trim and slender friend.

As far as the bringing of prisoners to trial was concerned, the chief agent of the Committee of General Security had been given a perfectly free hand by the decree of the 27th Nivose. At first, therefore, he had experienced no difficulty when he desired to keep the Englishman in close confinement for a time without hurrying on that summary trial and condemnation which the populace had loudly demanded, and to which they felt that they were entitled to as a public holiday. The death of the Scarlet Pimpernel on the guillotine had been a spectacle promised by every demagogue who desired to purchase a few votes by holding out visions of pleasant doings to come; and during the first few days the mob of Paris was content to enjoy the delights of expectation.

But now seventeen days had gone by and still the Englishman was not being brought to trial. The pleasure-loving public was waxing impatient, and earlier this evening, when citizen Heron had shown himself in the stalls of the national theatre, he was greeted by a crowded audience with decided expressions of disapproval and open mutterings of:

"What of the Scarlet Pimpernel?"

It almost looked as if he would have to bring that accursed Englishman to the guillotine without having wrested from him the secret which he would have given a fortune to possess. Chauvelin, who had also been present at the theatre, had heard the expressions of discontent; hence his visit to his colleague at this late hour of the night.

"Shall I try?" he had queried with some impatience, and a deep sigh of satisfaction escaped his thin lips when the chief agent, wearied and discouraged, had reluctantly agreed.

"Let the men make as much noise as they like," he added with an enigmatical smile. "The Englishman and I will want an accompaniment to our pleasant conversation."

Heron growled a surly assent, and without another word Chauvelin turned towards the inner cell. As he stepped in he allowed the iron bar to fall into its socket behind him. Then he went farther into the room until the distant recess was fully revealed to him. His tread had been furtive and almost noiseless. Now he paused, for he had caught sight the prisoner. For a moment he stood quite still, with hands clasped behind his back in his wonted attitude—still save for a strange, involuntary twitching of his mouth, and the nervous clasping and interlocking of his fingers behind his back. He was savouring to its utmost fulsomeness the supremest joy which animal man can ever know—the joy of looking on a fallen enemy.

Blakeney sat at the table with one arm resting on it, the emaciated hand tightly clutched, the body leaning forward, the eyes looking into nothingness.

For the moment he was unconscious of Chauvelin's presence, and the latter could gaze on him to the full content of his heart.

Indeed, to all outward appearances there sat a man whom privations of every sort and kind, the want of fresh air, of proper food, above all, of rest, had worn down physically to a shadow. There was not a particle of colour in cheeks or lips, the skin was grey in hue, the eyes looked like deep caverns, wherein the glow of fever was all that was left of life.

Chauvelin looked on in silence, vaguely stirred by something that he could not define, something that right through his triumphant satisfaction, his hatred and final certainty of revenge, had roused in him a sense almost of admiration.

He gazed on the noiseless figure of the man who had endured so much for an ideal, and as he gazed it seemed to him as if the spirit no longer dwelt in the body, but hovered round in the dank, stuffy air of the narrow cell above the head of the lonely prisoner, crowning it with glory that was no longer of this earth.

Of this the looker-on was conscious despite himself, of that and of the fact that stare as he might, and with perception rendered doubly keen by hate, he could not, in spite of all, find the least trace of mental weakness in that far-seeing gaze which seemed to pierce the prison walls, nor could he see that bodily weakness had tended to subdue the ruling passions.

Sir Percy Blakeney—a prisoner since seventeen days in close, solitary confinement, half-starved, deprived of rest, and of that mental and physical activity which had been the very essence of life to him hitherto—might be outwardly but a shadow of his former brilliant self, but nevertheless he was still that same elegant English gentleman, that prince of dandies whom Chauvelin had first met eighteen months ago at the most courtly Court in Europe. His clothes, despite constant wear and the want of attention from a scrupulous valet, still betrayed the perfection of London tailoring; he had put them on with meticulous care, they were free from the slightest particle of dust, and the filmy folds of priceless Mechlin still half-veiled the delicate whiteness of his shapely hands.

And in the pale, haggard face, in the whole pose of body and of arm, there was still the expression of that indomitable strength of will, that reckless daring, that almost insolent challenge to Fate; it was there untamed, uncrushed. Chauvelin himself could not deny to himself its presence or its force. He felt that behind that smooth brow, which looked waxlike now, the mind was still alert, scheming, plotting, striving for freedom, for conquest and for power, and rendered even doubly keen and virile by the ardour of supreme self-sacrifice.

Chauvelin now made a slight movement and suddenly Blakeney became conscious of his presence, and swift as a flash a smile lit up his wan face.

"Why! if it is not my engaging friend Monsieur Chambertin," he said gaily.

He rose and stepped forward in the most approved fashion prescribed by the elaborate etiquette of the time. But Chauvelin smiled grimly and a look of almost animal lust gleamed in his pale eyes, for he had noted that as he rose Sir Percy had to seek the support of the table, even whilst a dull film appeared to gather over his eyes.

The gesture had been quick and cleverly disguised, but it had been there nevertheless—that and the livid hue that overspread the face as if consciousness was threatening to go. All of which was sufficient still further to assure the looker-on that that mighty physical strength was giving way at last, that strength which he had hated in his enemy almost as much as he had hated the thinly veiled insolence of his manner.

"And what procures me, sir, the honour of your visit?" continued Blakeney, who had—at any rate, outwardly soon recovered himself, and whose voice, though distinctly hoarse and spent, rang quite cheerfully across the dank narrow cell.

"My desire for your welfare, Sir Percy," replied Chauvelin with equal pleasantry.

"La, sir; but have you not gratified that desire already, to an extent which leaves no room for further solicitude? But I pray you, will you not sit down?" he continued, turning back toward the table. "I was about to partake of the lavish supper which your friends have provided for me. Will you not share it, sir? You are most royally welcome, and it will mayhap remind you of that supper we shared together in Calais, eh? when you, Monsieur Chambertin, were temporarily in holy orders."

He laughed, offering his enemy a chair, and pointed with inviting gesture to the hunk of brown bread and the mug of water which stood on the table.

"Such as it is, sir," he said with a pleasant smile, "it is yours to command."

Chauvelin sat down. He held his lower lip tightly between his teeth, so tightly that a few drops of blood appeared upon its narrow surface. He was making vigorous efforts to keep his temper under control, for he would not give his enemy the satisfaction of seeing him resent his insolence. He could afford to keep calm now that victory was at last in sight, now that he knew that he had but to raise a finger, and those smiling, impudent lips would be closed forever at last.

"Sir Percy," he resumed quietly, "no doubt it affords you a certain amount of pleasure to aim your sarcastic shafts at me. I will not begrudge you that pleasure; in your present position, sir, your shafts have little or no sting."

"And I shall have but few chances left to aim them at your charming self," interposed Blakeney, who had drawn another chair close to the table and was now sitting opposite his enemy, with the light of the lamp falling full on his own face, as if he wished his enemy to know that he had nothing to hide, no thought, no hope, no fear.

"Exactly," said Chauvelin dryly. "That being the case, Sir Percy, what say you to no longer wasting the few chances which are left to you for safety? The time is getting on. You are not, I imagine, quite as hopeful as you were even a week ago,... you have never been over-comfortable in this cell, why not end this unpleasant state of affairs now—once and for all? You'll not have cause to regret it. My word on it."

Sir Percy leaned back in his chair. He yawned loudly and ostentatiously.

"I pray you, sir, forgive me," he said. "Never have I been so d—d fatigued. I have not slept for more than a fortnight."

"Exactly, Sir Percy. A night's rest would do you a world of good."

"A night, sir?" exclaimed Blakeney with what seemed like an echo of his former inimitable laugh. "La! I should want a week."

"I am afraid we could not arrange for that, but one night would greatly refresh you."

"You are right, sir, you are right; but those d—d fellows in the next room make so much noise."

"I would give strict orders that perfect quietude reigned in the guard-room this night," said Chauvelin, murmuring softly, and there was a gentle purr in his voice, "and that you were left undisturbed for several hours. I would give orders that a comforting supper be served to you at once, and that everything be done to minister to your wants."

"That sounds d—d alluring, sir. Why did you not suggest this before?"

"You were so—what shall I say—so obstinate, Sir Percy?"

"Call it pig-headed, my dear Monsieur Chambertin," retorted Blakeney gaily, "truly you would oblige me."

"In any case you, sir, were acting in direct opposition to your own interests."

"Therefore you came," concluded Blakeney airily, "like the good Samaritan to take compassion on me and my troubles, and to lead me straight away to comfort, a good supper and a downy bed."

"Admirably put, Sir Percy," said Chauvelin blandly; "that is exactly my mission."

"How will you set to work, Monsieur Chambertin?"

"Quite easily, if you, Sir Percy, will yield to the persuasion of my friend citizen Heron."

"Ah!"

"Why, yes! He is anxious to know where little Capet is. A reasonable whim, you will own, considering that the disappearance of the child is causing him grave anxiety."

"And you, Monsieur Chambertin?" queried Sir Percy with that suspicion of insolence in his manner which had the power to irritate his enemy even now. "And yourself, sir; what are your wishes in the matter?"

"Mine, Sir Percy?" retorted Chauvelin. "Mine? Why, to tell you the truth, the fate of little Capet interests me but little. Let him rot in Austria or in our prisons, I care not which. He'll never trouble France overmuch, I imagine. The teachings of old Simon will not tend to make a leader or a king out of the puny brat whom you chose to drag out of our keeping. My wishes, sir, are the annihilation of your accursed League, and the lasting disgrace, if not the death, of its chief."

He had spoken more hotly than he had intended, but all the pent-up rage of the past eighteen months, the recollections of Calais and of Boulogne, had all surged up again in his mind, because despite the closeness of these prison walls, despite the grim shadow of starvation and of death that beckoned so close at hand, he still encountered a pair of mocking eyes, fixed with relentless insolence upon him.

Whilst he spoke Blakeney had once more leaned forward, resting his elbows upon the table. Now he drew nearer to him the wooden platter on which reposed that very uninviting piece of dry bread. With solemn intentness he proceeded to break the bread into pieces; then he offered the platter to Chauvelin.

"I am sorry," he said pleasantly, "that I cannot offer you more dainty fare, sir, but this is all that your friends have supplied me with to-day."

He crumbled some of the dry bread in his slender fingers, then started munching the crumbs with apparent relish. He poured out some water into the mug and drank it. Then he said with a light laugh:

"Even the vinegar which that ruffian Brogard served us at Calais was preferable to this, do you not imagine so, my good Monsieur Chambertin?"

Chauvelin made no reply. Like a feline creature on the prowl, he was watching the prey that had so nearly succumbed to his talons. Blakeney's face now was positively ghastly. The effort to speak, to laugh, to appear unconcerned, was apparently beyond his strength. His cheeks and lips were livid in hue, the skin clung like a thin layer of wax to the bones of cheek and jaw, and the heavy lids that fell over the eyes had purple patches on them like lead.

To a system in such an advanced state of exhaustion the stale water and dusty bread must have been terribly nauseating, and Chauvelin himself callous and thirsting for vengeance though he was, could hardly bear to look calmly on the martyrdom of this man whom he and his colleagues were torturing in order to gain their own ends.

An ashen hue, which seemed like the shadow of the hand of death, passed over the prisoner's face. Chauvelin felt compelled to avert his gaze. A feeling that was almost akin to remorse had stirred a hidden chord in his heart. The feeling did not last—the heart had been too long atrophied by the constantly recurring spectacles of cruelties, massacres, and wholesale hecatombs perpetrated in the past eighteen months in the name of liberty and fraternity to be capable of a sustained effort in the direction of gentleness or of pity. Any noble instinct in these revolutionaries had long ago been drowned in a whirlpool of exploits that would forever sully the records of humanity; and this keeping of a fellow-creature on the rack in order to wring from him a Judas-like betrayal was but a complement to a record of infamy that had ceased by its very magnitude to weigh upon their souls.

Chauvelin was in no way different from his colleagues; the crimes in which he had had no hand he had condoned by continuing to serve the Government that had committed them, and his ferocity in the present case was increased a thousandfold by his personal hatred for the man who had so often fooled and baffled him.

When he looked round a second or two later that ephemeral fit of remorse did its final vanishing; he had once more encountered the pleasant smile, the laughing if ashen-pale face of his unconquered foe.

"Only a passing giddiness, my dear sir," said Sir Percy lightly. "As you were saying—"

At the airily-spoken words, at the smile that accompanied them, Chauvelin had jumped to his feet. There was something almost supernatural, weird, and impish about the present situation, about this dying man who, like an impudent schoolboy, seemed to be mocking Death with his tongue in his cheek, about his laugh that appeared to find its echo in a widely yawning grave.

"In the name of God, Sir Percy," he said roughly, as he brought his clenched fist crashing down upon the table, "this situation is intolerable. Bring it to an end to-night!"

"Why, sir?" retorted Blakeney, "methought you and your kind did not believe in God."

"No. But you English do."

"We do. But we do not care to hear His name on your lips."

"Then in the name of the wife whom you love—"

But even before the words had died upon his lips, Sir Percy, too, had risen to his feet.

"Have done, man—have done," he broke in hoarsely, and despite weakness, despite exhaustion and weariness, there was such a dangerous look in his hollow eyes as he leaned across the table that Chauvelin drew back a step or two, and—vaguely fearful—looked furtively towards the opening into the guard-room. "Have done," he reiterated for the third time; "do not name her, or by the living God whom you dared to invoke I'll find strength yet to smite you in the face."

But Chauvelin, after that first moment of almost superstitious fear, had quickly recovered his sang-froid.

"Little Capet, Sir Percy," he said, meeting the other's threatening glance with an imperturbable smile, "tell me where to find him, and you may yet live to savour the caresses of the most beautiful woman in England."

He had meant it as a taunt, the final turn of the thumb-screw applied to a dying man, and he had in that watchful, keen mind of his well weighed the full consequences of the taunt.

The next moment he had paid to the full the anticipated price. Sir Percy had picked up the pewter mug from the table—it was half-filled with brackish water—and with a hand that trembled but slightly he hurled it straight at his opponent's face.

The heavy mug did not hit citizen Chauvelin; it went crashing against the stone wall opposite. But the water was trickling from the top of his head all down his eyes and cheeks. He shrugged his shoulders with a look of benign indulgence directed at his enemy, who had fallen back into his chair exhausted with the effort.

Then he took out his handkerchief and calmly wiped the water from his face.

"Not quite so straight a shot as you used to be, Sir Percy," he said mockingly.

"No, sir—apparently—not."

The words came out in gasps. He was like a man only partly conscious. The lips were parted, the eyes closed, the head leaning against the high back of the chair. For the space of one second Chauvelin feared that his zeal had outrun his prudence, that he had dealt a death-blow to a man in the last stage of exhaustion, where he had only wished to fan the flickering flame of life. Hastily—for the seconds seemed precious—he ran to the opening that led into the guard-room.

"Brandy—quick!" he cried.

Heron looked up, roused from the semi-somnolence in which he had lain for the past half-hour. He disentangled his long limbs from out the guard-room chair.

"Eh?" he queried. "What is it?"

"Brandy," reiterated Chauvelin impatiently; "the prisoner has fainted."

"Bah!" retorted the other with a callous shrug of the shoulders, "you are not going to revive him with brandy, I imagine."

"No. But you will, citizen Heron," rejoined the other dryly, "for if you do not he'll be dead in an hour!"

"Devils in hell!" exclaimed Heron, "you have not killed him? You—you d—d fool!"

He was wide awake enough now; wide awake and shaking with fury. Almost foaming at the mouth and uttering volleys of the choicest oaths, he elbowed his way roughly through the groups of soldiers who were crowding round the centre table of the guard-room, smoking and throwing dice or playing cards. They made way for him as hurriedly as they could, for it was not safe to thwart the citizen agent when he was in a rage.

Heron walked across to the opening and lifted the iron bar. With scant ceremony he pushed his colleague aside and strode into the cell, whilst Chauvelin, seemingly not resenting the other's ruffianly manners and violent language, followed close upon his heel.

In the centre of the room both men paused, and Heron turned with a surly growl to his friend.

"You vowed he would be dead in an hour," he said reproachfully.

The other shrugged his shoulders.

"It does not look like it now certainly," he said dryly.

Blakeney was sitting—as was his wont—close to the table, with one arm leaning on it, the other, tightly clenched, resting upon his knee. A ghost of a smile hovered round his lips.

"Not in an hour, citizen Heron," he said, and his voice flow was scarce above a whisper, "nor yet in two."

"You are a fool, man," said Heron roughly. "You have had seventeen days of this. Are you not sick of it?"

"Heartily, my dear friend," replied Blakeney a little more firmly.

"Seventeen days," reiterated the other, nodding his shaggy head; "you came here on the 2nd of Pluviose, today is the 19th."

"The 19th Pluviose?" interposed Sir Percy, and a strange gleam suddenly flashed in his eyes. "Demn it, sir, and in Christian parlance what may that day be?"

"The 7th of February at your service, Sir Percy," replied Chauvelin quietly.

"I thank you, sir. In this d—d hole I had lost count of time."

Chauvelin, unlike his rough and blundering colleague, had been watching the prisoner very closely for the last moment or two, conscious of a subtle, undefinable change that had come over the man during those few seconds while he, Chauvelin, had thought him dying. The pose was certainly the old familiar one, the head erect, the hand clenched, the eyes looking through and beyond the stone walls; but there was an air of listlessness in the stoop of the shoulders, and—except for that one brief gleam just now—a look of more complete weariness round the hollow eyes! To the keen watcher it appeared as if that sense of living power, of unconquered will and defiant mind was no longer there, and as if he himself need no longer fear that almost supersensual thrill which had a while ago kindled in him a vague sense of admiration—almost of remorse.

Even as he gazed, Blakeney slowly turned his eyes full upon him. Chauvelin's heart gave a triumphant bound.

With a mocking smile he met the wearied look, the pitiable appeal. His turn had come at last—his turn to mock and to exult. He knew that what he was watching now was no longer the last phase of a long and noble martyrdom; it was the end—the inevitable end—that for which he had schemed and striven, for which he had schooled his heart to ferocity and callousness that were devilish in their intensity. It was the end indeed, the slow descent of a soul from the giddy heights of attempted self-sacrifice, where it had striven to soar for a time, until the body and the will both succumbed together and dragged it down with them into the abyss of submission and of irreparable shame.

CHAPTER XXXVI

Submission

Silence reigned in the narrow cell for a few moments, whilst two human jackals stood motionless over their captured prey.

A savage triumph gleamed in Chauvelin's eyes, and even Heron, dull and brutal though he was, had become vaguely conscious of the great change that had come over the prisoner.

Blakeney, with a gesture and a sigh of hopeless exhaustion had once more rested both his elbows on the table; his head fell heavy and almost lifeless downward in his arms.

"Curse you, man!" cried Heron almost involuntarily. "Why in the name of hell did you wait so long?"

Then, as the prisoner made no reply, but only raised his head slightly, and looked on the other two men with dulled, wearied eyes, Chauvelin interposed calmly:

"More than a fortnight has been wasted in useless obstinacy, Sir Percy. Fortunately it is not too late."

"Capet?" said Heron hoarsely, "tell us, where is Capet?"

He leaned across the table, his eyes were bloodshot with the keenness of his excitement, his voice shook with the passionate desire for the crowning triumph.

"If you'll only not worry me," murmured the prisoner; and the whisper came so laboriously and so low that both men were forced to bend their ears close to the scarcely moving lips; "if you will let me sleep and rest, and leave me in peace—"

"The peace of the grave, man," retorted Chauvelin roughly; "if you will only speak. Where is Capet?"

"I cannot tell you; the way is long, the road—intricate."

"Bah!"

"I'll lead you to him, if you will give me rest."

"We don't want you to lead us anywhere," growled Heron with a smothered curse; "tell us where Capet is; we'll find him right enough."

"I cannot explain; the way is intricate; the place off the beaten track, unknown except to me and my friends."

Once more that shadow, which was so like the passing of the hand of Death, overspread the prisoner's face; his head rolled back against the chair.

"He'll die before he can speak," muttered Chauvelin under his breath. "You usually are well provided with brandy, citizen Heron."

The latter no longer demurred. He saw the danger as clearly as did his colleague. It had been hell's own luck if the prisoner were to die now when he seemed ready to give in. He produced a flask from the pocket of his coat, and this he held to Blakeney's lips.

"Beastly stuff," murmured the latter feebly. "I think I'd sooner faint—than drink."

"Capet? where is Capet?" reiterated Heron impatiently. "One—two—three hundred leagues from here.

I must let one of my friends know; he'll communicate with the others; they must be prepared," replied the prisoner slowly.

Heron uttered a blasphemous oath.

"Where is Capet? Tell us where Capet is, or—"

He was like a raging tiger that had thought to hold its prey and suddenly realised that it was being snatched from him. He raised his fist, and without doubt the next moment he would have silenced forever the lips that held the precious secret, but Chauvelin fortunately was quick enough to seize his wrist.

"Have a care, citizen," he said peremptorily; "have a care! You called me a fool just now when you thought I had killed the prisoner. It is his secret we want first; his death can follow afterwards."

"Yes, but not in this d—d hole," murmured Blakeney.

"On the guillotine if you'll speak," cried Heron, whose exasperation was getting the better of his self-interest, "but if you'll not speak then it shall be starvation in this hole—yes, starvation," he growled, showing a row of large and uneven teeth like those of some mongrel cur, "for I'll have that door walled in to-night, and not another living soul shall cross this threshold again until your flesh has rotted on your bones and the rats have had their fill of you."

The prisoner raised his head slowly, a shiver shook him as if caused by ague, and his eyes, that appeared almost sightless, now looked with a strange glance of horror on his enemy.

"I'll die in the open," he whispered, "not in this d—d hole."

"Then tell us where Capet is."

"I cannot; I wish to God I could. But I'll take you to him, I swear I will. I'll make my friends give him up to you. Do you think that I would not tell you now, if I could."

Heron, whose every instinct of tyranny revolted against this thwarting of his will, would have continued to heckle the prisoner even now, had not Chauvelin suddenly interposed with an authoritative gesture.

"You'll gain nothing this way, citizen," he said quietly; "the man's mind is wandering; he is probably quite unable to give you clear directions at this moment."

"What am I to do, then?" muttered the other roughly.

"He cannot live another twenty-four hours now, and would only grow more and more helpless as time went on."

"Unless you relax your strict regime with him."

"And if I do we'll only prolong this situation indefinitely; and in the meanwhile how do we know that the brat is not being spirited away out of the country?"

The prisoner, with his head once more buried in his arms, had fallen into a kind of torpor, the only kind of sleep that the exhausted system would allow. With a brutal gesture Heron shook him by the shoulder.

"He," he shouted, "none of that, you know. We have not settled the matter of young Capet yet."

Then, as the prisoner made no movement, and the chief agent indulged in one of his favourite volleys of oaths, Chauvelin placed a peremptory hand on his colleague's shoulder.

"I tell you, citizen, that this is no use," he said firmly. "Unless you are prepared to give up all thoughts of finding Capet, you must try and curb your temper, and try diplomacy where force is sure to fail."

"Diplomacy?" retorted the other with a sneer. "Bah! it served you well at Boulogne last autumn, did it not, citizen Chauvelin?"

"It has served me better now," rejoined the other imperturbably. "You will own, citizen, that it is my diplomacy which has placed within your reach the ultimate hope of finding Capet."

"H'm!" muttered the other, "you advised us to starve the prisoner. Are we any nearer to knowing his secret?"

"Yes. By a fortnight of weariness, of exhaustion and of starvation, you are nearer to it by the weakness of the man whom in his full strength you could never hope to conquer."

"But if the cursed Englishman won't speak, and in the meanwhile dies on my hands—"

"He won't do that if you will accede to his wish. Give him some good food now, and let him sleep till dawn."

"And at dawn he'll defy me again. I believe now that he has some scheme in his mind, and means to play us a trick."

"That, I imagine, is more than likely," retorted Chauvelin dryly; "though," he added with a contemptuous nod of the head directed at the huddled-up figure of his once brilliant enemy, "neither mind nor body seem to me to be in a sufficiently active state just now for hatching plot or intrigue; but even if—vaguely floating through his clouded mind—there has sprung some little scheme for evasion, I give you my word, citizen Heron, that you can thwart him completely, and gain all that you desire, if you will only follow my advice."

There had always been a great amount of persuasive power in citizen Chauvelin, ex-envoy of the revolutionary Government of France at the Court of St. James, and that same persuasive eloquence did not fail now in its effect on the chief agent of the Committee of General Security. The latter was made of coarser stuff than his more brilliant colleague. Chauvelin was like a wily and sleek panther that is furtive in its movements, that will lure its prey, watch it, follow it with stealthy footsteps, and only pounce on it when it is least wary, whilst Heron was more like a raging bull that tosses its head in a blind, irresponsible fashion, rushes at an obstacle without gauging its resisting powers, and allows its victim to slip from beneath its weight through the very clumsiness and brutality of its assault.

Still Chauvelin had two heavy black marks against him—those of his failures at Calais and Boulogne. Heron, rendered cautious both by the deadly danger in which he stood and the sense of his own incompetence to deal with the present situation, tried to resist the other's authority as well as his persuasion.

"Your advice was not of great use to citizen Collot last autumn at Boulogne," he said, and spat on the ground by way of expressing both his independence and his contempt.

"Still, citizen Heron," retorted Chauvelin with unruffled patience, "it is the best advice that you are likely to get in the present emergency. You have eyes to see, have you not? Look on your prisoner at this moment. Unless something is done, and at once, too, he will be past negotiating with in the next twenty-four hours; then what will follow?"

He put his thin hand once more on his colleague's grubby coat-sleeve, he drew him closer to himself away from the vicinity of that huddled figure, that captive lion, wrapped in a torpid somnolence that looked already so like the last long sleep.

"What will follow, citizen Heron?" he reiterated, sinking his voice to a whisper; "sooner or later some meddlesome busybody who sits in the Assembly of the Convention will get wind that little Capet is no longer in the Temple prison, that a pauper child was substituted for him, and that you, citizen Heron, together with the commissaries in charge, have thus been fooling the nation and its representatives for over a fortnight. What will follow then, think you?"

And he made an expressive gesture with his outstretched fingers across his throat.

Heron found no other answer but blasphemy.

"I'll make that cursed Englishman speak yet," he said with a fierce oath.

"You cannot," retorted Chauvelin decisively. "In his present state he is incapable of it, even if he would, which also is doubtful."

"Ah! then you do think that he still means to cheat us?"

"Yes, I do. But I also know that he is no longer in a physical state to do it. No doubt he thinks that he is. A man of that type is sure to overvalue his own strength; but look at him, citizen Heron. Surely you must see that we have nothing to fear from him now."

Heron now was like a voracious creature that has two victims lying ready for his gluttonous jaws. He was loath to let either of them go. He hated the very thought of seeing the Englishman being led out of this narrow cell, where he had kept a watchful eye over him night and day for a fortnight, satisfied that with every day, every hour, the chances of escape became more improbable and more rare; at the same time there was the possibility of the recapture of little Capet, a possibility which made Heron's brain reel with the delightful vista of it, and which might never come about if the prisoner remained silent to the end.

"I wish I were quite sure," he said sullenly, "that you were body and soul in accord with me."

"I am in accord with you, citizen Heron," rejoined the other earnestly—"body and soul in accord with you. Do you not believe that I hate this man—aye! hate him with a hatred ten thousand times more strong than yours? I want his death—Heaven or hell alone know how I long for that—but what I long for most is his lasting disgrace. For that I have worked, citizen Heron—for that I advised and helped you. When first you captured this man you wanted summarily to try him, to send him to the guillotine amidst the joy of the populace of Paris, and crowned with a splendid halo of martyrdom. That man, citizen Heron, would have baffled you, mocked you, and fooled you even on the steps of the scaffold. In the zenith of his strength and of insurmountable good luck you and all your myrmidons and all the assembled guard of Paris would have had no power over him. The day that you led him out of this cell in order to take him to trial or to the guillotine would have been that of your hopeless discomfiture. Having once walked out of this cell hale, hearty and alert, be the escort round him ever so strong, he never would have re-entered it again. Of that I am as convinced as that I am alive. I know the man; you don't. Mine are not the only fingers through which he has slipped. Ask citizen Collot d'Herbois, ask Sergeant Bibot at the barrier of Menilmontant, ask General Santerre and his guards. They all have a tale to tell. Did I believe in God or the devil, I should also believe that this man has supernatural powers and a host of demons at his beck and call."

"Yet you talk now of letting him walk out of this cell to-morrow?"

"He is a different man now, citizen Heron. On my advice you placed him on a regime that has counteracted the supernatural power by simple physical exhaustion, and driven to the four winds the host of demons who no doubt fled in the face of starvation."

"If only I thought that the recapture of Capet was as vital to you as it is to me," said Heron, still unconvinced.

"The capture of Capet is just as vital to me as it is to you," rejoined Chauvelin earnestly, "if it is brought about through the instrumentality of the Englishman."

He paused, looking intently on his colleague, whose shifty eyes encountered his own. Thus eye to eye the two men at last understood one another.

"Ah!" said Heron with a snort, "I think I understand."

"I am sure that you do," responded Chauvelin dryly. "The disgrace of this cursed Scarlet Pimpernel and his League is as vital to me, and more, as the capture of Capet is to you. That is why I showed you the way how to bring that meddlesome adventurer to his knees; that is why I will help you now both to find Capet and with his aid and to wreak what reprisals you like on him in the end."

Heron before he spoke again cast one more look on the prisoner. The latter had not stirred; his face was hidden, but the hands, emaciated, nerveless and waxen, like those of the dead, told a more eloquent tale, mayhap, then than the eyes could do. The chief agent of the Committee of General Security walked deliberately round the table until he stood once more close beside the man from whom he longed with passionate ardour to wrest an all-important secret. With brutal, grimy hand he raised the head that lay, sunken and inert, against the table; with callous eyes he gazed attentively on the face that was then revealed to him, he looked on the waxen flesh, the hollow eyes, the bloodless lips; then he shrugged his wide shoulders, and with a laugh that surely must have caused joy in hell, he allowed the wearied head to fall back against the outstretched arms, and turned once again to his colleague.

"I think you are right, citizen Chauvelin," he said; "there is not much supernatural power here. Let me hear your advice."

CHAPTER XXXVII

Chauvelin's Advice

Citizen Chauvelin had drawn his colleague with him to the end of the cell that was farthest away from the recess, and the table at which the prisoner was sitting.

Here the noise and hubbub that went on constantly in the guard room would effectually drown a whispered conversation. Chauvelin called to the sergeant to hand him a couple of chairs over the barrier. These he placed against the wall opposite the opening, and beckoning Heron to sit down, he did likewise, placing himself close to his colleague.

From where the two men now sat they could see both into the guard-room opposite them and into the recess at the furthermost end of the cell.

"First of all," began Chauvelin after a while, and sinking his voice to a whisper, "let me understand you thoroughly, citizen Heron. Do you want the death of the Englishman, either to-day or to-morrow, either in this prison or on the guillotine? For that now is easy of accomplishment; or do you want, above all, to get hold of little Capet?"

"It is Capet I want," growled Heron savagely under his breath. "Capet! Capet! My own neck is dependent on my finding Capet. Curse you, have I not told you that clearly enough?"

"You have told it me very clearly, citizen Heron; but I wished to make assurance doubly sure, and also make you understand that I, too, want the Englishman to betray little Capet into your hands. I want that more even than I do his death."

"Then in the name of hell, citizen, give me your advice."

"My advice to you, citizen Heron, is this: Give your prisoner now just a sufficiency of food to revive him—he will have had a few moments' sleep—and when he has eaten, and, mayhap, drunk a glass of wine, he will, no doubt, feel a recrudescence of strength, then give him pen and ink and paper. He must, as he says, write to one of his followers, who, in his turn, I suppose, will communicate with the others, bidding them to be prepared to deliver up little Capet to us; the letter must make it clear to that crowd of English gentlemen that their beloved chief is giving up the uncrowned King of France to us in exchange for his own safety. But I think you will agree with me, citizen Heron, that it would not be over-prudent on our part to allow that same gallant crowd to be forewarned too soon of the pro-posed doings of their chief. Therefore, I think, we'll explain to the prisoner that his follower, whom he will first apprise of his intentions, shall start with us to-morrow on our expedition, and accompany us until its last stage, when, if it is found necessary, he may be sent on ahead, strongly escorted of course, and with personal messages from the gallant Scarlet Pimpernel to the members of his League."

"What will be the good of that?" broke in Heron viciously. "Do you want one of his accursed followers to be ready to give him a helping hand on the way if he tries to slip through our fingers?

"Patience, patience, my good Heron!" rejoined Chauvelin with a placid smile. "Hear me out to the end. Time is precious. You shall offer what criticism you will when I have finished, but not before."

"Go on, then. I listen."

"I am not only proposing that one member of the Scarlet Pimpernel League shall accompany us to-morrow," continued Chauvelin, "but I would also force the prisoner's wife—Marguerite Blakeney—to follow in our train."

"A woman? Bah! What for?"

"I will tell you the reason of this presently. In her case I should not let the prisoner know beforehand that she too will form a part of our expedition. Let this come as a pleasing surprise for him. She could join us on our way out of Paris."

"How will you get hold of her?"

"Easily enough. I know where to find her. I traced her myself a few days ago to a house in the Rue de Charonne, and she is not likely to have gone away from Paris while her husband was at the Conciergerie. But this is a digression, let me proceed more consecutively. The letter, as I have said, being written to-night by the prisoner to one of his followers, I will myself see that it is delivered into the right hands. You, citizen Heron, will in the meanwhile make all arrangements for the journey. We ought to start at dawn, and we ought to be prepared, especially during the first fifty leagues of the way, against organised attack in case the Englishman leads us into an ambush."

"Yes. He might even do that, curse him!" muttered Heron.

"He might, but it is unlikely. Still it is best to be prepared. Take a strong escort, citizen, say twenty or thirty men, picked and trained soldiers who would make short work of civilians, however well-armed they might be. There are twenty members—including the chief—in that Scarlet Pimpernel League, and I do not quite see how from this cell the prisoner could organise an ambuscade against us at a given time. Anyhow, that is a matter for you to decide. I have still to place before you a scheme which is a measure of safety for ourselves and our men against ambush as well as against trickery, and which I feel sure you will pronounce quite adequate."

"Let me hear it, then!"

"The prisoner will have to travel by coach, of course. You can travel with him, if you like, and put him in irons, and thus avert all chances of his escaping on the road. But"—and here Chauvelin made a long pause, which had the effect of holding his colleague's attention still more closely—"remember that we shall have his wife and one of his friends with us. Before we finally leave Paris tomorrow we will explain to the prisoner that at the first attempt to escape on his part, at the slightest suspicion that he has tricked us for his own ends or is leading us into an ambush—at the slightest suspicion, I say—you, citizen Heron, will order his friend first, and then Marguerite Blakeney herself, to be summarily shot before his eyes."

Heron gave a long, low whistle. Instinctively he threw a furtive, backward glance at the prisoner, then he raised his shifty eyes to his colleague.

There was unbounded admiration expressed in them. One blackguard had met another—a greater one than himself—and was proud to acknowledge him as his master.

"By Lucifer, citizen Chauvelin," he said at last, "I should never have thought of such a thing myself."

Chauvelin put up his hand with a gesture of self-deprecation.

"I certainly think that measure ought to be adequate," he said with a gentle air of assumed modesty, "unless you would prefer to arrest the woman and lodge her here, keeping her here as an hostage."

"No, no!" said Heron with a gruff laugh; "that idea does not appeal to me nearly so much as the other. I should not feel so secure on the way.... I should always be thinking that that cursed woman had been allowed to escape.... No! no! I would rather keep her under my own eye—just as you suggest, citizen Chauvelin... and under the prisoner's, too," he added with a coarse jest. "If he did not actually see her, he might be more ready to try and save himself at her expense. But, of course, he could not see her shot before his eyes. It is a perfect plan, citizen, and does you infinite credit; and if the Englishman tricked us," he concluded with a fierce and savage oath, "and we did not find Capet at the end of the journey, I would gladly strangle his wife and his friend with my own hands."

"A satisfaction which I would not begrudge you, citizen," said Chauvelin dryly.

"Perhaps you are right... the woman had best be kept under your own eye... the prisoner will never risk her safety on that, I would stake my life. We'll deliver our final 'either—or' the moment that she has joined our party, and before we start further on our way. Now, citizen Heron, you have heard my advice; are you prepared to follow it?"

"To the last letter," replied the other.

And their two hands met in a grasp of mutual understanding—two hands already indelibly stained with much innocent blood, more deeply stained now with seventeen past days of inhumanity and miserable treachery to come.

CHAPTER XXXVIII

Capitulation

What occurred within the inner cell of the Conciergerie prison within the next half-hour of that 16th day of Pluviose in the year II of the Republic is, perhaps, too well known to history to need or bear overfull repetition.

Chroniclers intimate with the inner history of those infamous days have told us how the chief agent of the Committee of General Security gave orders one hour after midnight that hot soup, white bread and wine be served to the prisoner, who for close on fourteen days previously had been kept on short rations of black bread and water; the sergeant in charge of the guard-room watch for the night also received strict orders that that same prisoner was on no account to be disturbed until the hour of six in the morning, when he was to be served with anything in the way of breakfast that he might fancy.

All this we know, and also that citizen Heron, having given all necessary orders for the morning's expedition, returned to the Conciergerie, and found his colleague Chauvelin waiting for him in the guard-room.

"Well?" he asked with febrile impatience—"the prisoner?"

"He seems better and stronger," replied Chauvelin.

"Not too well, I hope?"

"No, no, only just well enough."

"You have seen him—since his supper?"

"Only from the doorway. It seems he ate and drank hardly at all, and the sergeant had some difficulty in keeping him awake until you came."

"Well, now for the letter," concluded Heron with the same marked feverishness of manner which sat so curiously on his uncouth personality. "Pen, ink and paper, sergeant!" he commanded.

"On the table, in the prisoner's cell, citizen," replied the sergeant.

He preceded the two citizens across the guard-room to the doorway, and raised for them the iron bar, lowering it back after them.

The next moment Heron and Chauvelin were once more face to face with their prisoner.

Whether by accident or design the lamp had been so placed that as the two men approached its light fell full upon their faces, while that of the prisoner remained in shadow. He was leaning forward with both elbows on the table, his thin, tapering fingers toying with the pen and ink-horn which had been placed close to his hand.

"I trust that everything has been arranged for your comfort, Sir Percy?" Chauvelin asked with a sarcastic little smile.

"I thank you, sir," replied Blakeney politely.

"You feel refreshed, I hope?"

"Greatly so, I assure you. But I am still demmed sleepy; and if you would kindly be brief—"

"You have not changed your mind, sir?" queried Chauvelin, and a note of anxiety, which he vainly tried to conceal, quivered in his voice.

"No, my good M. Chambertin," replied Blakeney with the same urbane courtesy, "I have not changed my mind."

A sigh of relief escaped the lips of both the men. The prisoner certainly had spoken in a clearer and firmer voice; but whatever renewed strength wine and food had imparted to him he apparently did not mean to employ in renewed obstinacy. Chauvelin, after a moment's pause, resumed more calmly:

"You are prepared to direct us to the place where little Capet lies hidden?"

"I am prepared to do anything, sir, to get out of this d—d hole."

"Very well. My colleague, citizen Heron, has arranged for an escort of twenty men picked from the best regiment of the Garde de Paris to accompany us—yourself, him and me—to wherever you will direct us. Is that clear?"

"Perfectly, sir."

"You must not imagine for a moment that we, on the other hand, guarantee to give you your life and freedom even if this expedition prove unsuccessful."

"I would not venture on suggesting such a wild proposition, sir," said Blakeney placidly.

Chauvelin looked keenly on him. There was something in the tone of that voice that he did not altogether like—something that reminded him of an evening at Calais, and yet again of a day at Boulogne. He could not read the expression in the eyes, so with a quick gesture he pulled the lamp forward so that its light now fell full on the face of the prisoner.

"Ah! that is certainly better, is it not, my dear M. Chambertin?" said Sir Percy, beaming on his adversary with a pleasant smile.

His face, though still of the same ashen hue, looked serene if hopelessly wearied; the eyes seemed to mock. But this Chauvelin decided in himself must have been a trick of his own overwrought fancy. After a brief moment's pause he resumed dryly:

"If, however, the expedition turns out successful in every way—if little Capet, without much trouble to our escort, falls safe and sound into our hands—if certain contingencies which I am about to tell you all fall out as we wish—then, Sir Percy, I see no reason why the Government of this country should not exercise its prerogative of mercy towards you after all."

"An exercise, my dear M. Chambertin, which must have wearied through frequent repetition," retorted Blakeney with the same imperturbable smile.

"The contingency at present is somewhat remote; when the time comes we'll talk this matter over.... I will make no promise... and, anyhow, we can discuss it later."

"At present we are but wasting our valuable time over so trifling a matter.... If you'll excuse me, sir... I am so demmed fatigued—"

"Then you will be glad to have everything settled quickly, I am sure."

"Exactly, sir."

Heron was taking no part in the present conversation. He knew that his temper was not likely to remain within bounds, and though he had nothing but contempt for his colleague's courtly manners, yet vaguely in his stupid, blundering way he grudgingly admitted that mayhap it was better to allow citizen Chauvelin to deal with the Englishman. There was always the danger that if his own violent temper got the better of him, he might even at this eleventh hour order this insolent prisoner to summary trial and the guillotine, and thus lose the final chance of the more important capture.

He was sprawling on a chair in his usual slouching manner with his big head sunk between his broad shoulders, his shifty, prominent eyes wandering restlessly from the face of his colleague to that of the other man.

But now he gave a grunt of impatience.

"We are wasting time, citizen Chauvelin," he muttered. "I have still a great deal to see to if we are to start at dawn. Get the d—d letter written, and—"

The rest of the phrase was lost in an indistinct and surly murmur. Chauvelin, after a shrug of the shoulders, paid no further heed to him; he turned, bland and urbane, once more to the prisoner.

"I see with pleasure, Sir Percy," he said, "that we thoroughly understand one another. Having had a few hours' rest you will, I know, feel quite ready for the expedition. Will you kindly indicate to me the direction in which we will have to travel?"

"Northwards all the way."

"Towards the coast?"

"The place to which we must go is about seven leagues from the sea."

"Our first objective then will be Beauvais, Amiens, Abbeville, Crecy, and so on?"

"Precisely."

"As far as the forest of Boulogne, shall we say?"

"Where we shall come off the beaten track, and you will have to trust to my guidance."

"We might go there now, Sir Percy, and leave you here."

"You might. But you would not then find the child. Seven leagues is not far from the coast. He might slip through your fingers."

"And my colleague Heron, being disappointed, would inevitably send you to the guillotine."

"Quite so," rejoined the prisoner placidly. "Methought, sir, that we had decided that I should lead this little expedition? Surely," he added, "it is not so much the Dauphin whom you want as my share in this betrayal."

"You are right as usual, Sir Percy. Therefore let us take that as settled. We go as far as Crecy, and thence place ourselves entirely in your hands."

"The journey should not take more than three days, sir."

"During which you will travel in a coach in the company of my friend Heron."

"I could have chosen pleasanter company, sir; still, it will serve."

"This being settled, Sir Percy. I understand that you desire to communicate with one of your followers."

"Some one must let the others know... those who have the Dauphin in their charge."

"Quite so. Therefore I pray you write to one of your friends that you have decided to deliver the Dauphin into our hands in exchange for your own safety."

"You said just now that this you would not guarantee," interposed Blakeney quietly.

"If all turns out well," retorted Chauvelin with a show of contempt, "and if you will write the exact letter which I shall dictate, we might even give you that guarantee."

"The quality of your mercy, sir, passes belief."

"Then I pray you write. Which of your followers will have the honour of the communication?"

"My brother-in-law, Armand St. Just; he is still in Paris, I believe. He can let the others know."

Chauvelin made no immediate reply. He paused awhile, hesitating. Would Sir Percy Blakeney be ready—if his own safety demanded it—to sacrifice the man who had betrayed him? In the momentous "either—or" that was to be put to him, by-and-by, would he choose his own life and leave Armand St. Just to perish? It was not for Chauvelin—or any man of his stamp—to judge of what Blakeney would do under such circumstances, and had it been a question of St. Just alone, mayhap Chauvelin would have hesitated still more at the present juncture.

But the friend as hostage was only destined to be a minor leverage for the final breaking-up of the League of the Scarlet Pimpernel through the disgrace of its chief. There was the wife—Marguerite Blakeney—sister of St. Just, joint and far more important hostage, whose very close affection for her brother might prove an additional trump card in that handful which Chauvelin already held.

Blakeney paid no heed seemingly to the other's hesitation. He did not even look up at him, but quietly drew pen and paper towards him, and made ready to write.

"What do you wish me to say?" he asked simply.

"Will that young blackguard answer your purpose, citizen Chauvelin?" queried Heron roughly.

Obviously the same doubt had crossed his mind. Chauvelin quickly re-assured him.

"Better than any one else," he said firmly. "Will you write at my dictation, Sir Percy?

"I am waiting to do so, my dear sir."

"Begin your letter as you wish, then; now continue."

And he began to dictate slowly, watching every word as it left Blakeney's pen.

"'I cannot stand my present position any longer. Citizen Heron, and also M. Chauvelin—' Yes, Sir Percy, Chauvelin, not Chambertin ... C, H, A, U, V, E, L, I, N.... That is quite right— 'have made this prison a perfect hell for me.'"

Sir Percy looked up from his writing, smiling.

"You wrong yourself, my dear M. Chambertin!" he said; "I have really been most comfortable."

"I wish to place the matter before your friends in as indulgent a manner as I can," retorted Chauvelin dryly.

"I thank you, sir. Pray proceed."

"... a perfect hell for me,'" resumed the other. "Have you that? ... 'and I have been forced to give way. To-morrow we start from here at dawn; and I will guide citizen Heron to the place where he can find the Dauphin. But the authorities demand that one of my followers, one who has once been a member of the League of the Scarlet Pimpernel, shall accompany me on this expedition. I therefore ask you'—or 'desire you' or 'beg you'—whichever you prefer, Sir Percy..."

"'Ask you' will do quite nicely. This is really very interesting, you know."

"... 'to be prepared to join the expedition. We start at dawn, and you would be required to be at the main gate of the house of Justice at six o'clock precisely. I have an assurance from the authorities that your life should be in-violate, but if you refuse to accompany me, the guillotine will await me on the morrow.'"

"'The guillotine will await me on the morrow.' That sounds quite cheerful, does it not, M. Chambertin?" said the prisoner, who had not evinced the slightest surprise at the wording of the letter whilst he wrote at the other's dictation. "Do you know, I quite enjoyed writing this letter; it so reminded me of happy days in Boulogne."

Chauvelin pressed his lips together. Truly now he felt that a retort from him would have been undignified, more especially as just at this moment there came from the guard room the sound of men's voices talking and laughing, the occasional clang of steel, or of a heavy boot against the tiled floor, the rattling of dice, or a sudden burst of laughter—sounds, in fact, that betokened the presence of a number of soldiers close by.

Chauvelin contented himself with a nod in the direction of the guard-room.

"The conditions are somewhat different now," he said placidly, "from those that reigned in Boulogne. But will you not sign your letter, Sir Percy?"

"With pleasure, sir," responded Blakeney, as with an elaborate flourish of the pen he appended his name to the missive.

Chauvelin was watching him with eyes that would have shamed a lynx by their keenness. He took up the completed letter, read it through very carefully, as if to find some hidden meaning behind the very words which he himself had dictated; he studied the signature, and looked vainly for a mark or a sign that might convey a different sense to that which he had intended. Finally, finding none, he folded the letter up with his own hand, and at once slipped it in the pocket of his coat.

"Take care, M. Chambertin," said Blakeney lightly; "it will burn a hole in that elegant vest of yours."

"It will have no time to do that, Sir Percy," retorted Chauvelin blandly; "an you will furnish me with citizen St. Just's present address, I will myself convey the letter to him at once."

"At this hour of the night? Poor old Armand, he'll be abed. But his address, sir, is No. 32, Rue de la Croix Blanche, on the first floor, the door on your right as you mount the stairs; you know the room well, citizen Chauvelin; you have been in it before. And now," he added with a loud and ostentatious yawn, "shall we all to bed? We start at dawn, you said, and I am so d—d fatigued."

Frankly, he did not look it now. Chauvelin himself, despite his matured plans, despite all the precautions that he meant to take for the success of this gigantic scheme, felt a sudden strange sense of fear creeping into his bones. Half an hour ago he had seen a man in what looked like the last stage of utter physical exhaustion, a hunched up figure, listless and limp, hands that twitched nervously, the face as of a dying man. Now those outward symptoms were still there certainly; the face by the light of the lamp still looked livid, the lips bloodless, the hands emaciated and waxen, but the eyes!—they were still hollow, with heavy lids still purple, but in their depths there was a curious, mysterious light, a look that seemed to see something that was hidden to natural sight.

Citizen Chauvelin thought that Heron, too, must be conscious of this, but the Committee's agent was sprawling on a chair, sucking a short-stemmed pipe, and gazing with entire animal satisfaction on the prisoner.

"The most perfect piece of work we have ever accomplished, you and I, citizen Chauvelin," he said complacently.

"You think that everything is quite satisfactory?" asked the other with anxious stress on his words.

"Everything, of course. Now you see to the letter. I will give final orders for to-morrow, but I shall sleep in the guard-room."

"And I on that inviting bed," interposed the prisoner lightly, as he rose to his feet. "Your servant, citizens!"

He bowed his head slightly, and stood by the table whilst the two men prepared to go. Chauvelin took a final long look at the man whom he firmly believed he had at last brought down to abject disgrace.

Blakeney was standing erect, watching the two retreating figures—one slender hand was on the table. Chauvelin saw that it was leaning rather heavily, as if for support, and that even whilst a final mocking laugh sped him and his colleague on their way, the tall figure of the conquered lion swayed like a stalwart oak that is forced to bend to the mighty fury of an all-compelling wind.

With a sigh of content Chauvelin took his colleague by the arm, and together the two men walked out of the cell.

CHAPTER XXXIX

Kill Him!

Two hours after midnight Armand St. Just was wakened from sleep by a peremptory pull at his bell. In these days in Paris but one meaning could as a rule be attached to such a summons at this hour of the night, and Armand, though possessed of an unconditional certificate of safety, sat up in bed, quite convinced that for some reason which would presently be explained to him he had once more been placed on the list of the "suspect," and that his trial and condemnation on a trumped-up charge would follow in due course.

Truth to tell, he felt no fear at the prospect, and only a very little sorrow. The sorrow was not for himself; he regretted neither life nor happiness. Life had become hateful to him since happiness had fled with it on the dark wings of dishonour; sorrow such as he felt was only for Jeanne! She was very young, and would weep bitter tears. She would be unhappy, because she truly loved him, and because this would be the first cup of bitterness which life was holding out to her. But she was very young, and sorrow would not be eternal. It was better so. He, Armand St. Just, though he loved her with an intensity of passion that had been magnified and strengthened by his own overwhelming shame, had never really brought his beloved one single moment of unalloyed happiness.

From the very first day when he sat beside her in the tiny boudoir of the Square du Roule, and the heavy foot fall of Heron and his bloodhounds broke in on their first kiss, down to this hour which he believed struck his own death-knell, his love for her had brought more tears to her dear eyes than smiles to her exquisite mouth.

Her he had loved so dearly, that for her sweet sake he had sacrificed honour, friendship and truth; to free her, as he believed, from the hands of impious brutes he had done a deed that cried Cain-like for vengeance to the very throne of God. For her he had sinned, and because of that sin, even before it was committed, their love had been blighted, and happiness had never been theirs.

Now it was all over. He would pass out of her life, up the steps of the scaffold, tasting as he mounted them the most entire happiness that he had known since that awful day when he became a Judas.

The peremptory summons, once more repeated, roused him from his meditations. He lit a candle, and without troubling to slip any of his clothes on, he crossed the narrow ante-chamber, and opened the door that gave on the landing.

"In the name of the people!"

He had expected to hear not only those words, but also the grounding of arms and the brief command to halt. He had expected to see before him the white facings of the uniform of the Garde de Paris, and to feel himself roughly pushed back into his lodging preparatory to the search being made of all his effects and the placing of irons on his wrists.

Instead of this, it was a quiet, dry voice that said without undue harshness:

"In the name of the people!"

And instead of the uniforms, the bayonets and the scarlet caps with tricolour cockades, he was confronted by a slight, sable-clad figure, whose face, lit by the flickering light of the tallow candle, looked strangely pale and earnest.

"Citizen Chauvelin!" gasped Armand, more surprised than frightened at this unexpected apparition.

"Himself, citizen, at your service," replied Chauvelin with his quiet, ironical manner. "I am the bearer of a letter for you from Sir Percy Blakeney. Have I your permission to enter?"

Mechanically Armand stood aside, allowing the other man to pass in. He closed the door behind his nocturnal visitor, then, taper in hand, he preceded him into the inner room.

It was the same one in which a fortnight ago a fighting lion had been brought to his knees. Now it lay wrapped in gloom, the feeble light of the candle only lighting Armand's face and the white frill of his shirt. The young man put the taper down on the table and turned to his visitor.

"Shall I light the lamp?" he asked.

"Quite unnecessary," replied Chauvelin curtly. "I have only a letter to deliver, and after that to ask you one brief question."

From the pocket of his coat he drew the letter which Blakeney had written an hour ago.

"The prisoner wrote this in my presence," he said as he handed the letter over to Armand. "Will you read it?"

Armand took it from him, and sat down close to the table; leaning forward he held the paper near the light, and began to read. He read the letter through very slowly to the end, then once again from the beginning. He was trying to do that which Chauvelin had wished to do an hour ago; he was trying to find the inner meaning which he felt must inevitably lie behind these words which Percy had written with his own hand.

That these bare words were but a blind to deceive the enemy Armand never doubted for a moment. In this he was as loyal as Marguerite would have been herself. Never for a moment did the suspicion cross his mind that Blakeney was about to play the part of a coward, but he, Armand, felt that as a faithful friend and follower he ought by instinct to know exactly what his chief intended, what he meant him to do.

Swiftly his thoughts flew back to that other letter, the one which Marguerite had given him—the letter full of pity and of friendship which had brought him hope and a joy and peace which he had thought at one time that he would never know again. And suddenly one sentence in that letter stood out so clearly before his eyes that it blurred the actual, tangible ones on the paper which even now rustled in his hand.

But if at any time you receive another letter from me—be its contents what they may—act in accordance with the letter, but send a copy of it at once to Ffoulkes or to Marguerite.

Now everything seemed at once quite clear; his duty, his next actions, every word that he would speak to Chauvelin. Those that Percy had written to him were already indelibly graven on his memory.

Chauvelin had waited with his usual patience, silent and imperturbable, while the young man read. Now when he saw that Armand had finished, he said quietly:

"Just one question, citizen, and I need not detain you longer. But first will you kindly give me back that letter? It is a precious document which will for ever remain in the archives of the nation."

But even while he spoke Armand, with one of those quick intuitions that come in moments of acute crisis, had done just that which he felt Blakeney would wish him to do. He had held the letter close to the candle. A corner of the thin crisp paper immediately caught fire, and before Chauvelin could utter a word of anger, or make a movement to prevent the conflagration, the flames had licked up fully one half of the letter, and Armand had only just time to throw the remainder on the floor and to stamp out the blaze with his foot.

"I am sorry, citizen," he said calmly; "an accident."

"A useless act of devotion," interposed Chauvelin, who already had smothered the oath that had risen to his lips. "The Scarlet Pimpernel's actions in the present matter will not lose their merited publicity through the foolish destruction of this document."

"I had no thought, citizen," retorted the young man, "of commenting on the actions of my chief, or of trying to deny them that publicity which you seem to desire for them almost as much as I do."

"More, citizen, a great deal more! The impeccable Scarlet Pimpernel, the noble and gallant English gentleman, has agreed to deliver into our hands the uncrowned King of France—in exchange for his own life and freedom. Methinks that even his worst enemy would not wish for a better ending to a career of adventure, and a reputation for bravery unequalled in Europe. But no more of this, time is pressing, I must help citizen Heron with his final preparations for his journey. You, of course, citizen St. Just, will act in accordance with Sir Percy Blakeney's wishes?"

"Of course," replied Armand.

"You will present yourself at the main entrance of the house of Justice at six o'clock this morning."

"I will not fail you."

"A coach will be provided for you. You will follow the expedition as hostage for the good faith of your chief."

"I quite understand."

"H'm! That's brave! You have no fear, citizen St. Just?"

"Fear of what, sir?

"You will be a hostage in our hands, citizen; your life a guarantee that your chief has no thought of playing us false. Now I was thinking of—of certain events—which led to the arrest of Sir Percy Blakeney."

"Of my treachery, you mean," rejoined the young man calmly, even though his face had suddenly become pale as death. "Of the damnable lie wherewith you cheated me into selling my honour, and made me what I am—a creature scarce fit to walk upon this earth."

"Oh!" protested Chauvelin blandly.

"The damnable lie," continued Armand more vehemently, "that hath made me one with Cain and the Iscariot. When you goaded me into the hellish act, Jeanne Lange was already free."

"Free—but not safe."

"A lie, man! A lie! For which you are thrice accursed. Great God, is it not you that should have cause for fear? Methinks were I to strangle you now I should suffer less of remorse."

"And would be rendering your ex-chief but a sorry service," interposed Chauvelin with quiet irony. "Sir Percy Blakeney is a dying man, citizen St. Just; he'll be a dead man at dawn if I do not put in an appearance by six o'clock this morning. This is a private understanding between citizen Heron and myself. We agreed to it before I came to see you."

"Oh, you take care of your own miserable skin well enough! But you need not be afraid of me—I take my orders from my chief, and he has not ordered me to kill you."

"That was kind of him. Then we may count on you? You are not afraid?"

"Afraid that the Scarlet Pimpernel would leave me in the lurch because of the immeasurable wrong I have done to him?" retorted Armand, proud and defiant in the name of his chief. "No, sir, I am not afraid of that; I have spent the last fortnight in praying to God that my life might yet be given for his."

"H'm! I think it most unlikely that your prayers will be granted, citizen; prayers, I imagine, so very seldom are; but I don't know, I never pray myself. In your case, now, I should say that you have not the slightest chance of the Deity interfering in so pleasant a manner. Even were Sir Percy Blakeney prepared to wreak personal revenge on you, he would scarcely be so foolish as to risk the other life which we shall also hold as hostage for his good faith."

"The other life?"

"Yes. Your sister, Lady Blakeney, will also join the expedition to-morrow. This Sir Percy does not yet know; but it will come as a pleasant surprise for him. At the slightest suspicion of false play on Sir Percy's part, at his slightest attempt at escape, your life and that of your sister are forfeit; you will both be summarily shot before his eyes. I do not think that I need be more precise, eh, citizen St. Just?"

The young man was quivering with passion. A terrible loathing for himself, for his crime which had been the precursor of this terrible situation, filled his soul to the verge of sheer physical nausea. A red film gathered before his eyes, and through it he saw the grinning face of the inhuman monster who had planned this hideous, abominable thing. It seemed to him as if in the silence and the hush of the night, above the feeble, flickering flame that threw weird shadows around, a group of devils were surrounding him, and were shouting, "Kill him! Kill him now! Rid the earth of this hellish brute!"

No doubt if Chauvelin had exhibited the slightest sign of fear, if he had moved an inch towards the door, Armand, blind with passion, driven to madness by agonising remorse more even than by rage, would have sprung at his enemy's throat and crushed the life out of him as he would out of a venomous beast. But the man's calm, his immobility, recalled St. Just to himself. Reason, that had almost yielded to passion again, found strength to drive the enemy back this time, to whisper a warning, an admonition, even a reminder. Enough harm, God knows, had been done by tempestuous passion already. And God alone knew what terrible consequences its triumph now might bring in its trial, and striking on Armand's buzzing ears Chauvelin's words came back as a triumphant and mocking echo:

"He'll be a dead man at dawn if I do not put in an appearance by six o'clock."

The red film lifted, the candle flickered low, the devils vanished, only the pale face of the Terrorist gazed with gentle irony out of the gloom.

"I think that I need not detain you any longer, citizen, St. Just," he said quietly; "you can get three or four hours' rest yet before you need make a start, and I still have a great many things to see to. I wish you good-night, citizen."

"Good-night," murmured Armand mechanically.

He took the candle and escorted his visitor back to the door. He waited on the landing, taper in hand, while Chauvelin descended the narrow, winding stairs.

There was a light in the concierge's lodge. No doubt the woman had struck it when the nocturnal visitor had first demanded admittance. His name and tricolour scarf of office had ensured him the full measure of her attention, and now she was evidently sitting up waiting to let him out.

St. Just, satisfied that Chauvelin had finally gone, now turned back to his own rooms.

CHAPTER XL

God Help Us All

He carefully locked the outer door. Then he lit the lamp, for the candle gave but a flickering light, and he had some important work to do.

Firstly, he picked up the charred fragment of the letter, and smoothed it out carefully and reverently as he would a relic. Tears had gathered in his eyes, but he was not ashamed of them, for no one saw them; but they eased his heart, and helped to strengthen his resolve. It was a mere fragment that had been spared by the flame, but Armand knew every word of the letter by heart.

He had pen, ink and paper ready to his hand, and from memory wrote out a copy of it. To this he added a covering letter from himself to Marguerite:

This—which I had from Percy through the hands of Chauvelin—I neither question nor understand.... He wrote the letter, and I have no thought but to obey. In his previous letter to me he enjoined me, if ever he wrote to me again, to obey him implicitly, and to communicate with you. To both these commands do I submit with a glad heart. But of this must I give you warning, little mother—Chauvelin desires you also to accompany us to-morrow.... Percy does not know this yet, else he would never start. But those fiends fear that his readiness is a blind... and that he has some plan in his head for his own escape and the continued safety of the Dauphin.... This plan they hope to frustrate through holding you and me as hostages for his good faith. God only knows how gladly I would give my life for my chief... but your life, dear little mother... is sacred above all.... I think that I do right in warning you. God help us all.

Having written the letter, he sealed it, together with the copy of Percy's letter which he had made. Then he took up the candle and went downstairs.

There was no longer any light in the concierge's lodge, and Armand had some difficulty in making himself heard. At last the woman came to the door. She was tired and cross after two interruptions of her night's rest, but she had a partiality for her young lodger, whose pleasant ways and easy liberality had been like a pale ray of sunshine through the squalor of every-day misery.

"It is a letter, citoyenne," said Armand, with earnest entreaty, "for my sister. She lives in the Rue de Charonne, near the fortifications, and must have it within an hour; it is a matter of life and death to her, to me, and to another who is very dear to us both."

The concierge threw up her hands in horror.

"Rue de Charonne, near the fortifications," she exclaimed, "and within an hour! By the Holy Virgin, citizen, that is impossible. Who will take it? There is no way."

"A way must be found, citoyenne," said Armand firmly, "and at once; it is not far, and there are five golden louis waiting for the messenger!"

Five golden louis! The poor, hardworking woman's eyes gleamed at the thought. Five louis meant food for at least two months if one was careful, and—

"Give me the letter, citizen," she said, "time to slip on a warm petticoat and a shawl, and I'll go myself. It's not fit for the boy to go at this hour."

"You will bring me back a line from my sister in reply to this," said Armand, whom circumstances had at last rendered cautious. "Bring it up to my rooms that I may give you the five louis in exchange."

He waited while the woman slipped back into her room. She heard him speaking to her boy; the same lad who a fortnight ago had taken the treacherous letter which had lured Blakeney to the house into the fatal ambuscade that had been prepared for him. Everything reminded Armand of that awful night, every hour that he had since spent in the house had been racking torture to him. Now at last he was to leave it, and on an errand which might help to ease the load of remorse from his heart.

The woman was soon ready. Armand gave her final directions as to how to find the house; then she took the letter and promised to be very quick, and to bring back a reply from the lady.

Armand accompanied her to the door. The night was dark, a thin drizzle was falling; he stood and watched until the woman's rapidly walking figure was lost in the misty gloom.

Then with a heavy sigh he once more went within.

CHAPTER XLI

When Hope Was Dead

In a small upstairs room in the Rue de Charonne, above the shop of Lucas the old-clothes dealer, Marguerite sat with Sir Andrew Ffoulkes. Armand's letter, with its message and its warning, lay open on the table between them, and she had in her hand the sealed packet which Percy had given her just ten days ago, and which she was only to open if all hope seemed to be dead, if nothing appeared to stand any longer between that one dear life and irretrievable shame.

A small lamp placed on the table threw a feeble yellow light on the squalid, ill-furnished room, for it lacked still an hour or so before dawn. Armand's concierge had brought her lodger's letter, and Marguerite had quickly despatched a brief reply to him, a reply that held love and also encouragement.

Then she had summoned Sir Andrew. He never had a thought of leaving her during these days of dire trouble, and he had lodged all this while in a tiny room on the top-most floor of this house in the Rue de Charonne.

At her call he had come down very quickly, and now they sat together at the table, with the oil-lamp illumining their pale, anxious faces; she the wife and he the friend holding a consultation together in this most miserable hour that preceded the cold wintry dawn.

Outside a thin, persistent rain mixed with snow pattered against the small window panes, and an icy wind found out all the crevices in the worm-eaten woodwork that would afford it ingress to the room. But neither Marguerite nor Ffoulkes was conscious of the cold. They had wrapped their cloaks round their shoulders, and did not feel the chill currents of air that caused the lamp to flicker and to smoke.

"I can see now," said Marguerite in that calm voice which comes so naturally in moments of infinite despair—"I can see now exactly what Percy meant when he made me promise not to open this packet until it seemed to me—to me and to you, Sir Andrew—that he was about to play the part of a coward. A coward! Great God!" She checked the sob that had risen to her throat, and continued in the same calm manner and quiet, even voice:

"You do think with me, do you not, that the time has come, and that we must open this packet?"

"Without a doubt, Lady Blakeney," replied Ffoulkes with equal earnestness. "I would stake my life that already a fortnight ago Blakeney had that same plan in his mind which he has now matured. Escape from that awful Conciergerie prison with all the precautions so carefully taken against it was impossible. I knew that alas! from the first. But in the open all might yet be different. I'll not believe it that a man like Blakeney is destined to perish at the hands of those curs."

She looked on her loyal friend with tear-dimmed eyes through which shone boundless gratitude and heart-broken sorrow.

He had spoken of a fortnight! It was ten days since she had seen Percy. It had then seemed as if death had already marked him with its grim sign. Since then she had tried to shut away from her mind the terrible visions which her anguish constantly conjured up before her of his growing weakness, of the gradual impairing of that brilliant intellect, the gradual exhaustion of that mighty physical strength.

"God bless you, Sir Andrew, for your enthusiasm and for your trust," she said with a sad little smile; "but for you I should long ago have lost all courage, and these last ten days—what a cycle of misery they represent—would have been maddening but for your help and your loyalty. God knows I would have courage for everything in life, for everything save one, but just that, his death; that would be beyond my strength—neither reason nor body could stand it. Therefore, I am so afraid, Sir Andrew," she added piteously.

"Of what, Lady Blakeney?"

"That when he knows that I too am to go as hostage, as Armand says in his letter, that my life is to be guarantee his, I am afraid that he will draw back—that he will—my God!" she cried with sudden fervour, "tell me what to do!"

"Shall we open the packet?" asked Ffoulkes gently, "and then just make up our minds to act exactly as Blakeney has enjoined us to do, neither more nor less, but just word for word, deed for deed, and I believe that that will be right—whatever may betide—in the end."

Once more his quiet strength, his earnestness and his faith comforted her. She dried her eyes and broke open the seal. There were two separate letters in the packet, one unaddressed, obviously intended for her and Ffoulkes, the other was addressed to M. le baron Jean de Batz, 15, Rue St. Jean de Latran a Paris.

"A letter addressed to that awful Baron de Batz," said Marguerite, looking with puzzled eyes on the paper as she turned it over and over in her hand, "to that bombastic windbag! I know him and his ways well! What can Percy have to say to him?"

Sir Andrew too looked puzzled. But neither of them had the mind to waste time in useless speculations. Marguerite unfolded the letter which was intended for her, and after a final look on her friend, whose kind face was quivering with excitement, she began slowly to read aloud:

I need not ask either of you two to trust me, knowing that you will. But I could not die inside this hole like a rat in a trap—I had to try and free myself, at the worst to die in the open beneath God's sky. You two will understand, and understanding you will trust me to the end. Send the enclosed letter at once to its address. And you, Ffoulkes, my most sincere and most loyal friend, I beg with all my soul to see to the safety of Marguerite. Armand will stay by me—but you, Ffoulkes, do not leave her, stand by her. As soon as you read this letter—and you will not read it until both she and you have felt that hope has fled and I myself am about to throw up the sponge—try and persuade her to make for the coast as quickly as may be.... At Calais you can open up communications with the Day-Dream in the usual way, and embark on her at once. Let no member of the League remain on French soil one hour longer after that. Then tell the skipper to make for Le Portel—the place which he knows—and there to keep a sharp outlook for another three nights. After that make straight for home, for it will be no use waiting any longer. I shall not come. These measures are for Marguerite's safety, and for you all who are in France at this moment. Comrade, I entreat you to look on these measures as on my dying wish. To de Batz I have given rendezvous at the Chapelle of the Holy Sepulchre, just outside the park of the Chateau d'Ourde. He will help me to save the Dauphin, and if by good luck he also helps me to save myself I shall be within seven leagues of Le Portel, and with the Liane frozen as she is I could reach the coast.

But Marguerite's safety I leave in your hands, Ffoulkes. Would that I could look more clearly into the future, and know that those devils will not drag her into danger. Beg her to start at once for Calais immediately you have both read this. I only beg, I do not command. I know that you, Ffoulkes, will stand by her whatever she may wish to do. God's blessing be for ever on you both.

Marguerite's voice died away in the silence that still lay over this deserted part of the great city and in this squalid house where she and Sir Andrew Ffoulkes had found shelter these last ten days. The agony of mind which they had here endured, never doubting, but scarcely ever hoping, had found its culmination at last in this final message, which almost seemed to come to them from the grave.

It had been written ten days ago. A plan had then apparently formed in Percy's mind which he had set forth during the brief half-hour's respite which those fiends had once given him. Since then they had never given him ten consecutive minutes' peace; since then ten days had gone by how much power, how much vitality had gone by too on the leaden wings of all those terrible hours spent in solitude and in misery?

"We can but hope, Lady Blakeney," said Sir Andrew Ffoulkes after a while, "that you will be allowed out of Paris; but from what Armand says—"

"And Percy does not actually send me away," she rejoined with a pathetic little smile.

"No. He cannot compel you, Lady Blakeney. You are not a member of the League."

"Oh, yes, I am!" she retorted firmly; "and I have sworn obedience, just as all of you have done. I will go, just as he bids me, and you, Sir Andrew, you will obey him too?"

"My orders are to stand by you. That is an easy task."

"You know where this place is?" she asked—"the Chateau d'Ourde?"

"Oh, yes, we all know it! It is empty, and the park is a wreck; the owner fled from it at the very outbreak of the revolution; he left some kind of steward nominally in charge, a curious creature, half imbecile; the chateau and the chapel in the forest just outside the grounds have oft served Blakeney and all of us as a place of refuge on our way to the coast."

"But the Dauphin is not there?" she said.

"No. According to the first letter which you brought me from Blakeney ten days ago, and on which I acted, Tony, who has charge of the Dauphin, must have crossed into Holland with his little Majesty to-day."

"I understand," she said simply. "But then—this letter to de Batz?"

"Ah, there I am completely at sea! But I'll deliver it, and at once too, only I don't like to leave you. Will you let me get you out of Paris first? I think just before dawn it could be done. We can get the cart from Lucas, and if we could reach St. Germain before noon, I could come straight back then and deliver the letter to de Batz. This, I feel, I ought to do myself; but at Achard's farm I would know that you were safe for a few hours."

"I will do whatever you think right, Sir Andrew," she said simply; "my will is bound up with Percy's dying wish. God knows I would rather follow him now, step by step,—as hostage, as prisoner—any way so long as I can see him, but—"

She rose and turned to go, almost impassive now in that great calm born of despair.

A stranger seeing her now had thought her indifferent. She was very pale, and deep circles round her eyes told of sleepless nights and days of mental misery, but otherwise there was not the faintest outward symptom of that terrible anguish which was rending her heartstrings. Her lips did not quiver, and the source of her tears had been dried up ten days ago.

"Ten minutes and I'll be ready, Sir Andrew," she said. "I have but few belongings. Will you the while see Lucas about the cart?"

He did as she desired. Her calm in no way deceived him; he knew that she must be suffering keenly, and would suffer more keenly still while she would be trying to efface her own personal feelings all through that coming dreary journey to Calais.

He went to see the landlord about the horse and cart, and a quarter of an hour later Marguerite came downstairs ready to start. She found Sir Andrew in close converse with an officer of the Garde de Paris, whilst two soldiers of the same regiment were standing at the horse's head.

When she appeared in the doorway Sir Andrew came at once up to her.

"It is just as I feared, Lady Blakeney," he said; "this man has been sent here to take charge of you. Of course, he knows nothing beyond the fact that his orders are to convey you at once to the guard-house of the Rue Ste. Anne, where he is to hand you over to citizen Chauvelin of the Committee of Public Safety."

Sir Andrew could not fail to see the look of intense relief which, in the midst of all her sorrow, seemed suddenly to have lighted up the whole of Marguerite's wan face. The thought of wending her own way to safety whilst Percy, mayhap, was fighting an uneven fight with death had been well-nigh intolerable; but she had been ready to obey without a murmur. Now Fate and the enemy himself had decided otherwise. She felt as if a load had been lifted from her heart.

"I will at once go and find de Batz," Sir Andrew contrived to whisper hurriedly. "As soon as Percy's letter is safely in his hands I will make my way northwards and communicate with all the members of the League, on whom the chief has so strictly enjoined to quit French soil immediately. We will proceed to Calais first and open up communication with the Day-Dream in the usual way. The others had best embark on board her, and the skipper shall then make for the known spot of Le Portel, of which Percy speaks in his letter. I myself will go by land to Le Portel, and thence, if I have no news of you or of the expedition, I will slowly work southwards in the direction of the Chateau d'Ourde. That is all that I can do. If you can contrive to let Percy or even Armand know my movements, do so by all means. I know that I shall be doing right, for, in a way, I shall be watching over you and arranging for your safety, as Blakeney begged me to do. God bless you, Lady Blakeney, and God save the Scarlet Pimpernel!"

He stooped and kissed her hand, and she intimated to the officer that she was ready. He had a hackney coach waiting for her lower down the street. To it she walked with a firm step, and as she entered it she waved a last farewell to Sir Andrew Ffoulkes.

CHAPTER XLII

The Guard-House of Rue Ste. Anne

The little cortege was turning out of the great gates of the house of Justice. It was intensely cold; a bitter north-easterly gale was blowing from across the heights of Montmartre, driving sleet and snow and half-frozen rain into the faces of the men, and finding its way up their sleeves, down their collars and round the knees of their threadbare breeches.

Armand, whose fingers were numb with the cold, could scarcely feel the reins in his hands. Chauvelin was riding close beside him, but the two men had not exchanged one word since the moment when the small troop of some twenty mounted soldiers had filed up inside the courtyard, and Chauvelin, with a curt word of command, had ordered one of the troopers to take Armand's horse on the lead.

A hackney coach brought up the rear of the cortege, with a man riding at either door and two more following at a distance of twenty paces. Heron's gaunt, ugly face, crowned with a battered, sugar-loaf hat, appeared from time to time at the window of the coach. He was no horseman, and, moreover, preferred to keep the prisoner closely under his own eye. The corporal had told Armand that the prisoner was with citizen Heron inside the coach—in irons. Beyond that the soldiers could tell him nothing; they knew nothing of the object of this expedition. Vaguely they might have wondered in their dull minds why this particular prisoner was thus being escorted out of the Conciergerie prison with so much paraphernalia and such an air of mystery, when there were thousands of prisoners in the city and the provinces at the present moment who anon would be bundled up wholesale into carts to be dragged to the guillotine like a flock of sheep to the butchers.

But even if they wondered they made no remarks among themselves. Their faces, blue with the cold, were the perfect mirrors of their own unconquerable stolidity.

The tower clock of Notre Dame struck seven when the small cavalcade finally moved slowly out of the monumental gates. In the east the wan light of a February morning slowly struggled out of the surrounding gloom. Now the towers of many churches loomed ghostlike against the dull grey sky, and down below, on the right, the frozen river, like a smooth sheet of steel, wound its graceful curves round the islands and past the facade of the Louvres palace, whose walls looked grim and silent, like the mausoleum of the dead giants of the past.

All around the great city gave signs of awakening; the business of the day renewed its course every twenty-four hours, despite the tragedies of death and of dishonour that walked with it hand in hand. From the Place de La Revolution the intermittent roll of drums came from time to time with its muffled sound striking the ear of the passer-by. Along the quay opposite an open-air camp was already astir; men, women, and children engaged in the great task of clothing and feeding the people of France, armed against tyranny, were bending to their task, even before the wintry dawn had spread its pale grey tints over the narrower streets of the city.

Armand shivered under his cloak. This silent ride beneath the laden sky, through the veil of half-frozen rain and snow, seemed like a dream to him. And now, as the outriders of the little cavalcade turned to cross the Pont au Change, he saw spread out on his left what appeared like the living panorama of these three weeks that had just gone by. He could see the house of the Rue St. Germain l'Auxerrois where Percy had lodged before he carried through the rescue of the little Dauphin. Armand could even see the window at which the dreamer had stood, weaving noble dreams that his brilliant daring had turned into realities, until the hand of a traitor had brought him down to—to what? Armand would not have dared at this moment to look back at that hideous, vulgar hackney coach wherein that proud, reckless adventurer, who had defied Fate and mocked Death, sat, in chains, beside a loathsome creature whose very propinquity was an outrage.

Now they were passing under the very house on the Quai de La Ferraille, above the saddler's shop, the house where Marguerite had lodged ten days ago, whither Armand had come, trying to fool himself into the belief that the love of "little mother" could be deceived into blindness against his own crime. He had tried to draw a veil before those eyes which he had scarcely dared encounter, but he knew that that veil must lift one day, and then a curse would send him forth, outlawed and homeless, a wanderer on the face of the earth.

Soon as the little cortege wended its way northwards it filed out beneath the walls of the Temple prison; there was the main gate with its sentry standing at attention, there the archway with the guichet of the concierge, and beyond it the paved courtyard. Armand closed his eyes deliberately; he could not bear to look.

No wonder that he shivered and tried to draw his cloak closer around him. Every stone, every street corner was full of memories. The chill that struck to the very marrow of his bones came from no outward cause; it was the very hand of remorse that, as it passed over him, froze the blood in his veins and made the rattle of those wheels behind him sound like a hellish knell.

At last the more closely populated quarters of the city were left behind. On ahead the first section of the guard had turned into the Rue St. Anne. The houses became more sparse, intersected by narrow pieces of terrains vagues, or small weed-covered bits of kitchen garden.

Then a halt was called.

It was quite light now. As light as it would ever be beneath this leaden sky. Rain and snow still fell in gusts, driven by the blast.

Some one ordered Armand to dismount. It was probably Chauvelin. He did as he was told, and a trooper led him to the door of an irregular brick building that stood isolated on the right, extended on either side by a low wall, and surrounded by a patch of uncultivated land, which now looked like a sea of mud.

On ahead was the line of fortifications dimly outlined against the grey of the sky, and in between brown, sodden earth, with here and there a detached house, a cabbage patch, a couple of windmills deserted and desolate.

The loneliness of an unpopulated outlying quarter of the great mother city, a useless limb of her active body, an ostracised member of her vast family.

Mechanically Armand had followed the soldier to the door of the building. Here Chauvelin was standing, and bade him follow. A smell of hot coffee hung in the dark narrow passage in front. Chauvelin led the way to a room on the left.

Still that smell of hot coffee. Ever after it was associated in Armand's mind with this awful morning in the guard-house of the Rue Ste. Anne, when the rain and snow beat against the windows, and he stood there in the low guard-room shivering and half-numbed with cold.

There was a table in the middle of the room, and on it stood cups of hot coffee. Chauvelin bade him drink, suggesting, not unkindly, that the warm beverage would do him good. Armand advanced further into the room, and saw that there were wooden benches all round against the wall. On one of these sat his sister Marguerite.

When she saw him she made a sudden, instinctive movement to go to him, but Chauvelin interposed in his usual bland, quiet manner.

"Not just now, citizeness," he said.

She sat down again, and Armand noted how cold and stony seemed her eyes, as if life within her was at a stand-still, and a shadow that was almost like death had atrophied every emotion in her.

"I trust you have not suffered too much from the cold, Lady Blakeney," resumed Chauvelin politely; "we ought not to have kept you waiting here for so long, but delay at departure is sometimes inevitable."

She made no reply, only acknowledging his reiterated inquiry as to her comfort with an inclination of the head.

Armand had forced himself to swallow some coffee, and for the moment he felt less chilled. He held the cup between his two hands, and gradually some warmth crept into his bones.

"Little mother," he said in English, "try and drink some of this, it will do you good."

"Thank you, dear," she replied. "I have had some. I am not cold."

Then a door at the end of the room was pushed open, and Heron stalked in.

"Are we going to be all day in this confounded hole?" he queried roughly.

Armand, who was watching his sister very closely, saw that she started at the sight of the wretch, and seemed immediately to shrink still further within herself, whilst her eyes, suddenly luminous and dilated, rested on him like those of a captive bird upon an approaching cobra.

But Chauvelin was not to be shaken out of his suave manner.

"One moment, citizen Heron," he said; "this coffee is very comforting. Is the prisoner with you?" he added lightly.

Heron nodded in the direction of the other room.

"In there," he said curtly.

"Then, perhaps, if you will be so good, citizen, to invite him thither, I could explain to him his future position and our own."

Heron muttered something between his fleshy lips, then he turned back towards the open door, solemnly spat twice on the threshold, and nodded his gaunt head once or twice in a manner which apparently was understood from within.

"No, sergeant, I don't want you," he said gruffly; "only the prisoner."

A second or two later Sir Percy Blakeney stood in the doorway; his hands were behind his back, obviously hand-cuffed, but he held himself very erect, though it was clear that this caused him a mighty effort. As soon as he had crossed the threshold his quick glance had swept right round the room.

He saw Armand, and his eyes lit up almost imperceptibly.

Then he caught sight of Marguerite, and his pale face took on suddenly a more ashen hue.

Chauvelin was watching him with those keen, light-coloured eyes of his. Blakeney, conscious of this, made no movement, only his lips tightened, and the heavy lids fell over the hollow eyes, completely hiding their glance.

But what even the most astute, most deadly enemy could not see was that subtle message of understanding that passed at once between Marguerite and the man she loved; it was a magnetic current, intangible, invisible to all save to her and to him. She was prepared to see him, prepared to see in him all that she had feared; the weakness, the mental exhaustion, the submission to the inevitable. Therefore she had also schooled her glance to express to him all that she knew she would not be allowed to say—the reassurance that she had read his last letter, that she had obeyed it to the last word, save where Fate and her enemy had interfered with regard to herself.

With a slight, imperceptible movement—imperceptible to every one save to him, she had seemed to handle a piece of paper in her kerchief, then she had nodded slowly, with her eyes—steadfast, reassuring—fixed upon him, and his glance gave answer that he had understood.

But Chauvelin and Heron had seen nothing of this. They were satisfied that there had been no communication between the prisoner and his wife and friend.

"You are no doubt surprised, Sir Percy," said Chauvelin after a while, "to see Lady Blakeney here. She, as well as citizen St. Just, will accompany our expedition to the place where you will lead us. We none of us know where that place is—citizen Heron and myself are entirely in your hands—you might be leading us to certain death, or again to a spot where your own escape would be an easy matter to yourself. You will not be surprised, therefore, that we have thought fit to take certain precautions both against any little ambuscade which you may have prepared for us, or against your making one of those daring attempts at escape for which the noted Scarlet Pimpernel is so justly famous."

He paused, and only Heron's low chuckle of satisfaction broke the momentary silence that followed. Blakeney made no reply. Obviously he knew exactly what was coming. He knew Chauvelin and his ways, knew the kind of tortuous conception that would find origin in his brain; the moment that he saw Marguerite sitting there he must have guessed that Chauvelin once more desired to put her precious life in the balance of his intrigues.

"Citizen Heron is impatient, Sir Percy," resumed Chauvelin after a while, "so I must be brief. Lady Blakeney, as well as citizen St. Just, will accompany us on this expedition to whithersoever you may lead us. They will be the hostages which we will hold against your own good faith. At the slightest suspicion—a mere suspicion perhaps—that you have played us false, at a hint that you have led us into an ambush, or that the whole of this expedition has been but a trick on your part to effect your own escape, or if merely our hope of finding Capet at the end of our journey is frustrated, the lives of our two hostages belong to us, and your friend and your wife will be summarily shot before your eyes."

Outside the rain pattered against the window-panes, the gale whistled mournfully among the stunted trees, but within this room not a sound stirred the deadly stillness of the air, and yet at this moment hatred and love, savage lust and sublime self-abnegation—the most power full passions the heart of man can know—held three men here enchained; each a slave to his dominant passion, each ready to stake his all for the satisfaction of his master. Heron was the first to speak.

"Well!" he said with a fierce oath, "what are we waiting for? The prisoner knows how he stands. Now we can go."

"One moment, citizen," interposed Chauvelin, his quiet manner contrasting strangely with his colleague's savage mood. "You have quite understood, Sir Percy," he continued, directly addressing the prisoner, "the conditions under which we are all of us about to proceed on this journey?"

"All of us?" said Blakeney slowly. "Are you taking it for granted then that I accept your conditions and that I am prepared to proceed on the journey?"

"If you do not proceed on the journey," cried Heron with savage fury, "I'll strangle that woman with my own hands—now!"

Blakeney looked at him for a moment or two through half-closed lids, and it seemed then to those who knew him well, to those who loved him and to the man who hated him, that the mighty sinews almost cracked with the passionate desire to kill. Then the sunken eyes turned slowly to Marguerite, and she alone caught the look—it was a mere flash, of a humble appeal for pardon.

It was all over in a second; almost immediately the tension on the pale face relaxed, and into the eyes there came that look of acceptance—nearly akin to fatalism—an acceptance of which the strong alone are capable, for with them it only comes in the face of the inevitable.

Now he shrugged his broad shoulders, and once more turning to Heron he said quietly:

"You leave me no option in that case. As you have remarked before, citizen Heron, why should we wait any longer? Surely we can now go."

CHAPTER XLIII

The Dreary Journey

Rain! Rain! Rain! Incessant, monotonous and dreary! The wind had changed round to the southwest. It blew now in great gusts that sent weird, sighing sounds through the trees, and drove the heavy showers into the faces of the men as they rode on, with heads bent forward against the gale.

The rain-sodden bridles slipped through their hands, bringing out sores and blisters on their palms; the horses were fidgety, tossing their heads with wearying persistence as the wet trickled into their ears, or the sharp, intermittent hailstones struck their sensitive noses.

Three days of this awful monotony, varied only by the halts at wayside inns, the changing of troops at one of the guard-houses on the way, the reiterated commands given to the fresh squad before starting on the next lap of this strange, momentous way; and all the while, audible above the clatter of horses' hoofs, the rumbling of coach-wheels—two closed carriages, each drawn by a pair of sturdy horses; which were changed at every halt. A soldier on each box urged them to a good pace to keep up with the troopers, who were allowed to go at an easy canter or light jog-trot, whatever might prove easiest and least fatiguing. And from time to time Heron's shaggy, gaunt head would appear at the window of one of the coaches, asking the way, the distance to the next city or to the nearest wayside inn; cursing the troopers, the coachman, his colleague and every one concerned, blaspheming against the interminable length of the road, against the cold and against the wet.

Early in the evening on the second day of the journey he had met with an accident. The prisoner, who presumably was weak and weary, and not over steady on his feet, had fallen up against him as they were both about to re-enter the coach after a halt just outside Amiens, and citizen Heron had lost his footing in the slippery mud of the road. His head came in violent contact with the step, and his right temple was severely cut. Since then he had been forced to wear a bandage across the top of his face, under his sugar-loaf hat, which had added nothing to his beauty, but a great deal to the violence of his temper. He wanted to push the men on, to force the pace, to shorten the halts; but Chauvelin knew better than to allow slackness and discontent to follow in the wake of over-fatigue.

The soldiers were always well rested and well fed, and though the delay caused by long and frequent halts must have been just as irksome to him as it was to Heron, yet he bore it imperturbably, for he would have had no use on this momentous journey for a handful of men whose enthusiasm and spirit had been blown away by the roughness of the gale, or drowned in the fury of the constant downpour of rain.

Of all this Marguerite had been conscious in a vague, dreamy kind of way. She seemed to herself like the spectator in a moving panoramic drama, unable to raise a finger or to do aught to stop that final, inevitable ending, the cataclysm of sorrow and misery that awaited her, when the dreary curtain would fall on the last act, and she and all the other spectators—Armand, Chauvelin, Heron, the soldiers—would slowly wend their way home, leaving the principal actor behind the fallen curtain, which never would be lifted again.

After that first halt in the guard-room of the Rue Ste. Anne she had been bidden to enter a second hackney coach, which, followed the other at a distance of fifty metres or so, and was, like that other, closely surrounded by a squad of mounted men.

Armand and Chauvelin rode in this carriage with her; all day she sat looking out on the endless monotony of the road, on the drops of rain that pattered against the window-glass, and ran down from it like a perpetual stream of tears.

There were two halts called during the day—one for dinner and one midway through the afternoon—when she and Armand would step out of the coach and be led—always with soldiers close around them—to some wayside inn, where some sort of a meal was served, where the atmosphere was close and stuffy and smelt of onion soup and of stale cheese.

Armand and Marguerite would in most cases have a room to themselves, with sentinels posted outside the door, and they would try and eat enough to keep body and soul together, for they would not allow their strength to fall away before the end of the journey was reached.

For the night halt—once at Beauvais and the second night at Abbeville—they were escorted to a house in the interior of the city, where they were accommodated with moderately clean lodgings. Sentinels, however, were always at their doors; they were prisoners in all but name, and had little or no privacy; for at night they were both so tired that they were glad to retire immediately, and to lie down on the hard beds that had been provided for them, even if sleep fled from their eyes, and their hearts and souls were flying through the city in search of him who filled their every thought.

Of Percy they saw little or nothing. In the daytime food was evidently brought to him in the carriage, for they did not see him get down, and on those two nights at Beauvais and Abbeville, when they caught sight of him stepping out of the coach outside the gates of the barracks, he was so surrounded by soldiers that they only saw the top of his head and his broad shoulders towering above those of the men.

Once Marguerite had put all her pride, all her dignity by, and asked citizen Chauvelin for news of her husband.

"He is well and cheerful, Lady Blakeney," he had replied with his sarcastic smile. "Ah!" he added pleasantly, "those English are remarkable people. We, of Gallic breed, will never really understand them. Their fatalism is quite Oriental in its quiet resignation to the decree of Fate. Did you know, Lady Blakeney, that when Sir Percy was arrested he did not raise a hand. I thought, and so did my colleague, that he would have fought like a lion. And now, that he has no doubt realised that quiet submission will serve him best in the end, he is as calm on this journey as I am myself. In fact," he concluded complacently, "whenever I have succeeded in peeping into the coach I have invariably found Sir Percy Blakeney fast asleep."

"He—" she murmured, for it was so difficult to speak to this callous wretch, who was obviously mocking her in her misery—"he—you—you are not keeping him in irons?"

"No! Oh no!" replied Chauvelin with perfect urbanity. "You see, now that we have you, Lady Blakeney, and citizen St. Just with us we have no reason to fear that that elusive Pimpernel will spirit himself away."

A hot retort had risen to Armand's lips. The warm Latin blood in him rebelled against this intolerable situation, the man's sneers in the face of Marguerite's anguish. But her restraining, gentle hand had already pressed his. What was the use of protesting, of insulting this brute, who cared nothing for the misery which he had caused so long as he gained his own ends?

And Armand held his tongue and tried to curb his temper, tried to cultivate a little of that fatalism which Chauvelin had said was characteristic of the English. He sat beside his sister, longing to comfort her, yet feeling that his very presence near her was an outrage and a sacrilege. She spoke so seldom to him, even when they were alone, that at times the awful thought which had more than once found birth in his weary brain became crystallised and more real. Did Marguerite guess? Had she the slightest suspicion that the awful cataclysm to which they were tending with every revolution of the creaking coach-wheels had been brought about by her brother's treacherous hand?

And when that thought had lodged itself quite snugly in his mind he began to wonder whether it would not be far more simple, far more easy, to end his miserable life in some manner that might suggest itself on the way. When the coach crossed one of those dilapidated, parapetless bridges, over abysses fifty metres deep, it might be so easy to throw open the carriage door and to take one final jump into eternity.

So easy—but so damnably cowardly.

Marguerite's near presence quickly brought him back to himself. His life was no longer his own to do with as he pleased; it belonged to the chief whom he had betrayed, to the sister whom he must endeavour to protect.

Of Jeanne now he thought but little. He had put even the memory of her by—tenderly, like a sprig of lavender pressed between the faded leaves of his own happiness. His hand was no longer fit to hold that of any pure woman—his hand had on it a deep stain, immutable, like the brand of Cain.

Yet Marguerite beside him held his hand and together they looked out on that dreary, dreary road and listened to of the patter of the rain and the rumbling of the wheels of that other coach on ahead—and it was all so dismal and so horrible, the rain, the soughing of the wind in the stunted trees, this landscape of mud and desolation, this eternally grey sky.

CHAPTER XLIV

The Halt at Crecy

"Now, then, citizen, don't go to sleep; this is Crecy, our last halt!"

Armand woke up from his last dream. They had been moving steadily on since they left Abbeville soon after dawn; the rumble of the wheels, the swaying and rocking of the carriage, the interminable patter of the rain had lulled him into a kind of wakeful sleep.

Chauvelin had already alighted from the coach. He was helping Marguerite to descend. Armand shook the stiffness from his limbs and followed in the wake of his sister. Always those miserable soldiers round them, with their dank coats of rough blue cloth, and the red caps on their heads! Armand pulled Marguerite's hand through his arm, and dragged her with him into the house.

The small city lay damp and grey before them; the rough pavement of the narrow street glistened with the wet, reflecting the dull, leaden sky overhead; the rain beat into the puddles; the slate-roofs shone in the cold wintry light.

This was Crecy! The last halt of the journey, so Chauvelin had said. The party had drawn rein in front of a small one-storied building that had a wooden verandah running the whole length of its front.

The usual low narrow room greeted Armand and Marguerite as they entered; the usual mildewed walls, with the colour wash flowing away in streaks from the unsympathetic beam above; the same device, "Liberte, Egalite, Fraternite!" scribbled in charcoal above the black iron stove; the usual musty, close atmosphere, the usual smell of onion and stale cheese, the usual hard straight benches and central table with its soiled and tattered cloth.

Marguerite seemed dazed and giddy; she had been five hours in that stuffy coach with nothing to distract her thoughts except the rain-sodden landscape, on which she had ceaselessly gazed since the early dawn.

Armand led her to the bench, and she sank down on it, numb and inert, resting her elbows on the table and her head in her hands.

"If it were only all over!" she sighed involuntarily. "Armand, at times now I feel as if I were not really sane—as if my reason had already given way! Tell me, do I seem mad to you at times?"

He sat down beside her and tried to chafe her little cold hands.

There was a knock at the door, and without waiting for permission Chauvelin entered the room.

"My humble apologies to you, Lady Blakeney," he said in his usual suave manner, "but our worthy host informs me that this is the only room in which he can serve a meal. Therefore I am forced to intrude my presence upon you."

Though he spoke with outward politeness, his tone had become more peremptory, less bland, and he did not await Marguerite's reply before he sat down opposite to her and continued to talk airily.

"An ill-conditioned fellow, our host," he said—"quite reminds me of our friend Brogard at the Chat Gris in Calais. You remember him, Lady Blakeney?"

"My sister is giddy and over-tired," interposed Armand firmly. "I pray you, citizen, to have some regard for her."

"All regard in the world, citizen St. Just," protested Chauvelin jovially. "Methought that those pleasant reminiscences would cheer her. Ah! here comes the soup," he added, as a man in blue blouse and breeches, with sabots on his feet, slouched into the room, carrying a tureen which he incontinently placed upon the table. "I feel sure that in England Lady Blakeney misses our excellent croutes-au-pot, the glory of our bourgeois cookery—Lady Blakeney, a little soup?"

"I thank you, sir," she murmured.

"Do try and eat something, little mother," Armand whispered in her ear; "try and keep up your strength for his sake, if not for mine."

She turned a wan, pale face to him, and tried to smile.

"I'll try, dear," she said.

"You have taken bread and meat to the citizens in the coach?" Chauvelin called out to the retreating figure of mine host.

"H'm!" grunted the latter in assent.

"And see that the citizen soldiers are well fed, or there will be trouble."

"H'm!" grunted the man again. After which he banged the door to behind him.

"Citizen Heron is loath to let the prisoner out of his sight," explained Chauvelin lightly, "now that we have reached the last, most important stage of our journey, so he is sharing Sir Percy's mid-day meal in the interior of the coach."

He ate his soup with a relish, ostentatiously paying many small attentions to Marguerite all the time. He ordered meat for her—bread, butter—asked if any dainties could be got. He was apparently in the best of tempers.

After he had eaten and drunk he rose and bowed ceremoniously to her.

"Your pardon, Lady Blakeney," he said, "but I must confer with the prisoner now, and take from him full directions for the continuance of our journey. After that I go to the guard-house, which is some distance from here, right at the other end of the city. We pick up a fresh squad here, twenty hardened troopers from a cavalry regiment usually stationed at Abbeville. They have had work to do in this town, which is a hot-bed of treachery. I must go inspect the men and the sergeant who will be in command. Citizen Heron leaves all these inspections to me; he likes to stay by his prisoner. In the meanwhile you will be escorted back to your coach, where I pray you to await my arrival, when we change guard first, then proceed on our way."

Marguerite was longing to ask him many questions; once again she would have smothered her pride and begged for news of her husband, but Chauvelin did not wait. He hurried out of the room, and Armand and Marguerite could hear him ordering the soldiers to take them forthwith back to the coach.

As they came out of the inn they saw the other coach some fifty metres further up the street. The horses that had done duty since leaving Abbeville had been taken out, and two soldiers in ragged shirts, and with crimson caps set jauntily over their left ear, were leading the two fresh horses along. The troopers were still mounting guard round both the coaches; they would be relieved presently.

Marguerite would have given ten years of her life at this moment for the privilege of speaking to her husband, or even of seeing him—of seeing that he was well. A quick, wild plan sprang up in her mind that she would bribe the sergeant in command to grant her wish while citizen Chauvelin was absent. The man had not an unkind face, and he must be very poor—people in France were very poor these days, though the rich had been robbed and luxurious homes devastated ostensibly to help the poor.

She was about to put this sudden thought into execution when Heron's hideous face, doubly hideous now with that bandage of doubtful cleanliness cutting across his brow, appeared at the carriage window.

He cursed violently and at the top of his voice.

"What are those d—d aristos doing out there?" he shouted.

"Just getting into the coach, citizen," replied the sergeant promptly.

And Armand and Marguerite were immediately ordered back into the coach.

Heron remained at the window for a few moments longer; he had a toothpick in his hand which he was using very freely.

"How much longer are we going to wait in this cursed hole?" he called out to the sergeant.

"Only a few moments longer, citizen. Citizen Chauvelin will be back soon with the guard."

A quarter of an hour later the clatter of cavalry horses on the rough, uneven pavement drew Marguerite's attention. She lowered the carriage window and looked out. Chauvelin had just returned with the new escort. He was on horseback; his horse's bridle, since he was but an indifferent horseman, was held by one of the troopers.

Outside the inn he dismounted; evidently he had taken full command of the expedition, and scarcely referred to Heron, who spent most of his time cursing at the men or the weather when he was not lying half-asleep and partially drunk in the inside of the carriage.

The changing of the guard was now accomplished quietly and in perfect order. The new escort consisted of twenty mounted men, including a sergeant and a corporal, and of two drivers, one for each coach. The cortege now was filed up in marching order; ahead a small party of scouts, then the coach with Marguerite and Armand closely surrounded by mounted men, and at a short distance the second coach with citizen Heron and the prisoner equally well guarded.

Chauvelin superintended all the arrangements himself. He spoke for some few moments with the sergeant, also with the driver of his own coach. He went to the window of the other carriage, probably in order to consult with citizen Heron, or to take final directions from the prisoner, for Marguerite, who was watching him, saw him standing on the step and leaning well forward into the interior, whilst apparently he was taking notes on a small tablet which he had in his hand.

A small knot of idlers had congregated in the narrow street; men in blouses and boys in ragged breeches lounged against the verandah of the inn and gazed with inexpressive, stolid eyes on the soldiers, the coaches, the citizen who wore the tricolour scarf. They had seen this sort of thing before now—aristos being conveyed to Paris under arrest, prisoners on their way to or from Amiens. They saw Marguerite's pale face at the carriage window. It was not the first woman's face they had seen under like circumstances, and there was no special interest about this aristo. They were smoking or spitting, or just lounging idly against the balustrade. Marguerite wondered if none of them had wife, sister, or mother, or child; if every sympathy, every kind of feeling in these poor wretches had been atrophied by misery or by fear.

At last everything was in order and the small party ready to start.

"Does any one here know the Chapel of the Holy Sepulchre, close by the park of the Chateau d'Ourde?" asked Chauvelin, vaguely addressing the knot of gaffers that stood closest to him.

The men shook their heads. Some had dimly heard of the Chateau d'Ourde; it was some way in the interior of the forest of Boulogne, but no one knew about a chapel; people did not trouble about chapels nowadays. With the indifference so peculiar to local peasantry, these men knew no more of the surrounding country than the twelve or fifteen league circle that was within a walk of their sleepy little town.

One of the scouts on ahead turned in his saddle and spoke to citizen Chauvelin:

"I think I know the way pretty well; citizen Chauvelin," he said; "at any rate, I know it as far as the forest of Boulogne."

Chauvelin referred to his tablets.

"That's good," he said; "then when you reach the mile-stone that stands on this road at the confine of the forest, bear sharply to your right and skirt the wood until you see the hamlet of—Le—something. Le—Le—yes—Le Crocq—that's it in the valley below."

"I know Le Crocq, I think," said the trooper.

"Very well, then; at that point it seems that a wide road strikes at right angles into the interior of the forest; you follow that until a stone chapel with a colonnaded porch stands before you on your left, and the walls and gates of a park on your right. That is so, is it not, Sir Percy?" he added, once more turning towards the interior of the coach.

Apparently the answer satisfied him, for he gave the quick word of command, "En avant!" then turned back towards his own coach and finally entered it.

"Do you know the Chateau d'Ourde, citizen St. Just?" he asked abruptly as soon as the carriage began to move.

Armand woke—as was habitual with him these days—from some gloomy reverie.

"Yes, citizen," he replied. "I know it."

"And the Chapel of the Holy Sepulchre?"

"Yes. I know it too."

Indeed, he knew the chateau well, and the little chapel in the forest, whither the fisher-folk from Portel and Boulogne came on a pilgrimage once a year to lay their nets on the miracle-working relic. The chapel was disused now. Since the owner of the chateau had fled no one had tended it, and the fisher-folk were afraid to wander out, lest their superstitious faith be counted against them by the authorities, who had abolished le bon Dieu.

But Armand had found refuge there eighteen months ago, on his way to Calais, when Percy had risked his life in order to save him—Armand—from death. He could have groaned aloud with the anguish of this recollection. But Marguerite's aching nerves had thrilled at the name.

The Chateau d'Ourde! The Chapel of the Holy Sepulchre! That was the place which Percy had mentioned in his letter, the place where he had given rendezvous to de Batz. Sir Andrew had said that the Dauphin could not possibly be there, yet Percy was leading his enemies thither, and had given the rendezvous there to de Batz. And this despite that whatever plans, whatever hopes, had been born in his mind when he was still immured in the Conciergerie prison must have been set at naught by the clever counter plot of Chauvelin and Heron.

"At the merest suspicion that you have played us false, at a hint that you have led us into an ambush, or if merely our hopes of finding Capet at the end of the journey are frustrated, the lives of your wife and of your friend are forfeit to us, and they will both be shot before your eyes."

With these words, with this precaution, those cunning fiends had effectually not only tied the schemer's hands, but forced him either to deliver the child to them or to sacrifice his wife and his friend.

The impasse was so horrible that she could not face it even in her thoughts. A strange, fever-like heat coursed through her veins, yet left her hands icy-cold; she longed for, yet dreaded, the end of the journey—that awful grappling with the certainty of coming death. Perhaps, after all, Percy, too, had given up all hope. Long ago he had consecrated his life to the attainment of his own ideals; and there was a vein of fatalism in him; perhaps he had resigned himself to the inevitable, and his only desire now was to give up his life, as he had said, in the open, beneath God's sky, to draw his last breath with the storm-clouds tossed through infinity above him, and the murmur of the wind in the trees to sing him to rest.

Crecy was gradually fading into the distance, wrapped in a mantle of damp and mist. For a long while Marguerite could see the sloping slate roofs glimmering like steel in the grey afternoon light, and the quaint church tower with its beautiful lantern, through the pierced stonework of which shone patches of the leaden sky.

Then a sudden twist of the road hid the city from view; only the outlying churchyard remained in sight, with its white monuments and granite crosses, over which the dark yews, wet with the rain and shaken by the gale, sent showers of diamond-like sprays.

CHAPTER XLV

The Forst of Boulogne

Progress was not easy, and very slow along the muddy road; the two coaches moved along laboriously, with wheels creaking and sinking deeply from time to time in the quagmire.

When the small party finally reached the edge of the wood the greyish light of this dismal day had changed in the west to a dull reddish glow—a glow that had neither brilliance nor incandescence in it; only a weird tint that hung over the horizon and turned the distance into lines of purple.

The nearness of the sea made itself already felt; there was a briny taste in the damp atmosphere, and the trees all turned their branches away in the same direction against the onslaught of the prevailing winds.

The road at this point formed a sharp fork, skirting the wood on either side, the forest lying like a black close mass of spruce and firs on the left, while the open expanse of country stretched out on the right. The south-westerly gale struck with full violence against the barrier of forest trees, bending the tall crests of the pines and causing their small dead branches to break and fall with a sharp, crisp sound like a cry of pain.

The squad had been fresh at starting; now the men had been four hours in the saddle under persistent rain and gusty wind; they were tired, and the atmosphere of the close, black forest so near the road was weighing upon their spirits.

Strange sounds came to them from out the dense network of trees—the screeching of night-birds, the weird call of the owls, the swift and furtive tread of wild beasts on the prowl. The cold winter and lack of food had lured the wolves from their fastnesses—hunger had emboldened them, and now, as gradually the grey light fled from the sky, dismal howls could be heard in the distance, and now and then a pair of eyes, bright with the reflection of the lurid western glow, would shine momentarily out of the darkness like tiny glow-worms, and as quickly vanish away.

The men shivered—more with vague superstitious fear than with cold. They would have urged their horses on, but the wheels of the coaches stuck persistently in the mud, and now and again a halt had to be called so that the spokes and axles might be cleared.

They rode on in silence. No one had a mind to speak, and the mournful soughing of the wind in the pine-trees seemed to check the words on every lip. The dull thud of hoofs in the soft road, the clang of steel bits and buckles, the snorting of the horses alone answered the wind, and also the monotonous creaking of the wheels ploughing through the ruts.

Soon the ruddy glow in the west faded into soft-toned purple and then into grey; finally that too vanished. Darkness was drawing in on every side like a wide, black mantle pulled together closer and closer overhead by invisible giant hands.

The rain still fell in a thin drizzle that soaked through caps and coats, made the bridles slimy and the saddles slippery and damp. A veil of vapour hung over the horses' cruppers, and was rendered fuller and thicker every moment with the breath that came from their nostrils. The wind no longer blew with gusty fury—its strength seemed to have been spent with the grey light of day—but now and then it would still come sweeping across the open country, and dash itself upon the wall of forest trees, lashing against the horses' ears, catching the corner of a mantle here, an ill-adjusted cap there, and wreaking its mischievous freak for a while, then with a sigh of satisfaction die, murmuring among the pines.

Suddenly there was a halt, much shouting, a volley of oaths from the drivers, and citizen Chauvelin thrust his head out of the carriage window.

"What is it?" he asked.

"The scouts, citizen," replied the sergeant, who had been riding close to the coach door all this while; "they have returned."

"Tell one man to come straight to me and report."

Marguerite sat quite still. Indeed, she had almost ceased to live momentarily, for her spirit was absent from her body, which felt neither fatigue, nor cold, nor pain. But she heard the snorting of the horse close by as its rider pulled him up sharply beside the carriage door.

"Well?" said Chauvelin curtly.

"This is the cross-road, citizen," replied the man; "it strikes straight into the wood, and the hamlet of Le Crocq lies down in the valley on the right."

"Did you follow the road in the wood?"

"Yes, citizen. About two leagues from here there is a clearing with a small stone chapel, more like a large shrine, nestling among the trees. Opposite to it the angle of a high wall with large wrought-iron gates at the corner, and from these a wide drive leads through a park."

"Did you turn into the drive?"

"Only a little way, citizen. We thought we had best report first that all is safe."

"You saw no one?"

"No one."

"The chateau, then, lies some distance from the gates?"

"A league or more, citizen. Close to the gates there are outhouses and stabling, the disused buildings of the home farm, I should say."

"Good! We are on the right road, that is clear. Keep ahead with your men now, but only some two hundred metres or so. Stay!" he added, as if on second thoughts. "Ride down to the other coach and ask the prisoner if we are on the right track."

The rider turned his horse sharply round. Marguerite heard-the clang of metal and the sound of retreating hoofs.

A few moments later the man returned.

"Yes, citizen," he reported, "the prisoner says it is quite right. The Chateau d'Ourde lies a full league from its gates. This is the nearest road to the chapel and the chateau. He says we should reach the former in half an hour. It will be very dark in there," he added with a significant nod in the direction of the wood.

Chauvelin made no reply, but quietly stepped out of the coach. Marguerite watched him, leaning out of the window, following his small trim figure as he pushed his way past the groups of mounted men, catching at a horse's bit now and then, or at a bridle, making a way for himself amongst the restless, champing animals, without the slightest hesitation or fear.

Soon his retreating figure lost its sharp outline silhouetted against the evening sky. It was enfolded in the veil of vapour which was blown out of the horses' nostrils or rising from their damp cruppers; it became more vague, almost ghost-like, through the mist and the fast-gathering gloom.

Presently a group of troopers hid him entirely from her view, but she could hear his thin, smooth voice quite clearly as he called to citizen Heron.

"We are close to the end of our journey now, citizen," she heard him say. "If the prisoner has not played us false little Capet should be in our charge within the hour."

A growl not unlike those that came from out the mysterious depths of the forest answered him.

"If he is not," and Marguerite recognised the harsh tones of citizen Heron—"if he is not, then two corpses will be rotting in this wood tomorrow for the wolves to feed on, and the prisoner will be on his way back to Paris with me."

Some one laughed. It might have been one of the troopers, more callous than his comrades, but to Marguerite the laugh had a strange, familiar ring in it, the echo of something long since past and gone.

Then Chauvelin's voice once more came clearly to her ear:

"My suggestion, citizen," he was saying, "is that the prisoner shall now give me an order—couched in whatever terms he may think necessary—but a distinct order to his friends to give up Capet to me without any resistance. I could then take some of the men with me, and ride as quickly as the light will allow up to the chateau, and take possession of it, of Capet, and of those who are with him. We could get along faster thus. One man can give up his horse to me and continue the journey on the box of your coach. The two carriages could then follow at foot pace. But I fear that if we stick together complete darkness will overtake us and we might find ourselves obliged to pass a very uncomfortable night in this wood."

"I won't spend another night in this suspense—it would kill me," growled Heron to the accompaniment of one of his choicest oaths. "You must do as you think right—you planned the whole of this affair—see to it that it works out well in the end."

"How many men shall I take with me? Our advance guard is here, of course."

"I couldn't spare you more than four more men—I shall want the others to guard the prisoners."

"Four men will be quite sufficient, with the four of the advance guard. That will leave you twelve men for guarding your prisoners, and you really only need to guard the woman—her life will answer for the others."

He had raised his voice when he said this, obviously intending that Marguerite and Armand should hear.

"Then I'll ahead," he continued, apparently in answer to an assent from his colleague. "Sir Percy, will you be so kind as to scribble the necessary words on these tablets?"

There was a long pause, during which Marguerite heard plainly the long and dismal cry of a night bird that, mayhap, was seeking its mate. Then Chauvelin's voice was raised again.

"I thank you," he said; "this certainly should be quite effectual. And now, citizen Heron, I do not think that under the circumstances we need fear an ambuscade or any kind of trickery—you hold the hostages. And if by any chance I and my men are attacked, or if we encounter armed resistance at the chateau, I will despatch a rider back straightway to you, and—well, you will know what to do."

His voice died away, merged in the soughing of the wind, drowned by the clang of metal, of horses snorting, of men living and breathing. Marguerite felt that beside her Armand had shuddered, and that in the darkness his trembling hand had sought and found hers.

She leaned well out of the window, trying to see. The gloom had gathered more closely in, and round her the veil of vapour from the horses' steaming cruppers hung heavily in the misty air. In front of her the straight lines of a few fir trees stood out dense and black against the greyness beyond, and between these lines purple tints of various tones and shades mingled one with the other, merging the horizon line with the sky. Here and there a more solid black patch indicated the tiny houses of the hamlet of Le Crocq far down in the valley below; from some of these houses small lights began to glimmer like blinking yellow eyes. Marguerite's gaze, however, did not rest on the distant landscape—it tried to pierce the gloom that hid her immediate surroundings; the mounted men were all round the coach—more closely round her than the trees in the forest. But the horses were restless, moving all the time, and as they moved she caught glimpses of that other coach and of Chauvelin's ghostlike figure, walking rapidly through the mist. Just for one brief moment she saw the other coach, and Heron's head and shoulders leaning out of the window. If his sugar-loaf hat was on his head, and the bandage across his brow looked like a sharp, pale streak below it.

"Do not doubt it, citizen Chauvelin," he called out loudly in his harsh, raucous voice, "I shall know what to do; the wolves will have their meal to-night, and the guillotine will not be cheated either."

Armand put his arm round his sister's shoulders and gently drew her back into the carriage.

"Little mother," he said, "if you can think of a way whereby my life would redeem Percy's and yours, show me that way now."

But she replied quietly and firmly:

"There is no way, Armand. If there is, it is in the hands of God."

CHAPTER XLVI

Others in the Park

Chauvelin and his picked escort had in the meanwhile detached themselves from the main body of the squad. Soon the dull thud of their horses' hoofs treading the soft ground came more softly—then more softly still as they turned into the wood, and the purple shadows seemed to enfold every sound and finally to swallow them completely.

Armand and Marguerite from the depth of the carriage heard Heron's voice ordering his own driver now to take the lead. They sat quite still and watched, and presently the other coach passed them slowly on the road, its silhouette standing out ghostly and grim for a moment against the indigo tones of the distant country.

Heron's head, with its battered sugar-loaf hat, and the soiled bandage round the brow, was as usual out of the carriage window. He leered across at Marguerite when he saw the outline of her face framed by the window of the carriage.

"Say all the prayers you have ever known, citizeness," he said with a loud laugh, "that my friend Chauvelin may find Capet at the chateau, or else you may take a last look at the open country, for you will not see the sun rise on it to-morrow. It is one or the other, you know."

She tried not to look at him; the very sight of him filled her with horror—that blotched, gaunt face of his, the fleshy lips, that hideous bandage across his face that hid one of his eyes! She tried not to see him and not to hear him laugh.

Obviously he too laboured under the stress of great excitement. So far everything had gone well; the prisoner had made no attempt at escape, and apparently did not mean to play a double game. But the crucial hour had come, and with it darkness and the mysterious depths of the forest with their weird sounds and sudden flashes of ghostly lights. They naturally wrought on the nerves of men like Heron, whose conscience might have been dormant, but whose ears were nevertheless filled with the cries of innocent victims sacrificed to their own lustful ambitions and their blind, unreasoning hates.

He gave sharp orders to the men to close up round the carriages, and then gave the curt word of command:

"En avant!"

Marguerite could but strain her ears to listen. All her senses, all her faculties had merged into that of hearing, rendering it doubly keen. It seemed to her that she could distinguish the faint sound—that even as she listened grew fainter and fainter yet—of Chauvelin and his squad moving away rapidly into the thickness of the wood some distance already ahead.

Close to her there was the snorting of horses, the clanging and noise of moving mounted men. Heron's coach had taken the lead; she could hear the creaking of its wheels, the calls of the driver urging his beasts.

The diminished party was moving at foot-pace in the darkness that seemed to grow denser at every step, and through that silence which was so full of mysterious sounds.

The carriage rolled and rocked on its springs; Marguerite, giddy and overtired, lay back with closed eyes, her hand resting in that of Armand. Time, space and distance had ceased to be; only Death, the great Lord of all, had remained; he walked on ahead, scythe on skeleton shoulder, and beckoned patiently, but with a sure, grim hand.

There was another halt, the coach-wheels groaned and creaked on their axles, one or two horses reared with the sudden drawing up of the curb.

"What is it now?" came Heron's hoarse voice through the darkness.

"It is pitch-dark, citizen," was the response from ahead. "The drivers cannot see their horses' ears. They wait to know if they may light their lanthorns and then lead their horses."

"They can lead their horses," replied Heron roughly, "but I'll have no lanthorns lighted. We don't know what fools may be lurking behind trees, hoping to put a bullet through my head—or yours, sergeant—we don't want to make a lighted target of ourselves—what? But let the drivers lead their horses, and one or two of you who are riding greys might dismount too and lead the way—the greys would show up perhaps in this cursed blackness."

While his orders were being carried out, he called out once more:

"Are we far now from that confounded chapel?"

"We can't be far, citizen; the whole forest is not more than six leagues wide at any point, and we have gone two since we turned into it."

"Hush!" Heron's voice suddenly broke in hoarsely. "What was that? Silence, I say. Damn you—can't you hear?"

There was a hush—every ear straining to listen; but the horses were not still—they continued to champ their bits, to paw the ground, and to toss their heads, impatient to get on. Only now and again there would come a lull even through these sounds—a second or two, mayhap, of perfect, unbroken silence—and then it seemed as if right through the darkness a mysterious echo sent back those same sounds—the champing of bits, the pawing of soft ground, the tossing and snorting of animals, human life that breathed far out there among the trees.

"It is citizen Chauvelin and his men," said the sergeant after a while, and speaking in a whisper.

"Silence—I want to hear," came the curt, hoarsely-whispered command.

Once more every one listened, the men hardly daring to breathe, clinging to their bridles and pulling on their horses' mouths, trying to keep them still, and again through the night there came like a faint echo which seemed to throw back those sounds that indicated the presence of men and of horses not very far away.

"Yes, it must be citizen Chauvelin," said Heron at last; but the tone of his voice sounded as if he were anxious and only half convinced; "but I thought he would be at the chateau by now."

"He may have had to go at foot-pace; it is very dark, citizen Heron," remarked the sergeant.

"En avant, then," quoth the other; "the sooner we come up with him the better."

And the squad of mounted men, the two coaches, the drivers and the advance section who were leading their horses slowly restarted on the way. The horses snorted, the bits and stirrups clanged, and the springs and wheels of the coaches creaked and groaned dismally as the ramshackle vehicles began once more to plough the carpet of pine-needles that lay thick upon the road.

But inside the carriage Armand and Marguerite held one another tightly by the hand.

"It is de Batz—with his friends," she whispered scarce above her breath.

"De Batz?" he asked vaguely and fearfully, for in the dark he could not see her face, and as he did not understand why she should suddenly be talking of de Batz he thought with horror that mayhap her prophecy anent herself had come true, and that her mind wearied and over-wrought—had become suddenly unhinged.

"Yes, de Batz," she replied. "Percy sent him a message, through me, to meet him—here. I am not mad, Armand," she added more calmly. "Sir Andrew took Percy's letter to de Batz the day that we started from Paris."

"Great God!" exclaimed Armand, and instinctively, with a sense of protection, he put his arms round his sister. "Then, if Chauvelin or the squad is attacked—if—"

"Yes," she said calmly; "if de Batz makes an attack on Chauvelin, or if he reaches the chateau first and tries to defend it, they will shoot us... Armand, and Percy."

"But is the Dauphin at the Chateau d'Ourde?"

"No, no! I think not."

"Then why should Percy have invoked the aid of de Batz? Now, when—"

"I don't know," she murmured helplessly. "Of course, when he wrote the letter he could not guess that they would hold us as hostages. He may have thought that under cover of darkness and of an unexpected attack he might have saved himself had he been alone; but now—now that you and I are here—Oh! it is all so horrible, and I cannot understand it all."

"Hark!" broke in Armand, suddenly gripping her arm more tightly.

"Halt!" rang the sergeant's voice through the night.

This time there was no mistaking the sound; already it came from no far distance. It was the sound of a man running and panting, and now and again calling out as he ran.

For a moment there was stillness in the very air, the wind itself was hushed between two gusts, even the rain had ceased its incessant pattering. Heron's harsh voice was raised in the stillness.

"What is it now?" he demanded.

"A runner, citizen," replied the sergeant, "coming through the wood from the right."

"From the right?" and the exclamation was accompanied by a volley of oaths; "the direction of the chateau? Chauvelin has been attacked; he is sending a messenger back to me. Sergeant—sergeant, close up round that coach; guard your prisoners as you value your life, and—"

The rest of his words were drowned in a yell of such violent fury that the horses, already over-nervous and fidgety, reared in mad terror, and the men had the greatest difficulty in holding them in. For a few minutes noisy confusion prevailed, until the men could quieten their quivering animals with soft words and gentle pattings.

Then the troopers obeyed, closing up round the coach wherein brother and sister sat huddled against one another.

One of the men said under his breath:

"Ah! but the citizen agent knows how to curse! One day he will break his gullet with the fury of his oaths."

In the meanwhile the runner had come nearer, always at the same breathless speed.

The next moment he was challenged:

"Qui va la?"

"A friend!" he replied, panting and exhausted. "Where is citizen Heron?"

"Here!" came the reply in a voice hoarse with passionate excitement. "Come up, damn you. Be quick!"

"A lanthorn, citizen," suggested one of the drivers.

"No—no—not now. Here! Where the devil are we?"

"We are close to the chapel on our left, citizen," said the sergeant.

The runner, whose eyes were no doubt accustomed to the gloom, had drawn nearer to the carriage.

"The gates of the chateau," he said, still somewhat breathlessly, "are just opposite here on the right, citizen. I have just come through them."

"Speak up, man!" and Heron's voice now sounded as if choked with passion. "Citizen Chauvelin sent you?"

"Yes. He bade me tell you that he has gained access to the chateau, and that Capet is not there."

A series of citizen Heron's choicest oaths interrupted the man's speech. Then he was curtly ordered to proceed, and he resumed his report.

"Citizen Chauvelin rang at the door of the chateau; after a while he was admitted by an old servant, who appeared to be in charge, but the place seemed otherwise absolutely deserted—only—"

"Only what? Go on; what is it?"

"As we rode through the park it seemed to us as if we were being watched, and followed. We heard distinctly the sound of horses behind and around us, but we could see nothing; and now, when I ran back, again I heard. There are others in the park to-night besides us, citizen."

There was silence after that. It seemed as if the flood of Heron's blasphemous eloquence had spent itself at last.

"Others in the park!" And now his voice was scarcely above a whisper, hoarse and trembling. "How many? Could you see?"

"No, citizen, we could not see; but there are horsemen lurking round the chateau now. Citizen Chauvelin took four men into the house with him and left the others on guard outside. He bade me tell you that it might be safer to send him a few more men if you could spare them. There are a number of disused farm buildings quite close to the gates, and he suggested that all the horses be put up there for the night, and that the men come up to the chateau on foot; it would be quicker and safer, for the darkness is intense."

Even while the man spoke the forest in the distance seemed to wake from its solemn silence, the wind on its wings brought sounds of life and movement different from the prowling of beasts or the screeching of night-birds. It was the furtive advance of men, the quick whispers of command, of encouragement, of the human animal preparing to attack his kind. But all in the distance still, all muffled, all furtive as yet.

"Sergeant!" It was Heron's voice, but it too was subdued, and almost calm now; "can you see the chapel?"

"More clearly, citizen," replied the sergeant. "It is on our left; quite a small building, I think."

"Then dismount, and walk all round it. See that there are no windows or door in the rear."

There was a prolonged silence, during which those distant sounds of men moving, of furtive preparations for attack, struck distinctly through the night.

Marguerite and Armand, clinging to one another, not knowing what to think, nor yet what to fear, heard the sounds mingling with those immediately round them, and Marguerite murmured under her breath:

"It is de Batz and some of his friends; but what can they do? What can Percy hope for now?"

But of Percy she could hear and see nothing. The darkness and the silence had drawn their impenetrable veil between his unseen presence and her own consciousness. She could see the coach in which he was, but Heron's hideous personality, his head with its battered hat and soiled bandage, had seemed to obtrude itself always before her gaze, blotting out from her mind even the knowledge that Percy was there not fifty yards away from her.

So strong did this feeling grow in her that presently the awful dread seized upon her that he was no longer there; that he was dead, worn out with fatigue and illness brought on by terrible privations, or if not dead that he had swooned, that he was unconscious—his spirit absent from his body. She remembered that frightful yell of rage and hate which Heron had uttered a few minutes ago. Had the brute vented his fury on his helpless, weakened prisoner, and stilled forever those lips that, mayhap, had mocked him to the last?

Marguerite could not guess. She hardly knew what to hope. Vaguely, when the thought of Percy lying dead beside his enemy floated through her aching brain, she was almost conscious of a sense of relief at the thought that at least he would be spared the pain of the final, inevitable cataclysm.

CHAPTER XLVII

The Chapel of the HOly Sepulchre

The sergeant's voice broke in upon her misery.

The man had apparently done as the citizen agent had ordered, and had closely examined the little building that stood on the left—a vague, black mass more dense than the surrounding gloom.

"It is all solid stone, citizen," he said; "iron gates in front, closed but not locked, rusty key in the lock, which turns quite easily; no windows or door in the rear."

"You are quite sure?"

"Quite certain, citizen; it is plain, solid stone at the back, and the only possible access to the interior is through the iron gate in front."

"Good."

Marguerite could only just hear Heron speaking to the sergeant. Darkness enveloped every form and deadened every sound. Even the harsh voice which she had learned to loathe and to dread sounded curiously subdued and unfamiliar. Heron no longer seemed inclined to storm, to rage, or to curse. The momentary danger, the thought of failure, the hope of revenge, had apparently cooled his temper, strengthened his determination, and forced his voice down to a little above a whisper. He gave his orders clearly and firmly, and the words came to Marguerite on the wings of the wind with strange distinctness, borne to her ears by the darkness itself, and the hush that lay over the wood.

"Take half a dozen men with you, sergeant," she beard him say, "and join citizen Chauvelin at the chateau. You can stable your horses in the farm buildings close by, as he suggests and run to him on foot. You and your men should quickly get the best of a handful of midnight prowlers; you are well armed and they only civilians. Tell citizen Chauvelin that I in the meanwhile will take care of our prisoners. The Englishman I shall put in irons and lock up inside the chapel, with five men under the command of your corporal to guard him, the other two I will drive myself straight to Crecy with what is left of the escort. You understand?"

"Yes, citizen."

"We may not reach Crecy until two hours after midnight, but directly I arrive I will send citizen Chauvelin further reinforcements, which, however, I hope may not necessary, but which will reach him in the early morning. Even if he is seriously attacked, he can, with fourteen men he will have with him, hold out inside the castle through the night. Tell him also that at dawn two prisoners who will be with me will be shot in the courtyard of the guard-house at Crecy, but that whether he has got hold of Capet or not he had best pick up the Englishman in the chapel in the morning and bring him straight to Crecy, where I shall be awaiting him ready to return to Paris. You understand?"

"Yes, citizen."

"Then repeat what I said."

"I am to take six men with me to reinforce citizen Chauvelin now."

"Yes."

"And you, citizen, will drive straight back to Crecy, and will send us further reinforcements from there, which will reach us in the early morning."

"Yes."

"We are to hold the chateau against those unknown marauders if necessary until the reinforcements come from Crecy. Having routed them, we return here, pick up the Englishman whom you will have locked up in the chapel under a strong guard commanded by Corporal Cassard, and join you forthwith at Crecy."

"This, whether citizen Chauvelin has got hold of Capet or not."

"Yes, citizen, I understand," concluded the sergeant imperturbably; "and I am also to tell citizen Chauvelin that the two prisoners will be shot at dawn in the courtyard of the guard-house at Crecy."

"Yes. That is all. Try to find the leader of the attacking party, and bring him along to Crecy with the Englishman; but unless they are in very small numbers do not trouble about the others. Now en avant; citizen Chauvelin might be glad of your help. And—stay—order all the men to dismount, and take the horses out of one of the coaches, then let the men you are taking with you each lead a horse, or even two, and stable them all in the farm buildings. I shall not need them, and could not spare any of my men for the work later on. Remember that, above all, silence is the order. When you are ready to start, come back to me here."

The sergeant moved away, and Marguerite heard him transmitting the citizen agent's orders to the soldiers. The dismounting was carried on in wonderful silence—for silence had been one of the principal commands—only one or two words reached her ears.

"First section and first half of second section fall in, right wheel. First section each take two horses on the lead. Quietly now there; don't tug at his bridle—let him go."

And after that a simple report:

"All ready, citizen!"

"Good!" was the response. "Now detail your corporal and two men to come here to me, so that we may put the Englishman in irons, and take him at once to the chapel, and four men to stand guard at the doors of the other coach."

The necessary orders were given, and after that there came the curt command:

"En avant!"

The sergeant, with his squad and all the horses, was slowly moving away in the night. The horses' hoofs hardly made a noise on the soft carpet of pine-needles and of dead fallen leaves, but the champing of the bits was of course audible, and now and then the snorting of some poor, tired horse longing for its stable.

Somehow in Marguerite's fevered mind this departure of a squad of men seemed like the final flitting of her last hope; the slow agony of the familiar sounds, the retreating horses and soldiers moving away amongst the shadows, took on a weird significance. Heron had given his last orders. Percy, helpless and probably unconscious, would spend the night in that dank chapel, while she and Armand would be taken back to Crecy, driven to death like some insentient animals to the slaughter.

When the grey dawn would first begin to peep through the branches of the pines Percy would be led back to Paris and the guillotine, and she and Armand will have been sacrificed to the hatred and revenge of brutes.

The end had come, and there was nothing more to be done. Struggling, fighting, scheming, could be of no avail now; but she wanted to get to her husband; she wanted to be near him now that death was so imminent both for him and for her.

She tried to envisage it all, quite calmly, just as she knew that Percy would wish her to do. The inevitable end was there, and she would not give to these callous wretches here the gratuitous spectacle of a despairing woman fighting blindly against adverse Fate.

But she wanted to go to her husband. She felt that she could face death more easily on the morrow if she could but see him once, if she could but look once more into the eyes that had mirrored so much enthusiasm, such absolute vitality and whole-hearted self-sacrifice, and such an intensity of love and passion; if she could but kiss once more those lips that had smiled through life, and would smile, she knew, even in the face of death.

She tried to open the carriage door, but it was held from without, and a harsh voice cursed her, ordering her to sit still.

But she could lean out of the window and strain her eyes to see. They were by now accustomed to the gloom, the dilated pupils taking in pictures of vague forms moving like ghouls in the shadows. The other coach was not far, and she could hear Heron's voice, still subdued and calm, and the curses of the men. But not a sound from Percy.

"I think the prisoner is unconscious," she heard one of the men say.

"Lift him out of the carriage, then," was Heron's curt command; "and you go and throw open the chapel gates."

Marguerite saw it all. The movement, the crowd of men, two vague, black forms lifting another one, which appeared heavy and inert, out of the coach, and carrying it staggering up towards the chapel.

Then the forms disappeared, swallowed up by the more dense mass of the little building, merged in with it, immovable as the stone itself.

Only a few words reached her now.

"He is unconscious."

"Leave him there, then; he'll not move!"

"Now close the gates!"

There was a loud clang, and Marguerite gave a piercing scream. She tore at the handle of the carriage door.

"Armand, Armand, go to him!" she cried; and all her self-control, all her enforced calm, vanished in an outburst of wild, agonising passion. "Let me get to him, Armand! This is the end; get me to him, in the name of God!"

"Stop that woman screaming," came Heron's voice clearly through the night. "Put her and the other prisoner in irons—quick!"

But while Marguerite expended her feeble strength in a mad, pathetic effort to reach her husband, even now at this last hour, when all hope was dead and Death was so nigh, Armand had already wrenched the carriage door from the grasp of the soldier who was guarding it. He was of the South, and knew the trick of charging an unsuspecting adversary with head thrust forward like a bull inside a ring. Thus he knocked one of the soldiers down and made a quick rush for the chapel gates.

The men, attacked so suddenly and in such complete darkness, did not wait for orders. They closed in round Armand; one man drew his sabre and hacked away with it in aimless rage.

But for the moment he evaded them all, pushing his way through them, not heeding the blows that came on him from out the darkness. At last he reached the chapel. With one bound he was at the gate, his numb fingers fumbling for the lock, which he could not see.

It was a vigorous blow from Heron's fist that brought him at last to his knees, and even then his hands did not relax their hold; they gripped the ornamental scroll of the gate, shook the gate itself in its rusty hinges, pushed and pulled with the unreasoning strength of despair. He had a sabre cut across his brow, and the blood flowed in a warm, trickling stream down his face. But of this he was unconscious; all that he wanted, all that he was striving for with agonising heart-beats and cracking sinews, was to get to his friend, who was lying in there unconscious, abandoned—dead, perhaps.

"Curse you," struck Heron's voice close to his ear. "Cannot some of you stop this raving maniac?"

Then it was that the heavy blow on his head caused him a sensation of sickness, and he fell on his knees, still gripping the ironwork.

Stronger hands than his were forcing him to loosen his hold; blows that hurt terribly rained on his numbed fingers; he felt himself dragged away, carried like an inert mass further and further from that gate which he would have given his lifeblood to force open.

And Marguerite heard all this from the inside of the coach where she was imprisoned as effectually as was Percy's unconscious body inside that dark chapel. She could hear the noise and scramble, and Heron's hoarse commands, the swift sabre strokes as they cut through the air.

Already a trooper had clapped irons on her wrists, two others held the carriage doors. Now Armand was lifted back into the coach, and she could not even help to make him comfortable, though as he was lifted in she heard him feebly moaning. Then the carriage doors were banged to again.

"Do not allow either of the prisoners out again, on peril of your lives!" came with a vigorous curse from Heron.

After which there was a moment's silence; whispered commands came spasmodically in deadened sound to her ear.

"Will the key turn?"

"Yes, citizen."

"All secure?"

"Yes, citizen. The prisoner is groaning."

"Let him groan."

"The empty coach, citizen? The horses have been taken out."

"Leave it standing where it is, then; citizen Chauvelin will need it in the morning."

"Armand," whispered Marguerite inside the coach, "did you see Percy?"

"It was so dark," murmured Armand feebly; "but I saw him, just inside the gates, where they had laid him down. I heard him groaning. Oh, my God!"

"Hush, dear!" she said. "We can do nothing more, only die, as he lived, bravely and with a smile on our lips, in memory of him."

"Number 35 is wounded, citizen," said one of the men.

"Curse the fool who did the mischief," was the placid response. "Leave him here with the guard."

"How many of you are there left, then?" asked the same voice a moment later.

"Only two, citizen; if one whole section remains with me at the chapel door, and also the wounded man."

"Two are enough for me, and five are not too many at the chapel door." And Heron's coarse, cruel laugh echoed against the stone walls of the little chapel. "Now then, one of you get into the coach, and the other go to the horses' heads; and remember, Corporal Cassard, that you and your men who stay here to guard that chapel door are answerable to the whole nation with your lives for the safety of the Englishman."

The carriage door was thrown open, and a soldier stepped in and sat down opposite Marguerite and Armand. Heron in the meanwhile was apparently scrambling up the box. Marguerite could hear him muttering curses as he groped for the reins, and finally gathered them into his hand.

The springs of the coach creaked and groaned as the vehicle slowly swung round; the wheels ploughed deeply through the soft carpet of dead leaves.

Marguerite felt Armand's inert body leaning heavily against her shoulder.

"Are you in pain, dear?" she asked softly.

He made no reply, and she thought that he had fainted. It was better so; at least the next dreary hours would flit by for him in the blissful state of unconsciousness. Now at last the heavy carriage began to move more evenly. The soldier at the horses' heads was stepping along at a rapid pace.

Marguerite would have given much even now to look back once more at the dense black mass, blacker and denser than any shadow that had ever descended before on God's earth, which held between its cold, cruel walls all that she loved in the world.

But her wrists were fettered by the irons, which cut into her flesh when she moved. She could no longer lean out of the window, and she could not even hear. The whole forest was hushed, the wind was lulled to rest; wild beasts and night-birds were silent and still. And the wheels of the coach creaked in the ruts, bearing Marguerite with every turn further and further away from the man who lay helpless in the chapel of the Holy Sepulchre.

CHAPTER XLVIII

The Waning Moon

Armand had wakened from his attack of faintness, and brother and sister sat close to one another, shoulder touching shoulder. That sense of nearness was the one tiny spark of comfort to both of them on this dreary, dreary way.

The coach had lumbered on unceasingly since all eternity—so it seemed to them both. Once there had been a brief halt, when Heron's rough voice had ordered the soldier at the horses' heads to climb on the box beside him, and once—it had been a very little while ago—a terrible cry of pain and terror had rung through the stillness of the night. Immediately after that the horses had been put at a more rapid pace, but it had seemed to Marguerite as if that one cry of pain had been repeated by several others which sounded more feeble and soon appeared to be dying away in the distance behind.

The soldier who sat opposite to them must have heard the cry too, for he jumped up, as if wakened from sleep, and put his head out of the window.

"Did you hear that cry, citizen?" he asked.

But only a curse answered him, and a peremptory command not to lose sight of the prisoners by poking his head out of the window.

"Did you hear the cry?" asked the soldier of Marguerite as he made haste to obey.

"Yes! What could it be?" she murmured.

"It seems dangerous to drive so fast in this darkness," muttered the soldier.

After which remark he, with the stolidity peculiar to his kind, figuratively shrugged his shoulders, detaching himself, as it were, of the whole affair.

"We should be out of the forest by now," he remarked in an undertone a little while later; "the way seemed shorter before."

Just then the coach gave an unexpected lurch to one side, and after much groaning and creaking of axles and springs it came to a standstill, and the citizen agent was heard cursing loudly and then scrambling down from the box.

The next moment the carriage-door was pulled open from without, and the harsh voice called out peremptorily:

"Citizen soldier, here—quick!—quick!—curse you!—we'll have one of the horses down if you don't hurry!"

The soldier struggled to his feet; it was never good to be slow in obeying the citizen agent's commands. He was half-asleep and no doubt numb with cold and long sitting still; to accelerate his movements he was suddenly gripped by the arm and dragged incontinently out of the coach.

Then the door was slammed to again, either by a rough hand or a sudden gust of wind, Marguerite could not tell; she heard a cry of rage and one of terror, and Heron's raucous curses. She cowered in the corner of the carriage with Armand's head against her shoulder, and tried to close her ears to all those hideous sounds.

Then suddenly all the sounds were hushed and all around everything became perfectly calm and still—so still that at first the silence oppressed her with a vague, nameless dread. It was as if Nature herself had paused, that she might listen; and the silence became more and more absolute, until Marguerite could hear Armand's soft, regular breathing close to her ear.

The window nearest to her was open, and as she leaned forward with that paralysing sense of oppression a breath of pure air struck full upon her nostrils and brought with it a briny taste as if from the sea.

It was not quite so dark; and there was a sense as of open country stretching out to the limits of the horizon. Overhead a vague greyish light suffused the sky, and the wind swept the clouds in great rolling banks right across that light.

Marguerite gazed upward with a more calm feeling that was akin to gratitude. That pale light, though so wan and feeble, was thrice welcome after that inky blackness wherein shadows were less dark than the lights. She watched eagerly the bank of clouds driven by the dying gale.

The light grew brighter and faintly golden, now the banks of clouds—storm-tossed and fleecy—raced past one another, parted and reunited like veils of unseen giant dancers waved by hands that controlled infinite space—advanced and rushed and slackened speed again—united and finally torn asunder to reveal the waning moon, honey-coloured and mysterious, rising as if from an invisible ocean far away.

The wan pale light spread over the wide stretch of country, throwing over it as it spread dull tones of indigo and of blue. Here and there sparse, stunted trees with fringed gaunt arms bending to prevailing winds proclaimed the neighbourhood of the sea.

Marguerite gazed on the picture which the waning moon had so suddenly revealed; but she gazed with eyes that knew not what they saw. The moon had risen on her right—there lay the east—and the coach must have been travelling due north, whereas Crecy...

In the absolute silence that reigned she could perceive from far, very far away, the sound of a church clock striking the midnight hour; and now it seemed to her supersensitive senses that a firm footstep was treading the soft earth, a footstep that drew nearer—and then nearer still.

Nature did pause to listen. The wind was hushed, the night-birds in the forest had gone to rest. Marguerite's heart beat so fast that its throbbings choked her, and a dizziness clouded her consciousness.

But through this state of torpor she heard the opening of the carriage door, she felt the onrush of that pure, briny air, and she felt a long, burning kiss upon her hands.

She thought then that she was really dead, and that God in His infinite love had opened to her the outer gates of Paradise.

"My love!" she murmured.

She was leaning back in the carriage and her eyes were closed, but she felt that firm fingers removed the irons from her wrists, and that a pair of warm lips were pressed there in their stead.

"There, little woman, that's better so—is it not? Now let me get hold of poor old Armand!"

It was Heaven, of course, else how could earth hold such heavenly joy?

"Percy!" exclaimed Armand in an awed voice.

"Hush, dear!" murmured Marguerite feebly; "we are in Heaven you and I—"

Whereupon a ringing laugh woke the echoes of the silent night.

"In Heaven, dear heart!" And the voice had a delicious earthly ring in its whole-hearted merriment. "Please God, you'll both be at Portel with me before dawn."

Then she was indeed forced to believe. She put out her hands and groped for him, for it was dark inside the carriage; she groped, and felt his massive shoulders leaning across the body of the coach, while his fingers busied themselves with the irons on Armand's wrist.

"Don't touch that brute's filthy coat with your dainty fingers, dear heart," he said gaily. "Great Lord! I have worn that wretch's clothes for over two hours; I feel as if the dirt had penetrated to my bones."

Then with that gesture so habitual to him he took her head between his two hands, and drawing her to him until the wan light from without lit up the face that he worshipped, he gazed his fill into her eyes.

She could only see the outline of his head silhouetted against the wind-tossed sky; she could not see his eyes, nor his lips, but she felt his nearness, and the happiness of that almost caused her to swoon.

"Come out into the open, my lady fair," he murmured, and though she could not see, she could feel that he smiled; "let God's pure air blow through your hair and round your dear head. Then, if you can walk so far, there's a small half-way house close by here. I have knocked up the none too amiable host. You and Armand could have half an hour's rest there before we go further on our way."

"But you, Percy?—are you safe?"

"Yes, m'dear, we are all of us safe until morning-time enough to reach Le Portel, and to be aboard the Day-Dream before mine amiable friend M. Chambertin has discovered his worthy colleague lying gagged and bound inside the chapel of the Holy Sepulchre. By Gad! how old Heron will curse—the moment he can open his mouth!"

He half helped, half lifted her out of the carriage. The strong pure air suddenly rushing right through to her lungs made her feel faint, and she almost fell. But it was good to feel herself falling, when one pair of arms amongst the millions on the earth were there to receive her.

"Can you walk, dear heart?" he asked. "Lean well on me—it is not far, and the rest will do you good."

"But you, Percy—"

He laughed, and the most complete joy of living seemed to resound through that laugh. Her arm was in his, and for one moment he stood still while his eyes swept the far reaches of the country, the mellow distance still wrapped in its mantle of indigo, still untouched by the mysterious light of the waning moon.

He pressed her arm against his heart, but his right hand was stretched out towards the black wall of the forest behind him, towards the dark crests of the pines in which the dying wind sent its last mournful sighs.

"Dear heart," he said, and his voice quivered with the intensity of his excitement, "beyond the stretch of that wood, from far away over there, there are cries and moans of anguish that come to my ear even now. But for you, dear, I would cross that wood to-night and re-enter Paris to-morrow. But for you, dear—but for you," he reiterated earnestly as he pressed her closer to him, for a bitter cry had risen to her lips.

She went on in silence. Her happiness was great—as great as was her pain. She had found him again, the man whom she worshipped, the husband whom she thought never to see again on earth. She had found him, and not even now—not after those terrible weeks of misery and suffering unspeakable—could she feel that love had triumphed over the wild, adventurous spirit, the reckless enthusiasm, the ardour of self-sacrifice.

CHAPTER XLIX

The Land of Eldorado

It seems that in the pocket of Heron's coat there was a letter-case with some few hundred francs. It was amusing to think that the brute's money helped to bribe the ill-tempered keeper of the half-way house to receive guests at midnight, and to ply them well with food, drink, and the shelter of a stuffy coffee-room.

Marguerite sat silently beside her husband, her hand in his. Armand, opposite to them, had both elbows on the table. He looked pale and wan, with a bandage across his forehead, and his glowing eyes were resting on his chief.

"Yes! you demmed young idiot," said Blakeney merrily, "you nearly upset my plan in the end, with your yelling and screaming outside the chapel gates."

"I wanted to get to you, Percy. I thought those brutes had got you there inside that building."

"Not they!" he exclaimed. "It was my friend Heron whom they had trussed and gagged, and whom my amiable friend M. Chambertin will find in there to-morrow morning. By Gad! I would go back if only for the pleasure of hearing Heron curse when first the gag is taken from his mouth."

"But how was it all done, Percy? And there was de Batz—"

"De Batz was part of the scheme I had planned for mine own escape before I knew that those brutes meant to take Marguerite and you as hostages for my good behaviour. What I hoped then was that under cover of a tussle or a fight I could somehow or other contrive to slip through their fingers. It was a chance, and you know my belief in bald-headed Fortune, with the one solitary hair. Well, I meant to grab that hair; and at the worst I could but die in the open and not caged in that awful hole like some noxious vermin. I knew that de Batz would rise to the bait. I told him in my letter that the Dauphin would be at the Chateau d'Ourde this night, but that I feared the revolutionary Government had got wind of this fact, and were sending an armed escort to bring the lad away. This letter Ffoulkes took to him; I knew that he would make a vigorous effort to get the Dauphin into his hands, and that during the scuffle that one hair on Fortune's head would for one second only, mayhap, come within my reach. I had so planned the expedition that we were bound to arrive at the forest of Boulogne by nightfall, and night is always a useful ally. But at the guard-house of the Rue Ste. Anne I realised for the first time that those brutes had pressed me into a tighter corner than I had pre-conceived."

He paused, and once again that look of recklessness swept over his face, and his eyes—still hollow and circled—shone with the excitement of past memories.

"I was such a weak, miserable wretch, then," he said, in answer to Marguerite's appeal. "I had to try and build up some strength, when—Heaven forgive me for the sacrilege—I had unwittingly risked your precious life, dear heart, in that blind endeavour to save mine own. By Gad! it was no easy task in that jolting vehicle with that noisome wretch beside me for sole company; yet I ate and I drank and I slept for three days and two nights, until the hour when in the darkness I struck Heron from behind, half-strangled him first, then gagged him, and finally slipped into his filthy coat and put that loathsome bandage across my head, and his battered hat above it all. The yell he gave when first I attacked him made every horse rear—you must remember it—the noise effectually drowned our last scuffle in the coach. Chauvelin was the only man who might have suspected what had occurred, but he had gone on ahead, and bald-headed Fortune had passed by me, and I had managed to grab its one hair. After that it was all quite easy. The sergeant and the soldiers had seen very little of Heron and nothing of me; it did not take a great effort to deceive them, and the darkness of the night was my most faithful friend. His raucous voice was not difficult to imitate, and darkness always muffles and changes every tone. Anyway, it was not likely that those loutish soldiers would even remotely suspect the trick that was being played on them. The citizen agent's orders were promptly and implicitly obeyed. The men never even thought to wonder that after insisting on an escort of twenty he should drive off with two prisoners and only two men to guard them. If they did wonder, it was not theirs to question. Those two troopers are spending an uncomfortable night somewhere in the forest of Boulogne, each tied to a tree, and some two leagues apart one from the other. And now," he added gaily, "en voiture, my fair lady; and you, too, Armand. 'Tis seven leagues to Le Portel, and we must be there before dawn."

"Sir Andrew's intention was to make for Calais first, there to open communication with the Day-Dream and then for Le Portel," said Marguerite; "after that he meant to strike back for the Chateau d'Ourde in search of me."

"Then we'll still find him at Le Portel—I shall know how to lay hands on him; but you two must get aboard the Day-Dream at once, for Ffoulkes and I can always look after ourselves."

It was one hour after midnight when—refreshed with food and rest—Marguerite, Armand and Sir Percy left the half-way house. Marguerite was standing in the doorway ready to go. Percy and Armand had gone ahead to bring the coach along.

"Percy," whispered Armand, "Marguerite does not know?"

"Of course she does not, you young fool," retorted Percy lightly. "If you try and tell her I think I would smash your head."

"But you—" said the young man with sudden vehemence; "can you bear the sight of me? My God! when I think—"

"Don't think, my good Armand—not of that anyway. Only think of the woman for whose sake you committed a crime—if she is pure and good, woo her and win her—not just now, for it were foolish to go back to Paris after her, but anon, when she comes to England and all these past days are forgotten—then love her as much as you can, Armand. Learn your lesson of love better than I have learnt mine; do not cause Jeanne Lange those tears of anguish which my mad spirit brings to your sister's eyes. You were right, Armand, when you said that I do not know how to love!"

But on board the Day-Dream, when all danger was past, Marguerite felt that he did.

15071468R00342

Made in the USA
Middletown, DE
22 October 2014